KU-637-054

Climate change denialism may be more about fear and inertia than genuine belief. We have to give governments of the world something they're more afraid of to make them act.

Seraphina Rose
Chief Scientific Advisor
The Circle

Back a wounded animal into a corner, make them feel threatened? Don't expect a reasonable reaction.

Cassandra Penn
Elder and Seer
The Circle

RED
SKY
BURNING

WALTHAM FOREST LIBRARIES

904 000 00702107

Also by
TERI TERRY

THE CIRCLE TRILOGY
Dark Blue Rising
Red Sky Burning
Black Night Falling (coming soon)

THE *DARK MATTER* TRILOGY
Contagion
Deception
Evolution

THE *SLATED* TRILOGY & PREQUEL
Slated
Fractured
Shattered
Prequel: *Fated*

Mind Games
Dangerous Games

Book of Lies

TERI TERRY

RED SKY BURNING

Book 2 of The Circle Trilogy

Hodder
Children's
Books

HODDER CHILDREN'S BOOKS

First published in Great Britain in 2021 by Hodder & Stoughton

1 3 5 7 9 10 8 6 4 2

Text copyright © Teri Terry, 2021

The moral rights of the author have been asserted.

*All characters and events in this publication, other than those clearly
in the public domain, are fictitious and any resemblance to
real persons, living or dead, is purely coincidental.*

All rights reserved.
No part of this publication may be reproduced, stored in
a retrieval system, or transmitted, in any form or by any means, without
the prior permission in writing of the publisher, nor be otherwise circulated
in any form of binding or cover other than that in which it is published
and without a similar condition including this condition being
imposed on the subsequent purchaser.

A CIP catalogue record for this book
is available from the British Library.

ISBN 978 1 444 95510 1

Typeset in Bembo Schoolbook by Avon DataSet Ltd,
Arden Court, Alcester, Warwickshire

Printed and bound in Great Britain by Clays Ltd, Elcograf S.p.A

The paper and board used in this book
are made from wood from responsible sources.

WALTHAM FOREST LIBRARIES		
904 000 00702107		
Askews & Holts	23-Jul-2021	
JF TEE		

Part 1

Denzi

1

I didn't see it coming. Nobody did.

I say that, but there was *something* that last night: a tightness in my chest, a pressure, inside and out, that made breathing feel like an effort even when I was still.

I couldn't sleep and I thought it was the relentless weather. Hot, humid, the air not moving at all, and OK, it *was* summer, but it shouldn't have been that hot in England. At least that's what they say, but it's mostly what I remember growing up: hot, endless summers, the only relief in the sea. I'm sure that has a lot to do with why I'm a swimmer.

So, I couldn't sleep, and I remember wondering why I hadn't told Tabby everything. Not about that Penrose Clinic she was worried about – I didn't know anything about it yet, then – but in relation to the other things she told me that were seriously weird. The way she, Isha and Zara had never even trained before, but were discovered and brought there – to the elite summer swim school. It was meant to be training for future stars of the sport; that they'd never even competed before didn't make any kind of sense. And also that between the three of them and Ariel, two of their parents were geologists and two worked for oil and gas companies. I'd said my dad was a politician – true, he's an MP in London – but didn't mention my mother.

I don't, generally – mention my mother. I don't even call her

3

that. It felt too weird saying 'Mum' or even 'Mother' to a stranger, so I've always just called her by her first name, Leila. I see her so seldom that she seems kind of like a story I've been told rather than one I've lived. But I could have told Tabby that Leila was on the other side – that she was part of Big Green in Washington DC, the umbrella environmental group that stands against oil and gas companies like Industria United.

So, lying awake, thinking, I decided I would tell Tabby about her the next day. And we could ask some of the other swimmers about their backgrounds, see if these parallels continued. And if they did, try to work out *why* – what it meant. This was a puzzle, and nothing gets my attention more than not understanding how something fits together.

But then there was a knock at my door.

2

Who could it be?

I squint at my tracker in the dark: 2.40 a.m.

There's another light *tap tap*.

I get up and open the door.

Becker? If there is anyone I wasn't expecting to see standing there at this time of night, our running trainer is it.

His hair is rumpled like he's just got up.

'Sorry to wake you, Denzi. You've got a call – Director Lang's office downstairs. Come on.'

A call. When we're not allowed our own phones, and only get to use theirs for one call home a week? And in the middle of the night?

'What the hell? Has something happened?'

He shrugs. 'I don't know. She just asked me to get you.'

I follow Becker down the stairs, through the front lobby and down a hall to the director's office.

He taps once, opens the door.

She's there at her desk – Christina Lang, the director of the swim school – and, OK, maybe I should be wearing more than my boxers. But she only looks concerned, and my gut is clenching.

'Denzi, take a seat. Here you go.' She passes me the phone.

'Hello?'

'Denzi?' It's Dad. *Relief* floods through me to hear his voice,

5

followed by panic at all the other things that could have happened.

'What's wrong?'

'It's your mother. I don't know how serious it is – we haven't got all the details yet – she's been involved in an accident. Oliver called from the hospital. They're asking you to go.'

'*What*? What kind of accident?'

'She was knocked off her bike by a car. That's all I know.'

'Shit.'

'Yeah. Well, it's totally up to you, I promise. What do you want to do?'

And I'm sitting there, not saying anything – not knowing what to say. She's never been there for me, so why should I? But what if . . . this the last time I will ever see her?

'Denzi? If you're not sure what to do, consider this. In my experience, if you are ever in doubt about whether to do something or do nothing, it's usually the things you don't do that you regret.'

And I know he's talking about something else completely, yet . . . he's right.

'I'll go,' I say.

'All right. Jax has been checking flights. We can get you on a seven a.m. direct to Washington, DC if you can get to Heathrow in time. Can I speak to Christina again?'

'Thanks, Dad.'

I hand the phone back to her. They're talking details while my mind is reeling: my mother? An accident?

Director Lang hands the phone back to me.

'Dad?'

'All sorted. We'll meet you at the airport with your passport; Jax is packing you a few clothes and things, too.'

'Thanks.'

We say goodbye and I hang up.

'All right, Denzi,' Director Lang says. 'Go get dressed and be out front in ten minutes. Becker will drive you to Heathrow.'

'Thanks. Both of you: thanks.'

We don't talk much on the way. It's almost three a.m. when we leave; Becker's sat nav says three hours. Will that leave enough time to get through security for a seven a.m. flight? But there's hardly any traffic and we make it there in nearer two and a half.

He pulls up in front of departures.

'Thanks again,' I say.

'No problem. Though this'll be the first morning *ever* I've not made the six a.m. run. Hope everything is OK, kid.'

I get out, rush into departures and, as I do, wonder about Becker. I've never liked him much, mostly because he seems to pick on weaker runners. Maybe away from training he's all right.

I find Dad and Jax.

'Quick, they'll close the gate soon,' Dad says. 'I've checked you in; here's your boarding pass, passport, cards and cash, and your mobile. I've charged it. There's a driver and car arranged to meet you there; he'll have a sign with your name at arrivals, OK? I've texted you Oliver's number in case you need it.'

Dad gives me a hug; Jax does too.

Jax hands me a small bag. 'Only packed a carry on, no time to check anything,' he says.

'Go, go,' Dad says. 'We'll wait a while in case you miss it. Text me. Love you.'

'You too.' I start to rush towards security.

7

'Call us when you get there,' Jax calls out.

'Will do!' I turn, wave as I go through and out of their sight.

Security is even slower than usual and, once I'm through, the gate is about as far away as it could be. I run full tilt to get there. A woman in flight-crew uniform is pulling the door closed.

'Please! My mother has been in an accident. I have to get on this plane.'

She hesitates, then opens it again. 'All right. You'll have to hurry.' I hand her my passport and boarding pass to be scanned.

'Thank you,' I say and rush up the tunnel to the plane.

I'm shown to my seat and sink into it before it registers – this is business class? God. It must have cost a fortune last minute like this.

I text Dad. Made it. Thanks for the posh seat.

Hope it's all OK. Call whenever you need or want to.

Thanks.

I turn my phone to airplane mode, do up my seat belt. They start the usual inflight safety stuff.

I'd been so focused on worrying about catching this flight that now that I'm here, I'm remembering *why*.

Is she all right? I didn't ask Dad if they knew anything else. They'd have told me if they did, wouldn't they?

But if she isn't all right . . . what if I'm too late?

I can't think about that now and force my thoughts away, back to what I've left behind.

Tabby. I should have given Becker a message for her; I hope they'll tell her where I've gone. Not sure anybody else will notice I'm not there, except maybe Dickens, the school cat.

So much for summer swim school and being in the next Olympics. I guess that's something else I can blame on Leila. Then I feel guilty for thinking that when I don't know if . . . well. I carefully don't think about that any further.

I hope Dad really *is* OK with me making this trip. Whatever went wrong between my parents all those years ago, he's never really been able to tell me. I mean, he's gay, which would be enough to end things once he'd worked it out, but somehow I sense there is more to it. Not that he's trying to keep things from me; it's more like he can't bear to talk about it.

We taxi to our runway. The engines power up and we're speeding down it now, then lurch as we climb into the sky. The mad pace of my heart gradually slows.

My mind is still spinning. I usually can't sleep on planes; I'm not great at getting to sleep anywhere, really – even at home it takes ages. But exhaustion has me.

I'm gone.

3

I come out of passport control and look for the promised driver holding a sign with my name. They're not there.

Don't panic – maybe they're stuck in traffic. I scan back and forth across the crowd. People are being met all around me with hugs and flowers, or drivers in hats. I hang back, wondering what I'll do if no one turns up. Call Leila's husband, Oliver? I can't get a taxi; no one said which hospital.

Then there's a girl walking towards me. She's tall, stunning with that white sundress against dark skin. I haven't seen her for years so it's hard to be sure, but is that my stepsister, Apple? Actually, Apple Blossom, but she once twisted my arm behind my back and told me she'd kill me if I ever called her that again. Yes, it must be her: she's waving.

'Denzi! Hi! Welcome to the USA.' A big smile.

'Hey, Apple. I was expecting a driver. Is everything OK?'

'As far as I know. I volunteered to come get you. I had to get out of there; I hate hospitals,' she says, and I'm remembering now that her mum died of breast cancer. She hesitates. 'Your mom is in a coma.'

I swallow. 'She's in a *coma*? Is she going to be all right?'

Her smile goes. 'Honestly, they don't know. Let's get you there.'

4

It's like a TV hospital drama. Leila is hooked up to machines that beep, and Oliver is holding her hand.

'Thanks for coming, Denzi,' he says.

'Tell me what happened.'

'Car knocked her off her bike. She had a helmet on but still has a head injury, though from what they can tell it is only minor – they don't know why she's not regained consciousness.'

He lets go of her hand, stands. Rolls his shoulders like he hasn't moved in hours. 'Look, have a moment with her. I'll be back soon.' He leaves with Apple.

I sit in the chair by her bed. Her face is pale, bruises down one side. A bandage across her forehead.

Her face: it's so still. There are lines there now, around her eyes, that I don't remember. Grey streaks in her hair. It was, what – four years ago? – the last time I saw her. I was thirteen. She was on a work trip to London. We had lunch and it was weird, awkward; I'd felt like she only did it because it was something she *should* do rather than something she wanted to. Though maybe I put what I was feeling on to her; I don't know.

I can't even work out how I feel right now. Though if she died and I hadn't come, I'd have felt guilty. Is that the only reason I'm here?

Sitting here, watching her breathe, I know it's more than that.

There has always been this sense of something *missing* – especially when I was younger. I'd see my friends and cousins with their mums, and wonder why my mum didn't want me. She left me with Dad when I wasn't even a year old, and to make the break more thorough and complete, left the country, too.

And I never asked her *why* she was never there for me. I think I have a right to know her reasons – I'm old enough for her to be straight with me now.

And I guess that's how I feel: I want her to live, so I can ask her why.

But that isn't the only reason. Can you lose something you've never had? I don't know, but I don't want to lose her again. Not like this.

Later we go for a walk in the hospital grounds, Apple and me. It's a hot, still day; even hotter here in D.C. than England has been lately, or maybe it's just the contrast between air-conditioned private hospital and the outdoors. I can't shake this weird feeling that the world is holding its breath, waiting, like something is coming. It makes me edgy, jumpy, and – most of all – longing for the sea. To swim in salty depths so far and fast that this would all go away.

'I can't handle being in a hospital room for long,' Apple says. 'I was ten when Mom died; I'll never forget sitting there, watching her die. Waiting for it to be over.'

'Were you close?'

'Of course we were, she was my mom! Oh. Sorry.'

'It's fine. How do you get on with Leila?'

She shrugs. 'OK, I guess? I never felt she was trying to replace

12

my mom – she's not the momsy type – but we get on all right most of the time.'

'What was your mum like?'

'Like sunshine. Not this sort,' she says, and gestures at the sun blazing relentlessly down on us. 'More like that first warm day in the spring. That probably sounds silly.'

'No. It doesn't.'

'Dad wasn't sure if you'd come.'

'She's still my mum.' I say the words, but don't feel them. My family has been Dad and Jax as long as I can remember: two dads, or is Jax kind of like my mum should have been? Doesn't matter, either way. And now I'm remembering I'd said I'd call when I got here.

'I forgot to call home. I should do it now, sorry.'

'It's fine.'

Apple goes back inside. I sit on a bench and dial home.

It rings once.

'Hello?' It's Jax.

'Hi, it's me.'

'How're things? What's happening?' And I tell him all I can – that she's in a coma, we don't really know – but I can sense something, some tension, behind his voice.

'Is Dad there?'

'No. Something's going on, not sure what it is this time. He'll be sad to have missed your call.'

'Tell him that I'm all right. And if there is any news, I'll call and let you know.'

We say goodbye. I wonder what is happening this time to have Jax sounding worried and Dad working late, if it is the usual

13

political crap or a crisis of some sort. As the Home Secretary, he's often part of COBRA, the group that meets when there are serious emergencies or threats – pandemics, terrorism or natural disasters, mostly. I check the BBC on my phone: nothing like that has made the news. At least, not yet.

I'll message Dad, I decide.

I open Signal – Dad doesn't like it if I text or call his mobile with mine; he says you never know who is watching or listening in. Signal is secure, though it's pointless most of the time because nobody I know uses it – apart from Dad and Jax.

Got here, she's in a coma – will let you know if anything changes. All ok with you?

I'm walking back when it vibrates.

Thanks for letting me know. And I'm ok, though things are . . . interesting . . .!

Which could mean just about anything.

Later, Oliver manages to convince Apple it's OK for her to go home. He tells me to go with her, but this is why I'm here, isn't it? So I stay.

He goes to get a coffee. A doctor comes in while he's gone, checks the equipment connected to Leila, does something to her IV bag.

'Why is she like this? Is she going to wake up?'

'We don't have all the answers with head injuries. But it may be that she's taking a rest, healing, that she'll wake up when she's ready. Try talking to her – it might help. Even if she doesn't respond, she may still be able to hear you.'

Once she's gone, the door shut behind her, I hesitate.

Glance to the door; Oliver isn't back yet.

I swallow and take her hand. 'OK, hi. It's Denzi. How're things? I guess you can't answer me. It's been a while. Um, so, school is going OK. I've mostly been focusing on swimming.' And I start to tell her how I love it, that it's the only place I feel at ease with myself and the world, my place in it. How happy I'd been to be invited to this elite training programme that was held at my school over the summer. It hits me that this may be the only time I can remember talking to her about anything important to me, and here she is, in a coma.

'Anyhow, that's me. But if you come out of this, we need to talk. There are things I want to ask you, and—'

Wait. Did she move? Her hand – it felt like it tightened a little in mine. Did I imagine it?

I hear the door open behind me and glance towards it: it's Oliver. I look back at Leila, staring at her, *willing* her to come back.

Her eyelashes move, her eyes – are they part open?

'I think she's coming around,' I say. Oliver rushes over as her eyes open and look into mine. Then to Oliver next to me.

She turns her head a little, winces. Licks her lips. 'What the hell is going on?' she says.

Oliver hits the call button and soon a nurse and a doctor come – a different one than before. Everyone is smiling, they're checking her readings, and Oliver is calling Apple. I stand back, watching.

When they're done Oliver goes to Leila, holds her hand.

The doctor smiles at me. 'You must be Leila's son from England.'

'Yes. I'm Denzi.'

15

'Maybe she was waiting for your arrival to come around,' the nurse says.

'Could it be because I was talking to her? Like that other doctor said to try?'

'Other doctor? What other—'

'Hey, remember me? The patient? When can I get out of here?' Leila says.

He turns to her. 'Not just yet. We need to check you out thoroughly, make sure everything is all right.'

Oliver asks questions about Leila's head injury; the doctor says it was unusual the way she woke up all at once, without changes in brain activity that normally happen first. That they need to do tests and scans.

Leila's eyes find mine. Did me talking to her have anything to do with her coming around? It couldn't. Could it? I'm looking at her and she's looking back, and even though neither of us is saying anything, it feels like the first time we've ever had an honest conversation.

5

'Here's to Leila!' Oliver holds out his wine glass and clicks it against Apple's and then mine. 'Scared me half to death, she did.' His phone vibrates. He looks at the screen and sighs. 'It's my editor. I better take this.'

He gets up, leaves the dining room. Apple reaches for the wine bottle.

'Leave it, Apple,' he calls, and her hand falls back.

'He has eyes in the back of his head,' she says.

I'm stifling a yawn.

'You must be tired.'

'Not too bad. I slept a bit on the plane. But what is it here? Ten. So, at home it's six in the morning.'

'Ouch. Are you going to stay a while?'

'I don't know. I'd like to get back to swim training as soon as I can, but I need to talk to Leila before I go.'

Oliver comes back. He's shaking his head.

'What is it this time?' Apple says.

'Some new lot of crazies have been sending letters about how they're going to destroy the world if we don't stop all forms of carbon extraction and emissions pronto. My editor is wondering if we should give them a story.'

'They've been sending *letters*?' Apple says. 'Does anyone actually do that any more?'

'Crazies and paranoid types who avoid phones and the internet, and that's about it,' Oliver says.

'Doesn't destroying the world to stop us destroying the world with climate change seem kind of, well, pointless?' I say.

'To be fair, it was more specific. They seem to be aiming for the US and the UK: said they will cause natural disasters in both countries.'

'How can disasters be natural if they make them happen?'

'Good point.'

'Why the US and the UK?' Apple says, her hand reaching for the wine bottle again until he whips it out of her reach.

'Why do you think?' Oliver says.

She shrugs and I answer. 'Because the UK is where the industrial revolution began. And the US mostly denies the problem even exists.'

He raises his eyebrows, nods. 'That's pretty much what the letter said.'

'Are you going to do a story on it?' Apple says.

'Only if something actually happens. Though we've been in touch with a few government contacts, and it turns out they've had the same letter today. All parties.' He shrugs. 'Crazies with a postal budget.'

A bit later I get shown to a guest room. Their house is *huge* – but everything in the US seems bigger, louder.

I take out my phone. I'd messaged Dad and Jax earlier about Leila coming round and they've both answered with some version of 'Isn't that great'. Nothing else since then.

I shouldn't call, it's early there still, but I'm wondering now

18

if what had Dad working late in the UK is the same thing Oliver's editor was phoning him about – he did say US and UK, didn't he?

I'll message instead of call. I open Signal, but even though it's secure I hesitate, not sure what to say. I don't want to tell Dad what Oliver said; maybe he wasn't supposed to tell us?

I settle on this: Going to sleep now, let me know if anything is happening.

I get into bed but my mind is too awake for sleep. I could blame it on jet lag, but getting to sleep has never been easy for me and lately it seems to be getting worse. I'm restless, uneasy, and it isn't just Leila's accident and changing time zones making me feel like this. Something is missing, something I need. I hadn't thought about it at first, what with everything going on, but leaving swim school when I did, I missed my sea day. Even though school was on the coast, training was in pools except for one day a week when we were taken to a beach – and I missed my slot.

I sigh and remember standing by the school fence with Tabby, staring at the endless blue below us. Both of us were hungry for the sea, but that wasn't all. Not on my part, anyway. I wanted to swim, yes, but not alone; I wanted Tabby to be with me, too.

I wish again that I'd told Becker to give her a message. She'll notice I'm not there and ask, won't she?

Unless she didn't feel the same way. Maybe I made up what I saw in her eyes because I wanted to see it. Nadya – the sports psychologist – came along then and interrupted us; maybe if she hadn't, I'd have done or said something. I don't know.

It seemed every time I was alone with Tabby, one of the staff just happened to come along. Almost like they were trying to keep us apart.

Now that's being both paranoid and trying to blame them for me not having the nerve to say how I feel to Tabby. Next time I see her, I'll do it.

For now, I try to put it out of my mind, to go blank. I close my eyes and pretend I can still see even though my eyes are shut. Strange things appear then disappear, tracing random paths in darkness. Fronds wave as if in a breeze, eyes peek out from behind, then vanish in the darkness . . .

It's a forest, the underwater kind. Seaweed tethered to rocks below drifts lazily with the currents, brushes against my skin. Makes me shiver.

I'm hiding.

Something searches for me, wants me, wants my flesh in its teeth.

If I'm hidden, then so is the searcher. Not being able to see where it is fills me with fear; I'll stumble into it, not be able to get away in time. I'm panicking, wanting to swim up and out.

No. Me breaking cover is what it wants. Stay hidden.

I swim deeper into the forest.

6

Wake up.

My eyes open but I'm disoriented, part of me still scared, hiding underwater in my dream, and part here, now. Flashes of light through the window dazzle my eyes, followed in an instant by a crash of thunder so loud my ears are ringing, even as after-images make me blink. A storm – a ferocious storm. Is that what woke me?

Or my phone – it's ringing, too.

I fumble for it. 'Hello?'

'Hi, Denzi.' It's Dad.

'What's up?'

'A hurricane has hit southern England.'

'*What*? Seriously?'

'Sorry to wake you, I . . .'

'What is it?'

'I just had to hear your voice, Denzi. It's your school: that whole stretch of coast. It's been inundated by storm surge. I'm so glad you weren't there.'

'Oh my God. Is everyone OK – did they get out?' *Tabby.*

'I don't know. I'll tell you if I can find out. That's not all, there's also been—'

There's a particularly massive crash of thunder that drowns out what he is saying. And then the line goes dead.

I look at the screen: no network.

I just sit there, stunned. One minute I was asleep, the next . . . this thing I can't get my head around. Did that really happen? Did Dad call and tell me . . . a hurricane, the school? Is Tabby OK? No, this can't be, it can't . . .

Get a grip. Look at your phone. Recent calls, and there it is: Dad did call, it wasn't a jet lag-induced-dream. There's still no network, so I can't call him back to find out what else he was going to tell me. Find a landline?

I flick the light switch; nothing. Power is out, too.

I look out the window to darkness – there are no lights anywhere, until massive streaks of lightning once again light up the sky. I've never seen lightning like this before – it goes on and on, with branches that stretch across the sky. All at once rain comes, lashing down and drowning the world.

'Denzi!' My name is being shouted down the hall.

I feel my way to my door and step into the hallway.

I hear someone swearing, then there is torch light, getting closer. It's Oliver, with Apple close behind him.

'Come on. We're going to the panic room.'

'The what?'

'Panic room! It'll be safer.'

There's another flash and his face . . . once I see it, I don't ask anything else, just follow him and Apple down the stairs. He looked completely freaked. We go through a door and then another one – it's heavy, reinforced? He pulls and bolts it behind us. Flicks some switches and there are lights.

'There's a generator,' he says.

He collapses into a chair, shaking his head.

'Dad, what is it?' Apple says.

'A hurricane. It's hit New York. Might be coming this way.'

'What the actual?' she says, then raises a hand to her shocked face. 'Emmie. My girlfriend. She's there – shopping with her mom.'

'There's also been a hurricane off the south coast of England,' I say. 'I was just talking to Dad when the phone cut off.'

The three of us look at each other and it's like we think the same thought, same moment.

Apple finds her voice first. 'Dad? Those letters. They said natural disasters in the US and the UK. Didn't they?'

'How could anybody cause a hurricane?' he says. 'Let alone two of them.'

'That's crazy. Isn't it?' I say.

The lights brighten. The power is back on.

'If it *is* possible,' Oliver says, 'I'm going to find out.'

7

Oliver lets us out of the panic room once he's checked and rechecked all the weather reports; the hurricane is meant to be slowing, faltering, and won't make it this far. He's called the hospital and everything is OK there, so Leila is all right, too. It's still pouring rain, but the thunder and lightning are first distant, then gone.

I'm on the sofa with Apple, news on. Mobile networks are back and I try to call Dad; it goes to message. He texts moments later that he's in a COBRA meeting; he'll try to find out what he can about school and get back as soon as he can.

'Any news?' Apple says, and I show her the text. 'What's COBRA?'

'An emergency meeting in the Cabinet Office Briefing Rooms. Must be about the hurricane.' I marvel that he's texting me in the middle of *that* – it'd likely be with the Prime Minister, key advisors.

She checks her phone again and shakes her head. Still no reply from her girlfriend in New York. Now and then she closes her eyes, lips moving without sound: praying, she says when I ask. Raised as I was without going to church, that kind of thing usually makes me feel uncomfortable, but not today.

The letter Oliver told us about last night is all over the news: every paper and TV station and government office received it yesterday. It was sent by a group calling itself The Circle; they said they were going to cause natural disasters in the US and the UK, and then – bam – the next day: two hurricanes. They are demanding immediate action to radically reduce emissions and stop all forms of extraction of oil and gas, or more disasters will follow. Eco-terrorists, they're being called.

'Can they really cause hurricanes?' Apple says. 'How?'

'I don't know,' I say.

'If they can, nowhere near the coast is safe.'

'I need to get home. Can I use your laptop?'

She gives it to me and I look for flights. 'There's nothing: flights are cancelled all over the area. Airports are shut because of high winds, flooded runways, or both.'

Apple edges her cold hand into mine. Hour after hour, we watch.

The footage is unbelievable. It must be bad enough in England, but hitting New York with a hurricane?

It's devastation.

They say it was a category four hurricane. Winds up to a hundred and fifty miles per hour blew out windows, took off roofs, tossed debris around like missiles, and that wasn't even the worst of it. The hurricane pushed storm surge into New York Harbour and the harbour acted as a funnel, making the water surge ever higher, almost like a tsunami. It being high tide made it even worse. Brooklyn and Staten Island were hit hard; the East River and Hudson River have merged over lower Manhatten. Highways, subways and railway tunnels are all flooded, tunnels and bridges unusable. Millions of people live there and they're cut off, trapped, while rain is still falling and waters rising.

And there was no time to warn anyone what was coming. There wasn't a tropical storm being tracked and its risk assessed to consider giving an order to evacuate. It's like the hurricane came from nowhere.

Apple checks her phone again. 'Still no reply,' she says.

'Maybe the network is down there.'

'Maybe.'

'When Dad called, he told me my school had been *inundated* – that was the word he used. That's where I'd be now if I wasn't here.'

What about everyone who was there? Did they get out? Especially Tabby. There was something about her, I can't even begin to explain why – I *need* to see her again. She can't be gone. Can she?

'We watch this,' Apple says, 'and it's horrible, it's real. It's just as horrible and real when it happens in the Philippines or Caribbean, but even though all the experts say climate change will make things like this happen more often and be worse, no one here does anything about it. Is that what this group, The Circle, is trying to get across?'

'I don't know. Maybe. Helluva way to make a point.'

'Maybe the only way. Make the effects of climate change feel more of a personal threat and governments might act. Anyhow, that's the sort of thing Leila would say.'

'Is it?'

'You really don't know her, do you?'

'I guess not.'

My phone rings; I glance at the screen and answer.

'Dad?'

'Hi, Denzi. I've only got a moment, just wanted to make sure you're OK?'

'Fine, just wanting to know about school. Any news?'

'Sorry, but it's not looking good. That part of the coast was completely flooded by storm surge. They're checking the area by boat and helicopter, looking for survivors. Everything is cut off. If I learn anything else I'll let you know.'

'Dad? There's a girl who was at swim school. Her name is Tabby – also known as Holly. I think Tabby is her middle name. I didn't get her surname. I really need to know if she's OK.'

'I'll see if I can find out.'

They've found some experts on hurricanes to interview on TV. They talk about how they're formed, speculate whether causing a hurricane deliberately is possible. They don't think it can be done – you can tell from what they say and don't say, even though they don't come right out and say so.

'But if hurricanes can't be caused on purpose, then how did this group send letters with their threats before they happened?' Apple says.

'Exactly. And they can't figure out why they didn't see them coming. There was no storm that gradually grew into a hurricane, it was just, *bam*, out of nowhere.'

I'm on Apple's laptop again, trying to make sense of it all. 'Hurricanes form when the surface water temperature is over 26.5 degrees Celsius – that's 79 degrees Fahrenheit. Water evaporates and condenses, there is low pressure at the centre and winds swirl around it. So, it seems that the main thing to do to make a hurricane is to heat a bunch of surface water.'

27

'Yeah, but how?'

'Ocean temperatures are already higher than they used to be because of climate change, but not high enough for hurricanes to form spontaneously where they did. Chemicals – like sodium – dumped in the water would heat it, but that doesn't sound like something they'd do if they want to protect the environment. The other possibility is microwaves.'

'Microwaves? You'd need a rather big microwave oven for that.'

'They think it can be done remotely.'

'This all sounds like science fiction, doesn't it?'

'Yeah. But either they caused the hurricanes, or they are better at detecting them than the government is, saw them coming and took the credit. Which seems most likely?'

Apple's phone beeps with a text. She pounces on it, grins widely. 'It's Emmie. She's OK, she's OK.' And then she's crying and I'm awkwardly patting her shoulder, happy for her but still wanting – *needing* – a moment like this of my own.

Tabby, where are you?

8

The roads are chaos. Even though the hurricane never stretched as far as DC, the thunderstorms at its edges have brought down trees and the heavy rain has flooded low-lying areas.

We haven't been able to visit Leila today because of this, but then, just before dinner she's home, in a taxi that has somehow made it through.

'What are you doing here?' Oliver says. 'Didn't they say you should stay for a few more days?'

'I checked myself out. They just want to be paid more of their astronomical rates! I'm fine, but I'd go crazy if I stayed there any longer.'

And she looks fine, she really does. You'd never know she'd been hooked up to beeping machines, unreachable, just a day ago. Even the bruises on the side of her face are almost gone, and the bandage is missing from her forehead.

Oliver and Apple fuss, get her to sit down. I hang back but her eyes find mine.

'So, I didn't imagine it: you *were* at the hospital, Denzi.'

'Yep. Came all the way to see you.'

'You said you wanted to ask me some things.'

'You heard what I said? All of it?'

'I think so. Mostly about swimming. You left training to come?'

29

'Yeah. But Dad called, said that school – that is both where I go to school term time, and where the summer swim training is held – has been flooded by storm surge. He's just glad I wasn't there.'

'So, he can thank me for that. First time for everything.' There it is – the hostility I always feel from her, and I get that it is directed at Dad and not me as such, but that isn't how it feels. What was I thinking, wanting to talk to her? Nothing has changed.

Before I can think what I should or shouldn't say, dinner is being brought in by Oliver.

After dinner, without discussion, we head to the sofas facing the TV news which has been on all day.

'I've got some news of my own for you,' Oliver says. 'I'm going to New York in the morning. Apple is in charge.'

She claps her hands. 'At last!'

'Only because Denzi will be leaving at some point and Leila might be concussed.'

'What will you be doing there?' I say.

'Disaster reporting, but focusing on its slimy underbelly.'

'Sounds like fun,' Apple says.

'Who do they help first?' Oliver says. 'The white, the rich, the photogenic. Who gets forgotten? The poor, the weak, people of colour like Apple and me. No matter the lip service paid to Black Lives Matter by the authorities, it needs to be shouted out again and again. I need to be there, to hold them accountable.'

'How do you know it will be that way?'

'I know.'

Leila holds up a hand for us to listen, turns up the TV with the remote.

'. . . and now from the White House.'

The President is at the big desk in the oval office, saying the usual stuff about sympathy and help for all those affected. Oliver makes gagging noises in the background.

'Now to this organisation calling itself The Circle. We don't know yet if they could have caused the hurricanes that struck New York and England so savagely, but rest assured, if they did, they will regret it. This is an attack not just on the great city of New York but on our entire way of life and all we Americans hold dear.'

He goes on with more of the same and Leila grabs the remote and mutes it.

'Not a single word – did you hear that? – not a single word about climate change, global warming, any of it,' she says.

'Do you think it's right to hold a gun to someone's head until they switch from fossil fuels to an electric car?' Oliver says.

'Of course not.'

'How about this: is it right to take away the only means families have to make a living, to feed their children? Even if it is in dirty industry?'

'How about if the dirty industry is poisoning their children and destroying any chance they have to live off the ruined land as they used to?'

'Is it right to stop poor countries from extracting their way out of poverty?'

Apple hands me a bowl of popcorn. 'This is better than the movies,' she says, in a low aside. Oliver throws a pillow at her

31

head, but she ducks and it goes over the back of the sofa.

'Yes. Stop them from extracting to save the world,' Leila says. 'Compensate them fairly for doing so.'

'That will never happen. It's not the American way; and I don't see the UK or the EU stepping up to that plate either.'

'They bloody well should, all of them.'

'They won't. Especially since they're either denying there is a problem, or ignoring it whenever it's inconvenient.'

Leila clenches her fists. 'It's this idiot in the White House and his idiot friends who insist that climate change was made up to attack the American way of life. What is that even supposed to *mean*?'

'Having it all and not giving a damn who it hurts?' Oliver says. He turns to me. 'What do you think of our president, Denzi?'

Caught. 'Well, ah . . .'

He laughs. 'Nothing you can say will offend in this house. Best be a little careful outside these walls, though, until you're home.'

'I just can't believe they really think climate change is a hoax,' I say. 'With the heat waves, the fires, the glaciers melting, the sea levels rising?'

'It's easy to believe what you want to believe,' he says. 'Besides, oil and gas lobbyists have been whispering nonsense in their ears for years.'

'Is that even legal?'

'Oh, yes. You can believe and say what you like on this side of the pond, and truth is a commodity to be bought and sold like any other. And it's hard to argue with an industry whose dollars have been keeping them in office with campaign contributions.'

'Again, is that even legal?'

'Well, there is legal, and then there is legal. There is always a way to get money where you want it, if you have enough of it to begin with.'

'Apart from the nonsense being whispered – even shouted – in important ears, more and more I'm not sure we've been handling the situation as we should,' Leila says. 'Trying to work within their framework according to their rules is not getting us anywhere. Whenever we think we've gone a step forwards – delayed a pipeline, banned fracking in sensitive areas – we go two steps back somewhere else.'

'Their framework is the only framework.'

'Then it needs to change.'

'Yes! Back to an all-out attack on our American way of life,' he says, and as I'm watching Oliver and Leila spar with words, I'm wondering what Leila was like with Dad. Dad has his own opinions on stuff but is never as direct as the way they are talking now. It's always quietly, softly, politely, even if no one else is listening.

Leila and Oliver *match*, in a way I can't see that Leila and Dad ever did. On paper the middle-class Brit who went to Oxford and the cynical American journalist might not sound like a good fit, but in reality their words sound the same in different accents. Both want to fight for change, to make a difference, and the reserved, English part of me is uneasy with that, even as the rest of me wishes I was the same. Am I too much like Dad and not enough like Leila?

If I am, whose fault is that?

My phone vibrates in my pocket, and I take it out – it's Jax.

Hey you, your dad asked me to check flights. Looks like things are

33

open again tomorrow, can get you on one that leaves early evening. Is that ok or do you want to stay for a while?

I don't hesitate for long. Even without swim school to go back to, I don't want to be here any longer than I have to be. I still want − *need* − to swim. But most of all, I want to go home.

Early evening tomorrow sounds good.

OK, will book and email details.

They come through soon after.

I wait for Oliver and Leila to both be drawing breath at the same time and jump in. 'They've booked a flight home for me tomorrow at six,' I say. 'Is that OK?'

'A.m. or p.m.?' Apple says.

'P.m.'

'I can take you,' she says.

Do I imagine this or does Leila look disappointed?

It's late at night and I'm on my phone, looking at everything I can find online about the hurricane that hit the south coast of England. The news here focused pretty exclusively on New York.

The maps on the news sites show that school was bang in the middle of the part of the coast worst affected by the hurricane and storm surge. Huge areas are still cut off.

The thought of the sea climbing that cliff and flooding the school? It just seems so unbelievable.

Tabby could be all right. People escape things in ways you can't believe all the time, and it's not like she can't swim.

My phone beeps.

There's a text from Theo, a classmate; he's in most of my A-levels. Nice enough, but the sort who insists on knowing everything about everybody, which makes me never want to tell him anything.

Are you ok, mate? Heard about the school. Weren't you there this summer for swimming training?

I relent and answer.

I'm fine. Wasn't there when it happened.

Go on the school chat and tell everyone, all right? People have been worried. Also about all the school staff who were there over summer.

Guilt hits me. I'd been so focused on the swim school and Tabby I hadn't been thinking of all the staff – maintenance, kitchens, grounds – who are there during both term time and summer.

I go to the school website and log in.

There's a short post from Mr Khan, the head teacher. He says that the entire school grounds have been flooded by storm surge; they don't have a full picture yet of the extent of damage or who was there or what happened to them. More updates are promised when they know more.

And I'm surprised how many messages there are to me. I don't fit in to any of the cliques, really, but so many people knew I was there and are worried that I'm touched.

Really sorry for not checking in sooner. I'm fine, I wasn't there. I answer over and over again, then post the same to the chat page.

I go back to news about the hurricanes, but then, tired of all the misery, I start looking up hurricane survivor stories. In the mix are several links: *Girl Rescued by Dolphins. Miracle Dolphin Girl. Lucky to be Alive: Girl Saved by Dolphins.*

They all have some variation of the same story: that an unconscious girl was saved by dolphins and rescued from the sea by a fisherman. It happened some miles east along the coast from the school. There are uncertain photos, blurry, in the rain, that seem to show a girl being supported in the sea by a row of dolphins. Surely that can't be? Someone's photoshopped this for their fifteen minutes of fame.

The girl isn't named and the photo quality isn't great, but if I squint at it . . . well. It *could* be Tabby. She has the right proportions, the same long, dark hair.

But maybe I'm just clutching at hope – wanting a miracle, no matter how unlikely, on a day when they're in short supply.

The sun – so intense. The railing is hot where I lean on it, looking below, at gentle waves lapping against the supports. There is salt on my lips and the taste is like a drug. Now I'm holding the railing tight to stop myself from climbing on to it and diving down, down, from the pier.

I'm about to make myself walk back down the pier to the shore, to get in the sea the safe way, when they come. The pod of dolphins surfaces some distance out, dives down and disappears. And I'm hoping they will come this way, and waiting, waiting, and then – below – so close, they surface again. One turns, seems to look up at me as I look down at him: a challenge?

Up and over the railing, I hurtle through the air, down, down, down . . . but now the sea is gone. I'm falling, falling, into nothingness.

9

I get the summons after breakfast the next morning.

'Denzi? Come on, let's talk,' Leila says, and I follow her down a hall and through a door to what looks like a cross between an office and a gym. There are a few chairs and she points at one and sits on the other.

She must see me looking around at the gym stuff. 'I like to think on the treadmill,' she says. 'Or on my bike, but maybe I'll stick to the stationary one for a while.'

'Are you still feeling OK?'

'Well, oddly enough, yes. I don't think what happened to me even rates as high as being a mild concussion. I was there on the side of the road, knocked off my bike. I'd banged my head; without a helmet, things would have been different for sure, but I was honestly feeling just fine. The driver insisted on calling an ambulance. Then somewhere on the way to the hospital, I fell asleep. And then I woke up when you were talking to me. That's all it seemed like to me – that I'd had a nice, long nap. I don't even have a headache or anything.'

'Well, I'm glad you're all right.'

'Thanks. So. What did you want to talk about?'

And I'm unsure what to say, or how to say it – or if I even still want to.

'Just say whatever is on your mind. Something your dad never managed,' she says, with such an acid tone that I can't not react.

'Look, I get that you got divorced and both of you have moved on. But you are always so hostile about Dad and it seems to include me, too.'

She grins. 'Thought that would make you talk.'

I'm surprised. She did that on purpose?

'Hmmm. Well, I guess I just want to know *why*. Why you left. Not Dad, I get that, but you left me too. You went so far away you almost never saw me. Why?'

'Hasn't your dad ever talked to you about this?'

I shake my head. 'Not really. Somehow, he can't.'

Both her hostility and smiles are gone; there is just sadness. 'I find it hard to talk about, too. But I'll try. Did your dad ever tell you that we tried and tried for a baby, but no luck?'

I shake my head.

She sighs. 'And then came IVF. That failed, too. But what it did do was completely mess around with my body, my mind. The hormones and stuff; the hoping, then the failure. It was awful. And then your dad found this new clinic to try. And I didn't want to; I'd had enough. But he talked me into it somehow. And that time, it worked – I got pregnant.'

'Were you happy then?'

'Yes. But it felt weirdly like it wasn't me, wasn't my baby. And I was sick the whole time. And everyone said, when the baby comes, it'll all be worth it.

'And you were perfect. Beautiful. And I loved you.' Her eyes glisten and she blinks, hard. 'But I couldn't cope with being a mother. The doctors said I had postpartum depression. I think they got it wrong: it was more like PTSD – post traumatic stress disorder – from the IVF and the rest of it.

'Anyhow, I was a mess, on all these tablets and kept feeling worse and worse. But the most awful part of it was that I was a failure at the one thing your dad wanted. And that was when I found out about Jax.'

My eyes widen. This, I wasn't expecting. 'Dad was seeing Jax when you were still together? When I was a baby?'

'Yes. I confronted him; he denied it. At first. Later he said he never meant for it to happen, that it was just who he was. That it had taken him a while to understand. But rightly or wrongly, I felt that your dad had tricked me to give him a child, so I left him with you and got as far away as I could. But that wasn't fair to you, Denzi. And I'm sorry.'

A tear spills and runs down her cheek and she rubs it away, and I feel like I should reach out to her – hold her hand or something – but can't bring myself to do it. I'm so shocked at what she said about Dad that I don't know what to say.

'Maybe I shouldn't have told you.' She shakes her head. 'Denzi, that is just my side of things. Talk to your dad about it, OK?'

'Thanks. And I will.'

I'm reeling from what she said, the emotion with which she said it, but at the same time something niggles at the back of my mind: IVF . . . Tabby. What was that clinic she mentioned, the one she thought was also at the swim school?

'What was the clinic you went to called?'

'The Penrose Clinic.'

10

My plane rushes down the runway, lifts off.

Apple's insistence that I keep in touch is still in my ears. She seemed upset to see me go, and I was surprised to feel a wrench inside, too. We never got along when we were younger and I wasn't there for long this time, but with everything – the hospital, Leila being in a coma, the hurricanes and us both worrying about people – it felt, I don't know, *intense*. I've never minded being an only child, but maybe having a sister, even a far-away stepsister, could be a good thing.

DC disappears below and I'm waiting, *longing*, for the moment when blue sea stretches out below us. There's an ache inside at being away from it for so long. But as we ascend, we go through clouds and soon all I can see below is grey.

I sigh, sit back and think through what Leila said about Dad and Jax. Part of me insists she's lying, she must be, that Dad wouldn't do that – cheat on her with Jax when she'd had this baby he wanted and was so unwell.

But everything she said felt real.

And it was the Penrose Clinic, the same clinic Tabby's parents went to; the same clinic Tabby thought was hidden at the swim school. Even if she was mistaken about that, what are the chances of us both being there, both being IVF babies from the same clinic?

It could be some weird coincidence, but somehow, I don't believe it. Coincidences can happen, sure, but when I put it together with the other coincidences – the weird way so many parents of the swimmers were involved one way or another in the oil and gas industry, how at least three of them were scouted out of the blue without having trained before – it's too much to believe it all happened by random chance.

It's almost like somebody set out to *collect* us, to bring us together.

It sounds ridiculous when I frame it like that. Why would anyone do that?

The one thing I want to do is talk to Tabby about it. I'd felt that there was some part of the story about herself that she wasn't telling; it might make all this fit together and make some kind of sense.

Maybe that is something I can't do, may never be able to do, and the emptiness that I feel inside to think I may never see Tabby again has nothing to do with solving these riddles.

Where are you, Tabby?

Part 2
Tabby

11

It's a long journey and I mean to use it to think things through, but it's hard to organise my thoughts. When I try to think about the horror I saw at the school – what it *was*, and what it might mean – I can't face it, not yet.

I'm past tired and into exhausted, and my head still feels muddled from being drugged in the hospital. So many stations are closed because of floods, wind damage, storm surge – or all three – that getting anywhere, even places not directly affected, is complicated. When I found out it was going to take a train and four buses to get from Bristol to Tintagel, I almost cried.

One step at a time.

I'm on the third bus now, the one to Bude where I make the last change. It's harder to be anonymous on a half empty bus than on a busy train; I carefully keep my eyes away from my fellow passengers and hope they'll do the same.

I don't know Bude, but as we get closer we are nearing the sea; I can feel it. When we finally pull in and get off the bus, I can taste it.

I rush down the road and now my eyes can see it, too. I don't remember when my next bus is; I don't care.

It's a sandy beach, crowded on a hot evening like this: swimmers, sunbathers, parents with little kids playing in the sand.

I falter a moment, remembering building sandcastles with Cate. Knocking them over and starting again.

I shake my head. Cate wasn't my mother; I may have thought she was for most of my life, but she wasn't. And she's gone: I have to rely on myself.

Shoes off, I hold them in one hand and walk on the hot sand down to the water's edge. It's so calm, it's hard to believe what happened on the south coast just days ago – the thundering rain, winds, storm surge – and so many people died. Simone, too. My real mother, even though I didn't know her for long. And what happened to everyone at the swim school?

There were so many who could be lost: friends, like Ariel, and many others I'd never even spoken to. But there is one in my mind above all the others: Denzi. He'd disappeared before the hurricane. I can only hope he was safely away, but the pain from thinking that something could have happened to him makes me want to disappear into the sea and never come back.

No. I push it away for later and focus on here. Now.

I step in, just far enough to have waves lap at the tops of my ankles, then another step, and another, until the water is halfway to my knees. I have to concentrate to stop myself from running forwards, diving under.

I feel . . . *exposed* on the land. Even just having my feet in the sea like this makes me feel a little better. And a little cooler, too. The sun is beating down and my clothes stick to my skin. I shake the scarf off my head, shove it in my backpack.

What would people make of it if I did what I want, clothes, backpack and all? Just dived under, and then later wandered back to get on a bus, dripping wet?

Not the way to stay unnoticed.

I reach into my pocket for my travel details. Only one more bus, I can do this.

But only if I hurry.

12

I'm breathless when I get to the bus just as the doors are closing. The driver sees me, my hands together in a *please* gesture. He shakes his head but opens the door.

'You're late. I've only let you on because it's the last bus.'

'Thank you, I appreciate it.'

'And?' A long pause, a sigh. 'Where are you going?'

'Oh. Sorry. Tintagel.' I buy a ticket, sit down. Only remembering then that I'd taken the scarf off my hair when I was at the beach and it's still tucked in my bag.

I can't help feeling like everywhere I go, there are eyes – looking at me, assessing me, maybe remembering me well enough that if a photo ends up on the news, like the last time I was missing, they might say, 'Hey, I saw that girl on the bus the other day.'

Just wearing a scarf isn't enough. I need to do something to change the way I look.

Anyhow, it isn't the police I'm worried about the most. Wading in the sea seems to have revived me enough to face what I've been skirting around in my thoughts all day.

That night. The darkness, the dread. The sound. *Thump-thump. Thump-thump.* It drums in my memory now along with my heartbeat.

The *thing* making the sound.

Banging against the bars of her underwater cage with a rock. *Thump-thump.* Not a girl, not a fish: something in between. I force myself to focus, to remember: her human-like face, deformed arms, the rest covered in scales, not skin.

Blank eyes in a face that I knew: Ariel. My friend. Part of them alike enough to be twins, but the rest? I shudder.

The Penrose Clinic and The Circle are entwined like snakes – I know it. Cate was murdered before she could tell anyone. And now they're after me.

What am I going to do?

Most people would say, go to the police. But raised as I was by Cate – always on the run, never trusting authority? I flinch to even think it.

There was that DCI – Palmer was his name. He came to tell me Cate died, and later, to ask me about The Circle. He seemed OK, and he wouldn't have come to ask me about The Circle if he was involved with them, would he?

No. I can't do it. Cate was murdered in prison. How can I trust the same won't happen to me?

Cate, I miss you so much.

I'd been angry when I found out she'd taken me away from my parents. After so many years apart I was only just starting to get to know my real mum and dad; even if I couldn't bring myself to call them that, I was starting to understand what they could mean to me. But Simone – my mum – she's gone.

I try to push that away, to not think about it, but it's too late: I'm caught in my memory and can't escape. Our car swept off the road by storm surge from the sea. Filling with water. How she fought and struggled to get us out. Until she *stopped*. Still, silent. Eyes staring but not seeing, and I thought I'd be joining her soon.

Somehow I survived, woke up in a hospital bed with no idea how I got there. Then I saw that news story about a girl who was rescued by dolphins: is that possible? Was it really me? I wish I remembered what happened.

And what about my dad, Ali? He was missing after our house flooded, presumed drowned. What about everyone at swim school? Did any survive? Would I have drowned if I'd stayed? Ariel, Zara, so many others whose names I didn't even know; I'm sick to think they might all have died. And what about Denzi and Isha? Neither of them were there those last days. I'd been told sometimes swimmers choose to leave, and that made sense for Isha – after she nearly drowned in a tank during training – but not Denzi.

I'd been convinced he wouldn't leave voluntarily without telling me; that we had this connection, that he cared. Maybe I'm kidding myself and imagined it. At least if I did, that could mean that he chose to leave, that he is safe.

Focus: think.

I found the missing piece of the puzzle – *why* Cate took me from my parents – when I saw the Penrose Clinic four-leaf clover on Elodie's shoulder. Elodie, Simone's mum, my grandmother – I thought she cared about me, that I could rely on her, but I was wrong. She was even drugging me in the hospital so I couldn't remember things or tell anyone. I fought against it, managed to get away. To run.

And now I'm going back to Cornwall, to one of the places I lived with Cate. To Jago, my friend. Will the police think to look for me there?

They're busy just now – so much has happened, people are dead and missing in high numbers from the hurricane. If I can change my appearance – my hair – that might be enough to fool anyone who sees a missing-person photo. Last time I had my arm in a cast, but now there's nothing like that to make me stand out in a crowd. Small places do notice newcomers more, so I'll be something they're used to – a backpacker, walking the coastal path. At least the parts of it that aren't under water.

And what about The Circle?

Now that Cate is gone I might be the only one who knows that the Penrose Clinic is a front for The Circle.

They were looking for me just hours ago. The proof was there: Malina, one of the swim school coaches, chasing me at Bristol station – it was sheer luck I got away. Malina, who had The Circle's tattoo on her shoulder.

Well, maybe I'm hoping they'll think I'm not dumb enough to come back here.

That makes me smile at myself. So, I am – just dumb enough – but I've got to be careful now in all other ways. Stop running for buses or acting weird on busy beaches. Stay out of sight until I find Jago.

And then?

And *then*: I'll go from there. I'll work out what to do, with or without his help.

13

It's evening when I step off the bus in Tintagel. Still hot. I trudge along the familiar road, through the village, to the rocky lane that leads to the castle. Despite how tired I am, I start to breathe easier, to walk faster. I know exactly the place where I'll first see the sea and without meaning to, I'm rushing, half running.

There.

Blue sparkles below, as far as for ever; as near as now if I hurry. It's a still day, the surface like glass from this distance. Nothing like the stormy seas just days ago on the south coast, but not even that can make me hesitate.

I *want, need,* to feel the sea. Not just dipping my feet in like I did earlier, either. It's been too long. It's so hard to resist, to make myself think of anything else, but I can't rush headlong to the beach by the castle. It's a popular place; too many people will be there.

This is what I must do: take a right on the coastal path and walk. It's only a few miles. Go past the busy places to our beach – mine and Jago's. Wait for the tide coming in and people leaving, and swim there tonight. It's somehow right that it should be there.

I set out, holding myself to a slow, measured pace. Drinking in the view as I go. Breathing in and tasting air that moments ago may have kissed the surface of the sea; breathing out so it may do so again.

This section of the path cuts inland and then back to wander around the curve of the coastline. Other walkers – kids, dogs – go past now and then, the numbers dwindling the further I go.

The sun is getting lower in the sky when I finally reach the steep steps down to our beach. It's probably an hour or two before sunset. The tide is coming in – soon the sandy beach will be completely underwater, but that doesn't matter to me.

I head down the steps, trying to take care on the uneven stone, although I can't help but rush. It's so close.

There are just a few people on the beach: a couple lying on the sand to one side, a man with a dog to the other. The couple are getting up now and shaking their towels. The man is throwing a ball for the dog into the water and it bounds after it, splashing with great excitement, grabs the ball and runs back to him for it to be thrown again.

I hang well back, go off to the side away from the steps, and scramble up sun-warmed rocks. I make myself wait, but it's *so* hard.

I want to be in the sea in a way that goes beyond my need for anything else – food, sleep, I can do without. This, I can't. Why am I this way? I always just accepted that I am different to other people – that it's the way I am, like how some people are tall and some have green eyes. When it was me and Cate on our own, things made sense. Now that I've seen more of the world, I'm not so sure.

And it's not just how I feel about it, either. I can hold my breath for a very long time – twenty minutes or more – and sometimes when I swim, I'm not myself. It's like something inside of me changes and takes over. Malina told me it was dangerous.

That if I forget who I am I may forget to breathe, too – and I've done that. I had to be dragged up to breathe by some of my friends. I could have died. I couldn't remember what happened, not in the way memory usually works – it was more feelings, colours. But it was like part of me wanted to stay underwater for ever.

Half girl – half fish.

I shudder. I'm nothing like what I saw, yet . . . *no. Not now.* I can't think about this in any sort of rational way when I'm waiting like this for what I need.

The couple leaves.

Does that dog ever get tired of chasing his ball? He doesn't seem to, but eventually his human has had enough and they start up the steps.

They're soon out of sight.

I don't want to be seen going for a swim by anyone above. The last thing I need is for some well-intentioned walker to call the coastguard if they see me disappear too long under water.

I wait, breathing in tune with the sea. The sun is beginning to set. The tide has reached its highest point and is starting to turn. I stash my backpack, shoes, between some rocks, clamber down to the water's edge, shivering even though it is still hot. It's like I have a fever and now that it is so close to breaking, I want to draw out this feeling.

Be careful, Tabby, I remind myself. *Remember who you are.*

The water, so deliciously silken and cool on my feet, ankles. The current is pulling at my legs as I go deeper, tempting me, and there is nothing holding me back now.

I breathe out fully, in fully, then dive under the waves, push

54

away from the rocks and let the current have its way.

Further, deeper; skimming along sand that is beach at low tide, then rocks and out of the cove. Joy courses through me. The water is colder, swifter, out of the sheltered cove. Is it the drop in temperature that jolts my awareness?

Be reasonable. Stay safe. I surface and breathe, surprised to see how far out I've got on one breath when I'm so weary.

OK. Back we go.

I swim across the cove at an angle so I'm not fighting the current head on, then turn and do it again and again. In this way I zigzag closer to the shore until I can stand and walk out of the water, regret in every step at what I'm leaving behind and what I am now: exposed on the earth again.

I glance at the path above and have to squint to see. It's past dusk now. Even assuming anyone is walking by above this late, I doubt they can see me if I can't see them.

I clamber up the still-warm rocks to my stuff, every sense alive, as if that swim was what I needed to shake off the last effects of whatever drugs Elodie was giving me to keep me quiet in the hospital. I'm awake, alert. Listening, feeling – my heart beating, the rough warm rock, the movement of air on my skin. *Poised*, too, to deal with any threat.

I'd been so focused on getting here that I haven't thought much further ahead. To find Jago I need to watch this beach; I need to do it without drawing attention to myself. But right now, more than anything, I need sleep.

Before it gets too dark to see at all, I climb back up the stone steps to the path above.

What now?

Off the coastal path nearby there are fields, separated by dry stone walls. There is no real cover – it's too open, really, unless I walk further – but somehow I'm unwilling to leave this area behind.

Instead I climb over a stone wall dividing fields at a low point, drop to the other side. Feel my way along in gathering shadows to a dip in the ground.

I bought a second-hand tarp on my way to the station in Bristol. I take it out of my pack, spread it on the ground. I search through my bag for my bottle of water, sandwiches, to have a picnic in the darkness, leaning against the wall.

I still feel keyed up, on high alert, as if some danger is nearby. What? A curious seagull, maybe? A few mosquitos? It's being out here on my own in the dark, that's all it is. I've camped rough more than a few times before, but always with Cate. Never alone.

I make myself lie down on the tarp, pull it around me, use my pack as a pillow. It's too warm really even for the tarp, but I feel too exposed when I try to push it away.

I can hear Cate's voice now, as if she were here: she'd say, *Play pretend*, and we'd imagine ourselves where we wanted to be. But my imagination won't keep me safe from Elodie and The Circle.

Cate always said that if I'm uncertain of what path to take, the four points of our compass will show me the way:

Sun . . . Sea . . . Earth . . . Sky

I focus on each in turn.

The earth supports me under the sky; the sun is on its night-time quest and will be back in the morning, leaving the moon in its place. Though the sea is too far to touch and see, it whispers music to me still. It is there, steady, always.

Try again. Cate's voice in my mind. *A different sort of pretend.*

I think about it for a while. OK. This tarp is actually a cloak of invisibility. No one is here, and even if someone was, they can't see me. Right?

Eyes closed, I imagine myself invisible.

I'm here, but no one can see me. It's the cruellest exile from all that I love. Even in the sea I only experience it fully if she lets go, and tonight she fought against it.

She could know me, I think, if she wanted to — but she doesn't want to. Why?

She should: she wants what I want.

Somehow, I will find a way to reach her, and show her this.

14

Wake up.

I open my eyes, awake in an instant, heart pounding. Was there a sound?

Laughter, voices, footsteps; I'm afraid to look out from my tarp to see who is there.

They get gradually louder, and then move away again.

Ah. That must be people on the coastal path.

I peek out into bright sunshine; by the sky it is around mid-morning. I must have been tired: I slept for ages.

I scan the fields around me; there are no signs of a farmer or anyone else.

Sit up, stretch. I'm stiff, uncomfortable, as if I've slept on the ground all night. Funny, that.

I get up, pull my hands through my hair. Scarf back on. Fold up the tarp and shove it in my bag, then walk along the stone wall to the low point where I climbed it last night.

I listen carefully, not wanting to be caught doing this. I can't hear anyone. I look over the wall in both directions: no one is in sight. I climb over the wall quickly to the path.

What now?

First, the beach. Jago *could* be there, right now. He used to meet me there after school in the afternoon, but it's summer holidays now. I've got no idea what he's doing – he might have a summer job. Or what if his family has gone away?

No. Don't think that.

What if that other group of teenagers who were here the last time I was here come, what then? Don't think about that either, I tell myself, but it's too late.

I'd been with Jago, talking, when they came up. They said some things that made me angry, and I left. Some of them stayed and fought with Jago, though I didn't know about that until later. The rest followed me.

I ran up the steps. They caught me, forced some awful spirit down my throat. I got away, ran up the path to the road without looking. I was hit by a car. Arm broken and taken to a hospital.

Everything followed on from that.

Cate arrested for kidnapping me. Going home to my birth parents, Simone and Ali.

Cate and Simone are both dead now. I flinch inside. Ali probably is, too. Even if he isn't, I can't go to him, not with Simone's mum Elodie in the mix.

Stop it, just stop it, Tabby. Focus on what needs doing, not the things you can't change.

There are a few people on the beach I can see from above; it's too far to tell for sure if Jago is one of them, though I doubt it. There are couples with kids, a few people on their own. One with a dog. At least there aren't any groups like that day.

I can't stop myself; I head down the steps.

When I get to the bottom for a closer look, Jago isn't there. I knew that really, didn't I?

Shoes off, I walk across the sand to the water's edge. I wade in until the highest point of the waves reaches up to my knees, falls back and rises again. I want to dive in like I did last night, but not with this many people about, watching.

I sit on the sand, legs stretched out. My feet are soon dry enough and I'm reaching for my shoes when there are running footsteps – a child, a boy, maybe six or seven years old. He stops in his tracks, staring.

'You've got funny feet. Do they help you swim?'

I look up, both dismayed and surprised. No quack, quack noises?

'Maybe. I don't know.'

There's a woman looking over.

'They're magic,' I say. 'It's a secret, OK?'

He grins. 'OK.'

'Robin?' a voice calls, and he runs back.

Well, if there is a better way to shout 'Tabby is here' than my webbed toes, I can't think what it is. I hope he'll keep the secret.

15

My stomach is rumbling by the time I get to the Spar in Boscastle.

I came here instead of Tintagel even though it is further away; I was in Tintagel yesterday and don't want to be seen over and again by the same people in case it makes them remember my face.

I must shop carefully; I don't know long the money I got for selling Simone's bracelet will last. Water bottles are heavy but I can't do without them. Basic food that'll keep, like crackers and peanut butter, apples, tins of tuna – the kind with a pull tab. Scissors for my hair.

I'm queueing to pay when I see the stand with the local newspaper, and there, on the front cover? Me. It's a photo from the welcome home party Simone and Ali had soon after I got there, and I'm clean, hair brushed and totally dressed up. Don't think I look much like that now, but I can't rely on no one recognising me – not when I was recognised before from photos in a newspaper. That time it was blurry, from CCTV, but I was still recognised. And OK, then I was wearing the same clothes as in the photos and had one arm in a cast, but even so.

How am I going to stay out of sight and find Jago at the same time?

I need some binoculars. When all I want to do is run and hide, I force myself to wander around, checking more shops.

Some touristy type shop sells cheap kids' ones. I try them. Not great but I think they'll do. I'm waiting to pay for them and a floppy sun hat, sunglasses and an 'I Love Cornwall' T-shirt – maybe a better sunny-day disguise than a scarf – when I hear a voice, one I know.

It's *her*, the girl who was with that group at the beach: the ones who chased me the last time I saw Jago. She works here? But the person ahead in the queue is asking her to show some jewellery in a cabinet. She goes to do that; another woman is at the counter.

I pay quickly and go.

I find public loos and lock myself in a cubicle. Shaking. Would she have recognised me? I don't know. If she did, and she saw that photo in the paper . . . *no*! Don't think about it.

Has anyone else had enough of a look at my face to recognise me from that photo?

Maybe on that last bus to Tintagel.

I gather my hair into a high ponytail on the top of my head. We never went to the hairdresser's. Cate used to call this a unicorn cut when she did it for me, but that was never more than a trim, an inch or two. Even when we were trying to look different, to not be seen, she never did what I'm about to do. Today I need a drastic change.

I take out the scissors I bought and start cutting into my thick hair just above where it is gathered together. It's hard, and not just because the scissors aren't very sharp and my hands are shaking. My long, dark hair is part of *me*. Something I hide behind, and having less of it will make me feel more exposed.

At last I finish hacking my way through it. Bet that looks *amazing*.

I hold my hair in my hands: there it is, maybe fifty centimetres – no longer part of me.

I make myself flush it away, hoping it won't back up the system. Put on my new T-shirt and shove the old one in my bag. Come out, wash hands and face, look in mirror.

Ugh. I tidy my hair with my hands as best I can, and it feels *wrong* – my fingers barely go through it and then nothing is there. I study myself in the mirror. It's *awful* and weird and something is choking inside me.

Get over it. It's just hair.

I do look different, right? And that's the whole point.

I put on the sunhat to hide it, and the sunnies too: there. I couldn't look more like a tourist. I'm either a master of disguise, or totally kidding myself.

That afternoon I use the binoculars to scan the beach every hour or so from different points along the path above, hoping no one is looking up and wondering why. Each time I *will* Jago: please be there. Each time I'm disappointed. And apart from needing to find him, I want, so much, to go back down to the beach myself. Being this close – able to see and taste it in the air – is torture. I'm hot, a bit queasy, my thoughts muddled, like a fever is taking hold; the cure is just there, down below me.

But I can't go to the beach and swim all day, every day, and stay unnoticed.

Just this once I could though, couldn't I?

My feet are heading for the way down before I get control.

No, *wait*.

Stay hidden until night.

16

When everyone, including the sun, has finally gone, I slip down the steep steps like a ghost. Stash my pack down deep between some rocks, and walk to the water's edge.

It has only been hours, really, so my need to be in the sea is not as urgent as last night. Even so, everything inside me has been waiting for this. But unlike yesterday, I don't want to draw the moment out. I want to disappear.

Down, down, under water; further, faster. Deeper. It's even harder than it was yesterday to stay in control, to remember who I am and what I need to do: to make myself go up to breathe.

When I finally do, I'm so far from the shore that I'm startled.

This is dangerous. What if I forget? But I don't want to go back, not yet. I stay on the surface, swimming lazily back and forth.

Danger.

There – on the shore. A light.

It moves along the path above, then starts bobbing down – someone is coming down to the cove in the dark.

Why?

It could be teenagers, or someone who fancies night fishing – anything. But it's not easy in the dark even with a torch, and the beach is mostly underwater with the tide coming in, so why would anyone bother?

Fear twists in my gut. The Circle: could they have traced me to this beach? I was known to come here when I lived nearby with Cate. Even if no one remembers, it must be on an official record somewhere; I was running from this beach when I got hit by a car. Malina or anyone else from The Circle must know about the connection I have to the sea. They'd be the only ones to think to come looking for me here, in the dark.

Unless whoever it is has nothing to do with me. I try to convince myself, but don't believe it.

I stay far out, watching, waiting. The light bobs around the cove, as if someone is looking for something. I'd wedged my pack down between some rocks; I hope it is hidden well enough. Everything I have is in that pack.

After a while the light bobs back up the steps and along the path, until it finally disappears.

I start for the shore. The tide is still coming in a little so there isn't as much of a rip as last night, so I get into the cove more easily and directly, but then, at the last minute, go left – to the far side of the cove, where rocks should block any view of me getting out of the water. What if there was more than one of them, they found my pack, and one of them stayed behind in the dark to wait for me to come back for it?

I'm crouched in shallow water behind rocks, shaking, afraid to go forward or back, to even move.

Be calm. Listen, move carefully, out of sight.

I breathe easier, waiting for my heart rate to slow, and *listen* with all of my senses. Not just my ears: the pattern of air on my skin as it moves, the feel of the water, the rock on the earth.

Nothing.

I creep forwards so slowly I'm barely moving, against the rocks, staying low. Out of the water now, exposed – the fear is coming back.

Calm washes through me again: *listen, move.* I almost flow around the rocks, so slowly, every sense alive and listening.

Gradually I get closer to where I stashed my pack. Again, listening with all of me, even stilling my breathing a moment to see if anyone else breathes.

I go behind the rock concealing my pack. Listen again. Slowly, cautiously, moving towards it. It's still there, as I left it. There is *relief*, then more caution. Is someone watching from a distance?

I move slowly, still listening. I check all around. Finally satisfied no one is here I stand up and breathe easier, looking to the sea and the rocks around me, bare shadows in starlight. Feeling . . . *bemused*, as if I'd been out of myself, watching the way I moved and felt. I didn't know I could move like that, so controlled and quiet. I didn't know I could listen like that, either.

I retrieve my pack, start up the rocky steps silently, stopping to listen as I near the top. Nothing.

I go along the path to my wall, over it to my sleeping place. Tarp out, lying down. Eyes open and looking at the sky.

OK. I got away with it this time. It was just luck I wasn't on the beach when they came; luck they didn't find my pack. The torch moved around a lot; they were being thorough, though perhaps looking for a hidden person made them less likely to find a dark pack in shadows between rocks.

Will they come back?

I can go somewhere else to swim at night, but I have to be

near here during the day to watch for Jago. And what if they're watching the whole coastline?

Who do I think I am, that I can do anything against a group like this? They have money, people, resources. They caused *hurricanes*; I can't even imagine how they could do that. Finding one girl on her own shouldn't be much of a challenge for them.

Cate is in my mind again. *Feeling sorry for yourself is a waste of energy.* Well, true, but I'm guessing she never imagined this.

Or did she?

Before the police took her away, one of the last things she said to me: *It's too soon, you're not ready.* Did she always know I'd find myself in this kind of position?

I sigh. She was right. I'm not ready.

But these things I know:

I might be the only one who knows about the link between the Penrose Clinic and The Circle. If that is true, I may be the only one who can stop them and make them accountable.

Not just for what they've done to the world with their hurricanes or whatever else they may threaten, but whatever it is they've done to *me*.

Maybe if I can work out what that is, I'll be closer to understanding them and what they plan to do next. And what I can do to stop them.

Somehow I have to do these things before they find me.

Stealth is an important skill.

And so, the first lesson is to hide from threats, real or imagined: stay unseen.

The second is speed: get away.

67

The third: only fight when sure of victory.
Or if there is no other choice.
No other choice . . .

17

Wake up.

My eyes open. There is something warm? Warm breath. Panting, sniffing.

A dog: black and white and in my face.

'Good boy. Ssssh,' I say, and look around. There is a jeep kind of thing moving on the field in the distance.

A farmer?

The dog looks back to him and puts his head back. *Arrrrroooo!* Or, *Look what I found*, in dog.

I scramble up, grab my pack and bolt for the low point on the wall.

'Hey!' a voice calls out, but I'm over now and run. It's only a bit later that I realise I've left my tarp behind.

I'm keyed up. Everything in me says, *Danger: get away from here.* The photo in the paper, the lights at the cove last night, the dog in the field. But I need to find Jago; I need some help.

And if I leave, where can I go?

I don't want to live like we used to, Cate and I. Always on the run and looking over our shoulders. I want a normal life, but I can't just try to disappear like we used to, knowing what I know about The Circle.

But getting caught won't help, either.

One more day.
One more chance.

18

It's late that afternoon when I finally see Jago through my binoculars – on the beach where he used to meet me. He's skipping stones into the water. It's all I can do to not run to him, but there are other people there: a young couple with a toddler, a few teenage girls sitting on the sand laughing at something on a phone, someone with a dog. None of them look particularly worrying, but that is too many eyes to risk it.

So I hang back, out of sight part way up the path I know Jago will take when he leaves, the one that leads to the road where I got hit by a car. And I wait.

I start counting backwards from a thousand, trying to still the nervous excitement in my stomach. Then forwards, then backwards again.

Finally there are sounds on the path. Someone is coming this way – is it Jago? But then there is the high voice of a young child; a woman's voice answers. I hide away from the path: the couple with the toddler come past.

Counting: 135, 134, 133 . . . 1, 2, 3, 4 . . . 876, 877, 878—
Wait. Someone else is coming.

This time there are no voices; it sounds like single footsteps. No dog. I wait, peering through the trees. One person, dark hair. He turns a little and I'm sure: it's him.

I rush forwards.

'Jago!'

He turns. First there is shock, in his wide, open eyes, then a big smile.

'Tabby? Is that really you?'

He's close now, his arms are around me and mine are around him in a hug that we both hang on to, tight. There are tears in my eyes that I've found him, my friend, at last.

My hat falls off and I reach down for it, self-conscious about my hair.

He grins and touches my hair before I can cover it up. 'Trendy cut,' he says.

'Yeah, right.'

'I've been so worried about you – with that storm,' he says. 'I kept trying to call. And then you were in the paper and people have been looking for you again. What happened? What's going on?'

I pull away and hold his eyes in mine. 'I need your help. But you promised, remember? Not to tell anything about me to anyone, no matter what.'

Concern crosses his face. 'Something is really wrong, isn't it?'

'Yeah. But you have to keep your promise, or I'm going.'

'I will, I promise.'

'Thanks,' I say, and then hear voices below: someone else is coming up the path from the beach. 'I don't want us to be seen together. Can we meet somewhere later?'

We hurriedly arrange a time, a meeting place. A quick goodbye and he's gone.

72

19

I hide the rest of the day, minutes feeling like hours. Why didn't I go with Jago this afternoon? What if he doesn't turn up – how will I find him again? As the sun moves slowly across the sky, I think of every possible reason there could be for him to not turn up, some reasonable, most not.

Finally, the sun is low enough in the sky to set out. I make myself walk at a normal pace on the coastal path towards Boscastle. There's a bench, he said; he'll be there, and I thought I knew where it was but now I'm questioning it. What if we wait in different places?

When I finally approach the place I think he meant, someone is there, sitting on the bench. The light is gone, and I'm squinting: is it him?

Then he turns and his face is caught in the moonlight: it's Jago. I smile; happy, *relieved*, and it's like those feelings let all the others come out in a rush: distress and fear, Simone-shaped pain, worry for Denzi, Ariel and Ali, and everyone else who might have been on the coast when the hurricane hit. And now I'm shaking, trying not to cry as I sit next to him.

'Hey, hey, whatever it is, it'll be all right,' he says, and his arms go around me, and I want to believe him so much, but I don't.

I breathe, in and out, in and out; hold the tears away, get

73

back control. Pull away a little and shake my head. 'It isn't all right, it can't be. You don't know.'

'Tell me, and we'll work it out together.' His brown eyes are steady on mine. And I know we can't work everything out just by talking, but he's my friend, he's here. He wants to listen. It feels so good to see him and not be alone. But he doesn't know what helping me might even mean.

What am I going to tell him? Everything, part of it, or none at all? I could make up some story, something close to the truth – about my evil grandmother and having to get away from her. It could be safer for Jago to know nothing.

But maybe I owe him the truth, at least as much of it as I can bear to tell.

'It's kind of a long story,' I say.

'Start at the beginning?'

'That's further back than you might think. But I'll try.' I swallow, trying to organise my thoughts.

'My parents wanted a baby but couldn't have one. They tried IVF and that failed, too. But then they found this new clinic – the Penrose Clinic. Have you heard of it?'

He shakes his head.

'It was another type of IVF, and it worked: they had me.

'You know that Cate took me away from my parents when I was three. She raised me like she was my mum.' The tears are threatening to come back, and I blink furiously. 'Before the police took Cate away, one of the last things she said to me was, "Beware The Circle."'

'Woah. The eco-terrorists?' Jago says. 'The ones who say they caused the hurricanes?'

74

'Yes. And you know what happened to Cate. I think she was killed by The Circle because she knew things about them. She had this tattoo, of four circles – just the same as the symbol they use. She'd had it removed and there was just a scar, but I remembered seeing it later. She'd left me a drawing of exactly the same symbol where I'd find it, and wrote "Beware The Circle" underneath. I think she took me from my parents to protect me from them.'

I give him an outline of what happened this summer. How I saw the door with the Penrose Circle symbol on it at the swim school, The Circle's logo hidden within it. I keep back what I found behind their locked doors, not sure if I can bear to say it out loud – if that would make it more real. Or if he'd even believe me if I did. I tell him that I ran away; ended up in hospital after being caught in storm surge. That I escaped the hospital, was chased through the station by Malina from swim school. That I think they're still looking for me.

'I don't understand all of this yet,' I say. 'But I think that somehow the Penrose Clinic is a front for The Circle. I'm afraid that some part of what they're doing or planning involves me, though I don't understand why or what it is. Or maybe they're just trying to track me down because I know too much.'

'Wow.'

'Yeah.'

'That's a lot to figure out. How about for now we work out where to go next? Do you need a place to stay?'

'I've been camping but can't go back to where I was – someone saw me there.'

'I know a place you might be able to stay for a while – with a friend. His parents are away. Should I call him?'

He wants to involve someone else? I'm alarmed and caution says no, but the rest of me is saying *yes*. I need somewhere to rest, to hide. To recover a little from everything that has happened, and to work out what to do next.

'I don't know what to do.'

'It's up to you how much of all this you want to tell him, and he won't mention you're there if we ask him not to. Trust me, he's all right.'

And I do trust Jago. Maybe at least partly because I have nowhere – no one – else to go to.

'Should I call him to set it up?' he says.

'Yeah. OK, thank you.'

20

Once we leave the footpath near Boscastle, I follow Jago at a distance, not wanting to walk up the road together where we might be seen, even in the dark. His friend, Sascha, has a car and will be waiting for us. It's blue: he told me the registration number and where it'll be.

My feet are going slower as I get closer.

I see the car up ahead, pulled in on the side of a back street just where Jago said it'd be. I slip into shadows for a minute, two, three. There is something inside of me that demands caution, stealth, and I give in to it, waiting to see if anyone is following behind.

No one appears.

When I get close to the car Jago gets out. 'I was getting worried,' he says, and opens the back door for me. I get in.

'Hi, mystery girl! I'm Sascha,' the driver says, turning in his seat with a big grin, and it's the kind that makes you grin back. He looks a little older than us, and he must be tall; his arms and legs seem to overfill the front of the car. Purple and blue dyed ends stick out in his unruly, fair hair. 'Specialist subjects include mixology, the art of illusion and rescuing damsels in distress.'

'Hi, and thanks. I'm Tabby.'

'Before we go, first I have a very important question,' he says, and pauses. 'Pizza, burgers, or fish and chips?'

It smells so good. I want to pick it up with my hands, sink my teeth into the fish, but I try to make myself go slow with a knife and fork.

'Hungry?' Jago says.

'Yes.'

'I can't cook,' Sascha says.

'He really can't,' Jago quips.

'I can!' I say. 'I will cook for you tomorrow.'

'Yay! You can stay. At least until my parents get back in September. So, I know Jago said you're not up for questions just now, and that's fine. But I did see a photo in the paper that looked a lot like you – though with long hair.'

I hesitate. But there is no point in trying to deny it, is there? 'Yeah, that's me. I put it in a ponytail and then cut it off.'

'That'll explain why it's a bit jagged.'

'I was trying to change how I look.'

'Then you've succeeded. But I could dye your hair? And even it out a little? Oh. And a makeover!'

'Really? That'd be great!'

'Are you sure? I mean, look at *his* hair,' Jago says, and Sascha laughs and reaches across and ruffles Jago's.

'I'll get the stuff before you change your mind,' Sascha says, gets up and goes down the hall.

Jago is smiling and I smile back at him. Happy to be here, with him and Sascha. Even more happy to not be out there, alone.

Then Sascha is back with some tubes of stuff that he mixes together in a few little plastic tubs.

'Ready?'

'What colour will it be?'

'I'm not entirely sure; I mixed a few together. More fun that way, don't you think?'

'Uh, yes. Sure. Do it.'

An hour later I've rinsed it out, had a shower and promised not to look in the mirror. Sascha has found me some stuff to wear, said it's his sister's and that no, she won't mind – she's at her boyfriend's for a few days.

I come out in a short jean skirt and a little black top and they both whistle.

'Sit here,' Sascha says. Next to him, laid out like surgical instruments – a brush, scissors, hair dryer.

He pulls my hair every which way and trims some bits here and there. Then dries it, using the brush to hold it out strand by strand.

'Can I look yet?'

'No! Make-up next.'

And he has me close my eyes, puts stuff around them, then on my face.

'OK, ready. Here's a mirror.' He hands it to me with a dramatic flourish.

Wow. My hair: it's got streaks that are kind of a bluey-green. And my eyes – like cat's eyes with eyeliner. And these clothes, too. Nobody would ever recognise me done up like this; I barely recognise myself.

'Well? What do you think?'

'It's amazing! Thank you!'

'Let's go out to celebrate!' Sascha says. 'No one will know it's you, I promise.'

'I'm not sure that's a good idea,' Jago says, a slight frown between his eyes, but I don't want to stay in and hide, not tonight. The girl who hides alone is no more; she's been replaced by someone who has friends and streaked hair and goes out.

'Yes! Let's go,' I say.

'Only if you're sure?' Jago says, and I nod. 'OK then, you need a different name. What should it be?'

'I don't know,' I say, mind blank.

'Pick a book at random,' Sascha says. He spins me around and points me towards the bookshelf.

I pull a book off the shelf.

'Perfect,' he says. 'The author's name is Naomi Klein, so you'll be Naomi. OK?'

'Naomi.' I say it, testing it out, then smile.

'My turn,' Sascha says and takes the mirror, quickly puts dark eyeliner on. Silver sparkle around his eyes. 'Jago?'

'No, thanks.'

Sascha goes to change his shirt.

'Are you sure you're OK with going out, Tabby?' Jago says. 'Do you need to sleep?'

I shake my head, feeling a bit wired, like I do sometimes when I overbreathe and hold my breath until I'm going light-headed, but it feels amazing at the same time. In the mirror I see someone else, and I like her.

21

The pub is crowded. It's Friday night, Jago says; I'd completely lost track of the days of the week. There are hellos called out as we squeeze in, go through to the back and then outside. Sascha goes to the bar and comes back a while later carrying soft drinks – but then he takes out a flask from inside his jacket. He puts some in two of the glasses, then looks a question at me. I nod, and he pours some in my glass, too.

'Are you sure you want that?' Jago says.

And I am, because I'm not me. I'm someone called Naomi with amazing hair and a short skirt who goes to pubs and drinks something out of a flask.

I try a few cautious sips: it's cola, but with a kick. The bubbles tickle my nose and I'm giggling and having some more.

And there are more people outside now and everyone is happy and chatting about what people are doing, what party is on tomorrow. Sascha is in the centre of things, Jago is quieter.

A few girls come outside and I stiffen. One of them is that girl from the beach – the day I broke my arm – the one I saw in the shop in Boscastle. I turn away, afraid she'll recognise me, but they're talking to another group of boys, backs towards us, and I start to relax.

A blond boy who says he is Ethan is there next to me now and saying how pretty I am, and I'm not even embarrassed.

I smile back and say he is pretty, too – because he is – and he laughs.

He puts his hand on my back, under my top, and I'm confused, pulling away but he's still coming closer.

'Leave her alone.' It's Jago.

'She yours?'

'Push off.'

There's tension now and people are looking over, and I'm scared there's going to be a fight, that it'll be my fault.

But then Sascha is there and says something I don't hear and Ethan laughs, moves away with Sascha, and the tension is gone.

'Thanks,' I say to Jago. 'I didn't know what to do.' My cheeks are burning. I'd felt like I was one of them, but I'm not, am I?

'It's all right. But I think maybe we should go,' Jago says, but then that girl is there, at Jago's shoulder.

'Hey, J, how're things?' she says, and he's startled, glances at me and I turn away, look down, pretend to adjust my skirt.

'Who's this?' she says. 'Hi. I'm Flick.'

Trapped, I turn. Glance at Jago. 'This is Naomi,' he says.

'Have you moved here?'

I shake my head. 'Just visiting for a while.'

She's looking at me, head tilted like she's thinking, as if there is something about me she's not sure of. Then the girl she came with is coming out with drinks and she turns to her.

'Let's get out of here,' Jago says, and then he's waving at Sascha, who comes over to us again.

'Home time? Spoilsports.'

We walk back to the car and my head is reeling. I'd been so happy to be there and be somebody else. But first Ethan and then that girl – Flick? – reminded me: I'm not like the rest of them. I never will be.

'Do you think she recognised me?' I say to Jago.

'No way. You look so different. And if she had, she'd have said. Flick's not good at subtle.'

The way she looked at me makes me less sure, but I can't seem to think straight. I need something to clear my head and there is only one thing that works.

'Can we go down to the harbour before we go back?' I ask.

'Good idea,' Sascha says. We get in and he turns the car around, heading back down to near where we left the coastal path to meet Sascha earlier.

There is a bobbing light down below us on the road.

Two people are walking with an Alsatian on a lead. His nose is to the ground, pulling them along.

I swallow. That's just where I walked earlier. Is he following my trail?

Jago must be thinking the same thing. 'Get down, Tabby,' he says, but I'd already started to, the need to hide automatic, and duck down low in the back seat, away from the window, as we go past them. 'Shit,' he says, a moment later.

'What's happened?' I say.

'They went straight to where we were parked before. Then stopped short, like they lost the trail and started looking all around.'

'You think they're looking for Tabby?' Sascha says.

'Maybe. Let's get out of here.'

22

'This is unreal,' Sascha says. 'Why would the police have a sniffer dog out trying to find somebody at night like that?'

My head is throbbing now. 'If they were looking for me, it might not have been the police.'

'Who, then?' Sascha says.

I look between the two of them. My head aches, and I'm trying to remember how much I told Jago, to work out if I should tell him more – and if I should tell Sascha anything. And I want to confide in them both *so much*, but I don't know if I should.

'I don't know what to do. Maybe it's better for you if you don't know.' Tears well up in my eyes and I blink, but one still goes down my cheek.

'Is it the mob?' Sascha says. 'Organised crime: you've stolen the contents of their safe and now they're coming to get you?

'Or . . . a diamond heist! There was one in the news in London recently. Are you a cat burglar? Is your pack really full of diamonds?

'No, wait, I know: there were rumours of an unidentified flying object – a flying saucer – on Bodmin. That's it, I know it: you're actually an alien.'

And I'm grinning more with each crazy idea, and then I'm laughing, too, but there are still tears in my eyes and laughing becomes crying – about having to hide, being scared what will happen to me if I get caught. But maybe the tears are even more from the agony that we didn't go to the harbour, we couldn't with people out with a dog looking for me. And it's where I want to be, now – in the sea. The only place I truly feel hidden and safe. The disappointment from almost being there and then having it taken away is too much to bear.

Jago is next to me now, arm around my shoulders, and Sascha is handing me tissues and they're both looking so concerned, and somehow that makes me want to cry even more.

Finally, I manage to force myself to breathe slowly until I'm in control.

'Sorry,' I say.

'No problem,' Sascha says. 'Though you've totally wrecked that brilliant make-up job I did earlier. And I expect Jago has told you this, but I'm really good at keeping secrets.'

'He is,' Jago says.

'OK.' I nod, steady myself further. 'It's complicated. But I've found out some things about The Circle, and I think they're after me.'

'The terrorists who caused the hurricanes?' Sascha says, his eyes wide, and I nod.

'They're linked to an IVF clinic somehow – the Penrose Clinic. The one my parents used to have me. My nanny – Cate – took me away from my parents when I was three. She raised me like she was my mum. And I thought she was, but she wasn't. I only found out when the police caught us and arrested her, saying that she'd kidnapped me.'

'OMFG,' Sascha says. 'For real?'

'Yeah. But before the police took Cate away, one of the

last things she said to me was, "Beware The Circle." And then Cate was killed in prison.' Sascha's eyes open even wider and I pause again. The tears are threatening to come back, and I blink furiously.

Jago takes my hand. 'I'm so sorry,' he says.

'It's not your fault, Jago.'

Sascha is looking between us, not understanding why he said that.

'I told the police Tabby called me,' Jago says. 'I thought she needed rescuing. It's because of me that they caught up with them, and Cate died.'

'They would have found us eventually, Jago.'

'You have to go to the police about all of this,' Sascha says.

'I can't. I haven't got any proof. And I don't trust them, not after what happened to Cate,' I say, but that isn't the only reason. Cate always said never trust anyone in authority. Everything inside me protests at even *thinking* about going to the police.

'So do you think it was them – The Circle – with the dog, following your trail?' Jago says. 'How would they have known where to look for you to start with?'

'I was camping in a field near the beach and this morning a farmer saw me. Maybe he called the police, or they found out some other way that a girl was spotted there? I left my tarp behind: it would have had my scent for the dog.'

'There's something I haven't told you yet,' Jago says. 'The reason I went to the beach this afternoon. A policewoman came and talked to me, asked if I'd heard from you, and of course I hadn't seen you yet then. But I wondered if they had a reason to be looking for you around here, so I went to the beach in case you turned up. Was she even really a policewoman?'

'I don't know.'

'What next? If you can't go to the police, what do you do?'

'I'm not sure,' I say, but even as I say the words, something is shifting inside of me. Maybe it was talking about all of this, first alone with Jago and again now. Focusing on The Circle and the clinic feels the wrong way around. What they did to me has to tie into all of this, I feel it in my gut. Even though just thinking about it makes me uncomfortable, maybe the answers I need are hidden inside of me.

'What aren't you telling us?' Jago says.

'I don't know. I mean there might be something else, but I can't . . .' I shake my head. 'I need to think.'

'So is the key thing here so far – the bit you know about The Circle that you think no one else may know – is that they're connected somehow with this Penrose Clinic?' Sascha says.

'Yes. Maybe I can try to find out stuff about them online, how it all links together?'

They exchange a glance.

'Ren. You need Ren,' Jago says. 'She's a good friend and a genius with that kind of stuff. She's got a blog that has all this conspiracy stuff on it. This is right up her street.'

'I don't know if I want anyone else involved.'

'Maybe the more people that know about that clinic and The Circle, the better,' Jago says.

That sinks in, and I nod. 'You might be right.'

'Look, it's late. Get some sleep. And we'll talk about it again in the morning.'

Sascha shows me to his sister's room, finds me a big T-shirt to

87

sleep in. I come out from washing my face and Jago brings me a glass of water, Sascha behind his shoulder. 'Take Mr Ted. He's great for helping you sleep. Trust me.'

He hands me a giant pink teddy bear.

'Thanks. Goodnight.'

They go, shut the door. I shrug the T-shirt on and get into bed, Mr Ted between me and the door. No matter how much there is to think about, just curling up in an actual bed on clean sheets feels *so good*. And they're both here, too; I'm not alone.

Part of me doesn't trust this feeling; it says run, hide. But how can I when it looks like either the police or The Circle has got dogs out sniffing for me?

And I think I really do trust Jago and Sascha. It feels . . . *different*, to think maybe someone besides Cate has my back, that I have friends. Different, but good.

It feels strange that I feel both like I know Jago really well, and don't know him at all: he has friends and this whole other life I know nothing about. I think he was right that I can trust Sascha. But what about Ren?

I'm glad that policewoman – or whatever she was – questioned Jago before he saw me. I'm not sure he could have hidden it from them if he knew I was in the area. But is it only a matter of time before they try him again? And if they're suspicious, to check out his friends, like Sascha, too?

Maybe they're right about telling more people; they said that Ren has a blog. She could get information out, couldn't she?

Feeling like I'm not alone any more feels good – it feels *right*. But there are still so many things I didn't tell them, like that half girl/half fish in the tank under the clinic at the school. The dreams

I have; the way I can hold my breath for so long when I swim. My fear that I'm another one of their experiments.

What would Jago think if he knew?

The kin are everything. We stay together, always. A threat to one is a threat to all.

We cannot run from this, even if it means death.

It's what we are.

Through her eyes, I'm beginning to understand things I didn't before. About her world, and people. And how sometimes those that should be kin are more like sharks.

My kin saved us when we were trapped in that metal box in the sea.

Would her kin do the same, and save mine?

I have to show her to remind her what they did.

She sleeps and I take her back in her dream – to when they came. They moved the metal box, smashed the glass out the back. When we would have given up, made us fight to crawl out. Then, when we were almost gone, they carried us up – to the surface. To the place between sea and sky, to breathe.

And so we lived. And so we live, still.

She should remember. She MUST remember!

Part 3

Denzi

23

I scan the crowd at arrivals until I spot a familiar face and a wave. It's Jax. Dad isn't here.

'Hey, you, welcome home,' he says, leans in for a hug like he always does, and if there is the briefest of pauses before I hug him back, he doesn't seem to notice.

'Where's Dad?'

He rolls his eyes. 'Where do you think? Haven't seen him for five minutes since you left. And how was your trip, was it all right? Apart from, you know, Leila. And hurricanes.'

'She was in a coma, remember?'

'Sorry. She's all right now?'

'Yeah. She seems to be.'

We head for the car park and as we walk, I glance at Jax. 'I had some good talks with Leila before I left.' Do I imagine it, or does he stiffen when I say that?

Then he shakes his head, as if dismissing whatever he was thinking. 'That's a good thing,' he says. 'No matter what – family is family. Like we are. Right?'

'Right.'

'Now, if you're not too jet-lagged, we can meet your dad on the way home – he'll get out for a quick coffee, he said.'

'Yep. Let's do it.'

★ ★ ★

We're across London and at a table before Dad makes it in.

'It's so good to see you,' he says. He's exhausted. There are shadows under his eyes, stubble on his face that would normally never be there during work hours.

'You too,' I say, and it is, despite or because of everything. He gives me more of a proper hug than he usually would in a public place, and I remember how he called me that night in Washington – so upset to think that if I hadn't left swim school when I did, I could have been swept out to sea.

A waitress comes over with my tea, their coffee, ordered while we waited for Dad.

'How is Leila?' Dad asks.

Is this the moment to ask about all the things Leila said – about Jax? About why she left the way she did? No. Save it for when we're on our own. 'She seems fine. They're not sure why she was in a coma.'

'I'm glad she's doing well. Sorry I couldn't make it to the airport earlier.'

'Doesn't matter. I guess you've been busy.'

A rueful smile. 'You could say that. Are you all right?'

'I don't know. I still can't believe what's happened – a hurricane in England? At my school? It just doesn't seem real. And to think I could have been there when it did – and of all the people who were, and what may have happened to them? I can't get my head around it.' I can't bring myself to ask what I most want to know. I'm afraid of the answer: has he found out anything about Tabby?

'You're not alone in struggling to take it all in,' Dad says. 'A hurricane of that magnitude here is completely unprecedented.'

'Do you think it's true? What The Circle say they did?'

'What do you think?'

'Well, if they didn't cause the hurricanes, it's a ridiculous coincidence that they happened in such an unusual way in two places at about the same time after their threats. But how?'

'Exactly. That is pretty much what we've been arguing about for days.'

'What's going to be done about it?'

He shakes his head. 'You know I can't talk about that.' He glances at his watch, has a gulp of too-hot coffee. 'Sorry, I have to go shortly. But first, I looked into that girl you asked me about. Is this her – Tabby, also known as Holly?' He shows me a photo on his phone.

'Yes,' I say. And my stomach is twisting. I feel sick, scared what he is going to tell me, want him to stop before he says anything else.

'Her full name is Holly Tabitha Heath. She'd already left the school when the hurricane hit. Her mother was driving her home when their car got caught in storm surge. She nearly drowned; unfortunately, her mother didn't survive.'

'Oh my God,' I say, the relief that Tabby is OK and the shock of her mother's death vying for my reaction. 'Where is she now?'

'Well, that's the thing. She ran away from a hospital in Bristol – nobody knows.'

'What? She's missing?'

'I'm afraid so. She's on a long list of missing persons the police are trying to deal with after the hurricane.'

'I wonder why she ran? Where she went?'

'Is this girl special to you?' Jax asks.

I hesitate, uncomfortable, then say, 'I don't know. Maybe she either is, or could be.'

'I'll see if I can nudge for more information,' Dad says. 'But everything is overstretched just now.'

'At least you know she survived the hurricane,' Jax says.

'Yeah. Thanks, Dad.'

Sitting here with Dad and Jax, wrapped in their care and concern, I know that whatever happened to make things the way they are, they are my family. The only family that has always been there for me, and that counts. I couldn't imagine either of them ever leaving me for any reason the way Leila did. My eyes are stinging to think what Tabby must have been through and is going through, having lost her mother; how I would feel if something happened to Dad or Jax.

'Hey. I love you two, you know that?' I say.

Dad's eyes mist. In public? He really *is* tired. Jax sweeps us both into a hug as Dad gets up: time to go.

'Come on, boy, let's get you home,' Jax says. 'Any chance you can make it for dinner?' he says to Dad.

He shakes his head. 'I'll be late, if at all. Sorry.'

When we get home, I'm exhausted – somewhere past the point of needing sleep – and all I want to do is binge watch the news. Every channel, back and forth, even though they keep repeating stuff. Official death tolls. The displaced, the missing. Like Tabby. Were the hurricanes *really* caused on purpose? Could they – would they – do it again if their demands aren't met?

My phone beeps now and then. There are texts from friends from school, from my trainer in London. I can't deal with them now, not yet.

But then there is one from Apple: Still awake?

This one I answer. More or less.

Is that girl you were worried about all right?

And I don't know what to say. I sigh. I don't, generally, share much of how I feel about stuff. With anybody, outside of Jax and Dad, and even with them not very much. But even though this feels new, Apple is my sister. Besides, she's far enough away that it somehow seems all right.

I don't know. Tabby went missing from a hospital after the hurricane.

Oh no. Not knowing things SUCKS.

Yep. Unless knowing is worse.

I'll pray for her. If that's OK.

I'm a total atheist, but there are moments when it seems sensible to back the other team. Just in case.

It's more than OK. Thanks.

Besides, Tabby is alive. Or at least she was, and there's no reason to think any different.

I'm starting to spot the loop in the news – the stories they repeat in varying sequence when they're reporting on a disaster and can't think of anything new to say while they wait for something else to happen or not happen. Footage of the hurricanes, storm surge and floods are interspersed with the latest aftermath from England and New York. As they play out on the screen, I remember Oliver was going to New York. He's newspaper not TV so he's not likely to appear on camera in any of what I'm watching, but I wonder what he is seeing that isn't on the 'some viewers may find this distressing' sequence with the blurred-out faces.

Is Oliver still in NY?

Yes. He called a few hours ago – he's all right. Do you have the news on now? President is about to be on.

As I'm reading her text, the BBC switch to live from the US – the White House. The President is going to make a statement.

'Jax? You might want to watch this,' I call out, and he comes in from his study down the hall.

I text Apple: We're all ears.

The camera focuses in on a face that is both loved and despised, in the US and around the world. I'm more in the despising camp.

'Fellow Americans, the recent hurricanes and their fallout inflicted a horrible toll on the brave people of the city and state of New York, as well as on our friends in the United Kingdom. We're doing everything we possibly can to support American victims and their families, and we will rebuild – I promise you that.

'Now, there's something I need to tell you. There has been endless speculation in the media about whether this group calling itself The Circle had a hand in causing these hurricanes as they claim. Let me tell you that there is a great deal of doubt as to whether there is any truth in that whatsoever. But know this: we will never submit to threats or bow down to any group that threatens Americans or our way of life. Whether they had anything to do with the hurricanes or just want to scare people by riding on its coat-tails, we're working tirelessly to bring them to justice.'

'OK then,' Jax says. 'Wonder if we knew what they were going to say before they said it?'

'Hmmm. One way or another, bluff called. But is it a bluff?' I say, and there is a sick feeling inside me. If The Circle really were behind the hurricanes, how will they react to what the President said and didn't say?

My phone vibrates again: it's Apple. Leila is spitting. Nothing said about the climate emergency. Laterz, I'm going shopping with Emmie to work off the stress.

We're eventually told that the Prime Minister will make a statement tomorrow morning. Is that what is keeping Dad out still? Or maybe it is just in reaction to the US.

We eat dinner in front of the TV. I stay there when Jax goes to work in his study; he wanders back near midnight and suggests bed. I shake my head, say I want to stay put, something else might happen and I want to watch. He comes back a moment later, turns down the lights and hands me a pillow and blanket for the sofa.

'Thanks,' I say, but have no thoughts of sleep. I never seem able to sleep as much as most people do, but whenever there is anything at all to think about, it usually deserts me completely.

Or, worse: makes me wish I had kept both my eyes open.

I'm searching. Underwater, and I don't know what I'm looking for. Deep under the waves where the sky is a memory, the sun too distant to reach this watery underworld of hidden, drowned things.

Searching, despite the fear that the finding will be worse than not finding. Some things are best left undisturbed, lost in the dark.

I go deep enough to catch glimpses of the dead. If I try to look straight at the horror, they vanish from view; they can only be seen on the periphery, by looking away. The staring eyes – those not yet eaten by fish and other scavengers. Bloated skin. Haloes of hair that drift around their faces. And I'm trying to think who they were – if I recognise any of them – but I can't. The dead are the dead.

I should be one of them. I will be, soon.

Cold hands reach for mine . . .

24

Trainers on, I run. As far and as fast as I can. It's early – so early that Hyde Park is nearly empty. Just a few joggers and dogwalkers and any I see I overtake and leave behind.

God, those dreams. Every time I closed my eyes they were there. What happened in them was bad enough, but it was the *feeling* all through – of dread so strong and immobilising, I felt like a fly stuck in glue. Wanting to escape but struggling to even move. I've always had insane dreams but lately it feels like they're getting worse, like I'm caught inside a horror movie I can't escape. Sometimes – like last night – I'm even aware that I'm dreaming, but I can't wake up.

Running, swimming – these are the things I know. What I *need* – especially the swimming. It's almost like I can't breathe right when out of the water. When I'm swimming – especially in the sea – everything feels right inside me in a way it doesn't anywhere else. No matter how much effort I'm putting in to go further and faster, some part of me is *still* inside: calm, centred. It's like it is my safe place, one where I can be who I am. It's also what I need to focus and think clearly, and I need to work out how to try to find Tabby. So this afternoon, I'll swim. And hope that something comes to me in the water.

Until then, running is the next best thing, but running is more about pushing myself to exhaustion – so just going on takes all my attention, and I can't think about anything else, not even how much I miss the sea.

There hasn't been enough running and swimming lately to banish whatever it is that hides in my dreams.

Ha. That really *does* sound like something from a horror movie. Get a grip, Denzi.

Further, faster, longer. Exhaustion is close, and I glance at my watch. Just enough time to get home and shower before the UK government's latest dance on TV.

The Prime Minister comes out of the door of Downing Street, the proper expression for the occasion – serious, grave – in place. I don't like her. Anyone who can summon emotions on their face at will has to be viewed with distrust. It's part of the job, Dad would say, and has nothing to do with whether she's good at it – just how long she can keep it. As to whether the PM is any good at her job, Dad won't be drawn. Even when it is just me and Jax he won't say what he really thinks about her.

Dad believes in systems, structure, reports; careful thought and analysis; action only when all the facts are known. The situation with The Circle must be hell for him.

The PM smiles just enough to show warmth and concern, but not too much to be accused of lacking sympathy for victims.

'Good morning. In the days since the tragic events of the hurricanes both in England and in New York, the question has been asked again and again: did the threats from a group calling itself The Circle lead to this tragic loss of life and destruction of property on a scale not seen in either country's past? We've already told you that our scientific advisors doubt the feasibility of what they've claimed. We are and have been discussing these matters with our close allies and friends in the United States.' There is a pause while she looks at the camera, as if into the eyes of every journalist there, every voter watching this on the BBC.

'Our government remains committed to addressing the current climate emergency as a matter of utmost urgency. The supposed actions of this group have not, and will not, change our resolve.

'Thank you.'

She makes her way back to the door of number ten and disappears inside.

Jax and I exchange a glance. 'So, is she basically saying it doesn't matter if The Circle did or didn't do anything, because of course we plan to solve the climate crisis regardless?' I say.

'I think so.'

'And last night, did the US president say something like, it doesn't matter what they did or didn't do because we're ignoring all that climate change rubbish regardless?'

'Ha! Something like that was implied, I suspect.'

'And this utmost urgency line here: they make these statements, but what is our government actually *doing* about the climate emergency?'

'At least they admit there is one,' Jax says. 'As to the rest of it, you've got me. Ask your dad, if you ever see him again. Any plans for the day?'

'Going for a swim.'

'When you get back, there's something we need to talk about. Your school has been in touch. It'll be closed for at least the next school year, so in the meantime we need to find you another school for September. They're asking other independent schools

103

with space to help out in the short term without the usual interview and application processes. I've got a list. Only two with swimming programmes, though.'

'School. Like that's important?'

Jax raises an eyebrow.

'I mean, it is, but with everything that has happened it doesn't *feel* like it.'

'I get that. But you need to think about these things anyhow. I'll email the links – have a look when you get back, all right?'

25

I plunge into the beckoning water of the Serpentine Lido at Hyde Park. Wanting to be outside, under the sky, I came here instead of the usual training centre. Or maybe it was because I didn't want to go where people know me, might want to talk. All I want to do is swim.

As the water closes around me my head starts to clear, the fatigue from my disturbed night and morning run are gone.

I push for speed, watching to avoid other swimmers. The hot weather has brought them out today, but as if they sense I need the space, most stay away.

The longer I swim, the less I think about deeper waters, of cold hands that seek to grasp. The more I think of things I can do to find Tabby.

I will find her.

I need to see her again.

Going by the sun, it is hours later when I finally get out of the pool. Swimmers have been thinning out, leaving the water, and a vague sense has reached me even as I did lengths that something is going on. Now I see the police, people packing up to go even though the sun is still bright in the sky.

And there is a rumbling sort of noise – not far away.

Still wet, I pull on my T-shirt and walk towards the sound.

A policewoman intercepts me. 'It's probably best to leave the park the other way today,' she says.

'What's happening?'

'A demonstration. Climate protestors. We're advising people to keep clear.'

'Why?'

'For your safety.' She gives me a look, then goes to intercept a family that are heading in the same direction.

For my safety? Curious, I ignore what she said. Climate protests are peaceful. Passive resistance is about the worst they do, stopping traffic and doing their best to paralyse central London every Friday for as long as I can remember.

But it's not Friday.

I don't have far to go – a crowd is growing on the north-east edge of Hyde Park, centred around Speakers' Corner.

But it's not Sunday either, the day speeches and debate normally take place here.

In the midst of them is a step ladder, the type with a podium frame on top. A boy – fourten or fifteen – is climbing its steps and soon stands there. His face is familiar; his name escapes me, but he's been one of the poster kids of the climate movement for a while. He's surrounded by a sea of the young and not so young holding signs: 'There is no planet B.' 'The sixth mass extinction is NOW.' 'Save our future.'

And I'm uneasy, the way I always feel when confronted by these messages. Is it as bleak as they say? If it is, why isn't anyone doing something about it? Maybe those with the power to change things are the same as me – afraid to focus on it too closely, afraid to understand what is happening.

Someone hands a megaphone up to the boy, and I move closer to listen.

'Thank you for coming today on such short notice!' he says.

There are cheers around him, angry shouts from further away.

'We heard it from the Prime Minister this morning: we are in the midst of a climate emergency! She said it's urgent, but they've said that before. What have they done?'

Cries of 'Nothing', 'Stuff all' and ruder versions of the same come from the crowd around him.

'Science tells us we're at a tipping point. If we don't act, right *now*, it'll be too late. We have to make them take this seriously.'

The crowd is pushing in. More people have arrived but these ones don't have signs, and now they're yelling things of their own: 'Go back to school!' 'Terrorists in training!' 'Get a life!'

The mood is ugly and getting uglier. The boy with the megaphone is saying something again but it's drowned out by the shouts.

The police are at the edges, trying to get between the two groups but there aren't enough of them.

Then things are being thrown. The ladder is knocked over. I lose sight of the boy and try to push through, to go help, but can't get through the wall of bodies – the stink of sweat, the close heat, the crush, the anger and panic.

Riot police in full gear with shields are here now, and that's it, I'm getting out of this. I push my way back through the edges of the crowd and away, but my ears are still full of shouting, people crying out. There's nothing I can do, is there? I hesitate, not wanting to walk away if I can help.

Then I see a boy, maybe ten, with an older girl – he's almost dragging her – her eyes are closed and her head is bleeding.

'Hi. Can I help?'

'My sister, something hit her, hurt her head.' He's scared, struggling not to cry.

'It's OK, I'll help you. Let's get her out of here.'

I carefully pick her up, carry her limp body. She's only maybe fourteen years old, light. Finally we reach a park exit. As we go through, there's a flash in my eyes – cameras – voices. I ignore them and get around to a police car on the road next to the park. Paramedics come and the girl is soon in an ambulance to be taken to hospital. It pulls away, her brother's 'Thank you' still in my ears.

Then there's another camera in my face, a microphone. I push them away and run.

26

Back home I'm showering – there's blood on my skin from that girl and now I'm feeling sick and retching in the running water, stomach empty.

Once out I pick up my phone.

I message Dad and Jax on Signal. Hey. I'm all right but got caught in the Hyde Park riot after my swim. Might have been photographed helping an injured girl but wasn't involved. Not sure anyone knew who I am.

The landline rings soon after. An aide of Dad's, Melanie, is on the line.

'OK, Denzi, we're glad you're all right. Now tell me exactly what happened.' I run through it. 'All right. I wonder if we should do a story with this ourselves and head them off?'

'Oh God, please don't!'

'I'll talk to your dad.'

I can't stop myself from looking at all the online news. It doesn't take long to find it: a photo of me carrying that girl. My face is turned just away from the camera and the image isn't that clear. It's captioned, 'Unidentified teen helps girl injured in climate protest.' I'm relieved they don't know who I am, but then I feel guilty for even thinking that when it goes on to say that the girl is in a critical condition at hospital.

What the actual is happening? Are kids protesting against climate change really getting hit by missiles thrown by thugs, here, in London?

I read more reports, not believing what I see on some of the news sites. They're calling it a violent protest, blaming it on those kids. That's not what happened. It was the ones who came to crash the protest that caused it all.

The police knew – they must have. The way that policewoman said to get away for my own safety – they knew something was going to happen. So why didn't they stop it?

I put the TV news on. There's footage of the protest that became a riot and when I see it and think that I was there, it feels both unreal and unbelievable. They say that the Home Secretary – Dad – will be making a statement. It's more balanced on the BBC. Speculation is that anger against the supposed actions of The Circle has become anger at climate protestors generally. They seem to be reasoning – if you can call it that – that anyone concerned about the climate must be a terrorist.

All I can see is that boy on the podium, knocked over. The injured girl and her brother.

And all I can feel is that what The Circle wanted has backfired. How will they react to this?

Later I give in to hunger and devour sandwiches Jax left for me hours ago. Next to them is a note with a smiley face pointing at my laptop – he wants me to look at schools, something that feels even less important now.

I take my laptop with me to the sofa. I'd been thinking while I was swimming what I could do to try to find Tabby.

Now that Dad has told me her full name, I can search for her properly: 'Holly Tabitha Heath'.

A recent newspaper article comes up, from a local paper in Cornwall: the title is 'Missing Girl', and there is a photo of Tabby with her name. It says she is also known as Tabby Seymour, that she went missing from Bristol and may have ties to Northern Cornwall.

Is she from Cornwall? Her accent wasn't. But thinking of it now I couldn't pick her accent as being from anywhere in particular, really.

The photo: she's done up like she was going to some posh red-carpet thing. She looks amazing in a dress, even though it doesn't seem like her somehow. Of course, I've never seen her in anything but swimming and running gear, that kind of stuff.

I stare at her face on the screen. There is a half-smile for the camera, but her eyes look guarded.

Maybe the first clue to finding her is understanding *why* she ran away.

The last time we spoke she was freaked about seeing a Penrose Clinic symbol she recognised on a door, hidden away downstairs in the sports medicine building. Dad said her mum was driving her home, so she was leaving swim school. Does that mean she found out something more about the Penrose Clinic being there? Something that upset her enough to leave?

Wherever Tabby has gone – would she still be in touch with friends online? I search for Holly Tabitha Heath on every social networking platform I can think of: nothing. She doesn't exist. Then I try Holly Heath, Tabby Heath, Tabitha Heath, and Tabby Seymour, her also-known-as from the newspaper story. There are hits but none of them look anything like her.

Either she's never been on these kinds of sites, she uses a different username, or she has deleted her accounts.

What about her family – will there be some clues there?

Dad said Tabby's mother died. I look for names of the confirmed dead from the hurricane and storm surge online. The list is so long, and my stomach twists, trying to take it in – the immensity of what has happened. So many lives lost. Many more left behind to grieve.

Focus. I search surnames: there are two with the surname Heath. One I rule out as the first name is Thomas. The other is Simone Jean Heath (née Penn).

Simone Heath is all over the internet. Lawyer, not currently practising. Husband Alastair Heath, a VP with Industria United. Tabby wasn't kidding when she said her dad works in oil and gas – that's the biggest company of them all. He was reported missing at the family home on the coast of Dorset after the hurricane.

One parent dead, one missing. What was Tabby running from? Why?

The only thing I have to go on is the Penrose Clinic. Taking together the weirdness of their presence at school and Tabby's reaction to it, my gut is telling me there must be something there.

I type 'Penrose Clinic' into the search box.

Pages of hits come up, starting with their website.

It's not what I expect. All I know about it is that Tabby and me were both IVF babies from this clinic, but there's nothing about IVF on their website. It's all about research – the main focus seems to be medical genetics. Stuff like finding the causes of inherited diseases, diagnosis, genetic counselling. Nothing about making babies in test tubes.

There's a list of addresses in places like London, Berlin, Los Angeles; I'm not surprised to see there isn't a listing for the basement of the sports med building at school.

What does all this mean?

If the clinic changed focus from IVF to medical genetics, why? Leila failed at IVF with the NHS, went to Penrose, had a baby. If they had an edge in what they were doing, why would they stop doing it?

Unless they haven't stopped, and it just isn't on the website. But then how would they get patients? How did my parents end up going there if it isn't advertised?

Or maybe they do the IVF part of the business under a different name now. I try searching for private IVF, and woah: there are so many private fertility clinics, even just in the UK. I glance through some of the names, websites, but there is no way to know if one of them is somehow associated with Penrose.

I go back to my original search for the Penrose Clinic, and look beyond their website. The search throws up the usual mishmash of the relevant and irrelevant, but even the relevant bits – the ones that probably *are* about the Penrose Clinic – don't yield much of interest. There are references to fundraising, scientists and doctors who work with them in some capacity or another, reports on their work in scientific publications. I scroll through them one after another, but nothing seems to shed any light on why Tabby would need to run away.

I can't give up; I won't. And what happened today in the park has if anything made me more focused, more determined.

It's made me think of the 'what ifs'.

What if I'd been the one hit on the head and taken to hospital? What if Tabby needs help? What if I'm the only one who can help her?

I have to find another way.

The answer is obvious, really. There are two people I know who must be able to tell me about this clinic: my parents.

It seems weird that Dad never told me I was an IVF baby. It's kind of why I *exist*, so you'd think it might have been mentioned.

Was it all just part of him never talking about what happened with him and Leila?

Leila said I should ask him about the things she told me. Part of me shies away from venturing into Dad's no-go areas, but Leila was right. And now it goes beyond wanting to know his side of things: I need to know what he knows about the Penrose Clinic.

Phone out, I send a message on Signal: Dad, we need to talk. When can I see you?

27

'Got home as soon as I could,' Jax says. 'Are you all right?'

'Ish. It was pretty intense.' I give him the rundown of what I saw and heard.

'So glad you weren't hurt. You need to think: run *away* from trouble, not towards it.'

'I couldn't *not* help.'

'I know. Just want you to stay safe. Have you heard from your dad?'

I shake my head. 'No, Melanie. She said—'

The landline starts to ring and Jax goes to answer it.

'Hello?

'Who's calling?

'He's not available at the moment. Why do you want to speak to him?

'I see. No, I don't think so. Bye.' He's rolling his eyes as he hangs up the phone.

'What was that about?'

'Some reporter who wants you to make a statement about your involvement in the Hyde Park riot.'

'Involvement? I wasn't *involved*.'

'I know. They just want some dirt on your dad. Best get back to him or Melanie.'

I pick up my phone, but as I do, it vibrates with a message.

It's Dad. I'll be there within the hour.

It's actually just over an hour when the front door opens, but there is a sinking feeling inside when I see it isn't just Dad: Melanie is with him. I'm not going to be able to get into personal stuff with her here.

Jax tells them about the reporter who called and they're not surprised. Is that why Dad came home – to talk about *managing* the story, as Melanie calls it, not because I messaged him?

'We'll issue a statement,' Melanie says, 'saying why you were at the park, that you just went to see what was happening and then helped that poor injured girl. Don't speak to the press, all right? Don't post about it online, either.'

'Fine with me.'

'Now there is something else I have to tell you. The girl you helped has very sadly died, which will make the press more hungry to get to you, I'm afraid.'

She's still talking but I've stopped listening. I didn't even know her, but I'm shaking. I was washing her blood away in the shower, and now she's dead?

Jax is there, a hand on my shoulder. 'You did what you could, Denzi. More than many people would have done.'

Now I'm angry. 'I've got some questions of my own. The police were obviously expecting problems. Why didn't they stop it from happening in the first place? Then that girl would still be alive.'

'Denzi, think,' Dad says. 'Can you imagine the response if we tried to close down a climate protest?'

'So you *did* know?'

116

'That there might be trouble? We had an idea. There was a strong police presence to deal with any objection to the protest, but unfortunately we were overwhelmed by numbers that weren't expected.'

'Isn't it your job to expect the unexpected?'

Before he can say anything else – before I can take it back, say I'm sorry – his phone is ringing and he glances at the screen, sighs. 'I have to take this.

'Yes?

'What?' He's swearing. 'Yes, as soon as possible.'

He ends the call. 'Sorry, we have to go. Denzi, I know you wanted to talk but it'll have to be later. Please: say nothing to the press or anyone else, all right? And stay in. Don't answer the phone or the door for now.'

Jax is shaking his head. 'Do you have to go? Can't it wait?'

'No, it can't. If you want to know why, I expect the BBC will fill you in.'

They cross swiftly to the door, but then Melanie turns back to us and her face brightens. 'Whatever it is, it'll take the heat off you, Denzi, if they're focused on something else.'

Huh. Something has happened – from Dad's reaction, something not good – and she's smiling about *that*?

And despite whatever it is, all I can think about is Tabby. When will Dad's talking *later* be?

Jax has the remote, points at the TV. The door is only just closing behind them when the story hits.

'Breaking news. The organisation calling itself The Circle has sent detailed demands to all major networks and newspapers in the UK and internationally, as well as governments around the world. If significant moves aren't made towards an enforceable international accord on halting climate change within specified parameters and timeframes, they threaten unnamed targets who, in their words, are either complicit in climate change or block initiatives to address it.'

'Uh oh,' Jax says. 'What does that mean? More hurricanes?'

'Or maybe, as it talks about targets, it'll be something else – more directed?'

We watch. Later Jax orders pizza and we watch some more. I keep checking my phone for a message from Dad saying he's on his way home, but nothing. Meanwhile the news reports are all speculation. What does it mean? Who will be targeted? But if addressing the climate emergency is so urgent, why don't they just do what is asked anyhow?

The UK threat level is raised from substantial to severe. The UN security council is having an emergency meeting tomorrow.

My phone vibrates: it's Apple. So here we go: what next?

Dunno. Maybe your president should watch over his shoulder, he's got to be on the list.

DON'T call him MY president.

Sorry.

Did you know that you're famous?

??

She sends a link. It's the same photo of me as before, carrying that girl in Hyde Park, with a new caption: 'Good Samaritan now identified as Denzi Pritchard, son of Home Secretary Pritchard.'

And underneath: 'Denzi Pritchard, a promising swimmer, was caught up in the riot upon leaving the Serpentine Lido this afternoon. He helped an injured girl who later sadly died in hospital.'

I show it to Jax.

'So, that sounds like Melanie's version of events at least,' he says. 'Though no guarantees it'll run the same everywhere.' He does a search, soon finds another article that he reads out: '"What was Denzi Pritchard, son of Home Secretary Pritchard, *really* doing at the Hyde Park riot?" It's followed by so-called witnesses saying you were part of the rabble yelling and throwing things.'

'It's not true.'

'That's never stopped them before.'

'Should we tell Dad?'

'I'm sure Melanie has it flagged up and is aware. And she was probably right, anyhow – that there is too much going on for anyone to focus on you for long.'

'Huh. Hope so – even though I wish what is going on, wasn't.'

I'm feeling claustrophobic. I want to run, but Dad said not to go out, and I know Jax would veto if he knew. Instead I yawn, say I'm heading upstairs. Wait until he turns off the TV and I hear their door open, shut. The shower come on.

I slip out the back way in running kit. Hood up, I'm just another runner. As a few miles go by I start to feel more myself, despite all the crazy in the world, and able to think things through.

Fact: there's nothing I can do about The Circle and their threats, just worry like everybody else. Put it aside for now.

Also fact: my name and photo are out there, and there's nothing I can do but wait for it to blow over.

Doing nothing doesn't sit well; I need to *do something*.

Focus: on finding Tabby, and on the Penrose Clinic.

28

It's after midnight by the time I'm showered, back in my room with the door shut.

It's still evening in Washington, DC. I text Apple first – ask her if Leila is there, tell her I want to talk to her. She says she's home, in her office, and gives me the number.

It rings twice.

'Leila Klein.'

'Hi. It's Denzi.'

'Denzi?' Her voice – surprise. Well, I guess I've never called her before. 'It's good to hear from you. Apple said you got home OK.'

'Yeah, no dramas. There is something I want to ask you about now, though.'

'What's that?'

'It's that clinic you mentioned. The Penrose Clinic. I've been trying to find out stuff about it but not coming up with much.'

There is a slight pause. 'What do you want to know?' she says.

Her voice. Is it guarded?

'It's because of a friend, really. She was a Penrose baby, too – that's what she called it. She never really explained what, but she thought there was something not right about them. And then when you mentioned the same clinic, I was curious. But when I look them up online there isn't much about them other than research they're doing. And nothing at all about IVF.'

'Well, let me think. It was a long time ago, and a time and place I haven't wanted to dwell on. Not because of you!' she adds, hastily.

'I understand. But anything you can remember?'

'Well, it was *very* expensive. Your dad handled it, but there was paperwork – forms to sign, a lot of that. Have you asked your dad? About this, and that other stuff we talked about?'

'Not yet. He's been tied up with work with everything going on. But I will.'

'Do that. A university friend of his told him about the clinic and that's how we ended up there. It wasn't advertised or anything, as far as I know. I remember feeling *uneasy* with the place, and not just because I didn't want to undergo more IVF. It's hard to explain, but I felt a bit like I was being handled. And there were endless scans and tests after I was pregnant; they didn't just go, "Congratulations and bye" They were interested in *everything*. I found it intrusive. I wanted a home birth and then found out we'd signed something early on about having the baby in a private hospital in London. Though that was just as well with all the problems at the last minute.'

'What sort of problems?'

'There was some kind of immune reaction – because of our blood types being different, I think? I ended up having an emergency C-section, with all the drama. But we were both fine at the end of it all so they must have known what they were about.'

'Was there any follow-up after I was born?'

121

'Just the first months. As far as I know.'

Because then you were gone, I think. 'But not like an ongoing study or anything? My friend said there was with her.'

'I don't think so, but ask your dad. There were a few times I was asked to go to one of the US branches of Penrose for checks, and was told that if I did I could have free ongoing healthcare. I told them to get stuffed.'

Wow. She really didn't like them, then – healthcare costs the earth in the US, and she turned down free?

We talk a bit more, about other stuff – she asks about what happened at Hyde Park, so either Apple told her or she found out another way.

After she says goodbye I still sit there, holding my phone. Thinking.

Nothing Leila said reassures me in any way. Instead, I feel even more strongly:

Something is up with this Penrose Clinic, I know it – I can feel it in my gut. But what could it be? What made Leila hesitant to talk about it, and Tabby run away?

My head is aching. Today has been too much, all of it. I lie down, close my eyes, try to sleep. My mind hops from one thing to another, nothing making sense, everything spinning . . .

I slice through the water. Wary of the deep places, I stay near the surface. The transition between sea and air is so close that I could reach out at will, have part of me in one zone, part in the other; I can almost convince myself they can merge and become one world. That the fight between the two can end in harmony.

But that is a fantasy. There will be no rest until one wins.

122

And so I swim. Desperate both to dive down deep, and to fly through the air. Held between, instead.

I'm nobody's pawn. I will *choose.*

But not yet.

29

My head is pounding when my eyes open the next morning. I feel like I've gone ten rounds with someone bigger than me. That dream was so weird, and it felt like it was running on a loop all night long.

I shower and have some breakfast, but still feel groggy. I shake it off, determined: today is the day. I'll work out what the hell is going on.

When I pick up my phone, I see missed calls, messages. Dad and Melanie. I groan: what now?

There is also a link messaged from Melanie, one I'm tempted to ignore. I sigh. I guess it's better to know?

I click on it and it takes me to a news site. And there I am, going out the back door in my hoody late last night. Captioned, 'Where is the son of the Home Secretary sneaking out to late at night?' Another photo, captioned, 'Back almost 90 minutes later.' Speculation again as to my involvement in the Hyde Park riot. Inferring I was out planning more mayhem.

God. I message Dad: I went for a RUN last night. That's all, and if they followed me, they'd know that.

Then I'm creeped out. Was it just someone watching the house, camera in hand, or did they? *Follow* me?

This distraction I don't need, and I push it away.

Focus.

I couldn't find out much about the Penrose Clinic, so I'll see if I can find out anything about swim school. The clinic was there – in the CSME, the sports medicine building. Swim school must be involved somehow.

First, I go back to the school website, to see if there is any more information about what happened there after the storm surge.

There's another post from Khan, the head teacher, listing school staff who are missing, and those confirmed dead – kitchen staff, gardeners, caretakers. People I probably saw all the time during the school year but never really knew, and that seems so wrong now.

Then I find an external link for the swim school.

It takes me to a missing-persons page; it's not an official one of the swim school. Instead it looks like it was set up by parents of some of the swimmers. They're getting together, demanding answers about what happened to their children. I'm lost in reading pleas for information. Photos of the missing – so many of them – with messages from parents, friends.

There's a post and photo of Zara. I'd come in last on purpose once to run extra laps so she wouldn't have to. Her face smiles on the screen. Missing. Messages from her parents, school friends.

Ariel is here, too. I wasn't sure of her – she was so *out there* with people, and extroverts always make me uncomfortable. But she was Tabby's friend, and she's missing. There are so many messages under her image, it's like everyone who ever met her is her grieving best friend.

There are also some posts – very few – from people marking themselves as safe, like a boy I recognise vaguely who was in a different swimming group; Con is his name. And Isha, too, another friend of Tabby's. She'd gone home before the hurricane.

I hesitate, then put up a post of my own – marking myself as safe.

Scanning through I find another marked-safe post, this one from Becker – our running coach. I hadn't thought of him and I really should have after he drove me to the airport in the middle of the night.

Maybe he knows something – *anything* – about the school and the clinic. Or Tabby.

His post has a link, and soon I know a few more things about him. His full name is Andrew Morrison Becker, and he owns a private gym in London

Maybe I should step up my training.

30

'No way. Denzi?'

It's Becker, looking thinner and with stubble on his face, but it's definitely him.

'Hi.'

'What are you doing here?'

'Looking for a new gym.'

He raises an eyebrow like somehow he isn't convinced. He takes over the tour from someone named Jenny who had started to show me around, points out the cardio equipment and the weights room; tells me about their classes and membership.

Finally he ushers me towards an office and we sit down in chairs both sides of a desk.

'Glad you're OK,' Becker says.

'Thanks. You too.'

'How was your mum in the States?'

'She was in a coma when I got there, but she came out of it and is fine now.'

'That was a lucky escape for you. Not being at the school, I mean.'

'I know. If it wasn't for that accident she was in . . .' I shrug.

'Should I bother going through the gym membership forms, or do you want to tell me why you're really here?'

'I want to know what happened. Were you there? When the hurricane came?'

He shakes his head. 'I would have been if it wasn't for one of the girls doing a runner the night before.'

'Who?'

'She was a friend of yours, I think. Tabby?'

'What happened?'

He hesitates, then shrugs. 'I don't suppose it matters much now. I don't know why she left or how, but she did. Her fitness tracker triggered an alarm because her pulse rate was really high. Traced it to that black cat.'

'Dickens?'

He nods. 'He had her tracker around his neck. There was a search of the school and grounds; she couldn't be found. A few of us were sent out of school to try to find her – I was checking bus stops and train stations, that sort of thing. I drove to Taunton station in case she'd hitched there; that's around where I was when the hurricane hit. Just thought it was a normal sort of storm – found out the truth soon after. Roads were closed, phone lines and mobile networks down. It was unreal.'

'And Tabby?'

He shakes his head. 'I don't know where she was – hidden someplace at the school we couldn't find her, maybe? If so, chances are . . .' His voice trails off.

I'm smiling to think of her putting her tracker on the cat, and shake my head. 'I can tell you some of what happened to her. Her mum picked her up and was taking her home. They got caught up in storm surge. Her mum drowned, but Tabby survived. She was taken to a hospital in Bristol.'

'That's some good news about Tabby, then. Apart from her mother.'

'Well, sort of.' I explain what Dad told me, how she's missing again. 'Look, I really want to find her, make sure she's all right. Do you know anything about why she might have left the school? Maybe it has something to do with why she's gone off again. Was it something about the school?'

Again, there's something there, some reluctance on his part to talk, and that in itself makes me more suspicious of the whole place.

'Please.'

'It hardly matters what I say any more, does it? Now that most of them are dead or missing. I always felt there was something going on there, something under wraps. There were all these endless NDAs I had to sign to even get through the gates, but they paid so over the odds that I went anyhow. Everything I've got is sunk into this gym and it's been struggling. Six weeks away for good pay I couldn't pass up.'

'NDAs? What are they?'

'Non-disclosure agreements, promising to never talk about the place or methods used. Threat of legal action if you did. There was a definite us and them in the staff, also. Us on the outside, not involved in whatever it was. Them on the inside, like the director, Malina, most of the swim coaches.

'I convinced myself the secrecy was all about the training methods, that they didn't want other trainers or coaches to learn about. But there really was over-the-top security. And some of the training they did?' He shakes his head. 'It didn't make sense and, believe me, I know a few things about training.

'When Tabby disappeared, I didn't think it through at the time. I thought we were just looking for her, to make sure she was OK.

'But afterwards? This may sound a bit crazy. But there was something about the way they reacted to her being missing. It made me wonder if she knew something, and they found out what it was.' He shakes his head. 'But that wouldn't explain why she's run away again now, since she'd already got away from the school.'

'Becker, did you ever hear the rumours about there being a secret way to the sea under the CSME building?'

'Don't think so. But maybe that's why there were locked doors; it'd probably be dangerous.'

'Locked doors?'

'One of the physios told me. Under the CSME. He kept seeing people coming and going so, being curious, went to investigate. Locked doors at the bottom of both stairwells. Not just ordinary locks, either – the sort you have to swipe with a security pass.' Becker frowns. 'He left soon after he told me about that.'

Locked doors down a stairwell: that's where Tabby said she saw the Penrose Clinic symbol.

'Look, you're not going to tell anybody any of this, are you?' Becker says. 'I did sign the NDA. I shouldn't be talking.' He looks more nervous than he should. With most of them missing and presumed dead now, why could it possibly matter?

'Of course not. Can I just ask you one more thing? Have you ever heard of the Penrose Clinic?'

He shakes his head. 'Don't think so. Should I have?'

★ ★ ★

On the Tube home I'm thinking about what Becker said. He was nervous, as if talking about the place was going to come back at him. That is making me feel on edge too, and then I wonder if I've been snapped going in and out of the gym? If anyone is following me now? Just for the hell of it, I get on and off trains, make random changes – taking anyone who could be there on a merry dance – but all the while I'm getting more and more worried about Tabby.

If Becker is right and Tabby knows something, are they still looking for her, too? What would they do if they find her before I do?

Who even is this *they* behind the them and us split at the school that Becker told me about? Maybe whoever they were and whatever they were doing there doesn't matter any more – not if they were all there when the hurricane came and didn't survive.

But I can't take that risk.

Next moves? Talk to Dad about Penrose; see if he knows anything useful.

And try to contact Tabby's friends.

31

My phone is ringing as I go up our steps, unlock the door.

The call comes through Signal – it's Dad. I shut the door, then answer. 'Hello?'

'Where have you been?'

'I was checking out a new gym.'

'What's wrong with the usual place?'

'Nothing. Anyhow, decided not to join the new one.'

'Denzi, we need to know where you are.'

'Why? Don't you trust me?'

Dad sighs. 'Of course I do. And I know you like your independence, but just check in, all right? It'd help me answer unexpected questions as to your whereabouts, like I got last night.'

'Sorry about that. Is everything OK?'

'It will be. I've got to go. Stay in, all right?'

He says goodbye and is gone before I get the chance to say anything else.

I'm through the door, annoyed for more than one reason. I need to talk to him about Penrose and Tabby: when will I get the chance?

I start to message him on Signal, then think, no. I'll send more than one message if I text instead.

Dad, I really need to talk to you. To ask you about the Penrose Clinic.

There's a pause. Then a reply: I'll get some time at home as soon as I can.

Laptop. Sofa. I point the remote at the TV and switch to the BBC.

The PM is talking about the UK spearheading an international climate task force, one with power to impose rules, sanctions, like The Circle is demanding. She's careful to say that it was what was being planned, anyhow. Already the idea has guarded comments of support from some world leaders, but all say some variation of 'the details will have to be considered carefully'. Other more negative reactions follow also – from the US, some of their allies.

Assuming it is even set up, they'll talk and talk and do nothing useful if key countries aren't involved, won't they?

I mute it and go back to the swim school page.

Tabby's friend: Isha. She marked herself safe and said that she'd left the school before the hurricane, though not exactly when. Maybe she knows something about what happened with Tabby.

I find Isha's post and send her a friend request, along with a message saying who I am, that I was at the swim school.

A message comes back within minutes: What do you want?

To talk about Tabby.

There's a pause, and then: I think I remember you. Didn't you sit with Tabby and Ariel at meals?

Is this a test? No, you did. I was off to the side reading books most of the time.

She accepts my friend request. OK, Denzi, it's you. Sorry to be so careful. My parents have been on my case about security with all the threats just now – as my mum works in oil & gas. Do you know what happened to Tabby? She's not on the missing or safe lists from swim school.

I don't know for sure. I give her the basics that Dad had told me, adding in Becker's details without the source.

Wow. So she's run away twice?

Yes, that's what I understand. I don't know why she ran, though. Have you got any ideas?

There was something she was worried about. She'd gone out to check it at night and I wore her tracker for her. But they worked it out and came to my room. I was sent home. I wanted to go home anyhow, but I was worried about Tabby and they wouldn't tell me anything.

She'd gone to check something at night . . . it must be the Penrose Clinic door. She'd said she was sure, but I bet she wanted to double check what she saw – that's it, isn't it? And then sometime after that . . . she put the tracker on Dickens and vanished.

It has to have something to do with the Penrose Clinic.

Isha, have you ever heard of the Penrose Clinic?

She doesn't answer for so long that I'm worried she's gone.

Isha? Are you still there?

Yes, and yes – I have heard of it. Why?

Tabby told me she was a Penrose baby. I didn't know it then, but so was I.

She doesn't answer. Finally I message her again: Isha?

I don't know if it is safe to talk about this here.

Safe? What do you mean?

Look, I know this is meant to be encrypted, but delete this chat after anyhow, ok?

134

I will, I promise.

OK. I'm a Penrose baby, too. So was Zara.

What? Seriously?

I don't like talking about this on here. Can we get together and talk in person?

Of course. Are you near London?

Brighton.

I'll get a train there, I message back, wondering if this will clear the Dad radar or if I should even tell him. What if he says not to go?

How about we meet at the end of the pier? Is tomorrow any good?

Yes. What time?

Noon?

OK. See you then.

We exchange numbers. I do as she asked, delete the chat at my end knowing she's doing the same.

This is so unbelievably *weird*.

Late that night I'm pacing in my room, feeling caged. I'd go for a run again, but do I want to be back in the news? And if I message Dad what I'm doing like he asked, he'll veto it. Won't he? And then I'll have to decide whether to do as I want anyhow. I don't want to risk a big blow-up when I still need to talk to him.

Everything keeps going back and forth in my mind.

Four Penrose babies – Tabby, me, Isha, and Zara – at swim school. A branch of the Penrose Clinic hidden there behind locked doors. Leila and Becker both being guarded about what they would say. Becker and his us/them and NDAs. Isha being so afraid to chat: what is she scared of? I'm hoping she'll tell me when we meet tomorrow, but I'm not sure she will.

There's a tap on my door.

'Yeah?' I call out.

Jax peers in. 'I saw the light under the door – guess you can't sleep either. Have you been watching the news?'

I shake my head. 'Has something happened?' I ask, alarmed.

'Yes and no. Come see.'

All over the world, reports are coming in as the sun comes up, starting in Australia, then moving along date lines. Circles – four of them, two rows of two, edges just touching – appearing in all sorts of places. On the sides of oil tankers. Coal burning energy plants. Offices of all the big oil companies, and that's not all – also at the homes of CEOs and VPs of the same companies. As the word spreads, some are found where it is still night, like the offices of Industria United in London, North Sea oil platforms. Even the sides of a storage facility in the Shetland Islands.

Some are in stark red paint. Some places they're like crop circles in the grass – including the manicured lawns of the White House.

So far, the UK parliament is untouched – is that because of their talk of setting up a task force that everyone knows will never happen?

One that is hard to understand are the big red circles on the side of the building that houses the offices of Big Green in Washington – where Leila works.

And nowhere did anyone see anything, and in places like the White House it's hard to imagine *how* this could be done without anyone noticing.

So, The Circle talked about targets, and here they are, marked up for the world to see.

We watch as reporters around the world scramble to bring footage from far and near, until Jax starts yawning sometime after midnight, orders us both up to bed.

In my room the walls feel too close and I'm restless, pacing back and forth. The windows are open but it's still stifling, like the air is too warm and heavy to breathe.

Are the circles a random symbol or do they mean something?

Back and forth, again, and again: around and around. I swim along the walls of my prison looking for a way out that I know isn't there, but I can't stop.

Yesterday – today – tomorrow: they are all the same, no matter which way I go.

Around and around . . .

32

I wait until I'm on the train to message Dad, so it is too late for him to say no: Brighton for a sea swim today, I won't be late. All that comes back is, Have fun.

I'm watching scenery rush past the window, and as it does another sort of rush goes through me: the sea is getting closer. It's been days since I've been near it and the closer the train gets to Brighton, the stronger the call.

That day, running with Tabby: standing by the gates over the cliff. Both of us staring at the sea in the same way. I never felt as . . . *connected* to a girl as I did at that moment. It wasn't how she looks, though even after a run she looked amazing, standing there, that long dark hair. Those eyes. The way they looked at the sea, and then at me. It was almost like she wanted the sea, and me, just as much as I did.

I shake my head. Just because I'm daft like that about the sea I shouldn't think anyone else is the same, at least, not just from that one moment. But it *felt* that way.

I'm beyond worried about Tabby. Is she safe? It's been days since she disappeared in Bristol. Where has she gone?

And Isha: what is she afraid of? Not trusting chat encryption, wanting to talk in person like this?

Whatever this is all about – I want to *know*.

* * *

I walk down from the station to the seafront – more of a jog than a walk, as much as I can through the waves of people, all heading in the same direction. The sun is relentless. Why didn't I come early enough for a swim before meeting Isha?

I drink the sea in with my eyes when I get to the beach, then reluctantly start walking along the pier. The taste of the sea in the air will have to do for now.

When I reach the end of the pier, I'm ten minutes early. I scan heads and faces but she's not here yet.

There are fishermen casting. Kids with ice cream. A scoop of chocolate falls off one kid's cone and he howls until his mother gives him hers. The sea below is calm, and it's hard to imagine what it did so recently around the coast when everything is so normal here.

There is commotion now – fingers point out to sea, at flashes of silver: dolphins! My heart seems to jump with them, fall down back into the water. They carve up again as a group and splash down and it's all I can do to stop myself from diving from the pier to join them. Goosebumps run up and down my arms: that dream I had, in Washington, that I dived off the pier to join dolphins but then fell and fell. My head spins and I step back from the railing a little.

Five past now. More people surge to see the dolphins and still I'm scanning faces, waiting.

Quarter past. Most of the crowd has gone, either in the water or seeking shelter from the sun. I'm chewing my bottom lip, wanting to do both. Worried. Where is she?

I check my phone: no message or anything saying she'll be late. Maybe she forgot, or decided not to come. Though she doesn't strike me as the sort who would no-show without letting me know.

Twenty past, and I text: Hi, it's Denzi. I'm here, hope haven't missed you?

There's no answer.

Another twenty minutes makes forty minutes late. I text again. Hi, are you ok? I'm going to wait til one then go for a swim. I'll be back here at two.

It's one and still no answer. I walk back up the pier and then along the seafront to the left, walking quickly to get past some of the crowd. Put my phone in a waterproof case and zip it into my swim shorts pocket, shuck off T-shirt and trainers. Walk across the shingle to the water's edge. Some part of me is still worrying about Isha, but more is focused on each step getting closer and closer to the sea, until – at last! – I'm in it. Feet . . . ankles . . . calves. When it is up to near my waist, I dive under.

It's cold after the heat of the sun on my skin and all at once I feel completely awake, alive. The tension I was holding inside about so many things – including waiting for this moment – strips away. All I am is here, now. Swimming as far and fast under water as I can.

When I finally break the surface to breathe, I've come so far out I'm startled. Maybe all that crazy apnoea training at the swim school actually did do something for us.

I swim lazily along the line of the beach, away from the pier, back towards it and repeat. Finally – reluctantly – I kick back for the shore. It must be getting near two by now.

As I get out of the water into the sun my worrying about what has happened to Isha returns. I get my phone out. There's still no reply, but I pull on my T-shirt and trainers, and head up to the end of the pier. Wait another hour, have another swim, look around one more time. There's no sign of her.

I head for the train station and home.

On the train, I'm looking at the swim school page again: Isha's post is gone. I deleted our chat so I don't have her username – I'd just taken the link from the page. I hunt for her but come up with nothing. She might have been set to private so I can't find her without a link.

I'm even more uneasy now about her not turning up. Has something happened to her?

What was her surname? I saw it when I messaged her and I try to picture how it was on the screen. A short surname. Something Asian, maybe? No matter how I try, I can't remember.

I try searching for 'Isha – swimmer'; then 'Isha – Brighton – swimmer'. Random stuff comes up; nothing that seems to be about her or any details.

Maybe Dad could work out who she is, check with her family that she's OK? I'll include that on the growing list of things we need to talk about.

I still can't believe that there were four Penrose babies that I know of at the school: Tabby, missing. Zara, missing. Isha – who knows what has happened to her. And me. If there were four of us, who knows if there were even more?

But *why*? What does it mean?

There's a sick feeling, deep in my gut, that echoes the miles as the train pulls away from the sea.

33

When I get home, Jax has left lasagne to heat up and a note. He's out, Dad was home earlier – I've missed him. And he's back at work, in COBRA meetings. Translation: he can't take calls. It ends with, 'Stay home after dark'.

Huh. What am I – ten?

I'm halfway through the lasagne when it hits me: there was another swim school survivor marked as safe on that page where I found Isha: Con. Maybe he's a Penrose baby too? I could ask him, see what he says.

I finish eating and load the dishwasher, not sure what to do.

I don't know Con; I barely recognised him from his photo. I don't think we've ever even spoken. How do I bring up the subject?

Just do it.

I go back to the swim school missing persons page to find his post. There's a message pinned at the top of the page: it says the last of the roads to the school that were shut have been cleared. Some of the parents are going to meet tomorrow and go there. They want to see for themselves what happened and are ignoring official instructions to stay away.

What will they see? I both want to know, and to never go there again – a place where so many died.

I find Con's message and click reply.

Hi, Con. Not sure we've spoken but I was at the swim school this summer. There's something I want to ask you if that's ok.

I check messages over and over again. It's an hour later when an answer pings in.

Hi, Denzi, I remember you. You left a few days before the hurricane I think? I went home a day later. My little brother broke his leg in a trampolining accident and was asking for me.

Poor kid, is he ok?

Fine – milking it now and demanding constant beck and call. Can't believe what happened back at swim school. So many friends – gone.

I know.

Not that I had many of them as friends, exactly, and now they're gone and there isn't another chance, it feels wrong. I never bothered, and now it's too late.

What was it you wanted to ask?

Here goes. This may seem a weird out of the blue kind of question – but have you ever heard of the Penrose Clinic?

A pause. Yes. Why do you ask?

I was an IVF baby with them. Turns out there were at least three others at swim school who were, too. Just seems really weird.

No way. That's beyond weird. Look, I've been told not to talk about this. But . . . so am I! A test tube creation from Penrose, that is. Does that make five of us?

Yes. Who said not to talk about it?

My mum. Apparently, it was a bit hush-hush. They couldn't afford the treatment and got it for free as part of a research thing, you know? Part of the deal was to keep quiet. But she told me about it a few years ago, thought I should know. You won't tell anyone what I said about it?

Of course not.

That's super-weird though. That there were five of us at swim school. What are the chances?

Later I'm thinking of just that: the chances of five us being there just randomly happening to be Penrose babies.

Maths isn't my favourite subject, but I did OK at the statistics part we did last year. If the fifty of us at swim school were random from the population at large, what is the chance of five of us being IVF? A little online research suggests the per cent of live births resulting from IVF is something like two – more than I would have thought. So, if there was a two per cent chance that one of us there was IVF, then the chances of five of us being IVF is 0.02 multiplied by itself five times.

Which comes out to just about zilch. Something like *one chance in three million*. Given that the two per cent is based on all IVF and that I have no idea how many IVF babies came from the Penrose Clinic or if we're even included in official figures, the chances are likely to be much less than one chance in three million.

If I accept that it was basically impossible for five Penrose babies to have just happened to be there at the same time, then *why* did it happen?

There are only two reasons I can think of. The first is that, for reasons unknown, the organisers of the swim school went out looking for Penrose babies and invited us there for the summer. That's maybe backed up by the fact that Tabby and Isha had both been scouted without having trained before, though it doesn't explain why Penrose babies seem to be particularly good swimmers.

Which brings me to the other possibility: what if there is something about being a Penrose baby that makes you a very good swimmer? Then perhaps we were either found because we were good swimmers, or they went looking for us knowing we'd be good swimmers.

Assuming it is even possible, did they set out to create babies that would grow up with these skills? But *why* would anyone do that? It seems extreme if the only aim was to coach gold-medal winning Olympic swimmers.

There's clearly secrecy around the Penrose Clinic's IVF. Isha was scared to even talk about it. Leila and Becker said there were NDAs. Con was specifically told not to. What was it he said? I look back at our chat: . . . *got it for free as part of a research thing . . . Part of the deal was to keep quiet*.

Another thing: if there were five Penrose babies there this summer, maybe there were more? Given it wasn't drawn to our attention, I'm guessing they don't want it known. So even if it was just the five of us, how could they be sure we wouldn't find out?

I guess it isn't the sort of thing that comes up as a conversation starter: 'Hi, I was an IVF baby, were you?' seems unlikely. Tabby only mentioned it because she saw that door; Isha was hesitant to even talk about, so I'm guessing she would never have told Tabby or me without it being raised by us first. Con, ditto – if I hadn't asked him outright, he'd been told not to talk about it, so why would he?

The Penrose Clinic website doesn't even mention IVF: are they keeping it some sort of secret now, or has it always been that way? Their website says they do research in medical genetics; nothing about babies and—

Wait. What I know about the five of us, and what this clinic does – do they go together? What if – I swallow, acid in my throat to even think it – what if we were part of their research?

If they mucked around with our genes – it's *got* to be so illegal. Is that why the NDAs and secrecy?

I need help figuring this out.

Phone out, I message Dad, and do it his way, on Signal. I really need to talk to you – soon.

It's an hour or so before he messages back. Sorry I missed you earlier. Hands full at the moment – how about tomorrow?

I know you're busy, but this is important.

There's a pause. I'll check into something and message back.

Ten minutes later: A car will come for you at nine.

34

'Jax sends a care package.' I put a box on the desk, packed in haste when Jax got back just before nine. 'Mostly biscuits, I think.'

'Thanks for bringing it,' Dad says.

'I didn't think at first they'd let me bring it in. It's mad getting in here. Worse than an airport.'

'I know, security has really been stepped up. It's good to see you, Denzi. Sorry I haven't been around much since you've been back.'

'I understand,' I say, and I do, but that doesn't make it feel any better, knowing I'm so far down the list. Which is childish, I tell myself. Dad opens the box, holds it up to me and I take one. Chocolate chip. YUM.

'Is this your dinner?' I say.

'Let's see: carbohydrate, dairy, nuts for protein. Why not? Now as to why you're here: Jax told me you'd said you had some good chats with Leila when you were away, and then you texted me about the Penrose Clinic. What did she tell you?' He's looking at the biscuits instead of me, takes another out. Focuses on which bit to eat first and yes, they're good but not that good. He's *nervous*, and seeing that makes me feel strange, uncomfortable. It isn't right for my dad to be nervous of talking to me about anything.

Leila and what she told me isn't why I came here today, but I can't let it go.

'Leila told me to talk to you, to get your side of things.'

'Did she? What else?'

He's fishing – to see what I know – before he says anything. I've lived long enough with a dad as a politician to read the signs.

I shake my head. 'You go first.'

He sighs. 'If you know about Penrose you must know about the IVF treatments?' I nod. 'Leila was very unwell after you were born; she couldn't deal with being a mother. I couldn't deal with her. I'm sorry I haven't talked to you about this before. I should have.'

'Is it true that you and Jax – while you were still married to Leila?'

'Yes. It wasn't my finest hour.'

'She thought you tricked her – to have a baby.'

'I know. She told me that when she left. It's not true, I promise you. It wasn't until I met Jax – well. Sometimes you meet the right person and – that's it. You'll understand that one day if you don't now. But although I didn't handle things the right way, I never planned it to happen like it did, either. A few years later, I tried to get Leila more involved in your life. She wouldn't talk to me, and I can't say I blame her.'

He's uncomfortable – uneasy – but I know him. He's telling the truth about this now.

And I'm remembering thinking how Leila and Oliver belonged together; and Jax and Dad do, too. Maybe things have worked out the way they should for them, but what about me? I don't even know how I feel.

'Are we OK?' Dad says.

'I don't know. Yeah. Probably. But that isn't why I'm here. I want to ask you about the Penrose Clinic.'

'What about it? Why?'

'Well, it's probably going to sound a bit crazy, but here goes. That girl I had you look into – Tabby – was also a Penrose baby. She's still missing. I think something about the Penrose Clinic might be behind why she ran away, and it has something to do with the swim school.' I quickly run through how Tabby saw a hidden door at the school with the Penrose Clinic symbol; that she went back to look for it at night, and then ended up leaving.

'Seems an odd place to find the Penrose Clinic. Is this just based on something Tabby thought she saw on a door?'

'Well, I know that she went back to double check the door before she left. I don't know if she learned any more.'

'If she went to double check, she wasn't sure what she saw. And you don't know what she found when she did so. And anyway, even if it was what she thought – you don't know why she left. There could be any number of reasons.'

Dad's voice, what he is saying – all sound so reasonable, I'm starting to question what I thought. But he hasn't heard the rest.

'Listen, there's more. Since then I've found there were more Penrose babies, like us, there this summer. I was meant to be meeting one of them, Isha, today, but she didn't show, and her post has disappeared from the swim school page online. I'm worried about her.'

'There's probably a simple explanation for that: maybe she remembered she had a boyfriend and thought she shouldn't, or found something else to do and didn't tell you. And just how many Penrose babies were there this summer?'

'Including me, five that I know of; there may have been more. That isn't random, it can't be. Something seems very odd about all of this. Can you find out if Isha is OK? And has there been any news of Tabby's whereabouts? And what about the rest of the swimmers – were more of us Penrose babies?'

Dad has his politician face on just now, the one that says he's listening, but there is no reaction to what I've said. He's hiding something; I know it, and we're not talking about what happened with Leila any more. Why would he do that?

'If there is something going on with Penrose, I have a right to know: you decided to have me with them. It was your choice, not mine. Tell me what you know.'

He shakes his head. 'You're making this all sound dark and mysterious, and it isn't. It was an IVF clinic like any other. And it is going back a few years; it's not something I've thought of for a while.'

'Did you have to sign something saying you wouldn't talk about it?'

His eyes open a little wider: surprised? 'There were NDAs – non-disclosure agreements. Leila signed as well; she isn't supposed to talk about the Penrose Clinic, though I don't suppose talking to you counts. What has she told you so I know where we are?'

'I guess the way she put it was that she felt uneasy with them – like she was being handled, I think she said.'

'That's fair; she did. But I didn't. I think that was part of her mental illness beginning to manifest then that made her feel that way. What else can I tell you? It was a specialist international

150

clinic, with branches in major cities around the world. Their technology was beyond what the NHS could offer – seemed to offer hope to failed IVF patients, such as Leila. I understand there were some patents pending at the time. Hence the NDAs. There's nothing unusual about that.'

'Don't you think it's weird that there were so many of us that were Penrose babies at the same swimming school?'

'It seems a pretty crazy coincidence, but sometimes things like that happen. What was it on the news a few months ago – identical twins who had never met after being adopted and living in different countries ending up at the same university, on the same course? Sometimes strange things happen.'

I'm looking at him, about to give him the stats I worked out, when there's a buzz on his phone. He answers, 'Yes, on my way,' then hangs up.

'Look, I understand you're worried about your friends. I'll see if there is any news about Tabby, and check into Isha to reassure you. And I'll look into the other swimmers from the summer, see if there is a way to find out if there were more Penrose babies there; I expect not, but just to put your mind at rest. So leave it to me, all right? I have to go now; I'll walk you out. The car is waiting for you.'

We head out of the office door and down the hall, and I glance at him as we walk. I didn't tell him my suspicions that Penrose did something to us that changed us. If I'm honest, I couldn't bring myself to say it out loud; it'd be proof positive to Dad that I've lost the plot. Or maybe, it's more because I don't want to think about it too closely.

He said he'd look into everything, which is what I wanted to hear, but I'm still uneasy. There's something there, something he isn't saying. I can feel it. What could it be?

Home and again unable to sleep, I keep thinking through it all. Finally I give up and go back to the swim school page, and click on the pinned post – the one about going to the school tomorrow. There's a list of who is going – I check it, wondering if Con is going, but his name isn't there. Maybe he doesn't know about it?

I look for Con's post, but I can't find it. It's been taken down, just like Isha's. Seeing that makes the hackles go up on my neck.

I go back to our chat; it says, Con has left this conversation.

What the hell?

Something weird is going on, and it all links back to the swim school. Could I find out anything if I go there?

I go back to the post about tomorrow and add a comment: I was there this summer and want to come. Does anyone have room for one more?

It's almost three a.m. before another insomniac answers: it's Becker.

I do.

35

'What are you up to today, then?' Jax says over fried eggs on toast. It's early, not much past six, and he's looking at what I'm wearing. Usually this time of day, if I appear at all, it'd be in running gear, not a shirt and jeans like I have on this morning.

'Ah . . .'

'Out with it.'

'OK. There's some of the parents of kids that are still missing from swim school meeting up and going there. To see what happened to the place. I want to go.'

'Oh God. Are you sure that is wise?'

'No. I just feel like I have to go, see it for myself.'

He looks back at me for a while, then nods. 'Do you want me to take you? I can't today, I've got meetings all day. I could try to cancel them, or we could go on our own tomorrow?'

'Look, it's all right. I've got a lift from one of the coaches.'

'Are you sure?'

'Yes. But not sure what Dad will make of it. If I tell him . . .'

'Promise not to get in any trouble? And give me this coach's name, number, that sort of thing?'

'Absolutely.'

'Leave your dad to me.'

'Thanks, Jax.'

★ ★ ★

I get to Becker's gym just as he's coming out, yawning, car keys in hand.

'Hey, kid. We seem destined to go on road trips.'

'Really appreciate it.'

'This way,' he says, gestures. His car is around the corner and we get in. 'Last chance to change your mind – are you sure you want to come?'

'Yes. How about you?'

He shrugs and grins. 'Not sure, still going. Just feels like something I have to do.'

'Same.'

Like when we were going to the airport in the middle of the night, he drives too fast and we don't talk much on the way. As city becomes motorway and then quieter roads and countryside and the well-known way to school gets us closer and closer, I'm remembering.

My first trip to this school with Dad and Jax. Boarding here for the first time, aged eleven, and I was freaked to be left there, alone, knowing no one. I almost asked them to take me home instead. Something made me keep it inside, though I think Jax knew: he asked me, before they went, if I was sure. And I wasn't but said I was.

I was happy enough going there each year since then – years that seemed slow at the time but, looking back, came and went.

And my last trip this way – I'd had a few days home between end of term and swim school and it was weird to be going back in the summer, but I couldn't turn down the opportunity even if it meant not really having holidays. It felt strange at first being here with this bunch of kids who weren't usually at school – not to mention there being girls also. I was on my second last year of school and knew the place inside out, but it was all new to most of them.

Tabby stood out from the others, right from the first time I saw her. She didn't have this veneer of confidence most of them did, but more than that: it was like everything she thought and felt was *there*, on her face. And though she was more like sixteen than eleven, I saw echoes in her of how I felt my first time being left at school.

And now she is God knows where, the school was flooded, so many people are missing and dead – here and all along the coast. And I'm on the road to the centre of the place it all happened. The same place so much of my life has happened. It's just . . . unreal.

Now Becker is taking the last turn and we're almost there. 'OK, kid?' he says.

'Yeah, I think so.'

As the road dips down we start to see signs of what happened – bedraggled fields, misplaced things like a rubbish bin sideways just off the road, pieces of wood and what looks like a shed roof. Garden and household things and general rubbish pushed to the sides when the road was cleared.

One more bend.

There it is: the school. From above it now, it looks much like it always did, but as we get closer we see the truth. We left early but already there are a few cars pulled up in front of the gates, people standing around, some with arms around each other. A police car also. We pull in behind one of the cars and get out.

A policewoman walks over to us. 'I'm sorry, but the site is still being searched, and it isn't safe. You can't go any further.'

There's a sign on the gates. Gates which must have been built to last as they're still standing, but the fences are mangled further along. There is junk, broken glass, around the main building below. Tents: is that like forensics – have they found bodies? And now my stomach is twisting like I'm going to be sick and I breathe in, out, in, out, until it passes.

What did I think I could learn from coming here? I can't even go through the gates.

People are putting flowers in the fence and now I think I should have brought something, too, but what do flowers mean to the dead?

'Both of us – we could have been here,' Becker says. 'In some ways it'd have been easier for me if I was. I keep thinking I could have done something, anything.'

A man and woman are coming towards us.

'Did you have someone in your family at the school?' the woman asks.

Becker shakes his head. 'I worked here – I was the running coach.'

'And I was a student,' I say.

'Maybe you knew our daughter? Zara.'

We both nod.

'I'm so sorry. Such a nice girl. She didn't like early morning running much, though,' Becker says.

'That doesn't surprise me,' Zara's dad says. 'But swimming? She was like a fish. Coming here was her dream come true. How could it end like this? I still can't believe . . .' His voice trails away.

'*Don't*,' Zara's mum says. 'They'll find her – she's somewhere, alive, and they'll find her. I know it. How could she drown, the way she swims?'

And I get it. Unless a body is found and identified as being their daughter, they'll deny it as long as they can. They'll hope.

More parents arrive; some brothers and sisters, too. And they all have the same baffled pain, denial. How could this have happened?

I can't take any more and after a while tell Becker I'm going for a walk. There's a footpath that runs along fields and then drops down closer to the school, but it hasn't been cleared. It's a bit of a struggle to go along, pushing junk out of the way – stuff swept here from who knows where.

When the path dips down by the school there are segments of the fence down, some panels missing. A way in: can I find out anything that will help me find Tabby?

I'm out of sight of the gates, the people there. Without stopping to think if it is a good or bad idea, I slip through a gap in the fence.

This is part of where we used to run with Becker – along the perimeter of the grounds. The CSME – where Tabby saw the Penrose door – isn't far.

I set off at a fast jog, having to slow to get around parts of trees. Roof tiles. All sorts.

When I get to the gap in the hedge that leads to the CSME, and look through, all I see is rubble. The rambling old building is completely destroyed. If there were any clues to why Tabby ran away from this place hidden here, they're gone. Another dead end.

I'm disappointed even though I don't know what I thought I was going to find: if the building was still standing and the doors were locked – with security doors, as Becker said – I wasn't going to get anywhere.

I should head back before anyone spots me or notices I'm missing. But I'm about halfway down to the gates above the cliffs and sea, where I stopped with Tabby. It's the place I think of the most when I remember being with her.

There's no one around; it's not far.

Down the dip to where the view of the sea comes in and—

I stop, shocked.

The fence and gate are gone, and it's like a chunk of the coastline has fallen, or been eroded, or whatever you want to call it: the sea has cut itself a new, wider bay. The water is relatively calm today. I stare at it, unable to imagine what it would have been like on that day. The head teacher said on the school website that repairs will take a year or more but is there any way I want to come back here, knowing what happened?

There is more debris around me now and I'm remembering the policewoman saying they're still checking the site. Have they been here, looking for – I swallow – bodies? I don't believe in ghosts – at least, I don't think I do – but there is something about being here that has me thinking, or feeling, different. If they haven't checked around here yet there could be bodies still, and now I'm backing away, wanting to get back to Becker.

There is a light touch on the back of my leg. Startled, I spin around, fists up as if they would be any use against what I was thinking. At first I don't see anything, but then there is movement in the long grass across from me.

Dickens? He's low in the grass, backing away. I must have scared him, spinning around like that.

'Dickens, it's all right. It's me, Denzi.' I sit on the grass and hold out a hand. He's nervous, but comes closer, a little at a time, until he sniffs my hand then looks disappointed there's no treats on it.

'Sorry, didn't know I'd see you.' He comes closer and I stroke him. He leans into my hand.

'I wish you could talk. You could tell me why Tabby put her tracker on you that day, couldn't you?'

He tilts his head as if he's thinking about what I said, then comes closer still, half sits on my lap for more strokes. I can feel he's much thinner than he was.

'You were meant to be the mouser, but you lived on treats from everyone really, didn't you?'

He's snuggling into me.

'How about this: come home with me? We live in London so it's different to what you're used to.'

He licks my hand with his rough tongue. I shift him up into the crook of my arm, stand awkwardly while holding him – thinking if I let go, he might run off – but he seems content to ride with his head looking over my shoulder.

I walk back to the breach in the fence, go through and then towards the front gates.

Some of the cars have left, a few others have come. There are more flowers, cards, too, stuck to the fence and gate. Becker looks over.

'Ah, there you are. And is that the school cat?'

'Well, he was. Dickens said he'll try being my house cat for a

159

while. Is it OK to take him home in your car?'

He shrugs. 'What the hell. But any mess in my car and you're cleaning it.'

We set off soon after. Dickens curls into a ball on the back seat.

'If only that cat could talk,' Becker says, echoing what I thought earlier.

'How did he survive?'

'Don't know. He's down one of his nine lives for sure.'

I text Jax. There's someone coming home with me.

Intriguing. What's her name?

He's a he – Dickens. I take a photo and send that too. He was the school cat. He needs feeding up and a place to stay, I hope that's ok?

We'll see how it goes.

36

'We'll see how it goes, you said.' I'm raising my eyebrows: it looks like Jax has bought out the pet shop on his way home. 'Do we need all this stuff?'

'It's what was recommended. Also they said not to let him out until he's been here at least a few weeks and knows it as home.'

'What about— Oh.' Jax is holding up a cat litter tray, one with a roof. Dickens eyes it suspiciously then looks up at me and meows with a definite *no-way* tone. We both laugh.

'Are you hungry, little fellow?' Jax says. He strokes him, then waggles a tin and goes for a tin opener. The phone rings on his way and he holds the tin out to me while he answers.

I open it and wrinkle my nose. 'Smells like cat food for sure,' I say. Dickens' front paws are half up my legs and his nose is twitching. I find a bowl, put it in and he's started to eat before it is all the way down on the floor, purring as he tucks in. What else? Water. Another bowl.

Jax is back, phone down. 'It's a good news, bad news thing. Your dad is coming home for dinner!'

'And what is the good news?'

'Don't be cheeky. He's bringing someone. In an hour. And there's no time to get catering.'

★ ★ ★

After veg peeling duty, I have a quick shower while Dickens sniffs every corner of my room. When I come out he's curled up and fast asleep on my pillow.

I take his photo. There's one thing I can do at least: show it wasn't impossible to survive what happened there. I go to both the school page and then the swim school missing page and post a photo of Dickens, captioned, 'School cat found today, alive and well. He's making himself comfy at ours.'

There are more posts and photos on the swim school missing page from today: of the school, zoomed in from the gates. Of flowers and tributes left there also. And I'm thinking of Zara's parents, the desperation in her mother's voice, when I hear the door downstairs. Voices. Dad, and a woman?

I start down the stairs, but when I see who is there, stop short.

Jax has got there first, giving me a moment to recover as I go down the rest of the way.

Dad introduces them. 'Christina. It's lovely to meet you,' Jax says, and he and Christina – *Director Lang*, from swim school – exchange a double air kiss. What is *she* doing here?

She turns to me. 'Denzi. It's so good to see you again. How is your mother?'

'Ah, she's fine, thanks,' I say, trying to keep the shock from my face.

'What would everyone like to drink?' Jax says, and leaves to fetch wine a moment later.

'Denzi, I just had to come speak to you,' she says. 'Such a terrible tragedy, the loss of so many young lives – coaches and school staff, too. So appalling. It's understandable if you – or any of the others that have survived – are having trouble coming to grips with all of it.'

'You weren't there?'

'No. I feel guilt for that every day. I'd had a day out to attend to some appointments in London. Not that there was anything I could have done if I had been there but go down with the ship, as they say.'

'I, for one, am very glad neither of you were there,' Dad says.

Jax returns with the wine. He pours glasses and hands them around, including half a glass for me, but I don't want it, not with her here. I'm not sure what it means but I don't like it.

'Come, sit with me,' she says, and then I'm trapped next to her on the sofa. 'I understand from your dad you've been worried about some of your friends. I want to set your mind at rest, as much as I can, so I've looked into a few things.

'You were supposed to be meeting with Isha and she didn't show, is that right?' I glance at Dad. He told her that?

'Uh, yeah?' I say – no point in denying.

'She had to go stay and help out with her aunt who is having some health problems. Her mum says she forgot to take her phone; she saw your messages and told Isha. Isha says she's very sorry she didn't make it. Her family, though, is very protective of Isha and might not want her meeting a boy now they know about it. So if you don't hear from her, don't worry.

'Also, that boy, Con – his parents were concerned about the time he's spending online. Teenagers these days! – and have imposed an internet ban for a while.

'Finally, Tabby. The poor girl. The authorities are really concerned about her safety. She's had such a tough time, and I'm

163

sorry to say, she has had ongoing struggles with her mental health. I've been given the OK to share this with you by her family, otherwise I couldn't, of course. She has delusions that she and only she can save the world. Part of this is spotting conspiracies against her that don't exist. If you hear anything from her, you must let me know. Here's my card,' she says, and hands it to me, and I manage to stay calm, to take the card. Even as I'm thinking, *I don't believe anything you've said*.

'Shouldn't I call the police instead?' I say, pushing her, to see what she'll say.

'That's what I'd do, obviously, but I can give them some insight on how to handle the situation. All right?'

Jax is back again with canapés, saving me having to answer. Conversation moves to other topics.

Dad went to *her*? I went to him for help, confided in him, concerned something wasn't right about both the Penrose Clinic and the swim school, and he goes to the director of the swim school. What was he thinking?

At dinner they're chatting about old times, mutual friends, and at first I'm not paying much attention but then some pieces slot into place. Leila said it was a friend of Dad's that got them involved in the Penrose Clinic: was it Christina?

'Did you know each other from university?' I ask Dad.

'Yes. Cambridge: Trinity College.'

'You're the friend of Dad's my mum – Leila – mentioned. Aren't you?'

'What friend do you mean?' she says.

'The one who told Dad about the Penrose Clinic. Which led to me, you know, being here, and all that.'

Surprise is quickly replaced on her face by something like amusement. There is a glint in her eyes. Does she knows I'm on to her? Maybe I shouldn't have said that. 'It's so long ago, I'm not sure I remember. Do you, Monty?'

Dad turns to pour wine and shakes his head at the same time.

Later I'm relieved when she's finally standing, saying goodbye. Heading for the door along with Dad, who says he has a late meeting. I catch movement out of the corner of my eye – Dickens. At the top of the stairs looking down, staring at Christina as she puts on her coat. His fur is on end, bristling, as if he likes her as much as I do.

As the door closes behind them, I wonder if she realises the slip she made. I never mentioned Con to Dad, did I? And I only noticed today that his post was missing – it might have been like that for a while, but I didn't know it. So how did she know he's one of the ones I'm worried about?

I'm sure by the way they both reacted that she *is* the friend Leila mentioned who got them going to the Penrose Clinic to have me all those years ago. Does that mean that Christina is involved in both the clinic and the swim school?

She said Isha is at her aunt's and not to worry if I don't hear from her again. She said Con has been banned from the internet by his parents. She also said Tabby is mentally unwell, to call if I see or hear from her.

I don't believe any of it, but if she's lying, why? And what really happened to Isha and Con? At least going by the way she stressed to contact her if I hear from Tabby, she doesn't know where Tabby is.

'You're looking pensive,' Jax says as we load the dishwasher. It's tempting to confide in him about all this and see what he thinks, but I know that anything I say will go back to Dad – does that mean on to Christina, too? That Dad involved her feels like a betrayal.

Up in my room I go back online, searching again for anything about the Penrose Clinic. I go through page after page but don't find anything interesting I didn't before.

I don't know what else I can do to learn any more about them. But maybe I know somebody who can help: Oliver. He's an investigative journalist, after all. OK, he is in the US. But going by their website, Penrose has branches there, too.

I have Oliver's number from when Leila was in the hospital. I hesitate. Going to Dad didn't go well. But the last thing Oliver – or Leila, if he confides in her – would do is tell Dad. They do not communicate.

It's early afternoon there. I find his number and hit call before I can change my mind.

It rings a few times, then he answers. 'Hello?'

'Hi, Oliver? It's Denzi.'

'Hi, how're things?' he says, a note of surprise and worry in his voice to hear mine.

'Everything is fine. But there's something I'm trying to find out about and was hoping you could help.'

'Finding stuff out is what I'm best at. What is it?'

'The Penrose Clinic. The one Leila went to in order to have me.'

'Leila mentioned you'd asked her about it. Why the interest?'

'A weird coincidence that has turned into an unbelievable coincidence.'

'Tell me.'

So I do. About how there were at least *five* Penrose babies at swim school out of fifty of us. There could easily have been more, but I don't know how to find out now that most of the others are missing, presumed dead. And Tabby seeing the Penrose symbol on the door, then running away – twice.

Oliver whistles. 'What the hell? That can't be random – five of you there?'

'Look, I've done the maths. The chances of that happening randomly is way less than one in three million. And that's not all.' I explain about Isha failing to show, and Isha and Con both disappearing online.

'That does sound odd, but there could be any number of reasons.'

'Why would two teenagers, at about the same time, with the same swimming background and Penrose history, both cut themselves off from the internet? Come on.'

'It's suspicious enough to warrant a look, I'll give you that. What do you think it all means?'

'Honestly, I have no idea. I'm just worried about my friends. Also, I'm wondering if both Dad and Leila know more than they'll say about this clinic.'

'Hmmm. Well, I won't get between you and Leila, or side with one over the other. But you've made me curious. Leave it with me, and I'll see what I can find out.'

Part 4
Tabby

37

My eyes open wide. The sun is just coming up – is it the light that woke me?

I listen intently but hear nothing worrying, just trees moving slightly in the breeze outside, distant cars. Birds. And all the while I'm listening part of me is still in my dream.

I was in the sea, in the car, where Simone died. I almost did, too.

I would have, but *they* saved me: the dolphins came, and they saved me.

We called them.

Who is *we*?

How is that even possible?

I haven't been able to remember what happened, yet somehow, when I'm asleep, it's *there*.

It must be pure fantasy – it's not real, it can't be.

Can it?

What about that news report I saw on TV in the hospital in Bristol? A girl rescued by dolphins, supported in the sea, delivered unconscious to a fisherman. It looked like me in the photos, but they weren't clear enough to be certain.

So, did what I dream about really happen, or did my unconscious make it all up to fit the news story?

Even though it seems too crazy to even think it could be true . . . it felt so real.

* * *

I get up a few hours later. The house is still quiet. I make tea, then go through the fridge and cupboards. They are pretty bare, but I come up with enough ingredients to make pancakes.

I mix the batter and when I start to cook the first batch, the smell of food must do magic: Sascha and Jago appear almost instantly to eat them.

'These are amazing,' Sascha says. 'Thank you!'

'It's the least I can do. And I've been thinking, about stuff you said last night. Tell me more about Ren.'

'Well, she's a little odd, but clever with computers and into weird conspiracy theories,' Jago says. 'She's always finding crazy stuff online.'

'Can she keep secrets?'

'I think so.'

'You don't *know* so if you only think so.'

'She's legendary. Trust us,' Sascha says.

I'm not sure what being legendary actually *means*, but agree – as long as they won't tell her any more than what I'm comfortable with once we meet.

Sascha gets his phone out.

'Ren, hi. Listen, this is between us, right?

'OK. I've got something – someone – who may know some things about The Circle. Are you interested?

'Save the questions.

'Yes, OK. See you then.'

'Well?' Jago says.

'We're to meet at hers in an hour.'

172

38

'You have to promise me something, first,' I say. 'That you won't tell anyone anything I'm about to tell you unless I agree.'

Ren is raising a pierced eyebrow, sceptical. 'Well. It's hard to make that promise without knowing *why*. For example, if you told me a bomb was going off in our school tomorrow, I'd call the police. Or if you told me you were going to kill yourself, I'd try to stop you or tell someone who could.'

'No bombs, no suicide, I promise.'

'OK then, if there is nothing like that – then I promise. And I'll admit that I'm more than a little curious.'

'All right,' I say. And actually, I *do* believe her, and not just because Jago and Sascha vouch for her. If she thinks that much about a promise and what it means before she makes it, then I believe her when she does.

I tell her everything that I told Jago and Sascha about the links between the Penrose Clinic and The Circle, and about Cate's circle tattoo, and Malina's, too. How Cate died. Her eyes open wider, her mouth hangs open. Then she shakes her head. 'I mean, seriously?'

'All of it is true.'

'And these tattoos – do they look just the same as the symbol The Circle has been using?'

'That's what I was told; I drew them, and a police detective who came to ask me about The Circle said it looked the same.'

'Haven't you seen it on the news?'

I shake my head, look to Jago and then back to Ren. 'I've been a bit out of touch. What's happened?'

'More letters and threats were made a few days ago, and this symbol appeared like magic in loads of places linked with dirty fuel around the world. I'll show you.'

She turns back to her computer, goes to news channels. Images of the circles – small and large – either painted, carved or scorched on surfaces or grass. Places like the offices of oil and gas companies, political groups and institutions. Even the lawn of the White House. And some are at the homes of private individuals, like those with controlling interests in some of these dirty companies.

Could Ali – *Dad* – have been targeted like this if he wasn't missing? I'm horrified to think so, even knowing what he is and what he does as a VP of Industria United. There is a pang of guilt inside that I haven't tried to find out if he's been found. I've been avoiding thinking about it, afraid to have confirmed what I fear: swept out to sea and he's no swimmer, so how could he survive? I push it away to think about later: focus on *now*.

'Does that mean these places marked by the circles are all targets?'

'That's the theory. What about the symbol – is it the same?'

'Yes. It looks just like the tattoos.'

'Obvious question next: why don't you go to the police?'

I shake my head. 'Cate died in police custody. And anyhow, I have no proof. Who is going to believe me?'

'Then what is your plan? Assuming you have one.'

'Find out as much as I can about The Circle and the Penrose Clinic, and go from there.'

'I can already tell you there's *nothing* out there on this Circle group. Until the letters that were received the day before the hurricanes, no one had ever heard of them. Since then, everyone – me included – has been looking for information online that just isn't there, and while there is speculation all over the place, there is nothing concrete about who or what they are.' She leans back in her chair, runs a hand through spiky red hair. 'But this Penrose Clinic, either on its own, or combined with The Circle? Let's see what we can find.'

She's started to turn back to her computer when there is a beep and Sascha takes his phone out of his pocket, glances at the screen. 'Uh oh,' he says.

'What is it?' Jago says.

'Hang on, got to make a call.

Sascha leaves the room. We can hear his voice but not what he is saying, and then he comes back in.

'That was a mate. Police have been door knocking, asking if anyone saw a car parked near the link to the coast path early evening yesterday. He saw my car but didn't tell them, just called to say what is going on. And that's not all. They've also been showing a photo of that missing girl from the newspaper, he said. That must be you.'

There's a twisting feeling in my gut. They'll catch up with me; it's only a matter of time. Isn't it? I hug my arms around myself, as if that could keep them away.

Jago's warm hand is on my shoulder. 'If one person saw and recognised Sascha's car, someone else probably has, too, and they

175

might tell the police or whoever it was pretending to be the police,' he says. 'You can't go back to Sascha's.'

'I know,' I say, miserable at the thought. Being there with them had felt so *safe*, but how could it now?

Then Jago and Sascha are looking at Ren, but she shakes her head. 'The parentals have given me an overnight-guest ban while they're away.'

'When was the last time you did what they told you to do?' Sascha says.

'They told me not to get a stud in my tongue, and I didn't.'

'Show us your tongue!' he says, and she sticks it out: it's got a ring through it and they both laugh. It has the sound of something they say to each other all the time.

'Point taken.' She's looking at me, and sighs. 'Don't make a mess or empty the fridge and you can stay for a few days while we try to figure all this out.'

'Are you sure it's—'

'Say yes before I change my mind.'

'Yes! And thank you.'

Ren turns back to her computer. 'Now be quiet or go away.'

39

Jago has borrowed Ren's bike to go check in at home. Since then the TV is on and Sascha keeps changing channels. I start to tune out, to try to think things through. No matter how I try to make sense of things, to think about what I should do next, I keep coming back to this: The Circle has left its symbol *all over the world*.

No matter where I go, they'll always be there.

That is both terrifying and makes things easier at the same time. There is no point in even thinking about trying to dodge all of this and go to ground: they'll always be there.

'Ren?' Sascha calls out. 'Come look at this.'

He turns the sound up – BBC – as Ren comes in.

'Breaking news: the organisation calling itself The Circle has sent a new message to news networks and governments around the world, as follows:

'The Earth cannot wait for governments of the world to act. The sun in the sky over the slowly poisoned earth and seas cannot wait. We've sent details of how the hurricanes were caused for your scientists to verify: stop denying the facts. Stop denying that our planet is dying. Act or face the consequences.

'We understand that detailed information has been sent to

relevant scientific institutions and that these will be examined as soon as possible.'

Experts and commentators come on screen next with what they think about all of it and after a while Sascha turns it down again.

'Are they going to do something awful – another hurricane?' I say.

'Maybe,' Ren says. 'It's all guesswork though, isn't it? No one knows what they are planning.'

'Have you found out anything?' Sascha says to Ren.

'Nothing linking Penrose and The Circle, nothing new on The Circle. But the Penrose Clinic – there's so little information on them or what they do that it's actually a bit weird. There's stuff about fundraising and worthy-sounding research projects into genetic diseases, and nothing at all about IVF. I'll keep digging, though.' She looks around the room. 'Where's Jago?'

Sascha looks at his phone, frowns. 'He said he had to check in at home for a bit, but he really should be back by now. I'll call him.' Then, 'It's going to message . . . *Where are you, mate? Give us a call,*' he says.

We watch the news some more. Scientists say they're analysing what was sent. Commentators speculate; politicians dodge saying anything real. It's heading past dinner time and still no word from Jago. Ren texts him also; no reply, and I can tell they are worried, too. There's a creeping sense inside me. Something has happened, I know it, but what?

Then Sascha's phone pings. He looks at the screen and grins. 'It's Jago. He says, *Sorry, something came up. Order pizza: my treat.*'

40

Jago arrives on Ren's bike just as the pizza delivery car pulls in. He comes in, pizza boxes held in front like trophies.

Sascha whoops and takes them, puts them on the table, and something smells good, but even though I'm relieved to see Jago I'm not reassured. There's something – some worry – I can see on the set of his face, in the way his smile isn't quite to his eyes.

'What's happened?' I say.

'Food first,' Jago says. 'I'm starving.'

Sascha opens one of the boxes and he and Ren dive in, and I watch. Not sure I'm hungry, especially with wondering what Jago is going to tell us after 'food first', or even if I were hungry, whether this is something that I eat. The whole vegan thing has gone out the window with the dairy and fish I've had lately: what would Cate think? But this pizza is something else again – there looks to be some kind of meat on it, and that feels a step too far.

Jago opens another box. 'Vegetarian, this one. Better?'

There's peppers, courgette, tomatoes; I reach for a piece gingerly. Sniff it, try a bite. Take another bigger one. 'It's good,' I say.

'Haven't you had pizza before?' Sascha says.

I shake my head no, and the way he looks at me now is like that's even weirder than everything else he's heard from me these last few days.

'So, we're suitably mollified by pizza,' Ren says once most of it is gone. 'What kept you?'

'Well, I kind of had to go see Flick,' Jago says.

Flick? *That* girl?

'Why?' Sascha says.

Jago takes his phone out. 'She texted me this. *I remember where I've seen your friend Naomi before – but that isn't her name, is it?*'

My stomach falls. I'd been afraid she might recognise me from that day at the beach, but Sascha and Jago kept saying how different I looked now – convinced me she wouldn't.

'And?' I say. 'What did she have to say?'

'She has worked out who you are – the girl from the beach a while ago, and in the papers as a missing person. But I think I've convinced her to keep it to herself for now.'

'What – did you promise her your first born?' Sascha says.

Jago rolls his eyes but looks uneasy enough that I wonder *how* he went about convincing her.

'What does *for now* mean?'

'Look, I know the first time you met Flick was pretty shit. But she isn't all bad. We were friends until the last few years. She's with this crowd – well, you met some of them. But she's had a tough time with her stepdad and kind of gone off the rails. Drugs and stuff.'

'Do you trust her?' I say.

He shrugs his shoulders. 'Not completely. But I do know she definitely won't go to the police. Whether she'll keep quiet apart from that? I don't know.'

'If she talks, the word might get around,' Ren says. 'But no need to panic just yet. Nobody apart from us knows that Tabby is staying here, do they? But if Flick says anything and includes you, Jago, the police might end up back on your doorstep. Maybe you should stay away from here for a while.'

41

Ren has made up a sofa bed for me in a spare room upstairs. Lent me a tablet when I asked if I could look some stuff up. I know she's done this already and knows how better than I do, but I can't help wanting to try myself.

But first and foremost is Ali – my dad. He's been there at the back of my mind and I want to know what has happened to him, even though I'm afraid to find out.

I put 'Alistair Heath' in the search box. Hesitate, finally press enter.

Relief floods through me: he's all right. Missing from his flooded home, found clinging to wreckage at sea a few days later. Mourning his wife, searching for his missing daughter.

I want, *so much*, to go to him – to show him I'm all right. But I can't: what about Elodie? I'd be walking straight into a trap.

I push that aside. Next search: 'Penrose Clinic'. I find their website, and there is stuff about research but nothing about IVF; other links seem to be mostly about research and fundraising, much like Ren summed up earlier. I go through them, one after another, just in case there is something – anything – that Ren missed. Clicking links, scanning words and images, and I'm going so fast it almost doesn't register.

A photo of one of the founders of the clinic – Dr Seraphina Rose – at a fundraiser, shaking hands with some benefactor who has made a donation. Just behind and to one side of Dr Rose is a teenage girl, looking like she'd rather be anywhere else. I look and look again, unable to believe or process what it might mean. It's from a few years ago, so she's younger and looks a little different – her hair is longer – but it really looks like Ariel.

I read the rest of the article; there is nothing to say who is standing in the back of the photo.

I do another search, this time on Dr Seraphina Rose. There's fundraising stuff. Scientific articles. Loads of information, but nothing about any daughter.

Next search? 'Ariel Rose'.

Top of the list is a recent photo of a girl smiling and holding a swimming trophy, and this time there is no doubt at all: she doesn't just look like Ariel. She *is* Ariel.

But Ariel told me she'd never heard of the Penrose Clinic. Yet there she was at a Penrose fundraiser close to a woman with the same surname, who must be her mum.

She lied. If she lied about that, who knows what else she might have lied about?

Why did she lie?

Will I get a chance to ask her, or did she perish in the flooded school?

Though if the Penrose Clinic and The Circle are linked, then her mum is involved somehow. Surely she wouldn't let her own daughter drown.

Horror dawns inside me as I put this together with the girl-fish I saw with Ariel's face. Who knows what this Dr Rose might do if was she experimenting on her own children.

The floods might have washed away any proof of what she's

done. That girl-fish was the extreme, but what about us? Did they use the hurricane to destroy what they had created – girls like Ariel? And me.

They're trying to find me, but maybe it isn't because of what I know. Maybe it is because of what I *am*.

What now? Should I tell Jago and the rest about all of this?

A logical part of me says yes, I should: how can they help me – or even know how – if they don't know the whole story? But my instincts scream *no*. This is me, who and what I am: it is mine, not for sharing.

This I need to work out, myself.

But there is still something niggling in the back of my mind – something about the news earlier?

I go back to the BBC website, thinking I want to look again at those Circle symbols that appeared and where they were, but as soon as I go there it's all about breaking news:

Smoke and fire. Flames reaching for the sky or spreading above or even below ground. Some of the places marked by The Circle with their symbols earlier are burning: company offices, remote oil fields, a coal burning plant in Australia. Even the White House lawn.

There can be none of the doubt that followed the hurricanes of who is responsible: they marked their targets before they acted.

But *how* could The Circle have done this without being stopped, or, at least, observed? Some of the fires were set in what must be very secure, guarded locations, but nobody saw a thing.

The US response is swift: there can be no negotiation with terrorists. Not said, but all between their words, is that they won't take part in an international climate accord. They don't want to be seen to be doing what terrorists want, even if it is what they *should* be doing anyway.

Some fires are already out of control, like in Australia: it's day there now, but the smoke is so thick the sky is dark except where flames show red against it. The earth is tinder-dry from heat and drought, and fire is an animal – charging, destroying, *consuming* everything in its path.

The sea can't burn but oil platforms can, and one does in the North Sea, flames shooting high into the night sky. An environmental disaster, the newsreader says.

How can The Circle say they want to stop global warming and then do things like this?

I finally turn off the tablet, wrap my arms around myself. It's so hot and humid tonight; I feel like I'm there, one of the places I saw burning in the news.

I close my eyes but can still see flames, red and bright – as if they've also burned on to my retinas, left scars that will never go away.

Sun . . . Sea . . . Earth . . . Sky . . .

The sun burns in the sky and on the earth.

Sun . . . Sea . . . Earth . . . Sky . . .

What of my promises to honour and protect them?

I missed making my promise this year, and panic to think what that might mean.

Sun . . . Sea . . . Earth . . . Sky . . .

The chant is louder and louder but still flames burn with heat so intense, it's as if my very blood boils in my veins. There is only one answer, one way to make it stop.

Plunge into the sea. Down, down to darkness, cold. Still. The depths where almost nothing can live.

I can't.

Can I?

Something unnamed hides, deep in a seaweed forest, in fronds of green swaying in the current.

Both drawn and repelled, I swim deeper into darkness, searching. I will find it, I must. There is no choice.

The kin come. They shadow my movement; are they trying to help me find what is hidden?

One comes close enough to touch. She seems to stare right inside me, and there is something about here, now, this moment: it's important. There is an almost understanding inside of me, but then I shake my head, turn away. Swim for the surface but no matter how fast I go it is never fast enough.

I can't get away from what I am.

42

I open the back door as quietly as I can and step out into the darkness.

It's about two a.m. and I should be asleep. Once I woke up, that dream was running through my mind over and over again. The fever is back; all I can think of is plunging into the cool depths of the sea. But should I be wandering around on my own when The Circle might be out looking for me, complete with a sniffer dog? Probably not, but there is no way I can stop myself. The sea is calling and nothing else matters.

I set off at a jog through Boscastle, down the hill to the sea. The closer I get the faster I go, blood rushing and pounding through my body like waves on the rocky shore.

As I near the sea I slow to a walk. The salt on my lips is better than chocolate. It's not merely taste and smell, it is *more*: all the indefinable fragments of sense and memory that together say, this is *me*.

It's *who I am*, and I've been denying it for too long – not the joy the sea brings me, but the understanding. The *why* I am the way I am.

I slip into the water and the touch on my skin makes me shiver. Not with cold, but anticipation, longing.

Sometimes before, I've felt like there is a switch inside me – if it flips, I'm gone. Something else takes over, just like it does sometimes in my dreams. Malina taught me to visualise a silver rope – to tie myself to reality so I couldn't switch off; to struggle for control against part of myself.

Malina, who now tries to hunt me down.

Was she right about this?

I can't fight against myself, not if I'm trying to understand who and what I am. But what if I forget too much? Forget to breathe?

I dive under.

The cool water caresses my body and I swim out, down, further and deeper. Determined but scared, and fear wants to deny whatever this is, push it aside or be pushed aside myself. I don't need Malina's rope if I stay aware, but still there is a sense of struggle – a mental arm wrestle inside of me.

Let go.

I need to be who I am – *all* of me.

Stop struggling.

I relax, stay here and aware.

There is a moment – a pause – a sense of *something* else that had been fighting inside me, letting go too.

Then the water around me . . . changes. I see as I did before underwater; at the same time everything I feel, see, smell and taste becomes something else, more vibrant, alive. There is both wonder – I didn't know it could be like this – and exhilaration and triumph, both mine and not mine. It wraps around me, inside, like a mental hug.

At last we are one!

There are distant sounds and vibrations in the sea – the signature of a pod we know.

We call them and they come: the kin. They swim alongside and all around and then it's like my dream – one dolphin comes close enough to touch, seems to stare inside of me. But this time, instead of swimming away, I hold out one shaking hand. She nudges against my hand, pushes it. Looks me in the eyes and nudges me again. And my hand is drawn to first stroke her, then to the dorsal fin on her back – to hold on.

As if that is what she was waiting for, she soars at speed through the water, taking me along – to the place between here and there. As we break the surface and she flies through the air, I let go, land with an undignified splash and breathe in deep. She's laughing – I swear she is! Moonlight plays on her silvery skin. The rest of the pod join us, rising as one and defying gravity to fly before diving down deep. And I have my ride again, holding tight. We soar through the water as if we are a bird in open sky.

Somehow, they are part of me.

No, that's not quite right. They are part of *us*.

It's the joy I've been longing for – the *why* no matter how fast I swim it is never fast enough.

The kin. Why did I call them that? I don't know.

They are our kin.

This thought is both mine and not mine, but instead of fear that would push away, now there is wonder.

It was the dolphins that saved me. Wasn't it? That wasn't just a dream I had before, it was a memory.

We called them; they saved us.

Us; yes. We are a plurality, like twins that wear the same skin. Both close, alike, and completely different.

Silver shadows that swim in the deep glimmer as if they have their own light. We surface as one to breathe; my skin is pale in moonlight, so different to theirs.

Weak, fragile.

We have other strengths.

Yes. We are strong together.

How long we play in the water like this I don't know, but the sky is starting to lighten. I swim slowly for the shore, dolphins all around. I pause, treading water. One by one they touch my outstretched hand and then turn back to deeper water.

Anguish rips through me, loss and loneliness so intense it's crushing. My limbs feel too heavy to leave the water. Somehow I stand, stagger towards the shore, and as I do part of me bleeds away in torment until it is gone.

The pain of loss is so intense I drop to the rocky ground, arms and legs drawn in tight around me, tears running down my face. Rocking myself and trying to get control.

Finally I manage to untangle myself, sit, stare out at the sea.

The dolphins breach once – slice an arc through the air – and then they are gone. They were waiting to make sure we're OK, weren't they?

We?

What happened?

I'm alone again: just Tabby. But in the water I am something *more*. There was this other presence inside me and once we stopped fighting each other for control – the way Malina told me to – it was like we shared my body, my thoughts. That's not right: *our* body, *our* thoughts, part alien, animal, yes – but so close together that I didn't know where one began and one ended.

I've edged close to understanding this in my dreams, as if

my unconscious mind has a better grasp of reality. But tonight, it wasn't a dream. I was awake, alive – more than I have ever been before.

But only in the sea?

On land, I am bereft.

43

I walk back to Ren's. The will to run is gone now that I'm going further away from the sea instead of closer to it.

Now I'm away from the water I'm questioning what happened, how it felt. There was something inside me that is both of the sea and part of me. A separate consciousness? That's not quite right – more like two halves of a whole, that can come together or be separate. Now the pain of leaving the water has subsided, there is a strange energy – euphoria – running through my whole body, making me feel light enough to float away.

We swam with *dolphins*. So fast – flying! And they came when we called them, too, and the whole experience was . . . *joyful*. Yes; that's the right word. I found what has always been missing, and it was there, inside of me, all along.

This is mad, impossible. There must be something wrong with me if I think that these things are true – they can't be.

I have to go back, experience it again. Before I even finish the thought my body has turned to walk back to the sea.

I make myself stop. It's early morning, people will be around soon. I can't go back and risk being seen. But each step away from the sea is a struggle.

The sun is rising properly by the time I get to Ren's, to the back door I'd left unlocked. But when I reach for the handle, it won't turn. I'm locked out? I hesitate, then give the door a light tap.

Ren opens it almost immediately. 'Where've you been? I thought you'd done a runner.'

'Why would I?'

She shrugs. 'I don't know. Where were you?'

'The sea. I went for a swim.' I reach to straighten my hair, tangled and dried in salt.

'Why?'

'Needed some air,' I say, uncomfortable with her questions, the way she's looking at me like she somehow knows I'm hiding something.

'In the water?'

'Why so many questions?' I say, not wanting to share anything of what happened – not now, maybe not ever.

'Something tells me there is more to you, to this situation – as crazy as it may already be – and I'm curious what it could be.'

There's a tap on the door before I can think what to say.

Ren raises an eyebrow and nods at me, as if to say *later*, and opens the door. It's Jago.

He's surprised to see me, then smiles widely. 'Thank God you're all right.' He hugs me.

'Why wouldn't I be?' I look between the two of them. 'Has something happened?'

'She just got back,' Ren says to Jago. 'Tell her. I'll put the kettle on.'

'What is it?' I say.

'A few hours ago, someone broke in at Sascha's,' Jago says.

'He'd gone to pick up Erin, his sister, after I went home – she'd had an argument with her boyfriend. She was asleep in her room. The one you slept in. She woke up, thought she'd heard something. Her door opened – she said she could see the figure of a woman outlined in the light from the hall. She pretended to be asleep, stayed still. Whoever it was crept across the room, stood next to her bed a moment, then left.'

'Maybe just a burglar?' Ren says, but I can tell by the way she says the words, that isn't what she thinks, and neither do I.

'Sascha said nothing was taken,' Jago says. 'It was like they went to the bed to see who was there, and then left.'

'You think it was somebody looking for me?'

'It's possible. Erin – once she got over being too scared to move – woke Sascha; they called the police. Whoever it was had got through a security door somehow; they both swear it was locked.'

'If whoever it was went there looking for Tabby, they're not the police,' Ren says. 'They don't generally break in at night looking for a missing person, or at least, if they do, they don't then sneak away quietly afterwards.'

'Definitely not the police,' Jago says. 'Sascha said the police were baffled why anyone would break in and not take anything. He got the feeling they were looking at both of them suspiciously, as if they'd made it up. Then when Sascha called me and Ren, Ren checked and said you weren't here, that she didn't know where you might have gone. I thought maybe whoever it was came here, too.'

'I'm so sorry you were worried. I went swimming; thought I'd be back before anyone noticed. Is Erin OK?'

'Freaked her out right back to her boyfriend's house, which Sascha says is a result.'

'How would anyone know to look for me there?'

'Maybe someone else remembered seeing Sascha's car where that sniffer dog lost your trail,' Jago says. 'Maybe they have been following me, or my friends. I don't know. I came here a roundabout way on my bike, double backed on myself a few times – felt like a bit of an idiot doing it. But I'm pretty sure no one followed me here.'

'If you need to go out again, spare key is here,' Ren says to me, pointing to a drawer. 'Not that it looks like locking doors slows them down much.'

'Don't,' Jago says. 'Stay safe.' And I can see he is waiting for me to say it – that I won't slip away at night again on my own. But I can't promise that.

Ren hands both of us mugs of tea and even though it is still scalding hot, downs half of hers at once. 'God. This is too early since, you know, I was up half the night finding out stuff about the Penrose Clinic.' She grins.

'You did?' I say. 'What?'

She sinks into a chair at the dining table and we join her. 'Something very odd. I found a reference that an investigation into the Penrose Clinic was started about ten years ago, by the GMC – the General Medical Council. They investigate allegations of misconduct by doctors, stuff like that. But then . . . nothing. It wasn't dismissed, or completed – it just vanished.'

'That's interesting,' Jago says. 'Do you know why it was started? Why it disappeared?'

'Well, the second question is easier to answer than the first.

I expect someone in power leaned on someone to make it go away. Not easy with the GMC, by the way – it'd have to be someone with a lot of clout to make that happen.'

'And the first question?' I ask, uneasy. Did someone find out what they were doing – what I am? Maybe the authorities already know; this someone in power that Ren mentioned does, anyhow, and I don't like to think somebody might have known things about me a long time before I did.

'Don't know yet,' Ren says. 'I've got a few ideas of places to look. We'll see what I can find. In the meantime, what do you think, Tabby? Why might Penrose have been under investigation?'

'I . . . I don't know.'

'Maybe it was in relation to the IVF side of what they did, so they made a deal to drop that and just go on with research in genetics? That'd explain why there isn't anything about them and IVF that I can find.'

'Hmmm.'

'In which case, maybe there was something going on with their IVF that was dodgy.'

'Yeah, I guess. I think I need a shower – is that OK?' Ren and Jago are both looking at me, as if they see I want to get away from her questions, to run and hide.

But Ren tells me where the towels are and points me towards the stairs. As I go up, they're still talking, voices too low to hear, as if they dropped down a notch so I couldn't.

I've asked Ren to find out stuff and now I'm scared she will – that they'll know what hides inside of me, even as the certainty of what happened in the sea last night is fading.

I need to go back to the sea.

44

That afternoon I borrow Ren's tablet again. Maybe we haven't found much about the Clinic or The Circle because we're not looking for the right things; maybe answers are hidden in what I haven't told them.

Like how even now, just hours from my swim, I'm desperate to return to the sea – to go there again, to feel what I did. I can't stop this hunger or contain it – it's like I'm burning inside and the only way to stop the pain is to plunge back into the sea.

I haven't explained any of this to Ren or Jago – somehow I can't. I may be a freak. Who wants to be friends with a freak?

Last night felt like my dream: I called the dolphins and there they were. Is that why they came when I was trapped in the car underwater, somehow freed me, saved my life?

But that brings back being in the car, Simone – Mum – drowning in front of me, and a flurry of fear and pain. I concentrate on remembering last night to push that away. The speed, the feeling – of wonder, joy – and . . . *rightness*. We were always meant to swim together like we did. Simone said even when I was small I wanted to swim with the dolphins, that she had to hold me back.

Will the sense of being complete – all of me, together – return in the sea? Will the dolphins come again if we call them? I want to try. I want to go there and do it *now*, and it's all I can do to hold myself back.

Instead I open the tablet, search for images of dolphins, imagining this one or that was my friend last night. I follow links to websites about dolphins and I'm looking for images, idly scanning through some of the words.

Dolphins are – of course! – mammals. Like me. Warm-blooded, oxygen-breathing, live young at birth. How do they live in the sea and still breathe when they need to?

They can hold their breath about as long as I can, which is way over normal for a human. But if dolphins can hold their breath for, say, twenty minutes, does that mean that is the longest they can ever sleep? That they have to wake up to surface and breathe?

No way. Seriously? There are goosebumps on my neck, my spine. *Dolphins sleep with one eye open*, like Simone said I do; they keep part of their brain awake and part asleep, so they know when they need to breathe.

Half awake, half asleep – a way I've often felt. Knowing when I was asleep if there was any worrying noise, for example, I'd wake myself up. I do that all the time.

Sometimes when I'm asleep I hold my breath. Don't breathe again until I wake up. Just thinking about it makes me feel short of breath and I close my eyes, concentrate on breathing – in slowly, hold, out slowly, repeat. Trying to settle. Everything feels out of whack: all I can focus on is the sea and my insane need for it.

The sea is taking over, but it is one of four: *sun, sea, earth, sky*. I concentrate on the litany, the four points of the compass, one after another – and the agony inside me starts to ease, at least a little.

There is something bothering me about the four words – the four points of the compass. What is it?

I frown, trying too hard and it won't come.

I close my eyes, slow my breathing. Try to let my mind wander.

When it comes to me I open my eyes wide in surprise: The Circle. Their message that they sent out far and wide – the wording, what was it again? The second line: *The sun in the sky over the slowly poisoned earth and seas cannot wait.*

It's the four points of the compass: sun, sea, earth and sky, like Cate taught me. Not in the usual order but they're there, in the same sentence. Cate, who had a Circle tattoo. Are these words from The Circle?

I turn back to the tablet, and type in 'sun, sea, earth, sky', and hit enter.

So many hits. I sigh, look through a few pages of links. Nothing seems useful, but what was I expecting to find?

I add to the search: 'The Circle'.

There: the words are found together on some archaeological site. Something about ancient stones found in caves?

There is an image of a stone carving, cut into four by a cross. In each quadrant there are symbols that the caption says represent sun, sea, earth, sky.

There are hairs sticking up on my neck, a shiver going up my spine. Each of the four drawings is surrounded by a circle.

Four circles, in two rows of two: just like the symbol used by The Circle.

But this is ancient stuff, like drawings found on cave walls from long ago, before humans even were as they are now.

Does this mean The Circle has been around for thousands and thousands of years – maybe even longer?

Sun, sea, earth, sky: if I concentrate, the voices are there, stretching back and forth in time. But are some of them from so very long ago?

There are goosebumps on my arms, the back of my neck.

Yes. So long ago: faint words, whispered in my mind. Not like the strong sense of the other inside me when I'm in the sea; this is something different, more tenuous, as if stretching out to me from so many years ago takes so much effort it is barely a whisper.

I've had dreams before of voices in my head, all shouting to be heard; being one lost in many felt like a different sort of drowning. Cate stilled them in my dream, but they've never completely gone away. They are my background static; a buzzing fly I can usually choose to ignore, unless it comes straight for me.

If the four circles represent sun, sea, earth, sky, what Cate taught me was from The Circle. And even though she kept me safe and away from them for most of my life, has what I've been running from been hiding inside me, all along?

If so, to find The Circle, all I need to do is to look in a mirror.

45

'Interesting,' Ren says. 'It does look like the same symbol with four circles. How did you find it?'

'I did a search – "sun, sea, earth, sky" – with The Circle.' I hesitate, feeling uneasy explaining things that were part of my life with Cate, even though I'd convinced myself I had to show Ren what I found. 'It's the four points of our compass that Cate taught me. We promised to protect them.'

Her head tilts to one side. 'Protecting sun, sea, earth and sky sounds like an environmental aim – one way to protect them would be by stopping extraction, halting global warming. But why on a rock in a cave in Sweden? And it says here that it was estimated to be six thousand years old – well before the industrial revolution.'

'That's not all. Read through to the end. It's been linked to other findings.'

She focuses on the screen and the mix of wonder and shock I felt when I read the same words is still with me:

Nearly identical symbols have been found in other caves – either carved on slabs like this one, or as cave paintings – in countries, indeed continents, so far apart it is difficult to imagine the same group being responsible for them all. In any event they are separated widely in time, with the oldest ten thousand years old, the newest closer to two, and others at points between.

'That's a bit freaky,' Ren says. 'What do you think it means?'

'I don't know.' Shivers run up and down my spine. The Circle: sun, sea, earth, sky. Voices – past, present, future – chanting in my dreams.

Past and present I understand, to an extent at least. But the climate change news has been so bleak for so long that it is hard to see how the planet – people, plants, animals – can continue as a recognisable version of itself for much longer.

Is there a future? Is that what this is all about?

Ren quizzes me about things Cate taught me, the promises we made, and it is hard to talk about. Somehow it feels wrong – private, not for outsiders. And the way I feel now makes me think back to how Cate always said not to tell anyone about us. At first I'd put that down to her not wanting to get caught for having stolen me from my parents so many years ago; later, to her wanting to keep me safe from The Circle. But was there more to it?

I fake sleepiness and escape at last, back to the spare room. Close the door, flop on the sofa bed.

I don't want to be as I was before: afraid to trust anyone. Keeping everything inside. I sigh. Maybe I was starting to trust Simone and Ali. But Elodie was Simone's mother: once I knew that, could I have gone to Simone with any of this? I don't know.

Apart from Cate and, to a lesser extent, Jago, is there anyone I could trust with all my secrets?

Unbidden, one face swings into focus in my mind: Denzi's.

And I'm remembering that day, the Sunday morning run alone with him. We stopped by the locked gate to the sea, stood there, together, and there was something in his eyes that made me feel understood, as I am. Without hiding anything.

Ren's tablet is still here, and I flip the cover open. Wanting to search for information about Denzi, but how can I? I don't even know his last name.

Though he said he went to school there, not just swim school in the summer. Maybe there is something about him on the school website?

I search for the school site, click on the link. There's a message from the head teacher on the home page for the school, about it being closed for repairs for the next school year. About staff who died in the storm surge.

And there is also a link for family and friends of people missing from summer swim school . . . and survivors.

My hand reaches again to tap the link on the screen, but I hesitate, a sick feeling in my stomach. What if he's missing, too? They said he went home, but did he? Even if he did, if he lived along the coast someplace there – he might well have done since he went to school there – he might still have been caught up in the storm surge.

I'm thinking of all the people there, the ones I knew, the ones I didn't. Is knowing who survived and who didn't better than all this doubt?

I don't know, but unable to stop myself, I tap the link.

At the top is a pinned post about a trip family members of some of the missing made to the school gates. They left flowers, cards – attached to the fence – and *there, just there*, his face in profile. A huge smile takes over my face. It's Denzi. He was there. He's all right.

Tears well up in my eyes and the screen blurs. I fight to blink to see if there is anyone else in the posted photos I recognise, but the only one I find is Becker.

Missing-person posts line the page: so many faces, most I recognise even if I didn't know all their names.

Ariel is missing. Zara, too.

I can't find anything about Isha – does that mean she's all right?

There are so few posts marking someone as safe, but I find Denzi's.

Marked safe: Denzi Pritchard. That's his full name: Denzi Pritchard. And he's got Dickens, too? I'm so happy to see a photo of the school cat. I'd been worried something happened to him after I put my tracker in place of his collar. Even if it could have happened anyhow, it would have felt like it was my fault.

I search Denzi's name to see what I can find. There are links to newspaper articles.

He helped a girl who was injured in Hyde Park at a climate protest; that is so like him. When I read through the article, I'm caught in surprise. His dad is the actual *Home Secretary*? I mean, he said his dad was an MP, but not that he was in the cabinet and not just in any post, but as Home Secretary.

Beware of authority: Cate said that more times than I can count or remember.

Denzi's steady eyes in his profile image stare back at mine. Is knowing he is all right enough? Dare I risk contacting him, to at least let him know I'm OK?

There are footsteps coming this way in the hall, a tap on the door and I close the tablet.

'Yeah?'

Ren stands in the doorway. 'My parents called. They'll be home tomorrow night.'

'So I need to go.'

She shrugs. 'Not necessarily. But we'll need a story as to why you are here. We'll come up with something. I found out some more about that archaeologist who found that carving you showed me. She was discredited, and the whole thing revealed as a hoax.'

'Why would someone do that?'

She shrugs. 'Trying to get rich and famous, I guess? Anyhow, she admitted she faked the find.'

'But the circles symbol . . .'

'Well, they haven't got a monopoly on circles. And anyhow, these circles weren't on their own, they were drawn around the symbols. Probably it was just a random coincidence.'

Ren seems to think that is the end of it, but the chant is there, just below normal perception; if I listen for it, it is there – there all the time.

Sun . . . Sea . . . Earth . . . Sky . . .

46

Ren's spare key turns to lock the back door with a rasp and a clunk. I freeze: did anyone hear?

Get a grip: it was a tiny little noise, I know, but my senses feel magnified, turned up – every touch, sound. Even the streetlights are too bright.

I slip down the road, keeping to shadows when I can. Running even faster than last night.

Does this make any sense – going to the sea again so soon? It's only been a *day*. When I was at swim school we only went once a week, and yes, it was hard, but I could wait that long.

Maybe that was because I had no choice, but I don't think that is all there is to it. Something is changing inside me; the balance is shifting in a subtle way. There is nothing I can do to stop myself going there again tonight. I'm not fully in control of what I feel, what I do.

Even though the sun has been gone for hours, it's still hot, but I'm shivering. Goosebumps track up and down my arms and spine. I can hear the sea now, smell it.

And then . . . there it is.

See it, touch it, taste it.

I step into the water. Feet, ankles, legs, then dive under. Saltwater covers my skin and there is a brief moment of panic – it's not happening this time, I'm still alone – then a sense of bemusement.

Where else would I be?

I'm back to being me – *all* of me. The two halves together.

Yes. This is as we should be.

We call the kin, but as we do so, they are already here, as if they were watching and waiting for our return. There are more of them this time, but I recognise the ones I know from the night before. The same dolphin comes up to me. My hand on her dorsal fin – the mad race of joy through the sea. The speed and feeling of it is like nothing else; I'm buzzing but also completely at peace at the same time.

I'll never be able to swim alone again.

The night goes by in a blink. The sky is beginning to lighten, and I should go – get back before I'm missed. Before Ren and Jago are worried.

Goodbyes from the kin, in a look or gesture, a light touch. I swim to the shore. Feet on the ground.

The pain is there again as I step slowly out of the water, but it isn't as intense as last night.

Is that because this time, we know this isn't a one-off? That we'll be back here, together, again?

But do we have to wait until then? *Stay with me.*

Uncertainty. *This is not my world.*

But it is mine, and you are part of me.

I am always with you, even if I sleep. I'll be there if you need me as I have been before.

Instead of leaving in agony, this time it is softer, more gentle. A sense of gradual release, as if part of me is drifting to sleep inside.

I sit on the rocky shore, watch the sun rise over the water into low cloud that gives a display of red and pink streaks across the sky. Bemused by what happened, how I feel now, as if I'm glowing from the inside. I should go back to Ren's, but—

Danger.

Someone walks along the water's edge. A woman alone, and there is nothing about her to say she is anything but a walker who likes sunrises. I don't know her – I'd remember if I did. The rising sun lights up her long, red hair, like fire. Yet everything inside me is on alert, poised.

Behind us!

I listen intently, move my head a fraction to one side to localise the disturbance in the air. Someone behind me breathes, moves quietly, slowly, towards me. I can't run for the sea with the other woman there, and the one coming towards me cuts off escape the other way.

Wait. Listen. Let her get a little closer – far enough to evade but close enough that they can't change direction in time to cut me off, and then—

I spring to my feet and *run*. She is so close I feel the air move when she reaches out to grab me but misses.

I glance back and the shock of recognition almost makes me stumble. It's Malina – how did she find me here?

Run.

As far and as fast as I can. The woman on the beach is running, too, going wide to try to catch me between her and Malina, but I'm faster. The sounds of pursuit are lessening; I'm pulling away.

'Tabby, wait! Please. We want to help you.' Malina's voice,

as always, has something about it that makes me listen. But I don't have to do what she says, not any more.

Then there is another figure, closer and running in from the left – there are three of them?

Run. Too many to fight.

To fight? I wouldn't know how.

I do.

47

I run as fast as I can and after a while, when I look back, there is no sign of Malina or the other two.

What now?

I don't dare go straight to Ren's. They must have some way of tracking my movements, or how did they find me here, on this one beach out of all the endless miles of coastline?

It's very early still, no people around, and that makes me more nervous. I need to hide somewhere until Boscastle wakes up, until there are other people around to hide behind. I don't know what Malina would do to me if they catch me – I don't want to find out – but whatever it is, there isn't much they can do with other people around.

I hurry down quiet streets, looking for a place to hide. A footpath takes me between back gardens with fences along both sides. A tree near the footpath has branches that stretch over the fence. Look both ways: no sign of Malina or anyone else. I climb the tree, along the branch until I'm looking down on one of the gardens. No dogs or anyone in sight.

I lower myself to hang off the end of the branch, drop down.

Now to hide. The garden is overgrown – bushes, flowers all needing to be cut back or deadheaded. I push my way down between the fence and some bushes, getting caught by twigs, scratched.

There. No one will see me unless they push in here themselves.

But what if they bring that sniffer dog back to track me? What if they find me however they found me earlier, at that beach?

Rest. I'll watch and listen.

The panic, the running after a night in the sea: I'm exhausted. I drift off to sleep.

The sun is high in the sky when I open my eyes.

I push through to see, and study the back of the house carefully, watching for any movement in windows. I don't want to be seen.

It's clear.

I pull myself up from the bushes that sheltered me. Use a bench to climb over the fence, and back to the footpath behind. No one is in sight.

Smooth my hair and clothes as much as I can after a night in the sea and a morning in a garden, brush sand from my skin. Breathe in, out, in, out.

I walk until I'm near the centre of Boscastle and there are people walking this way and that. Someone with a dog but not a sniffer dog, just a bouncy small dog. No sign of Malina or the other two.

Plan?

Walk normally, make sure I'm not followed. Go back to Ren's. Get my stuff and go. I have to, don't I? They've got so close; they'll never stop searching until they find me.

I walk up the road, taking pains to look normal, calm; at the same time every sense is on overdrive. Listening to things I shouldn't be able to hear – conversations, whispers, movements in all directions.

Something is wrong; I taste it in the air. I don't know what it is.

I go around a corner, hurry across and stand deep in shadows by a doorway. Wait.

Malina comes around the corner, frowns, looks ahead and hurries on. She must have been following me; she'll come back once she realises she's missed me, won't she?

I hurry back the way I came, then take the busiest turn – people are all around me now. Half panicked. What should I do?

I stop and pretend to look in a shop window, studying reflections behind.

It's *her*. The red-haired one that walked along the water so I couldn't run for the sea. She's across the street. Phone in hand: calling Malina?

Run.

I dash between people, almost crash into someone and there are annoyed sounds behind as I clear a corner. Malina is ahead and I reverse, turn. Walk along with a group of pensioners. I'm cornered.

What now?

Dive into a shop.

48

'Well, if it isn't *Naomi*,' Flick says, and narrows her eyes. Of every shop and café, I had to go into hers.

I risk a glance back through the glass windows and see her again: Malina, and the other woman is with her now. Walking this way. I duck down behind some shelves of T-shirts and hope they didn't see where I went. I'm trapped if they did.

'What's wrong?' Flick says.

'I'm being followed. Please, can you help me?'

She walks towards the glass window. 'By two women, one ginger? In dark clothing, sunglasses? They're coming this way.'

I'm scared. What should I do? She turns back and my eyes plead with hers.

'Quick. Come behind here, duck down.' I do as she says, hiding behind the till and counter. The bell rings on the door as it opens. Flick walks towards them.

'Hello, can I help you?' she says.

'I hope so.' Malina's voice. 'There was a girl, with blue-streaked dark hair, in shorts. A blue T-shirt. I thought she came in here? She dropped her phone. I want to return it.'

Flick is leaning against the counter on the other side, putting herself between me and them. If they lean forward, they'll see me.

'Nope. Haven't seen anyone like that. Maybe next door?'

'We'll just have a look around while we're here.' There are

more footsteps and I'm pulling myself in as small as I can, barely breathing. They're checking the whole shop, aren't they?

After a while the bells ring as the door is opened again.

'Thank you, come again,' Flick says. And a moment later, 'Don't move until I say,' she says quietly. 'One of them is outside the shop still, looking around. I think the other one has gone in next door.

'OK, she's turned away. Quick and I'll let you out the back way – *now*!'

I get up, dash to the back of the shop with Flick. There's a security door – she taps the code, pulls me through into a room full of shelves piled high with T-shirts and hats and whatever else they sell.

'Thank you.'

She goes through to a door at the back. 'Wait. I'll have a look.' She opens it, looks through, then quickly shuts the door and turns the deadlock. 'One of them is around the back now. They didn't believe me, did they? Who the hell is after you? This is like James Bond.'

I'm shaking now, but she's grinning. She's loving this; it's a game, isn't it? Something to tell her mates. The bigger the drama, the better.

'Well, if you won't tell me, I bet Jago will. I got *ways* of making him talk.' She takes her phone out of her pocket.

'Jago? Your friend *Naomi* is hiding in the stock room at my work . . . Uh huh. Yeah. Someone is watching both front and back doors, too . . . OK. Bye.

'He's going to call back.'

A bell rings; she looks through the door and groans. 'Bloody customers,' she says, and goes through to the shop.

I watch through the glass panel in the door. Some older people browse the shop. Eventually they buy some postcards, leave. Flick is on her phone again. I can't hear what she is saying. She comes back in.

'OK, we've got a plan. I'm going to be you and Sascha is going to pick me up out front where it's busy with people. Then Jago will come later to the back door for you. OK?'

'That could work. Are you sure? Can you leave the shop? What if they catch you? They're not . . .' I pause, not sure how much to say. 'Nice.'

She shrugs. 'I'll lock up. And I can take care of myself. So, strip – we need to swap clothes.'

She's about my height, a little thinner. Her skirt is *tight*.

'I want that back,' she says. 'Don't rip it bending over! Oh, ugh. Have you been swimming in these?' She rifles a shelf, finds a scarf. 'Now to hide my hair.'

Her phone beeps. 'That's Sascha,' she says. 'Stay here until Jago taps on the back door. All right?'

'Thank you, Flick. So much.'

'It's all right,' she says, looking uncomfortable. 'Jago's cool. He says you're a friend, so . . .' She shrugs.

She goes through to the shop. The bell rings before she could have got to the front door – someone else is coming in?

'Felicity. OMG, what are you wearing? Why haven't you been out front? I got a call that you've been out back for ages.'

'Your friends got nothing better to do than spy on me, is that it? I need to take the rest of the day off.'

'Like hell you do. Leave now and that's it.'

'Stupid bloody cow. You can shove this job.'

'Just wait until I tell your mother.'

The bells ring as the door opens and closes. I peer through the glass of the stockroom door and can just see the blue of Sascha's car through the front window, Flick ducking into it. A squeal of tyres as he takes off.

Flick's boss – she's coming this way! I hurriedly duck down to hide behind some shelves. The door opens. There's a thud as if she's put something on the table. She's swearing under her breath. There's a pause, then: 'Hi, it's me. I've got to stay at the shop. That idiot niece of yours has taken off again. Uh huh. Yes, well you can tell your sister that this charity job is over.'

She stomps back out the door into the shop. I slump down on the floor.

Did it work? Will Malina and the others leave, thinking I've gone, try to follow Sascha's car?

How did they know where to find me this morning? I guess Malina knows what the sea means to me, but they came to the exact same beach. It's like she knew I'd be there.

Panic quickens inside of me. Where is Jago? I've got to get out of here.

I ease myself, stiff, to stand. Staying well back, I check through the window into the shop; she's at the counter with customers. I go to the back door. Flick could see one of the women from here, she said.

I hesitate, then turn the deadlock and open the door a crack, then a little more.

I look all around. No one is here. But they'll come back, won't they, when they realise they've been tricked?

216

Then my eyes are drawn to movement – at the end of the lane. Someone is turning in on a bicycle and heading this way. And I tense up, not sure whether to retreat back inside and lock the door, or run – but then it comes a little closer. It's not one of them, and the relief is so strong I sag back and lean against the door.

It's Jago.

49

'You weren't going to go off without me, were you?' Jago says.

'No. Well, only if you didn't come soon.'

'Are you OK?'

'Some version of it. Let's get out of here before they work out they've been tricked and come back.'

'We'll go to Ren's the back way, so no one sees us.'

Jago doubles me. It's not easy to sit on a bicycle seat in a short, too-small skirt, but I manage, tuck my feet up and he pedals, standing, behind. We get on the main road and the whole time I'm watching – does anyone seem interested? But besides a few looking at my legs no one seems to pay any attention.

The road rises sharply on the way to Ren's, and after a while we stop. Jago is breathing hard. 'Let's walk a bit,' he says.

We carry on, walking fast, with Jago pushing the bike.

'So, what's going on, Tabby? Ren said you'd taken the spare key. Until we heard from Flick – well. I've been – *all* of us have been – so worried about you. Where did you go?'

And I feel awful for making them feel that way. 'I'm sorry you were worried. I went for a swim. I meant to be back so early no one would notice, but they came to the shore and almost caught me. I hid in a garden, waited until people were up and around. I was going to go to Ren's then, but they saw me, and I hid in Flick's shop – I guess you know the rest.'

'Why go out on your own when you know they've been looking for you?'

I glance at Jago, and I owe him an explanation – I know I do – yet what can I say?

'It's hard to explain.'

He stops walking, turns to me. 'Try.'

I hesitate, and I know this isn't something that he'll understand. He's not like me. The sense of being so different – the *otherness* inside me – deepens; being apart and alone even when standing close to a friend.

'It's like I had to go there, to swim. I know that doesn't make sense to you. It's kind of like it's the only place I feel *myself*.' I glance nervously back down the road. 'Let's go?'

'All right,' he says, and we start back up the road, but I can tell he thinks there is something I'm not telling him. And there is, but how can I?

'Jago, I'm sorry. Thanks for the rescue.'

'No worries. Well, worries, yes, but that's OK.'

The road flattens enough to get back on the bike. We go a different way, a road that goes behind Ren's, Jago says. Then we get off the bike and go down a path between houses. There's a gate in a fence – we go through and across to another gate. I recognise the back of Ren's house.

He knocks once and Ren opens the door.

She whistles and eyes me up and down. 'Loving the outfit.'

'Yeah, well. It's Flick's.'

'Can't believe . . . I mean I can. Flick called, and said what happened, but . . .' She shakes her head.

'Are they all right?'

219

'Yes. Sascha drove around and around for an age – said a car was following them. Then finally they stopped at a pub and Flick took the scarf off so whoever was following could see it wasn't you. Apparently she did a big stage bow and a wave.' Ren rolls her eyes. 'Then they got lunch at the pub. Still there, I think.'

'Thank them for me.'

'Not going to do it yourself?'

I shake my head. 'I can't stay. They're too close; they'll find me here eventually.'

They start talking about places they could take me, other friends who might help, but that isn't right. I can't stay here and put Jago and more of his friends at risk.

The sense of otherness I felt earlier deepens, and I tune out, look inside. I need the kin, but can't risk going back to the sea, not now. If I can't do that, then more than anything I need to be with someone like me.

Denzi: he didn't know about Penrose, but he was like me. I'm sure of it.

But what about his dad? He's the Home Secretary. Can I trust Denzi when he basically lives with authority?

I need to see him. I have to. But not at his place – away, somewhere else.

'Look, thanks for trying but I need to leave this area completely,' I say. 'I've got a friend in London. I'll go there.'

'Who is it?' Jago says. 'Do they know about all this Penrose and Circle stuff?'

I hesitate. 'Some of it. And I'd rather not say who it is.' And the hurt on Jago's face that I've caused makes me falter. 'I trust you, I do. But if you don't know where I am and someone asks, you can be honest.'

'I don't like this,' he says.

'Can you stay with this friend?' Ren says.

'I don't think so, because of his family. I'll go to London and meet up with him somewhere.' I see Jago about to protest, and I hold up a hand. 'I'm sorry. I'm grateful for all you've both done for me. But I need to leave and I need to do it alone.'

I head for the stairs, for a quick shower and to grab my things. My mind is spinning with what I have to do – how to get there.

I'm back down in record time. 'Can you give Flick back her clothes?' I say.

'Sure. Might even wash them first,' Ren says, pulling a face as I hand them over.

'Tabby, I know you said you have to go to London on your own, but we've come up with a plan,' Jago says.

I start to shake my head but Ren says, 'Just listen and then decide. I've messaged a friend in London who says you can stay for a while. Don't worry, I haven't told him any of this or even your name – just that a friend needs a place to stay. So you can get to London, stay there tonight, contact your other friend the next day and take it from there. What do you think?'

'Who is he?'

'He's a blogger – I've known him for years. A bit intense but solid.'

And I'm looking at Ren and then Jago. This was the problem with my plan – where to stay. Do I let them solve it? I don't know what is the right thing to do, but I'm scared to be in London alone.

'Say yes and I'll let him know,' Ren says.

'OK, then yes. Thanks.'

'Wait a sec, Ren. Do you know this blogger IRL?' Jago says. I must look at him blankly. 'IRL – in real life.'

Ren shakes her head. 'Anyone like that is too traceable. Trust me, I trust him.'

'I'm coming with you,' Jago says to me.

I shake my head. 'You don't have to do that.'

'Yes, I do. I'll check the place out and make sure it's OK. Don't argue.' There is a set to his jaw that says he really means what he says. And I'm so happy not to go alone that I don't argue, even though there is an uneasy feeling inside. I shouldn't let him do this for me, but the words don't come.

'Lucky that trains to London from Bodmin started running normally again this week,' Ren says. 'I'll get a taxi to take you there.' She takes out her phone, books it on an app. 'It's on the way. I'll cover it.'

'Let me pay for it, I've got some money.'

'Keep it, you may need it. And don't worry about the taxi, it's on my dad's account. He probably won't even notice. And I've got something for you,' Ren says. 'Well, not a gift, it's a loan – give it back whenever, though.'

'What is it?'

She holds out the tablet she'd let me use yesterday.

'What, seriously? No, I can't possibly—'

'Take it – I hardly use it and it'll come in handy. And you can use it to keep in touch with us. We'll set you up.'

I watch as Ren makes up a profile for me and sets up an email address. From there she signs me up to Twitter, WhatsApp, a few other places, and shows me how to use them.

'There's something else we need to talk about before you go,' Ren says. 'When I first met you, you made me promise not to say anything you told me unless you said I could. I think it's time to talk: to get the word around online about the link between the Penrose Clinic and The Circle. And just maybe, if that happens, they won't be so intent on tracking you down to keep you quiet.'

I nod. 'You're right. It makes good sense. Do it.'

'Taxi is here,' Jago says.

50

It's a long enough drive to the station that I can sit back and think, and get more and more nervous.

This all feels too *easy*. Malina got so close: would she let me get away like this?

How do we talk about this with a taxi driver in the front?

'Do you fancy a walk?' I say to Jago.

He raises an eyebrow.

'It'd be good to get some fresh air before we get on the train for so long.'

'Whereabouts?'

'Excuse me?' I say to the taxi driver. 'Do you know if there are any footpaths near the station we could go for a walk?'

'There's footpaths all around. How long?'

'Maybe a mile or so?'

'There's a bridge car park with a footpath that leads straight to the station. Probably take less than half an hour – the footpath is above the River Fowey. Nice day for it.'

'Thanks, that sounds good.'

Not long after, he turns off the main road, pulls in to a small car park. He points out the footpath to take to the station. We're getting out and I see Jago giving him some money.

'Did you have to pay him?'

'Just a tip.'

'The fare must be huge. If I give you some money can you give it to Ren?'

'Don't worry about it, she's not.'

'But—'

'No buts. As to why we're here, I'm guessing you've had enough exercise, what with swimming at night and being chased about. You're worried they're watching the station?'

I nod. 'Sorry. You must think I'm paranoid.'

'It's understandable, especially after this morning. Come on; let's go.'

We walk down the footpath between the trees and it is beautiful, green — all the rain from the hurricane has made everything grow in overdrive, as if it knows this break from the drought won't last. But with each step, my anxiety grows. They must know after that near miss today that I'll try to leave. And where else would I go to get away from here?

My feet slow.

'Tired? Do you want me to carry your pack?' Jago says.

I shake my head.

'Look, when we get there, you stay out of sight. I'll go check the whole station and platforms and wave to you to come if it's all right.'

'And if it's not all right?'

'I won't wave; I'll come back to you.'

I shake my head. 'That won't work, for two reasons. To start with, you don't know who to look for.'

'So, describe them,' he says. And I try to put Malina and the other two women she was with into words.

'If there is anyone who fits that even vaguely, we'll leave and

225

think of something else to do. All right?'

'Then there is the second problem. If they recognise you as my friend – and they may well do, if it was one of them who pretended to be police and came to ask you if you knew where I was – then they'll try to follow you to me.'

'Good point.' He pauses a moment. 'How about this. If either of them is there, I won't come to you. I'll walk up the road away from the station to draw them away. Then you get the train; I'll make sure no one is following me and come on a later train and meet you in London. I can message you on Ren's tablet, right?'

I think about it for a while – finally I nod. 'OK,' I say.

'Anyhow, I expect I'll be waving and we'll be getting on the train together.'

'Hope so,' is all I say out loud, but my thoughts are swimming. Coming here with Jago feels *wrong*. I shouldn't have let him come with me; I shouldn't let him take any more risks for me. This is mine: my problem. I can't run away from it – it is who I am, how they made me – it isn't his battle. And if I said that out loud, he'd say it's because he's my friend. But the other half of that is I'm also *his* friend.

I can't do this any more – to Jago, Ren, Sascha. I don't want them caught up in this more than they already are, even Flick, especially as she doesn't know what this is about, who she is dealing with. It's not fair. If it's clear at the station, I'll have to convince Jago to let me get on the train alone.

When we near the station, I do as Jago says, and stay on the path in the trees. He walks down to the station while I watch from the shadows, and I don't see anyone alarming. A family with children. A man smoking out front. Another couple arrive, and none of them look anything like Malina or the other women.

Jago goes through the entrance to check the platforms. When he comes out a few minutes later I breathe a sigh of relief. I was being paranoid, everything is OK, and . . .

He doesn't wave.

51

I lean further back into shadows of trees. Jago heads up the road away from the station, but there is no one following . . .

A woman steps out of the entrance. A glance is all it takes: it's Malina. Another woman appears at her shoulder – she's the one with red hair I saw with Malina in Boscastle. They speak. Malina starts up the road behind Jago, and the other woman goes back inside the station.

This is what we didn't prepare for. What do I do?

Adrenalin floods through my body. It says *run*, do it now – get away – but what about Jago? If Malina catches up to him, what might she do? I don't know, and I'm sick to think anything could happen to him. But me getting caught trying to go to him won't help either of us.

Jago, I'm so sorry.

I run back the way we came so fast I'm almost flying, my feet seeming to barely touch the ground.

I pause when I reach the bridge where we joined the path. If they know the area they might come here. What do I do?

There's another marked path ahead. I take it. Fast and faster, settling into a pace beyond anything I could normally maintain.

The path takes me to a National Trust property – Lanhydrock, it's called. I slow, walk along the edges of the car park, thinking, while my heart rate gradually comes down.

I have to get away. I'm both scared and sad to think it, but it has to be alone. And the last thing I want is for Jago to get on a train to London, thinking he'll meet me there. That can't happen.

I take out Ren's tablet. It needs Wi-Fi – is there any? There is a café next to the car park and I walk there to check, but nothing picks up. I'm frowning at it when a man walks out and sees me.

'There's no Wi-Fi here,' he says, and looks at me closer. 'Is everything OK?'

'It's just I'm supposed to meet someone here and can't check what's happened to them without Wi-Fi.'

He hesitates. 'Look, you can connect to my phone if it's quick.'

'Really? Thank you. How do I do that?'

'Hotspot,' he says, looking surprised I don't know. He then proceeds to take the tablet from me to set it up.

'Thank you,' I say, and quickly go into messages like Ren showed me. Click on Jago. Bite my lip, what do I say and say fast?

I'm ok, got away. Not going to London on the train so don't go there. I'll get in touch later. You were followed, so take care. Thank you.

A message pings back from Jago almost instantly. Where are you??

I disconnect. There are tears in the back of my eyes, but I blink and try to look like they're not there.

'Thanks for that,' I say.

'Are they coming?'

'Yes, just running late.'

'Wait in the café?'

'I'm good here. Thanks again.'

He walks to his car. Gets in, drives out with a wave.

I walk back to the shade of trees beyond the car park. What now?

Despite what I told Jago, should I still go to London – to Ren's friend? She gave me his details – they're on the tablet in our messages. She said no one knows he is her friend, so there's no reason anyone would think to look for me there.

How? I don't know how to get anywhere from here if I don't get a train.

Hitch a ride? I have done this with Cate before, never on my own, and I'm scared to try. She was good at assessing people fast; I'm not sure I can do the same.

Unless I hitch a ride with someone without them knowing . . .

There are a few pickup-type four-wheel drives in the car park, open at the back. Could I hide in one of those?

But it could be going *anywhere*. What if it goes in completely the wrong direction?

Well, if I don't know where I'm going, then how could Malina begin to guess where to look? It'll get me away from her and her friends – then I can work out how to travel to London from wherever I am.

I walk over to one. It's so full of stuff, I'd have to take something out to even get in. Some people come out of the café and, startled, I walk on, hoping they didn't think I look suspicious. They get in a car and soon leave.

There's another pickup. I walk over to check, and the back is mostly empty.

A car comes in to park and I walk on. I look at my watch like I'm waiting for someone while the people get out of the car and leave. I walk back to the pickup.

In the back of it there's a fixed storage box, probably locked, and too small to hide in anyhow; another bag or something is strapped down with bungee cords next to it. I might be able to hide between them or behind the bag. I look around carefully. No cars are coming; no one on foot is heading this way. I clamber up and inside the back, dropping down low in case anyone comes while I check it out.

I undo the bungees, shift the bag, take off my backpack and squeeze it and me in behind the bag. Then I reach around to reattach the cords.

I'm not completely out of sight no matter how I wriggle around; if anyone has a close look, they'll spot me. It's the best I can do.

A few times I hear footsteps, voices, cars starting up, wheels crunching on shingle.

And I wait. The sun is shining and it's hot, crammed in like this against metal that seems hotter every minute. I'm not sure how much longer I can stay here, but then I remember Malina and that makes me think of two things.

One: I will wait because I must. They'll find me if I don't get away from this area.

Two: the way to forget how hot I am, to feel cool – something Malina taught me. I imagine myself on our beach, mine and Jago's, then I'm filled with a flurry of worry for Jago that I struggle to control.

Focus. I'm lying on the sand. Breathe: in and out, slow and then slower, in time with imagined waves. Relax: hands, feet . . . calves, legs, arms . . . neck, shoulders . . . core.

Breathe, so slow now . . . in . . . out . . . in . . . out, in time with imagined waves.

I'm drifting, *separating* from myself. The tide is coming in; it laps first against my feet, then my legs, bit by bit coming up further until I'm underwater.

Now, I swim . . . out to sea, to the cool, dark depths.

There's a twist of silver, a cord that holds me together; Malina said to do this. I don't need it, not any more.

I take it off my wrist and let it fall away.

And so we tumble through the waves. The kin come to play; they're in the water all around us. We come up to breathe when we need to but stay together, and the joy is complete. I want to stay here, but something pesters for attention inside of me.

Listen.

I open my eyes: in a rush I'm back in my body, in the pickup.

There are footsteps coming closer, voices – two women. Very close now and then a *beep beep*, the sound of doors being opened. I'm scared they'll see me but then the pickup moves a little as someone gets in. Doors close. The engine starts and soon we pull out, start up the road.

The road is uneven; the pickup bounces. It's jarring and uncomfortable, but I don't dare move or sit up in case one of them notices. Soon we're on a smoother road, going fast. I don't know where we are going, but after a while I know this: away from the sea. I can feel it getting further away, a wrench of loss deep inside, and even though it'd be a bad idea to go back, it hurts, so much.

Trusting that part of myself that watches to keep me safe – to bring me back when I need to act – I close my eyes.

I drift back to our beach, to the sea . . .

Sun . . . Sea . . . Earth . . . Sky . . .

Sun . . . Sea . . . Earth . . . Sky . . .

The voices are in harmony to start with but then something is changing – now it's more like a voice track dubbed over a film.

They start to separate, into distinct voices, all with their own point to make – shouting at me to listen, shouting over each other until I can't understand any of it.

They're out of synch, jarring, pulling me in all directions.

I curl up inside myself, hands over my ears but I can't keep them out. They're tearing me apart.

Cate, help me!

The thought – the plea! – is barely formed, and she is there.

Ssssh, Tabby, it's all right. I've got you.

Her arms are around me and the voices fade.

Part 5

Denzi

52

Please come. Eva's friends and family really want to meet you.

I read the message on my phone, as I have done so many times – to make me keep putting one foot in front of another.

Eva, the girl I carried out of Hyde Park, bleeding, her little brother alongside. I got her to the police and paramedics took her to hospital, but she still died. Hit by a bottle, her brother said to the paramedics – thrown by thugs. She didn't deserve this. All she did was go to a climate change protest.

She was only fourteen years old, but she stood up for something she believed in.

When have I done that? Staying out of stuff, being a loner, is who I am. If I'm honest, not always for good reason.

But I can change, can't I?

Now. I'll do it, now.

When I get there I'm afraid I've got the address wrong – it's not a church or a crematorium, it is more like the entrance to a park. Then I see a sign with Eva's name, the time. I go through a gate, take a winding path through trees to a garden. A large number of people are gathered there, standing in groups, talking.

A girl walks towards me.

'Denzi? I'm Hayden. I messaged you?' She's hesitant, her eyes are red but there is a shy smile for me. 'Thank you for coming.'

'Least I could do.'

'Well, it means a lot. Eva's parents want to meet you.'

She takes me to Eva's dad.

'Thank you for what you did for Eva.' His handshake, a strong grip. He's standing there, rigid, like he's trying to keep himself together, but how can he at his daughter's funeral? Fathers aren't supposed to outlive their daughters; that's not the way it should be.

Eva's mother, crying, hugs me. Her little brother is trying to be like his dad but his lower lip is trembling.

It's a humanist funeral: no hymns or readings. When it begins, everyone listens as one by one her friends and family say a few words. I start to get an impression of Eva, who she was. A good student with a crazy sense of humour who loved animals. That's what got her involved in climate protests to begin with – the thought of living in a world after the mass extinction without so many of them. Polar bears, her favourites. Retreating with melting ice, in a world that is changing.

And that's why we're here: a woodland burial. No embalming chemicals, tombstones or cremating fires: it's what Eva would have wanted, her father says. A small wicker coffin, covered in flowers. A burial in a meadow where Eva will become part of the nature she loved.

There are press outside when it is time to go, and I wonder if I should have told Dad I was going to be here.

Hayden catches up with me. 'We're meeting this afternoon to plan a climate event in Eva's memory. Will you come?'

I say *yes*, and there it is: more proof that I can change.

★ ★ ★

The meeting is at somebody's house in Harrow. Eva's brother – Ryan – is there. He said his dad didn't want him to go but his mum got involved and here he is now. He's probably the youngest; Hayden must be a little older than Eva, fourteen or so, and there are about thirty of us, most in mid to late teens. There are some faces I recognise – the boy who spoke at Hyde Park is there, his arm in a cast. Broken when he fell from the podium in the midst of the crowd. There are many faces from Eva's funeral also – her friends, more subdued than the others.

'Hi. Name, number, email?' A boy hands me a clipboard. I write it down.

Another step.

After a while someone whistles, and the chatter quietens down. 'Thanks for coming, everyone.' The boy with the broken arm – introduced as Bishan – is chairing things. 'This is for Eva. What should we do?'

People call out suggestions – a march, a sit-in, occupying public places – and they get big and then bigger with discussion.

'I think we're getting there. A flash march on Friday, beginning at central points around London. We'll shut down roads as we go. Finish in Hyde Park. Tell everyone to be ready and then post where and when at the last minute.'

And I'm uneasy. Does *flash* mean no advance planning or warning to anyone – the city, the police?

No protection if things go wrong.

'Denzi? Is everything OK?' It's Hayden. Her earnest face – so young. What risks should she take? It won't help Eva if her friends are hurt.

I wave an arm in the air. 'Hi. I have a question. Do you tell

239

the police?'

'Is that Denzi? Hi. Welcome aboard. We don't ask permission from the authorities, but they'll know something is being planned from all the build-up online. We won't give the locations out until the last minute.'

Serious. Dedicated. Determined to make a difference, to change things. Did The Circle start like this? And become something else when everything failed?

Even so, I want – *need* – to be part of this. There is unease inside at how the press will report it if they see me there; how Dad will react and if there will be implications for him politically. The old me would probably have run it past him before committing myself. But since I went to him for help about the Penrose Clinic and swim school, and my fears for Tabby and Isha, and he went straight to the director of the swim school – no. I'm not going to him about this; not to get back at him, but because I'm unsure of his motives in a way I haven't been before.

Anyhow, this isn't about Dad. It's about Eva. It's me. I have to do this.

Bishan calls for a show of hands to go ahead with the plan.

Every hand goes up, including mine. And despite my reservations, I can feel what they feel. A sense of something being *done*, and is that what this is really mostly about? Finding hope that things can change, before it's too late.

Later I'm walking home from the Tube, lost in thought. Reeling from the day, really – how it made me feel, the impact of it all. So maybe it takes longer to penetrate than it should: the sirens. In the distance and all around, getting louder. There are always

240

sirens somewhere in London, a usual backdrop to city noise – traffic, people – but this is more than any version of normal.

I get my phone out.

There are missed calls. And a message from Dad: Get home.

I check the BBC and what I see makes me stop walking as I look and look again. Unconfirmed reports of bombings – there have been explosions? Multiple targets in and around London. I flip to Twitter; images and footage I can't begin to take in flood my feed. Fires, burning. People running away, many hurt.

I shove my phone back in my pocket as if that will make it go away, then run the rest of the way home.

53

Dad is on his way out when I get home, his relief plain to see when I come in.

'Where have you been?' he says. 'Why don't you ever answer your phone?'

'Sorry, it was on silent. Just caught your message,' I say, only answering the second question and normally he'd be all over that, but this isn't *normally*.

'You've seen the news?'

'Explosions – bombs? – around London. Why? Who has done this?'

'We don't have many details yet. I'm heading in now. Stay home until further notice. Don't go *anywhere* – not to run or swim or anything else. You got that?'

Then he gives me a quick hug, and heads out the door.

Jax is on the sofa, news on, and I stand behind the sofa, caught – watching the screen and unable to look away.

'Hey,' he says.

'Hey.'

He turns and gestures for me to come around and I do, sit next to him on the sofa. Staring at the screen. Listening for answers, but they have none. The places targeted seem pretty random. Some involved casualties, some didn't – so it wasn't like they were set in places where they'd do either the most or the least harm to people – and still no one has claimed responsibility. Who would do this?

Where is Tabby? Is she all right? I've no reason to think she is anywhere around London, but the more things go wrong, the more I worry about her. Is she alone, scared, hiding? The world is dangerous enough for a girl alone; with all the news lately my fear for her is even more.

'This just in. Reports from the US that, following a series of explosions, Hoover Dam has been breached.'

'Oh my God. That's huge, isn't it?' I say.

They go to a US report – scenes from the air. Swirling rushing water on a scale that I can't take in.

They leave that story, go back to the studio. 'There are unconfirmed reports that the Three Gorges Dam in China – the largest dam in the world – has also been breached. We're seeking further details.

'Just in. The London bombings have now been linked to the Thames flood barrier. Key components of the capital's flood defences have been destroyed.

'Over to—'

The screen blurs, and then goes dark and silent.

'Lost the satellite signal maybe?' Jax says.

I take out my phone. The BBC is the same: a dark screen, and I show it to Jax.

Then words appear, scroll across the screen.

What the hell?

This is an update from The Circle to people and governments of the world.

> Global warming and rising sea levels threaten populations and wildlife around the globe. Homes and habitats are vanishing – and will continue to vanish – in low-lying areas: sacrifice zones to distant political and corporate greed.
>
> Now more of you know what it feels like to fear rising water.
>
> Take action now. Cease extraction; cut emissions.
>
> Before it is too late.

It's followed by a four-circles symbol. The screen goes dark and blank again, then a few seconds later the studio signal returns.

The newsreader – shock on her face she is struggling to hide echoes mine.

There's a pause, then, 'We understand that broadcast signals around the world have been interrupted by hackers. What you may have seen was the result. It was not broadcast by the BBC or any other news network.

'It has now been confirmed that, along with Thames flood defences and the Hoover Dam in the United States, the Three Gorges Dam in China has also been targeted. Explosions have breached the dam and millions of lives are in danger. Now back to our reporter near the Hoover Dam.'

We watch scenes from the US and later from China, then back to London. It feels like a disaster movie – it can't be real. They rush to get experts on the scale and extent of damage from the dams being breached, and it's beyond immediate flood damage: drinking water supplies, irrigation, hydropower too. This group claims to be environmentalists, but they've sabotaged clean power. They must know what will replace it; dirty power is the only quick fix to this devastation.

What has happened in London is not on the same scale, unless there is another storm – like, say, a hurricane – with huge rainfall and storm surge heading for a London without flood defences. That The Circle has caused hurricanes before doesn't seem to be in serious dispute any more.

Just who and what is this Circle, that they cause damage and death on such a scale? How can they begin to justify what they've done? How can they be here, in London, and in the US and China all at the same time? This isn't some small group of nutcases; this must have taken planning, organisation, resources.

We watch until I think I can't take it any more, and as if Jax feels the same he reaches for the remote, looks a question at me and, when I nod, turns it off.

The combination of Eva's funeral; the meeting after; worrying about Tabby; now this. Nothing feels *real*, and I'm unsettled, angry – like I want to argue with someone.

Dickens appears and rubs around my ankles. 'Hey, cat. Have you had your dinner?'

'Yes, he has,' Jax says.

'Treats, then. Cheese?'

I find it in the fridge, cut a few small pieces and hold out my hand. Dickens purrs and eats them neatly, one at a time, and there is something about him doing this that soothes me inside, just a little. The anger drains away and leaves something harder to handle behind. I settle back on the sofa; Dickens jumps up and sits on the top of it and licks my ear.

'Are you OK?' Jax says.

'Ish.'

'You went to the funeral?' I look at him. 'It was on the news. Saw you. Could have said and we'd have dusted off your dark suit. Or I could have come with you, if you wanted.'

'I checked the suit and I've got taller. Thought this was OK.' Black jeans, a dark shirt.

'Could take you shopping – want to schedule it?'

'I'm hoping I don't need to go to any more funerals.'

'Here's to that.'

'Here's to Eva.'

He holds up his coffee mug and I clink it with my tea.

Later I'm staring at the ceiling in my room. Sleep won't come. I can't stop thinking about the bombings, yet the scale of what has happened is hard to take in. Eva's funeral seems like it happened in another day, another time, yet now that I've met her family it's also more personal and immediate. There is nothing anyone can do or say to them to make their pain go away; it'll always be there. Just the same as the families who have lost people they love from the bombings today.

It's gone midnight and I haven't heard Dad come in yet – no surprise that he's working late. I want to corner him, ask him about Penrose again – find out what he was hiding. But I also need to know he's OK. I'd rather we were all home, under one roof. What if there are more bombings? What if the government is targeted?

Phone out, I send a message in Signal: Hey, Dad. Are you OK?

It vibrates a moment later. Fine. Still struggling to take in what has happened.

Same. Home soon?

Hope so. Get some sleep.

Easier said than done. I roll over and Dickens protests the movement by my feet. I hold out a hand and he comes up to sniff it, then realising there's no treat there, sighs and plonks himself down next to me. An ear scratch and he's purring.

'Really glad you're here,' I say, and he yawns, fish breath right by my nose. 'Well, most of the time.' He settles in the crook of my arm and gives me a narrow-eyed don't-move look, and closes his eyes.

I sigh. There's an ache deep inside me. Worry for Tabby and loss and pain from today are amplified by another kind of despair: not being able to go to the place I want – *need* – to be when things are wrong.

I shut my eyes and imagine myself *there*. At first, it's the beach where they took us once a week from swim school, but then, remembering what happened along that coast, I shift to Brighton.

Sometimes I can conjure up the feel, smell and taste of the sea, and imagining being there is almost enough. It's not working today.

Try again.

There were dolphins not far from the pier – carving out of the water into the air as one, disappearing again down deep. The excitement around me, too; everyone – children with ice cream, parents, teenagers on a walk, fishermen – stopped whatever we were doing or saying to just stand there and watch.

Remembering the dolphins makes me long for the sea even more.

Eva loved polar bears. I bet she loved dolphins, too. What is happening to the planet isn't somebody else's problem – it's mine, it's Dad's. Every one of us who lives and breathes on our earth has the same problem, and ignoring it won't make it go away.

It was Eva's, too, and she's gone. What The Circle has done is unlikely to have the impact they seem to want; it is just more distraction – noise – taking attention away from the real problems we all face.

If Eva's march still goes ahead on Friday, I have to be there.

The deep, the dark, calls me.

I dive down, down until the sun is a faint memory, far above. There is something I need, something I must find, but I don't know what it is.

I swim, searching, and I don't want to stop. But something is niggling, nagging away at me. Something I've forgotten? But the longer I swim the less I know what it is.

Then water rushes past – I'm jerked straight up as if I were a fish on a line – until I fly up out of the water in an arc and breathe in deep.

Oxygen: that was what was missing.

I plunge back down to the depths. Searching again . . .

54

Dad is there at breakfast with Jax when I come down and something eases a little inside. We are all safe and well, at least for now. But what about Tabby? With everything going on, I know Dad won't be home much; now might be the only chance I get to corner him with my questions for a while.

'I was listening for you last night, but didn't hear you come in. I need to talk to you,' I say.

I didn't even say what about, but he's uneasy, looks away to glance at his watch. 'Have some breakfast, first,' he says.

The news is on in the background while we eat and it's hard to look away. The threat level in the UK has been upgraded from severe to critical – the highest level. Dad tells me because of this I can't leave the house without a PPO, a personal protection officer. That any outings have to be booked with them a day in advance. That they've booked me in to be taken to swimming every day at nine, without even asking what I want to do.

A few fires still burn in London from yesterday's bombs, and there's a smog warning in place.

Jax snorts. 'Smog from the fires of so-called environmentalists.'

'That's not their only deal. It can't be,' I say.

'Why do you say that?' Dad says.

'Ending climate change can't be all that they want. If it was their be all and end all, they wouldn't destroy dams that provide hydroelectric power knowing that'll lead to more and more dirty energy being produced.'

'Terrorists, the lot of them,' Jax says.

'That's what they were saying when Eva was hurt.' They both look to me. 'The thugs who were throwing things – calling them terrorists. As if those kids were responsible for what The Circle has done.'

'Obviously they're not, but some of what they say sounds the same,' Dad says. 'Idiots generalise.'

'What is actually going to be done about climate change? When are we going to stop extraction and burning fossil fuels?'

'Well, it's complicated—'

'To kids like Eva, it wasn't complicated. Make a decision to change and stand by it.'

Dad shakes his head. 'Denzi, I understand how you feel, and in many ways I share your feelings. But we are working within a framework where the odds are against our viewpoint.'

'Then maybe it is time to change the framework.' Now I'm remembering someone who said almost the same thing when I was there, not long ago: Leila. *Mum.*

'Have you got the political bug?' Dad says. 'Find something else, something less soul-destroying. Go back to your swim training and leave the world to us to sort out.'

'Because you've been doing such a good job?' I say, then hastily add, 'I don't mean *you* specifically, Dad.'

'I know. Look, there may be something in the works that will sort a lot of problems out at once. I can't say anything else about it yet. Leave this alone. Go back to your training and think about your future.'

'My future? That's exactly what I'm thinking about.'

'Ding!' Jax says. 'Next round later? I'm heading for the shower. Will you still be here when I come down?' he says to Dad.

Dad shakes his head. 'I have to go soon.'

'But not just yet,' I say, as Jax heads for the stairs. 'Time to talk, remember?'

'Yes, of course. What's on your mind?'

'You. Your friend, Christina. And Penrose. When I told you I was worried about Tabby and Isha and something going on at the swim school with the Penrose Clinic, you went to her.'

'Of course. She's the one who could answer the questions,' he says, in a tone of voice that is reasonable, reassuring; the way he'd speak to the cameras about whatever political calamity is under scrutiny. Not the way he'd normally speak to me when we are alone.

'Think about it: if there is something dodgy going on, is she going to level about it? And Dad, I've known you for seventeen years and fifty-six days. No matter how good you think you are at hiding how you feel, I know there is something you know, something you are hiding about this clinic. What is it?'

He shakes his head. 'You need to leave this alone.'

'Why?'

'Because I'm asking you to.'

'Not good enough.'

'You're worse than PM's Question Time during a pandemic.'

'And?'

He sighs. There is a level of worry in his eyes that makes me even more concerned about what he is hiding.

'Dad, if there is something you know about this clinic and

251

how I was born, you have to tell me. It's about *me* – I have the right to know.'

There is indecision playing on his face and he finally shakes his head. 'OK. Straight up, here's the story. Penrose were using some . . . *procedures* that the medical profession as a whole didn't agree with. It was the only way to have you, my own child; something I wanted more than anything. Despite how annoying you can be.'

'Huh. What procedures? Why didn't the medical profession agree with them?'

'In order for Leila to have a viable pregnancy, they had to make some changes in the genes in the fertilised egg; this kind of thing goes against both international moratoriums and UK laws on editing human genes. If this came out . . . well. I might be unemployed.'

'What changes? What did they do to me?'

'Just what they had to do for Leila to carry a child to term – that is all. And that is all I have to say on this. But know this: if the press find out about it and that I knew, my political life will be on the line. You need to stop asking questions about this clinic. Don't talk about it with anyone – even Jax.' He glances again at his watch. 'I have to go; are we done?'

I'm looking back at him and I still have so many questions. His political life – is that the most important thing to him in all of this? What about *my* life – and what it could mean to me to know more about how I was born? I'm no nearer to finding Tabby and have even more reason to worry for her. Did she find out something about this clinic that threatens their dirty secrets?

'Yes. We are. Done.'

We're looking back at each other's eyes, and it's like something between us has changed that can never be the same again. He looks away first. Stands, starts to walk for the door.

He turns back. 'I almost forgot to tell you. Christina Lang called yesterday. She said there have been sightings of your friend Tabby in Cornwall, that she may be heading for London. If you hear from Tabby, you'll let Christina know, won't you? Despite what you may think, she is genuinely very worried about her.'

Is she worried about Tabby, or about what Tabby might know?

Yet one of the knots of tension inside of me lets go, just a little: Tabby is OK, at least she was when she was seen.

As for the rest of it, Dad doesn't wait for an answer. He didn't mean it as a question; he thinks I'll do what I'm told, like I usually do.

But maybe my framework needs to change, too.

55

There's a knock at the door at exactly nine: the PPO is right on time to take me to training. It rankles inside that I'm here, ready. I'm still trying to come to terms with everything Dad said earlier and how I feel about it, yet here I am, doing what he wants me to do.

'That'll be your chariot,' Jax says, and then must register some of my feelings from my face. 'Go. This is what you want to do anyhow, right?'

Jax doesn't know, does he, or why would Dad have specifically told me not to talk to him about Penrose? What would he think if he did and that Dad was keeping it from him? And then I just want to get away, not think about secrets that I know and he doesn't.

'Sure. Right.'

I open the door.

A woman stands there, not in uniform. Long red hair glints in the morning sun, but that is her only warmth. She isn't smiling.

'Denzi?'

'Hi.'

'I'm Stacey Linden. I'm hoping you looked out to see who was here before you opened the door? I was holding up my official ID to the peep hole.' It's in her hand. 'Always check ID before opening the door.'

'OK, sure. Sorry.'

We get into her car out front, and yes, it's easier than walking up the road to the Tube and changing twice, but it feels weird, not getting around on my own.

Apart from her ID lecture, she is a woman of few words. We're soon at the training centre. She walks me to the doors, says she'll be back for me at noon. Gives me a card with her number if anything changes.

Once I'm in the pool all the irritation at how I had to get here dissolves. I really have been wanting this, needing it – relentless training. Length after length. It's the next best thing to being in the sea to think things through, or to stop thinking completely.

Even though I know thinking is what I should be doing, I can't stop myself from going for the latter: pushing for speed and pushing again, but I can never go fast enough to leave it all behind me. Not like I did in my dream last night.

Remembering the dream makes me feel like I did then, swimming underwater for too long, holding my breath – forgetting to surface. When I woke up, I was gasping as if I'd been holding my breath in my sleep. Thinking of that makes me feel like I haven't got enough oxygen now. I pull in to the side of the pool, leaning on the side with my arms and holding my head above water, but this vague sense of panic at not being able to breathe is still there. Finally I haul myself out and sit on the side of the pool.

Other swimmers are still going back and forth in the lanes. I glance at the time; it's nearly noon and time for my lift home.

'Denzi? Is that Denzi Pritchard?'

A girl is walking towards me and she seems to know who I am, but I'm none the wiser as to why or where.

She's smiling. 'It *is* you.'

She sits next to me on the side of the pool, feet in the water.

'Uh, hi,' I say.

She rolls her eyes. 'You don't know who I am, do you?' She shakes her head. 'You really do live in a world all your own. I'm Jess. From summer swim school, yeah?'

I'm searching my memory. There was a girl named Jess in Tabby's group I think – tall, long blonde hair. Like she has, and now I'm matching her face to my memory.

'Sorry. I'm not great with names.'

'I don't think we've spoken before, so you're forgiven.'

'Do you train here regularly? I don't think I've ever seen you here.' Even though it took me a moment to place her, she stands out.

She shakes her head. 'I've moved in with my aunt. She's near here, so.' She shrugs. 'Good club?'

'Yes. Just normal stuff though.'

'Normal?'

'Like none of that swim school apnoea training and so on.'

'Yeah, that was a bit on the side of weird. Anyhow, I'm glad you're OK.'

'You too. Were you there? When the storm hit?'

She hesitates. She looks away and then up to my eyes. 'Yes. But I don't want to talk about it, OK?'

'Sorry. Of course.'

'I've got to go.' She gets up, starts to walk away. If she was in Tabby's group, she might know something – anything – about why Tabby ran. Does not wanting to talk about the storm extend to other things at swim school?

Remembering the state of the place when I found Dickens, being there when it was ripped apart must have been terrifying. I could have been there. So could Tabby.

Maybe Jess knows something – anything – about those last days at swim school that I missed, that may give me some clue about Tabby and why she ran.

'Jess?' She turns. 'Will you be here again tomorrow?'

She hesitates, nods. 'Same time, same place.'

'See you then.'

56

That afternoon I'm restless, pacing around the house. I want to go out for a run, and I want to go alone. Dad said not to go anywhere without a PPO, and I sigh. Get out my phone and send Stacey a text.

Hi, it's Denzi Pritchard. Can I go for a run from home? Asking for permission makes me feel even more like I'm caged than I did before.

My phone soon vibrates with her reply. Can't be there so you'll have to stay in. And in general we need a day's notice.

How about tomorrow then? I send back.

There's a pause before she answers.

We'd have to approve the route in advance, have an extra officer along. With everything going on in London we haven't got the person-power to cover it just now.

Great. Just great.

Best we've got at home is an exercise bike; I hate staring at a wall when I could be outside. I get on it anyhow, put the incline right up and have barely begun when my phone starts to ring.

It's Oliver?

'Hello?'

'Hey, Denzi. How're things?'

'Kind of annoying. You?'

'Worse than annoying. I'm heading for the Hoover Dam

area; I'm at the airport now. But the reason I'm calling is that I've had a few interesting conversations lately about the Penrose Clinic. What is up with them?'

'I was hoping you could tell me,' I say. So here I am, talking to a journalist about Penrose. Dad would be horrified, even though the journalist in question is married to my mother. Or maybe that makes it even worse. But I'm not backing away from this now.

'Whatever it is, somebody wants it to stay a secret. I've been warned off.'

'Warned off? By who?'

'Can't go into that. I just wanted to tell you: leave it alone,' he says, and his words sound so much like Dad's.

'I can't do that.'

'Well . . . if you're sure. There is something I've found out.'

'What's that?'

'There's an ex-employee of the Penrose Clinic that has said a few things about them online, years ago. I got in touch. I'm sure he knows something, but he refused to talk on the phone. Until this Hoover Dam thing hit I was going to fly to London to talk to him. But I can't now.'

He was going to fly all this way? He must think this is important – maybe even if I called him off because of what Dad said, he wouldn't let it go.

'Can I do it?'

'I don't know what is behind all of this. But I definitely get the feeling there may be unpleasant people involved. Leila would have my head on a plate if I let you.'

'And?'

He laughs. 'I'm a good judge, and I think you have a sensible head on your shoulders. The guy works in a pub; I'll tell you where if you want to check him out. I could call him and say you'll be coming, but somehow I think you'll have better luck getting things out of him if you surprise him.'

He tells me the guy's name, the pub's address, and I scribble down the details.

'Be careful,' he says.

'I will be. What about you?'

He laughs again. 'I'm always careful. Give me a call if you find out anything. Bye.'

From what I've picked up about Oliver, he likes stories that some people would rather not be told. He probably gets warned off all the time – that he even bothered to mention it to me shows he's really concerned. Yet he still trusted me enough to tell me about this ex-employee, to be able to judge for myself what to do and how to talk to him. More trust than Dad has shown in me lately.

Or is that fair? Dad didn't want to tell me – I almost made him. It's because of that that I'm caught in the thick of all of this and it almost makes me wish I didn't know.

But if any of this will help me find Tabby, to protect her, I have to do it.

57

Last time I went out when I wasn't supposed to, there were photos of me in the news. That time I was slipping out the back way in a hoody for a run; it's hard not to look suspicious slipping out the back way in a hoody at night.

I study the street out the window. It's school knocking-off time; a few kids walk past. One of our neighbours pulls in across the road. A dog walker, an older couple holding hands. No hidden press photographers or government cars that I can see.

I brazen it out the front door, walking like I know what I'm doing. I head for the Tube, half expecting Dad or Stacey to pop out in front of me and demand to know where I'm going.

Tube station. Platform. I go the wrong way a few times, doubling back on myself, but don't see anyone taking an interest. One last Tube to Harrow and the pub.

It's on a backstreet that has seen better days.

Inside it's worn and tired, and even though smoking hasn't been allowed in pubs for years, there is still a vague taste of cigarettes in the air, as if it has soaked permanently into the walls and chairs.

It's a real drinkers' pub, with a half dozen solitary drinkers staring at their glasses. I'd stand out if anyone bothered to look up.

'Is Doug here?' I ask the woman at the bar.

'Starts at six.'

I order a soft drink. Not long to wait.

I settle in a corner, thinking about what to say to Doug and how to say it. Oliver said surprise might work best – so should I just come straight out with it and ask him about Penrose? But the being careful part may be to not let anyone else hear it.

The door opens and a man comes through. If it is Doug, he's almost half an hour early.

He nods at the woman at the bar and heads for a 'Staff Only' door. I get up and get there as he does.

'Hi. Are you Doug?'

'Maybe. Who wants to know?'

'I was hoping I could talk to you about a place you used to work.'

'I've got nothing to say.' He pushes at the door, starts to go through.

'Wait. I was born because of the Penrose Clinic,' I say, keeping my voice low.

He hesitates, turns and looks at me. 'You were one of their IVF babies?'

I nod. 'Yes.'

'You might not want to know.'

'*Please*. It's important to me.'

His face softens; he sighs. 'All right. Come through.' I follow him into a storeroom, across to another door. An office. 'Sit there. I'll be back in a minute.'

A minute passes, another, and just as I'm worrying that he's left, he comes back with a pint in his hand. He sits down across from me.

'So, what do you want to know?'

'Anything you can tell me about the Penrose Clinic and their IVF.'

'The Penrose Clinic ruined my life. They hired me twenty odd years ago as a lab scientist to help set up the IVF part of their business. They paid over the odds with no long hours and extra shifts like I had in the NHS: it seemed like a dream job. There were some dodgy things going on, though.'

'What kind of dodgy things?'

'Once we were up and running, the way they did some of the protocols seemed overly complicated. And something just didn't feel right, in my gut, you know? But I never expected what I found.' He downs half the pint in one go. 'They were doing extra procedures with fertilised eggs before they were implanted. I challenged them about it, and next thing you know they made up some crap about me drinking on the job and I got sacked. They wrecked my reputation to such an extent that my career was completely over. Even had their lawyers chasing me with their non-disclosure agreements, threatening if I said anything. But they needn't have bothered: no one would listen to what I had to say about it.'

'Extra procedures – like what?'

'All of their customers were really well off – rich and then some. I managed to get a look at payment details: some of them were paying huge sums of money, way more than they should have. I bet they were paying more to get what they wanted. A girl or a boy? Blonde or dark hair? Extra smart, maybe, or beautiful, or whatever they thought was important? Designer babies, that's what I think. All completely unethical and illegal.'

And he's looking at me, as if he's trying to judge what I am that could have been designed to order. Dad made it sound like whatever they did was about making the IVF work, nothing else. But did he know more than he said?

'What I want to know is why the sudden interest? I got this call from some journalist in the US a few days ago; now you're here. Look, I've said too much. Get outta here. Go.' He gets up, clutches his now empty pint glass. He goes through the door and I follow.

'What are you afraid of?' I say.

He glances back. 'That clinic was *connected*, you know?'

I step out of the pub on to the street, reeling from what he told me. Doug's version goes beyond anything Dad said: which is true?

It's hard to fathom that Dad would order a designer baby. He was so into the idea of having his own child, so why would he let them change my DNA, make me something different? Somehow it doesn't add up.

Or maybe I'm just trying to convince myself because I don't believe he would do something like that – both to me, and because it's illegal.

I'm not any closer to finding Tabby, and I'm even more worried about her now. Did she find out about the clinic's illegal procedures? Is knowing their dirty secret dangerous?

And now, I know it, too.

Be careful, Oliver said, and I'm hyperaware of everything and everyone around me. It's crowded, almost six; people hurrying home from work or to work or whatever else they need to do and

264

paying no attention at all to me. I'm being completely paranoid, aren't I?

Then a flash of something catches my eye across the road – something red. Red like Stacey's hair is red? I turn, study the rush of commuters, but don't see her or anyone else with red hair. There's a girl with a red scarf – that must be what it was.

Get a grip, I tell myself and go down the steps to the Tube.

That night, I'm staring at the ceiling, thinking it all through. Maybe Doug made up the designer baby thing, but why? Maybe so he has someone to blame for losing his job. He may well have been drinking on the job back then, like he was today. But even though what he told me went beyond what Dad admitted to, it's similar enough to make me think Doug was telling the truth.

It's weird to think someone may have changed something that is part of me before I was even born. What could it be? I'm sure if Dad could have made requests it would have been something like me being a genius, and I'm not much above average in school. The only thing that stands out about me is how good a swimmer I am, but Dad isn't into sports of any sort. He's always seemed faintly surprised that I am.

The swim school was full of people like me; at least five of us were Penrose babies. It's beyond weird to even think it, but did they actually do something to make us good swimmers? Our parents couldn't have all asked for that, surely – why would they?

If that's the case, maybe whatever was designed about us wasn't for our parents. But then . . . *why*?

My instinct had been that Tabby running away had to have something to do with the Penrose Clinic. With all I've found out since then, that conviction is even stronger.

Christina told Dad Tabby might be heading for London, but I'm not any closer to finding her.

What now?

The only thing I can come up with is to talk to Jess at swimming tomorrow. See if she knows anything about Tabby's last days at the school – in case there are any clues there. But I won't tell her anything about the Penrose Clinic or the designer-baby thing. Maybe it *is* dangerous to be talking about it, and it isn't fair to get her involved.

Should I call Oliver, tell him what Doug said? If the whole designer-baby thing is true and Dad is involved, what would happen if the story gets out?

I need to think this through some more. And maybe give Dad another chance to tell me everything.

I'm swimming. Around and around and around again. The wall curves endlessly, holding the water in, the people, out.

They stare at me through the glass and I can't get away from their eyes.

I'm trapped. The water is salt as it should be but it's not the sea.

All I can do is swim around and around and around . . . and dream of breaking the glass.

Then the water would drain away, and without it I can't survive.

Around and around and around . . .

58

I start with backstroke the next morning – it's easier to watch for Jess. She arrives about half an hour later. I wave, swim over to the side as she's getting in.

'Hi,' I say.

'Hi yourself.'

'Glad to see you again. Look, I was hoping we could talk?'

She tilts her head to one side. 'Maybe later. Time to train.' She crosses to the fast lane. 'Race you?'

She pushes off and takes off in a front crawl – fast. She can swim. Of course everyone at swim school could, but not many of the girls could push me. Tabby could, so can Jess. I stay in the lane behind her, telling myself that I'm holding a bit in reserve, that I could overtake her if I wanted to.

I'm not sure if I'm kidding myself or not.

It's not far off noon. I have to get out soon and haven't got Jess to stop long enough to talk to her, though the *push, push* of our swimming has been an antidote for what I'm missing. It's not the same as being in the sea, not even close, but so long as I go as hard as I can, I stop thinking about it.

I stop, wait for Jess to loop back to me.

She grins. 'Are you giving up?'

'Never. I've got to go soon. I was hoping we could talk.'

'We could get some lunch over the road? I've been eyeing up that Italian for a while.'

'Sounds good,' I say, even as I'm wondering how Stacey will react. But what is she going to do: drag me out of the restaurant?

'Meet you out front in ten,' she says.

I get there before she does. Phone out: message to Stacey. I'm having lunch across the road from the pools. Won't need picking up for a few hours.

An answer comes almost immediately. OK. How about 2/2:30? Text when you're ready.

That was easier than I expected. Maybe that's the secret: don't ask, *tell*.

Jess comes out not long after me, wet hair swept back in a ponytail. 'Look, I know it was my idea, but I should warn you that I'm not great company at the moment.'

'Doesn't matter, it's just lunch. I don't know about you, but I'm *starving* after training.'

'Hmmm, well I could devour a gallon of spaghetti just now.'

'Sounds good to me: bring on the carbs!'

She hesitates, then smiles, follows me out the door.

We get there, scan the menu, order. Just as I'm wondering how to ask her about Tabby, she tells me why she's not herself. Her parents – they're missing. They lived in Devon and were never found after their house was swept away by storm surge. And that's why she's staying with her aunt in London.

I'm so sorry – it's all I can say. I can't imagine what that is like. And I can't. It's not like Eva being buried by her parents, but Jess would never have imagined she could lose both her parents at once, especially at our age.

'I just wish I'd been home for the summer, that we'd had that time together,' she says. 'I'm not sure how I even feel about swimming any more, but it's like I do it because it's what I know. I don't know who I am without it.'

'I get that. I feel kind of the same. It's like the only normal thing left in my life.'

'But we're not that normal about swimming, are we?' she says. 'I mean, not to most people. I'm literally *dying* to go to the seaside. I'm not used to being away from it for so long.'

'I'm just the same. That was the thing that was so cool about the summer – everyone was like us. There is a page set up by parents about those who are missing from swim school – have you seen it? You can mark yourself as safe, too – so people know you're all right.'

She flinches. 'I don't want to. And I don't want to talk about it, either. All right?'

I can't pressure her, not after what she's been through. 'Sure,' I say.

We arm wrestle to pay the bill, and I win. I text Stacey, and we head for the doors to wait outside.

'Sorry to get heavy on you,' Jess says.

'Don't apologise.'

'Look. There are some things I do want to talk about – about the summer. I might need some time to get there, that's all.'

'That's OK. In the meantime, I had a thought. Do you want to skip training tomorrow and go to Brighton? To swim in the sea?'

'YAYYYYY!' she says and jumps up and down like a little kid.

'I take it that was a yes?'

She takes out a pen and grabs my hand, writes her number across it.

59

'Dinner in five!' Jax calls up the stairs. But when I head down, he's standing in front of the TV, news on.

'Now we return to the breaking news from the United States. Scandal has rocked Big Green, the consortium of key environmental groups that lobby for reduced emissions in Washington, DC. An anonymous whistle blower has leaked communications within the Big Green lobby that show a clear trail of agreements by Big Green to back off protests against environmentally sensitive developments. Allegations have also been made that payments to support Big Green's operations were in fact made indirectly by oil and gas giants such as Industria United and other key players. Over to our local reporter on the scene.'

'Whatever will happen next?' Jax says.

'Leila works for Big Green. But I know how she felt about the environmental stuff; there is no way she could be involved in any of this. Is it even true?'

I get my phone out, but hesitate. Probably there is a lot going on there just now. Instead of calling, I text – Apple, not Leila.

Hi. Are you all ok? What is happening over there with Big Green?

She answers straight away. Leila says it's all made up to discredit the environmental groups. Dad called – they've been arguing. He says it doesn't look that way, that maybe she wasn't aware of what was happening behind the scenes. There's press camped out front wanting to talk to her, talk of indictments and stuff.

Shit.

Yeah, it's hit the proverbial, that's for sure.

It isn't long before every climate change denialist is on the news: if the environmentalists can't be trusted, why believe anything they say? Then the British press are running with it: that the Home Secretary's ex-wife is increasingly under the spotlight in connection with the scandal.

There is speculation that international talks to set up a climate task force, one with teeth, will collapse.

How will The Circle respond to this?

There's a cold feeling in the pit of my stomach.

What about Eva's march on Friday? Things could go off in London; they shouldn't do it. I've barely finished thinking that when I get a text from one of the march organisers.

We've been talking about Friday. Now more than ever we need to stand up and show the world that we mean what we say. Anyone who wants to back out – that's fine – but Eva's march is a go. If you're with us, be in Central London by 10 a.m. and await instructions by text.

Not much later another text comes, this time from Eva's friend, Hayden. Hi. Are you still going? I am. Could we meet before?

She's scared. I can almost feel it in what she says and doesn't say. She's scared, but she's still going.

There is only one answer I can give:

Yes and yes.

60

There are too many things to worry about. Tabby. Leila. The Circle's next move, the fallout from their last ones. Climate change, the fate of the whole planet. Hayden and the rest of these idealists set on staging this march. How I'm even going to get away to go to it. But right now, none of that matters.

We're like little kids on Christmas morning, Jess and me. Not talking much on the train, both of us lost in our own thoughts, but grinning in a crazy way as we pull into Brighton.

'Thank you for this,' Jess says. 'It was a brilliant idea.'

Now that we're off the train we don't hurry, we walk – stroll – through the crowds of people. Drawing it out. Making it last.

There – the sea. We walk closer until we're on the beach, then down the shingle to the water. Away from the pier. Trainers off, T-shirts, shorts, left with our towels. To the water's edge, slowly. Standing there as a wave drops back, then another returns to touch our feet – a tease to draw us further. A step, another. Ankles, calves, knees, and then, like she can't stand it any more, Jess shrieks and runs in until she can dive under.

I follow more slowly until it's too much and I dive in and I'm there, too. Swimming underwater along the seabed. She's just ahead and we're racing for real now. I'm gaining bit by bit until we're next to each other and we stop, go up to breathe. Treading water, and then there is movement that draws my eyes.

We both see them at once.

Dolphins!

One of them comes *close* and swims around us, looks at us as if he is curious who and what we are. He circles back to the others. They turn together, rise out of the water as one and without discussion we follow behind. They dive down deep and disappear, then surface all around us.

Jess's eyes are wide with wonder. Mine, too.

They move just beyond us and we swim towards them; they move again and so do we. They could easily get away but return again and again; it's like we're playing a game. This way, then that, then back again.

Finally they swim faster, further out, and we can't follow. They disappear into the distance. We wait a while but this time they don't come back.

I glance at the sky, startled to see how far the sun has moved across. We've been in the sea for hours.

'Had enough?' I say.

'Never. But yeah, we should get out I guess.'

We swim slowly, lazily, for the shore.

We find a quiet spot away from others to sit and watch the sun start to go down. I'd texted Stacey and Jax that we're running late and I'm surprised there aren't any objections. I'd been surprised yesterday, too, when Stacey didn't seem to mind me going to Brighton on the train with Jess – she just wanted to take me to and from the station. Maybe busy Brighton is less alarming to her than a jog around London streets. Or maybe it's that I'm rarely here but often there, if anyone is trying to find me. Either way I don't care, so long as I can keep coming here when I need to.

'Jess?'

'Hmmm?'

'There's something I was hoping you could help me with.'

She turns to me, head tilted to one side. Sleepy eyes from the sun and swimming. And I don't want to upset her, take her away from this. She's been through a lot.

'It's OK,' she says, as if she can see the struggle going on inside of me. 'What is it?'

'Tabby. I think she was in your group?' She nods. 'She's missing.'

'So many are.' A shadow crosses her face.

'Not in the same way. Listen.' And I tell Jess that Tabby had run away before the hurricane hit, survived being swept to sea, but then ran away from a hospital. 'She's still missing, and I want to find her.'

'Wow. Do you know why she ran?'

'I was hoping there might be something – anything – that happened at the school after I left that might shed some light on it. Is there anything you can think of?'

'Let me think,' she says. 'I did get the sense that *something* was up – I'm not quite sure what. Especially the morning before the hurricane; all the staff and coaches seemed kinda stressed out. And one of the boys said he'd overheard staff saying someone had broken in to the CSME. Oh, do you think it was Tabby? Maybe she ran because they worked out it was her?'

'Why would she do that?' I say, not wanting to admit that I think that is exactly what Tabby did.

'I don't know, but there was something about the place that

just wasn't quite right. I could feel it.' She's hesitating, as if there is something she's not sure whether to say.

'Please, if there is anything you know that could help me find Tabby, tell me.'

She looks at me sideways. 'You really care for her, don't you?'

'She's a friend.'

'Yeah, right. No worries on that score with me, mate. OK, there is something else. I had a really odd conversation with Isha. She'd asked me if I was an IVF baby, from some particular clinic – Pen-something. Pen-flower? No that's not it, let me think . . .'

I'm looking at her and remembering how I decided not to raise the clinic with her, to keep her away from knowing anything about it, but she already does.

'Penrose? I think that was it,' she says. 'Have you heard of it?'

'Um, yeah. I was an IVF baby from Penrose. Did she say why she was asking about it?'

'She didn't say; I don't know. Thought it was a weird question.'

'Are you? A Penrose baby?'

'And now you're asking, too? No.'

'Thing is, I wasn't the only Penrose baby at swim school.'

'Who else?'

'Isha, Zara, Con and Tabby. And they're only the ones I know about.' I tell her how I found out about each of them, what Becker had to say about the swim school. And that Tabby saw the clinic's symbol on a door under the CSME.

She frowns. 'But why would the clinic be hidden away? Why would they be there at all? I don't understand.'

'Me neither. And why were there so many that were IVF

276

babies from the Penrose Clinic at swim school? How come we were all such good swimmers, brought together in one place?'

'What do you think?'

'I honestly don't know,' I say, not sure how far to go with what I tell Jess. She knows about the clinic, but is the dangerous part the genetic meddling Doug said they were doing? I'll keep that to myself. 'But I think the reason Tabby ran away has something to do with the Penrose Clinic.'

'It does seem pretty strange that there were so many IVF kids from there this summer, but maybe it was just some kind of weird coincidence?'

I shake my head. 'Too unlikely.'

'That's what coincidences *are* – unlikely things that happen anyhow.'

'Is there anything else you can think of that happened at the swim school those last few days? Anything about Tabby?'

She shrugs. 'I don't think so. It was just all the usual – train, train, and then, to add some variation, training again.' She glances at her phone. 'That reminds me. What time did you say that train is?'

We have to run and just catch it. The train is crowded, no chance to talk any more, and I'm thinking through all the things Jess said. I'd half expected her to say she was a Penrose baby, too. That she isn't doesn't change that it's almost impossible for five of us being there to happen randomly, but it does show there isn't anything definite about there being any more of us.

She didn't say anything about what happened when the hurricane hit. What was it she said – that so many are missing?

So many teenagers, like us: lost to the sea.

Zara's parents – they couldn't believe she was gone, not when she could swim like she could.

And there is a niggle inside me about exactly that. Is Jess the *only* one who survived who was there when the hurricane hit? Those marked safe – Isha, Con, Becker, me – all left before. Though Jess didn't want to go to the swim school page and mark herself safe, maybe because she can't bear to see the names and faces of the missing; she might not be the only survivor who feels that way. But even still: there were so many missing posts. So many strong swimmers, lost to the sea. It's not just Zara's parents who can't believe this. It seems unreal.

I could have been there – if Leila hadn't had that accident, or I decided not to go to her, I would have been. So much happens by chance.

Con, too: his little brother was in an accident or he would have been there also.

Weird, isn't it: similar reasons both of us weren't there – an accident to someone in our families?

Is this another coincidence to examine?

Leila was knocked off her bike by a car. Sounds like she wasn't badly hurt – there'd have been no reason for me to go, if she hadn't slipped into a coma.

A coma that the doctors couldn't explain.

She'd come back after I spoke to her – like that doctor suggested – and the way it happened, so soon after, it had made me think that me talking to her reached her somehow.

Now something else is niggling, some memory, and I'm casting back, trying to work out what it is that is bothering me.

When she woke up and the other doctor and nurse came,

I spoke to the doctor and mentioned what the other doctor had said.

And he said, *what other doctor?*

But then Leila was talking and we didn't finish that conversation.

What if . . . her coma wasn't a weird medical thing. What if it was caused – so I would go there. And once I was there, that other doctor – she did something to her IV, didn't she? – did something to stop it.

Now I'm shaking my head at myself. My imagination. That's crazy, isn't it?

Going back to Jess being the only one I know of who was there when the hurricane came and survived. Does it make any sense to think that none of the others – strong swimmers, all of them – managed to swim and save themselves? That only Jess made it?

I want to ask her what she thinks, how she survived when others didn't, but that isn't a conversation for a crowded train. Then when we get off the train in London, Stacey is there, waiting for me.

'Bye. See you tomorrow,' Jess says.

61

Late that evening I'm in my room. Dad was working late; Jax and I had dinner but I was distracted. I couldn't – still can't – get my head around the day. The whole experience of the beach, the sea, the dolphins. Jess, too.

But that's not the only thing I'm worrying about: Eva's march is tomorrow.

Laptop out, I check the news. It's not good. Since the latest actions of The Circle and the collapse of Big Green, the backlash against anyone protesting about climate change is increasing.

After a while I can't keep reading the news; each headline is bleaker than the one before it. I feel sick in my stomach to think what happened to Eva; to think it could be even worse tomorrow. That trying to honour her life could lead to more violence.

I hear the front door open and close downstairs. I glance at the clock; it's after midnight. Is that Dad?

I get up, head down the stairs. He's in the kitchen with Jax, making tea.

'Ah, hello, Denzi. Shouldn't you be asleep?'

'Shouldn't you?'

He shrugs, and I see the shadows under his eyes. He often works late but doesn't look as exhausted as this.

'Is something wrong?' I say.

'It's not right, anyhow.'

'What's happening?'

'You know I can't tell you much.' But then he shrugs again. 'It'll hit the news tomorrow anyhow. The proposed ICI – international climate initiative – we've been trying to set up? Not going to happen, at least not in a useful form. Too much disagreement on scope and powers, and now the US has pulled out completely.'

'Why?'

'The voice of climate-change denialists just keeps getting stronger.'

'Because of the collapse of Big Green? Or The Circle?'

'Both. They've given credence to not trusting the climate change lobby or anything they say, and more popular support to the deniers.'

He and Jax head up to sleep soon after, waving me along ahead of them.

Back in my room, door closed, I'm thinking that none of us said what I'm sure we were all thinking:

How will The Circle react to this news? What will they do next?

There's a cold knot of dread deep in my gut.

Phone out, I keep refreshing the news pages, in case any other disaster movies come true. My eyes close now and then; I almost fall asleep then wake up. Hit refresh again.

It's dawn when a new story drops in – from the US. They have CCTV of interest in the Hoover Dam investigation. They're releasing it now, hoping someone can identify a girl wanted for questioning.

There's a brief video. A girl – short dark hair – with a large backpack. She's facing away from the camera but there is something about the way she moves, something familiar. Her head turns to one side; her face is caught in profile.

I play it again and again, watch it almost frame by frame. Her hair is shorter and the footage isn't clear, yet the more I look the more I'm sure:

It's Ariel.

Part 6
Tabby

Part 5

lobby

62

Wake up.

My eyes open. I'm confused, disoriented. I'm one place in my mind – spinning in beautiful blue – and physically here in another. I want to go back.

A door slams shut, and the sound pulls the rest of me to the here and now in a rush. All at once I feel my true body, and it isn't good: I'm hot, so dry my tongue is stuck in my mouth. My head aches – *everything* aches.

Another door, voices. A *beep beep*. Footsteps move away, but there are other sounds, all around. Distant traffic. Nearby vehicles moving slowly. Other voices and footsteps. I wait as long as I can bear without moving but the sounds continue. Wherever I am, it's busy and I'm unlikely to get out from the back of this pickup unseen.

I shift around cautiously enough to lift my head, push on the bag that is against me. I reach across it to a bungee cord that is hooked on the pickup frame and struggle to make it loose enough to come off. When it finally unhooks, it snaps back and hits my arm, and I bite back a cry. I rub my arm and wriggle around until I can reach further and undo the other strap. I sit up properly.

So, we're parked in the middle of a big car park. There is a trolley return opposite – must be a supermarket. Hopefully the owners of the pickup are busy shopping and won't return in a hurry.

I stretch, move around enough to get circulation back in my stiff body and legs. A woman is going by with a full trolley and I wait until she is past, then put on my backpack and stand up, climb down out of the pickup. When my feet are both on the ground my legs buckle, and I hold on to the side of the vehicle until it passes and I can stand again.

A couple going past glance at me curiously but don't say anything, keep walking with their trolley.

I was right; there is a big supermarket across the car park. I wonder where I am? I need the loo, water and Wi-Fi, and that's a safe bet to have all three.

The very large tea in front of me in the supermarket café is next to my second bottle of water – the first was down in one. I take out the tablet.

Wi-Fi – yes! I sign in as a guest.

I go to the group chat that Ren set up for the three of us; there are messages from Jago, asking if I'm all right. I bite my lip. He must be so worried. I've worked out from the signs at the front that I'm in Salisbury, which is a good distance away from Bodmin station; it must have been hours since my last message. I'm thankful the pickup I was hiding in got closer to London instead of further away, even though the increased distance from the sea is a steady pain inside.

I post a reply. Hi, I'm fine. Hitched a ride to Salisbury.

He answers almost instantly. Tabby, you're really all right?

Yes, I promise: I'm fine. I couldn't go back to get the train – there

286

were two of them, and only one followed you; the other stayed at the station. How about you – how did you get away?

Sascha picked me up. What are you going to do now?

Think I'll get the train to London from here, and go to Ren's friend.

I'm not sure you should. There's been bombings in London. US and China, too.

What??

London flood defences. Hoover Dam. Some huge dam in China. Massive damage and loss of life, and The Circle is claiming responsibility.

I'm staring at the screen. Why? Why would they do that? And the people who did these things are trying to find me. I'm scared, but I have to make it *stop* – somehow. No matter how tempting it is to run back to my friends, it wouldn't be safe for them, or for me.

I can't go back to Cornwall. They'll find me – they know where to look.

Don't go to London on your own. I'll come and meet you first.

No, don't. You'll likely be followed. I'll be fine.

There is a pause before he answers. Then, Will you message as soon as you get there?

I will, I promise. Is Ren's friend still expecting me?

I haven't told Ren what happened at the station, so he should be. Haven't been able to get in touch with her – she's not answering phone or email. Her parents were due back so she's probably busy with them.

OK. I should go, need to find the train station. Thanks for everything.

Take care Jx

I need to work out my next move but can't stop myself going to news sites, and what I see makes me feel sick inside. London has got off lightly – at the moment. What if there is another hurricane and no flood defences?

But the footage from the breached dams – the floods, people swept away. Drowning. Homes and businesses destroyed. And my stomach twists, bitter acid at the back of my throat. I'm there, underwater, caught again in a car – with Simone, watching her struggle. Then her wide, still eyes. My heart is racing, I can't breathe . . .

Be still.

I push the images away. That happened; it is over now. Simone died, but I'm still alive, and I need to carry on.

I make myself close down the news and go to a map site. It looks like I'm about a two-mile walk to Salisbury station; then one train to London.

I memorise the way to the station as best I can, buy some food and more water on the way out of the supermarket and set out.

It's evening now but the sun is still intense; if it's possible, I'm soon even hotter than when I was sandwiched in the back of the pickup. Though I could manage it then by switching off, going to a dream beach. I can't do that while I'm walking, but just thinking about it makes me start to feel a little better.

I lose my way a few times and have to ask for directions, but finally I get to the train station.

There are security, police, in the concourse. On the platforms. Watching, checking. It's an alert or something – because of the bombings? They're not looking for me, that's what I tell myself, but it's hard not to turn around and run.

This is what I need to do.

Not all the trains are running. I get a ticket for one that is, trying to keep my face turned away from the police, the CCTV.

288

It's hard to be in a train station and not to think of Malina chasing me at Bristol station, then turning up at Bodmin Parkway, too – I keep thinking she'll suddenly appear. But there are no signs of her or anyone else paying attention.

There are only minutes until my train leaves and I rush to the platform, then on to the train. It's busy but I still find a seat by a window to stare out of as we set off. My eyes are closing. I was awake all night; the only sleep I've had was a few hours hiding in a garden this morning, and then in the back of the pickup – if that counts as sleep.

Now I'm drifting; random images flit through my mind, out of order. The sea last night. The dolphins. Malina, closing in. Jago.

The kin.

Both the dolphins and friends like Jago are part of me, but at the same time, none of them are what I am – who I am. The feeling of *otherness* I felt with Jago earlier, when I couldn't tell him how I felt about the sea, intensifies. I'd felt so alone, and it felt wrong. I'm not meant to be like this.

Apart from Cate, the only time I can remember feeling completely understood and connected with somebody was with Denzi: that day we stopped by the gates when we were running, and both looked at the sea the same way.

Now I'm remembering how everyone in my swim school group was that first time we went free swimming in the sea: the silent tension in the air on the way, the joy when we got there. Something connects us all, but is it the same thing? I know Isha and Zara were Penrose babies and it had seemed so unreal that we were in the same place, but what if we *all* were?

If The Circle encompasses the Penrose Clinic, then they knew the hurricane was coming. Would they have let them all drown? I don't know because I don't know *why* we were made as we are. If there was some purpose behind it, it wouldn't make sense to let them die.

Unless they're covering their tracks – getting rid of the evidence of what they did.

But what about Denzi?

I told him about the Penrose Clinic; I'm sure he was truthful when he said he didn't know what it was. Maybe he is a Penrose baby, but doesn't know about it – I only found out recently, after all.

What next? Things can't go on the way they have been. I keep reacting to things, situations. Running away. I need to *act* not react. Take control of who and what I am, work out what it means – both to me, and to the Penrose Clinic. Why are they so intent on tracking me down? Were others at the school like me? What does it all have to do with The Circle that Cate warned me about?

I need to find out before they catch up with me again.

63

It's late when I get to London; the moon has taken over the sky. The sea is so far away that its absence is a constant ache that makes it hard to think beyond what I lack.

Maybe if I have something to eat and some sleep this tired fogginess will go away.

I have a quick snack in a café by the station, then head for the Underground. Ren told me which line, where to change, to go to her friend's place, but when I get there the station is closed. There are signs – the Tube is shut still because of the bombings.

I find a map in a bus shelter: I can walk. It's about five miles and I set out at a fast pace.

As I go, it's like earlier today in the taxi with Jago – the closer I get to where I'm going, the more uneasy I begin to feel. Around me people rush in this direction, that – many on their own, like me, others with friends, or holding hands. Many of those on their own are probably going home to someone, and my solitude in the midst of so many is more instead of less.

I find another map in a bus shelter; his house isn't far away. I walk there, slow and then slower.

Something feels *wrong*. What is it?

I get to the right street but go past, keep walking.
Think.

Malina keeps finding me. How?

Was it really as obvious as I thought earlier for Malina to be waiting for me at Bodmin Parkway station, or did they somehow know that was where I'd go?

The only ones who knew were Jago and Ren. I trust them – they'd never pass information along about me. I'm sure of it.

But what if somehow that is what is happening without them knowing?

I walk further on, find another café – one with Wi-Fi.

I open the chat; there's a message from Jago, asking if I got here OK. I scroll back through the messages before, see where Ren sent the train times, her friend's name and address.

What if somehow Malina can see what is here? My stomach twists in a knot. Then they know where I'm going; they're probably watching for me there now.

Or maybe I'm wrong. Maybe it was just luck and guesswork that had them at the station in Bodmin at the right time.

I hesitate, then go to the group chat. Reply: Hi both, I'm in London! Got here no problems and found Ren's friend's place. He's all right and the guest room is great. I'm so ready for some sleep. Tx

I hesitate. It feels so wrong to lie to my friends, but how else can I know for sure?

I press *send*.

Now what?

I head for Ren's friend's place.

Careful. Quiet. Stealth.

I walk near to a group of girls about my age, as if I'm with them, keeping them between me and the road. They turn and this time I shadow someone on their own. It's around this corner.

What am I expecting? I don't even know.

Then a police car goes by, turns up the street. Another one is already there.

There's a lane lined with trees, and I fit myself against a tree in shadows where I can just see the house, the police. *Listen* with all of me.

'Open the door! It's the police.'

The door opens; a man peers out. 'What's going on?'

'We have reason to believe you're harbouring an underage runaway.'

'What? Of course not.'

'Well, you won't mind if we take a look, then.'

They're not waiting for an answer or to show a warrant; two push inside. Another waits by the door, and with a shock I see her red hair. She turns her head just enough for me to be sure: it's the woman who was with Malina. The one who waited at Bodmin when Malina followed Jago.

I step back, turn away – go up to the end of the road. Turn. Walk. Turn again, and again, moving away from the area gradually.

My heart is pounding – *thud-thud, thud-thud* – drums of fear as I walk into the night.

64

I walk, not stopping until I'm so tired I can barely put one foot in front of the other. I must have gone miles and have no idea where I am. It's late, almost midnight, but there are still people everywhere. London may not sleep but I'm desperate for it.

Instead I find a late night café, more tea.

What now?

There is Wi-Fi, messages from Jago. Still nothing from Ren. He'd answered me before, asking me to check in again before I go to sleep. A few more messages follow, worried for me when I don't answer.

I don't believe – can't believe – that either of them have been telling Malina and her friends anything about where I am. So how did they know to go to that house, and why did they do so just after I told Jago I was there? Somehow, they must be seeing these messages.

So, do I answer him, and just be careful what I say?

I'm not sure if it is a good idea, but I can't leave him worried like that.

Hi, Jago, I'm ok but police went to Ren's friend's house. I was watching before I went in and got away before they saw me.

He starts typing an answer immediately; must have been watching and waiting for me. Omg. Are you sure you're ok?

Yes, I promise.

But how did they know to go there?

I don't know. Could they somehow see what we're saying here?

There's a long pause before he answers.

Maybe the tablet or Ren's computer have been hacked. Turn it off in case they can trace it. But first there is something else to tell you. I kept calling Ren's when she didn't answer and finally, late, her dad answered. She's been in a car accident.

Oh no, is she ok?

I don't know. I'll try to find out more tomorrow.

I should go. Don't worry about me; I've got a plan. Bye Tx

I am worrying, be careful Jx

Tablets can be hacked? Traced? I do a quick search and what I read scares me. I turn it off but is that enough? I can't just abandon it; it's Ren's.

I so hope she is OK.

Was it just a random accident, or did Malina or one of the others have something to do with it? Ren said she was going to tell people online about the relationship between Penrose and The Circle. Maybe they found a way to stop her before she had a chance.

Fear — for me, for Ren, for Jago and everyone who has ever helped me — makes me want to twist into myself and hide, go somewhere they can never find me.

But what if I'm the only one who knows the things I know?

I can't lose it now. I have to find a way to stop them. Make them pay for what they've done.

I leave the café, find a train station nearby. I write Ren's name and address on the back of the tablet and take it to the office.

'Do you have a lost and found?'

'Yes, what have you got?'

'I found this tablet. It looks like it's got a name and address on the back.'

'Thanks.'

I leave the station, start walking again. Now what?

I told Jago I had a plan, but that was more to reassure him than anything else. All I've got is to contact Denzi, arrange to meet him. I'm so glad I hadn't done that already on Ren's tablet, that I didn't tell them Denzi's name or anything else about him.

But I can't do anything about contacting Denzi in the middle of the night. I can't walk all night, either. I can't camp out in a park in London like I did in Cornwall – here, night fears would be real.

A car goes past then slows down until I catch up.

'Hey, darling, want a ride with us?'

I ignore them, keep walking and instead of driving on they go slowly next to me, keeping pace.

'Come on, it'll be fun.' And they're laughing, saying rude things about my legs.

There isn't anyone else around me now and they're still there, following, and I'm scared.

Ahead – on the other side of the road – pavement leads between some buildings; there is no road next to it to drive along.

I change direction, run back then across the road and up to the pavement, and run and run – past buildings, to another street and another, for how long I don't know.

Now I'm on a back street. It's dark, quiet.

There is a sudden noise behind me and I spin around, then

almost laugh at myself. It's a cat – staring down at me from a fence post. Get a grip.

Then his eyes shift to something over my shoulder.

Danger.

I turn around – two boys stand there. I'm trapped between the two of them and a fence.

One of them smiles; a knife glitters in his hand.

'Give us your bag and you won't get hurt.'

I start to take my pack off my shoulder, but it's all that I have. Then there is this *rush* – adrenalin, anger, something *else* – all through my body. Everything in and around me changes: the darkness is less, the way I move is more. I spin around, fast, kick the one without the knife hard in the gut and feel the point of impact jar through my body. As he falls to the ground the other one is reaching towards me with his knife, too slow; I slam my bag into his knife hand. It clatters to the ground and when he reaches for it, I stomp, hard, on his hand. There is a sickening, crunching noise and he screams.

I *run*, leaving cries of pain behind me. Footsteps pound behind me but soon drop away, and as I run something *changes*, again. The night looks as it did before and my fear takes over again.

This time instead of a back street I head for sounds of traffic. A busier road. Not many people are walking around this late, but there are enough of them that I feel safer, and I stop, breathing hard, at a bus stop. My hands are shaking, energy gone. Shock and fear are taking over and I'm gripped by an overwhelming longing for the sea, a cool, dark hiding place. Here I feel so exposed.

I don't know how to fight; whatever possessed me to take such a risk? I could have been stabbed. *How* did I even do that? The echo of breaking bones and screams are in my ears still, acid in my throat, and I struggle to stop myself from throwing up. I did that? Hurt somebody so bad they screamed? He might have stabbed me if I hadn't, but the feeling of power and violence running through me was so alien.

The other half of me, that is usually only truly there in the sea, took over – did those things – while I watched. I swallow. The not-human half.

Humans, though, are violent all the time; to themselves, to the earth, to forests and animals and every form of life. Animals, though? They use it to eat, to protect, to defend.

Who am I to say my human half is any better than the animal half?

A night bus comes maybe ten minutes later. The others waiting start getting on and after a small hesitation I drop back, crouch down and duck through the middle doors while they are still queueing to get on – all the while waiting for the driver to call out, for others on the bus to react – nothing. A few passengers who must have seen me ignore what I did.

I'll stay on the bus until it stops, I decide. After the bus starts again I make my way down the aisle and then up the stairs to the top. It's quieter here. There's a girl and boy kissing at the back. A man on his own. The rest is empty, and I take a seat somewhere between them.

I'm shaking still and I'm not sure if it's more fear or tiredness. Those first men in that car – what would they have done if I hadn't got away? I don't know. Probably nothing besides be obnoxious, but I don't know. But going down back streets at night wasn't a good idea. I need to be smarter.

It's a long while before I calm down enough for my fatigue to set in. My eyelids are doing that dance where they close, my head drops but the movement wakes me up. Open eyes and repeat.

I must drift off for a while because the next time I look up the boy and girl aren't there any more. There is a woman on her own, two teenage boys and the same man as before.

My bag? Where's my bag?

I have a moment of panic then see it's slipped from the seat to the floor. What if someone had taken it? The rest of my money, a few odds and ends of clothes, are in there – it's all I have.

I put it between me and the window, double wrap the strap tight around my arm. If I drift off again it should wake me if it moves or someone tries to take it. London streets go by my window as I try to stay awake.

Sun . . . Sea . . . Earth . . . Sky . . .

My promise and all the promises stretch back over so many years. Voices – past, present – say the four points of our compass over and again, and the voices merge in time:

Sun . . . Sea . . . Earth . . . Sky . . .

But then we shift forwards. There is a wrongness *in time, so vast that I don't understand.*

The voices that surround me fade, until only mine remains . . .

65

An early morning café. Breakfast, tea, and I start to feel more awake.

The night bus had got to its last stop not long after I finally fell asleep and had that nightmare, one I'm still having trouble shaking off. Then there'd been an hour or so of darkness to walk around in before the sun started to brighten the sky. As it came up my spirits rose with it.

OK, last night was scary; I'm lucky I didn't get hurt. And before that, hearing about the bombings and nearly getting caught by Malina and her friends in Boscastle, Bodmin and London – all in one day – packed in a lot of stress. But each time I got away: so that is Tabby three, Malina zero. And they don't know where to look to find me in London, do they? It's a big city.

The more I think about it, the more I am certain: working out who and what I am is key to why The Circle are trying so hard to find me. It must somehow be important to what they are doing. And the best way to work myself out is to find someone else like me, and I'm sure that is Denzi. There's no other way I can explain what we felt together when looking at the sea.

Find Denzi, and then go from there.

I ask around and am told there are computers that can be used in a library not far away. I kill time until it is open.

Sign on to a computer.

I go back to the school website and find the link to the swim school missing page. Hunt down through all the posts until I spot Denzi's found post.

I click on his name, then on 'Send Message'.

Staring at the screen, I think about what to say and how to say it. I won't use my name, but he needs to know it's me. I think about it for a while, then begin to type.

Part 7

66

Denzi

I head downstairs for an early breakfast after a sleepless night. I watched that bit of CCTV on the news over and over. Should I call the police? Tell them that Ariel, a girl who went missing in the hurricane in England, somehow reappeared in the US and had something to do with the Hoover Dam explosions? It sounded beyond crazy, and the more I looked at the face on the screen the less convinced I was that it was actually her. But if there were any chance, shouldn't I call the police and let them decide?

Finally, I texted Becker, asked what he thought. Another insomniac – he answered minutes later. He agreed it looked a bit like Ariel, but he was sure it wasn't her – something about the shape of her nose not being quite right. He added that it'd be cruel to her family to think she might be involved, might still be alive. I looked one more time and decided he was right.

I'm not hungry, but today is the day of Eva's march. I don't know what might happen but I'd best eat in case I need some energy.

I'm on a second round of toast with peanut butter when my phone beeps – a message. Pick it up, glance at the screen then do so again.

There's a message from . . . Cat Dickens? As if on cue, he comes into the kitchen to inspect his empty bowl, then gives me a narrow-eyed look for my failure. I'm pretty sure he can't type out breakfast requests, so who is it?

I open the message.

Hi, Denzi. Thinking of the suitcase on the stairs, loners in the garden, the hidden way to the sea. Hope we can talk again soon.

The cat name, the loner, the case – it's Tabby. It has to be! It was only sent minutes ago, and I'm flooded with relief: she's OK. But why is she on the run, sending this cryptic message? Why was Oliver warned off? What is with all the crazy coincidences? What the hell is really going on with the Penrose Clinic and the rest?

I answer.

Hi, Cat, we need to talk. Tell me where and when, or call. I give my mobile number.

I stare at the screen, willing her to answer or my phone to ring.

One minute, two . . . a message pings in.

I'm not sure how to get around this, but I'm scared messages and phones are hacked.

She's there – she's still there. She's afraid to answer? Well, OK. As son of a security-conscious politician, this is one thing I do know about.

Sign up for Signal. It's secure – I promise – all end-to-end encrypted. And message me there.

I wait – but nothing comes back, not in messages or Signal. Five minutes, then ten tick slowly by.

It's time: I have to get ready before Stacey gets here.

All I can do is keep checking for a reply as I go.

67

Tabby

I read Denzi's messages over and over again. He didn't ask why I called myself Cat Dickens or said all that stuff so he'd know who I was. Just a simple, to the point, *We need to talk*. He knows something is wrong, doesn't he? And then he suggests Signal, whatever that is.

But before I look into that, I have two questions.

How do I know with absolute certainty that it really is him? That someone in The Circle hasn't hacked into his account and is pretending to be him?

Second question: if it really is Denzi, can I trust him? I wouldn't have contacted him in the first place if I didn't think so, but now that I've done it, I'm scared. What if I got him wrong? What if I tell him everything and he doesn't believe any of it, thinks I'm bonkers and turns me in to the authorities?

I sigh. One thing I do know: I don't want another night walking around London or on a night bus, needing sleep but afraid someone might hurt me, steal my stuff. I don't need a lot of sleep, but even so I can only go without it for so long. I'm feeling unwell, wrong in the head – it's hard to think straight. Worse than I should feel from just a night or two of not sleeping – how many times have I done that before and been OK? But then I was swimming. That's what I need to feel better.

But I'm here now, and there isn't a beach in easy reach; just buck up. *Focus*.

The other problem is that my money will run out at some point. And I'm convinced I need to find someone like me to help me work out what I am, what it means, and that that someone should be Denzi.

OK. But how do I know it really is him, not someone pretending?

There is something about the words he used that sounds like him, but I need to come up with a place to meet him where I can make sure it is him before getting too close.

What next?

I'm uneasy. If Ren's tablet or computer were hacked, is anything online safe?

I look up Signal, read about it, and it sounds like it should be OK to use. This end-to-end encryption means no one can tap into our messages or what we say.

But I can't use it. Not without a phone number: you have to have one to sign up.

My computer time is almost up. I quickly write down Denzi's number, erase history and leave the library behind.

I walk and think about how to handle the situation. Not much later I find myself in a mobile phone shop buying the cheapest smart phone they have. That and topping it up takes most of what is left of my money from selling Simone's bracelet. This has to work; I have nothing to fall back on now.

Once out I find a quiet bench. Find Signal, set it up.

OK, this is it: *do it*.

I enter Denzi's number. Think for a while – write a message. Read it over and over, then press 'Send' before I can change my mind.

68

Denzi

I wait inside the pool centre, out of sight of the doors in case Stacey doesn't leave straight away after dropping me out front. Hayden texted earlier – said to meet her at Trafalgar Square, one of the starting points for the protest march that will be posted to the world soon.

Just when I'm thinking that's long enough and start for the doors, Jess comes through.

'Denzi! Are you waiting for me?' A grin and a raised eyebrow.

I shake my head. 'You've caught me: about to duck out of training today.'

'Why?'

I hesitate, then draw her to the side as some other swimmers come through the doors. 'There's a climate protest march, in memory of Eva, the girl who died after Hyde Park. I'm going.'

'Wow. That is so cool. Can I come?'

'Don't. There may be trouble. There's been so much aggro against environmental groups lately – it might be worse than when Eva was hurt.'

'I want to come,' she insists. 'I'll go find it on my own so you might as well take me along.'

I shake my head. 'Are you sure?'

'Yes!'

'OK, then. I'm meeting some of the others at Trafalgar Square.'

We head out, start walking for the Tube. As we go I tell her that we're meeting Eva's friend, Hayden – how I know her.

'There's something else we need to talk about,' Jess says. 'You know how you thought Tabby running away might have something to do with the Penrose Clinic? I know you're worried about her, but it might not be for the right reasons.'

'What do you mean?'

'I didn't tell you this yesterday, because I had to think about whether I should or not. It was told in confidence. But I think you need to know. Tabby really wasn't well – mentally, I mean. She had this crazy childhood – she was kidnapped when she was three, raised more or less on the run by someone who she thought was her mother. Just months before swim school the woman who kidnapped her was killed. Tabby, well, she couldn't deal with it all – she had delusions that people were after her. So her running away is probably because of all of that.'

'Seriously? How do you know?'

'She told me.'

We're at the Tube now, too many people around us to talk as we start going down the stairs to the platform, and I'm reeling from what Jess said. I can't believe it. And the stuff about being kidnapped – it is so out there.

Though maybe that'd explain why Tabby had two names – Tabby and Holly – and seemed really flustered when she'd told me Tabby and then realised what she said. And there *was* something different about her – something about the things she said and did, with, I don't know, an *innocence* about other people

310

and the world. Could what Jess said about how she grew up explain it?

I didn't know Tabby for long, but she didn't strike me as the sort of person who shares loads of personal stuff easily, any more than I usually would. So why would she have told all that to Jess? I can't remember even seeing them say hello. Apart from me, the only people I ever saw Tabby talk to were Ariel and Isha.

And delusions? Could Tabby be mentally ill?

I try to think it through, not automatically reject it. If what Jess said is true about Tabby's background, she's been through a lot, and OK, yes, sometimes Tabby did seem to be struggling with things. But something about what Jess said doesn't ring true. And if Tabby was having delusions, she'd think they were real, wouldn't she? So she'd hardly tell Jess they were delusions.

But why on earth would Jess make something like that up?

We meet by Nelson's Column.

Hayden is already there, a friend along with her. It's always busy at Trafalgar Square but even more so today. The crowd is growing, coalescing, around us: mostly teenagers, some younger, some older. Many of them have bags with them that now reveal signs. Placards. Hayden says she made one for me: '4 Eva 4 Ever: Act Now on Climate Change'. I take it and thank her.

More people come, and more.

'It's online everywhere now,' Hayden says, excitement on her face, in her voice, as she shows me her phone. 'Look! It's all tagged #4Eva4Ever. That was mine – I came up with it.'

Hayden's friend takes our photo, Jess alongside, to post online. The press will jump on me being here, won't they? And that reminds me of something else I have to do. A message on Signal, to Dad and Jax. I'm sorry to worry you but I had to go to Eva's march. I'll get in touch later.

Jess is looking at me. 'Texting my dads. Told them I skipped training so they don't panic if anyone notices I'm not where I should be.' And even as I explain, I think, *Why so curious, Jess?*

There is a banner being unfurled to go first, someone with a megaphone organising us to follow behind. There's an air of excitement – both upbeat and serious at the same time – when we start out. We fan out from the square on to the road, stopping traffic as we go. More and more join us as we start to head up Pall Mall.

My phone vibrates in my pocket.

There's a message on Signal from an unknown number. I'm in London – where can we meet, somewhere public? I need more help with my case. Don't tell anyone and come alone.

Tabby.

'My dad,' I say to Jess. Tabby asked me not to tell anyone, so I won't. But I'm not sure why I'm lying to Jess, either; I didn't need to tell her who it was from, so why did I lie?

Then I reply: Just left Trafalgar Square on this climate protest march. We're heading for Hyde Park. How about there?

69

Tabby

A climate protest march, Denzi said. There'll be crowds of people, won't there? Walking, and likely not too fast. I'll get to the park first and find a place we can meet, somewhere I can be out of sight and watch – make sure it really is Denzi.

I reply: I'll head to the park, find a place to meet and let you know where.

The Tube is running again, and it's London-busy and then some. The platform I need is absolutely packed – hot, crowded, and my head is spinning. I don't feel right, like maybe I've caught something, but it doesn't feel like any cold or fever I've ever had. I have to fight to make myself stay on the platform, not retreat.

I push on to the next Tube that comes. When the doors shut it is so full that bodies are pressing all around. I'm feeling even more faint, like if it weren't impossible rammed in like this, I'd fall over.

When we get there and the doors open, I can't get away from the crowd – it seems almost everyone gets off with me at Marble Arch. There are loads of kids and teens, most in school uniform – all excited, talking – and I hear some of them say that they're going to Speakers' Corner. Are they here for the march – is that where Denzi will be going, too?

When I step out of the Tube exit to the street I have to push through the crowd to get some space around me. My vision blurs and I stand, one hand on a bench until it passes. That's when I see the police: one car pulled in, and another. More on foot. The panic is instant, making me want to run, but that would just draw attention to myself. I manage to walk past them calmly, head turned away, telling myself that they're not looking for me, they're here for the protest.

I find a map of the park posted up near the entrance and decide to head across Hyde Park to Kensington Gardens. Hopefully that will be far enough away from Speakers' Corner that the police and crowds will not spill over.

With a few likely places in mind, I walk, fast. There are crowds of people and they're all going the other way; it's like swimming against the current to get through them. It's a little quieter by the time I reach the bridge over the Serpentine, a dividing point between Hyde Park and Kensington Gardens. I start to cross it when my eyes are caught by the Lido, my heart by a memory.

Cate brought me here once, years ago. I must have been five or six, and it seemed a magical place: a stretch of the Serpentine Lake sectioned off for outdoor swimming in the middle of London.

The blue water shimmers; it's so close. I'm feeling so unwell, faint and sick. I need to swim, I have to. It's the only thing that will make me feel better.

But what about finding a place to meet Denzi?

If he's caught in all those crowds of people he won't get here for a while, will he? And my feet refuse to take me anywhere else.

I walk over, pay to get in. It's busy; no free lockers. Take off T-shirt and shorts – my swimsuit is on underneath, always – a habit I can't break even when not near the sea. I look around, put my stuff on the bank near the lifeguard, next to some other towels and bags. Not deep enough to dive, I walk in from the edge.

Cool. Wet. *Blissful*, even though it's fresh, not saltwater. As water closes around me some of the tension eases inside. I walk further to deeper water and stand there, just breathing a moment. Then dive under and swim: along the bottom to the far end and back again. Even though I feel so much better than I did a short time ago it is still frustration. The water – it's not deep enough, cold enough.

I don't know how long I swim underwater – often underneath other swimmers, surfacing only occasionally. Going back and forth. Again and again, lost in the feeling of swimming at last. But I'm aware enough that something nags for attention: Denzi. I need to tell him where to meet.

I find the will to make myself get out of the water, slow and reluctant. I go back to near the lifeguard where I left my pack and then panic – where has it gone?

There are more bags and things here now – I look through them and find mine, half covered by someone's towel. I breathe a sigh of relief, take my clothes out. Glance up and there are curious eyes watching me – because of how I swam, maybe? It's not a good way to avoid drawing attention. I hurry away, pulling T-shirt and shorts on over wet suit as I go back the way I came.

I hurry up and down different paths, assessing and rejecting different places, and then I see the statue of Peter Pan. In front of it is Long Water, the narrow part of the lake that connects to the Serpentine with its Lido; behind there are trees and bushes where I can hide. I wait for a few tourists with cameras to walk away, then slip into the trees. This will do.

I go further into the green and take out my phone.

I'll wait by the Peter Pan statue.

Another moment, an answering text: I'll come as soon as I can. A question – do you know this girl, the blonde one?

A photo follows.

Denzi is there, talking to a younger girl with dark hair – both are holding protest signs – and there is a blonde girl next to his shoulder.

I frown. Why is he asking? She looks familiar – I think she was at summer swim school, but I never spoke to her and don't remember her name.

Don't know her name, was she there this summer? Is something wrong?

70

Denzi

If Tabby isn't even sure who Jess is in that photo I forwarded, she definitely hasn't told Jess her life story, has she? But why would Jess lie about it? Unless . . . it's true, and Tabby is the one with a shaky grip on reality. But everything inside me refuses to believe it.

I need to talk to Tabby: that is the only way I'll know for sure.

So what do I do now? Exactly as she asked. Go to meet her alone, and tell no one.

We're almost at Hyde Park. The crowd has swelled so much around us along the way that we're barely managing a slow walk. Someone with a megaphone has started a chant: 'For Eva, for ever; For Eva, for ever . . .' It gets louder and louder as more people join in.

I duck down and pretend to tie a shoelace.

And quickly text Tabby: Nothing to worry about. I'll come alone.

As I straighten Jess turns back just in time to see the phone in my hand.

'For Eva, for ever; For Eva, for ever . . .'

'Is everything OK?' she says.

'Fine,' I say, and I put the phone back in my pocket. We're crossing the road to the park now; it's been closed by police. There are groups of protestors coming from different directions and converging here; as everyone comes together our pace slows even more. We're almost at the centre of the throng.

'For Eva, for ever; For Eva, for ever . . .'

Bishan with his broken arm is on another podium ladder – a taller, sturdier-looking one than he was knocked down from the last time. People swirl around us, getting closer and closer, trapping us in the centre, and I'm just tall enough to be able to see that there are police along the edges of the protest. There is another crowd forming and trying to push in. Are things about to go wrong like they did the last time? But it looks like the police are here in number and keeping the groups apart, containing things – at least for now.

'For Eva, for ever; For Eva, for ever . . .'

Bishan holds up a hand for quiet and the chant dies away. Someone below passes him a megaphone.

'Thank you all for coming! This march was organised to remember Eva: a passionate young climate protestor who so tragically died after receiving injuries during a protest not far from where we stand now. Nothing would stop her from fighting for the climate, the animals she loved, the planet that is our home. And so we continue this fight.'

Hayden and her friend are wedged close in front of me, Jess to one side, other people all around. How am I going to get away to go to Tabby?

Bishan continues, outlining plans of action I only half hear as I try to ease through the Kensington Garden side, bit by bit, but it's impossible to do so without drawing attention to what I'm doing. I'll have to wait until this is over to get away on my own.

But then a ripple of noise grows and takes over – towards

the road. I can't see much from here, just that there is some kind of disturbance.

Then there are shouts. *Screams.*

Bishan on his ladder is looking over everyone's heads and horror crosses his face.

The crowd all start to move away from the road, pushing and shoving and trying to get away from whatever is happening.

I shield Hayden and her friend in front of me to protect them as much as I can as the crowd heaves around us – pushing us forward – into people who can't move away fast enough. Jess is on one side of me, but then the crowd shifts and she's pulled away. Hayden trips but I keep her upright. The pressure behind us increases, but finally, the people ease away in front of us and we can walk, then run to get away.

Tears streak Hayden's face. 'What's happened?'

'I don't know, I couldn't see . . .'

Then Jess, Bishan, and a few others that I remember from Eva's funeral come up behind us.

'Did you see what happened?' I ask Bishan.

'A car – it rammed into the crowd. People were hurt, I don't know how badly.'

I turn to Hayden. 'You're both all right?' She nods. 'Stay here. I'm going back to see if I can help.'

'I'm coming,' Jess says.

'Don't. Stay here with the others.'

'You can't stop me,' she says, and there is something on her face, not quite right – though what *right* is supposed to be in a situation like this I don't know.

I run back towards the noise: crying; screaming. Everyone is running the other way but I get through, Jess not far behind.

A policeman stops me.

'Please. Can I help?' I say.

He looks at me, looks again, like he knows who I am. He shakes his head. 'Paramedics are here, more are coming. You would only get in the way.'

My phone vibrates, and again. Two Signal messages.

Dad: Are you all right?

Tabby: What's happening? Are you ok – still coming?

I answer both with yes just as Jess catches up.

It's time to go to Tabby. I can't help here, and I'm desperate to see her.

'Go back to the others, I've got something to do,' I say to Jess.

She shakes her head. 'I came here with you – don't leave me on my own.'

And she's right – things could kick off again. I need to go to Tabby alone, but I can't abandon Jess.

I'll see her safe, first.

We walk back until the others are in sight. 'There they are,' I say, and while she's looking towards them I turn, and run. Fast.

I glance back. *What?* She's chasing after me. Why would she do that?

I weave in and out and around people randomly. Put on a burst of speed, then wind through some trees and stop. Have I lost her?

I count down a few minutes, then look back the way I came. No sign of her. This is doubly weird – why would she try to run me down like that?

Keeping my head down, I head for Kensington Gardens.

71

Tabby

Sirens and distant cries of pain fill my ears and I want to run, hide. My heart is beating fast and adrenalin that needs to do something, anything, floods my body.

Caution, stealth. *Stay quiet, hidden.*

Denzi said *yes.* He'll be here soon.

I force my breathing to go slower; my heart rate slows, too. I'm against a tree in shadows, just able to see between branches. People across Long Water are running, hurrying away. Some rush past on this side also.

And then, all at once, he's here. Denzi. Caught in sunlight next to the statue of Peter Pan, looking all around.

I step part way out of the trees and he turns to the movement.

'Tabby?' he says and comes closer. I pull him into the shadows. We hug and his heart is beating fast, he's been running and scared but he is strong, solid. Here.

He pulls away, holds me at arm's length, studying me. 'I almost didn't recognise you.'

I touch my hair self-consciously, forgetting he hasn't seen me since Sascha's makeover. 'Was trying to look different – guess it's working.'

'What's going on?' he says.

'I have some things to tell you, some of it pretty unbelievable. I need help working out what to do next.'

'All right. Let's get out of here. Come back to mine?'

I shake my head. 'Someone might think to look for me there. Is there somewhere else quiet where we can talk?'

'Let's get away from here and then find a place. I think we need to walk the long way around to leave the park and get away from everyone.'

'What happened back there?'

He's shaking his head and there is shock in his eyes. 'A car rammed into the protest. It looked like a lot of people were hurt.'

'You tried to help.'

'Yes. Police sent me back, then I came here. Wait, I've got to text—'

'Nothing about me!'

'No. Just to let my friends know I'm OK and going.'

'That blonde girl?'

'Well, she's with the others but I'm not sure she's a friend – she may have been using me to try to find you. I can't work out what is going on. Can you tell me?'

'We'll talk. I'll tell you everything,' I say, and I mean it. I held back with Jago and his friends, kept some things to myself. But Denzi is one of us; I'm sure of it.

He's kin.

72

Denzi

Tabby holds my hand. And it's not like a boy-girl kind of thing, it's more like she's scared and needs something to hold on to. Maybe I do, too.

I keep glancing at her as we walk. I almost didn't recognise her with the shorter, crazy dyed hair – but the more I look, the more it suits her. And she's thinner, pale under her tan. Darkness in her eyes.

We walk quickly along the path towards the Lido, then go right when the path branches, heading further away from Hyde Park and towards the southern boundary of Kensington Gardens. The sounds of distress fade but the sirens are still loud, some getting closer, some further – taking the injured away? From the little I saw there were many injured, maybe dead, and I shudder inside, try to push it away – to concentrate on *now*.

We are nearing the Albert Memorial when Tabby stops short, pulls me back into shadows.

'What's wrong?'

'That girl whose photo you sent me – the blonde one. She's by the road.'

I glance back in time to see Jess ducking into a car – a government car, like the sort I get driven around in.

Then someone gets out of the car. It's Stacey? But why would Jess be with Stacey? Stacey starts to cross the road towards us.

'Run,' Tabby says.

'What? Why?'

Not waiting to answer, Tabby is off – pelting down the path back into the park, and I follow. Glance back over my shoulder: Stacey is running, too. She's chasing us?

Tabby is running faster than I've seen her manage before, and I can barely keep pace. Stacey looks fit but soon drops off behind us, but Tabby doesn't slow until we're nearly at the northern boundary.

'What's going on?'

Tabby can't speak she's breathing so hard, bent over. 'Do . . . you . . . know . . . that . . . woman?' she finally gasps out, a word at a time.

'She's a personal protection officer. Works for the government.'

Tabby shakes her head. 'That's . . . that's not all she is. Let's get out of here.'

'Are you all right?' Her breathing is slowing to near normal but she's even paler, her eyes unfocused.

'No time. Let's go.'

'Tabby?'

She looks at me. Slowly her eyes focus on mine. 'We have to go. Now.'

We approach one of the northern boundary gates. Tabby motions for me to stay back. Looks through, then curses under her breath.

'She's just coming – in her car. Let's go back.' Tabby starts to run along a different path now – the one that leads to the Peter Pan statue. She slows as we reach Long Water. 'Something isn't right. We can outrun her, but we can't get away if she cuts us off from leaving the park each time. She came exactly to where we were.'

'Lucky guess?'

'Doubt it. It's like we're being tracked somehow – like we were by the trackers we had to wear at swim school.'

Fitness trackers – like phone fitness apps. 'Maybe it's my phone?'

'Quick: throw it in the water.'

'What? No way. Look, the only ones authorised on my phone to be able to trace it are my dad and Jax, his partner. And that woman – Stacey – is assigned to protect me. She's probably worried, that's all.'

Tabby shakes her head. 'I'll leave you behind if I have to. Get rid of your phone. Please.' And she's scared, her voice desperate.

'OK. How about instead we stash it and watch what happens?'

'I don't know! All right. Do it – fast.'

We scatter some leaf litter over my phone at the edge of the path by the water, then disappear deep into the trees to watch and wait. Tabby is leaning against me – I'm holding her up. She's trembling? I touch her forehead. Hot – like feverishly hot.

Not long after, Stacey walks down the path, looks around. She's talking to someone on the phone. Then a woman appears from the other direction, and there is something about her, she's familiar somehow – oh my God. It's Malina? From swim school. What is she doing here?

They are searching along the edge of the path and soon find my phone. Stacey swears, says something to Malina. Malina throws my phone into the water.

Finally they walk off together the way Stacey came.

What the hell?

73

Tabby

I'm swaying on my feet. 'Need to sit a moment,' I say, and almost fall to the ground. I lean back against a tree, breathing deeply, but it's like I can't get enough oxygen.

'What's wrong?'

'I don't know.' I'm looking through my pack for my water bottle but it's empty and my head is spinning. I lie back on the grass.

'I'll get some.' He sprints off before I can stop him.

Concentrate on breathing, slow and steady. I try the Malina trick to cool myself down but can't focus enough for it to work, and I'm scared Denzi won't come back, that they'll see him and stop him.

But soon I hear his voice. My eyes are closed.

He's easing me up and I drink deep from his bottle, then pour the rest over my head.

'Maybe you've got heat stroke? You need to see a doctor.'

I shake my head no. I'd felt unwell earlier but better after swimming in the Lido. Was it running as fast as I could that has done this to me? I don't think so. Whatever this is, it's beyond exhaustion. There is something wrong with me – I can feel it – nothing to do with heat stroke. I don't need a doctor or medicine: I need the sea. I need it *soon*.

'I'll get help,' he says.

'No! Please. I'll be all right. I just need the sea – I need to swim in the sea. Then I'll be fine.'

He's worried, but there is also a glimmer of something in his eyes.

'You understand, don't you? You feel the same if you're away from it. You're one of us.'

'One of what?'

'I promise I'll explain everything, on the way. Please.'

'On the way to the sea?'

I nod.

'OK. Where should we go?'

'What is the closest?' Denzi suggests Brighton. He says he goes there all the time. I shake my head, wanting a place neither of us has been to before – where no one would think to look for either of us. We settle on Hastings, and he checks train times on my phone.

We wait a while, then walk the other way – back towards the Albert Memorial. It's not long since we almost left the park there before, but when we were running, then hiding and watching, it was like time slowed down. I was in that strange place where I could move very fast or not at all, as required. Run or stay hidden. The other half of me took over and kept me safe, but then, after, I felt worse than I did before – even worse than before the first time I went to swim from Ren's. Another dip in the Lido wouldn't be enough now.

Now I know we're on the way to the sea – even though it'll take a while to get there – I feel well enough to keep going.

My need for the sea is like an addiction, and it's getting worse.

74

Denzi

We are heading towards Gloucester Road and the Tube, walking slowly, Tabby half leaning on me. Is taking her to the sea instead of a doctor the right thing to do?

All around us people are stopped, huddled in groups. Talking, speculating, looking towards the parks or at their phones for news. I can't believe what happened at the protest, and it's like too many things around me don't make sense. The *world* doesn't make sense.

We get the Tube, change once. Not saying much with the usual crowds of people everywhere. We get to Charing Cross just in time to catch the next train. My phone pay is at the bottom of a lake, but we manage to come up with enough cash between us for tickets. Tabby is insistent that I don't call anyone, let them know I'm OK.

Am I?

I don't know.

We hurry to the platform and Tabby's pace matches mine, but she's looking even worse.

The train isn't very busy and we find seats together just as it pulls away from the station. No one is directly in front or behind us.

Tabby collapses into the seat. Her head is leaning back against it, her eyes looking up to mine.

'Thank you, Denzi.'

'How are you feeling?'

'Better,' she says again, but I'm plagued by doubt, that I should have insisted we get her checked by a doctor. But I couldn't make her, could I?

'What's going on, Tabby?'

'I don't even know where to start.'

'Is it about the Penrose Clinic?'

She nods and looks around, lowers her voice. 'And The Circle.'

My eyes widen. 'The terrorist group?'

'Yes. They're linked, and I found out. I've been running from them ever since. But I think they're after me for more than that. It's not just what I know – it's who I *am*. If I'm right, it's who you are, too.'

Who we are? And I know – don't I? What she means. Penrose babies. Made to be different.

Like me.

75

Tabby

Denzi holds my hand. He listens. He doesn't say, that can't be, I don't believe you, you're making this up. All the things I was afraid he'd say.

I tell him everything. About Cate. Beware The Circle. Her death. The Penrose symbol on the door; the circles hiding within. The terror hiding beneath: the girl-fish. Simone's death. Elodie's betrayal. Going to Jago; Ren's accident, and how scared I am for her and Jago. Almost getting caught in Cornwall and again in London. Everything to this moment.

When I'm done he's quiet, and I'm afraid he is thinking the things I was scared he'd say out loud.

'Denzi? Are you OK?'

He meets my eyes. 'I don't know. It's a lot to take in.'

'It's all true.'

'And you knew – before I did. That I'm a Penrose baby.'

'I guessed so, yes.'

'When I'd been trying to work out how to find you, I'd thought the reason you ran had to have something to do with the Penrose Clinic. I spoke to someone who used to work there. He said they were doing illegal procedures, mucking around with genetics – making designer babies.'

'I knew it must be something like that. But it's scary to hear you confirm it, just the same.'

'And that *thing* you saw. Why would anyone cross a fish and a girl?'

'I don't know. That's not the weirdest part of it, though. Her face – she looked like Ariel.'

'Like *Ariel*? Seriously?'

'Yes. And I found out something else about Ariel, online from some stuff about fundraising. Ariel's mother is Dr Rose, one of the founders of the Penrose Clinic. But when I'd asked Ariel if she'd heard of the Penrose Clinic, she said no. She must have lied.'

He's shaking his head. 'I thought I recognised her, convinced myself I was wrong, but now—'

'Recognised who? Ariel?'

'Yes. Can I show you something online?' he says, and I give him my phone. He does a search, brings up a video on a news site. 'Watch this.'

A girl with a backpack, not very clear – it's CCTV? And then she turns. 'She's had her hair cut, but it's Ariel. But I thought she was missing after the hurricane? And why is she on the news?'

'She was wanted for questioning in connection with the Hoover Dam bombings.'

'*What*? She wouldn't do that.'

'You probably thought she wouldn't lie to you either, but she did.'

I watch it again and again. 'Yes. It's her, I'm sure of it.'

'Ariel: she's the proof. Of the link between Penrose and The Circle.'

76

Denzi

Tabby's eyes have closed. She's leaning against me. Her breathing deepens, steadies. Asleep.

Everything she's told me – it can't be true, it can't.

She believes it. Every word.

She's delusional – that's what Christina and Jess said. So many things she told me about her life are the same as what Jess said – how did she know it if Tabby didn't tell her?

I shake my head. I'm looking for an out: a reason to reject things that I *know* are true, in a way that is beyond rational thought. It is raw, and real.

What have they done to us? *Why*?

Then our train arrives, and I can smell the sea. Nothing else matters.

77

Tabby

We start the short walk from the station to the beach. My head is light, as if I'm floating, the ground so far below that I have vertigo. If I were to fall I'd never get up again, so I hold tight to Denzi's hand. Neither of us have been to Hastings before but we don't need to ask the way – with every step we are closer to what we need. I can feel the presence of the sea, a secret joy quickening inside me.

When the water is in sight, everything inside me is *screaming* to run straight into the waves. Yet, somehow I know that waiting is part of what will make Denzi understand, or, more – help him believe what he must already know.

We walk down the shingled beach to the water's edge. Stand next to each other, *breathing* – for the salty tang, the taste, more than for oxygen.

'Now?' Denzi says. He's poised, I can feel it.

'Let's wait a little longer, get away on our own.'

We set out along the water's edge – going left – to the far end of the beach. Then we find a path to walk along the coast, through parkland, trees – sometimes blocking the view, sometimes framing it – and my head is even lighter. I'm giddy as if I'm flying there on a seagull's back.

After a while there's another path down to a rocky beach. There are only a few people there – a couple with a dog, some children and parents. We walk along past them to one end of the beach.

'Being so close to the sea, and waiting,' I say. 'How does it make you feel?'

He doesn't answer, so I try:

'It doesn't fit into words. I *need* the sea and it's beyond my need for anything else – I can go without food or sleep much easier. This, I can't. It's getting harder than it used to be – I don't know why. It's in my thoughts and . . . *under* them, too, in places I don't know by thinking, more like . . .' I pause, searching for meaning.

'*Feeling*. Not thinking, feeling.'

'Yes, that's almost it – except maybe, instead, it's a different kind of thinking?' It's hard to tear my eyes from the sea but I do so, look up to Denzi just as he does the same, turning to me. We are mirrors of the same anguish, longing. And wonder – to see it in each other as well as ourselves.

'I thought – I *felt* – this in both of us, that day by the gate, behind the school,' he says.

'Me, too.'

'Afterwards I thought I must have imagined it. That no one has this . . . *infection*, the same as me.'

'You are not alone,' I say, gently.

'But what does it— '

'No. Don't analyse, not now. Don't think, *feel*.'

'Now? Can we go in, *now*?' Denzi says again.

I shake my head. 'Patience. We should wait for the sun to be gone,' I say, though I have none of it myself. It is as much my physical weakness as any resolve to wait that stops my steps. 'Let's sit for a while?'

Denzi helps me down so I don't fall. And for a moment my head spins, vision goes dim and it feels like I'm about to pass out.

Focus: not just on the sea.

Sun . . . Sea . . . Earth . . . Sky . . .

I blink, and my vision clears.

The sun dips oh-so-slowly. With its last rays we tuck our shoes and things in my bag, and stash it out of sight between some rocks.

Denzi takes my hand and we walk to the water's edge.

78

Denzi

Tabby's hand, the beach, the sea – they've come together, made me drunk. I'm on a precipice, about to fall, tilting on an axis at right angles to all I know. Everything is *changing*. Part of me is afraid; part thinks I'm crazy. Most of me doesn't care.

'You are not alone.' She says it again as before; her words resonate inside me, as if I've heard them before and somehow know I will do so again.

We step into the water. Her hand in mine sets the pace. Each step is exquisite and slower than the one before, and my heart beats in time with the waves, with Tabby.

As the sea reaches more of my body it's pain and joy at once. When the water reaches my waist, Tabby stops, turns to me – and she seems to shine, as if lit up from the inside. Her smile is luminous.

'Remember,' she says. 'Remember me, and you. Don't lose yourself, not completely. Do you understand?'

I do and I don't, but she seems to know.

'It's all right,' she says. 'You will. Ready?'

We dive under the waves.

Swim, fast, underwater. Along the seabed and out, out, out. Despite how unwell Tabby looked earlier, our speed matches without effort – we swim side by side. The joy is *almost* complete. Like so many times before, I feel that no matter how I try I can never swim fast enough.

Not like I can in my dreams.

Then Tabby slows, so I do also, to match her. Slower again. She turns to me under water, treading now to stay in place. Her hair floats all around her, her eyes wide. She tilts her head to one side, smiles, and then – and then . . .

Dolphins. Circling around us. So close. One brushes against Tabby, nudges her and Tabby reaches out, strokes the dolphin, puts her hand on its dorsal fin – and then they're off together, carving through the water.

There is a nudge on my arm – another dolphin. We stare back at each other and I'm so full of wonder I'm shaking. He swims a circle around me, comes back, nudges me again. I do as Tabby did: stretch out a wondering hand, lightly touch his side then reach up to his dorsal fin. As if he was waiting for this, he takes off, pulling me along with him. The rest of the pod, the dolphin with Tabby, too, have circled back to join us and we rush through the water together.

There is joy in my blood, rushing in my ears, and something is happening *inside* of me – as if all my life I've been dreaming, and now I'm finally awake. No, that's not it. It's like Tabby said: I'm dreaming and I'm awake at the same time, losing connection between what is real and what isn't. I'm not in my feeble body any more: I'm one of them.

The kin.

And I want to stay here, in this moment, in the sea, for ever.

Then we go up, up, to surface, and cut through the air and with breathing I'm slammed back into my own body – lose my grip on my new friend – fall to the sea, alone.

Remember. Something is tugging on my hand. My vision is fractured; there is skin, eyes, blue-green streaked hair, all unconnected. Then it changes, becomes Tabby. Treading water next to me. Dolphins are surfacing and playing in the water all around.

'Denzi? Are you all right?'

Denzi. Yes, that is who I am. And I'm aware, alive – human. I pull Tabby closer; my arms go around her waist. I kiss her and there is a moment when I'm not sure that was the right thing to do, but then her arms are around me and she's kissing me back and I've never been kissed like this before. In the wild sea, under the stars, in the night.

79

Tabby

The sky is beginning to lighten; dawn will be soon. It's morning, already? How is that possible?

Swimming with the dolphins and Denzi is something that I've waited for, for ever – what we were always supposed to do. The night has sped by. That it is almost over is unbearable.

We swim for shore with a dolphin escort. As the water gets shallower, they turn to go back out to sea, each with a touch, a nudge, to say goodbye.

Feet on the sand. Walking in, slowly, but we stop when the water is still lapping against our feet and ankles. Wanting to draw out this connection.

'You look amazing,' Denzi says, then looks again – reaches to my hair. Holds out a bit of seaweed, and I laugh.

After a night in the sea, the sickness and fever I felt yesterday are gone. 'I feel amazing, too.'

We watch the sunrise, sitting on the beach. We should be exhausted after swimming all night but I'm the opposite, full of a strange energy. Denzi's arms are around me, I'm leaning in to him – to the wonder of having him close like this.

He leans down, kisses my neck and a shiver goes through my whole body that is so exquisite it's almost unbearable. I turn my head and then he's kissing me again.

'As nice as this is, I think we need to talk some more,' he

says, finally.

'Yeah. I suppose.'

'Stop looking at me like that, then.'

'Like what?'

'Like *that*.'

'I'll look at the sea, instead.' I half turn away again, my back against his chest. His arms tighten around my waist.

'What happened last night?'

'We swam, we met the kin.'

'The kin – you mean, the dolphins?'

'Yes. Our kin, I think.'

Yes.

He's silent for a while, taking in what I've said. I spent too long not understanding, pushing it away – trying to split myself in two and denying my other half. The only thing that made it all right was that first time I swam with the kin. I knew I had to bring him to them, that it's the only way.

'Have you ever felt like you're awake and asleep at the same time?' I say. 'That's what dolphins do: they have a split brain, half awake and half asleep. So they can swim in the sea as they sleep, the other part of them keeping watch, reminding them to breathe, that kind of thing. Sometimes I've felt like I switched to something else and couldn't remember what happened – maybe it was one part of my brain taking over while the rest slept.'

He nods. 'That makes sense.' He tilts his head, thinking. 'Could that be part of the reason for the weird dreams? Like sometimes, when I dream they are my dreams; sometimes they feel like dreams to me, but are actually from this other half of me that is awake while I sleep?'

'Wow. I never thought of it quite like that, but I think you may be right. It makes sense. Though there are some dreams I have, that don't seem to fit either of those categories; they feel more like they are other voices in time. But I can remember dreaming like I'm swimming in circles, back and forth – as if I was a dolphin trapped in a tank.'

'No way. I've had a dream like that, too,' Denzi says, and there are goosebumps on my spine. We've had the same dream? Denzi looks kind of freaked to think so, too.

'Are you OK?' I say.

'I don't know what I *am*, how can I be OK? But somehow, right now, I am.'

'Me, too. But I want to know *why* we are this way. I feel like there is something I almost understand but can't put in words, even to myself.'

'Let's put together what we know and see if we can work it out?'

'OK.'

'Everything started with IVF and the Penrose Clinic,' Denzi says. 'That we think we were some sort of designer babies.'

'Yes: they gave us something that makes us in some ways like the kin – like dolphins. So we can hold our breath like dolphins, communicate with them somehow.'

'And swim!'

'Yes. And I think somebody must have thought they were doing something they shouldn't; Ren, that girl I told you about? She found out that an investigation was launched by the GMC into Penrose about ten years ago, but then it vanished like it never was.'

'*Why* would they change us like that? If we can answer that, the rest might start making sense.'

We're both silent a moment. 'Add more pieces to the puzzle,' I say. 'The clinic is also The Circle. The Circle are eco-terrorists, attempting to blackmail the world to stop global warming.'

'And we thought most of those like us drowned, but it looks as if at least Ariel survived, and she may have been involved in blowing up Hoover Dam.'

'So, we have dolphins and drowning or not drowning, and— Wait.' I pull away a little from Denzi and turn so we are eye to eye. 'What did they say? The Circle. When the dams were destroyed?'

'Something like . . . make more know what it feels like to fear rising seas?'

'Maybe we are their back-up plan. Try to force humanity to stop global warming, but if it doesn't work and the seas continue to rise, we can live in the sea.'

We're silent a moment. 'No one asked us if we wanted this. Why would Ariel help them blow up a dam? Jess seems to be with them as well. What about the rest? Were they all part of The Circle already?'

'Maybe . . . that is the real reason Cate took me away. Not so much to protect me from The Circle, but to keep me out of it.'

'Though no one has ever tried to recruit me. But the big question for now is, what do we do? We need to go to the police.'

'I'm afraid of them. Cate died in their custody: The Circle must have a presence there.'

'So we need to get the word out wide enough that there

is nothing to gain by making us disappear. And then go to the police.'

'How do we get the word out like that?'

'My stepdad – Oliver – is a journalist, in the States. He's been looking into Penrose already for me; he's the one who told me where to find that ex-employee who told me about designer babies. Oliver also said he'd been warned off, though not by who. Maybe we could call him, tell him what we know, see what he thinks about getting the story out?'

A journalist, a big story – the biggest *ever* story. How could he resist?

'Yes. Let's try him if you think we should. But I told you that Ren was going to blog about all of this but then ended up in a car accident. I don't know for sure if The Circle were behind that, but they might have been – to keep her quiet. So, do you still want to involve your stepdad in this?'

'He's used to stepping on toes and still getting on with stuff. I think we should call him. And then we have to go to the police, right?'

'OK. But how? Is it safe to use my phone?'

'Is it registered to your name?'

'No. I bought it for cash, didn't give my true name. All I've used it for is to message you on Signal.'

'That should be OK then.'

Somehow I'm not as scared to go to the police as I was before. Is it because Denzi will be there, too? He's not an anonymous runaway who could disappear: he's the son of a politician. But it's not just that. He makes me feel braver, just by being himself.

'OK. There is this police detective in London who came to

talk to me when Cate died; I'd told him she had warned me about The Circle, but neither of us knew what that meant then. So later, after the hurricanes and The Circle claiming responsibility, he came to ask me about The Circle again. He wouldn't have done that if he was involved with it. I think we could trust him.'

'Let's do it.'

80

Denzi

We walk back to Hastings, put the last of our money together and find a café for some breakfast. There are people all around while we wait at our table, so talking about anything important isn't an option. We're silent with each other but it's the kind of silence that feels OK. And it gives me a moment to think.

I'm reeling from everything that's happened, the things that have been said. But most of all this: were we designer babies – engineered to be the way we are? Did my parents know about it? And I'm half, I don't know, *horrified*, to think there may be DNA in every cell of my body that isn't human. But I'm also . . . relieved. That's it, isn't it? It's like there's been a mystery inside me all my life, and now, I get it.

That first day we met I'd told Tabby I was a loner, but was that really out of choice? I've always felt this sense of being different to other people and it's made me struggle to relate, to trust. All at once that is gone. Tabby is here: I'm not alone any more.

She nudges me. 'Food is here,' she says. Plates have been brought without my noticing. 'Are you all right?'

I nod. 'Just thinking.'

Once we've eaten we go sit on the beach, well away from anyone. Without my phone I don't have any numbers, so I use Tabby's phone to do some searches to track down Oliver. I get to an assistant at his newspaper, say I'm Apple's boyfriend, leave my number. Within a few moments he calls back.

'So, who is this really?' Apple has a girlfriend, not a boyfriend.

'Hi, it's Denzi.'

'Are you all right? Your dad phoned Leila to see if we'd heard from you.' Wow. Dad, calling Leila? Unprecedented stuff, but then I guess I have been missing since attending a protest march yesterday. They must all be worried, and guilt stirs inside at being the cause.

'Listen. Don't tell anyone I've called, at least not yet,' I say. 'I've got the story of the century for you.'

'What is it?'

'I told you I was looking for a friend who'd run away from swim school, then later from a hospital? She found me. She's been on the run from the Penrose Clinic; she knows things they don't want to get out. The clinic is a front for The Circle.'

'Hang on. Seriously? The Circle – the ones who cause hurricanes, blow up dams and make threats?'

'Yes.' I run through everything as concisely as I can; Oliver asks questions now and then. When I get to our suspicion that the clinic has been meddling with genetics to make designer babies, he asks what they've done, and why. Somehow I can't bring myself to tell him what we think they've done to us; I just say we don't know.

'All right. I'll look into this. Now call your dad. And what about the police?'

'We want the word to get out before we go to the police. Same for Dad.'

'I'll have to tell him you've called, that you're all right.'

'Think about it. If you do – if they find out I've called you – that could put them on to you.'

Silence. 'Smart ass. OK, you've got a day before I tell them if you haven't by then – so I've got a day, too. I'll see what I can find out, but this has to go straight up to my editor now.'

'The more who know the better. Do it.'

'Are you all right on your own another day?'

'We're fine.'

'Take care of yourself.'

'You, too.'

I end the call. Tabby is against me – she's been listening in. 'He sounds pretty cool,' she says.

'Actually, he is.'

'So, I guess the next move is to call the police.'

'Yeah. Are you OK?'

'Not really. But you're right – Oliver is, too. We have to do it.'

'Let's see if we can track down that detective you know, see if we can arrange to meet him tomorrow. What's his name?'

'DCI Palmer. I don't know his first name. But don't tell him I'm going to be there, or your name, either. They'll find out.' She's scared, I can see it.

'We have to say enough that he's going to want to find out the rest.'

'How about not saying anything about The Circle or the clinic. Say you've got information on the death of Catelyn Green that you'll only tell him in person – something like that? He seemed to be in charge of that investigation.'

'If that isn't enough?'

She hesitates. 'How about that you have information on my whereabouts, but don't say you're with me. Use my name as he knows it – Holly Heath.'

I find a number for the Metropolitan Police, ask to speak to DCI Palmer; there is more than one of them. I ask for the one who was investigating the death in custody of Catelyn Green. I'm put on hold.

There's a click. 'The one you want is DCI Theodore Palmer. I'll put you through.'

It goes to voicemail.

'Hi. I've got information about the death of Catelyn Green and also the whereabouts of Holly Heath.' I give the number.

Then we wait. Tabby leans against me, looking out to sea and I wrap my arms around her again like before. The feel of her, her closeness, and the sea – again, I feel as if I'm half drunk. Close my eyes and breath in deep and I can taste salt, sand, Tabby – all merged into one.

When the phone finally rings, we both jump.

I answer. 'Hello?'

'DCI Palmer here. Who is this?'

'That doesn't matter right now. I've got some information for you – about Catelyn Green and Holly Heath.'

'Go on.'

'No, not on the phone. Can we meet up tomorrow?'

'Sure. Come to the station.'

'No. Can you come to me?'

'Where?'

I look at Tabby, who is listening; she nods. 'Hastings,' I say.

'Look, I'm busy. Why not just tell me now?'

'Can't do that. Tomorrow. I promise you, it's worth the wait.'

There's a pause. 'Where in Hastings?'

'I'll tell you in the morning.'

'Fine. I'll call when I'm on the way.'

'Don't mention this to anyone else. There may be police involvement.'

There's another pause on the other end.

'You'd better not be wasting my time.' There's a click as the call ends.

'He sounded annoyed,' Tabby says, having listened in again. 'Do you think he'll come?'

'I expect so; he'll be curious. But if he doesn't, we'll call him back, maybe tell him a little more.'

'What next?'

'Oliver has his day. Tomorrow, we meet up with DCI Palmer.'

'And today?'

'Today is for us.'

81

Tabby

We head the same way we did when we got here last night. This time we check a tourist map, so we know where we are: back up East Hill from Hastings, then to the country park and onwards.

We look for likely places to meet Palmer, ones where we can watch for him from a distance and get away if anything is wrong. We finally decide to tell him the beach in Hastings. We can escape faster to the sea than anywhere else.

We walk along coastal paths with cliffs below, far-ranging views on a clear, sunny day. Denzi's hand is in mine when the path allows it, or he walks behind me when not. We stop often, his arms around me, both of us gazing at the sea.

'Another swim?' he says.

'We probably shouldn't until the sun goes,' I say. 'Swimming with dolphins might attract attention.'

'Is that why we waited until we were on our own and it was getting dark last night?'

'Partly.'

'Only partly?'

'I wanted to draw it out. Make you see and feel what it was that we both have.'

'It worked,' he says, and kisses me again.

When the sun is high in the sky we find a shady spot in a

wooded glen away from the path. Lie down in the grass in each other's arms, using my pack as a pillow.

Denzi's breathing soon deepens: is he asleep?

Birdsong all around. Surf, out of sight below us but close enough to hear and taste. Denzi's warm breath on my skin. Shade enough to hold the sun at bay. I can almost forget everything else, and pretend: we are just an ordinary girl and boy. Nothing depends on what we do or say but each other.

Memory of last night stirs in my mind: the wild sea – the kin – are part of us. And despite *all the stuff*, would I ever want to give that up? If I had a magic wand and could make it all go away – be like everybody else – I'd be as bereft as if all my senses failed at once. It is almost like there is a whole different way to be and feel that is so much a part of me, that if that half of me died, the other half would soon follow.

The world and its sounds, smells, sensations, begin to drift in and out of my mind – sometimes here, sometimes fading away. The ground and the sense of being here with Denzi so close do the same, until they disappear . . .

Sun . . . Sea . . . Earth . . . Sky . . .

The four points of our compass; the promises made to protect and honour them every year. With Cate, yes, but it wasn't just us. Promises stretch far back in time; more voices join every year. Voices in harmony, merging in time:

Sun . . . Sea . . . Earth . . . Sky . . .

Time is a circle: there is the future, too. But when I look forwards, the voices that surround me fade until only mine remains.

There is fear, darkness. A crime so beyond anything imaginable that

351

my shock is complete.

This: this is why, the voices say. You'll see . . .

82

Denzi

When I wake, she's not in my arms.

'Tabby?' I say, and there is no answer. Panic starts to build inside. They've found her, taken her away.

I scramble to my feet, heart beating too fast.

'Tabby?' I say again, louder, and this time she answers – her voice is faint, back towards the path – and I'm so filled with relief that tears start at the back of my eyes.

Honestly. Get a grip, Denzi.

I walk through the trees to the path, to Tabby. She's standing where the view is the best and widest: sea and sky. The sun has shifted – it's early evening. We must have slept for ages.

'Hi,' I say. She turns towards me but then I gather her into my arms so we're both facing the sea. She settles in, leans against me.

'Is everything all right?'

'Beyond the usual, you mean?' She sighs. 'I don't know. I had this dream – at least something like a dream. It's like one I've had before, but worse this time. When I woke up, I felt completely freaked out. I can't seem to shake it off.'

'Do you want to talk about it?'

'I think so, but it'll take some explaining. Let's go down to the beach?'

Hand in hand we follow the path along the coast and then

down to the beach. There are just a few people – a woman walking a dog. A couple with two kids that look to be packing up their stuff. Soon we have the beach to ourselves. We sit where we did last night, and now I'm remembering how it felt, waiting, waiting, to go to the sea. I feel the same way today but without the sense of panic, or desperation – whatever it was. Now it's more like being hungry instead of starving.

'I'm listening,' I say, and gather her hand in mine.

She meets my eyes but hers are troubled.

'Have you ever heard about the four points of the compass? Not north and south and so on: the internal compass inside of you. The sun, sea, earth and sky.'

'I don't think so.'

'Cate taught me. We honoured all four, promised to care for and protect them, a promise that we renewed every year; a balancing of mind, body, spirit with sun, sea, earth and sky. Cate and I used to do it on my birthday, or what she said was my birthday: the twenty-first of June. But I missed it this year and haven't felt right about it since then.'

'This was an environmental sort of pledge?'

'I guess so, but it goes beyond that. It's hard to explain, but it was important to who we were. Who I am, now. Also, part of it was to keep the four in harmony and not honour one above the others. Which was hard for me, as the sea is always my centre.'

'Was that what you dreamed about?'

'Partly. This next bit is going to sound weird.'

'It's OK, I'm getting used to weird with you.'

'Huh. I hear voices sometimes, in dreams, and also when I'm awake. More and more often lately.'

'Voices?' I say and I'm feeling uneasy again, remembering what Jess and Christina said – about Tabby being mentally ill – but push my doubt away. I have to believe in her; we're in this together.

'Yes. Mostly they chant the four over and over again: sun, sea, earth, sky; sun, sea, earth, sky. This is going to sound even weirder, but it's like they stretch backwards and forwards in time. Like I'm connected to people who lived and have yet to be born, all at once.'

There are prickles up and down my spine and the unease must be reflected on my face.

'You think I'm crazy.'

'No, I don't. Not unless I am, too.'

'You hear the voices?'

'Not saying those words. But a sense of time being connected like that: past, present future. Like they're not in a straight line; more like time is a circle.'

'Yes. *The Circle*. I told you Cate had their tattoo on her ankle. I think she was part of them, and the things she taught me come from them.'

'That doesn't necessarily follow, though. It could just be her thing.'

She shakes her head. 'That's not all. I found this article online, written by an archaeologist. She'd found symbols carved and painted in caves and other places all over the world; symbols that represent sun, sea, earth and sky, arranged in quadrants around a cross. I saw her photographs: the cross looked like a compass. And each of the four symbols had a circle drawn around it, edges just touching. Just like Cate's tattoo.'

The goosebumps up and down my spine are there again, and more so.

'How old were these images she found?'

'Different ages, but some many thousands of years.'

'I've never heard about this before.'

'She was discredited, her career ruined. But that could have been a cover-up, so people wouldn't learn about this group.'

'Do you think these symbols mean that The Circle has been around for thousands of years, all over the world?'

She nods. Swallows. 'It's their voices in my dreams, stretching backwards and forwards in time. But then, in my nightmare this afternoon, all the future voices were silenced, leaving only mine.' Her face is pale. 'What does that mean?'

'It was a dream. It doesn't have to *mean* anything.'

She shakes her head. 'It wasn't just a dream; I'm sure of it. I think something bad is going to happen. I think it might be because I didn't renew my promise this year.'

I wrap my arms around her, hold her. Tell her everything will be OK, and even if it isn't, it's not her fault.

She's pulling away, shaking her head. 'I should have promised again. I didn't.'

'If you think it's important, can you do it now?'

'I don't know. It's just . . . I've always done it with Cate. Never alone. I miss her, so much.'

'You're not alone. I'm here. I'll promise with you.'

'Really? Are you sure?'

No. But words once said can't be taken back. Much like a promise.

83

Tabby

We stand on the sand – on the Earth – under the sun in the sky. The sea lapping against our feet.

Holding hands. I smile at Denzi. *Relieved*, so much, that he didn't think I was bonkers. Surprised I could tell him all of this, when even mentioning sun, sea, earth and sky to Ren and Jago had felt wrong. Is it because Denzi is the same as me? I don't know. Or maybe it's because of these feelings we have for each other, but they are too new to even know what they are. Or maybe, more, that I don't want to examine or question how we feel – not yet.

'Thank you, Denzi. Are you sure you want to do this?'

'Yes.'

'All right. These are the words.' I say each familiar phrase, pause so Denzi can repeat. As I do my voice becomes more sure, stronger:

If you close your eyes to avoid seeing what is before you, it is still there. If you close your ears to what is taught, the student fails, not the teacher. If you don't feel what is outside of you because all you do is look inside, you will always be alone.

We promise: to look, listen and feel with all of our senses; to protect sun, sea, earth and sky with all that we are, all that we were, and all that we may yet be.

As we speak, time seems to shift and swirl around us. A kaleidoscope of promises stretches backwards in time, but time goes forwards, too. I feel it stretch, become thin. *Yet to be* feels tenuous, uncertain.

Can the circle of time be broken?

84

Denzi

Tabby's hand is warm in mine. Without discussion we return to our spot on the beach.

When I said I'd promise with her it was an impulse – to help her, to stay close to her, maybe? I don't know. Maybe because if it is important to her, then it is to me. I didn't fully understand what it all represents, and I still don't.

But the words we said *meant something* deep inside me, in a way I've never felt before. It was like how my stepsister Apple is with praying – an impulse I've never had or really understood. Yet what we did today wasn't like religion, not in that kind of sense. It was more to do with feeling . . . *grounded*, in the natural world.

And the feeling of time around us as we spoke: what was that? I shake my head, unable to put into words what I don't understand.

I'm so focused on my thoughts that when Tabby nudges me I'm startled.

'The sky,' she says, her words a whisper. 'The sunset: look.'

The sun is lower in the sky – streaks of red radiate across the horizon even though there are no clouds I can see. As we watch, they stretch further into the sky, seem to grow, coalesce into each other until much of the sky is a deep, fiery red.

It's like nothing I have seen before. It's magnificent, glorious.

Neither of us says anything more; we're both staring in wonder. Drinking it in.

The sun sinks further – or it must, as the light is growing dimmer – but it can't actually be seen or pinpointed any more: the red is burning across all of the sky.

The light recedes bit by bit until it is gone – leaving after-images in the darkness.

It was amazing. Beautiful. *Wrong*.

85

Tabby

Darkness is complete – the stars and moon are hiding tonight – and still neither of us has said a word about what we saw together.

I'm uneasy without knowing why. Is it that I've watched the sun set all my life, but it has never been quite like that?

Denzi finally nudges me.

'Wow,' he says.

'And then some. What was it?'

'A seriously spectacular sunset,' he says, but his voice – it isn't *right*.

'It felt wrong. I don't know why.'

'Same for me. But there is one thing I do know: tomorrow we've got stuff to do.'

'Stuff? Like meeting with a DCI kind of stuff?'

'Yes, that's it. Tonight, on the other hand?'

I smile as he gets up, helps me to my feet. 'Tonight? What did you have in mind?'

Without answering we're walking to the water together. The touch on my feet as water laps against my skin makes me shiver without being cold. We walk further into the sea.

'Ready?' Denzi says.

'Yes.'

We dive under the waves.

Swim out, out. Further, deeper. Faster but not fast enough.

Then the kin come again: we fly together! In the sea, and the air. There is *here* and *now* and I push any thoughts of *yet to be* away.

86

Denzi

By the time we leave the sea, the sky is starting to lighten. I feel heavy, clumsy, on the sand without the sea to support me. We sit next to each other.

'I could have stayed out there for ever. Never come back,' Tabby says.

'I know what you mean. Not sure how that'd work, though. I mean, it'd be nice to have something to eat and a sleep now and then.'

'S'pose so.' A pause. 'It feels like we've been here together for both for ever and a moment. I don't want this to end.'

I slip an arm around her, a hug. 'Me neither.'

Time is a circle; we're spinning around the same place at the same time – a still moment within a storm. I shake my head. I'm getting all philosophical or something. It's this place, the dolphins, Tabby. All in the same orbit or orbited the same – now.

She stirs, pulls away. 'Look at the sky,' she says. 'The light – the sun – is in a shroud.'

The sky is a faint grey; it's light enough to see properly now but the sun isn't burning through. 'Some rain on the way, maybe?'

'It's not that kind of cloud.' She's looking at the sky, biting her lower lip. 'Something feels wrong, like it did last night.'

I'm uneasy. I hadn't wanted to think about that sunset last

night; had wanted to go to the sea and forget. 'What – like another hurricane sort of wrong?'

'No, nothing like that. Then it was hot, still. Sunny until the last. There was like a pressure building inside me – though that could have been all that was happening. Anyhow, this feels very different.'

'Let's check the weather on your phone?'

She reaches across for her pack, stashed by some rocks. Fishes out her phone and hands it to me.

I go to BBC Weather. 'Well, today it's meant to be the usual: hot, sunny, no mention of cloud cover. They've got it wrong.'

'The sun always shines, even if we can't see it. When it is night and the Earth is in the way; when it is clouded over in the day. If it is eclipsed, too. Still it shines.'

'Yes; you can take off in thick cloud cover and once you go high enough, there it is.'

'Take off? Do you mean, in a plane?'

'Yes. Haven't you flown?' She's shaking her head and I'm trying to imagine how different her life has been to mine. Despite that, how we fit together.

I'm looking at the BBC home page now. 'There have been loads of photos sent in of spectacular sunsets last night. There have been comments about it all over the place – not just Europe: North America, Australia, Africa, Asia. Pretty much everywhere. Meteorologists are struggling to explain it.'

'Some things can't be explained.'

She nestles closer to me. I touch a hand to her chin. 'Like this,' I say. Then we're kissing and again it is both for ever and a moment.

Her phone rings and we jump apart.

'The DCI?' I say and push to answer the call. 'Hello?'

'Palmer here. I'll be in Hastings in an hour. Where do I find you?'

'The beach, by Hastings Old Town. Yes. See you there.'

'So, it's time to go,' Tabby says.

'Are you OK with this – meeting Palmer?'

'It's the right thing to do – but I'm scared. I wish I were braver.'

'What – you? You must be the bravest person I know, all that you've done. And being on your own for so long.'

'I'm really not. I've just done what I have to.'

'Do you want me to go on my own and check him out first?'

'No. You don't know what he looks like, and anyhow, I want us to stay together. I just wish we could stay where we are. Just *stop*: not move or do anything, but stay by the sea.'

'Another time. We'll come back here, together. Won't we?'

'Of course.' She hesitates. 'Let's make this our place. If we lose each other, we'll come back. Meet here.'

'At sunset: for a swim.'

'Just before sunset. On the twenty-first of June. We renew our promise. Then swim.'

'Hopefully before then, but sure.'

She smiles now.

'Time to get going?' I stand, hold out a hand. Help her up.

We brush sand off our clothes.

'Wait,' I say, and turn to face her. Run my fingers through her hair, straightening it. Take out a bit of seaweed like I did yesterday, show it to her and drop it on the sand.

She manages a laugh. 'Better now?'

'Yes.'

We walk up the beach towards the footpath.

87

Tabby

I tell myself that everything is going well. Denzi is here with me; Oliver is on the job to get things out to the press; the DCI is on his way; the sea is nearby if we need it. But the sky is still this strangely deadened grey-white, and dread is growing inside me.

Caution.

I glance up at Denzi, and his skin, too, looks wrong in this light. I look at my hand and so does mine. It's all I can do not to run to the water and disappear, but he thinks I'm brave. I don't want to prove him wrong.

Look. Listen. Feel.

Every sense is on overdrive, to hear, see, smell – it all combines into a crushing level of sensory detail – and even though there is nothing I can point to that is worrying me, something is wrong. I feel it in my gut.

The voices, the ones inside me: they're loud, getting louder: *Sun . . . sea . . . earth . . . SKY . . . Sun . . . sea . . . earth . . . SKY . . .* thundering inside my head as my heart beats.

My feet slow, then stop.

Denzi turns, looks back. 'Tabby? Is something wrong?'

I raise my hand for quiet, trying to listen – to hear over the voices. And then there is movement beyond him, by the rocks to our right. Then to our left, someone breaks cover. It's Stacey.

'Run!'

One step, two, faster and faster we run, back down the beach to the sea. Denzi is a few steps behind me and then there is sound – like something crashing to the ground – and I look back over my shoulder. Denzi is lying on the ground, limp and still. My steps falter but now Stacey and the other woman are coming for me.

Even as my heart twists with agony and part of me is immobilised by fear, the other part is in control. I run faster, faster – into the water – dive under and swim away from the shore. Tears are washed from my face, my salt mingling with the sea.

Deeper and further from the shore I swim, and now the kin are here. They swim around me, agitated as if they feel what I feel. I hold one hand to a fin, and we carve through the water at a speed I can't reach on my own. Out, out, to sea.

Pain, fear, and confusion battle inside of me. I shouldn't have left Denzi; it's wrong to leave kin who need help.

But if they had both of us – no one would know what we know. I have to go on, alone, don't I?

Not alone.

The kin are all around me. But now they're not just agitated, they're full of fear.

As one we turn and swim first one way, then another, and we're closer and closer to each other. I'm getting buffeted and bruised, and there is something, *there*, in the water, something around us, and the kin are thrashing as we're drawn together.

It's a net: we're caught in a net.

Get around it – get out. The sides of the net – it's pulling up through the water and the kin are panicking. They'll all drown.

I use my hands and feet to climb up the side of the net even as we're about to be yanked from the sea.

I reach the surface in time; I could get away.

No.

'Stop!' I scream out the word before I even breathe.

The movement of the net below me stops and I'm looking up now – at a boat. The net was being drawn up to it. There are faces above, looking down.

'Let them go!' I say.

'If you come up, we'll release the net,' a voice calls down.

A rope is thrown down to me. I grip it and I'm pulled up, up, out of the water. Up over the side and I sprawl on to the deck. The net is loosened and the kin are free. Scared and some are hurt, but free.

'Tabby, it's so nice to welcome you aboard.'

It's Malina.

88

Tabby

I've been pushed into a cabin below decks and towards a shower, told to get on with it or someone will do it for me. I wash. There are clean clothes set out when I'm done, and I put them on, feeling dazed, numb, aching with bruises and scrapes – and unable to process what has happened.

Denzi – lying on the beach.

How did they find us there?

And again, in the sea. With the kin. We swam straight into their trap.

The kin and their panic in the net; we didn't see it until it was too late. Freedom is theirs at the cost of mine.

The door is locked, and I pound on it but there is no answer.

There's a porthole. There, through the glass? Some of the kin. Peering in at me, with a faintly disapproving air, like I shouldn't have given myself up.

But then we might have all died.

This is their way – I know it. The kin are all for one and one for all: they'd never leave Denzi like I did. If I hadn't done that, they wouldn't have all been risked in the net.

The door opens and I turn towards it. It's Malina, two other women behind her.

'I hope you're feeling better?' Malina says.

I ignore the question. 'What happened to Denzi?'

'That is not your concern.'

'Tell me. Please.'

She shakes her head. 'You need to focus on yourself for a while now. I'm glad we finally got you back so we can treat you. You may not realise, but you are very, very ill. Missing out on what we called vitamins – then nutritional supplements – has meant a relapse in your condition.'

So I was right to suspect their tablets. I frown. 'My condition? What do you mean?'

She tilts her head to one side. 'It is part of being one of us. You need help with individuation: keeping yourself separate from the multitude of voices, past and present.'

My eyes widen. 'The voices? Sun, sea, earth and sky?'

'Yes. Once you have been trained properly you can deal with this on your own. For now, you need help. I hope we're not too late.'

She gestures and one of the other women comes forward; she has a needle in her hand.

'I'm not one of you. Leave me alone!'

I back against the wall but there is nowhere to go.

The needle comes closer and when I try to push it away the other two of them hold me, push me down on the bed. The one with the needle pulls up my sleeve while the others hold my arm in place.

'No. Please don't do this. No!'

There is a sharp jab in my arm.

The needle is withdrawn; they let me go.

'Now you must rest, Tabby,' Malina says.

They leave the room; there is the click of the door locking.

371

I'm rubbing at my arm and scared and it's like the walls are closing in on me – like I have Isha's claustrophobia – and if I don't get out *now*, back to the sea, something bad will happen. Or has it happened already – is it this drug?

Even as I'm panicking, something else is taking over. A sense of calm – artificial and imposed, but I can't fight it – floods through me.

I'm so tired . . .

Sun . . . Sea . . . Earth . . . Sky . . .

The voices say the same words they usually do, but they aren't in synch. It is both jarring and deafening.

What have you done?

Voices, full of fury – focused on me.

But then they gradually fade away. Fall silent.

All that is left is darkness.

89

Tabby

I open my eyes, disoriented by my dreams so much that it takes reality a moment to find me.

My head feels *wrong* – like something is missing – but I can't examine that too closely just now. Malina is sitting calmly next to me.

'How are you feeling?' she says.

I don't answer her, sit up in bed and the movement brings *pain*. I gasp, take inventory. Arms and legs all there and working – just bruises, scrapes from the net.

'How did you find me? Here, and in Cornwall, too?'

'The dolphins. We worked out that you seem to have an affinity for them – whether you are drawn to them or they to you. We monitored for unusual sightings near shore in Cornwall, and there you were. We tagged and tracked the pod of dolphins after that, so followed them to this area, checked the beaches and waited at sea also in case you escaped. Once you were with them in the water we found you easily enough.'

'And Denzi?' I can't bring myself to finish the question.

'He is not your concern,' she says, repeating what she said before, and I'm trying to read into her words what that might mean. And I flinch away from even thinking it, from knowing that anything that has happened to him is my fault.

'Why go to so much trouble to find me?'

'As difficult as you have been, you are important to us.'

'By us, you mean The Circle. Don't you?'

She smiles. 'Just so. I knew you'd made that connection. We've taken measures to contain this.'

'Measures? What do you mean?'

'Just what we had to do to keep it out of the news.'

I stare at her, dismayed. Has everyone who ever tried to help me been subject to *measures*? Did they cause Ren's accident, to stop her from blogging about them? And what about Jago, Sascha – are they safe? And Denzi, and his stepdad Oliver, too. And I'm desperate to ask her about all of them, but don't dare. If she doesn't know about Oliver, I'm not going to tell her.

'You killed so many people in the hurricanes – including Simone – and then the bombings, too. And what about Cate? Was that The Circle?'

She frowns. 'What happened to Cate was unexpected. We weren't behind it. As for the rest, sometimes doing the right thing requires some wrong along the way.' Her face – it's full of such sadness, regret, too. But being sorry doesn't make it right. 'I know Cate schooled you in the promises: to protect sun, sea, earth and sky. This is our pledge; it is something we don't take lightly. Action had to be – still has to be – taken, to fulfil our obligations. No matter the consequences.'

'What gives you the right to decide who lives or dies?'

'Our adversaries. Decisions about who lives or dies – where sacrifice zones will be – are made every day by governments, oil and gas companies, other huge corporations. To stop them we have no choice but to play their game. Come with me now. There's something I need to show you. If I just tell you about it,

374

you might not believe me, and it's important you understand.'

She gets up, opens the door and I consider refusing, telling her to get stuffed, but curiosity has me.

We go up the steps to the deck. Maybe I can get away, go over the side, but just as I think that, a few more women flank us. My stomach lurches to see and smell the sea, so close but too far away.

'You have honoured the sea over the other elements for too long,' Malina says, and I'm startled – similar words I'd heard many times from Cate. 'Look up, instead. What do you see?'

Look up? All that is there is the sky. But it is still that uniform grey-white, deadened and flat. I'm uneasy again, as I was with the red skies that came the night before.

I frown. 'I don't understand the weather.'

'That's one way of putting it. Come.' She has me sit next to her on a bench.

'Have you heard of geoengineering?'

I shrug, don't answer, though I've heard of it somewhere. Something about artificially changing the climate?

'What you see in the sky now – what you likely saw in the red skies at sunset last night – has been geoengineered. Some governments and the biggest oil companies have collaborated. They held a press conference on this earlier today. They've injected huge quantities of sulphur-containing chemicals into the atmosphere, enough to mimic the biggest volcano ever known many times over.'

'Why would they do that?'

'It's like putting sunscreen on the whole planet – blocking enough of the sun's rays to mitigate global warming. They plan

375

to continue with more and more, to reduce global temperatures back to preindustrial levels.'

My mind is spinning. Blocking the sun with chemicals in the atmosphere? What else will that do?

'That's crazy.'

'Yes. It is.'

'Does that mean they'll keep extracting and burning fossil fuels and think it doesn't matter any more? Won't all the carbon released still poison the seas?'

She's nodding. 'Exactly. The seas will be poisoned like they're poisoning the skies. And that's not all. Crops will grow slower with less light. Changing rainfall patterns will cause crops to fail in some places and do better in others. The line between who has and has not will become more marked; many people will starve so others can feast. Wars will likely follow. It is the beginning of the end.'

'You're making this up.'

'I wish I were.' There is such sorrow on her face. 'Tabby, I know you don't trust me. I understand that. I've got a tablet – look for yourself.'

She logs in and hands it to me. She watches while I quickly check the usual news sites, and they are all reporting a press conference that was held at the London offices of Industria United. And there, on the screen: photographs – video, also – of the VP who announced what they have done. He looks proud; he says by lowering world temperatures they're saving the planet, halting the mass extinction. That this is the age of man – the Anthropocene.

I stare in shock at the screen, replay the video over and again, trying to take it in. Both what they've done, and who was in charge of the whole project. This Vice President of Industria United – is it really him?

Yes. His name is on the bottom of the screen: Alistair Heath. My dad. He did this?

I remember him telling Simone that they were doing something that would fix things. Stop climate change. That he couldn't tell us about it yet.

They waited until they had done it to hold their press conference, so no one had time to object.

Every news site carries the story, though reactions to what has been done vary depending on which experts they consult. Some herald it as a triumph of man over nature; others as the start of a coming apocalypse. Most are somewhere in between, with a wait-and-see kind of stance.

When I've had enough I look up. Malina's eyes – they are wet with tears. One trickles down her cheek.

'Tabby, this is why. Don't judge what we've done – or what we may yet do – without all the facts.'

90

Tabby

That night there is only darkness. No matter how wide I open my eyes, *nothing* is there. Other senses come into play: a sense of dread, twisting, deep in my gut; the ghosting of goosebumps up and down my spine; taste and smell, too, even if just blood from a bitten tongue.

They all say, *this is real*. People like my father did this to us, to the earth and sky. Their chemicals are as a death shroud, covering us all. Now they think they can extract and burn as they like without cooking the planet.

And this is supposed to be *better*?

What gave them the right to steal the sun? The moon and the stars, too – all of them. The universe is gone, and we are so alone.

And now I think I am beginning to understand why The Circle did the things they did, with their hurricanes, fires, floods. I still think it was wrong, but on the scale of wrongdoing it pales next to plunging us all into days of half-light, nights of darkness.

And I'm their prisoner. Even now I'm watched by Malina and the others, though what they think I'm going to do, I don't know. Throw myself from the deck of their ship into unseen sea in the middle of nowhere? It used to be my refuge, but my crazy need for the touch of salt water on my skin has gone, even as my tears remain.

The kin won't come for me no matter how I wish it. Something has changed inside of me; it's Malina's injection, I'm sure of it, and even though the pain that comes with my obsession has gone I'd give anything to have it back. To feel like *me*, not this deadened version, a shadow of myself. Half alive under a half-dead sky.

That Malina doesn't understand the full effect of the drug I've been given is plain. She thinks all it does is silence the voices until I learn how to deal with them; she doesn't understand what else is inside of me, and I'm not going to tell her.

I don't know where we are going. Malina told me they are taking me to learn about The Circle, my heritage. That I am one of them whether I want to be or not; that it's in my blood.

She still won't tell me about Denzi. It's the not knowing that is killing me, slowly, inside. Is he alive – hurt and alone? Or has he gone beyond to join the others I've lost? To even think it makes me gasp with pain, want to pull myself into a ball on this deck and howl.

I fight for control, for outer calm. No one knows where I am, what has happened to me. There will be no rescue. I'm going to have to take care of myself.

What I must do is this. Learn all I can, make them believe I can control the voices on my own and don't need their drugs any more. Then I will be me again: *whole*, and able to stand on my own against them.

For now, it is time to play a game. One where they believe I'm on their side, will think and do as they wish. Find out what I can about The Circle and their plans, then escape. Tell the world.

Learn their secrets, and then betray them.

Acknowledgements

Red Sky Burning was written from beginning to end during a pandemic, often in lockdown and always shielding.

Writers must be alone to write – I do, at any rate – but not like this. I've had more time and less will. It's taken a veritable army of family, friends and colleagues to keep me going and almost sane – thank you, everyone!

My writing was more muddled than usual: thanks to Tig Wallace and everyone at Hodder for helping me sort it out, and to Michelle Brackenborough for another stunning cover.

Special thanks to my tribe, the Slushies – Nick Cross, Kathryn Evans, Addy Farmer, Candy Gourley, Paula Harrison, Maureen Lynas, and Jo Wyton – you all rock! Our group has been a lifeline, especially with regular appearances by babies, puppies, and kittens. We've had every crisis you could think of between us, and somehow got through them all together.

Enthusiasm and encouraging words from readers on social media really makes a difference, too! Especially when there are no events to go to. I'm @teriterrywrites on Twitter and Instagram.

Finally, I'd be lost without Graham and Scooby. Thank you for keeping me at least partly in the real world.

photo by Debra Hurford Brown

TERI TERRY

is the bestselling author of the *Slated* trilogy and
prequel, *Fated*, the *Dark Matter* trilogy, and of
Mind Games, *Dangerous Games* and *Book of Lies*.
Her most recent works are *Dark Blue Rising* and
Red Sky Burning, the first two books in *The Circle*
trilogy. Her books have been translated into
seventeen languages and won prizes at home
and abroad.

Teri hates broccoli, loves all animals — especially
her dog, Scooby — and has finally worked out
what she wants to do when she grows up.

STAY UP-TO-DATE WITH TERI

🅕 @TeriTerryAuthor

🐦 @TeriTerryWrites

📷 @teriterrywrites

teriterry.jimdo.com

TABBY'S SEARCH FOR
ANSWERS CONCLUDES IN

BLACK
NIGHT
FALLING

COMING SOON

'Teri Terry is a master of the thriller'
Scotsman

THE *DARK MATTER* TRILOGY

AVAILABLE IN PAPERBACK, EBOOK AND AUDIO

THE *SLATED* TRILOGY

TERI TERRY
THE EPIC BESTSELLING TRILOGY

SL**A**TED

Can you know the truth if your mind has been wiped?

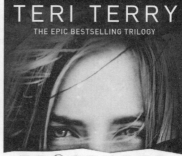

TERI TERRY
THE EPIC BESTSELLING TRILOGY

FR**A**CTURED

In a world full of danger, who can you trust?

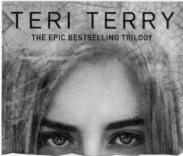

TERI TERRY
THE EPIC BESTSELLING TRILOGY

SH**A**TTERED

Everything she thought she knew was a lie...

THE PREQUEL

TERI TERRY
MULTI AWARD-WINNING AUTHOR OF *SLATED*

F**A**TED

One girl. One deadly choice.

AVAILABLE IN PAPERBACK, EBOOK AND AUDIO

'A gripping thriller'
Bookseller

ALSO BY TERI TERRY

AVAILABLE IN PAPERBACK, EBOOK AND AUDIO

'(An) excellent psychological
and supernatural thriller'
BookTrust

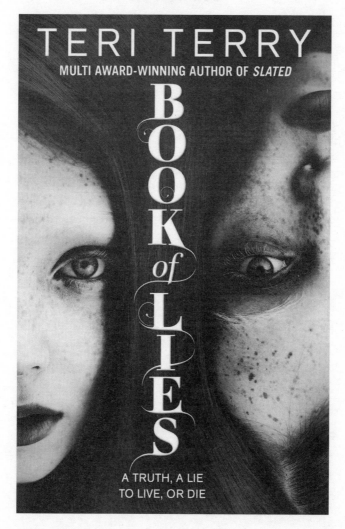

AVAILABLE IN PAPERBACK, EBOOK AND AUDIO

KU-637-016

Communication and Clinical Effectiveness in Rehabilitation

Frances Reynolds BSc DipPsychCouns PhD

Senior Lecturer in Psychology, Department of Health and Social Care, Brunel University, Isleworth, UK

ELSEVIER
BUTTERWORTH
HEINEMANN

EDINBURGH LONDON NEW YORK OXFORD PHILADELPHIA ST LOUIS SYDNEY TORONTO 2005

ELSEVIER
BUTTERWORTH
HEINEMANN

© 2005, Elsevier Limited. All rights reserved.

No part of this publication may be reproduced, stored in a retrieval system, or transmitted in any form or by any means, electronic, mechanical, photocopying, recording or otherwise, without either the prior permission of the publishers or a licence permitting restricted copying in the United Kingdom issued by the Copyright Licensing Agency, 90 Tottenham Court Road, London W1T 4LP. Permissions may be sought directly from Elsevier's Health Sciences Rights Department in Philadelphia, USA: phone: (+1) 215 238 7869, fax: (+1) 215 238 2239, e-mail: healthpermissions@elsevier.com. You may also complete your request on-line via the Elsevier homepage (http://www.elsevier.com), by selecting 'Customer Support' and then 'Obtaining Permissions'.

First published 2005
  Reprinted 2006

ISBN 0 7506 5665 4

British Library Cataloguing in Publication Data
A catalogue record for this book is available from the British Library

Library of Congress Cataloguing in Publication Data
A catalogue record for this book is available from the Library of Congress

Notice
Knowledge and best practice in this field are constantly changing. As new research and experience broaden our knowledge, changes in practice, treatment and drug therapy may become necessary or appropriate. Readers are advised to check the most current information provided (i) on procedures featured or (ii) by the manufacturer of each product to be administered, to verify the recommended dose or formula, the method and duration of administration, and contraindications. It is the responsibility of the practitioner, relying on experience and knowledge of the patient, to make diagnoses, to determine dosages and the best treatment for each individual patient, and to take all appropriate safety precautions. To the fullest extent of the law, neither the publisher nor the editors assumes any liability for any injury and/or damage.

The publisher

 your source for books, journals and multimedia in the health sciences

www.elsevierhealth.com

Working together to grow
libraries in developing countries
www.elsevier.com | www.bookaid.org | www.sabre.org

ELSEVIER   BOOK AID International   Sabre Foundation

The
publisher's
policy is to use
**paper manufactured
from sustainable forests**

Printed in China

Communication and Clinical Effectiveness in Rehabilitation

To Dad

For Elsevier:

Senior Commissioning Editor: Heidi Harrison
Development Editor: Robert Edwards
Project Manager: Gail Wright
Design Direction: George Ajayi

Contents

Acknowledgements

Extract from *This Game of Ghosts* by Joe Simpson published by Jonathan Cape: used by permission of The Random House Group Limited.

Extract from *C Because Cowards Get Cancer Too* by John Diamond published by Vermilion: used by permission of The Random House Group Limited.

Extract from *Lucky Man* by Michael J. Fox published by Ebury: used by permission of The Random House Group Limited.

Extract from *At the Will of the Body* by Arthur W. Frank © 1991 by Arthur W. Frank and Catherine Foote: reprinted by permission of Houghton Mifflin Company. All rights reserved.

Chapter 1

Introduction: taking a research-guided approach to communication

A physiotherapist and an occupational therapist are working with a patient who is well known to them as he has been in the in-patient rehabilitation programme for some time. Ben has a spinal cord injury, and has made good progress in mobilising using a wheelchair. Today, Ben seems quiet, unmotivated and averts his gaze. The more senior therapist outlines the day's programme in a cheerful, up-beat way. The more junior therapist notes the patient's nonverbal behaviour, its change since their last session together, and comments: 'You seem a bit downcast today. Is there something you would like to talk about before we begin today's programme?'

This scenario, based on a patient's experience, suggests that skilful communication is not necessarily mastered with age and seniority. Nor does an empathic response necessarily take time away from treatment. Indeed, an empathic understanding between therapist and patient may maximise the use of the time they spend together and the effectiveness of treatment.

Recent years have seen many new trends within the National Health Service (NHS) including an increasing emphasis on the need for health professionals to build collaborative partnerships with patients and to work cooperatively in multidisciplinary or interprofessional teams. Communication skills are now recognised to have a vital part to play in effective health care, maximising the outcomes of medical care and rehabilitation. The education of health professionals therefore needs to encompass more than technical expertise and knowledge. Furthermore, health care has been radically affected by a new emphasis on evidence-based practice, which encourages all practitioners to consult and appraise available evidence in order to formulate interventions capable of achieving the best outcomes.

Two central questions are addressed throughout this book. Can therapists take an evidence-based approach to communicating with their patients? Will a 'tutored' approach, based on communication theory, research evidence, clinical sensitivity and personal reflection, enhance the relationship between therapist and patient, and ultimately maximise the effectiveness of therapy?

The material presented will help occupational therapy and physiotherapy students to develop the insights, knowledge and skills that will enhance their communications with patients and colleagues. Students of other health disciplines will also find much of the material relevant. Many of the exercises, together with the recommended reading, further references and theory, may also be of interest to those with more clinical experience. We will mainly focus on the needs of patients in the physical rehabilitation setting. However, many of the issues that arise are common to other settings too.

A four-pronged approach to learning about communication is taken, in which you are encouraged to:

- Increase your sensitivity to patients' communication needs in the health care setting
- Consider theoretical models of skilful communication
- Consult evidence about the skills and strategies that increase the effectiveness of communication
- Practise reflective awareness of personal communication skills.

You will need to integrate these different aspects of knowledge and skill in order to achieve more effective, patient-centred communications in your clinical practice.

This chapter introduces you to the following terms and topics:

- What is 'communication'?
- Communication skills: why are they vital tools for physiotherapists and occupational therapists?
- Why do health professionals sometimes communicate poorly with patients?
- How may skilful communication influence patients?
- Communication and clinical effectiveness
- Evidence-based practice and clinical effectiveness
- Improving communication through research-guided practice

- How can you find relevant research evidence about patients' communication needs?
  - Books on communication in health care, health psychology, illness and disability
  - Journal articles
  - Electronic databases
  - Reviewing the evidence
- Other sources of evidence and information relevant to communication:
  - The clinical setting
  - Internet sites
  - Autobiographies of people living with illness/impairment
  - Films, novels and poems
- Observing and practising interpersonal skills
- Communicating with colleagues
- Conclusion.

Later chapters expand on these topics.

Communication remains an art as well as a science. Common sense certainly does not supply all the answers, and no book can provide adequate rules or 'recipes' that guarantee successful interactions either with patients or colleagues. There are difficulties in applying a strictly evidence-based approach, as we will see later. Hence you will need to develop reflective self-awareness, by analysing how your own attitudes and interactive style promote or inhibit certain types of communication. You will need to plan strategies for managing difficult encounters, and will need to be prepared to learn from mistakes. The book will encourage you to continue to seek out evidence about effective communication strategies to apply not only in your current situation, or during your next clinical placement, but throughout your career. Given the complexity of human encounters, your communications with patients and colleagues cannot realistically become 'perfect'. Yet communications based on education and reflection will almost certainly be more effective than 'untutored' attempts.

In conjunction with reading about communication skills theory and evidence, therapy students are strongly advised to carry out practical work, including the practise of interviewing and listening skills. Dickson et al (1997) suggest that communication skills are acquired in similar ways as other skills (such as driving a car). Learning occurs through preparation, active practise of specific skills and feedback from others, in addition to reading and reflection. Everyday encounters outside of the clinical setting can also provide opportunities for observation and further considerations about effective and ineffective communication strategies.

USE OF THE TERM 'PATIENT' IN THIS BOOK

The term 'patient' has generally been used in this book, although it admittedly carries certain unwanted meanings, including connotations of passivity and powerlessness. In some people's view, the term conjures up images of people who are waiting gratefully to receive the treatment that is organised and delivered by medical and therapy staff. The term has been associated with the biomedical model of care, which has traditionally focused upon treatment of the body machinery, neglecting the person's subjective experiences, active coping strategies and preferences (Reynolds 1996). Although the term 'patient' comes with unwanted baggage, other terms are not entirely satisfactory either. 'Client' is preferred by some health professionals, but it too connotes undesirable images, for example of the market-place and a customer buying services. 'User' is adopted in some health (particularly mental health) settings, as the term implies greater autonomy, power and choice than 'client'. However, 'user' arguably generates negative images of manipulation, and also perhaps suggests a 'voluntary' status, which does not do justice to the complex dilemmas, suffering, and resourceful coping strategies of so many people living with physical and mental illness. We really need a new term for people who are working in collaborative partnership with health professionals, particularly for those people with long-term illness and impairment who form the majority of the case-load of most National Health Service (NHS) therapists in the UK. Nevertheless, given that 'patient' remains the most widespread term for people participating in physical rehabilitation, this term will be adopted in this book, albeit with reservation.

WHAT IS 'COMMUNICATION'?

In everyday life, a person who is described as a 'good communicator' may be thought likely to be good at explaining information. You may anticipate that good communicators are persuasive and eloquent, adept at giving others verbal direction or advice, and clear about their own needs within the encounter. These are all information-giving or 'sending' skills, which rely primarily on speech. However, there is much more to communication than speaking and information-giving. The word 'communication' is derived from a Latin root, meaning 'to share'. Other similar words such as 'commune' and 'communion' have 'sharing' at their core. Hence to communicate well is both to give and receive information, in an interchange between persons. Successful communication depends on the receiver not only understanding the message that the sender intended, but also confirming this. In addition to 'sending' or 'initiating' skills, good communication relies on 'receiving' skills such as careful listening, and attention to the complex matrix of verbal and nonverbal cues that people exchange in conversation. It requires empathy to assess what the other person's needs and meanings may be within the communication. In the clinical setting, a therapist has not provided a clear explanation unless the patient has successfully understood the information. Neither can therapists be regarded as good at communicating if they forge ahead without noticing (and acting upon) the patient's nonverbal cues, such as signs of confusion, anxiety, unwillingness to take on board further information, and so on.

Successful communication depends upon a shared agenda in which each person in the interaction substantially agrees upon the information that has been exchanged and is satisfied with the focus of the interaction (Dickson et al 1997). In addition to the information that is carried verbally, that is in the form of spoken and written language, many messages are conveyed nonverbally. Facial expressions, eye contact and direction of gaze, gestures, tone of voice, posture, orientation and distance in relationship to the other person in the encounter all carry potent messages, even though few of these messages are 'sent' deliberately (Knapp & Hall 2002). For example, nonverbal messages convey whether we understand what is being said, our attitudes towards the task and each other, our mood state, and our social status. Some psychologists (e.g. Argyle et al 1971, Argyle 1990) point out that nonverbal cues have particular potency. Particularly in situations where verbal and nonverbal messages apparently conflict in meaning, people tend to trust the nonverbal cues rather than the spoken word. Perhaps they believe nonverbal behaviour is less well controlled and therefore more capable of revealing the other person's genuine attitudes and feelings. However, contrary to the message given in some 'pop psychology' books, it is not always easy to understand other people's nonverbal cues. In isolation, they are fundamentally ambiguous, and can often only be decoded through sensitivity to the wider communication context. You can explore this issue in the following exercise:

ACTIVITY Explore some possible meanings of nonverbal behaviour

Your patient, Ben, avoids eye contact during his encounter with you.
- Interpret the meanings of this nonverbal communication in as many ways as you can.
- If possible, compare your ideas with those of others.

Lack of eye contact carries a multitude of meanings, as do other forms of nonverbal behaviour. For example, it can signal depression, anxiety, or shame. Some people stop making eye contact in an encounter when they are listening intently, for example if they have a hearing impairment and are lip-reading. People also tend to look away when they are trying to formulate what they wish to say. Some people withdraw eye contact when they are bored, perhaps as a signal to end the conversation. Patterns of gaze and eye contact are also governed by cultural norms, as well as by individual mood. In some cultures it is considered impolite to make eye contact when communicating with a person of the opposite sex, or with a person perceived to have higher social status. Furthermore, lack of eye contact may reflect a lack of social skills, either through upbringing, or because of a disorder such as autism. This exercise illustrates that there are no simple communication 'recipes' – either for decoding others' messages, or for creating our own. We require sensitivity to the wider context, and need to consider numerous aspects of the encounter simultaneously. A communication strategy that works well with one patient will not necessarily be appropriate for another patient with different needs or expectations.

COMMUNICATION SKILLS: WHY ARE THEY VITAL TOOLS FOR PHYSIOTHERAPISTS AND OCCUPATIONAL THERAPISTS?

For therapy students who are immersed in the difficult study of anatomy, physiology and pathology, it may be tempting to dismiss the study of communication skills as an 'optional extra'. Indeed, for far too long health professionals have tended to assume that 'common sense' will be a sufficient resource to guide their interactions with patients and colleagues in the clinical setting (Dickson et al 1997). However, if we reflect on occasions when we have been patients interacting with health care professionals (such as doctors, nurses, dentists, and therapists), we usually find certain examples of poor practice. In these cases, we need to ask why 'common sense' so readily deserted the health professional.

ACTIVITY Personal experiences of poor communication

- Either on your own, or in discussion with others, reflect on an example of poor communication that you have experienced as a patient, when you consulted with a healthcare professional.
- Analyse what (for you) went wrong, and how you would have liked the encounter to have been conducted.
- Why do you think that the health professional made the errors that you noticed?

Certainly, not all student therapists (or even qualified therapists) communicate in satisfactory ways with their clients. Rebeiro (2000), for example, interviewed two clients in a mental health setting, and found that both had felt excluded from decision making and from having a real sense of partnership with their occupational therapists. Henkin et al (2000) asked physiotherapy students enrolled on a graduate degree programme to complete a social skills inventory, a questionnaire designed to measure communication competence. These researchers found that these students' scores were on average lower than those provided by a general cross-section of college students. The questionnaire received some validation as the physiotherapy students who expressed most concern about their communication skills tended to obtain lower scores. Studies such as these suggest that communication skills training needs to be included in the pre-qualification curriculum. However, we must be cautious about generalising these findings to the UK. Both studies were carried out in North America, and were based on small samples. Neither study gathered objective observations of the therapists in interaction with their patients. Nevertheless, taken together with other studies of patients' experiences, the findings suggest that therapists should not be complacent about their skills for interacting with patients.

Patients tend to judge the quality of their health care on the basis of their relationships and communications with therapists and other health professionals, rather than by judging their technical expertise (Gerteis et al 1993). Their views and needs in relation to communication will be considered in detail in Chapter 4. According to the complaints made by patients, the most frequent mistakes that health professionals make during consultations with patients include:

- Poor listening, lack of interest and limited empathy
- Interrupting the patient
- Maintaining a narrow focus on the physical complaint, and avoiding the patient's psychological concerns, and questions
- Providing insufficient (or confusing) information about the condition or treatment
- Failing to acknowledge the personal impact of the disease/injury on the patient and the family
- Conveying patronising attitudes
- Taking a prescriptive approach to treatment, rather than a partnership approach.

(See discussions also by Dickson et al 1997, and Gerteis et al, 1993, for further details.)

In general, patients dislike being treated as cases and wish to be treated as people. They prefer relating to health professionals who appear to be caring and interested in their welfare. These affective (socio-emotional) dimensions of health care influence patients a great deal, and can even affect health, recovery and coping, as we will see in Chapter 5.

ACTIVITY

- Compare the problems outlined above with your own negative experience of communicating with a health professional (identified in the previous activity).
- Consider whether your difficulty is included, or whether you would like to extend the list.

WHY DO HEALTH PROFESSIONALS SOMETIMES COMMUNICATE POORLY WITH PATIENTS?

Key problems arise from the following aspects of the health professional's training and working environment:

- An educational curriculum that equips students with the knowledge and skills for treating physical dysfunction, but that gives less attention to the wider psychological and social aspects of illness.

- An overcrowded and heavily assessed curriculum during training that focuses more on 'measurables' than on the more subtle skills of insight, empathy, self-reflection and communication competence.
- Academic and clinical educators who assume – without evidence – that good communication will happen automatically.
- Lengthy socialisation in the health professional role leads to the deliberate or careless use of jargon and advanced technical language with patients. Whether deliberate or unintentional, such use of unfamiliar language has the effect of alienating and disempowering patients.
- Familiarity with certain diseases/injuries leads the health professional to regard these as 'routine' rather than as a unique personal challenge for each patient.
- Hierarchy, high professional status and a heavy workload may lead some health professionals to regard their patients as 'objects' of treatment, rather than as people bringing their own resources to the rehabilitation process.
- Time pressures may encourage a narrow focus on physical rehabilitation and lead to the neglect of the patient's wider needs for information and support.

If you compare your own list of reasons for poor communication, perhaps you will extend the list given above. Whilst we need to recognise that many external pressures work against skilful communication with patients, patient partnership is now considered to be *central* to a quality service within the NHS, and is a core aspect of the standards of practice for physiotherapy and occupational therapy (Law et al 1995, Mead 2000, National Health Service Executive 1999). Therapists need good communication skills including listening, and explaining, if they are to work with patients in partnership. This will be explored in detail in Chapter 6.

HOW MAY SKILFUL COMMUNICATION INFLUENCE PATIENTS?

ACTIVITY Effects of skilful communication on a patient

Mrs Adam has recently undergone hip replacement surgery. Prior to discharge from hospital, she is referred to a physiotherapist and an occupational therapist.
- Regardless of the specific therapy intervention (such as provision of a raised toilet seat, or a set of recommended physical exercises) consider three ways in which skilful communication by the therapists with Mrs Adam will increase the likelihood of her making a good recovery from this operation.

There are many ways in which skilful communication assists patients, promoting the clinical effectiveness of all therapeutic interventions, and these will be considered in detail in later chapters. In the above activity, you might have considered some of the following benefits:

- Careful questioning, and attentive listening (as well as sharing information with other professionals through written clinical records) will enable the therapist to gain accurate information on which to base treatment. For example, in the case above, therapists need to find out about Mrs Adam's confidence to return home, her support systems, her home layout, and any other physical or social difficulties that might interfere with her rehabilitation.
- An empathic approach may help the patient to confide her fears and anxieties, enabling the therapist to refer her on to other professionals where necessary (for example, to social services).
- Clear explanation (for example, about exercises, what to do and what not to do in the first days and weeks) is likely to increase the patient's understanding of the reasons for the therapist's advice, encouraging adherence to treatment recommendations, and better morale, thereby maximising her recovery.

COMMUNICATION AND CLINICAL EFFECTIVENESS

Communication between therapist and patient has been described as the 'underground' practice that goes unnoticed and unreported (Fleming 1991 p. 1011). Yet good communication tends to have a considerable influence on patients' satisfaction with treatment (Ley 1988). Empathy and appropriate information giving can provide patients with additional means to cope with their health problems. Conversely, poor communication inevitably adds further stress to patients (and families) whose lives have already been changed by illness or injury. These are important considerations for all therapists who endeavour to provide a humane, ethical service to their patients in the rehabilitation setting. However, skilful communication has additional benefits. In some circumstances, research has shown that it increases the clinical effectiveness of medical care and therapy, helping to maximise the patient's degree of recovery and quality of life.

Clinical effectiveness has a variety of meanings (Benton 1999). In essence, effective treatment is successful, creating measurable change (for example, in the patient's ability to carry out activities of daily living). According to a Department of Health (1996) document, a clinically effective treatment does what it is intended to do, securing the greatest health gains from the resources available.

Returning to the case example above, skilful communication with Mrs Adam would help the therapists not only to devise a tailored intervention best suited to the patient's needs and limitations, but would help to motivate the patient to adhere to the recommended treatment, increasing the likelihood of a successful outcome. These issues will be further explored in Chapter 5.

EVIDENCE-BASED PRACTICE AND CLINICAL EFFECTIVENESS

All health professionals working in the NHS are being encouraged to critically assess the clinical effectiveness of their work with patients, and to provide, where possible, interventions for which there is an 'evidence-base'. In order to base their clinical work on best evidence, therapists need to have skills for finding out about the evidence that is available, and for critically analysing it in terms of quality and relevance. Therapists also need to be able to apply the evidence sensitively to their specific clinical problems (Hamer 1999). Evidence-based practice has been seen as a means of reducing the waste of time and resources associated with ineffective treatments (Sackett et al 1997).

Evidence-based practice has its roots in evidence-based medicine (EBM), an approach to decision-making about patients' treatment pioneered by the medical faculty at McMaster University in Canada in the 1980s. EBM challenged traditional medical practice which previously had been largely based on personal clinical experience and authority, by emphasising the use of scientific evidence, audit and reflective evaluation to increase the appropriateness and effectiveness of patients' treatments. Medical and therapy practitioners are being encouraged to formulate questions about the most appropriate treatment for a patient with a given condition, and then to search the research literature to determine which intervention out of those available is best supported by good quality evidence. Whilst it is most common for evidence to be reviewed in relation to patients with a shared condition, it is also possible to approach individual treatment planning in the same way (Tickle-Degnen 1998). EBP is difficult for many therapists to achieve because of limited training in research methods and philosophies, too little time to analyse and integrate research findings, as well as limited access to information resources (Metcalfe et al 2001, Turner 2001). Nevertheless, educational and training initiatives are gradually enhancing the evidence-based skills of health professionals.

Although there are many types of evidence about treatments, a convention has arisen among those advocating EBP to value the findings of randomised controlled trials above other research methods such as case studies and qualitative studies of patients' and therapists' experiences (Humphris 1999). In the simplest form of randomised controlled trial, two groups of patients are randomly selected for different treatments and their outcomes are compared. One group usually experiences a new form of treatment, whilst the other group either receives the usual pattern of care, or no intervention at all. The last option raises many ethical issues and is generally only included in the research design if patients are usually expected to join a waiting list for the conventional treatment. Their progress whilst on the waiting list is assessed, to provide a baseline against which to compare the progress of those receiving the newly developed treatment. This research design is not quite a genuine 'experiment' as several variables are usually varied simultaneously. For example, the different treatments being compared may be carried out in different settings, by different therapists, all of which introduce further variables into the situation. However, with large sample sizes, and the addition of further controls (for example, patients may not realise whether they are receiving the usual or new treatment), we may feel quite confident that the research design can offer robust evidence about the relative effectiveness of each treatment.

Example of a randomised controlled trial in the field of communication

LeFort and colleagues (1998) carried out a randomised controlled trial to assess whether a newly devised self-management programme for chronic pain achieved better results than a 'wait and see' approach. The patients had endured pain for more than three months, yet did not have any identifiable pathology, as is often the case with chronic pain. All of those participating in the trial were assessed in detail at the start and at the end of the programme. Patients who were randomly selected for the self-management programme received twelve hours of education and support over six weeks. The programme provided information about self-management techniques, as well as facilitating discussion, problem-solving and mutual support within the patient group. More than a hundred patients took part in eleven programmes, and a large number of assessments, including pain, level of disability, depression, dependency and life satisfaction were carried out. All patients (in both treatment and waiting list control groups) were re-asssessed about twelve weeks after the initial assessments, by a research assistant 'blind' to their treatment condition (to minimise bias). The researchers found that the patients who had received the self-management treatment package showed a statistically significant improvement in six of the ten assessments, compared with the control (waiting list) group. For example, they reported greater life satisfaction and less dependency as well as reduced body pain. They also reported greater self-confidence (self-efficacy) in managing their pain. However, all patients tended to remain *uncertain*, which the authors interpreted as linked to 'the amorphous nature of chronic pain itself and the lack of clear communication about chronic pain by many health professionals' (LeFort et al 1998 p. 304). The authors noted that the patients who had dropped out of the programme had been initially more distressed, and that this might suggest the need for a more specialised intervention for this group. Overall, the research was useful in clearly establishing that a psychoeducational programme complements the more conventional medical and physical therapies for chronic pain.

Studies such as these can be very powerful for revealing the effectiveness of one intervention over another. However, they often do not examine which components of the treatment were most associated with the various outcomes. For example, it is unclear in the study above whether different facilitators, with their possibly distinctive styles of interacting with the patient, achieved somewhat different outcomes, nor whether the dynamics in each patient group affected patients' motivation and attendance.

While evidence-based practice is clearly a rational approach that helps health professionals to make the best use of limited resources, it presents certain challenges, particularly if a strictly 'evidence-based' approach to communication is attempted. Firstly, EBP relies on the systematic review of all available evidence for an intervention, not just a single study. As indicated above, greater weighting is normally given to studies based on experimental, or randomised controlled designs. While a complete analysis of all relevant evidence is relatively straightforward for single interventions (such as establishing the suitability of a specific drug for a certain well-defined condition), it is much less clear whether and if such evidence is available to guide many day-to-day interpersonal encounters with patients. Therapists have many questions in relation to communication. These include:

- Is it better to support a verbal explanation to a patient with a written account such as a leaflet?
- Are there any established techniques for defusing an angry patient?
- Is there an effective way of motivating a patient who feels depressed about their progress?
- Do male and female patients with chronic conditions typically have different communication needs? Or not?

ACTIVITY

- Do you have some further questions about the most effective ways of communicating with patients?
- Can you envisage a research method that might help to answer your question(s)?

It is not straightforward to find clear, robust evidence to answer questions about the most effective ways of communicating with patients, as there have been relatively few studies addressing such issues explicitly. Secondly, the conventional 'hierarchy' of evidence is open to debate in relation to communication issues. Qualitative methods of research would seem particularly valuable for conveying insights into patients' needs and experiences of communication in health care. It is important to note, though, that evidence hierarchies and research values are currently being challenged, and some argue that EBP was never intended to be solely reliant on quantitative research findings (Jennings & Loan 2001). Humphris (1999) notes that the key issue in evaluating evidence is whether the research method is appropriate for answering the particular research question, rather than whether it adheres to an experimental design or not.

A further reason why EBP is difficult to achieve (in its purest form) in the field of communication is that relatively few studies are available which document the effects of *informal* communications on treatment outcomes. While planned educational 'packages' have received some research evaluation (as shown by the study by Lefort et al 1998, outlined above), everyday, less planned interpersonal exchanges between therapist and patient tend to remain part of the taken-for-granted and unexamined context of treatment. Explaining, listening, and motivating provide the matrix within which treatments are embedded. Their specific effects on the patient are often overlooked. Therapists' communication strategies are rarely considered as influences in their own right in studies evaluating treatment effectiveness. Furthermore, even where some evidence is available, a strictly evidence-based approach to communication remains difficult for a therapist to implement. This is because so many rapid decisions are required about how to communicate with patients and colleagues as each encounter unfolds. This perhaps places communication within the realms of art as well as science. Nevertheless, there are a number of thought-provoking research studies in this field which may be used to guide interpersonal strategies, and you are encouraged to make use of them.

RESEARCH-GUIDED PRACTICE

Because of the difficulties outlined previously, this book does not claim to offer a strictly 'evidence-based' approach to communication. Yet the book will strongly encourage you to be mindful of relevant research, and to continue consulting the research literature throughout your subsequent professional development. Jennings and Loan (2001) refer to this as 'research-based' rather than 'evidence-based' practice. In the following chapters, many references to relevant books and journal articles will be cited. Because relatively few research studies have been carried out on communication in physiotherapy and occupational therapy settings, relevant studies carried out by nurses and doctors will also be considered. Some of the journal articles and books selected are readily found in university and hospital libraries, and some articles are available in full-text versions via electronic databases such as CINAHL, Science Direct and Medline. This material will deepen your understanding of communication issues in health care, and will also increase your familiarity with research and evidence-based practice.

In order to understand more about how patients' treatment can be enhanced through engaging with the research literature, coupled with reflection on personal strategies of communication as well as sensitivity to patients' needs, consider the following scenario. If possible, discuss your ideas with others before reading on.

ACTIVITY Formulating and evaluating an approach to communication based on integrating research findings with clinical experience

Ann Jenkins is a therapist who works in a chronic pain management clinic. She is evaluating whether the multi-faceted therapeutic programme meets her patients' needs. In particular, she is considering whether the programme should be further developed in the light of evidence (e.g. Osborne & Smith 1998) that patients with chronic pain often feel disbelieved. In light of this evidence, she

decides, with the support of the interprofessional team, to provide the opportunity for patients to discuss and share experiences of disbelief and stigma in a group.
- How might she assess whether patients find this experience helpful or not?

Because any addition to the treatment programme carries some resource implications, it is important to assess whether an extra intervention is beneficial. In the example above, positive outcomes may be assessed subjectively – for example, by gathering feedback from patients as to whether or not they perceived the group discussion as helpful. More objective effects might also be evaluated. For example, the therapists may assess whether patients with chronic pain who have the opportunity to discuss their experiences of being disbelieved (or other negative social reactions) show more adherence to subsequent treatment, demonstrate improved coping or behavioural change, or reduce their ratings of pain intensity, compared with groups who have not taken part in this particular element of the programme.

If a therapist implements a fresh communication strategy (such as an educational intervention) on the basis of previous research findings, it is always a good idea to evaluate the outcomes. Each clinical situation is different. Patients' characteristics and health problems, as well as the therapist's levels of expertise, may differ from those found in previous research studies, making it uncertain that published findings will necessarily generalise. Therapists inevitably need to use their clinical reasoning skills as well as published evidence (Hamer 1999).

FINDING RELEVANT RESEARCH EVIDENCE ABOUT PATIENTS' NEEDS AND EFFECTIVE COMMUNICATION

In order to plan certain communication strategies (such as the use of a patient-centred educational package) and to decide whether a particular communication approach is likely to be effective or not, you will require a wide repertoire of skills and evidence. Reflections on personal performance, and informal feedback from colleagues, tutors or patients can greatly assist your professional development. However, theory about communication processes, and more formal research evidence, can also help you to extend your communication repertoire. There are many sources of theory, practical advice and research evidence about communication, and it is important to become familiar with strategies for accessing all of these.

Books on communication in health care, health psychology, illness and disability

Books within these categories are numerous, and can be found using any university library catalogue. Try typing in keywords such as communication, interpersonal communication, interactive skills, counselling skills, illness, disability. These should lead you to a wide range of relevant books. Also look out for books that report qualitative studies of patients' experiences of illness (e.g. Kleinman 1988, Radley 1993, Seymour 1998b), and books exploring the medical humanities (e.g. Kirklin & Richardson 2001). Some books and chapters are written by authors with personal experience of disability or illness. They often present a rich and reflexive analysis of research accounts (for example, of their interviews with disabled people), as well as personal experiences of social discrimination (e.g. see chapters in Corker & French 1999).

Journal articles

This book emphasises the wealth of clinical and research material about communication issues that is published in academic journals:

ACTIVITY Library based task

If you are a student in the early stages of your education as a therapist, do ensure that you are familiar with journals in your professional discipline. Consider examining at least four recent issues.

Suggested journals include:

- *American Journal of Occupational Therapy*
- *British Journal of Occupational Therapy*
- *Disability and Rehabilitation*
- *International Journal of Therapy & Rehabilitation*
- *Occupational Therapy Journal of Research*
- *Physical Therapy*
- *Physiotherapy Research International*
- *Physiotherapy Theory and Practice.*

Try scanning their contents pages and abstracts (article summaries) to check whether any articles address communication issues in therapy/ rehabilitation. Practise jotting down the titles of the relevant articles, the author and the other details that are required for a reference using a conventional format such as the Harvard style. This reference will allow you to return to the article if you so choose. You might read at least one article and note any finding that builds upon, or challenges, your current assumptions about effective communication in the clinical setting.

Electronic databases

These provide an excellent source of searchable evidence. Research into health care communication is catalogued in a variety of electronic databases, including AMED (therapy and complementary therapy literature), MedLine (which reviews mainly medical/therapy literature), CINAHL (mostly therapy and nursing literature) and PsycINFO (mostly psychological and social science literature). Some universities also provide access to other databases such as Science Direct, through which you can gain a huge variety of full-text research articles. Cochrane Reviews summarise the best evidence on many topics.

The catalogues are divided according to date of publication, enabling you to search only the most recent published research, or to examine research from a broader time period, depending on your requirements. Each database provides information about many articles, including in most cases, their abstracts (summaries). Some articles are available in 'full text' which can be read from the screen, printed out or downloaded on to disc. This book refers you to a number of these articles for further reading.

To access databases, you will need an 'Athens' user name and password, obtained through your university or hospital library. You will also need the **local instructions** for accessing the databases. Once you have logged on, you will be able to search one database, or several simultaneously. You can search for a broad topic (which will deliver many articles, often too many to search properly), or you can narrow your search in a variety of ways.

The basic search process is via 'keywords'. Once you have your username and password, try entering CINAHL and type in '*Communication skills*' (then request '*Perform search*'). The database will find a large number of articles and you can scan through their titles and (if relevant) their abstracts. To read most of the articles, you need to check whether they are available within your university/hospital library. However, the database provides the full text in some cases, enabling you to read the complete article straight from the computer. The titles are given in reverse chronological order, so that the most recently published articles are cited first.

If you have found too many articles to search through, then your search term is too general. One way of focusing your search is through the '*Combine*' option. To do this, type in another keyword that is relevant to your search, such as treatment *compliance* (or *adherence*) then click on '*Perform search*'. A large number of references will be located.

Click the icon button '*Combine*' (in the bar at the top), then the boxes next to each keyword, followed by '*Combine searches*'. The result represents the intersection between the two original sets, and contains only articles that refer (in this case) to *both* communication skills *and* adherence. By doing this, you will find a manageable set of references to examine further. To display the details of the references, you will need to click on '*Display*'. If you scroll through these, using the mouse and the '*Next citations*' buttons on the screen, you can examine the abstract of any article that interests you by clicking on the word '*Abstract*' that follows the reference. Practise saving selected references by clicking the mouse over the appropriate left-hand 'boxes' (e.g. the paper by Cameron 1996, on compliance). You will note that some articles, such as Cameron's, are available in full text.

It can be very practical to limit your search to full-text articles that you can read directly off the screen (or save to disc, or e-mail to yourself). As a further exercise, in CINAHL, type the keyword *'patient-centred'*, and click on the button *'Perform search'*. You will be invited to select from a further list. Click on *'Patient-centred care'*, then *'Continue'*, then *'Include all subheadings'*, then *'Continue'*. The database will indicate over 2000 references. This is too many to search through. If you wish to consult only full-text articles from this list, click on *'Limit'* (the icon on the bar at the top), then click on *'Fulltext available'*, then *'Limit search'*. The database will find you more than one hundred full-text articles on patient-centred care. These could form an important resource for any assignment on this topic, although clearly you cannot carry out a full-scale review of the research field in this way. If you ever need to carry out a more extended literature review, it is wise to check whether you gain further references by using the US spelling of key words (e.g. 'patient-centered'; communication 'behavior').

REVIEWING THE EVIDENCE

As well as reading about research into communication in the healthcare setting, you will need to develop skills for evaluating the appropriateness, adequacy and generalisability of the evidence. These skills will continue to develop throughout your training as a therapist, and you will become more proficient if you participate in further learning about research concepts and methods. If you are in the early stages of a therapy course, evaluation of research may seem difficult, and you may feel uncertain about whether and how the evidence can be applied in the rehabilitation setting. Nevertheless, each attempt to consider the limitations of theory and evidence will contribute to the development of your critical abilities.

If you are considering whether it is permissible to generalise the findings from one study to another setting (e.g. applying the results of a published study to your clinical encounters with patients), check the following:

- Are the patients/participants in the research study similar to the patients that you are planning treatment for? For example, are they of similar age, and background, and do they have similar clinical problems? If they are markedly different, work out whether and why you can still justify generalising the results of the study (for example, perhaps age and gender do not seem relevant to the published results).
- How big is the sample? Findings from a small sample may not be readily generalised (the evidence may be said to lack 'external validity').
- If an intervention study is described, is the nature of the intervention really clear? You might ask whether the intervention can be replicated in your setting. For example, if a study shows a particular leaflet to be effective in one setting, does this imply that a *different* leaflet would necessarily be useful in your clinical context?
- Are the findings clear? If, for example, two groups of patients undergoing different treatments are compared, are the differences between the groups substantial and unlikely to reflect chance factors? Were the two groups

similar at the outset, making it more justifiable to attribute change to the intervention?

- If a highly controlled experimental intervention has been described, can the findings really be generalised to the more complex natural setting of the hospital/community? Or would other variables become influential in a less controlled environment?
- What limitations have the authors pointed out? Can you identify further limitations in the research study?

Further questions to apply to the evaluation of research studies are suggested by Humphris (1999).

Qualitative studies generally explore the experiences of small groups of participants in depth, for example, through interviews and focus groups. Qualitative studies can be very helpful for providing direct accounts of patients' experiences. For example, Donovan and Blake (2000) analyse the comments of patients who were confused about the meanings of their doctors' reassurances about their arthritis. The researchers illustrate the themes that they inferred from the interviews with quotations from the patients. These offer much material for reflection, and for thinking deeply about patients' experiences of health care, which are perhaps key reasons for consulting published evidence. Quantitative studies tend to involve larger samples, and may gather objective data (such as blood pressure or distance walked in a fixed period), numerical measures from attitude scales, and reported ratings of change in mobility and self-care. Both quantitative and qualitative approaches to research have strengths and also limitations. If you wish to learn more about research in order to evaluate the results of studies into communication, useful introductory texts are Denscombe (1998) and French et al (2001).

OTHER SOURCES OF EVIDENCE AND INFORMATION RELEVANT TO COMMUNICATION

While formal research into therapist–patient communication (or communication within healthcare teams) can offer a useful guide to practice, it is not the only source of evidence. Insights into patients' needs and helpful communication skills and strategies can be gained from other forms of information such as:

- Personal observations in the clinical setting
- Internet sites
- Autobiographies of people living with illness/impairments
- Films, novels and poems depicting people's experiences of coping with illness and healthcare settings
- Reflections on one's own needs and experiences as a patient.

Observations in the clinical setting

In the clinical setting, therapists gain at first hand a wide variety of observations about their patients. They can use this information to improve their practice by taking time to reflect carefully on the treatment process, and any difficulties and conflicts that they encounter in achieving successful outcomes. Through becoming more aware of any unhelpful norms and patterns of behaviour in the clinical setting, the therapist can begin the process of challenge and change. Critical reflection on action is seen as an important tool for professional development (Johns, 2000). Audits of practice, and patient feedback can also provide information about the quality and appropriateness of services, including interpersonal communications. Critical reflection on practice, integrating research evidence, patient feedback and personal observation, seems likely to help therapists to develop a larger 'toolkit' of interventions, and to communicate more skilfully with each patient. One message of this book is that clinical practice is not only enhanced by evaluating the technical aspects of therapeutic interventions. Communication processes with patients also need to be subject to careful reflective appraisal, for clues as to what forms of information and support patients might need, and what can be improved.

Internet sites

There is a great deal of information to be acquired from the Internet. Increased understanding of patients' needs and perspectives can be gained from the sites serving people with diagnosed illnesses such as breast cancer, Parkinson's disease and multiple sclerosis. Through reading the information offered, and the views and experiences of site users, therapists can gain 'insider' information about illness that may help to increase empathy and sensitivity to patients' needs. You can find support groups and user sites by typing in search terms such as 'multiple sclerosis'.

There are other sources of web-based material relating to the 'medical' humanities. There are a variety of sites promoting arts and humanities relevant to the education of doctors, and much of the creative writing and artwork that is referred to on these databases would make a useful contribution to the reflective practice of occupational therapy and physiotherapy.

For example:

http://www.mhrd.ucl.ac.uk

Autobiographies of people living with illness/impairment

Several autobiographical works provide health professionals and students with insights into people's experiences of illness, disability and treatment. For example, John Diamond (1998) described his experience of cancer and subsequent radical surgery, vividly illuminating the impact that this disease had on his identity and day-to-day occupations, and emphasising the profound effects that communications with health professionals had on his well-being. Not all autobiographies describe chronic illness. Joe Simpson (1994) wrote about his experiences in recovering from a serious knee injury sustained whilst rock-climbing in the Andes. His book described several encounters with health professionals. Their poor communication skills clearly demoralised him and affected his confidence in the treatment that he was offered. His book provides an interesting case study of the effects that a sporting injury can have on a person's life and identity. More details are presented in an activity in Chapter 4.

Films, novels and poems

A range of films, novels and poems depict the experience of illness or health care, and some vividly portray communications between health professionals and patients. In medical education, there is a gradual recognition that the arts and humanities may increase empathy and insight into the diversity of human experiences. While films, novels and poems can be sensationalist or stereotyping in their portrayal of physical illness and mental health problems, some deal with these issues sensitively. Encounters between health professionals and patients are also regularly portrayed in television and film. However, you will certainly find some misleading examples, where callous, over-intrusive and unethical communications take place for dramatic effect, or where people's responses to illness seem far-fetched. Even in such cases, critical reflection on the encounters observed may increase your awareness of patients' likely needs in such settings, and may encourage you to formulate more appropriate professional responses.

There are a variety of web-sites listing useful resources of literature and art related to medicine and therapy. Also see Charon and Montello (1998), and Hunter et al (1995) for some further views and suggested resources.

You might also consult a variety of other literature that has been written by people with long-term health problems or impairments (e.g. see Saxton & Howe 1987). Tom Shakespeare (1999) offers a very interesting analysis of two films which address disability issues, namely *Breaking the Waves* and *Shine*. He brings both his personal experience of disability as well as an academic perspective to his analysis. His article includes discussion about some of the contrasting opinions that previous reviewers have expressed about these films, the general portrayal of physically or mentally disabled people in film, the use of non-disabled actors in disabled roles and the power of film to reinforce or challenge stereotypes. Shakespeare argues that film images can generate 'prejudicial attitudes towards disabled people' (p. 164). He also notes that disabled people are not necessarily in agreement about what constitutes a 'positive image' in cinematic terms. Readers are invited to engage in similarly critical reflections about the themes within films and literature that deal with experiences of illness and disability. Such reflections are likely to expose some of the taken-for-granted assumptions and stereotypes within the wider culture that readily undermine practitioners' communications with patients.

OBSERVING AND PRACTISING INTERPERSONAL SKILLS

Effective communication requires a range of skills that need to be developed through practice, in both the educational and clinical setting (Dickson et al 1997). While your knowledge about effective communication and your reflective self-awareness may increase through studying relevant research and autobiography, your communication behaviours are unlikely to change unless *practised* and *evaluated.* Some skills require 'hands-on' situations for learning, such as role play. Also, you may find it helpful to observe interpersonal skills and strategies in the encounters around you. Do practise unfamiliar skills (e.g. active listening, being assertive) and seek feedback from others about your performance. Despite the anxiety involved, you might find that the feedback obtained from videotaped interactions is really helpful for developing more effective communication skills. Dickson et al (1997) and Burnard (1991) strongly advocate such an active engagement in communication skills training. Certain studies (e.g. Caris-Verhallen et al,2000) support the effectiveness of videotaped feedback for improving communication skills.

COMMUNICATING WITH COLLEAGUES

Good communication skills are not only important for working with patients. Many occupational therapists and physiotherapists work with a variety of other professionals in multi-disciplinary teams, comprising medical staff, nurses, speech and language therapists, social workers and others, depending upon the speciality. Some teams take their collaboration further and work 'interprofessionally'. That is, colleagues from a variety of disciplines share information and establish common goals for the patient. Interprofessional working requires close collaboration among all colleagues to deliver a seamless service to the patient. There are many barriers to effective communication with colleagues, including status differences, poor understanding of each others' roles, and use of different theoretical models and terminology. Not only do these communication failures have a detrimental effect on therapists' job satisfaction within the health service, but ultimately, they can seriously undermine the patient's treatment, and impede recovery. Patients are often very aware of communication failures within teams, and form judgements about the quality of their care on this basis (Gerteis et al 1993). These issues will be further considered in Chapter 9.

CONCLUSION

This chapter has considered communication as a complex verbal and nonverbal exchange between people. Skilful communication is an integral part of the occupational therapy and physiotherapy process, needed at every stage of your work with patients. Teamwork among colleagues also depends upon a high level of interpersonal skills. Communication skills are not simply required to provide a humane, caring service to patients, but to maximise the effectiveness of therapeutic interventions, and to enhance patient satisfaction. There are various strategies for enhancing your awareness of communication processes and your interpersonal skills, and these will be considered in subsequent chapters. A person-centred attitude can be developed through considering patients' experiences of illness and health care, consulting relevant research and other evidence about effective communication strategies, practising unfamiliar skills, and engaging in critical reflection about your own personal experiences and performance.

The need to consult evidence has been emphasised, not only in relation to technical therapy skills and interventions, but also to identify the communication strategies that increase clinical effectiveness and patient satisfaction. Nevertheless, research evidence in this field is not extensive and does not necessarily give you a detailed guide to communicating with individual patients on specific issues. Given the range of research, and the many different types of communication that therapists engage in, this book cannot offer you a complete, systematic review on each topic. As discussed before, some approaches to evidence-based practice involve highly rigid procedures, including complex rules for comparing findings and evaluating whether evidence is robust or not. This book acknowledges that there are many gaps in our understanding of effective health communications. Moreover, when communicating with individual patients, there is a limit to how much one can follow general evidence-based guidelines, based on group studies and quantitative outcome measures. Clearly, each individual is unique, with particular needs, strengths and vulnerabilities. The central argument of this book is that effective professional communications require a good awareness of theory and research, and a wide repertoire of different communication skills (for teaching, motivating and developing rapport with patients). Both theory and skills need to be applied flexibly to the needs of each different patient. Also important is genuine respect for the individuality of the patient (or colleague), a high level of insight into patients' experiences of illness, and sensitivity to the moment-by-moment unfolding interaction.

Further reading

Greenhalgh T, Hurwitz B 1999 Narrative-based medicine: why study narrative? British Medical Journal 318(2 Jan):48–50

This is an interesting example of clinical decision-making during a doctor–patient interaction, based on a complex mixture of personal experience, attention to the specific details of the encounter and research-based guidelines for treatment. The article can be read in full-text form from MEDLINE, or from a paper copy of the *British Medical Journal.*

Cameron C 1996 Patient compliance: recognition of factors involved and suggestions for promoting compliance with therapeutic regimens. Journal of Advanced Nursing 24(2):244–250

This research paper reveals some of the ways in which communications between health professional and patient influence satisfaction and compliance with treatment. The article can be read in full-text format from the database CINAHL.

Donovan J, Blake D 2000 Qualitative study of interpretation of reassurance among patients attending rheumatology clinics: 'just a touch of arthritis, doctor?'. British Medical Journal 320(7234):541–544

This paper encourages awareness of the different meanings that a specific health problem may have for people, and their idiosyncratic ways of interpreting the communications that their health professionals intended to be reassuring. It is available in full text from the electronic database MEDLINE.

Diamond J 1998 C: because cowards get cancer too. Vermilion, London

There are many autobiographical accounts that provide insights into the experience of long-term illness and impairment, and the impact that communications with health professionals can have on coping. This account is thought-provoking.

Students can locate CINAHL, Medline and Science Direct through their university/hospital library website links. These sites cannot be accessed without going through the subscriber but most university and hospital libraries will provide this access.

Chapter 2

Models of health, illness and rehabilitation

The previous chapter outlined how skilful communication with patients depends upon more than common sense. Research evidence, sensitivity to patients' responses, and critical self-reflection have to be integrated if therapists are to address patients' complex needs more successfully in the rehabilitation context. Therapists who focus on the patient as a person, rather than as a condition, are embracing the patient-centred (or client-centred) approach to communication. However, Stewart et al (1995) point out that more is at issue than speaking and listening skills. Rather, a change in 'mind-set' is required. It is for this reason that this chapter explores various models of health, illness, disability and rehabilitation which influence the 'mind-sets' of therapists. The traditional models of illness, health care and rehabilitation need to be challenged if health professionals are going to shift from a clinician-centred to a patient-centred style of communication.

This chapter firstly discusses the more traditional biomedical model of illness and treatment, and then examines an alternative, namely the biopsychosocial model. The chapter acknowledges some of the academic, social and political influences that have challenged the dominance of the biomedical approach to health care during recent years. Other approaches to understanding illness and disability will also be considered, such as the social model, and the new classification system (ICF) recently developed by the

World Health Organization. The implications of these models for therapist–patient communication will be discussed throughout.

THE BIOMEDICAL MODEL OF HEALTH CARE

The biomedical model of illness and treatment dominated health care during the twentieth century until its last decade or so (McWhinney 1995). While it is most associated with the practice of medicine, it has also very much influenced professions 'allied to medicine' such as physiotherapy. Occupational therapists are distinctive in that they have traditionally espoused client-centred practice (Law 1998). Nevertheless, their work has inevitably been constrained – at least within the UK – by the domination of the biomedical model within the National Health Service.

What are the assumptions of the biomedical model? The model at its most extreme represents the patient as one who is passive in the face of ill-health, and awaiting a 'cure' by health professionals who have the necessary expertise. The diseased or injured body is therefore treated somewhat as a faulty car awaiting repair by expert mechanics. There is a strong focus on understanding the body machinery, with an emphasis on determining the pathogens, trauma and other factors that are disrupting its working. Taking the machine analogy further, the biomedical model of health presents illness/disease as opposite to health and well-being. This perspective did not always hold sway. The medical profession in its early development during the eighteenth century was mindful of the social and psychological effects of medical care and treatment but these aspects were largely forgotten during the explosion of scientific knowledge about the body in the twentieth century (McWhinney 1995). As advances were made in the understanding of biology and pathology, medical practitioners shifted their focus on to the faulty body 'machinery', and relegated to the background patients' experience of illness, the attitudes, beliefs and concerns which may influence coping and adaptation to illness, and the psychological and social resources that patients bring to the rehabilitation process. Because the biomedical model of care assumes that expert practitioners will act in the patient's best interests in order to cure disease or maximise functioning, the expressed needs and experiences of patients were traditionally seen as secondary to the practice of biomedicine. Doctors (and also other types of health professional) were permitted to wield authority, controlling their encounters with patients, for example, by asking numerous closed questions, and by interrupting when the patient strayed from the biomedical focus. This style of interacting clearly places the patient in a relatively powerless role (Clare 1991). Interactions may be described as 'clinician-centred'.

For many years, the biomedical model was perhaps reinforced by the remarkable advances in biological knowledge during the twentieth century, coupled with the discovery of new medications and technologies for 'curing' the body machinery of disease. It applies well enough to acute conditions that can be treated successfully, and that do not require long-term adaptation on the part of the affected person. However, certain social and political forces during the twentieth century, coupled with research in psychology, sociology and anthropology, gradually challenged the dominance and 'taken-for-grantedness' of the biomedical perspective, and suggested alternative ways of conceptualising health, disability and illness. These re-conceptualisations require changes in the patterns of interaction between health professionals and patients.

WHAT ARE HEALTH, DISEASE, ILLNESS AND DISABILITY?

Although the terms 'health', 'disease', 'illness' and 'disability' are regularly used by health professionals, their meanings are debated. Such debates should not be dismissed as 'simply academic', because our understandings of these terms fundamentally influence our approach to working with patients in rehabilitation.

ACTIVITY What is health?

- Read the case study of 'Ann' below, and rate Ann's level of health on a scale of 0-10 (ranging from 0 – not at all healthy, to 10 – extremely healthy).
- If you can, compare your view with another person's rating, and explore any difference of opinion.
- In coming to your decision, reflect on how have you defined 'health'? What, in your view, contributes to 'good health'?

Ann

Ann is 66 years old. She is married to a man who is ten years older, and she has two grown up sons. Ann has been a successful artist and illustrator, contributing to a number of children's books, as well as producing work for exhibition and sale. She is also interested in the history of childhood and toys and likes to spend time visiting relevant museums. Although she has semi-retired to spend more time with her husband, she continues to work on a part-time basis. Her savings and pension are small, and she relies on the income that she earns from her work. She also relishes her involvement in art, saying that she feels most alive when immersed in her drawings. She enjoys spending productive time in her studio.

Ann has had asthma all of her adult life. Her health fluctuates. She has been hospitalised almost every year with severe breathing problems, but when her health improves, she is an active, busy person. She is active in domestic tasks also, taking on the prime responsibilities for cooking and cleaning in the home. She has experienced some worsening pain in her back over the last nine months, and now finds it difficult to sit at her drawing board for more than a hour at a time. Recently, she fell down some stairs and sustained a Colles fracture of the right forearm. She can no longer drive, she needs help in the house, and finds it almost impossible to carry on with her artwork as she is right-handed.

Investigations since the fracture have revealed that Ann has marked osteoporosis (weakening of the bones). The cause of this disease is unknown but long-term use of steroid medication to control her asthma may have played some part.

What is health? And how should we best understand the effects of disease and injury on well-being? These questions are complex, and different perspectives offer different answers. As argued above, the traditional biomedical perspective has tended to focus on the physical workings of the body, in order to better understand the effects of disease and injury. Within this model, health is regarded as the ideal state of the body, in which disease and injury are absent. Ill-health tends to be understood as an organic malfunction brought about by various external assaults upon the body such as infection or injury, or through pathological processes (such as those associated with genetic factors) or ageing. In the example, above, if you focused upon Ann's diseases (asthma and osteoporosis) and injury (fractured wrist), you are likely to have rated her health as poor. If health and disease are seen as contrasting states of the body, it would be difficult to regard Ann as healthy. However, despite its powerful influence upon health care, the biomedical approach has certain limitations.

Because it takes a reductionist approach to disease and presents the anatomy and physiology of normal and abnormal states of the body as central to health care, the traditional biomedical perspective has rather neglected people's subjective experience of ill-health. It also encourages us to ignore people's intimate involvement in the process of rehabilitation and adaptation in chronic conditions. Kleinman (1988) argues that 'disease is the problem from the practitioner's perspective' (p. 5). This 'outsider' perspective has particularly unfortunate consequences in undermining attention both to the patient as a person, and to the therapist's need for good communication skills. Within traditional biomedicine, communication with the patient is seen primarily as a way of collecting data relevant to diagnosis, rather than as central to empathy and forming a relationship that will contribute to the effectiveness of treatment and rehabilitation (Brannon & Feist 1999). Arthur Frank (2001 p. 355), a sociologist with personal experience of cancer, argues that health professionals have to work 'outside the biomedical model' if they are to reduce their patients' suffering.

The limitations of a strictly 'reductionist' approach to health and health care are further illustrated by Frank, in reflecting on his own experience of illness:

> Medicine has done well with my body and I am grateful. But doing with the body is only part of what needs to be done for the person. What happens when my body breaks down happens not just to that body but also to my life, which is lived in that body. When the body breaks down, so does the life. Even when medicine can fix the body, that doesn't always put the life back together again. (Frank 1995 p. 8).

ACTIVITY   Appreciating the psychosocial impact of illness

- What do you consider may be the wider effects of disease/injury on Ann's life?
- Can you suggest one or two ways in which occupational therapists and physiotherapists may help Ann to put her life 'back together again'?

THE BIOPSYCHOSOCIAL PERSPECTIVE

The *biopsychosocial perspective* has been formulated (initially by Engel 1977) to encourage a more holistic understanding of the patient's complex experiences of health and illness. This perspective acknowledges not only the biological disorder, but also the psychological and social facets of disease and injury. It also redefines health, not so much as the absence of disease, but as a positive state of well-being. *Illness* is regarded as the health problem from the person's own subjective viewpoint, while *disease* refers to the objective state of the body. From this perspective, health professionals are expected to acquire some understanding of the patient's illness experience as well as the disease process itself.

The biopsychosocial perspective on health and illness accepts that illness is a complex experience for each individual patient, undermining not only physical functioning but penetrating into the person's valued roles, identity, and future plans. Frank (2001 p. 354) uses a metaphor to articulate the personal disruption and sense of isolation that for him was a central aspect of the cancer experience. He describes:

> ... my feeling of being disconnected from my life as I had been living it and from the lives of those around me. Suddenly, they (including my recently healthy self) were standing on one shore, and I was in a small skiff being carried toward an opposite shore. I could still call to them and they answered, but the distance separating us was growing rapidly.

If a more holistic, biopsychosocial perspective on the case study is taken, Ann may be regarded as enjoying many positive aspects to her health despite her asthma and osteoporosis. For example, she is active and busy for much of the time, immerses herself in creative work, continues with her personal and professional development and has numerous satisfying interests, as well as close family ties. If you regard health as a resource for 'doing', you may have rated Ann's health in the upper section of the 10-point scale when carrying out the previous activity. In this case, your concept of health may be similar to the description offered by the World Health Organization (1984):

> [Health is] the extent to which an individual or group is able ... to realise aspirations and needs; and ... to change or cope with the environment. Health is, therefore, seen as a resource for everyday life ... it is a positive concept emphasising social and personal resources, as well as physical capacities.

The biopsychosocial model suggests that each person will experience disease in an individual manner. For example, the experience of illness is shaped by whether the person assesses the condition as serious or life-threatening, and whether it seems likely to undermine quality of life, identity and plans. Well-being is also affected by the person's coping resources and social supports. In addition to the interventions of health professionals, the patient's own attitudes, self-management strategies and capacity to adapt are recognised as affecting long-term outcomes. In chronic back pain, for example, evidence shows that people's negative beliefs about the nature of their pain, the dangers of exercise, and their lack of perceived control over outcomes, can all conspire to increase physical disability in the longer term. In addition to personal beliefs and coping strategies, social support variables also modify the experience of illness and rehabilitation. People with higher levels of social support generally have better health, or regain health more successfully (see Chapter 7, and also Brannon and Feist 1999, and Steptoe and Wardle 1994, for further discussion).

Such wide differences in patients' needs, experiences, beliefs and coping suggest that health professionals will lose a lot of information that is relevant to the rehabilitation process if they focus narrowly on diagnostic categories and pathology rather than communicating in some depth with each patient about his/her experiences, beliefs, goals and coping strategies.

Nevertheless, any conceptual model has negative as well as positive aspects. In acknowledging the personal and social dimensions of illness and rehabilitation, there may be some risk of placing blame or an unwarranted responsibility on patients for recovery. Illness has always had moral connotations, being associated with 'evil' until the eighteenth century (Granshaw & Porter 1989). While healthcare professionals now tend to use 'illness' in neutral terms to describe the patient's experience of disease/injury, many patients themselves still perceive illness as inviting moral judgement, particularly moral exhortations to fight disease or 'rise to the occasion' and to be courageous (Frank 1997, Williams 1993). Some people with serious illnesses regard this as an additional burden. For example, John Diamond, when living with cancer of the throat and tongue commented:

> ... I despise the set of warlike metaphors that so many apply to cancer. My antipathy to the language of battles and fights has nothing to do with pacifism and everything to do with a hatred for the sort of morality which says that only those who fight hard against their cancer survive it or deserve to survive it – the corollary being that those who lose the fight deserved to do so. (Diamond 1998 p. 10)

Therapists clearly need to adopt a complex, person-centred perspective on health, illness and rehabilitation if they are to work sensitively with patients' own meanings.

WHICH SOCIAL AND CULTURAL FACTORS HAVE CONTRIBUTED TO THE DEVELOPMENT OF A BIOPSYCHOSOCIAL MODEL OF HEALTH, ILLNESS AND HEALTH CARE?

A variety of academic, social and political developments during the twentieth century have challenged the dominant biomedical model of health, illness and health care, and encouraged the adoption of a more holistic view. Once people started to regard illness and impairment as having social, cultural and psychological dimensions in addition to the physical, the stage was set for patients to play a greater role in promoting their own health, and to influence the treatment and rehabilitation process. Some of the factors which seem to have contributed to a conceptual shift away from the biomedical model are discussed below.

Sigmund Freud, unconscious processes and psychosomatics

Although his theories took some time to exert wider influence, and even now remain subject to great debate, Freud in the early part of the twentieth century raised the possibility that complex and largely hidden forces shaped behaviour, health and well-being (Jacobs 1998). He derived much of his theory of mind and behaviour through treating patients with impairments, such as a paralysis of a limb, or a difficulty in swallowing, that at first seemed to have a physical basis. Yet for these patients, medical investigations could not arrive at a physical pathology. Freud argued that their disturbances in functioning were 'hysterical conversion symptoms', attributable to psychological rather than to neurological factors or other physical disease. This re-conceptualisation provided some impetus for the subsequent more scientific studies of psychosomatic illness – that is, illness which does not clearly have a physical basis such as infection. As the twentieth century progressed, increasingly sophisticated psychological and psychosomatic research revealed the complex interplay between psychological, social and biological aspects of health. Many health psychologists and other researchers and therapists are now investigating the relevance of attitudes, emotional state and health behaviour to well-being, ill-health, and recovery from illness.

Freud, and other psychodynamic therapists, also heightened awareness that unconscious conflict may shape people's behaviour. From this perspective, we might interpret a patient's anger as perhaps revealing deeper issues, for example about dependence and powerlessness, rather than simply expressing a personal animosity towards the therapist. Insights into the role of unconscious conflicts have also led to an awareness among art therapists (and some occupational therapists) that patients can benefit psychologically from expressing painful feelings associated with illness, not only through words but through nonverbal means such as art (Malchiodi 1999). Moreover, research into relationships among stress, the immune system and health is beginning to support the argument that emotional verbalisation and social support benefit more than psychological well-being. Physical functioning can improve too. This is because long-term stress tends to impair immune functioning, to the detriment of health and recovery processes (Evans et al 2000). Therapists who can assist patients in managing the stress associated with illness and injury through communications which promote self-confidence and optimism may be helping them to maximise both their psychological and physical health.

Carl Rogers and client-centred therapy

Rogers was a psychologist, educator and counsellor who published a seminal book on client-centred therapy in 1951 (Rogers 1951, Thorne 2003). His work has had a profound influence on the practice of occupational therapy, and some forms of art therapy, as well as counselling. Through Rogers' experiences of counselling patients in psychological distress, he came to recognise that people brought more resources to solving their problems than they (and others) initially believed. He observed that people had a deep need for self-actualisation (or personal growth). Furthermore, he argued that the therapist could help clients or patients identify their goals, needs and resources primarily from attentively listening and reflecting back the key issues that they disclosed during the consultation, in an accepting, non-judgemental way. He suggested that therapists did not need to offer complex interpretations of their patients' disclosures. Nor did they need to offer advice. Rather, they were most effective when facilitating the client's own problem-solving.

Therapist qualities such as non-judgemental warmth, genuineness and empathy were seen as vital to the therapy process, as it was only under such conditions that the client would feel sufficient trust to disclose his or her deepest worries and needs, and gain sufficient support to begin solving his or her own problems. Rogers argued that people often experience psychological distress when they have suffered conditional love, especially during childhood. In this situation, the child feels as though love will only be given if certain behavioural patterns and achievements are displayed, for example by adopting the same interests as parents. Conditional love leads people to ignore their 'inner voice'. Their own goals and abilities may remain suppressed and unknown. Rogers argued that it was only when unconditional (non-judgemental) acceptance was experienced that the inner voice could be heard and acted upon. When such acceptance and respect were not forthcoming, the child would learn to ignore inner needs for fear of triggering the disapproval of parents. Thus within Rogers' model, unconditional acceptance becomes very central to the therapist–client relationship, offering the client a profoundly restorative or therapeutic experience. Working within an interpersonal climate of respect and trust, it is argued that the client is empowered to identify valued goals and meaningful strategies.

Rogers described his therapy as non-directive, as he endeavoured to follow the patient's agenda rather than his own. Above all, Rogers theorised that the quality of the client's relationship with the therapist depends upon the therapist's empathy, or ability to enter the client's own world of subjective experience.

ACTIVITY Comparing biomedical and client-centred perspectives

- Examine how the biomedical model and the client-centred perspective portray the optimal relationship between health professional/therapist and patient.
- Find as many contrasts as you can.
- Identify some strengths and limitations of each model.
- Critically reflect on the advantages and difficulties of applying a Rogerian, client-centred approach to occupational therapy or physiotherapy.

The Rogerian client-centred approach envisages that the therapist works in partnership with the client, rather than exerting power and authority. Client and therapist work together to identify the client's needs, resources and goals. A climate of trust encourages openness on both sides of the relationship. The therapist attempts – however imperfectly – to understand the client's world from the 'inside'. The biomedical perspective, on the other hand, prescribes a very different relationship. Here the therapist is seen as an expert, giving advice and treatment to a patient who is relatively passive. The relationship is a fairly distant one, and the therapist may see little need to appreciate the client's perspective. The focus remains on the physical body, rather than on the patient's other experiences such as loss, uncertainty and so on. While it may be seen as limited in focusing upon the physical body, the biomedical model can also be understood as having certain strengths. It acknowledges the health professional's considerable expertise. This clearly makes an important contribution to effective physical rehabilitation. It perhaps allows the therapist to manage stress through maintaining a certain emotional distance from the patient. The Rogerian approach may also have limitations in regard to the practice of physical rehabilitation. After all, it was initially developed on the basis of counselling practice, where listening, empathy and the therapeutic relationship could justifiably be seen as central to therapeutic change. It may be argued that physical rehabilitation, in contrast, depends upon a much wider variety of expert interventions. On the positive side, the Rogerian approach emphasises that the relationship between patient and therapist can have therapeutic properties in its own right. The approach also encourages attention to patients' personal needs as well as to their considerable resources. As we will see in subsequent chapters, patients' satisfaction and adherence to treatment tend to increase when therapists are person-centred in their approach. In rehabilitation (unlike some medical settings), therapists and patients work together for considerable periods. There is time to build a therapeutic relationship that can make a distinctive contribution to the effectiveness of therapy.

Demographic changes: ageing populations and the prevalence of chronic conditions

Another challenge to biomedicine, with its focus on physical impairment and 'cure', seems to have come about through demographic changes. The population consists of an increasing proportion of older people, and increasing numbers of the population have long-term disabling conditions which are not curable. For example, in the US it has been estimated that 49 million people reported chronic disabling conditions in 1991–2. This figure had risen to 54 million by 1994–5 (MMWR 2001). The leading causes of disability continue to be arthritis, back problems and cardiovascular disease. An approach to health care which focuses on cure (through medication, radiotherapy, surgery and so on) offers rather little to this large number of people living with chronic illness. Moreover, it is increasingly recognised that people with chronic illness require a range of personal and social resources to cope with their conditions on a day-to-day basis, if they are to attain a satisfactory quality of life. These issues are particularly relevant to physiotherapists and occupational therapists as it is these professionals, rather than medical specialists, who help many people with chronic conditions to regain function and hope for the future. Quality of life and personal coping strategies are clearly relevant to living with chronic illness and long-term impairments, and challenge the narrower biomedical approach to health care. Finding ways of working towards patients' goals, harnessing patients' values and motivation, and enhancing the patient's support networks are central to the rehabilitation of chronic conditions, and require therapists to develop a high level of communication skills. Such skills need to be developed not only through initial educational programmes but through the continuing professional development of all therapists.

Consumerism and the 'quality agenda' in the health services

Another challenge to biomedicine came about through the increasing power of the consumer movement. People gained increased rights as consumers in the latter part of the twentieth century, and started to challenge the paternalistic 'we know best' practices of businesses and public services including the NHS (Calnan & Gabe 2001). Political initiatives and changes in social policy in the UK gave patients more rights within the NHS, placed 'quality' on the agenda of management, and made public services more accountable (e.g. Department of Health 1992, 2000a). Patients as 'consumers' or 'users' of services gained more confidence to make complaints about poor treatment, and poor communication. Managers of health services have increasingly assessed patient satisfaction as an indicator of quality, although the validity of such assessments is open to dispute (Williams 1994). This is because, as Cleary and Edgman-Levitan (1997) argue, 'certain issues, such as being treated with respect and being involved in treatment decisions, aspects of care not included in many satisfaction surveys, are paramount issues for patients'.

Patients have also become consumers of health information, particularly since access to the Internet became commonplace. Kizer (2001 p. 1213) refers to this as the 'democratization of medical knowledge'. This information is enabling many to develop opinions about their own treatment and care, and to make more informed choices. While some health professionals have responded to this rise in patients' power and expertise with defensiveness (Wilson 1999), these developments can also be seen as facilitating the formation of partnerships between health professionals and patients.

Research into the psychosocial aspects of illness

Both quantitative surveys of patients' experiences, and sociological and anthropological theorising about the illness experience gathered pace through the 1980s and 1990s (e.g. Bury 1982, Charmaz 1983, 1991). Qualitative strategies of research into people's experience of illness and health care gained greater acceptance in the medical and health research community, and the findings may have created another impetus driving health care out from under the influence of the biomedical model. In 1988, Kleinman published a pioneering study of illness narratives, and showed through his careful analysis of patients' stories about their illness, treatment and coping strategies, that illness penetrates every point of a person's life. He showed that individual resourcefulness, the meanings that people place on their experiences of illness, and their social context all affect their adaptation and well-being. A variety of research studies of the chronic illness experience will be reviewed in the next chapter to explore its psychosocial aspects in more detail.

Self-advocacy by disabled people

A combination of consumerism and civil rights movements in the last half of the twentieth century presented a further challenge to the narrow focus of biomedicine on the body 'machinery'. Some disabled people disputed the right of medical doctors to exert so much influence over their lives, for example in deciding their entitlements to education, housing or social security benefits. The social control that institutions exercised over disabled people's lives has also been highlighted. For example, French (1993a p. 72) described her own experience at a residential school for blind children:

> Bravery and stoicism were demanded by the institution too; any outward expression of sadness was not merely ridiculed and scorned, it was simply not allowed. Any hint of dejection led to stern reminders that, unlike most children, we were highly privileged to be living in such a splendid house with such fantastic grounds – an honour which was clearly not our due … Not only were we compelled to deny our disabilities, but also the painful feelings associated with lifestyles forced upon us because we were disabled.

In the latter part of the twentieth century, disabled people (including people with learning difficulties) claimed their right to deserve a 'normal' life. Many who had been segregated in long-stay, isolated hospitals moved into community accommodation. Some celebrated their difference and rejected the notion that they were 'tragic' in any way, or that they necessarily aspired to any simple form of conventional 'normality' or 'independence' (French 1993b, Morris 1993). Physically disabled people began to advocate their entitlement to equal rights – to housing, transport, jobs and so on – and argued that it was not their physical impairments that prevented their full participation in the life of the community, but the social, environmental, attitudinal and institutional barriers to integration that they encountered on a daily basis (Oliver 1990, Swain et al 1998). Thus disability was radically re-framed within a 'social model' rather than in terms of an individual impairment-based or disease-based model.

Self-advocacy and the voices of previously silenced social minorities were heard more clearly towards the end of the twentieth century. A clear message was sent to health professionals that impairment and chronic illness affected more than the physical body. The prejudices, social discrimination and stigma experienced by many disabled people and people with chronic physical and/or mental illness fundamentally shaped the experience of illness or disability. As people who deserved as much status as those without physical impairments, disabled people advocated their rights to freedom of information, choice and the appropriate support that would enable them to participate in educational, work and leisure opportunities. They formulated the social model of disability as a radical alternative to the individualist, biomedical model. It can also be seen as a challenge to the biopsychosocial model.

THE SOCIAL MODEL OF DISABILITY

The World Health Organization (1980) put forward the *International Classification of Impairment, Disability and Handicap* (ICIDH). Impairment in this classification is defined as a lack or loss of a limb, organ or physiological process. For example, stroke may lead to loss of sensation and movement in one half of the body. Disability, within this classification, is defined in terms of functional losses. For example, the person may have difficulties in walking independently after stroke, or performing self-care activities. Returning to the case study above, if Ann cannot regain a full range of movement in her wrist, she may have difficulties in performing activities such as using a paintbrush, pen or cooking utensil, and may therefore be considered 'disabled' in terms of the ICIDH classification. Handicap within this classification is defined in terms of difficulties in maintaining social and occupational roles. This model is essentially individualistic, with disability seen as residing within the person.

In contrast, within the *social model of disability*, impairment is seen as a physical or functional loss (or lack of function, as in a congenital condition).

Disability refers to a variety of social processes whereby external barriers prevent people with impairments from participating fully in their chosen occupations and in the life of the community. The concept of 'handicap' is rejected entirely (partly because of its demeaning connotations). An early definition of disability proposed by the Union of Physically Impaired Against Segregation (1976 p. 14) described disability as:

> The disadvantage or restriction of ability caused by a contemporary social organisation which takes no or little account of people who have physical impairments and thus excludes them from participation in the mainstream of social activities. Physical disability is therefore a particular form of social oppression.

People who advocate the social model of disability have commented that impairment is not to be seen as individual tragedy. Instead, disability is seen as a form of social oppression, the result of non-disabled people applying unthinking and discriminatory attitudes and policies that curtail the participation of disabled people in mainstream roles and activities (Oliver 1993). Environmental, structural and attitudinal barriers make it harder for disabled people to participate in everyday life. Environmental barriers are very common and restrict access for disabled people (particularly those with mobility problems). For example, escalators may be a convenient way of reaching Underground trains for those who can walk, but this form of access closes the system to wheelchair users. Structural barriers encompass all the hidden and taken-for-granted ways in which organisations, businesses, transport and other systems operate, that prevent disabled people from participating on equal terms. For example, it may not be 'policy' in a business organisation to give out agenda notes in advance of a meeting, even though such a practice would considerably help anyone attending who has a visual impairment or dyslexia. Attitudinal barriers are created by negative social assumptions about disability, including stereotypes, and stigma.

The social model of disability is essentially owned by disabled people and challenges both the narrow focus on physical impairment and the paternalistic treatment policies derived from the biomedical model (Davis 1993). It portrays disabled people as requiring social action rather than individualistic treatments or 'cures'. The social model helped to revolutionise both conceptualisations of health and illness, as well as patients' status within health and social care. It can be seen as another cultural force encouraging the development of collaborative partnerships in the healthcare and rehabilitation process. This perspective also reminds health professionals that the problems of disabled people may be socially or politically imposed rather than issues for which health care or 'rehabilitation' necessarily has an answer. It challenges health professionals to think carefully about the goals of rehabilitation, and any assumptions that they hold about 'normality'.

ACTIVITY Disabling barriers

- Consider some of the disabling barriers (attitudinal, structural or environmental) that Ann may have encountered since developing osteoporosis and a wrist fracture.
- Try to identify some socially imposed restrictions that could make it harder for Ann to regain her previous lifestyle and levels of well-being.

Various structural barriers to equal participation by disabled people seem to be imposed by funding restrictions, which tend to be determined by the politics, values, and priorities of non-disabled people within government and the health and social care services. Poor levels of funding are endemic within rehabilitation services, and entrenched ageism within the NHS can also be disabling because it prevents many people, especially those categorised as 'older', from maximising their recovery from disease or injury (Seymour 1998a). For example, although intensive hand therapy provided by an occupational therapist could make an significant contribution in helping Ann regain her life as an artist and carer of her husband, the treatment may not be available locally. Waiting lists for physiotherapy may be unacceptably long. Prevalent social attitudes towards ageing and dependency can be disabling too (see discussion by Senior and Viveash 1998). Ageist attitudes can also prevent the older patient from participating fully as a respected partner in the decision-making and treatment process. Environmental barriers commonly influence life with a disabling condition. If Ann becomes more limited in her mobility through osteoporosis, she will almost certainly encounter a range of disabling barriers in the environment, such as inaccessible public transport systems, or adult education art classes that are scheduled to meet in upstairs rooms.

Disabled people are not necessarily ill or unhealthy. There is a common semantic confusion among these terms, that can further reinforce 'tragic' interpretations of disability, and encourage patronising attitudes on the part of health professionals. Iezzoni (1998) discusses some of the attitudinal and environmental barriers that she experiences, as a person with multiple sclerosis who uses a wheelchair.

ACTIVITY An autobiographical account of disability

- If you are interested in exploring a person's experiences of impairment, and the impact of disabling social forces, read the article by Iezzoni (1998) which is a full-text paper available through the electronic database MedLine, or in a paper copy of the *Annals of Internal Medicine*. The full reference is given at the end of the book.
- Summarise the disabling barriers that the author describes, and identify some of the strategies that she seems to use to overcome these barriers.

THE NEW ICF

The World Health Organization (2001) proposed a new model, namely the *International Classification of Functioning, Disability and Health*, usually abbreviated to the ICF. The new classification avoids the distinction, criticised in the previous model, between disability and handicap. Rather than portraying disability as a deviation from the norm, the ICF embraces more neutral terminology, seeking to avoid expressions that are demeaning to disabled people. Some, but not all, people in the Disability Movement value this new approach to classifying health and functioning. For example, Hurst (2003) argues that it represents a welcome shift away from the medical model of disability, and that the inclusion of environmental factors will help to create policies, systems and services that are more appropriate for disabled people. On the other hand, Wade and Halligan (2003) argue that the ICF is not person-centred enough, and needs to include more reference to people's own appraisals of their quality of life.

The ICF focuses on the 'barriers and facilitators that have an impact on a person's functioning', rather than on individuals (Schneidert et al 2003). It offers a classification of body structures, functions, activities and participation. Activities relate to tasks and actions such as self-care, mobility and so on, whereas participation relates to roles, community participation, and wider involvement in the social sphere. It is therefore a type of 'biopsychosocial' model, attempting to integrate in a formal way both medical and social perspectives. It recognises that social, environmental and personal factors as well as health conditions affect physical functioning, activity and participation. Some of the personal factors that can influence health and well-being include gender and coping style. Some of the social and contextual factors include support, services, home environment and technology. It can help therapists to work with patients/clients in partnership, to identify their various needs, problems and resources in a detailed, holistic way.

ACTIVITY Applying the ICF to Ann's case

- If you re-read Ann's case study, can you identify some impairments of body structure/function; some activity limitations/restrictions on participation; and some contextual factors that may affect her well-being?
- How might this holistic framework influence your communications with this patient?

(Some suggestions are given at the end of the chapter.)

PUTTING THE PATIENT FIRST: AN HOLISTIC, INTERPROFESSIONAL TEAM APPROACH

Whereas the biomedical model of health care places patients in a rather passive role receiving treatment from health professional experts, the biopsychosocial perspective and the social model have given the individual a more active role as participant in health care services. In tandem with such a radical shift in conceptualising the patient role, recent publications by the Department of Health (2000a, 2000b) have emphasised the need for the health care system to be responsive to patients' needs, by offering prompt, individualised treatment, and inviting patients' involvement in the planning and evaluation of services. In order to place the patient at the centre of the health care system, health professionals need to work together in an integrated, mutually respectful way. Such an approach by health professionals is increasingly advocated within the NHS as necessary to deliver patients a seamless and efficient service (Department of Health 1998a, 1998b, Harbaugh 1994). The biomedical model does not encourage such a degree of interprofessional co-operation.

From the patient's perspective, if professionals communicate with each other effectively, there are fewer repeated consultations, in which to answer the same questions or to receive the same advice. As well as being more convenient for patients, interprofessional working contributes to a more holistic approach to treatment, since the various functional, psychological and social needs of the patient can be more adequately addressed by different professionals. Harbaugh (1994 p. 17) argues: 'Recognising that people are *whole* people – embodied, thinking, feeling, relating and valuing people – the interprofessionally oriented helping professional is less likely to be satisfied with approaches that are aimed at fixing a part of the human problem'. Patients who observe that the professionals attending their care are communicating fully with each other, and share a good understanding of each others' roles, report feeling more secure and confident in their treatment, and more able to express their own opinions and needs (Miller 2001). Despite the advantages, there are many barriers to effective interprofessional team-working and these will be discussed in Chapter 9.

CONCLUSION

This chapter has discussed the biomedical model of health, impairment and disability, noting that it has tended to discourage frank and open communications between patient and health professional. Instead, health professionals within this model are seen as the experts who care for rather helpless patients. The social model, developed and owned by disabled people, emphasises the role of social and environmental barriers to participation in valued activities, and people's right to self-determination regardless of health problems and functional limitations. This model encourages health professionals to challenge any taken-for-granted notions of normality and rehabilitation, and to work towards the disabled person's valued goals. The social model questions the extent to which health and social care professionals should be involved in decision-making on the behalf of disabled people. It has encouraged an empowering approach, and positions disabled people as deserving of choice and control over their use of services, rather than as simply being in receipt of care. The biopsychosocial approach portrays health and illness as having many facets, including the physical, emotional and social. It encourages a person-centred approach to rehabilitation in which the expertise of both health professional and patient are shared, emotional issues raised by illness are acknowledged, and the person's own resources for adapting and coping with illness and impairment are harnessed. Therapists cannot achieve the degree of partnership required unless they adopt a flexible and sensitive approach to communication.

Applying the ICF to Ann: Suggested themes

Impairments in body function/structure
Include asthma and fluctuating respiratory difficulties; osteroporosis; Colles fracture; difficulties in grip and movement of wrist; back pain.

Activity limitation
Currently limited in artwork because of wrist fracture; back pain is affecting participation in artwork; fracture makes it difficult to carry out most activities including household tasks, and driving.

Contextual factors
An already small income is at risk from activity limitations; query level of support given by husband and sons; positive personal attitudes; query security of home environment.
(You could check the WHO (2001) book for the detailed codes that have been devised for specific conditions/problems.)

Implications for communication
The ICF suggests that a wide assessment of the patient is appropriate as her health and well-being are dependent on much more than her physical state. While Ann's personal and contextual factors seem quite favourable, key supports remain unknown. The husband and sons are quite shadowy figures in the case study. The ICF encourages us to find out about whether the people in the home context are supportive, or not. If the husband's own health is fragile, then the wrist fracture may have a serious impact on Ann's caring roles and responsibilities. We do not know whether the home is secure, or whether Ann's loss of income could threaten the loss of her home. The second scenario would have far-reaching effects on Ann's well-being.

Ann appears to be personally resourceful. Her coping strategies may include adapting her style of artwork whilst her wrist heals, or enlisting more help in the studio. The therapist will need to understand the place of art in Ann's life, if her goals are to be addressed appropriately in rehabilitation.

These many issues may be more appropriately addressed by several health professionals, but they will have to liase effectively if they are to share the information collected.

The case study illustrates that there is no 'routine' Colles fracture. Each person undergoing rehabilitation is unique in terms of personal characteristics and context, even when sharing the same medical diagnosis, and therapists' strategies of communication need to be flexible in response.

Further Reading

Iezzoni L 1998 What should I say? Communication around disability. Annals of Internal Medicine 129(8):661–665

This article is available in full-text format via MEDLINE.

Swain J, Finkelstein V, French S et al (eds) 1993 Disabling barriers – enabling environments. Sage, London

This classic book applies the social model to disability issues.

Chapter 3

Understanding patients' experiences of ill-health and health care

This chapter explores the diversity of people's experiences of ill-health and health care, through case examples, reflective exercises and research findings. As a health professional, you will need to develop empathy for the patient's perspective in order to take a collaborative, patient-centred approach to communication. The material presented will help you to regard each patient as an individual, rather than as a 'condition'. The aim of the chapter is to increase your sensitivity to the many stressful aspects of the illness experience, and to challenge certain stereotypes. Such insights will help you communicate more effectively with your patients. In this chapter, the following issues will be examined:

- Understanding illness from a stress-coping perspective
- Understanding illness as a biographical disruption
- Treatment and hospitalisation from the patient's perspective
- Some factors that influence a person's response to illness
- The illness experience: positive aspects amidst adversity.

ACTIVITY Adapting to multiple sclerosis

The following extract is taken from an interview with a young mother who has multiple sclerosis. She has some of the common problems associated with this chronic disease, including difficulties in walking, profound fatigue, and muscle pain.

• When you read her account, try to identify some of the other difficulties that she is confronting as a person with MS, and the coping strategies that she is using.

'Sometimes I am frightened about the disease and I have to get used to that and I have to make sure that I can continue to hold a family together and plan for a future ... I used to study but it got too painful sitting at the desk, so I have held back for a bit. But I'm thinking of volunteering to go down to a local school and do some reading with the children. Otherwise, you start thinking that you are a worthless sort of person and you are not doing anything that other people see as worthwhile. I had a big problem, thinking OK, I haven't got a lot of monetary value at the moment. I'm not completing my degree at the moment. Maybe people look at me and think that I am a failure. And I started to think maybe I was ... I think I was trying to take on too much at once. You can't judge yourself how you used to be before, how you look at other people and think they are doing this and that. What I am trying to learn is you get up in the morning and check how you are feeling. ... Maybe I can't decorate the room today, but maybe I could put a bunch of flowers in a vase so when the kids come home, the place can look beautiful and they will be happy to be here ... You can change and adapt a bit but that is something which is quite hard to do.'

UNDERSTANDING THE EXPERIENCE OF CHRONIC ILLNESS: SOME GENERAL ISSUES

As argued in the previous chapter, the biomedical model of illness applies quite well to acute illness. In short-term conditions, both health professionals and patients tend to focus on diagnosis, treatment, and the prospect of recovery. Although the health problem may be associated with a number of inconveniences, many patients cope well with these because they are essentially short-lived. However, long-term, or chronic, illness presents a wider array of intertwined experiences. These can be grouped as:

• Sensory (including symptoms such as pain and fatigue)
• Emotional (including anxiety, low mood, relief at gaining a diagnosis)
• Cognitive (such as worried thoughts, dwelling on worst case scenarios, comparing self negatively with others)
• Behavioural (for example, functional limitations, difficulties in ADL (activities of daily living, problems with mobility and balance, changes in sleep patterns)

- Social (such as role change from being a care-giver in the family to a recipient of care; encountering social stigma and discrimination)
- Self/identity (for example, altered self-image, changes in self-esteem)
- Moral (possible experience of shame and 'worthlessness', alienation, devaluation).

You might have noted some of these difficulties in your analysis of the interview extract above. Of course, whether or not an individual encounters these different experiences depends to some extent upon the person's own value systems, dispositions and coping strategies. However, social and cultural factors also influence the illness experience. For example, certain illnesses (such as HIV/AIDS) carry a greater social stigma within some cultures, perhaps marking the individual as blameworthy, and leading to ostracism (as noted in a study by Santana and Dancy 2000).

It is also important to recognise the heavy burden of suffering that many conditions impose (Charmaz 1999, Frank 2001). For example, severe pain, incontinence and mobility problems may provoke feelings of desperation and even thoughts about suicide. In addition, such difficulties and distress can permeate and undermine close social relationships. For example, some of the interviewees in a study carried out by Seers and Friedli (1996) described how their chronic pain had led to anger, intolerance and distancing within the family. Some feel obliged to protect their families from the worry of their illness. For example, a woman who had received treatment for breast cancer explained:

> That was a horrendous year, mastectomy, chemotherapy, radiotherapy. After months of treatment, I was feeling really battered. I'd still got three kids at home, old enough in some ways to be helpful, but in other ways I needed to protect them a bit. I wanted them to feel that their mum was riding above this. My husband was away a lot ... he couldn't talk about it that much anyway.

Clearly, health professionals need to be mindful of the enormous difficulties that some people (and their families) are facing in living with a chronic condition.

Nevertheless, while long-term illness can have a highly negative impact on life, there is evidence that some people construe its effects more positively. For example, although illness can bring about conflict and stress in personal relationships, some people also report that their relationships become more honest, open and supportive (Lyons et al 1995). Mohr et al (1999) found that some of their interviewees with multiple sclerosis described finding benefits within the illness experience, such as deepened social relationships, increasing spirituality and an enhanced appreciation of life. Such positive interpretations of the illness experience will be returned to later in this chapter.

Long-term illness creates many problems apart from functional limitations. Yet the biomedical perspective tends to overlook these, leading to a restricted focus within treatment, as emphasised by Kleinman (1988):

When chest pain can be reduced to a treatable acute lobar pneumonia, … biological reductionism is an enormous success. When chest pain is reduced to chronic coronary artery disease for which calcium blockers and nitroglycerine are prescribed, while the patient's fear, the family's frustration, the job conflict, the sexual impotence, and the financial crisis go undiagnosed and unaddressed, it is a failure (p. 6).

Since Kleinman's seminal work, a number of research studies have examined the wide-ranging effects of illness on people's lives. For example, Seymour W (1998) interviewed people with spinal cord injuries (and other pathologies causing paralysis) about their everyday lives and adjustment.

ACTIVITY The experience of spinal cord injury

- Before reading on, reflect on some of the ways in which spinal cord injury is likely to affect a person's life.
- Compare your list with the problems that Seymour's interviewees disclosed (outlined below).
- Which problems have you anticipated? Which problems surprise you?

Seymour (1998) described her interviewees' problems with mobility, access to the outside environment and incontinence. These probably represent the challenges that readers are most likely to anticipate resulting from spinal cord injury. People who are unfamiliar with the effects of spinal cord injury may be less aware of difficulties associated with expression of sexuality, changing roles, parenting, and altered body image (including loss of abdominal tone and restricted choice of clothing and footwear). Many also described barriers to work and other occupations, created not so much by their functional limitations but by the negative and stereotyped attitudes of others. Interviewees reported that health professionals sometimes focused too much on teaching a narrow range of skills for recovering independence, and overlooked their need to learn how to re-engage with their most valued pre-injury roles. One woman explained:

Obviously part of the rehabilitation process was to get me home … but it was very much an occupational therapy model of how I was going to manage stairs and how I was going to get to and from the bathroom. But never how was I going to manage to look after my baby. (Seymour, 1998: p. 71).

ACTIVITY Failure to agree on rehabilitation goals

The quotation above indicates that the rehabilitation process failed to address the patient's most valued goal, namely to look after her baby.
- Can you suggest some reasons why the health professionals concerned were apparently unaware of their patient's needs and goals?

UNDERSTANDING THE ILLNESS EXPERIENCE: ANALYSING A SPECIFIC CASE

ACTIVITY Analysing the different aspects of the illness experience

- Look again at the case study Ann, presented in Chapter 2, and identify as many different psychological and social aspects of Ann's illness as you can.

As indicated in the previous chapter, a variety of personal, contextual and physical issues are relevant to the experience of illness. The physical health problems described in the case example are quite common, but the issues that therapists would need to communicate about with Ann are far from 'routine'.

To give one example, osteoporosis affects large numbers of people. It particularly affects post-menopausal women, as reduced levels of oestrogen seem to be implicated in the loss of calcium from the bones. Bones are not solid objects but have a honeycomb structure inside, providing strength without excessive weight. In osteoporosis, there is a loss of this honeycomb structure, which increases the risk of fracture. Long-term use of steroid medication can contribute to bone loss. While this condition is statistically common, affecting about a third of women over 65 years, it presents a unique range of problems for each person who develops it (Lane et al 2000). Likewise, Colles fracture of the wrist is regularly treated in Accident and Emergency departments and health professionals may consider it to be relatively unproblematic.

Each patient is affected differently by long-term illness. In Ann's case, consider the personal implications of osteoporosis and wrist fracture. If she uses her right hand in her artwork, she may be very fearful of not making a full recovery. Any restriction in wrist movement may signify the end of her professional career as an artist. This poses risks for her familiar identity, her quality of life (recall that she described feeling most 'alive' when drawing), and, of course, her income. If her income falls, she may suffer additional restrictions on her activities during retirement. She may even fear losing her home. The fracture and diagnosis of osteoporosis may create additional uncertainty and anxiety about the future. Ann may fear the worsening of her condition over time, and further mobility problems should other fractures occur. After her fall, the world may not seem such a safe and secure place, and such fears may restrict her normal lifestyle (Hellstrom & Lindmark 1999, Reece & Simpson 1996). Pain may seem intractable, interrupting her artistic and domestic occupations, and reducing her sense of control over her life. We are told little about Ann's social circle, except that Ann's husband is considerably older. She may be anxious that her asthma and osteoporosis together will prevent her from looking after her husband should he become frail. If she has artist friends with whom she shares discussion of design or technique, any loss of professional identity may result in her feeling like a stranger in her social circle.

UNDERSTANDING ILLNESS FROM A STRESS-COPING PERSPECTIVE

Even mild acute illnesses can be stressful. In other words, the illness experience, in all of its physical, psychological and social aspects, is noxious, unwanted and inconvenient.

ACTIVITY Personal reflection on illness

- Consider the last minor illness or injury that you experienced, and identify some of the stressful aspects of this episode.

Insight into the illness experience has been enhanced through applying a stress-coping perspective. A popular framework for psychological research into stress is the transactional theory put forward by Lazarus and Folkman (1984). These authors argue that some events are not necessarily inherently stressful in themselves. Rather, the level of stress reflects our personal interpretation of the event. In order to understand the stressfulness of an illness, we need to appreciate how threatening the diagnosis or symptoms are for the person, the extent to which the illness intrudes into valued activities, and whether the person believes he/she has sufficient skills and resources to cope. We also need to acknowledge the influence of the context, including the amount of practical and emotional support that is available. A 'similar' diagnosis can therefore have different meanings for different individuals.

A good illustration is given by the research of Donovan and Blake (2000). These researchers carried out an interview study exploring patients' experiences of consultations with doctors at a rheumatology clinic, and their satisfaction with any reassurances that their doctor had given. One participant, who had witnessed her son suffering severe pain and functional limitation from rheumatoid arthritis, was very anxious on receiving the diagnosis herself. She readily imagined the havoc that the disease could cause her in the future. Although not discussed explicitly in this study, it seems likely that other patients who lacked this direct experience of arthritis in a relative would be less likely to consider 'worst case scenarios'. Some patients appeared much more readily comforted by the doctor's assurance that their disease was mild and under control. People with similar diagnosed conditions also vary widely in their beliefs about the effectiveness of medication, and in their estimations about the degree to which their self-image will be affected. They also differ in their readiness to confide their difficulties with others (Bath et al 1999).

ACTIVITY Evaluating a research article

The article by Bath et al (1999) is available as a full-text version in the electronic database CINAHL. It is a short paper based on interviews with people who have rheumatoid arthritis (RA).
- For this activity, access this article and summarise the various stressful experiences that accompany RA.
- Are any of the problems that the patients describe surprising to you?.
- Do you think that the problems described by these participants can be generalised?
(If you cannot gain access to this paper, some of the themes are summarised at the end of the chapter).

People's experiences of illness differ according to their values, interests, social support and many other variables. Their age and developmental stage may also influence the meanings of ill-health. Some children and adolescents who have lived with a chronic condition all of their lives appear stoical, regarding their health as 'normal' for them, and not wishing to be seen as a special case by their teachers and friends (Admi 1996). For others, the normal developmental changes in adolescence, such as awakening sexuality and growing need for independence, make chronic illness especially problematic.

ACTIVITY Jane: an adolescent with juvenile chronic arthritis

- Read the case study below, and consider what aspects of arthritis appear to be stressful for Jane.

Jane is 16 years old and has had juvenile chronic arthritis (JCA) since she was eight years old. She experiences stiffness and pain in her joints, particularly in her hips and knees, and also suffers from high levels of fatigue. At school, she often has difficulties on stairs, and rarely attends physical education lessons (P.E.). She has tried hard to keep up with her school-work, but fatigue has often curtailed her homework, and undermined her preparation for examinations. Her academic progress is somewhat below average. Perhaps because her condition makes physical activity difficult, Jane is rather overweight, and she is self-conscious about this. Jane would like to do a nursery nurse course at a college of further education, but she is concerned that flares in her condition will jeopardise her progress. She fears that her JCA may make it difficult for her to perform essential aspects of the nursing role such as holding infants safely. She is becoming increasingly moody at home, and uncooperative at school. Her mother is concerned that recently she seems to be more withdrawn. She rarely invites friends to the house any more.

While you need to be mindful that Jane's own view may be different, it is likely that you have identified a wide range of potential stressors in the brief case example:

- Pain
- Mobility problems
- Fatigue
- Uncertainty – associated with flares and periods of quiescence in the condition
- Limited participation in activities, including physical exercise
- Weight and self-image
- Limited choices (e.g. over college course; over time and effort that can be given to school-work; over the possibility and choice of a career)
- Sense of difference from peers, and fear of possible rejection.

These examples illustrate how illness typically presents each person with a diverse, possibly unique, set of stressors. Illness tends to take away control and choice. In chronic conditions, the person confronts a long-term process of adjustment and coping with the impact of the illness on lifestyle.

In the transactional model of stress developed by Lazarus and Folkman (1984), the degree of stress is not only determined by people's interpretations of the 'dangers' or threats inherent in the illness (or other adverse event) but by their appraisals of their coping resources. People tend to ask themselves whether their coping strategies are equal to the stressors that they are facing. Some people have confidence in their coping ability, perhaps because they have successfully dealt with a similar problem in the past, or because they have acquired skills from someone else who is successfully managing the problem. For example, a person newly diagnosed with MS may feel more confident about their own coping strategies if they have a friend or relative with the illness who is living a satisfactory lifestyle. Another person may be severely depressed by the prospect of a worsening illness. Coping resources also include social support and information. People with high levels of emotional and practical support appear to cope more positively with illness. Conversely, those living in an isolated or critical social context may encounter more difficulties in managing their illness (Manne & Zautra 1989). The transactional perspective on coping reminds us that people cope with medically similar illnesses in different ways, depending on their personal appraisal of the illness and their coping resources, including social support.

The stress-coping model proposes that people cope with stress through two major sets of strategies. Problem-focused strategies attempt to diminish the stressful nature of the event directly, whereas emotion-focused strategies seek to moderate personal responses to the stress. Problem-focused strategies for illness may include seeking medical help, practising exercises to recover physical function, and using appropriate aids and adaptations that enable participation in valued activities. Emotion-focused responses include venting anger, expressing anxiety, suppressing emotion through alcohol and other drugs, and seeking emotional support. Expressive emotion-focused strategies seem to be more useful than suppressive strategies. Some further examples are given later, when individual differences in the illness experience are considered in more detail. A number of studies suggest that the long-term use of emotion-focused strategies is associated with greater depression and activity restriction. For example, Pakenham (1999) found that certain emotion-focused strategies for dealing with multiple sclerosis, such as self-blame, avoidance, and wishful thinking, were maladaptive and associated with higher levels of distress.

UNDERSTANDING ILLNESS AS A BIOGRAPHICAL DISRUPTION

A sociological perspective has also enhanced understanding of the illness experience. In 1982, Bury suggested that illness should be regarded as a biographical disruption. Biography is essentially the person's life story. This includes not only an account of the past, and descriptions of personal characteristics and social roles. It also includes an imagined future. For example, some readers may aspire to become a parent, a senior practitioner or a marathon runner in the future. If serious illness and injury intervene, such plans and dreams are threatened, the self-image may be undermined, and the future then seems at best uncertain, and at worst hopeless (see Brock and Kleiber 1994, for one illustration).

Serious illness or injury, particularly if recovery is uncertain, casts us into an unfamiliar world, with new rules, and constraints. A person who has previously taken for granted a high level of control over daily life is likely to resent having their lifestyle choices, such as travel and employment, restricted by illness. Roles that were once valued may be difficult to perform, and previous aspirations may appear completely unattainable. For example, survivors of spinal cord injury face massive challenges, not only in their physical functioning, but also in their very sense of self. Men who have had a spinal injury often report feeling emasculated. Indeed, when a person is strongly committed to sports or athletics, any serious injury or illness may result in a prolonged challenge to the person's sense of self (Sparkes 1998). Even changes in style of clothing, resulting from hospital practices or the nature of the functional impairment, may threaten a person's identity. Bauby (1998) described his experience of 'locked-in' syndrome, a devastating condition resulting from a stroke in the brainstem that robbed him of almost all movement. In such a situation, one might think that choice of clothes had no relevance at all. Yet through wearing his own clothes rather than hospital attire, he felt more like his familiar self:

> Having turned down the hideous jogging-suit provided by the hospital, I am now attired as I was in my student days ... my old clothes could easily bring back poignant, painful memories. But I see in the clothes a symbol of continuing life. And proof that I still want to be myself (p. 25).

A recent study of stroke survivors confirms this view of stroke as threatening identity (Ellis-Hill & Horn 2000). Following stroke, the participants described themselves as having changed in a number of negative ways, regarding themselves as being less capable, less independent, less in control, less confident and of less value. Robinson (1990) analysed written narratives sent by people with multiple sclerosis, in which they described their experiences of living with illness. He inferred from these accounts that people with multiple sclerosis faced the task of integrating their illness into their self-image, and with extracting some positive meaning from the experience. Jensen and Allen (1994) offer a similar argument based on their review of a range of qualitative studies into the experience of illness. They suggest that people confront a key challenge when ill of re-defining their roles, goals and ultimately, their identity. Not all health professionals are aware of the ways in which long-term illness undermine people's fundamental sense of self.

Many health practitioners work in specialist units where, for them, the treated condition is a regular and unremarkable occurrence. In a large

---

ACTIVITY Further analysis of case studies

- Consider the two brief case examples below, and also re-read the description of Jane (above) who has juvenile chronic arthritis.
- Can you find three problems that these people share as a result of having an arthritis condition?
- Can you identify one or two ways in which their experiences of living with arthritis are different?

Charles Davis is 63 years old, and married with a grown-up daughter, and two grandchildren. He is approaching retirement as a managing director of a small business. In his spare time, he enjoys golf and he often goes to Spain for weekend golfing breaks. He also enjoys looking after his grandchildren on some of the weekends that he is at home with his wife. In the past year, he has developed noticeable symptoms of osteo-arthritis and is experiencing increasing pain in his knees and feet. His pain and mobility problems are beginning to make travel to work difficult, and his concentration at work is affected. He has not played golf for some months and misses his male golfing friends. He is concerned about whether he will need to take early retirement and how this will affect his pension, and his plans for an active retirement.

Meena Patel is a 56-year-old widow, with two sons of 17 and 18 years. She has osteoarthritis that is particularly affecting joints in the right hand. She is right-hand dominant. She first noticed mild symptoms five years ago, but now has pain more or less continuously, such that it is beginning to interfere with her ability to manage her work and her daily personal and home activities. Meena works as the head chef for a large company, running the staff restaurant. Her work involves a considerable amount of cooking, together with supervision of other chefs and kitchen assistants. She is having increasing difficulty with managing heavy containers with safety. Her symptoms are greatly aggravated at the end of the working day, such that the pain lasts all evening and is sometimes severe enough to disturb her sleep. Meena loves her job and is adamant that she will continue to work so that she can support her sons financially through university.

Accident and Emergency department for example, at least one elderly person will be treated for a stroke every day. In a rheumatology clinic, staff will assess and treat many patients who have rheumatoid arthritis. For this reason, the staff may gradually come to regard a condition as 'routine'. The patient will almost certainly not share this view. For example, a patient with rheumatoid arthritis, quoted by Donovan and Blake (2000), said:

> … I think that the doctor understands my problems, but they're not that dramatic to him. They are to me because I'm the one who is suffering. He doesn't think it's as desperate as I think it is. He thinks, 'you've got arthritis like millions of others'. But I've got to live with it … (p. 543).

Clearly, the people in these three case studies share problems that are typical of arthritis, namely pain, mobility limitations, and difficulties in everyday activities. They also experience uncertainty about the future. All experience some loss of choice (for example, over career options, or retirement date). However, even in these brief extracts, it is clear that the three individuals are facing some distinctive concerns. Illness for each person is experienced in distinct social contexts and has different effects on quality of life. Meena may be particularly concerned about her role as provider for her family, and her ability to support her sons through higher education. Her sense of herself as being a good mother, encouraging her sons to have high career aspirations, is under threat. Her deteriorating condition is also resulting in a physical inability to perform certain tasks at work. However, because of her senior position in the company, she may be able to delegate and thereby continue in her job. Charles may be concerned that his arthritis is making him a liability in his company, rather than an asset. He is used to having a high occupational status, and an income that enables him to pay for golf and other leisure activities. He also enjoys a wide social circle, based on his sporting interests. Since the appearance of his illness, these may all seem to him to be in great jeopardy. He may also be concerned that his role as a vigorous and lively grandfather is also under threat from his illness. Perhaps he experiences his relationships with his grandchildren (and his daughter) as changing. Jane, as discussed previously, is facing difficult academic and career choices, at a critical point in her development. She is reacting with moodiness to these problems. She also has problems with weight and self-consciousness, which are not easy to cope with for any adolescent in a Western culture. She seems to be reacting negatively to her sense of 'difference' from her peers at school.

Therapists also need to be aware that illness presents more than a disruption to an *individual's* biography. Through its effects on social roles and relationships, the disruptions ripple out through the family and social circle. For example, Charles' wife may also be extremely anxious about the future, and his daughter may miss his supportive care-giving to the grandchildren. If partners and family members are anxious and unsupported, they find it more difficult to help the person come to terms with their condition (Theobald 1997).

TREATMENT AND HOSPITALISATION FROM THE PATIENT'S PERSPECTIVE

In addition to the stress of illness itself, treatment and hospitalisation present further challenges. While entry into hospital can be greeted with relief and with an expectation of effective treatment, experiences such as staying away from home, medical investigations and invasive treatments may also be very stressful. Nichols (1995) has identified a number of stressful aspects of the hospital experience.

ACTIVITY Personal reflection on hospitalisation

- If you have had any direct experience of staying in hospital, or have visited friends or relatives in hospital, reflect on aspects of the hospital experience that can be stressful and disruptive to a patient's identity and sense of well-being.

Nichols (1995) has argued that many aspects of hospitalisation disrupt identity and well-being through encouraging passivity and helplessness on the part of patients. The institutional environment can all too easily strip a person of dignity. For example, patients may be distressed by the lack of control over their physical environment (Niven 1994). Staff may underestimate the patient's level of pain and provide inadequate pain relief (Hall-Lord et al 1998). Hospitals challenge dignity in multiple ways (for example, through requiring patients to wear nightwear during the day, or even worse, a hospital gown with a non-fastening back). Lack of privacy can also increase the stress of illness. Ward consultations are far from private even if held behind screened curtains. Patients from minority ethnic backgrounds (in particular) may find food and bathing facilities unsatisfactory. Excessive noise, especially during the night, can prevent sleep and this, in turn, can delay the healing process (Southwell & Wistow 1995). Some hospitals continue to have mixed sex wards, which can increase embarrassment, especially to patients who are facing stigmatising changes to their appearance or physical functioning. Any stay away from home can be stressful. Stress can increase if people are concerned about the adequacy of care available to family or pets at home, or about work responsibilities that are piling up in their absence.

Certain groups of patients may find the hospital environment particularly stressful. These include:

- People who have been admitted as emergency cases (without warning or preparation – such as people in road traffic accidents or suffering from stroke).
- People who have had traumatic experiences prior to admission (such as victims of violent assault).
- People with cognitive problems (associated with learning difficulties, dementia, or brain injury).

- Children, particularly those who are too young to understand what is happening to them, who have not been separated from parents before, or who are in pain.

Time to prepare oneself (e.g. for treatment such as surgery) and to make arrangements for the care of family and pets usually helps to reduce the stressfulness of hospital admission. However, health professionals need to be mindful of the difficulty in coping with hospitalisation if admission comes without warning. Difficulties such as not having the correct spectacles or a contact lens case may seem minor to staff, but are magnified in importance for a person already dealing with a major disjunction in his or her daily routine, as well as pain and uncertainty. Health professionals also need to be mindful of the patient's experience prior to admission. A hip fracture may seem a relatively 'straightforward' condition to treat from the health professional's perspective. However, it will seem far from routine to an elderly person who has fallen far from the reach of a telephone, and then become frightened and cold, unable to contact help for hours. People with cognitive problems can often function satisfactorily in their familiar home environment but are prone to becoming disoriented and anxious in the new setting of a hospital. Any difficulties in understanding the purpose of their stay or treatment are also likely to add to their burden of stress. Children tend to find hospitals stressful to the extent that they are subject to treatments, especially painful procedures, about which they have little understanding. Separation from parents is also likely to increase anxiety.

For day-case patients, and those attending therapy as out-patients, there are a variety of stresses including long waiting times, fear of the unknown, loss of income from having time off work, and inconvenient travel arrangements (Otte 1996). Pain associated with certain interventions may be a source of stress for some, as may the experience of being assessed and evaluated. Nevertheless, many patients express much satisfaction with such services, perceiving them as vital to achieving the maximum possible recovery. Therapists, nurses and medical staff can do much to alleviate the stress of hospitalisation and rehabilitation, through strategies such as appropriate information-giving (Nichols 1995). These strategies will receive further attention in later chapters.

SOME PERSONAL AND CONTEXTUAL FACTORS WHICH INFLUENCE PEOPLE'S RESPONSES TO ILLNESS

Individuals respond to and cope with illness and injury with a wide array of strategies, as documented by the growing research literature in this field. What is meant by 'coping' with illness? Coping refers to any action that is taken to deal with and minimise harm or threat. Coping with illness involves not only managing physical symptoms and dysfunction, but also the wider psychological, social and financial changes that often accompany illness (especially long-term illness). Although personal responses to illness seem at first sight to be a matter for the individual, it may be more productive to view coping as dependent upon a large set of interacting factors, comprising:

- Person variables
- Illness symptomatology
- Perceived treatment availability and effectiveness
- Social context
- Culture
- Environmental resources.

PERSON VARIABLES

People respond in very diverse ways to illness. Some responses are deliberate and controlled, but others are not. Furthermore, some responses are adaptive and contribute to quality of life while others have negative repercussions. In part, this diversity of responses reflects the varying personalities, needs, skills and vulnerabilities of different individuals. However, financial and social support resources are also relevant. Furthermore, cultural influences shape attitudes towards dependence, roles and obligations. All of these social and environmental variables shape a person's ways of coping with illness and injury.

ACTIVITY Personal reflection on coping with illness

- Consider your own personal responses to illness by reviewing how you deal with having a heavy cold (including symptoms such as having a sore throat, headache and blocked nose).
- Do you manage the symptoms by using over-the-counter medications, extra sleep, by taking time off from work or study, or by other strategies?
- Do you find yourself worrying about the meaning of sensations (such as headache)? Or do you usually minimise their significance?
- Is your attitude one of 'doing battle' with your cold? Or 'giving in'?
- Do you attempt to perform all of your daily activities in the 'normal' way, or do you take time out?
- What do you think influences your style of managing a respiratory infection?
- If possible, compare your reflections with those of another person, to identify ways in which your responses to a common illness are similar – or different.

Individual dispositions and attitudes

It appears that coping strategies may reflect long-standing personality traits, attitudes and learned habits. In particular, dispositions such as hardiness (Wallston 1989), sense of coherence (Antonovsky 1990) and self-efficacy (Holahan et al 1996) appear to help people cope positively with illness, and other adverse events. These variously named dispositions all tend to be associated with a strong sense of control, meaningfulness, optimism, and resistance to highly negative (or 'catastrophic') thoughts. There is abundant evidence that patients who fall prey to negative thinking, tend to be more depressed and tend to fare less well in coping with illness and rehabilitation. For example, Keefe et al (1989) showed that high levels of catastrophic thinking among people with rheumatoid arthritis was highly predictive of poorer rehabilitation outcomes one year later, and greater levels of impairment, even when other significant variables were controlled for. Conversely, optimism and a combative attitude seem on balance to promote increased well-being and adherence to treatment (e.g. Abbott et al 2001). In addition to general control beliefs, research suggests that patients' confidence in their ability to perform specific actions (self-efficacy) may be even more predictive of successful coping. For example, Bennett et al (1999) studied patients treated for a first myocardial infarction (heart attack). Those who had low self-efficacy concerning their ability to carry out exercise, and negative beliefs about the health benefits of exercise, were less likely to adopt health-promoting diet and exercise patterns in the subsequent three months. Beliefs in the possibility of personal control and influence over the course of illness appear to motivate coping and behavioural adaptation. On the negative side, for certain intractable illnesses, strong beliefs in control may at times give rise to frustration and self-blame.

Philosophical/spiritual/religious values

Finding meaning in adversity is an enormous resource for coping with stress, and for achieving a better quality of life. Antonovsky (1990) argues that people with a strong sense of coherence are more likely to find such meaning. Strong religious or spiritual values also help to provide people with a sense of hope and purpose, as well as enhancing their experience of emotional support during serious illness (Pargament 1997). Religious commitment appears to help people manage stress, resist depression, adjust to disability, and recover from surgery (Post et al 2000). In addition to religion, interests in philosophical or cosmological issues can also sustain a person through serious, life-threatening illness and provide a sense of self-transcendence (Do Rozario 1997). It is important for physiotherapists and occupational therapists to consider how they respond to patients who have religious or philosophical beliefs differing from their own. Post, Puchalski and Larsson (2000) put forward a number of suggestions that can help therapists convey respect for patients' beliefs without disowning their own personal beliefs.

Humour

Some patients cope with exceedingly difficult lives through humour. For example, several participants with degenerative amyotrophic lateral sclerosis (a disease of the motor system) referred to the importance of humour (Young & McNicoll 1998). Reeves et al (1999) noted how many people coping with HIV infection used humour. Perhaps for some people, humour is a customary way of gaining distance from stressful situations, including illness. Much further research is needed to understand the roots and benefits of this coping response.

Emotional vulnerability

Emotional vulnerability seems to account for some of the differences in people's responses to illness. High levels of anxiety and depression make illness particularly difficult to cope with, as does having an external locus of control (believing that external factors govern one's health, and that health is little influenced by personal actions). Some people appear to find the prospect of ill-health so anxiety-provoking that they deny the severity of symptoms, consequently delaying medical and other consultations. Denial can also lead to misperception of the information that health professionals provide concerning the diagnosis and illness. As these avoidant strategies appear to protect the person from overwhelming anxiety, they may be helpful in the short-term (Davidhizar & Giger 1998). However, prolonged denial may prevent the person from gaining access to effective treatment. It may also prevent family and friends from offering emotional and practical help. Some authors have suggested that the cognitive and emotional acceptance of illness improves self-management, whereas denial and avoidance behaviour are associated with poor treatment compliance (e.g. Abbott et al 2001). Acceptance and denial have an important role to play in influencing coping strategies.

Coping strategies

Individual differences in coping strategies have been discussed previously. The use of problem-focused strategies seems to require at least a measure of acceptance about illness. Then, for example, the person may seek information about the condition, evaluate advice about treatment options, and consider possible aids and adaptations. They may be more likely to practise recommended physiotherapy exercises regularly, and develop personal self-management strategies on the basis of what seems most effective, for example in relieving pain. (See Hammond 1998, for one discussion of self-management strategies in rheumatoid arthritis.)

Emotion-focused strategies include crying, becoming angry, using black humour and distraction. Some studies have shown that exclusive reliance on emotion-focused strategies for coping with illness is associated with negative emotional states such as anxiety and depression (Pakenham 1999). However, it is also important to recognise that emotional expression, especially during the early stages of illness, or during periods when symptoms worsen, may also be cathartic, permitting a healthy grief response. In grieving, the patient may go through a number of stages including denial, sadness, anger, bargaining, and acceptance. These do not necessarily follow in sequence, nor is acceptance necessarily achieved. Instead, it may be more realistic, as

Worden (1986) argues, to see grief as a complex emotional, cognitive and behavioural process of coming to terms with loss, enabling the person to move on with life.

Having a rich repertoire of coping strategies seems to promote greater well-being during chronic conditions, such as chronic pain (Haerkaepaeae et al 1996). However, rapid changes and instability in coping strategies may reflect greater emotional distress or desperation about a health problem (Schwartz & Daltroy 1999).

Maladaptive responses

People seem to use similar coping strategies for illness as they do to manage other stresses in their lives. For example, those who cope with stress in their lives through mind-altering medication (such as alcohol or illegal drugs) are particularly susceptible to coping with illness in the same way (Holahan et al 2001). Over-use of drugs can directly damage health, and may prevent the person from devising more adaptive problem-solving strategies. Other maladaptive strategies may include poor self-care (such as harmful eating or sleeping patterns), compulsive seeking of second opinions about the diagnosis and treatment, and not adhering to treatment recommendations. Patients sometimes report taking out their anger about their condition on their family, jeopardising family relationships and support (e.g. Seers & Friedli 1996).

ILLNESS SYMPTOMATOLOGY

Severe, intense or worrying symptoms present a particular challenge to a person's coping resources, because these symptoms intrude into everyday life, dismantle the person's familiar sense of self, and threaten the future. Illness can impose great suffering, through for example, intractable pain, disfigurement, and incontinence. Patients who regard their illness as uncontrollable and their treatment options as ineffective, not surprisingly may sink into profound helplessness, and become too demoralised to comply with treatment regimes. Some of the people with fibromyalgia pain and fatigue interviewed by Mannerkorpi et al (1999) described how they felt overwhelmed by their illness symptoms and unable to control their impact.

Intrusive illnesses also readily affect the person's sense of self as they permeate everyday activities and cannot easily be hidden from the view of others (Mullins et al 2001). Such conditions can also lead to shame and embarrassment. Negative judgements from others make it difficult for the person to maintain a positive attitude, or adopt self-management strategies.

General accounts of illness cannot convey the unique challenges posed by different diseases, such as multiple sclerosis, muscular dystrophy, diabetes, emphysema and arthritis. Therapists need to acquaint themselves with the different symptoms that their patients are confronting if they are to communicate with sufficient empathy. Broome and Llewelyn (1995) provide a number of helpful chapters exploring the psychological issues posed by a range of different health problems.

TREATMENT AVAILABILITY AND PERCEIVED EFFECTIVENESS

Perceived treatment availability and effectiveness also influence people's response to illness. When a condition is readily treatable, the person will have less concern that it is going to intrude forever into his or her life. Such confidence in treatment effectiveness improves commitment to treatment and behavioural adaptation. However, people do not always appreciate the evidence on which treatment effectiveness is judged. Adherence is often poor with treatments for illnesses that are relatively 'symptom-free' (such as high blood pressure), partly because the need for treatment is less obvious. Some patients interpret their symptoms in catastrophic terms and therefore find it difficult to believe that their treatment will be effective. Such doubts also seem to reduce adherence to the recommendations of therapists and medical staff (Horne 1997). In illustration, Petrie et al (1996) found that patients' attendance at cardiac rehabilitation was much poorer if they had negative beliefs about treatment effectiveness. Those believing initially that their heart attack was going to have major long-term consequences, and that treatment would have limited effectiveness, also tended to have more activity restrictions when followed up three and six months later. Patients who were initially optimistic about their prospects of recovery tended to return to work earlier. These outcomes were not simply accounted for by initial differences in the severity of the infarction. The findings indicated a profound role for individual beliefs about illness and treatment effectiveness in the recovery process. To maximise patients' co-operation, therapists need to provide careful explanation about the purpose and appropriateness of treatment. These issues will receive further examination in Chapter 8.

SOCIAL CONTEXT

Coping strategies and lifestyle choices do not simply reflect individual character traits (Maes et al 1996). People with high levels of practical and emotional support are more likely to resist depression and to adhere to treatment. Conversely, those living in an emotionally fraught or critical family context seem to cope less well, for example with rheumatoid arthritis (RA) (Manne & Zautra 1989). People enjoying a wider social network also tend to have more diverse social roles, obligations and rewards (e.g. as colleague, friend, brother etc). This diversity may be protective of well-being.

The social context can also have negative effects, limiting the person's effective self-management of illness through reinforcing the sick role. Parsons (1975) argued that the 'sick role' was a socially validated way of enabling people who were ill to abdicate their responsibilities for a period of time whilst they recovered their health (see discussion in Senior and Viveash 1998). However, if family members take over all of the responsibilities of a person (for example, someone who is suffering chronic pain), they may unwittingly reinforce the person's passivity. Even if the pain eventually subsides or becomes more manageable, the sick role behaviour is likely to continue, as it has been learned and rewarded over time. This process can lead the patient into an increasingly constricted, unsatisfying lifestyle, in which illness symptoms continue to be the main focus of attention.

CULTURAL FACTORS

Illnesses pose different challenges and elicit different responses depending on the value system of the culture in which a person lives. Some illnesses, such as HIV/AIDS, are more stigmatised in some cultures than others. Heckman et al (1998) compared the experience of people with HIV infection living in urban and rural areas of the US. They found that rural dwellers reported much greater social discrimination in relation to their illness. They experienced more anxiety and loneliness, and used more maladaptive coping strategies. In cultures that regard a particular illness as shameful or as a punishment for wrong-doing, people are unlikely to be open about their difficulties, or able to gain support.

People's understanding of the causes of their illness also differs from one culture to another. Sissons Joshi (1995) found that Indian patients with diabetes were more likely to blame themselves for their illness, attributing it to eating too much sugar in the diet, compared with patients in England. There also seemed to be cultural differences in the psychological need for explanation. People in England who had a meaningful way of accounting for their diabetes appeared to be better adjusted, but having a causal theory did not seem to influence the well-being of the Indian participants to the same degree. There has been very little research into the cultural dimensions of the illness experience, but clearly therapists require sensitivity to these.

Cultural issues also affect the illness experience through racism and prejudice. Evidence suggests that health professionals are not immune to prejudicial attitudes and that these can influence their behaviour towards patients with certain conditions. For example, Maxwell et al (1999) carried out a mixed-method questionnaire, interview and focus group study in the UK of patients with sickle cell disease (who tend to come from Afro-Caribbean or West African ethnic groups). The patients reported encountering high levels of disbelief from nursing staff about the pain that they were experiencing from their condition. They also regarded the consultation process as taking little notice of their needs, and (perhaps as a consequence) they received inadequate pain relief.

ENVIRONMENTAL AND STRUCTURAL RESOURCES AND BARRIERS

The presence of structural and environmental resources and barriers also affects the experience of illness. For example, positive policies towards illness and disability in the workplace help disabled people to continue in work for longer, whereas negative attitudes and policies led to earlier enforced retirement (Rumrill et al 1999). Financial security empowers choice (over the normal commodities of life, as well as enabling the purchase of suitable aids and adaptations in the home, useable transport, or private physiotherapy). Chronically ill and disabled people who face employment and financial difficulties, are less able to maintain their quality of life regardless of individual coping strategies. A wheelchair user in a study by Manns and Chad (2001) explained how her participation in wheelchair rugby was limited not by her personal physical limitations but by her inability to pay for a specialist sports chair. Leisure occupations, as well as paid work, are important for enhancing self-esteem, a sense of purpose, social contacts and opportunities for health-promoting physical activity. Yet they are readily curtailed by long-term illness (Wikstrom et al 2001). It is clearly unacceptable that financial and environmental barriers impose unnecessary restrictions on quality of life for so many disabled people.

THE ILLNESS EXPERIENCE: POSITIVE ASPECTS AMIDST ADVERSITY

Many people respond to illness in a variety of resourceful, indeed courageous ways, and report some positive experiences to have come out of adversity. Positive experiences include:

- Developing expertise about the illness and treatment options
- Commitment to health promotion strategies (appropriate diet, exercise, relaxation and other self-management methods)
- Setting of meaningful goals
- Enhanced social networks (e.g. joining organisations for people with similar health problems)
- Focusing on the needs of others
- Personal growth strategies – altering priorities and finding benefit in adversity.

Developing expertise

Many patients, especially those with long-term incurable conditions, become very knowledgeable about their conditions. Knowledge has both emotional and behavioural consequences, alleviating anxiety about the unknown, and enhancing the person's sense of control and choice – even in the context of serious progressive disease. It helps to combat depression, and increases commitment or adherence to rehabilitation, thereby maximising health outcomes. Health professionals have a vital role to play in providing patients with useable information, and this role will be considered later in Chapter 8. However, we must respect that some patients prefer 'not to know', and are willing to rely on the expertise of health professionals. This coping strategy also needs to be respected.

Health promotion strategies

A nutritious diet, regular physical exercise, adequate sleep, and meaningful occupations all help to maintain well-being, and prevent secondary conditions that can arise in disabled people such as pressure sores (Rimmer 1999). Many people with rheumatoid arthritis are committed to exercise believing it to be effective in controlling pain and reducing inflammation (Kamwendo et al 1999). A qualitative study of people living with stroke discovered that many regarded exercise as vital for maintaining mobility, giving structure to the day, keeping busy, and contributing to the active self-management of the condition (Pound et al 1999). Good nutrition plays an important role in controlling conditions such as diabetes. Many patients endeavour to maximise their recovery from illness through such health-promotion strategies, and encouragement from health professionals can be very empowering. Yet some disabled people perceive that health professionals could do much more to help them devise suitable exercise and other health promotion strategies (Godin & Shephard 1990).

Well-being is maintained not only through 'body maintenance' strategies but also through meaningful occupations. Long-term illnesses often restrict work and leisure activities, leaving people with empty days, and a loss of satisfaction with life and low self-esteem. People who retain (or acquire) satisfying work and leisure pursuits that can be accomplished despite their health problems may be better able to resist the 'master status' that serious illness exerts upon identity (Charmaz 1991, Reynolds & Prior 2003a, 2003b).

Setting meaningful goals

Some people cope with chronic conditions, such as back pain, by setting a series of manageable, meaningful goals. Indeed, this approach is foundational to most pain management treatment programmes, and helps the person to gain a sense of accomplishment even in the face of physical limitations (Mannerkorpi et al 1999). The person's goals do not necessarily need to focus on physical accomplishments, such as walking a certain distance. Well-being may be maintained, for example, through achieving goals such as joining a support group, beginning a new course or leisure pursuit, or finishing a valued project (Reynolds 1997).

Developing a social network

Social support is a well-recognised coping resource. The person may cope more positively with illness through enlisting the emotional and practical help of family, friends, and acquaintances who are in similar circumstances, such as a local support group.

ACTIVITY The role of support groups

- How might joining a support group help a person to cope with long-term illness?
- If Jane (see earlier case study) joined a Web-based support group for young people with JCA, how might she benefit?

Sharing experiences with others who have direct knowledge of the illness and its stressful aspects helps to reduce feelings of isolation and 'difference' (Gray et al 2000, Natterlund & Ahlstrom 1999). Support groups often have a practical function as well, in sharing coping strategies, and relevant information. Support groups also offer the person coping with illness the opportunity to be helpful to others, which can enhance self-esteem (Schwartz & Sendor 1999). Members often value the opportunity of being simply 'themselves', particularly if they usually feel that they have to be emotionally strong to avoid distressing family and friends (Lackner et al 1994).

ACTIVITY Evaluating a research article

Read the article by Natterlund and Ahlstrom (1999), which is available as a full-text article through the electronic database CINAHL. The authors report a phenomenological study that attempted to understand, in depth, 37 patients' experiences of support, without prejudging what these would be at the outset of the research. They used a number of open questions, and attempted through their process of analysing the interview material, to be faithful to the participants' own meanings. The article revealed how people with muscular dystrophy valued not only the support of peers, but also the supportive responses of staff.
- Summarise the benefits that patients described gaining from their support experiences.
- Compare their experiences to those that you identified in the previous activity.

Focusing on the needs of others

Some people appear to derive strength for coping with illness by focusing on the needs of others, for example, through raising money for charity, or through advocating on behalf of people in a similar situation. For example, a person with multiple sclerosis may spend time drawing the local council's attention to poor transport or access arrangements for disabled people, with a view not only to benefiting herself but improving opportunities for others. Some people offer others support (through befriending or counselling), and this has been shown to have positive effects on well-being (Schwartz & Sendor 1999). By focusing on serving the needs of others, the person may come to appreciate many qualities in his or her own life (Reynolds & Prior 2003b). Not all contributions relate to the needs of disabled people. One participant with multiple sclerosis interviewed by Reynolds and Prior (2003b p. 1237) described how she volunteered to hear children read at a local primary school:

> I suppose that the bottom line is that we'd all like to be out at work and doing the kind of working day that everybody always does, but that being the case ... you have to find other things that give you a sense of contributing ... it gives me a sense of achievement because [pause] it goes both ways, you get the sense of achievement because a little kiddy who's failing is beginning to achieve a bit.

Some people believe that they would not have made such a difference to the lives of others had it not been for their experience of illness. This perspective links to the pursuit of personal growth, described next.

Positive growth strategies

While most people anticipate that serious illness would be a wholly negative experience, studies are showing that some people interpret the illness experience as having had certain positive effects on their lives. For example, some people with multiple sclerosis describe their lives as having been positively transformed by illness, through developing, for example, more authentic social relationships, clarified spiritual values and an enhanced appreciation of life (Mohr et al 1999). About a third of women with breast cancer reported gaining closer relationships (Petrie et al 1999). Studies such as these show that confronting illness and mortality sometimes leads to a radical re-appraisal of previous values, and a rejection of 'consumerist' behaviour. Even people with very debilitating illness such as amyotrophic lateral sclerosis (which is similar in its effects to motor neurone disease) sometimes locate a valuable experience in the midst of loss. One participant interviewed by Young and McNicoll (1998) described his illness as a 'blessing', because it had helped him to become more honest and authentic. Reynolds (2003) found that some women with long-term health problems reported taking up artwork after the diagnosis of a serious condition (such as cancer), in order to fulfil life-long ambitions, as well as to cope with unstructured time and the worry of illness. Another participant with MS reflected on the opportunities that the illness had opened up for developing a more meaningful lifestyle:

> MS was a real catalyst. When I look back and see how my life was going, I was forty-five and my children were leaving home. In a job, which I did enjoy, but it was sort of seven days a week and I had time for nothing else ... MS has enabled me to open up my life in so many different directions. (Reynolds & Prior 2003b, p. 1236)

Such findings require more research, but they indicate that 'coping' involves more than illness management. If valued occupations can be maintained, or adapted to the constraints imposed by illness, then the person will continue to obtain satisfaction, self-esteem, social contacts and a sense of purpose. Such outcomes help the person to resist the biographical disruption that illness can otherwise impose (Bury 1982).

ACTIVITY Factors influencing coping strategies

The case study of Ann, initially presented in Chapter 2, is supplemented with further information below.
- Consider both accounts and identify some of Ann's responses to illness.
- What factors may have helped Ann to cope positively with the challenges that she was facing?
- What issues are raised for therapists who communicate with this patient?

When Ann first received the news of her osteoporosis, she spent many sleepless nights worrying about what the future would hold. She imagined how she might become increasingly prone to fractures, and encountered fearful images of 'crumbling bones'. Almost overnight, she felt herself to have become 'old', and the future seemed to promise only deterioration and decay. She could not bring herself to burden her husband with her worries, and felt panicky and depressed. She found it difficult to concentrate on anything other than illness. After some weeks, she confided her fears to a close friend, who suggested that she gain more information through the Internet. Her friend was also an artist and she suggested developing further skills in fabric dyeing and marbling which would not need the same level of dexterity as her ink drawings, and which would provide a satisfying occupation should the effects of osteoporosis interfere with her capacity to draw. Ann planned to enrol on a suitable course and started to look forward to developing her artistic talents in a new direction. With renewed hope, she also consulted with an occupational therapist regarding ways of adapting her art studio to her physical limitations. She also attended a series of physiotherapy sessions to find out which physical exercises would maximise her functional abilities.
(Some suggested answers to the questions above appear at the end of the chapter.)

CONCLUSION

A wide variety of issues have been explored in this chapter, to help you to consider the wider psychological, social and cultural aspects of the illness experience. For therapists to take a patient-focused approach to communication, they require considerable empathy with patients' individual perspectives on illness and disability. Close attention to patients' narratives during interviews and therapy help therapists to enter the patient's subjective world. They can better appreciate the specific difficulties that illness has introduced into the patient's life, the beliefs and strategies that the patient is drawing upon to manage illness and impairment, and the positive resources and supports that the patient can access. Such considerations help therapists to resist stereotyping their patients on the basis of factors such as age, gender and diagnosis, and help to shift the therapist away from the biomedical 'mind-set'. If therapists can encounter each patient as a person with a unique mix of strengths, goals and vulnerabilities, they are more likely to develop a working partnership, and tailor their rehabilitation to the patient's needs. There is a wealth of research into patients' perspectives, and the reference list provides many examples. Further specific reading is recommended below.

Further Reading

The following specific books and articles are recommended to enable a deeper appreciation of patients' experiences of illness, disability, treatment and rehabilitation.

Broome A, Llewelyn S (eds) 1995 Health psychology: processes and applications, 2nd edn. Chapman Hall, London
    This book provides a number of chapters which would give you a more in-depth understanding of the psychological experience of coping with conditions such as cardiac disorders, diabetes, neurological illness and chronic pain.
Mannerkorpi K, Kroksmark T, Ekdahl C 1999 How patients with fibromyalgia experience their symptoms in everyday life. Physiotherapy Research International 4(2):110–122
Natterlund B, Ahlstrom G 1999 Experience of social support in rehabilitation: a phenomenological study. Journal of Advanced Nursing 30(6):1332–1340
Seers K, Friedli K 1996 The patients' experiences of their chronic non-malignant pain. Journal of Advanced Nursing 24(6):1160–1168
Wikstrom I, Isacsson A, Jacobsson L 2001 Leisure activities in rheumatoid arthritis: change after disease onset and associated factors. British Journal of Occupational Therapy 64(2):87–92

Students of physiotherapy and occupational therapy are likely to have access to a range of professional journals. The Journal of Advanced Nursing provides many articles relevant to all health professionals, and its articles are provided in 'full-text' versions through the electronic database CINAHL.

Suggested answers to previous activities

Some themes arising in the research by Bath et al (1999)

You were invited to read this in an earlier activity. The researchers asked fifteen people with rheumatoid arthritis about their experiences. Not surprisingly, many referred to the problem of coping with pain, not only as a physical sensation, but also as a social issue. Not all friends and family members understood the reality of the chronic pain experience. Participants described problems with their medication (such as experiencing unpleasant side-effects, and failing to remember to take their tablets). Some patients battled with depression and loss of self-confidence (for example, associated with the disfiguring effects of the disease). Dependency, isolation and the uncertainties about how the disease might progress were also stressful for many participants. The condition also made work and other activities difficult, reducing choice, and affecting the financial security of families.

Ann, coping with ill-health: Some suggestions

The final activity asked you to consider Ann's coping strategies and some of the factors that may have contributed to her ultimately positive approach. Some suggestions follow:

At first, Ann responded to her health problems with enormous fear about the future. Her thoughts dwelled on worst case scenarios and her familiar sense of self was undermined. She felt alone and unsupported initially. However, a turning point came when she confided her fears to a friend, who was instrumental in encouraging a problem-focused strategy of coping. Ann began to gain useful information and developed new plans that would help to maintain her involvement in art. She accepted that the expertise of physiotherapists and occupational therapists could make a difference to her health and well-being.

It is not entirely clear why Ann responded in this positive way. Having social support seemed to make a difference. Other factors might include a feisty approach to life, creativity, and self-confidence, none of which were seriously eroded by illness. That she had control over a personal space (her studio) in the home environment could also be helpful in restoring her sense of self-efficacy. Therapists who are communicating with Ann would need to be very mindful of any ageist stereotypes, and the need to focus on goals that matter to Ann, especially her need to maintain her artistic skills.

Chapter 4

Patients' communication needs in healthcare settings

There is a great deal of evidence about patients' priorities and preferences when communicating with health professionals. Some of the main sources of information can be summarised as follows:

- Findings from surveys of patient satisfaction gathered after treatment, and other research into individuals' experiences of illness and health care.
- Autobiographical accounts of individuals recounting illness and treatment experiences.
- Observations of health professionals during more or less successful consultations with patients.

While each source of information has its own strengths and limitations, there is some consensus about the communications that are most helpful to patients in the healthcare and rehabilitation setting. These include:

- Partnership
- Empathy and support
- Information
- Control
- Realistic hope and reassurance.

Patients obviously expect appropriate expertise from their health professionals but they also place great importance on sensitive, informative, collaborative communications. Unfortunately, many believe that their interactions with health professionals lack these qualities. It appears that even minor improvements in the communication skills of health professionals can lead to marked increases in patient satisfaction (Ley 1988). Better communications, in turn, appear to result in other improvements in the processes of treatment, recovery and adaptation, as will be explored in the following chapter.

RESEARCH INTO PATIENTS' EXPRESSED NEEDS AND DISSATISFACTION DURING ENCOUNTERS WITH HEALTH PROFESSIONALS

Patient-centred (or patient-focused) care places the patient at the heart of the healthcare system. In order to offer patient-centred care, therapists, nurses and medical staff need to understand illness and impairment, as well as the system of health care and rehabilitation, not simply from the viewpoint of professionals, but from the perspectives of patients themselves. In the US, a series of focus groups of patients was conducted by the Picker/ Commonwealth program for patient-centred care (Gerteis et al 1993) to discover what patients really wanted from their communications with healthcare professionals. These themes were then explored further through more than 6000 interviews with patients, with a further 2000 of the patients' families and care partners also participating.

This research study established that patients believed that patient-centred communication involves the following:

- Respect for patients' values, preferences and expressed needs
- Co-ordination and integration of care among the health professionals involved
- Information and education
- Physical comfort
- Emotional support and the alleviation of fear and anxiety
- Inclusion of family and friends (for example in sharing information and decision-making)
- Well-managed transitions and continuity of care.

These preferences are also highlighted through other studies that sought to discover what patients regard as satisfactory and unsatisfactory about their health care. For example, Little et al (2001a) carried out a questionnaire study of patients prior to consulting their general practitioner (GP), about what they wanted from the consultation. A large majority wanted good communication (including the doctor listening to their concerns and offering clear explanation), partnership and health promotion. Only a quarter of the patients wanted a prescription for medication. Interestingly, the patients who felt more unwell and worried tended to place a higher value on having a patient-centred consultation. Younger patients, those not in paid work, and those attending the surgery more often, also expressed stronger needs for better communication. This perhaps indicates that patients who are more vulnerable appreciate receiving greater support. It is also possible that younger people are more consumer-oriented, with higher expectations about the extent to which health professionals should meet their needs.

Ogden et al (2002) carried out a questionnaire study that compared patients' and general practitioners' beliefs about the key components of patient-centredness. Patients and GPs shared certain beliefs. Both believed in the importance of sharing in decision-making, and the need for the doctor to be receptive to the patient's ideas about the cause and treatment of the problem. Both considered that the doctor needed to acknowledge the effect that the problem was having on the patient's life. Both agreed that the doctor needed to encourage the patient to speak openly, and to be aware of the patient's feelings. However, the perspectives of GPs and patients also diverged, with GPs tending to place more emphasis on the affective (emotional) quality of the relationship, whereas patients focused more on their need to receive information about all aspects of the illness, its likely course, treatment, side-effects, and so on.

Many surveys of patients' communication needs within the healthcare system have been carried out with medical patients, specifically focusing on their interactions with doctors. It is possible that doctor–patient communications, especially in hospital settings, are particularly constrained by the heavy pressures of insufficient time and mutual unfamiliarity. In hospital settings, consultations with doctors tend to be brief, and there may be little continuity or personalisation of care. These pressures are not always as extreme in rehabilitation contexts where patients usually have several treatment sessions. Also, as Klaber Moffat and Richardson (1997) point out, each therapy session may last for 30 minutes, rather than the five minutes or so allocated to medical consultations. In such cases, both therapist and patient have more time and opportunity to establish a relationship and to communicate openly with each other.

In physiotherapy and occupational therapy settings, there is evidence that patients place great value on collaborative communications. The features of patient-centred consultation that were highlighted by Gerteis et al (1993) in the medical setting, seem to be as important within the therapy process. For example, Darragh, Sample and Krieger (2001) interviewed 51 people with brain injury who had received occupational therapy, to elicit their views on the accessibility and effectiveness of the service. Participants regarded occupational therapy as helpful in developing their skills and in providing feedback on their progress. The participants highlighted the importance of the personal skills of the therapists, including their preparedness to communicate honestly and clearly, being supportive, respectful, listening fully, and offering understanding. May (2001) found that patients' satisfaction with a physiotherapy programme for back pain was strongly associated with their perceptions of the personal and professional manner of the therapists. Satisfaction was more likely to be expressed when physiotherapists had provided sufficient information, and when they had made the treatment a collaborative process. A somewhat similar relationship was found by McKinnon (2000) in a telephone survey of clients who had used occupational therapy services in Canada. The clients who expressed greater satisfaction with the service, tended to rate their therapists as having good communication and information-giving skills, as well as sound technical competence.

Partnership

Many patients report desiring greater partnership with health professionals and such involvement is supported by current NHS initiatives (see Holman and Lorig 2000, for one discussion). The Chartered Society of Physiotherapy regards the active involvement of patients as a core standard (Mead 2000). Law, Baptiste and Mills (1995) argue that partnership, as well as autonomy, enablement, accessibility and respect for diversity, are key features of client-centred occupational therapy.

A desire for active involvement or partnership in decision-making has been found in the majority of studies into patients' priorities in GP consultations (Wensing et al 1998). Little et al (2001a) factor-analysed the main concerns expressed by patients regarding their consultations with GPs, and found that partnership – as well as communication and health promotion – were valued by the large majority, especially those who were feeling more unwell, and worried.

In a genuine partnership, both parties bring strengths, skills and resources. Such relationships are also characterised by mutual respect and affirmation, rather than dependency, passivity or subservience (Thompson 2001). Although patients consult with health professionals in order to benefit from their expertise, many would welcome professionals in turn recognising their own knowledge, values and aspirations. Patients want to be trusted with information, and they want to be believed – for example about their experience of pain (Mead 2000). Patients and carers often express a desire to be informed so they can choose realistically among treatment options, and they have critical comments about therapists who make decisions without consultation.

Although partnership approaches are advocated by many patients with long-term health problems (Edwards 2002), it is important to acknowledge that some feel overwhelmed by the responsibilities involved. Particularly in the early stages of illness, during very serious illness such as cancer, or following severe trauma, some clients are so shocked or physically unwell that they prefer professionals to take control over the therapy process (see discussions by Coulter and Fitzpatrick 2000, Charles, Gafni and Whelan 1997). Further discussion of these issues will be found in Chapter 6.

From a patient-centred perspective, therapists need to be sensitive in their approach to patients, and prepared to change their role during the treatment process. The therapist may offer support and direct suggestions for treatment at some points, for example during an exacerbation of the patient's illness, but act more as an advocate or consultant at other points (Duggan & Dijkers 1999). A therapist who is well tuned to the partnership approach will be sensitive to the patient's expressed feelings and preferences, enabling patients to take on control and responsibility when they are ready to do so. Also, the health professional needs to balance their patients' needs for information with their need for hope and optimism, otherwise their coping strategies may be undermined (Coulter & Fitzpatrick 2000). The beneficial health outcomes of working in partnership will be discussed in the following chapter.

Emotional care and the socioemotional climate of the patient–professional relationship

Patients do not only desire a shared role in decision-making. For many patients, the socioemotional climate of the relationship with the health professional is a very important aspect of the treatment process. Whether their health problems are physical or psychological, all patients need 'emotional care' (Bennett 1993). It provides support and courage (Peloquin 1993).

Wensing et al (1998) reviewed the literature on patients' needs when consulting GPs, and found that the 'humane' aspects of care had profound effects on patients' satisfaction. Patients' ratings of satisfaction with their nursing care have also been highly correlated with their perceptions of nurses' kindness and empathy. Such ratings do not simply reflect the technical quality of care (Kadner 1994). For many patients, caring involves practitioners taking a holistic approach to their needs (Sourial 1997).

In serious conditions, such as cancer, the emotional support given by health professionals can make a great deal of difference to the coping process. A study of patients with multiple sclerosis who were receiving occupational therapy and physiotherapy found that participants who perceived their therapists to be friendly and caring tended to be much more satisfied with treatment (Roush 1995). Qualitative interviews with people who had experienced a brain injury further illustrated the support inherent in some therapist–patient relationships. The patients did not simply value acquiring skills during physical and occupational therapy. The experience of being cared for, and related to as a unique person, was also valued (Darragh 2001). For example, one participant said that the therapists:

> ... opened the Pandora's box of feelings and thoughts that I ... either never knew I had or had suppressed or hidden for so long. And they brought them out gently... they were able to connect with me. They really were. I'll never forget it (p. 194).

Yet not all patients have such fortunate experiences. Some health professionals are experienced by patients as cold, detached and uncaring. Peloquin (1993 p. 831) argues that some staff:

> engage in distancing behaviors and harmful withholdings: they are silent, aloof and brusque.

In the study by Darragh et al (2001), some participants with head injury commented negatively on practitioners' unwillingness to listen, and their dismissal of the patient's goals or ideas as 'absurd'. Some participants had felt insulted by professionals who had minimised their problems in relation to others who were deemed to have had a 'worse' head injury. According to one participant, his psychologist had argued:

> But you guys aren't having to deal with that much at all, you should see some of the other clients I've worked with (p. 197).

In making such a comparative judgement as an 'outsider', the professional had placed his own experience above that of the patient. He had also overlooked the unique set of problems faced by each of his patients, in the context of their injuries, plans, resources and vulnerabilities.

As a further example of differing standards of emotional care, Pound and Ebrahim (2000) observed the process of stroke rehabilitation and noted that some nurses lacked warmth towards their patients on a specialist stroke unit (although those employed on an elderly care unit were observed to be far more attentive). In trying to understand why such a poor socioemotional climate occurs in some settings, it is difficult to isolate the relative effects of individual lack of skill on the part of some health professionals from the cultures of care, or group norms, operating in different units. These can exert a strong influence on staff attitudes and behaviour.

Davis et al (2002) carried out focus group discussions with older adults who were living in their own homes or in retirement settings. All identified themselves as having arthritis. The participants discussed their personal strategies of managing pain, and the barriers that they encountered in adequate self-management. Many different strategies and barriers were revealed. In this context, it is notable that participants regarded poor relationships with health professionals as a significant barrier to the effective self-management of arthritis. Patients felt 'fobbed off' with medication, instead of having the opportunity of discussing alternative strategies of managing their own health and lifestyles. They also felt that their health professionals lacked empathy – the capacity to enter their lifeworld with sensitivity – and that they did not really try to understand their experience of pain. This view is shared by patients in many other studies. For example, a participant with arthritis interviewed by Donovan and Blake (2000 p. 543) reflected on what the clinician should offer:

> I'm not looking for sympathy … I think I want him to be aware, really, and a bit more concerned over my health and welfare.

Informational care

Bennett (1993) refers to patients' needs for 'informational care'. Many studies indicate that patients are often dissatisfied with the amount of information that they receive from health professionals. For example, Charles et al (1994) carried a telephone survey of about 4500 patients recently discharged from hospitals in Canada. Although the large majority believed that they had a relationship of trust with their health professionals, and had been involved in decision-making to their own satisfaction, a large minority also reported having received inadequate information. For example, about 36% reported not receiving information about what pain to expect after operations, or what danger signals to look out for. About 29% thought that they had not received clear guidance about when they could resume normal activities after leaving hospital.

Bruster et al (1994) carried out a patient satisfaction survey in the UK, enquiring into whether patients had experienced the various aspects of patient-centred communication as established by Gerteis et al (1993). More than 5000 patients were interviewed at home within a month of discharge from hospital. Compared with Charles et al (1994), the researchers uncovered an even higher proportion of complaints. For example, about 70% reported receiving no information about the warning signs they should look out for, and about 62% were unaware of when they could safely return to their daily activities.

Many of the studies that are critical of the quality and quantity of information-giving by health professionals have been carried out in medical settings. Nevertheless, similar findings have been obtained by research into the process of therapy. For example, May (2001) interviewed 34 patients with histories of back pain about their experience of physiotherapy. As found in so many medical studies, these patients valued therapists who provided information, and who made the treatment a consultative process. However, despite patients' priorities, several of the studies that have examined communications and treatment within the rehabilitation context show that information-giving is neglected. For example, Tyson and Turner (1999) carried out an audit of stroke rehabilitation services for an acute and community NHS Trust, surveying the views both of patients and staff, and also collecting outcome measures. They found that while the majority of patients were satisfied with the treatment that they had received, about a third of patients were dissatisfied. Some of their dissatisfaction related to the amount of therapy/ rehabilitation that they had been given, and patients' disappointment over the limited extent of recovery that had been achieved. Dissatisfaction was also related to patients' perceptions that they had received too little information. The questionnaires invited open-ended comments, and these revealed the importance of sound information for patients who are in the midst of crisis:

> When I was struck down by a stroke without warning I suppose I just felt so alone and lost and in need of professional advice and knowledge (Tyson & Turner 1999 p. 328).

ACTIVITY   Barriers to information–giving during rehabilitation

In response to Tyson's and Turner's study, it might be argued that some stroke patients are unrealistic about the extent to which they should expect full recovery from a devastating brain injury. Their dissatisfaction with treatment might spring from having over-optimistic expectations about treatment effectiveness, rather than any shortcomings in their health professionals' behaviour. Nevertheless, it would seem quite feasible for health professionals to alleviate other aspects of dissatisfaction, by offering more adequate information to patients and family members.

- Put forward some suggestions for why health professionals sometimes offer too little information to patients during stroke rehabilitation (and other forms of rehabilitation).

Tyson and Turner (1999) found that staff tended to present lack of time as a key factor that prevented information-giving. Yet lack of time may seem to be a poor 'excuse' for limited information-giving during rehabilitation as patients tend to receive care and treatment for extended periods, in which there are several opportunities to identify questions and share answers. Tyson and Turner (1999) put forward the following additional reasons: lack of staff, limited knowledge and awareness of stroke among staff, and the low priority afforded to stroke patients. It was also observed that treatment tended to focus only on the most basic activities of daily living and mobility, ignoring the patients' emotional and other needs. Limited skills for addressing emotional and behavioural problems were also admitted by some of the nurses surveyed. It is unclear whether limited resources, ageist attitudes, or poor awareness of the evidence supporting the effectiveness of intensive rehabilitation, played any part in the shortcomings observed in the giving of information by therapists. Other factors can inhibit professionals' willingness to share information with patients or to seek their views on goals and treatment. These will be explored in Chapter 8.

People with chronic conditions often express a strong need for information that would help them to manage their complex lives in a meaningful way, and to anticipate the future. They may develop a distrust of health professionals who present an excessively optimistic, pessimistic, or simplistic view of their condition, as noted by participants with a head injury (Darragh et al 2001). Information provides people with increased control, which in turn may be helpful for resisting depression. Despite the relative ease with which information can be given, many individuals express concern not only about being left in ignorance by health professionals, but about the conflicting advice that they have been given by different members of the multi-disciplinary team. For example, Edwards (2002) carried out a longitudinal interview study of patients undergoing orthopaedic operations, eliciting their views prior to surgery, a week or two after discharge from hospital and about two months later. Participants expressed a wish to manage their own rehabilitation (and their lives in general), but found that their efforts to do so were hampered by contradictory information. One participant illustrated this problem, saying:

> ... But when it comes to the actual weight-bearing, this time I asked would I be able to weight-bear, the nurse I saw in pre-admission said 'Yes, immediately after the operation', Mr Carter's registrar said 'No, not at all', and Mr Carter said 'Yes, after 4 weeks.' So there's three different answers to my one question! To me, that's quite important! Do I put weight on it or do I not! (Edwards 2002 p. 343).

Another patient revealed why it is so important for health professionals to share information:

> [It's] definitely important to find out everything. That's the only criticism I've got sometimes. I think – it's not that they fob you off, I don't think they realise how much information you need, because if you know what you're dealing with, you can deal with it ... Even if it's bad, even if you know it's going to be very painful, it's nice to know originally, because you then know what to prepare for (Edwards 2002 p. 343).

Another study of people coping with arthritis found that they, too, encountered similar difficulties obtaining information. Some perceived that the various health professionals needed to liase with each other much more effectively in order to give patients and families the information that they required to live with the condition. One said:

> The only thing that I personally would suggest is that when it's first diagnosed, someone, an adviser, comes along and says exactly what you can claim for from the social side, the medical side, the equipment side, the whole lot, not just their particular branch ... (Bath et al 1999 p. 37).

Health professionals may not necessarily pick up cues that patients need more information, or that they are ready to receive bad news. The debilitation and anxiety brought about by illness leaves many patients uncertain about the questions they would like answered. The status differences that some patients perceive between themselves and their health professionals leave them unassertive in their interactions and reluctant to ask questions. Hence it is vital that health professionals themselves take the responsibility to work proactively to ascertain the patient's information needs and understanding. Certain strategies for proactive information-giving will be explored in Chapter 8.

Hope and reassurance

As well as requesting better listening and attention to their individual stories of illness, patients also appreciate being supported emotionally, through the offer of realistic hope and reassurance. Hope has been described as a universal need for humans (Wong-Wylie & Jevne 1997).

Leydon et al (2000) interviewed 17 patients recently diagnosed with cancer. All mentioned hope in some form, and revealed the complex interplay between their strategies for maintaining hope and their strategies and desire for gaining information. At times, certain types of information were experienced as diminishing hope for the future, and patients then either halted their enquiries, or asked others to 'vet' new material to decide whether it was appropriate or not. As a further complication, for some patients, the pressure to seem brave and hopeful limited their ability to ask their practitioners questions, or to gain wider social support.

Wong-Wylie and Jevne (1997) gained insights into the influence of clinicians on the hope of patients with HIV infection. Participants saw hope-enhancing interactions as ones in which the clinician related to them as people rather than as cases. The clinician could also enhance hope through being welcoming, informing, encouraging and open to relationship (connecting). The opposite behaviours, interpreted as coldness, were experienced as diminishing hope. One described such a hope-reducing interaction as 'Here's this … here's that – bing, bang, boom, and you're out' (p. 41). Another poignantly revealed the power that a health professional can wield over their patients' sense of future:

> I felt that all the hard work I had done to try to educate myself had been a waste of time – I felt that she did not listen to me and treated everything I said in a very condescending way. Once again I had no control; no way of affirming the hope I felt that if I could regain control over my body, that maybe I could extend my life by making the healthy choices (p. 47).

There is evidence that hope is not only seen as desirable by patients but that it can lead to better health outcomes. These will be considered in the following chapter.

AUTOBIOGRAPHIES OF INDIVIDUALS RECOUNTING ILLNESS AND TREATMENT EXPERIENCES

The previous discussion has illustrated the myriad aspects of patient-centred care and has emphasised that a large number of research studies have illuminated the patterns of communication that patients prefer. This research contributes to an evidence-based guide to practice. However, we can also learn a great deal about people's communication needs during illness and health care by immersing ourselves in autobiographical accounts. For example, John Diamond (1998) wrote of his experience after an operation for cancer of the tongue (p. 158-9):

> … Nobody can tell you how it feels to be that post-operative person, the person who is lying there waiting for the new chapter to start and with no idea of how that chapter will read. I knew that everything that had

been done to me would have a permanent effect, but I couldn't say what that effect – on my constitution, my looks, my voice, my career, my persona – would be. I lay there and contemplated the new me and was frustrated by the shallowness of contemplation that was possible

In some autobiographies, the author describes encounters with health professionals that sadly illuminate how uncaring and distressing the traditional, biomedical approach to health care can be. For example, Joe Simpson (1994) provided a fascinating insight into a number of communication difficulties that he experienced during his lengthy treatment for a horrific knee injury. The injury had been sustained when he fell into a crevasse whilst mountain climbing. He described the behaviour of one consultant, Mr Kay, as follows (p. 207):

> He looked up brightly and said something inaudible to a junior registrar. They huddled forward, pointing to the X-ray with pen and spectacles. I leaned forward, trying to catch what they were saying. Mr Kay kept shaking his head, then he straightened, slid his spectacles into his pocket and turned to me.
>
> 'Well, it's a bad break. A tibial plateau fracture, quite rare I'm afraid, and it has left this piece sticking into the articular surface of the mortice.' He pointed to a spot on the X-ray.
>
> What the hell was he on about, I wondered, as I examined the fuzzy black and white image on the wall ...

Later in the account, Joe Simpson describes further experiences of this consultation (p. 208-209):

> They asked me to leave while they considered their options and return in a couple of hours. I sat morosely in a nearby pub. Although after the accident I had vowed never to climb again, it didn't feel right to have the choice taken away so harshly.
>
> Mr Kay seemed cheerful and confident on my return.
>
> 'Right, Joe. It is Joe, isn't it?'
>
> 'Yes.'
>
> 'Good, right! Well we have decided to try to break the displaced bone back into place.'

After demonstrating the technique (painfully) on Joe's good leg, the consultant added:

> 'The one problem, of course, is that after a three week gap it might not be possible to break the displacement. The bone will have hardened too much. If that is the case, we will have no choice but to fuse it.'
>
> 'And if it works, will my leg be back to normal?'
>
> 'No.' He said it confidently. 'In fact the outlook is pretty bad even if it does work.'

ACTIVITY Analysing an example of poor communication

- Identify the communication failures that occurred during the interaction described in the extract above.
- Check the list of patient-centred features that patients value in their communications with health professionals according to Gerteis et al (1993), and find how many are clearly present (or clearly absent) in the interaction that Joe Simpson recounts.
- How might these inadequate communications affect the patient's psychological state?

Many further examples of poor communications by health professionals are to be found in Simpson's book, and you are recommended to explore these further.

In the above extract, you may have noted the consultant's mystifying use of jargon, his apparent lack of awareness of the patient's vocation (mountain-climbing), his inability to recall the patient's name, and the withholding from the patient of any choice about treatment. The patient is excluded from the process of decision-making. Instead, it is carried out in a private discussion between doctors. The doctor leaves the patient without hope. The consultation is conducted strictly according to a biomedical discourse and thereby ignores the patient's own views, feelings and aspirations. This approach is likely to render the patient passive and helpless. Not surprisingly, when faced with such disempowering practices, the patient becomes angry and uncooperative. This emotional response, in turn, would most likely decrease any further commitment to the treatment and rehabilitation process. While the example focuses on the communication practices of a medical practitioner, similar problems can arise with any other health professional.

Like Joe Simpson, Oliver Sacks (1984) described being treated for a severe leg injury. He, too, experienced a range of uncaring, even unethical, encounters with hospital staff. One surgeon rejected any possibility that his operation had failed, even though Sacks could no longer feel or move his affected limb. The author vividly describes feeling stunned that the doctor saw no need to listen to his patient.

Although Sacks initially attributed the absence of caring to the defective personal qualities of the doctor, he went on to analyse how the conventional roles of Doctor and Patient within the healthcare system exert negative influences on the behaviour of each of them. He reflected that the health professional probably would not react in this way when interacting with people outside of the medical setting. The account provides much rich detail not only about the callousness of encounters that treat the patient solely as an injured body part, but also about the effects of such encounters on the patient's emotions, self-esteem and motivation. Such autobiographical accounts mirror the findings of certain research studies. For example, Charmaz (1991) discussed how health professionals can impose negative identities on disabled people through careless and demeaning comments. She observes that some patients feel driven to protect their self-image by not exposing themselves to derogatory healthcare consultations, even at the cost of ultimately cutting themselves off from important sources of help. Therapists may be tempted to discount such communication problems as only relating to physicians, and as simply reflecting traditional forms of medical training. It is unwise to assume, however, that therapists avoid these errors, as many studies show they do not.

There are also appreciative comments to be found in autobiographies about certain interactions with health professionals. Sacks (1984), for example, described individual members of staff who managed to be humane and caring. For example, a doctor who confided about his own experience of injury, and his subsequent surgery, helped to give Sacks more confidence. John Diamond acknowledged the quality of the emotional care as well as the curative treatment that he received for cancer:

> At the Marsden I want to grasp everyone – cleaners, professors of surgery, the rather distracted Chelsea women who volunteer to work in the outpatients tea shop – with a firm hand and look damply into their eyes. The Marsden really is how hospitals should be run: intelligently, flexibly, always engendering hope. In particular, I want to thank all the nurses ... who suffered without demur my temper tantrums ... (Diamond, 1998: p. 11)

Of course, autobiography as a source of evidence about illness and health experiences has its own strengths and limitations. Because the information is drawn from the experience of one individual, it may be regarded as anecdotal. A cautious reader might wonder if some authors even embellish or exaggerate their problems in the healthcare system in order to tell a more engaging story. On the other hand, some authors clearly have an altruistic mission to change practice for the benefit of others in similar situations, and to make information available that might help other people facing similar illnesses and impairments. An example is the book by McCrum (1998) about his experiences of recovering from a stroke at the young age of 42 years.

While representing 'only' one person's experience, autobiographical writing has the advantage of being less turgid and more readable than most research reports. Also, it must be acknowledged that conventionally 'scientific' surveys of patients' satisfaction with treatment can have their own biases. Some qualitative research studies are based on very small samples, making generalisation difficult. The main function of autobiography for enhancing communication skills is in sensitising readers to the 'insider's' experience of illness and health care, including the perspectives of family and friends (as in McCrum, 1998). It enables you to explore a person's experience of illness and health care first-hand in great depth. Formal research rarely offers such access to the complexity of life stories.

OBSERVATIONS OF HEALTH PROFESSIONALS DURING MORE AND LESS SUCCESSFUL CONSULTATIONS WITH PATIENTS

As well as exploring patients' own views of their interactions with healthcare staff, the degree to which communications are patient-centred can be examined by direct observation. Early studies showed, worryingly, that health professionals all too often interrupted patients within the first few seconds of an interview, even before they had finished their opening statement (Beckman & Frankel 1984, Frankel & Beckman 1989). Unfortunately, continuing problems in health professionals' willingness to listen are demonstrated in recent studies. For example, Barry et al (2001) recorded consultations between general practitioners and patients, and also interviewed each participant about their experiences. They noted diverse patterns of interaction. In some consultations, both patient and GP focused solely on medical discourse – the symptoms, required medication and so on. This agenda seemed to produce uncomplicated consultations with good outcomes when the patients presented with acute, straightforward health problems. In other consultations, patients attempted to refer to their own personal experiences, needs and ideas, particularly if they were living with a chronic condition. The authors refer to these communications as 'giving voice to the lifeworld'. In many cases, the GPs were observed to block or ignore such communications. Despite patients making repeated attempts to communicate their concerns, they were left with unanswered questions, and unacknowledged anxieties.

For example, one patient with a condition that made it painful for him to sit for any length of time or play sports could not manage to make the doctor 'hear' these concerns, despite repeated attempts. The doctor was more interested in discovering his medical history. The interaction followed the following pattern (intonation marks in the original have been removed):

P   I can't do any sports, I do a lot of travelling with work.
Dr   Sure, yeah.
P   And I just don't know where I am from one day to the next.
Dr   Did you go up to the outpatient clinic following on from that at all? Were you actually referred?
P   But with the travelling I'd – I do eight – over eighteen miles a day.
Dr   Sure, sure.
P   And that's just going to work and then if I have to travel from work ...
Dr   Hh, can I just take a look?

The mismatch between the agendas of each participant in the consultation continued to occur, as a later segment showed:

P   I'm having time off work with it and it's not ...
Dr   Do you have any trouble with antibiotics at all?

(Barry et al 2001 p. 496.)

ACTIVITY Analysing reasons for 'blocking' tactics

Such 'blocking' tactics, as seen in the extract above, are not confined to medical doctors.
- Put forward some reasons for why health professionals sometimes fail to hear their patients – why do they strongly resist entering their patients' 'lifeworld'?

Among the many pressures on health professionals that you will almost certainly have identified is lack of time, associated with busy, inflexible appointment schedules. This may indeed present one reason for their inattention to patients' stories. However, Barry et al (2001) also suggest that too many health professionals regard the patient's life experiences and perspectives as only really relevant to consultations about mental health matters. They noted that far less attention or empathy was offered to individuals with chronic physical problems, despite the obvious need that such patients have for information and support.

Whilst some observational studies have demonstrated what can go wrong in the encounters between patients and professionals, others have helped to highlight effective patterns of interaction. For example, Stewart et al (1995) described research studies into effective and ineffective patient–doctor interviews that were carried out by the Department of Family Medicine at the University of Western Ontario, Canada. While the research focused on medical consultations, the findings carry implications for patients' interactions with other health professionals. Analysis of about 1000 hours of audiotaped consultations led to the conclusion that the health professional was most effective when he/she elicited the patient's own concerns, agenda, and reasons for visiting the clinic. The authors' recommendations clarify the actions that health professionals need to take in order to communicate in a patient-centred manner. They emphasise that the following communications need to occur during consultations with patients:

- An exploration of both the disease and the illness experience.
- An attempt by the health professional to understand the whole person in their social context.
- The establishment of a shared agenda, including mutually agreed goals and shared definitions of the roles of patient and health professional.
- A wide treatment focus that encourages the patient in practising self-management strategies and health promotion.
- A willingness to use, reflect on, and enhance, the professional–patient relationship.

The authors also note that doctors (or other health professionals) need to be realistic about the time and resources available for their work with each patient.

However, as discussed in the previous sections, despite increasing emphasis on the importance of interpersonal skills by patients, researchers and clinical educators, observational evidence continues to be presented that health professionals do not always demonstrate these skills in practice.

CONCLUSION

What styles of interaction do patients desire when consulting with health professionals? What styles of interaction do professionals see as most effective? What are the defining characteristics of patient-centred communication? Looking at the information that has been presented here, it seems that there are both agreements and differences in patients' and professionals' views of patient-centredness. The contrasts perhaps reflect patients' and professionals' differing status as 'insiders' or 'outsiders' in the experience and management of illness. To conduct patient-centred consultations, health professionals have realised that they must elicit the patient's own perspective, goals and so on, and gain a deep understanding of the meaning of illness for the individual patient in his or her social context. They also need to share the decision-making process with the patient. There is increasing awareness among health professionals of the therapeutic influence of the professional–patient relationship, the value of motivating the patient's active involvement in health promotion to maximise outcomes, and the importance of gathering and integrating complex strands of biopsychosocial information. (Also see discussions of patient-centredness by Mead and Bower 2000, and Mead and Bower 2002). Not surprisingly, patients have somewhat different agendas within the encounter, looking to be heard, and to receive respect, support and relevant information, as well as wishing for a smooth-running, integrated care system that minimises their anxiety and inconvenience.

Although many aspects of health care influence patients' satisfaction, including accessibility, technical competence, and the physical environment, it is considered that the interpersonal aspects of care are particularly influential (Sitzia & Wood 1997). Possibly, patients' expectations are increasing in relation to the quality of care that they feel entitled to, and they are becoming more vocal in expressing dissatisfaction when communications are poor. We need to be cautious about whether surveys of patient satisfaction slightly over-emphasise the priorities that patients have regarding the interpersonal process of treatment, as there has been less detailed inquiry into their opinions about the more technical aspects of treatment content and effectiveness (Coulter & Fitzpatrick 2000). It is also possible that health and rehabilitation *outcomes* affect patients' satisfaction (when these are expressed retrospectively) and their recollections of the quality of their health care. For example, people who have made less recovery, suffering persistent difficulties in Activities of Daily Living (ADL), seem more likely to report dissatisfaction with their treatment (Jha et al 2002).

This chapter has established that patients generally prefer their health professionals to share power and responsibility, to offer information and empathy, and to regard them as whole persons with valued social roles and lives to lead outside of the treatment process. They do not find it acceptable or therapeutic to be regarded simply as 'conditions'. While patient-centredness is welcomed by patients as more humane and caring, questions remain whether such strategies result in any measurable, beneficial outcomes for patients. This is a particularly important issue as some health professionals argue that patient-centred consultations are likely to take longer and cost more resources than those directed autocratically by the professional. The following chapter will explore whether patient-centred treatments can maximise objective as well as subjective health outcomes, enhancing clinical effectiveness.

Further Reading

Dickson D, Hargie O, Morrow N 1997 Communication skills training for health professionals: an instructor's handbook, 2nd edn. Chapman Hall, London
This chapter has focused mainly on recent research into patients' views about the communications with health professionals that they find most helpful. This review contains some of the older, classic research, which may also be of interest to readers.

Mead N, Bower P 2000 Patient-centredness: a conceptual framework and review of the empirical literature. Social Science and Medicine 51:1087–2013
A clear review of the concept of patient-centredness. The journal Social Science and Medicine may be found in 'full-text' version through the electronic database Science Direct.

Barry C, Stevenson F, Britten N et al 2001 Giving voice to the lifeworld: more humane, more effective medical care? A qualitative study of doctor–patient communication in general practice. Social Science and Medicine 53:487–505
This paper, which reports on the differing agendas of doctors and patients, can also be found in the journal Social Science and Medicine via the electronic database Science Direct.

Chapter 5

Skilful communication and clinical effectiveness

The purpose of this chapter is to explore how patient-centred communications can enhance the effectiveness of treatment. There is increasing evidence that sensitive communications promote measurably better health outcomes. Nevertheless, the underlying processes remain uncertain and open to debate. A variety of explanations will be considered. We have seen from Chapter 4 that patients generally prefer to participate in caring and informative interactions with their health care practitioners. A wide range of research evidence has been presented showing that patients' satisfaction with their treatment depends to a considerable extent on the socioemotional climate that therapists establish, rather than their specific technical competence (which patients tend to take for granted, or find difficult to assess). People dislike and resent being treated as mindless objects simply because they occupy the role of 'patient' or 'client'. They find coping with illness and impairment more difficult when professionals fail to acknowledge that they are individuals with lives, families and aspirations outside the healthcare and rehabilitation context.

This chapter examines the positive health outcomes that research has linked to skilful communication in the clinical setting. However, to gain robust evidence in this field is challenging, and the chapter shows why this is so. Finally, a number of explanations are outlined that may account for how communication influences patients' health and well-being. This chapter emphasises measurable health benefits over and above patients' satisfaction with treatment. However, from the perspective of ethics and human rights, it should be emphasised that patients are fundamentally entitled to full information and respect regardless of whether or not this has any bearing on their objective degree of recovery or adjustment. Nevertheless, in a cultural context that emphasises evidence-based practice, it is unsurprising that some practitioners wish to see additional demonstrable benefits from adopting patient-centred communication strategies. Although respectful interactions do not necessarily take more time, there is a common perception that adding more education, support and shared decision-making to the therapeutic process will inevitably extend treatment sessions. In a situation of limited resources, some practitioners look for enhanced effectiveness to justify what they regard as extra input to their patients.

ASSESSING BENEFICIAL HEALTH OUTCOMES OF PATIENT-CENTRED COMMUNICATION – WHY IS THIS A DIFFICULT TASK?

Why it is difficult to provide really robust evidence that patient-centred communication provides additional benefits for patients over and above those gained from the technical side of therapy and medical care? To do this, we need to reflect on some difficult research issues that are at the heart of gaining evidence about the effects of patient-centred care.

Experimental research designs are usually considered the most capable of revealing causal influences. The classic design involves introducing a specific variable into a situation (the independent variable) and measuring its effects on another variable (the dependent variable). For example, the effects of a new treatment may be tested by comparing its outcomes against either a no-treatment condition (such as a waiting-list control group) or the current 'standard' treatment. True experimental designs tend to alter only one variable at a time, whilst controlling all others, in an attempt to isolate its specific effects on patients. As noted in Chapter 1, severe difficulties can be encountered in trying to apply the experimental research design to evaluating the effects of communication, except in cases where the communication variable being examined is very specific. The provision of a new information leaflet (for one example, see Peveler et al 1999) provides a good example of a simple communication intervention that can be evaluated using a classic experimental design. It is relatively straightforward to compare the outcomes (e.g. reports of pain levels, re-attendance at the clinic, anxiety) of patients who have received a new leaflet against patients who have not.

In normal clinical practice, however, patient-centred communication is multi-variate, and this makes it difficult to assess its effects. Therapists may use, for example, active listening skills, empathy, sensitive nonverbal responses, skilful questioning, validation of the patient's ideas, explanation, and many other forms of communication in a single therapy session. Furthermore, each interaction is unique, and therapists in the team may each have rather different, albeit effective, ways of communicating with patients. In such circumstances when many different processes are occurring simultaneously in a 'real world' setting, it is difficult to tease out their relative effects on patients' health and functioning.

As one consequence of the multi-variate nature of communication, even basic agreement about how to measure and categorise patient-centred interactions has not been reached. Many different ways of measuring health professionals' styles of communication with their patients have been developed. For example, Boon & Stewart (1998) located forty-four distinct measurement tools used by different researchers evaluating doctor–patient interactions.

Many assessments of health professionals' communication styles and outcomes rely on the decisions of external observers of the interaction rather than patients themselves. For example, some reviewers of health outcome research have chosen not to consider qualitative studies that explored patients' experiences of interactions with health professionals and the consequences that followed (e.g. Stewart 1995). Such exclusions risk diminishing our understanding of the outcomes of skilful communication, as perceived by patients.

Research into the effects of skilful communication on patients is also complicated because patients have different needs and vulnerabilities, and person-centred therapists recognise the need to adjust their approach to each individual. For example, some patients may welcome the opportunity to discuss their feelings about their illness or impairment, whereas others may prefer their therapists to focus on the practical aspects of therapy. Perhaps some prefer a practical focus because they find their feelings too raw to disclose, or because they already have good support systems in place, or because they characteristically resort to problem-solving strategies in stressful situations. Sensitive therapists will attempt to recognise each patient's needs at each point in the adjustment and rehabilitation process, adapting their communications accordingly. Given that classic experimental designs require a standardised input (independent variable), it becomes clear why it is difficult to evaluate the outcomes of flexibly implemented patient-centred communication strategies.

As a further research difficulty, traditional experimental designs commonly have a control group against which to evaluate the effects of the active treatment. For example in medical research, the effectiveness of a new drug is established by comparing its effects against an existing drug. Yet it is not always straightforward to decide what is a suitable experience for a control group in an evaluation of patient-centred interaction. It certainly seems unethical to have a comparison group of patients who are deliberately exposed to authoritarian, or insensitive communication.

Furthermore, in the classic form of 'single blind' or 'double blind' randomised controlled trials (RCTs), patients are left in ignorance as to their treatment condition. This is feasible when comparing the effects of an active versus placebo (dummy) medication, but we need to recognise that patients often have strong opinions about the communications that they receive in healthcare settings. It is difficult to keep patients 'blind' as to whether or not they are receiving empathic or informative communications. Indeed, when considering the nature and effects of patient-centred communication, patients' perceptions and opinions are a vital issue to take into account, and should not be dismissed as 'mere' placebo effects.

As a final problem to be considered, the experimental method fundamentally relies on a conceptualisation of the world in terms of cause and effect. While this may be a powerful way of understanding the impact of a physical intervention (e.g. a surgery technique) on the workings of the physical body, it seems to overlook the ways in which people actively construct and participate in their social worlds. For example, notions of cause and effect may not fully explain why a person who feels fully listened to and understood in the midst of crisis, finds courage and optimism, which in turn transforms their motivation to participate in therapy. Such psychological and social processes are not easily subject to measurement, and any health benefits that they promote are, for the same reason, difficult to verify.

Because of these various difficulties, research into the health outcomes of patient-centred communication has by necessity used a wide variety of methods, including patient self-report. Such a diversity of methods makes summarising the evidence a challenging task.

EXPLORING THE EFFECTS OF PATIENT-FOCUSED COMMUNICATION ON FUNCTIONING AND WELL-BEING: A CASE STUDY

Before reviewing the key health benefits of patient-centred communication that have been demonstrated by researchers, let us consider a particular case. You are invited to interpret how the young person in question might regain improved health and well-being if the multi-disciplinary team communicate with her in a collaborative, respectful, client-centred way.

ACTIVITY Katya: Struggling with the psychosocial aspects of cystic fibrosis

- After reading the following case study, suggest why Katya might be finding it more difficult to cope with her condition, taking into account not only disease factors, but also psychological and social issues.
- Consider the likely benefits for Katya's physical and psychological health if she works with a patient-centred, collaborative multidisciplinary team.
- Consider how and why such positive health outcomes might be achieved.

Katya is 17 years old, and lives with an inherited genetic condition, cystic fibrosis. Over the last year or so, Katya seems to be finding it harder to cope with her illness, feeling much more trapped by both the symptoms and the treatment. She takes regular medication and has a rigorous daily regime–of physiotherapy, and she is increasingly feeling more resentful of the intrusion of

> all this treatment into her life. Katya is studying for A Levels and is finding it increasingly difficult to carry her heavy bag to Sixth Form college, and to maintain sufficient energy to complete her homework. She intends to apply for university but is unsure whether to stay at home, where her physiotherapy arrangements could continue as before, or whether to move away like her other friends. Despite her worries, Katya does not want either teachers or peers to know about her difficulties. Her parents feel torn between asking the school or occupational therapy service to offer more support with her disability, and respecting Katya's wishes to keep her illness a private matter. Her parents also worry that Katya has begun to miss taking her medication.

During the discussion that follows, a range of evidence will be presented for positive health outcomes that follow on from patient-centred interactions. You may like to compare these with the outcomes that you have anticipated in the exercise above.

WHAT DIFFERENCE DOES PATIENT-CENTRED COMMUNICATION MAKE TO PATIENTS' HEALTH AND WELL-BEING?

Many studies that show that patients prefer collaborative, informative and caring interactions. But do such interactions really make a difference to rehabilitation? Some research, carried out mostly in medical settings, has attempted to assess the *health outcomes* of patient-centred communications (e.g. Brus et al 1998, Greenfield et al 1988, Little et al 2001b, Maly et al 1999; Mead et al 2002; l et al, 2000). In addition, a number of reviews have collated and critiqued these studies (McDonald et al 2002; Mead & Bower 2002, Stewart 1995, Stewart et al 2000). Some reviewers (e.g. Stewart et al 2000) acknowledge that the physical health benefits of effective communications are under-researched. Yet, on balance, their reviews conclude that there is convincing evidence that both informational and emotional care have positive effects on patients' adherence with treatment, on their coping strategies for illness, and their well-being. In some cases, patient-centred communications even seem to promote better physical recovery.

It is important, however, to note that most studies have focused on the outcomes of communications between doctors and patients, rather than interactions occurring in the therapy context. It may be argued that the addition of patient-centred communication to traditional biomedical forms of health care makes a more substantial and noticeable difference to patients. Also, consultations with doctors tend to be much more time-limited than patients' interactions with therapists. In the context of such highly focused, condensed medical interactions, it is possible that patient-focused strategies are especially enabling. Nevertheless, certain generalisations to therapist–patient consultations may be possible. Indeed, those advocating client-centred practice in counselling and occupational therapy have referred to the positive health outcomes that can be achieved with this form of communication (e.g. Lloyd & Maas 1992). In addition to increasing patients' satisfaction with the encounter, reviewers of research studies in this field suggest that there is sound evidence for six types of measurable benefit being associated with patient-centred interactions (McDonald et al 2002, Stewart 1995). It appears that such approaches to communication help patients to achieve:

- Improved adherence to treatment
- Better emotional health (including reduced anxiety and depression, and increased optimism)
- Improvements in symptoms
- Enhanced physical functioning
- Positive physiological changes (e.g. improvements in blood pressure and blood sugar levels)
- More satisfactory control over pain and more effective coping with other aspects of illness.

For example, Greenfield et al (1988) designed an intervention that helped patients with diabetes to participate more actively in their medical care. Compared with patients who received 'standard' educational materials, the authors found that the experimental 'active self-management' group had indeed managed to obtain more information from their doctors, and that they went on to gain better control over their blood sugar levels. The patients then went on to report fewer functional limitations. Rheumatoid arthritis is another disease that requires long-term self-management. Here, too, researchers have found that additional patient-centred education can promote better adherence with the various lifestyle changes that are a recommended part of treatment, including physical exercise, energy conservation and joint protection strategies (Brus et al 1998). These strategies cannot tackle the disease process itself but they yield valuable benefits in terms of promoting better functioning, optimism and subjective quality of life.

Patient-centred care does not only provide education in the form of information-giving. Self-management programmes are intended to promote in patients a better understanding of symptoms, additional ways of coping with feelings of anxiety and frustration, and effective strategies for managing problems such as pain. Perhaps it is not surprising that many studies have shown that patients gain in self-efficacy from these programmes and that their emotional well-being improves. Damush et al (2003) for example, carried out a randomised intervention comparing outcomes for patients with acute low back pain who underwent a self-management programme with those that received 'usual care'. They showed that the patients showed significant benefits in terms of emotional well-being and coping strategies from participating in the patient-centred educational programme.

While most studies of treatment outcomes focus on coping and psychological well-being, a few studies raise the possibility that interpersonal communications may even influence the process of physical recovery for certain patients. For example, Hawks et al (1995) provided a review of evidence concerning the health outcomes of patients who had received competent 'spiritual' care, defined as interactions that had assisted their search for meaning and purpose, self-awareness and relationships with others. Their review noted that patients' self-care, communications and adherence to treatment tended to improve from receiving such holistic interventions, and that in some cases, their physical health seemed to improve too.

Some studies have also demonstrated outcomes that may be considered advantageous from the view of health providers as well as patients, including reduced number of diagnostic tests, shorter hospital stays, and fewer re-admissions to hospital. For example, Stewart et al (2000) reviewed evidence suggesting that older patients who enjoy continuities in their relationships with medical staff are less likely to be hospitalised, thereby saving health service resources. For the older people themselves, fewer hospital admissions mean less stress and less risk of catching hospital-based infections.

It must be acknowledged that not all researchers have found links between patient-centredness and better health outcomes (Mead 2002). Furthermore, certain authors caution that the various improvements associated with patient-centred communications are in some cases quite modest (e.g. McDonald 2002). However, arguably even small gains are worthwhile from the patients' viewpoint. Mead and Bower (2002), who only reviewed quantitative investigations in primary care settings that met strict validity criteria, considered that the evidence about outcomes was mixed. Also, they noted that results could be biased by the likely non-participation in research of the least patient-centred physicians and the most distressed clients (for whom patient-centredness might be particularly valuable). Clearly, there is more research to be done, particularly in relation to therapist–patient interaction, where outcome studies are even more limited. Nevertheless, we can tentatively infer that therapists with excellent communication skills are helping their clients to achieve the maximum possible during rehabilitation.

FOCUS ON RESEARCH

One of the few studies to have examined outcomes of therapist–patient communications was carried out by Ambady et al (2002). They studied short 20-second segments of physiotherapists' nonverbal behaviour during interaction with older clients. The therapists' behaviour was rated on numerous dimensions, including dominance, aloofness, empathy, infantilising and enthusiasm. The patients were scored on their mobility, cognitive functioning, physical functioning, depression and self-esteem. The researchers found that therapists who were facially expressive tended to have patients who improved in terms of Activities of Daily Living (ADL), whereas those who were distant tended to have patients who declined in physical and cognitive functioning over the next few months. Clearly the reasons for such linkages between therapist behaviour and client outcomes are difficult to interpret, but a second study carried out by the authors showed that older patients were themselves highly sensitive to distancing behaviours (e.g. therapists who looked away or who seemed indifferent). Directions of cause and effect are always difficult to establish convincingly in correlational studies. It remains possible that clients who were having more difficulties in ADL were less rewarding to therapists. The therapists may have responded in turn with less warmth and enthusiasm. On the other hand, we might argue that the therapists' nonverbal behaviour affected the older patients' confidence and motivation to adhere to treatment recommendations, thereby influencing their health outcomes. As in many studies, the exact process connecting communication with outcome is open to debate.

Patient-centred care, in some cases, involves more than the individual patient. In contexts where the family is highly involved in providing care and support (for example, to elderly relatives, to children, or to family members with enduring cognitive or mental health problems), person-centred interactions between the multidisciplinary team and family appear to reduce stress. They can increase the family's involvement with the patient/ user of services (Pillemer et al 2003). Communication with the family can even encourage the patient to adhere more thoroughly to treatment recommendations. For example, Morisky et al (1985) showed that when families were given a programme of education about high blood pressure, their affected family members were subsequently far more likely to keep follow-up appointments, to manage their weight successfully and to maintain their blood pressure within advised limits. This was a well-designed experimental study in which some families received medical care plus the family education programme. Outcomes were compared against those achieved in families receiving the standard medical care alone. The beneficial effects of the educational programme were shown to be long-term, with the participants being followed up for three years.

Reviews such as that offered by Stewart (1995) examine a variety of studies that demonstrate improvement in health outcomes following collaborative, patient-focused communications. Yet a great deal of debate remains about how to account for such beneficial effects. Mead and Bower (2002) suggest that there is little solid evidence connecting specific aspects of communication (such as being aware of the client's perspective, or sharing power) with specific health outcomes. Maly et al (1999) make a similar point in an article that can be obtained in full-text from CINAHL. The study by Maly et al (1999) found that patients' physical functioning and self-reported health improved when they participated in an educational intervention that helped them to review their own medical notes and to ask appropriate questions of their physician. The patients appear to have been empowered to participate on more equal terms in the medical encounter. Yet the researchers comment at the end of the report that they could not fully explain how and why these improved health outcomes were achieved. Certainly patients did not simply become more compliant with their treatment. Possibly, they acquired greater self-efficacy for managing their condition, but again, the exact way in which this influences health and functioning is not obvious.

The remaining part of the chapter will examine the role of adherence to treatment and some of the other processes through which patient-centred communication may translate into positive health benefits for the patient.

HOW MAY PATIENT-CENTRED COMMUNICATIONS INFLUENCE HEALTH OUTCOMES?

We should not expect skilful, patient-centred communications to directly influence (or 'cure') the disease process, or impairment. Collaborative, respectful communications may lead to better health outcomes through a variety of other processes. There is strongest evidence that patient-centred interactions promote better outcomes through the following psychological and social processes:

- Adherence to treatment/advice
- Education and empowerment
- Tailoring treatment to the individual's goals and needs
- Stress reduction
- Increased support
- Wider repertoire of coping and self-management strategies
- Enhanced motivation, hope, and self-efficacy.

Any or all of these factors seem likely to maximise the effectiveness of technical and physical treatments. However, as cause and effect are difficult to specify with confidence, the remaining discussion must be regarded as speculative in places.

ACTIVITY Effects of client-centred communications with Katya

Return to your suggestions for the ways in which a collaborative, patient-centred approach by the MDT might have enhanced Katya's well-being, coping strategies and adherence to treatment.
- Did you anticipate any of the processes outlined above in the bullet points?
- Did you suggest any other possible influences?

Adherence to treatment/advice

In all forms of treatment that take place outside the closely supervised confines of a hospital, the patient needs to be an active and willing partner. Whether remembering to take medication, test blood glucose levels, use a splint at night, or practise certain physical exercises, the patient has to take on considerable responsibility for carrying out the treatment that health professionals have prescribed. However, there has been a large body of research showing that patients quite often have difficulty in adhering (or complying) with treatment. In more recent years, the term 'adherence' has come to be preferred over 'compliance'. 'Adherence' gives more weight to the role of the patient as an active decision-maker and a committed partner in treatment. Compliance suggests a passive subject who is directed or manipulated by more powerful authority figures. 'Non-compliance' seems to conjure up an image of wilful disobedience. In contrast, 'non-adherence' is more neutral in meaning. It sometimes refers to situations where the patient inadvertently fails to carry out treatment recommendations (perhaps because of misunderstanding the instructions, or forgetting). It can also refer to deliberate decision-making (for example, where the patient gives up treatment having considered its side-effects to be too uncomfortable, or because the perceived benefits are too limited to justify the intrusion of the regimen into daily life).

ACTIVITY Which occupational therapy and physiotherapy treatments rely on patients carrying out advice and instructions outside the hospital environment?

Occupational therapists and physiotherapists carry out some treatment interventions directly with patients in a hospital or clinic environment. Here, they can determine how well the patient is following advice, and can motivate patients who seem reluctant or forgetful. However, in many cases therapists rely on patients to motivate themselves and to carry out tasks and exercises in between therapy sessions.

- Draw up a list of interventions that will only be effective if patients are willing to follow professional advice outside of the hospital environment, and without supervision (for example, between appointments, or after discharge from hospital).

Ley (1988) offered a substantial review of research into relationships between patients' compliance/adherence with treatment, their satisfaction with healthcare communication, and other aspects of the treatment process. The review showed that many patients are inadequately informed about treatment choices and rationales, as well as lacking understanding about their own condition. Even simple instructions about the correct dose and frequency of medication are not always given (or understood by the patient). Ley also reviewed a number of studies showing that patients are prone to forgetting information – both about their health condition and their treatment instructions. His own research suggested that patients could retain only about five items of information per session. If more than this amount of information is given, proportionately more is forgotten (Ley 1979).

On the basis of his review of available evidence, Ley (1988) argued that patients who understand more about the treatment process will recall more information, and will be more satisfied with the consultation. Informative patient-centred consultations are likely to promote both better *recall* and better *satisfaction*. Both of these factors in turn encourage compliance/ adherence with treatment. For treatments of proven effectiveness, better adherence should lead to maximal patient recovery/functional outcomes.

Provision of individually tailored treatment

Patient-centred communication, according to many theories and assessment tools, includes the skilful gathering of information from the patient, the negotiation of a shared agenda, and the inclusion of the patient's own goals, ideas, and values in the planning of treatment. In occupational therapy, certain assessment tools such as the Canadian Occupational Performance Measure (COPM) have been formulated explicitly to help therapists address the patients' own problems in occupational performance, as well as their priorities and goals. The COPM also enables patients to evaluate their own performance in selected occupations and to rate their satisfaction with performance during and after treatment (Wressle et al 2003). Such an idiographic approach to assessment is highly compatible with patient- or client-centred communication, and its value in a multi-disciplinary setting requires further investigation.

ACTIVITY Why is an individually tailored treatment programme likely to lead to better outcomes?

Therapists are working with two clients who have had a spinal cord injury, at a similar level of the spine, with resulting paraplegia. One is a woman in her 40s, a college lecturer who was injured in a road traffic accident. The other is a young man of 20, a student, who sustained his injury playing rugby.

- Anticipate some possible differences between these two clients – in the physical, psychological and social resources and needs that each person brings to rehabilitation.
- What benefits are likely to follow on if the therapists tailor treatment to the individual's own needs, goals and resources, rather than providing a general 'off the peg' programme?

Note: Obviously for truly patient-centred practice, you would need to conduct sensitive assessments face-to-face with each person and gather a great deal more information. This exercise asks you to think about these issues in broad terms.

- As a further activity, if you are discussing your ideas with another student or colleague, you might reflect on any stereotypes – about middle aged female lecturers or young male rugby players – that are informing your answers to the questions above. It is worthwhile to be mindful of stereotypes as these can get in the way of truly client-centred communications when you work with disabled people in the clinical setting.

The effect of tailoring interventions to individuals and specific groups has been particularly examined in the field of health education and health promotion (Kreuter et al 2003). It has been observed that tailored interventions – in which information and activities are adapted to suit the patient's individual and cultural needs – can lead to better outcomes. Bulger and Smith (2000) discuss this concept in relation to empowering chronically ill people to manage their own condition. To give one example of a tailored intervention, Whitehorse et al (1999) reported that a culturally tailored Salsa aerobics program achieved remarkable success in helping low-to-moderate income Hispanic women reach satisfactory levels of physical activity (and therefore physical fitness). Non-tailored community programmes are observed to have disappointing attendances from such communities.

Motivation, almost by definition, seems likely to be strengthened when therapy focuses on goals and strategies that the person really values. We may also speculate whether patients develop a stronger bond with therapists who have the competence to tailor their interventions to the individual. Certainly the opposite case scenario seems likely, as we have seen earlier in Chapter 3, when a paraplegic woman's view of therapy was quoted (Seymour W 1998 p. 71). The participant was very critical about therapists who focused exclusively on basic issues such as teaching her transfers whilst neglecting the skills that were most valued by her – those that would enable her to resume looking after her baby. Individually tailored interventions seem likely to increase the experience of collaborative partnership between therapist and patient. Such appraisals are likely to increase motivation. In the scenario above, partnerships may be strengthened, if for example, the therapist appreciates that spinal cord injury is likely to pose somewhat different sets of problems depending on the person's age, gender, security of employment, leisure interests, sexual needs, and cultural representations of masculinity and femininity – and a host of other factors as well. The therapist also needs to be able to explore these issues sensitively with the patient. However, Kreuter et al (2000) caution that tailored materials really do need to match patients' behavioural, emotional and cognitive characteristics. Poorly tailored materials will not be as effective.

Whilst therapists may enhance motivation by tailoring the programme to the client's individual needs and goals, they also need to be mindful of their specific role and expertise. Client- or patient-centred physiotherapy and occupational therapy is a collaborative venture, neither exclusively directive nor non-directive. Neither patient nor therapist has sole responsibility in setting the agenda. Patients bring their knowledge of their goals and resources. Therapists offer informed advice on the basis of their skills, clinical experience and knowledge of the evidence about outcomes of treatment. Their relationship needs to be one of mutual respect if they are to communicate openly about feasible rehabilitation goals and strategies. Such negotiation seems to provide the foundation of patient-centred (or client-centred) therapy. According to a survey of 60 occupational therapists by Sumsion and Smyth (2000), the greatest barrier to client-centred practice was perceived to be differences in goals between therapist and client.

Stress reduction

Patient-centred communications have been widely observed to relieve disquiet, anxiety, and depression (Henbest & Stewart 1990). Stress reduction seems to be achieved through the practitioner's emotionally caring responses and through their provision of information and advice. More is at stake than 'simply' the relief of negative emotions. Research indicates that effective stress management may not only improve mental state but also physical well-being.

ACTIVITY Reflection on stress

- In this activity, reflect on your own experiences of anxiety (e.g. when facing an examination), anger (e.g. when frustrated by people or events) or depression/low mood (for example, on receiving some bad news). These states have certain distinctive psychological properties and effects on behaviour.
- Consider in detail some of the ways in which anxiety, anger and depression manifest themselves in your physical body, feelings, thoughts (cognitions) and behaviour.
- How might stress-related physical, emotional, cognitive and behavioural disturbances interfere with a patient's responses to therapy?

Anxiety states are associated with fears, apprehensions and uncertainty about the future (Rachman 1998). Anger tends to be triggered by uncontrollable events that thwart or frustrate us. It can sometimes be encouraged by the convenient presence of weaker 'victims' who can be blamed unfairly. Depression, on the other hand, tends to be associated with feelings of powerlessness, pointlessness, shame and negative thinking (Gilbert 1992).

Both the physical signs of stress (such as racing heart-rate, dry mouth, stomach cramps, and headache) and the negative thoughts, tend to interfere with concentration and learning. Hence stress can have negative effects on the learning that goes on during rehabilitation. Depression tends to be associated with negative thoughts, and feelings of lethargy, powerlessness or helplessness. The patient may feel low in self-efficacy, believing that the challenges ahead cannot be dealt with. Such feelings of defeat are likely to have a negative effect on rehabilitation outcomes.

Illness symptoms, including pain, are perceptual experiences, and to some extent, perceptions and interpretations are modifiable. Emotional states such as anxiety and depression appear to lead to more negative, indeed catastrophic, interpretations of bodily sensations, such as pain. Communications that help to challenge negative thoughts and that relieve any unwarranted anxiety can help patients to feel greater control over their illness symptoms. It appears that both informational and emotional forms of care are effective in this regard.

Communications may also serve to increase hope and optimism. Positive orientation to the future seems to be associated with greater functional recovery and better health. For example, Agarwal et al (1995) found that men who had an optimistic life orientation tended to make a better medical recovery from myocardial infarction, as well as enjoying greater perceived control, and less depression/anxiety in the month following their health crisis. Haerkaepaeae et al (1996) reported that patients with optimistic expectations achieved better outcomes from a chronic low back pain intervention. From a critical perspective, one might query whether optimism is really a causal influence. Perhaps it is simply associated with having less severe pain in the first place. However, even when Haerkaepaeae et al (1996) statistically controlled for the severity of functional problems (and work status) at the start of treatment, having optimistic expectations still predicted better outcomes.

Reductions in stress through patient-centred communication may have further benefits for the patient. In recent years, researchers have investigated the neurological and physiological basis of stress and established the field of psychoneuroimmunology (PNI). Much is now understood about the complexity of the immune system and its susceptibility to stress (see Evans et al 2000, for details). Acute stress tends to elevate certain aspects of immune functioning, for instance, raising numbers of circulating Natural Killer (NK) lymphocyte cells in the blood that have an important role in attacking virus-infected and cancer cells. During the course of evolution, this adaptation possibly conferred an increased probability of surviving short-term threats such as attacks by predators. However, stress that persists for lengthy periods appears to down-regulate the immune system, leading to lower levels of circulating lymphocytes, and secretory immunoglobulin A (a substance that defends mucosal surfaces, for example, in the nose and mouth). Chronic stress also leads to increases in cortisol levels. Research has discovered that chronic stress increases people's susceptibility to respiratory infection, leads to poorer antibody responses to vaccination (especially among people with high cortisol levels), and slower wound healing. The transactional model of stress proposes that stress occurs when threats exceed people's coping resources such as their skills and supports (as described in Chapter 3). PNI researchers have observed, in line with this perspective, that immune function seems to be worse among people who not only confront long-term stress (such as caring for a spouse with Alzheimer's disease) but who have fewer psychological resources such as low self-esteem and little social support. Immune system deficits may hold the key to explaining how psychological factors such as low self-esteem and depression increase risk of mortality, as shown by O'Connor and Vallerand (1998) in a prospective study of nursing home residents.

There is some evidence that emotional disclosure can lead to improved immune system functioning. James Pennebaker has conducted the main body of research in this intriguing area. He has used experimental methods to examine the ways in which writing (in private) about traumatic experiences affects immune function, compared with writing about neutral topics. Undergraduates have shown enhanced lymphocyte function, and reduced visits to a health centre in the six weeks following the intervention (Pennebaker et al 1988). Pennebaker and his colleagues suggest that the suppression of memories and feelings about a traumatic experience creates long-term stress, and that privately writing about such experiences can alleviate such stress, with beneficial consequences for immune functioning (Esterling et al 1999). They also regard nonverbal expression, for example through art and music, as likely to have an impact on health, particularly if accompanied by verbal processing (Berry & Pennebaker 1993). However, debate continues about the effects of emotional disclosure on immune functioning. Rosenberg et al (2002) found that writing about trauma in a prostate cancer group led to improvements in physical symptoms but not in immune system competence. We clearly need much further research to establish whether emotionally sensitive communications between health professionals and patients, leading to patient disclosures and the off-loading of distress, have any beneficial effects on the immune system. The possibility that the disclosure of highly stressful experiences could improve immune function and physical health is exciting, and its potential relevance to therapy is clear.

Education and empowerment

Mead and Bower (2002), argue that a distinct feature of patient-centred care is 'sensitivity to patient's preferences for information and shared decision-making' (p. 52). Some of the positive health outcomes that have been associated with patient-centred communications may come about through the provision of information. Does information empower choice and relieve some of the stress associated with illness and impairment? Before we look at some research studies that have linked information-giving to positive treatment outcomes, consider the following case study.

ACTIVITY Living in the aftermath of stroke

Martin is 55 years old and Head of Drama at a local secondary school. He suffered a stroke six weeks ago, and is making what his GP referred to as a 'good recovery'. However, Martin has not yet returned to work. He continues to have some problems with weakness on his right side, and some dysarthria (problems in coordinating the muscles involved in speech). His therapists note that he seems irritable and impatient during therapy sessions.
- What information might Martin need to cope with his health and mobility problems?
- How might information help Martin to maximise his recovery, to regain his emotional equilibrium, and to cope more effectively with his difficulties?

Patients have many questions in relation to illness, particularly sudden onset illnesses such as stroke. Questions about why they have become ill are common, as are questions about prognosis – how long they may take to recover, or return to former roles and activities. People also wish to know about their treatment options, and some wish to evaluate the evidence for the effectiveness of different treatments. They may seek first-hand information from others who share the same condition, for example to find out about their coping strategies, difficulties and quality of life. Information about other available supports, including disability benefits, pension entitlements, and employment options, may also be required.

Information empowers patients in a number of ways, enabling them to regain some control over events and choices. Patients who understand the illness, prognosis, and challenges ahead may be more motivated to adhere to treatment recommendations. Knowledge also helps to establish the person's status as an equal partner in the therapy process, rather than being relegated to the role of 'object' awaiting other people's treatment. It is central to 'biographical reconstruction', a process that was discussed in Chapter 3.

A central role of information in the rehabilitation process is to alleviate the state of uncertainty that is all too familiar to patients. It can thereby reduce unproductive anxiety, and in so doing, can harness the patient's full resources and commitment to the therapy process. Some patients go on to become experts in their condition and its treatment. Although some health professionals find such expertise threatening to their status and confidence, others welcome it as supporting the therapeutic alliance (Wilson 1999).

The role of information in promoting better health outcomes has been most intensively examined in relation to surgery. There is considerable evidence from well-controlled studies that show pre-operative education (especially about the sensations to expect after the operation) reduces post-operative ratings of pain, limits the use of analgesics, lessens anxiety, and promotes faster discharge from hospital (e.g. Egbert et al 1964, reprinted in the collection of papers edited by Steptoe and Wardle 1994). Such preparatory information-giving would appear to be a useful component of any treatment that could incur pain, such as certain physiotherapy exercises and manipulations.

Anxiety sensitises people to the experience of pain. Perhaps information helps to challenge patients' thoughts of 'worst case scenarios' and other concerns. It may also increase confidence in the treatment and recovery process, encouraging patients to develop greater self-efficacy for managing their symptoms. Self-care and personal coping strategies are central to living successfully with chronic illnesses. Evidence shows that information and understanding encourage better self-management strategies. Heisler et al (2002) illustrate this issue in relation to diabetes.

Information does not need to focus solely on medical matters such as prognosis, or treatment options. It can also be given in the form of tailored feedback about the patient's recovery pattern. This feedback can increase self-efficacy, and alleviate unnecessary worry. For example, in cardiac rehabilitation, feedback about the patient's physical state during exercise helps to reassure the patient (and partner) that the cardiac system is withstanding the extra effort without ill effect (Bennett 1993). Even negative information can be empowering. A brain-injured patient in the study by Darragh et al (2001) was grateful that a therapist had been honest with her about her limited prospects of returning to her highly skilled job. She said 'That was real hard to hear. But it was nice that somebody was finally honest with me too ... cause somebody finally understood' (p. 196). Such information, when given in an empathic way, can enable patients to commit themselves more fully to the challenging process of reconstructing their lives and identities. Clients have expressed much appreciation for the information and education received from therapists (e.g. McKinnon 2000), but further research in the rehabilitation setting is required.

Therapists need to be mindful that information can be presented in a number of ways, through written leaflets, tape recorded consultations, books, and web-sites, as well as through face-to-face verbal communication. Some suggestions for the effective use of these media will follow in Chapter 8.

Increased support

Health professionals often become important figures in the patient's support network. Lo (1999) for example, found that people with diabetes were much more likely to adhere to their difficult daily health regimens when they had not only good family support, but also positive rapport with their health professionals. Professionals do not need to take on sole responsibility for giving support. If they are attuned to the biopsychosocial approach to care, they can help patients to make use of – and extend – their own social networks. According to the transactional model (Lazarus & Folkman 1984), social support is an important resource or buffer that increases the person's capacity to withstand and cope with stress. People with larger social networks and good emotional support tend to be less depressed when confronted with serious long-term conditions (for example, see the study of people with arthritis by Penninx et al 1997a). Thus support may have important consequences for health, well-being and for treatment outcomes.

There are several distinctive types of social support. For example, Kahn and Antonucci (1980) suggest three main categories:

- Aid/instrumental support: comprising practical assistance, information, treatment, advice
- Emotional support: including empathy and caring
- Affirmation: including validation and acceptance, which strengthen identity and self-esteem.

When engaging in collaborative, person-centred relationships with patients, health professionals may offer all three types of support. Moreover, therapists may also help patients to expand their own support resources, for example

ACTIVITY How may social support promote coping and influence physical health?

Hilary is 72 years old, with COPD, chronic obstructive pulmonary disease, a severe respiratory condition. She can no longer walk for more than a few metres because of shortness of breath. Therapists are aware that Hilary is frustrated about the limiting effects of her illness on her lifestyle. She has a small but active support network. Her son lives close by and visits twice a week. He also brings her grocery shopping, does repair jobs in the house, and has bought her a computer with an Internet connection to enable her to have more contact with the outside world. Her daughter lives in another part of the country about 90 miles away. She telephones regularly and visits about once every two months. Hilary has two close friends who visit most days. They sometimes bring her a meal, or flowers, and they always bring conversation and laughter. Hilary enjoys their company and says that without them, she would probably stay in bed and 'give up'.

- If some of these supportive relationships were lost from this network, what effects might this have on Hilary's *physical*, as well as psychological, health?
- Can you suggest any ways in which Hilary might be able to extend her small social network?
- How may the patient benefit from receiving supportive communications from her therapists?

through the provision of group-based treatment programmes where appropriate, and by providing information about relevant support groups in the community.

Practical support in the form of assistance in the home and garden clearly helps to preserve the person's way of life. In the case above, it enables Hilary to stay in her own home. Furthermore, having support seems to help people to cope and deal with chronic pain and other symptoms more effectively. From the point of view of the transactional model of stress, support gives the person extra resources to deal with the demands of the situation, reducing the risk of feeling overwhelmed and defeated, and moderating the physiological stress response. Support also extends coping repertoires, through the sharing of experiences and strategies (for example, in support groups of patients who share a common diagnosis). Furthermore, support may encourage the individual to adhere to treatment through a sense of obligation or loyalty to co-supporters. Perceiving oneself as a valued member of a social network may encourage the person to take self-care more seriously. Positive social interaction also provides strong antidotes to the illness experience in the form of humour, sharing and other life-affirming experiences. However, a note of caution is required. People with chronic conditions, who receive more practical help than they desire, risk becoming more depressed, perhaps through loss of autonomy and control (Manne & Zautra 1989, Penninx et al 1998).

Both informational care and emotional care by therapists provide essential forms of support to patients when they are vulnerable and stressed. Such behaviour on the part of therapists also validates in patients a sense of being a respected person rather than a passive object receiving 'treatment'. Health practitioners probably offer support that is different in kind from that offered by families, but which is nevertheless highly valued. In particular, some patients with life-threatening illnesses strive to protect their families from worry, thereby losing opportunities to confide about their own fears (e.g. Sutherland & Jensen 2000). In such situations, health professionals can offer supportive listening, being able to face issues that close relatives find too painful. A study by Darragh et al (2001) illustrates this issue very well. The researchers carried out a qualitative interview study of people who had received a brain injury at least one year previously. Participants were asked about the qualities of medical and rehabilitation providers that they saw as relevant to their rehabilitation. While they recognised the importance of having meaningful goals, and learning new skills in rehabilitation, the relationship with the service provider was also valued. One way in which this relationship could be helpful was in allowing patients to speak about feelings and thoughts that they had not been able to confide to anyone else. Such disclosures may help the person to move forwards in their rehabilitation.

On the other hand, not all patients perceive their rehabilitation specialists to be emotionally supportive or holistic. Some patients have observed that therapists continue to subscribe to the medical model of treatment, and feel as though they have been treated primarily as objects during rehabilitation rather than as people (Lund & Tamm 2001). Some older men treated for coronary artery disease saw their health care professionals as offering limited tangible or emotional support, and considered that their relatives were more important in this respect (Yates 1995). However, therapists should not assume that relatives will inevitably offer emotional support, as substantial numbers of patients have few or no confidantes.

There are further reasons for health professionals to take patients' support needs seriously. Patients need to be encouraged to use and expand their social networks. This is because there is evidence that having a larger support network is predictive of greater objective physical health and longevity. A classic study was carried out by Berkman and Syme (1979). They surveyed a large representative sample of the general community-dwelling population in California and established that people with fewer social ties were more susceptible to death over a period of nine years. They found that the most isolated men were 2.3 times more likely to die within this period than the men with extensive social contacts. The risk for isolated women was even greater. These findings were not confined to a single survey. House et al (1988), for example, also showed that more socially integrated individuals had longer lives. A more recent study has shown that emotional support (but not instrumental support) is associated with increased longevity among older people (Penninx et al 1997b). Blixen and Kippes (1999) found that older people with osteoarthritis tended to rate their quality of life highly, and relied largely on their large social support networks rather than formal services.

Clearly health professionals cannot themselves supply all the support needs of patients. The evidence suggests that it is important to encourage patients to use and develop their support networks to achieve maximally effective rehabilitation outcomes and improved well-being.

There may be several processes linking social support to physical health. For example, supportive therapists, friends and family may encourage a more committed adherence to treatment, and better self-care. Berkman and Syme (1979) showed that people with more extensive social networks tended to use preventive health services more often. People who feel isolated are less likely to take part in health-promoting activities (such as cooking nutritious meals and taking exercise). Friends and family not only offer practical assistance in times of difficulty. Positive social relationships provide valued roles and pleasurable life-enhancing experiences. As discussed earlier, support may ultimately help to maintain immune function and therefore resistance to infection. Such relationships require much further research. Further detailed discussion about support issues is found in Chapter 7.

A wider repertoire of coping and self-management strategies

As suggested in the previous section, information, education, and social support all help the person to use and expand their own coping skills and strategies. All long-term health problems require the person to acquire strategies for managing the illness and also strategies for promoting quality of life, if adequate well-being is to be achieved (Bodenheimer et al 2002, Reynolds & Prior 2003b). Individuals can develop such strategies through personal experience and contacts with others who share the same condition. Nevertheless, health professionals can enhance the outcomes of rehabilitation through encouraging greater awareness of coping and problem-solving strategies, as well as by teaching new information. Head-injured participants in the study by Darragh et al (2001) were appreciative of therapists who showed them compensatory and coping strategies. Yet not all therapists include self-management programs in rehabilitation, and some seem to underestimate the day-to-day coping skills that patients require, concentrating on a narrow range of skills such as dressing and transfers (Seymour W 1998). There is some evidence that patients' engagement in health-promoting behaviours and ultimately their symptom management can be enhanced through participating in self-management programmes for chronic illness (Bodenheimer et al 2002). For example, a year after participating in a 7-week self-management programme for chronic illness, patients reported less fatigue, pain, role restriction and depression (Lorig et al 2001). Communications between therapists and patients that explore coping and self-management strategies as part of the therapy programme are likely to maximise health, mental well-being and functional outcomes. This issue is returned to in Chapter 8.

Enhanced self-efficacy

Self-efficacy is regarded as a key variable that differentiates people who succeed on a task and those who do not. Bandura (1997) argues that when people really value a certain goal or outcome, *and* feel capable of reaching it, their motivation is increased. This maximises their chance of success. Self-efficacy refers to the individual's belief that he/she can successfully engage in the required behaviour, even if obstacles are encountered along the way. Generalised efficacy beliefs relate to the individual's confidence in being able to manage most required behaviours. For example, some patients in cardiac rehabilitation may feel confident in being able to make all of the lifestyle adjustments that are recommended, including carrying out more physical exercise, giving up smoking and adopting a healthier diet. Bandura noted that many people have behaviour-specific self-efficacy beliefs, and these are particularly powerful determinants of behaviour (Bennett & Murphy 1997). For example, one person may feel confident about increasing their activity levels in cardiac rehabilitation but not feel able to give up smoking.

A large number of studies have shown that self-efficacy measures are correlated with people's success in making a wide range of behavioural changes in relation to their health, for example adherence to asthma self-management regimens (see Scherer and Bruce 2001, a full-text paper in CINAHL). Bodenheimer et al (2002), in a paper that can also be obtained in full-text from the database CINAHL, reviewed a wide variety of research findings showing that high self-efficacy is associated with better mental well-being in chronic illness (less anxiety, depression, hopelessness, pessimism), better pain control, and greater likelihood of making long-term behavioural changes.

It is not fully clear how and why self-efficacy should be such a strong predictor of positive behavioural change and well-being. Before considering a number of possible mediators, reflect on the following:

ACTIVITY Reflection on self-efficacy

Identify one or two behavioural changes that you would like to make. Consider the following – or another aspect of your lifestyle:
1. Eat more healthily
2. Give up smoking
3. Take more exercise
4. Get enough sleep
5. Stop being tetchy in the morning
6. Wash the dishes more frequently
7. Prepare essays well in advance rather than the night before a deadline.
- Consider how confident you feel about accomplishing these behavioural changes in the next month – express this confidence on a scale from 0-7.

- If you have high self-efficacy for your chosen behaviour, why do you think that statistically you have a greater chance of success?
- Conversely, if you feel low in self-efficacy, why might this predict failure in making the behavioural change?

There may be many reasons why people who are higher in self-efficacy are more successful, on average, in reaching their desired goals. For example, people high in self-efficacy may have:

- More past successes in reaching desired goals/changing the target behaviour, and therefore more of the requisite skills.
- Less emotional preoccupation, and more rational problem-solving approaches to difficult tasks.
- More energy/less fatigue (because they feel less depressed and helpless).
- A tendency to self-monitor whether they are successfully moving towards valued goals. Possibly those low in self-efficacy are not so mindful about their behavioural intentions as the ultimate goals are not particularly valued. This can lead to 'forgetting' about good intentions during daily activities.
- Characteristics such as better perseverance, and optimism (however, note that Bandura does not regard self-efficacy as a consistent personality trait – it is a construct that should be applied to specific behaviours or tasks).
- Internal motivation (rather than relying on external compliance with others' demands).

Marks (2001) recently reviewed research indicating that self-efficacy was an extremely important influence in the self-management of arthritis. Therapists who employ communication skills and strategies that help patients to feel more confidence in their ability to reach their goals are likely to maximise the outcomes of treatment. Some suggestions for working in ways that enhance the self-efficacy of patients will be provided in Chapter 8.

Cohesiveness and commitment

Further social processes operating within the partnership of patient and therapist may also confer positive health outcomes. In social psychology, it has been noted that individuals in highly cohesive groups and partnerships generally show more commitment to the group goals, perhaps because they do not want to let their colleagues down (e.g. Johnson & Johnson 2002). Participants in cohesive groups tend as a result to be more successful. Therapists who can build effective partnerships with patients may capitalise on such social motivation. On the other hand, patients who feel that treatment goals and strategies are simply imposed upon them may feel little responsibility towards the therapist, and make less effort.

CONCLUSION

There is a growing body of evidence that shows patient-centred communication to promote a wide variety of positive outcomes. These include improvements in adherence to treatment, recall of advice, satisfaction, emotional state, physiological markers, symptom reappraisal, pain control, and physical functioning. Most of the health outcomes research has focused on doctor–patient interaction, and not all has established clear, measurable benefits from patient-centred interaction. Nevertheless, the evidence and arguments are strong enough to suggest that all health professionals need to mindful of their patients' needs for emotional care, information, choice, self-management strategies, and support. Patients express great appreciation for therapists who relate openly and warmly, who recognise their difficulties, and who offer holistic approaches to rehabilitation. Although much more research is needed, there is suggestive evidence that positive health outcomes are facilitated by patient-centred interactions. In later chapters, some practical strategies for enhancing patient-centred, clinically effective communications will be presented.

Further Reading

Bodenheimer T, Lorig K, Holman H et al 2002 Patient self-management of chronic disease in primary care. Journal of the American Medical Association 88(19):2469–2475
This article shows the importance of supporting people's self-management strategies for chronic conditions.

Stewart M, Brown J, Donner A et al 2000 The impact of patient-centred care on outcomes. The Journal of Family Practice 49(9):796–804
This paper reviews a range of research examining the outcomes of patient-centred care, albeit in a medical context.

Scherer Y, Bruce S 2001 Knowledge, attitudes and self-efficacy and compliance with medical regimen, number of emergency department visits, and hospitalisations in adults with asthma. Heart & Lung: Journal of Acute and Critical Care 30(4):250–257
A clear account of a quantitative research study investigating relationships among patients' knowledge, attitudes, self-efficacy and compliance. The research focuses on asthma self-management, and will interest therapists who work with people who have respiratory disease. The research design may also be applicable to investigations of patients' self-efficacy and coping with other chronic conditions.

All three articles are easy to obtain, as they are available in full-text format from the electronic database CINAHL, as well as in the journals. Although the papers focus on medical encounters, the material will help you to consider how patient–centred communication may contribute to outcomes that are more effective from therapy and rehabilitation.

Chapter 6

Working in partnership with patients

We have seen from earlier chapters that social, economic and political changes over the last twenty or more years have encouraged many people to reject 'paternalistic' forms of health care. Many patients see themselves as entitled to active involvement in all decisions relating to their health. Recent NHS initiatives have embraced active patient participation and partnership as a means of enhancing satisfaction, better outcomes and improved quality of services (e.g. Holman & Lorig 2000, National Health Service Executive 1999, Farrell 2004). In earlier chapters, we have looked at patients' preferred styles of communicating with health professionals. We have also acknowledged that there is evidence showing that health outcomes are indeed maximised when health professionals work with patients in partnership, providing patients with the information that they need, offering emotional and other forms of support, and enhancing their self-efficacy and self-management skills. Some of the attitudes, skills and strategies that help to foster partnership working will be explored in this chapter. Some of the commonly encountered barriers to effective partnerships between health professionals and patients will also be acknowledged. The following topics are considered:

- Partnership approaches: the PACT model
- How can therapists establish better partnerships with clients?
- 'Therapist' factors that impede partnership working

- Stereotyping as a barrier to partnership working
- Stereotypes and social representations about ageing
- Gender stereotypes
- Stereotypes of disabled people
- Therapist skills that aid partnership: the core conditions
- Patient influences on partnership working
- Communication barriers: effects of language, culture and hearing impairment on partnership working
- Adjunctive influences on partnership working.

Clearly, communication skills cannot simply be acquired by reading (Dickson et al 1997). Active reflection on your attitudes and assumptions, together with the discussion and practise of the various suggested strategies, can all help to encourage a partnership-based approach to therapy. Above all, you are advised to take opportunities to receive feedback about your styles of interacting with others – either by studying video playback or by seeking comments from fellow students or colleagues. Although understandably such feedback can provoke anxiety, it can make a great difference to your self-awareness, and ultimately to your relationships with patients (Maguire & Pitceathly 2002). Caris-Verhallen et al (2000) found that communication skills practice with video playback helped nurses to communicate in a warmer and less patronising way with their elderly patients.

Without feedback, you may not realise that a communication style that you regard as practical and business-like has different meanings for others, perhaps making you seem brusque or detached. Conversely, you might persist communicating in a style that you believe conveys a caring attitude, without realising that other people usually find it patronising, or overly informal. Attitudes and feelings about others are often 'leaked' through our nonverbal behaviour with very little conscious awareness. Explicit feedback from others helps to give us an 'outsider' viewpoint, and ultimately enables us to acquire more control over our communications.

PARTNERSHIP APPROACHES

Partnership is central to many definitions of patient-centred (or client-centred) communication. For example, Stewart et al (1995) see partnership, which they term 'finding common ground' in relation to managing the health problem, as one of the six components of a patient-centred approach to care. Little et al (2001a) found that patients in primary care wanted good communication, partnership and health promotion during their consultations (not simply prescriptions). Partnership is central to occupational therapy definitions of client-centred practice (e.g. Law et al 1995, Mattingly 1988, Sumsion 2000), although Sumsion & Smyth (2000) report that partnerships are commonly threatened by therapists and patients failing to agree on the goals of treatment. Partnership has also been emphasised by a recent document from the Chartered Society of Physiotherapy which emphasises that patients are entitled to a greater involvement in treatment decisions (Mead 2000).

What is meant by 'partnership'? According to Gallant et al (2002), the term 'partnership' describes both a relationship and a process. They see partnerships between health professional and patient as essentially empowering the patient to take greater control over the tasks of managing illness, treatment or rehabilitation. A partnership relationship is essentially one of mutual respect and trust, with each partner acknowledging the useful resources that the other person brings to the joint venture. Therapists offer practical expertise or technical skills to the partnership, together with knowledge of the evidence about effective treatments. Patients bring knowledge of their values, resources, goals and so on. To work in partnership, each person needs to feel committed to sharing power, responsibility and accountability. Partnership is also a process that evolves over time. With changing circumstances, each partner may alter his/her roles and responsibilities. For example, with increasing experience, the patient may take on more of the self-management of a chronic condition, and the therapist may take on the role of consultant, to be called upon when needed. Above all, a partnership relationship avoids domination by one person over another, and is therefore not characterised by dependency, submissiveness or power struggles (Thompson 2001). The relationship is based on respectful strategies of communication, and the partners therefore do not manipulate, patronise or stereotype each other.

While some regard partnership-working as empowering, a word of caution is needed about the term 'empowerment'. Not all authors agree that health professionals 'empower' patients. The term may be criticised for implying that health professionals hold all of the power in the relationship, and that unless they are willing to bestow some of it on patients, the latter remain without power or influence. This image risks perpetuating the traditional 'deficit' stereotype of disabled people as weak, powerless, and tragic, and in need of some form of 'hand-out' from experts (Oliver 1998). In contrast, the 'partnership' concept emphasises mutual respect in the relationship and collaborative action, challenging the 'deficit' stereotype.

While at least two people engaging in communication are needed for a partnership to form, we might usefully consider successful partnerships as dependent upon four interacting factors. Each factor influences the success of the partnership (see Figure 6.1).

Figure 6.1 The PACT model of partnership

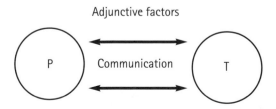

Adjunctive factors

P   Communication   T

Effective partnerships depend upon the:

- **P**atient – including state of mind, confidence, stage of adjustment to illness
- **A**djunctive factors – immediate environmental context, team culture, organisational resources, family support
- **C**ommunication processes – including verbal and nonverbal skills and strategies of each partner, barriers associated with partners' use of different languages or hearing impairment
- **T**herapist – including concept of own role, personal attitudes and stereotypes, self-awareness.

We need to recognise that this delineation of four partnership 'elements' has been made more for the convenience of a linear discussion, when in practice they interact in complex ways. We will consider each of these factors, starting with the therapist, as he/she has the greatest responsibility for ensuring effective collaboration. We will then move on to consider communication skills and barriers, the influence of patient characteristics and the effects on partnership exerted by adjuncts to the therapist–patient dyad (e.g. the team culture, physical environment, larger social networks, and so on). Some of the ways in which these elements of partnership interact will be considered throughout. For example, a 'patient' characteristic (such as depression) will have certain effects on the partnership depending upon the therapist's responding skills or empathy, and/or the support offered to both therapist and patient by the whole multi-disciplinary team. No factor can really be considered in isolation.

HOW CAN THERAPISTS ESTABLISH BETTER PARTNERSHIPS WITH CLIENTS?

To work in partnership with clients, rather than adopting a more traditional hierarchical, expert-led manner, is not without difficulties. The following broad strategies may be helpful:

- Conceptualise treatment as a joint venture/project, not one that is simply selected and administered by an 'expert'.
- Respect the patient as a valued person, with a unique biographical history and expertise to contribute to the partnership.
- Facilitate discussion about the psychosocial aspects of illness/injury.
- Silence your own internal talk – focus on the patient's story rather than your next question, judgement, or interpretation.
- Share information and skills.
- Be conscientious about negotiating mutually acceptable goals and treatment plans with the patient (rather than imposing them).
- Take the personal and professional development of communication skills seriously.
- Recognise that institutional policies and practices, as well as the traditional biomedical model of care, may work against partnership approaches to care, and challenge such inhibiting practices where possible.

Although these may seem to be quite straightforward strategies, many factors undermine partnership working. These will be explored next, and some positive strategies will be considered.

'Therapist' factors that impede partnership working

There are various reasons why some therapists find it difficult to share information and treatment decisions with patients, or to regard therapy as a joint or shared venture. These difficulties should not be attributed simply to 'personality' or other dispositions located within the individual. Lengthy education may in itself widen the social distance between therapist and patient, making it more difficult for the therapists to acknowledge the patient's legitimate forms of expertise. From three or more years of study, therapists acquire advanced technical knowledge which they may then find difficult to share. Mead (2000) reports that junior physiotherapists are more likely than their senior counterparts to regard themselves as the 'experts' on the most effective treatment, and to have stronger expectations that patients will accept their advice unquestioningly. With increasing experience and seniority, physiotherapists appear to shift towards forming active partnerships with their patients, becoming better able to provide patients with evidence about treatment options and effectiveness in order to support their informed decision-making.

Partnership working can also be threatened where health professionals fear dilution of their traditional power, and loss of status. Some therapists feel vulnerable to criticism by patients unless they occupy a dominant role (Hickey & Kipping, 1998). Some professionals defend the traditional, paternalistic model of care by arguing that it guides patients away from doing themselves harm. When treatment is based on shared decision-making and informed consent, the patient is more able to exercise the right to refuse an effective but unpleasant treatment, or to substitute a possibly ineffective 'complementary' therapy. Some professionals believe that partnership approaches are therefore problematic because their professional code of practice commits them to protect the patient's interest (Braye & Preston-Shoot, 1995). To involve patients in informed shared decision-making may require therapists to commit additional time to the consultation processes. Therapists also require communication skills for helping patients to weigh up the risks and benefits of different treatment options (Elwyn et al 1999).

ACTIVITY Why is power–sharing difficult?

- Suggest further reasons for why some therapists find it difficult to share power in the goal-setting and treatment process.
- Identify any personal barriers that might affect *your* ability to share power with patients.

Your list of reasons might include the following:

- Many therapists (particularly physiotherapists) have been socialised into the traditional biomedical model, which tends to cast patients into the role of passive recipient of treatment and care.
- Some therapists are socialised within the clinical setting into forming hierarchical relationships with their patients by a team or institutional culture that seeks to preserve the traditional social distance between health professionals and patients.
- Some therapists perhaps have emotional difficulties in dealing with uncertainty. There is much less ambiguity when therapists regard themselves as uncontested experts and direct their patients accordingly.
- Newly qualified therapists may have a relatively limited repertoire of intervention techniques. This in itself may lead to inflexibility, a problem that may be magnified by fears of being found 'wanting' if patients are invited to express their own needs and goals.
- Partnerships are beyond reach when therapists take a judgemental approach to their patients' problems, for example, perceiving the illness or injury to be self-inflicted (say, through obesity or smoking).

ACTIVITY Perceived barriers to partnership

This exercise encourages you to examine your own 'blind spots' or perceived barriers to forming partnerships with patients.

In the course of your clinical work, you will work with a diversity of patients. In not all cases will it be easy for you to engage in a genuine partnership.

- Look at the list below and rate how easy/difficult it may be for you to develop a working partnership with certain patients.
- If possible, share your views with another trusted person to find out whether you have identified similar or different barriers.

Obviously, the success of real partnerships depends upon many factors including the patient's own individual qualities as well as your own skills and attitudes. This activity asks you to reflect on these issues in broad terms.

- Use the following rating scale to determine your views about how easy/difficult it might be to work in partnership with each patient:

'I would find it: *Very easy – Easy – Unsure – Difficult – Very Difficult* to work with a patient who is ...'

a) Angry about his/her lack of progress
b) Depressed
c) Deaf
d) Of a different religious background
e) Very overweight
f) In the early stages of Alzheimer's disease
g) Suffering from an injury caused during a suicide attempt
h) Incontinent
i) Not able to speak English
j) Disfigured by serious burns

- Some health professionals lack appropriate confidence and interpersonal skills for eliciting patients' views and preferences – for example, because of limited clinical experience, or infrequent opportunities for communication skills training.

In some of the scenarios above, partnership working is threatened by elements of the PACT model other than the therapist's attitudes and values. For example, communication difficulties are quite likely to occur when the patient and therapist do not share a medium of communication (for example, when one, or both, has a hearing impairment or when each uses a different language). Where cultural and religious differences occur, the different values and expectations of patient and therapist may contribute additional difficulties to forging an alliance. Even in these cases, the therapist has the prime responsibility to address the difficulties that arise. But difficulties in collaborative working may also arise from the therapist's own unexamined social attitudes or stereotypes. Few people readily admit to having stereotyped ideas about others, yet stereotypes are widespread in the wider culture and mass media. Therapists need to increase their awareness of – and willingness to challenge – stereotypes, if they are to dismantle at least one major barrier to patient-centred communication.

Stereotyping as a barrier to partnership working

What is a stereotype? According to Colman (2001 p. 706), a stereotype is 'a relatively fixed and oversimplified generalisation about a group or class of people, usually focusing on negative, unfavourable characteristics'. Once believed to be typical only of the thought processes of authoritarian people, it is now recognised that stereotypes are widely used to make sense of complex social experiences. Unfortunately, they are quite resistant to disconfirmation. Stereotypes are attractive, it seems, because they form shorthand descriptions of groups and enhance our sense of predictability. They are comforting because they differentiate people into in-groups (who are like us, familiar and predictable) and out-groups (composed of people who are 'different' or 'other'). Age, gender, ethnicity and disability are all associated with certain negative stereotypes in our culture. If we are to avoid prejudice and overt discrimination, and build genuine partnerships with patients, we need to increase our awareness of these limiting social categorisations.

More recently, the concept of social representation has been developed (Potter 1996). According to this perspective, we borrow from the concepts and images circulating in conversation and the mass media to devise simplified ways of understanding and evaluating events and people. For example, in everyday life, when faced with an adolescent who is unable to express her feelings about a dramatic event, one person may borrow a 'potted' concept from psychoanalysis and describe the young woman as 'in denial'. Another person may draw upon a different concept from 'popular culture', applying a label such as 'uptight'. According to their social representations of the behaviour in question, the two people might react to the adolescent in different ways, and with different amounts of empathy. Potter (1996 p. 138) argues that social representations are 'built around a figurative nucleus which is a core image or picture'. A metaphor might also provide this core image.

Our social representations guide our opinions, which in turn may influence our actions. For example, if we believe in the unfortunately common mass media representations of 'schizophrenics' as unpredictable and dangerous people (perhaps using the core image of the 'homicidal maniac'), then we will fear and avoid anyone with such a diagnosis. If we are exposed to a social representation of this condition as a 'brain disease' that leaves its 'victims' deluded and isolated, then we may approach the diagnosed person with less fear. However, we are still unlikely to believe that people with such a diagnosis might learn effective ways of living with their condition. Potter gives an interesting example from a French research study of carers who had lodgers diagnosed with a mental illness living in their homes. The carers tended to represent mentally ill people as unclean, and perhaps it was no coincidence that they did not eat meals with their lodgers. Potter states (1996 p. 144) that the carers defended the exclusion of their lodgers from family mealtimes in the following way:

> Separate eating could be presented, not as a result of prejudice or fear, but as a consequence of the family's concerns about taste and hygiene.

The focus on cleanliness also perhaps helped the carers to categorise their lodgers' problems as a manifestation of 'normal behaviour' (as everyone can be placed along a continuum from extremely clean to extremely dirty), rather than as abnormal, unpredictable and anxiety-provoking. The shared social representation of mental illness had both positive and negative social consequences. It seemed to decrease anxiety in the carers but supported the continuing exclusion of the people with mental health problems from family activities.

So far, social representations may seem to you to be plucked at will from the mass media and other social sources of information. However, Potter argues that groups are partially defined through their shared social representations. Group members acquire common ways of interpreting their experiences. As part of their socialisation, health professionals do not only learn to share representations of illness and dysfunction. Other social representations become shared as well – for example, how to characterise the 'heart-sink' patient, or the 'compliant' patient. Let us now consider how certain stereotypes and social representations of major groups of patients may influence the possibility of partnership working.

Stereotypes and social representations about ageing

Age differences between therapist and patient can present certain barriers to effective partnership. Firstly, we have a number of ageist stereotypes in our culture, and they operate to increase the perceived difference or 'otherness' of older people (and also younger people such as children and adolescents). Secondly, when working with the very old or very young, therapists are more likely to liase with carers. With carers included in the partnership, it can be more difficult for the older/younger patient to make his or her own opinions and questions heard.

ACTIVITY Identifying age stereotypes

Which negative stereotypes of adolescents and older people have you encountered in the wider culture?
- Do you think that therapists usually resist such stereotypes when relating to people in these age groups?
- Anticipate one or two ways in which ageist stereotypes may disrupt partnerships between therapists and patients.

Stereotypes not only shape our perceptions, but also our behaviour. They can act as self-fulfilling prophecies in that our behaviour can influence others to act in ways that the stereotypes predict. For example, if we assume that older people do not expect to work in partnership, we may be quite directive and patronising in our behaviour towards them. In turn, such behaviour may socialise our older patients into passivity, thereby fulfilling the stereotype. There is some evidence for ageist stereotypes in the clinical setting. For example, Nieuwboer (1992) carried out an experimental study in which physiotherapists were shown videos of an older patient or a younger patient taking part in post-amputation gait training. The therapists had to formulate treatment plans for the two patients. Nieuwboer found that participants tended to express more negative judgements about older people's motivation for rehabilitation after amputation, and concluded that such attitudes might lead to the selection of less intensive or less specific treatments. This would result in poorer treatment outcomes for the older patients.

Stereotypes prevent us from knowing our patients as individuals with unique biographies. If, for example, we represent all older people as 'inevitably' having chronic physical illnesses or mental health problems, then we are likely to approach an older patient's health problem as 'routine' and unremarkable. Studies of older people with problems such as arthritis confirm that health professionals all too often adopt this approach (Donovan & Blake 2000). Such a social stereotype prevents the therapist from appreciating the unique, possibly devastating effect of the illness on the person, and his/her roles and lifestyle. It can also lead the therapist into ignoring the particular resources and objectives that each individual brings to rehabilitation.

ACTIVITY Exploring social representations of an older person

- Choose tabloid and broadsheet newspapers that have reported the same incident – for example, a speech by a high profile older politician, a crime against an older person, or a health story affecting older people (e.g. a 'flu' scare).
- Compare their accounts of this news item.
- Check for the social representations of old age and the ageist stereotypes that appear within the stories.

Each type of newspaper is likely to present rather different stereotypes. It will be unusual to find newspaper copy that is entirely free from clichés about age.

Gender stereotypes

Stereotypes about men and women abound in every culture. They can affect patients' attitudes to health professionals as well as health professionals' attitudes to patients. For example, patients appear to raise more psychosocial issues with female physicians. It is somewhat unclear whether patients do this because they stereotype female doctors as being more interested in such concerns, or because female physicians do indeed express more interest in the 'whole' person. Female doctors seem more likely to engage in partnership-building with their patients, and their patients similarly initiate more attempts to enlist their female doctors as partners (see review of research in this field by Hall and Roter 2002). Foss and Sundby (2003) found that gender is perceived as a highly relevant patient characteristic not only by physicians but by health professionals in general.

If we return to the issue of social representations, we can see that there are many different ways of representing female and male behaviour. Our use of language to describe a person's actions speaks volumes about our stereotypes and our willingness to classify behaviour as 'typically feminine' or 'typically masculine'. In turn, social representations of gender may influence the behaviour of men and women. In the following activity, two therapists describe a female patient who required a considerable period of rehabilitation following an orthopaedic operation.

ACTIVITY Exploring social representations of female behaviour

Two therapists have worked with Margaret, a 65-year old female patient, following her orthopaedic surgery. Their descriptions of her behaviour are given below.

- In these accounts, look for the various ways in which the patient is stereotyped. Cultural clichés and metaphors particularly reveal this. However, note that each therapist is 'buying into' a different stereotype of womanhood.
- Reflect on why the therapists might focus on the 'gender' aspects of the patient's behaviour.

- What are the likely consequences of the therapists' particular 'spin' on events for the quality of their working partnership with the patient?

Alan: Margaret was a real diva. She kept insisting that as she came in for her operation wearing high heels so she wasn't leaving until she could go out in her blessed high heels! I've met Barbie-type women before but not any who are 65 years old! I guess that she's always been a lady-who-lunches, got nothing better to think about than her appearance. It was really difficult, I found, to have much sympathy.

Rita: I admired Margaret's feisty spirit, although she did make life difficult at times. She was clearly a woman who had never let herself go. Probably always bossed her family around too! Clearly her children and grandchildren adore her. She was still very attractive and full of confidence, although she annoyed some of us with her insistence that she wasn't going to be satisfied with her recovery until back in her high heels. Still, I think that we need to recognise that even women of 65 have a right to want to look good.

In these accounts, each therapist draws on a number of negative female stereotypes or clichés – the 'diva', the 'lady-who-lunches', the 'Barbie', the 'battling granny', the woman who doesn't 'let herself go'. Some of these descriptions seem to accept women's traditional position as lower status people subject to the masculine gaze and approval. The attitudes of the second therapist possibly pose fewer barriers to partnership, but neither attempt to peer beneath the cultural stereotypes to enquire about the patient's own perspective and goals. Ageist assumptions are evident. For example, you might have noticed the second therapist's use of 'even women of 65 …'.

The ways in which such negative social representations of women militate against partnership-working are clearer if we hear the patient's own story:

ACTIVITY Margaret's story

- When you have read the extract below, consider any surprises that it presents to you.
- Would knowing more about Margaret's story help you to establish a better partnership with her? Why? Why not?

'I am nearly 66 years old and I retired last year as headmistress of a large school. I continue with a variety of positions on committees in the education field, and I think that I am appreciated for my experience and forthright manner. The orthopaedic problem brought me up sharp though, because I suddenly felt old after the operation. I became aware that my situation is rather precarious. If I can't manage the work, then I'll soon be de-selected from the committees. As a retired person, I am quite vulnerable to being sidelined anyway. If I was disabled too, the problem could be twice as bad. I have always worked and never really wanted to retire. It's partly my way of dealing with a fairly unhappy marriage,

> and partly my way of trying to make a difference to children's lives. Anyway, I joked with the therapists about not leaving until I was back in my high heels. I was utterly determined to get back to full mobility. I'm damned sure I am not going to be cast as a 'little old granny' going home to potter about. I am sure that doctors and therapists make these sexist assumptions when you're over 65. I have probably annoyed a few of them. They don't seem to appreciate assertiveness, particularly in their older patients. We are as keen to get back to our lives as the younger person, although many professionals don't realise this.'

Although stereotypically female qualities have been culturally devalued, social representations of masculinity can be equally problematic. For example, men are all too often represented as strong, and uncomplaining. Yet, as Wetherell (1996 p. 335) points out, a problem with this representation is that 'no man is ever big, strong and tough enough to match the cultural fantasy of the "real man"...'. Male patients who differ from the culturally most valued versions of masculinity may be subject to adverse comment, just as Margaret was subject to censure because she did not conform to the stereotype of the uncomplaining, grateful 'old lady' in the extracts above. Because cultural representations of gender also affect the self-concept, therapists need to be mindful that male patients may be less able to engage in partnership if they feel emasculated by their illness. Illnesses that affect physique, sexuality and mobility are particularly likely to threaten men's self-image, unless those affected can reformulate their image of positive masculinity. This issue has been explored in a qualitative study of men with prostate cancer by Stansbury et al (2003), and in an autobiographical account by Tepper (1999). Such a reformulation process may be particularly difficult for young men with a chronic illness who are at the stage of their development when they are establishing a valued personal and social identity (Williams 2000). While therapists need to be mindful of the challenges that illness can present to a person's gender identity, it is also important not to assume that the person is *necessarily* struggling with issues surrounding sexuality, femininity or masculinity.

Stereotypes of disabled people

Disabled people express concern about the negative stereotypes and images of disability that are portrayed in the mass media, including charity advertising (Morris 1993).

ACTIVITY Exploring social representations of disability

- Which negative stereotypes of disabled people circulate in the wider culture?
- Do you think that health professionals generally reject such stereotypes because of their extensive contact with disabled people?

Although it is tempting to believe that the education and caring dispositions of health professionals should immunise them against the negative stereotypes of disability operating in the wider culture, evidence suggests that this is not the case. Slevin (1991) gave an attitude questionnaire to school pupils, student nurses and qualified nurses, and found not only that participants expressed negative attitudes to older people, but that attitudes seemed to worsen once they had begun their nursing training. Gething (1992) carried out an experimental study in which a large number of health professionals (both students and qualified) rated a videotaped job applicant. Twelve different videos were presented, with the portrayed 'applicants' varying in gender, social skills and disability. The results suggested that health professionals tended to devalue wheelchair users both in terms of their perceived adjustment and perceived competence. French (1997) reviewed a number of studies that suggest the attitudes of health professionals are no more enlightened than those of the population at large.

Many of the relevant studies were published around ten years ago, and therefore it is tempting to argue that health professionals must surely have since developed greater awareness of disability issues. Yet some recent authors have challenged this assumption, suggesting that health professionals are prone to negative stereotypes of disability because they have little contact with disabled people *as equal status colleagues*. For example, Basnett (2001), a medical doctor who suffered a spinal injury later in his career, reflected on how the injury changed his views about disability. He observed that health professionals rarely encounter disabled colleagues in the work setting. Instead, they tend to see disabled people only as patients needing treatment. This perhaps diverts their attention away from the strengths, skills and resources of disabled people, and can perpetuate negative stereotypes. Basnett argues that with such limited experience '... health professionals can develop a view of disability that is at substantial variance from its reality for many disabled people' (p. 451).

Health professionals need to develop sensitivity to the variety of mostly negative stereotypes (or narratives) about disability that are prevalent in social discourse if they are to resist these. Thomas (1999 p. 50) refers to:

the 'personal tragedy' story; medical narratives about 'abnormality'... ; the 'shame of the imperfect body' story ... ; the 'it's best if you conceal imperfections' narrative; the 'dependency' story; the 'lives not worth living' narrative, and so on.

For therapists who lack any personal experience of illness or impairment, it is vital to gain a greater awareness of the social representations of disability and to challenge narrow preconceptions. One approach is to listen to the views and experiences of disabled people themselves, whether those stories are told by our patients, relatives or friends, by people interviewed by journalists, or in written autobiographies. The stories may surprise us, giving us access to experiences that we have never before considered. In the process, we may become more aware of the more subtle difficulties – and considerable resources – of disabled people. For example, French recounts her personal experience as a visually impaired person:

> Going out on windy days is more difficult. The wind makes a noise which obscures the small auditory cues which, though rarely appreciated until they are absent, are so helpful when walking about (French 1999 p. 21).

French also comments on the limited understanding shown by others, and their tendency to categorise her behaviour in an unthinking way as 'aberrant':

> Nobody interpreted my fear of walking over zebra crossings correctly, nor my dread of stepping near the edge of flower beds – and yet to me zebra crossings were steps to fall down and flower beds dark, bottomless pits (French 1999 p. 21).

The study of autobiographical accounts helps therapists to glimpse how the world seems from another person's perspective. Such experiences may help to increase empathy and challenge prejudice. We may also be horrified by disabled people's accounts of the ostracism and disempowerment that they have experienced at the hands of health professionals. Far from feeling like partners, some patients have been made to feel that they inhabit a different social universe from the staff in the hospital or rehabilitation setting. Oliver Sacks gives an example from his perspective as a neurologist with much experience of relating empathically to patients. He was shocked to find that other health professionals shunned him once he was admitted as a patient to hospital with a serious leg injury. They no longer treated him as an equal, even though his injury had not undermined in any way his knowledge or personality. Prejudices that are widespread in the wider culture have a tendency to permeate the medical and therapeutic setting, undermining the possibility of partnership.

If partnership-working is to become a reality, we need to remain open to patients' accounts of their social, emotional and physical difficulties and listen without judgement to their preferred coping strategies.

Therapist skills that aid partnership: the core conditions

At the heart of patient-centred care is a whole-hearted or unconditional respect for the person, including valuing of his or her unique experiences, goals, resources and needs. According to Carl Rogers (1967), a pioneer of client-centred therapy, therapists who offer three 'core conditions' are more likely to form a therapeutic alliance with their patients/clients. These are:

- Warmth and unconditional positive regard
- Genuineness
- Empathy.

The core conditions have been variously interpreted as therapist personality traits or dispositions, attitudes or communication strategies. Burnard argues that:

These personal qualities cannot be described as 'skills' but they are necessary if we are to use interpersonal skills effectively and caringly. They form the basis and bedrock of all effective human relationships (Burnard 1996 p. 45).

Unconditional positive regard or acceptance is respect that is given to the client/patient freely, 'without strings'. Rogers referred to this as 'prizing' the person, regardless of his/her particular interests, problems, skill, beliefs and so on. According to Rogers' theoretical perspective, the experience of receiving unconditional acceptance releases the person from feeling obliged to seek approval and the goals imposed by other people, and helps the person to identify personally meaningful goals. Such experiences may be especially liberating for disabled people. Many comment on the strong social obligation to 'pass' as 'normal' or to spend far too much time and energy on being 'independent', when accepting assistance on mundane tasks would in fact improve quality of life and release energy for more interesting occupations. However, not all therapists offer patients unconditional respect. There is evidence that patients all too often feel depersonalised and devalued within the medical and rehabilitation system (Peloquin 1993).

The second core condition of genuineness requires the therapist to come out from behind the professional façade. It involves relating to patients as people. One example of such genuineness is given in MacLeod (1993), from her observational study of nurses relating to patients in a ward setting. She quotes from her field notes, about an interaction between a female patient and nurse in which the patient discloses her worry that her husband, left to his own devices at home, is boiling the laundry by mistake:

As she gives the suppository [to the patient] Sister Hanna listens and shares a story of when she was in hospital having her youngest baby and her husband boiled the jeans, long before boiled jeans were in style (MacLeod 1993 p. 186).

MacLeod goes on to note:

This excerpt speaks of how the ward sisters are present with patients, acknowledging and preserving their sense of being with persons as well as patients. The ward sisters touch their patients' experiences, by the timing and pacing of their actions, by listening and by sharing themselves and their own experiences (p. 186-7).

Genuineness is generally regarded as a challenging task, as therapists need to avoid imposing any of their own negative feelings on patients. For example, they should be careful about burdening the patient with their own reactions such as sadness, or irritability.

Thirdly, Rogers argued that client-centred therapy depends upon the therapist's willingness and ability to offer empathy. It may help to clarify the meaning of empathy by saying what it is *not*. It is *not* sympathy, which involves imposing one's own feelings of pity or sadness on to the person who is ill. Sympathy can appear over-sentimental and burdensome, leaving patients with a desire to protect the health professional from emotional distress. It can also be patronising to disabled people. Many reject having a 'tragic' status imposed upon them (Oliver 1998). For example, an unthinking description of people as 'victims' of diseases such as multiple sclerosis, or as 'confined' to a wheelchair, might be intended to convey sympathy but the terms are understood by some disabled people as demeaning and disparaging (Morris 1991).

Empathy involves placing oneself in the client's shoes, trying to understand – however imperfectly – how the client may be experiencing illness or impairment in the broad context of his/ her life, family, work, and so on. It requires a willingness to suspend one's own judgements and assumptions about how the patient 'must' be feeling, and to listen carefully to all of the verbal and nonverbal information that the patient provides. It involves recognition that illness and pain have different meanings for each individual. Empathy sometimes involves a leap of imagination in order to glimpse how the world may look from the other's perspective. It is a far from passive process. As well as achieving an intellectual understanding, empathy involves sensitivity to one's own and the patient's feelings. Furthermore, it also involves communicating one's emerging understanding back to the patient, to invite correction of any errors, and to foster a genuine partnership. This process helps the client to acquire insights, and to feel heard (Maguire & Pitceathly 2002). The patient is likely to gain greater clarity about his or her personal needs and goals as a result.

Respect and empathy may be thought of as personal attitudes on the part of the therapist, but they also need to be *communicated* by the therapist and *experienced* by the patient. Respect and empathy will not be of much help to the patient unless they are clearly expressed by the therapist through verbal and nonverbal behaviour.

As well as demonstrating the 'core conditions', therapists use a wide repertoire of communication skills. These can be classified in many ways. For example, we may focus on verbal (word-based) ways of sharing information, and the nonverbal. Nonverbal cues include use of facial expression, eye contact, gestures, posture, orientation and distance between the partners, and paralinguistic voice qualities including tone, and emphasis. Nonverbal communication appears more prone to the unconscious leakage of emotions and attitudes, as people generally have less awareness and control over these behaviours. Communication skills have also been divided into task-oriented and socioemotional skills (Adams et al 1994, Klaber Moffat & Richardson 1997), and into sending (initiating) and receiving (responding) skills (Johnson & Johnson 2002). The appropriate phrasing of questions can be presented as an initiating skill, whereas active listening and empathy may be classified as responding skills. However, such a binary classification soon breaks down when we realise that sensitive questions (an initiating skill) may in effect be a profound *response* to information just disclosed by the patient. Also, active listening skills (receptive skills) may be used quite deliberately by the therapist to help the patient to initiate further disclosure and to encourage the patient's confidence and trust in the relationship.

As a first step to partnership, therapists need to communicate a deep respect for patients. This is partly accomplished through basic courtesies, for example, using the patient's preferred style of address; asking patients'permission before touching them; preserving the patient's dignity, for example when undressed; protecting privacy by not having sensitive discussions behind flimsy ward curtains.

Furthermore, respect is associated with acknowledgement of the patient's unique lifeworld. The therapist attempts to empathise with the patient, rather than following a pre-set, 'expert-led' agenda. Not all health professionals manage to do this, as the following activity explores.

ACTIVITY Analysing therapist–patient interaction

In an earlier activity, you considered how a patient might cope more effectively in the aftermath of stroke if given appropriate information. The extract appears again below.

- Examine the interaction between Martin (M) and his therapist (T), and note how each person is following somewhat separate agendas.
- Why do you think such misalignments in the agendas of patient and therapist occur?
- How might the therapist have responded to build more of a partnership or alliance with the patient? Suggest one or two verbal responses.
- Formulate a brief response that offers more empathy, showing the patient that you realise that he is anxious about returning to his post as Head of Drama.

Martin is 55 years old and Head of Drama at a local secondary school. He suffered a stroke six weeks ago, and is making what his GP referred to as a 'good recovery'. However, Martin has not yet returned to work, and continues to have some problems with weakness on his right side, and some dysarthria (problems in co-ordinating the muscles involved in speech). His therapists note that he seems irritable and impatient during therapy sessions.

M: The fatigue's really hitting me, I'm wondering if I'll ever be able to do a proper day's work again.

T: It's early days, you're making good progress.

M: You sometimes have to be able to work an 18-hour day to keep on top of a job like mine.

T: Have you been walking each day as we agreed?

M: Yes, but I can't see myself racing up and down the stairs at school. I have classes in two buildings, you know, some on the ground floor and some three flights up.

T: So what distance have you been walking each day?

Barry et al (2001 p. 495) gave the example of a physician and male patient following separate agendas in a consultation (an extract of an interaction sequence from this study was given in Chapter 4). In the research, the physician's reluctance to risk peering into the patient's lifeworld may have been associated with a view that the condition was simply 'routine' and manageable by medication. More fundamentally, the physician may have assumed that illness simply has a 'biological reality', and that its social and personal aspects are irrelevant to treatment (Mattingly 1988). Time pressures may also have restricted the clinician's focus to the biomedical aspects of the patient's condition. However, this response could readily suggest to the patient that his view was not relevant or wanted. Matthews et al (1993) point out that an empathic acknowledgement of the patient's fears and other feelings does not necessarily take much time. We need to acknowledge that the period available for consultation with patients is relatively brief. Yet it takes only a little time to respond in a caring way to a patient who has just described a health crisis or disclosed fears about the future. For example: 'That sounds like a frightening experience. Perhaps it will help if we look at ... ', or 'You seem very worried about .... Is there something you would really like to work on during therapy that would help you deal with these worries?' Even the briefest acknowledgement is better than none, and helps to build partnerships. However, Barry et al (2001 p. 497) note from their observations that health professionals often regard the patient's life experiences and perspectives as relevant only to consultations about psychological matters.

More positively, Crepeau (1991) presented a case example of an occupational therapist who made a successful attempt to enter the lifeworld of a male patient who had received a spinal injury. Crepeau argued that for therapy to be successful, the agendas (or schemata) of therapist and patient need to be brought together. This can be achieved in part by the therapist's willingness to accept and understand the patient's perspective. For example, an effort needs to be made to understand how this particular patient is experiencing his physical dysfunction. The therapist also has the responsibility for educating the patient about the knowledge and skills that she/he is bringing to the therapeutic process. Crepeau analysed several interactions between a therapist and a patient, who had a hand dysfunction. She showed how much information about the patient's hand function was being exchanged in both directions during the encounter. This helped to draw the pair together in a mutual problem-solving alliance. The analysis also focused upon the power dynamics involved in the interaction between therapist and patient, and how the successful partnership depended upon the therapist's willingness to share power in the situation. For example, she asked open questions, showed interest in the patient's account of his injury, and responded sensitively when the patient showed that he had become unwilling to pursue the topic of sexuality. On a lighter side, some teasing and joking within the interaction signified a strong and growing partnership between the pair.

For a therapist to foster a partnership approach, sensitivity is needed in regard to the psychosocial aspects of illness/injury, as well as preparedness to negotiate mutually agreeable goals and treatment strategies. Therapists need skills to help patients voice their own agendas, for example through using open questions and invitations. Some disabled people are all too aware of being given few choices during social encounters. For example, Stack (1999 p. 32) describes her own experience using a wheelchair:

> I have to stay firm in the knowledge of who I am and not be deflected by the constant barrage of other people's miscommunications ... 'I will put you over there ... ' (not where would you like to be?).

Rebeiro (2000) found echoes of this complaint in an interview study of patients with mental health problems, looking at their experiences of occupational therapy services. The clients reported that they had received prescriptive treatment rather than a meaningful choice of activity. The social distance between therapists and clients made collaborative partnerships difficult to achieve. However, while this is an intriguing study, the findings are based on only two clients' viewpoints. Talvitie (2000) carried out a more substantial observational study of thirteen patient–physiotherapist interactions. Videotapes revealed that the physiotherapists sometimes ignored the patient's perspective by giving instructions during practice of skills, when patients really needed to concentrate fully on maintaining their balance. However, the therapists showed more patient-centred skills when they provided appropriate encouragement for patients who felt despondent about their progress. This study was valuable in showing that therapists use many different communication skills during the course of treating patients, being patient-centred in some respects but less so in others.

Other research confirms that patients all too often lack influence during interactions with health professionals. For example, Barry et al (2000) discovered that patients often leave their consultations with physicians with unvoiced agenda items. Part of the communication failure may result from adjunctive or contextual factors such as time pressures. Patients' common beliefs that health professionals will not want to be bothered by 'too many' health issues or personal problems may also prevent full sharing. Nevertheless, therapists themselves can block expression of psychosocial issues and impede joint decision-making about goals and treatments by failing to show listening skills, by leaving no thoughtful silences in the encounter, by asking many closed questions (which encourage patients to confine themselves to brief yes/no responses) and by tightly controlling the agenda.

There are a variety of useful questions that help to elicit patients' concerns, together with their expectations about the therapy and the therapist's role. Platt et al (2001) give many examples, including:

> 'What sort of troubles are bothering you?... Tell me more about X, Y and Z.'
> 'Tell me a little about yourself as a person ... your work, who's at home, what goes on in your life?'
> 'What are you hoping for?'
> 'From what you have said, I imagine that this illness is very hard for you. Can you tell me what it's been like for you?'
> 'My role is X and I can see that you're hoping for Y, how best can we proceed?'

ACTIVITY Formulating questions that invite partnership

The above suggestions help you to think about the use of open questions and the open invitation 'Tell me about ... '.
- Formulate some further questions that would help a therapist to gain insights into patients' views of their illnesses, and their treatment goals, and that would therefore encourage a collaborative approach to therapy.
- If any of the above questions seem a little unsuited to your own way of communicating, find another way of phrasing them so that they would fit in better with your own personal style, while still serving the same purpose.
- If possible, swap the questions that you have formulated with someone else, and evaluate how effective they might be.

Therapists who wish to gain the patient's involvement in therapy as a joint venture may find it helpful to explore the use of assessment tools that are designed to encourage the patient to participate in goal-setting and treatment planning. Some occupational therapists, for example, use the Canadian Occupational Performance Measure (COPM), as it is designed to increase partnership-working (Wressle et al 2002). Goal attainment scaling provides another means by which therapists and patients can collaborate on setting goals and evaluating progress towards goals. Fisher and Hardie (2002) evaluated the effectiveness of goal attainment scaling in a multi-disciplinary pain management programme. They explained that this approach asks patients to identify which problems they wish to work on, and to plan specific, personally meaningful goals in relation to each problem area. The goals are very explicitly formulated. The researchers give the example of a patient deciding to work on a newsletter in the next six months, and setting a goal of ten pages of information. If the goal is achieved, the patient will score 0. If more is accomplished than the plan envisages, then the patient will score +1 or +2. Similarly, if less is accomplished than stated in the goal, the patient scores -1 (or -2 if the patient achieves less than the point at which treatment started). Fisher and Hardie (2002) report that the patients achieved significant improvements in mobility and activity. It would appear that such an approach to therapy encourages an alliance to form between therapist and patient, and that it harnesses the patient's motivation.

While therapists can do much to negotiate a shared agenda in their encounters with patients, partnership working is nevertheless constrained by numerous adjuncts to the therapist–patient dyad. For example, in settings where there are enormous time pressures, and limited cooperation among therapists and other health professionals in the wider team, it is much harder for effective partnerships to form at the therapist–patient level. We will return to these issues later.

PATIENT INFLUENCES ON PARTNERSHIP WORKING

Patients appear to vary in their willingness and desire to work in partnership with therapists. Reasons include:

- Their stage of adjustment post-injury or following the diagnosis of a serious illness
- Emotional barriers such as anger or extreme anxiety
- Cultural expectations that patient and health professional will occupy more 'traditional' roles
- Cognitive limitations.

We need to recognise that patients themselves sometimes feel overwhelmed by their condition, and ill-equipped to offer opinions. Particularly in the early stages of illness, during very serious illness such as cancer, or following severe trauma, some clients are so shocked or unwell that they prefer professionals to take control over the therapy process (see discussions by Coulter and Fitzpatrick 2000, Charles et al 1997). Patients who are new to hospital or recently diagnosed may feel intimidated by the problems that they perceive to lay ahead, and lack the confidence to ask questions or seek information. Patients who are angry about their condition, or who are frustrated by limited progress, may also feel disinclined to engage in partnership with their therapists.

Cultural factors and age also influence patients' values. Younger patients seem – as a group – to have a stronger preference for active participation in treatment decisions, at least in medical contexts (Charles et al 1997). Older people – again, as a group – perhaps have had longer socialisation into traditional forms of biomedical care, and appear to be more accepting of paternalistic treatment practices. Nevertheless, therapists need to be cautious about making generalisations. Many older individuals very much appreciate being offered greater control. Even when patients believe that they are not qualified enough to express opinions about interventions and goals, their accounts of their illness and lifestyle will nevertheless help the therapist to harness their strengths and to work towards meaningful goals. By facilitating such stories about the patient's personal life, the therapist helps the patient to feel respected and valued as a unique person. Mutual respect in turn contributes to partnership working.

Health professionals need to respond with flexibility to their individual patient's preferred type of therapeutic relationship.

Barriers to partnership can also arise from differences between the therapist's and the patient's own expectations about recovery. Patients may respond to unfamiliar, unanticipated physical dysfunction with what health professionals would regard as 'unrealistic' goals. For example, Hafsteinsdottir and Grypdonck (1997) reviewed studies of stroke patients and noted that there is often a wide gap between the goals of the patients and their health professionals. Many stroke patients, certainly at the outset of rehabilitation, are dissatisfied with anything less than full recovery. In this situation, if partnerships are to be successfully established, patients need a high level of support and education about their condition, and therapists need to be respectful of the unique resources and problems of each individual. Therapists also need to be willing to attend to each patient's unique capabilities, and adjust their expectations accordingly. Heim et al (1998) discuss the case of a whole team of therapists who eventually agreed to raise their expectations in response to an older patient who was adamant that he could make a good recovery if given a suitable prosthesis and intensive physical therapy. Despite the therapists' initially bleak projections, the patient indeed learned to walk independently with a walking aid.

Cognitive limitations (for example, among head-injured patients and those with dementia) also place certain difficulties on partnership working. The person may have limited insight into his or her own difficulties, making joint goal-setting problematic. Memory limitations may render usual strategies of information-giving ineffective. Therapists may have to work more extensively with the whole family or with professional carers, rather than forming a partnership exclusively with the patient. Regardless of the patient's cognitive ability, therapists need to be mindful of communicating respect. Some specialist ways of increasing support, information and self-management for people with cognitive problems will be considered in Chapter 8.

As indicated at the start of the chapter, the influence of the therapist and the patient in establishing an effective partnership cannot in practice be neatly distinguished. Each person's behaviour is given meaning by the other, and these interpretations affect the degree of 'meshing' that the partners can establish during interactions. For example, a patient's behaviour may seem assertive to one therapist but aggressive to another. The first interpretation increases the possibility of partnership working, but the second viewpoint undermines it. In turn, the patient is likely to feel respected and treated as an equal according to the first therapist's responses, but will probably feel judged and rejected in interactions with the second therapist. Depending upon the therapist's reaction, the patient's behaviour may change, and this can shape the quality of the emerging relationship for better or worse.

COMMUNICATION BARRIERS: EFFECTS OF LANGUAGE, CULTURE AND HEARING IMPAIRMENT ON PARTNERSHIP WORKING

Where communication barriers occur, they are likely to create problems for partnership working. Therapists and patients may find it particularly difficult to forge an effective alliance when they do not share a common language, when either has a hearing impairment, and where they cannot easily read each other's nonverbal communication (for example, because they have different cultural backgrounds).

ACTIVITY Reflecting on cultural and language barriers

Before reading on, consider the following case study. Decide upon some strategies that might help the therapist and patient to communicate more effectively.

Parveen migrated to the UK from India about a year ago to join her husband. She is being treated by therapists for gynaecological complications following the birth of her first child. Therapists consider that Parveen may be experiencing postnatal depression, but they have found it difficult to inquire about her condition as Parveen's husband has been translating for her during therapy sessions, and the therapists are not completely sure that he is conveying the full meaning of their questions or Parveen's replies. They are also unsure whether they understand her nonverbal communication correctly.

The communication problems described above are not uncommon. A recent study in a large inner city hospital in the UK (Brooks et al 2000) reported that about 19% of the annual admissions were people of South Asian backgrounds. The study examined this group's needs and views in relation to communication with staff, and their suggestions for improving the communication service. Of the sample of Urdu and Punjabi speakers recruited to the study, about a third could speak and understand English fluently, and a similar percentage had limited use of English. The researchers found that 31% were not able to speak or understand English. Some of this group relied upon relatives for translation, including children. However, this practice is generally regarded as unsatisfactory for a number of reasons (Smart & Smart 1995). When translating, relatives may edit the information being exchanged between professional and patient, especially when it is sensitive and potentially distressing or embarrassing. The intervention of relatives in the interaction between professional and patient breaches confidentiality. People can feel humiliated having to disclose personal information via relatives, and this problem appears to be worse in certain traditional cultures. Brooks et al (2000) found that just under half of the participants did not know about the availability of professional interpreters, and a similar proportion indicated that they would have liked an interpreter to help them with their communications with staff, in order to gain better information and support. The participants requested having more professional interpreters available and thought that they should be accessible throughout the day and night. They also requested having more Asian healthcare staff on the wards. Although a multi-cultural workforce might help to provide more culturally competent care to patients, the authors caution that bilingual speakers among the staff should not necessarily be relied upon to offer interpretation as this role may conflict with their existing work role. Also, professional interpretation requires specialist skills. The person needs to translate questions and answers accurately, without simplifying, editing or adding any personal views or assumptions to what is being said.

Given the influence of the therapeutic relationship, emotional support and information on patients' rehabilitation and well-being, rehabilitation services need to take the communication needs of non-English speakers seriously. We should expect more negative health outcomes when language barriers are not addressed, as communication quality influences not only satisfaction, but the patient's understanding, self-management skills and adherence to treatment. Poor quality interactions may even result in the patient having unnecessary hospital tests and receiving an inaccurate diagnosis.

How can therapists establish a more effective partnership with patients who use a different language? These strategies may be helpful:

- Learn about the values and beliefs of different cultures and religions, so that you have at least some understanding of the person's likely perspective on health, independence, mortality and so on, and can therefore work in a culturally sensitive and respectful way.
- If you work with colleagues who have different cultural backgrounds, make the time to learn more about cultural influences. You could discuss cultural differences in values, social behaviour and nonverbal communications (for example, in some cultures, extensive eye contact may be interpreted as threatening or disrespectful). Interactions with patients from diverse backgrounds can also present learning opportunities.
- Encourage the clinical team to invest in interpreters. As noted above, these can be drawn from staff members who have the appropriate language skills, but independent translators are generally more effective in helping patients to have their own voice in the interaction.

Certain similar barriers to open and effective communication with health professionals are encountered by people with hearing impairments. Hines (2000) carried out a national survey of hearing impaired patients who described their experiences of communicating with hospital staff. A large minority (37%) thought that the quality of professional communication was fair but with considerable failings, and 5% rated professional communications in entirely negative terms. Most of the patients considered that staff had insufficient communication skills for working with hearing impaired patients, and they believed that some made little or no effort.

One way for therapists to develop a more sensitive approach to communication is to gain insight into the experiences of people who are hearing impaired. Hogan (1999) points out that some people who become deaf believe that they inhabit a 'borderland'. Their impairment is not immediately visible to observers but neither can they participate easily in verbal interaction. Furthermore, some experience negative responses from others who take the view that the 'inability to communicate in various settings is a sign of personal failure' (Hogan 1999 p. 81). People who use sign language, instead of communicating verbally, report feeling even more ostracised. Hogan states the view of one research participant, who says:

> there was not much use in talking to a hearing service provider about being Deaf – what did they know about the everyday encounters faced by deafened people within a world hostile to the overall experience of disability? (p. 86)

What communication strategies may be helpful for interacting more effectively with hearing impaired patients?

- Be aware that people have to give *much* attention to the process of understanding verbal and nonverbal communications, if they have a hearing impairment (or if they are using an unfamiliar language). It is important to facilitate their attention and understanding as far as possible, so speak clearly, sit squarely in relation to the person so that your face is in full view, avoid fast or colloquial language, and minimise distractions (e.g. avoid a noisy environment, interruptions to the interview, or a messy background, including brightly patterned curtains). It is a good idea not to have your back to the window as the light background can throw your face into shadow, limiting the nonverbal cues and lip-reading opportunities that are available for the patient. It is very important not to obscure the mouth. Many patients in Hines' study reported that staff sometimes hindered communication quite unnecessarily by looking down at their notes or even holding their notes up in front of their faces.
- Be prepared to supplement communications with the patient in writing if this is a more effective medium (for example, patients who have developed a hearing impairment in later years can read and write perfectly easily). However, it is inappropriate just to hand out general leaflets. They are rarely read and should be considered to have a function only as back-up materials.
- Develop alternative communication skills in signing or Makaton (or other communication devices) for certain patients.
- Check with the patient that a hearing aid, if used, has not been mislaid or switched off.
- Be *prepared* for hearing impaired patients. In Hines' (2000) study, 17% of participants referred to the stressful experience of waiting for their names to be called in a reception area. Some felt anxious about being in the right position to be able to lip-read the person who was asking them to attend their consultation, and some felt anxious about asking other patients to help. Those who work in the rehabilitation setting need to greet patients with a hearing loss more appropriately.
- Avoid making negative judgements about the capabilities of hearing impaired (especially older) patients. Hines reports one patient who felt so poorly treated by staff that he pinned up a message over his bed on the ward: 'I am deaf, not daft' (p. 37).

Although it is probably difficult for therapists with good hearing to fully grasp the experience of hearing impaired patients, even a limited understanding enhances empathy. Individual needs vary in every case, so therapists need to be flexible in their approach. It is also important to understand that language barriers are not the 'fault' of the *individual* (e.g. the patient who is deaf or who uses another language). The difficulties that therapist and patient encounter result from a *system* failure, and therefore *system change* is usually required to dismantle the barriers. For example, there needs to be an organisational commitment to the provision of additional communication skills training for health professionals, and to pay for professional interpreters.

ADJUNCTIVE INFLUENCES ON PARTNERSHIP WORKING

Partnerships depend upon more than the attitudes and skills of two people working together. Many additional or contextual factors also play a role. For example:

- Team dynamics and institutional cultures influence the possibility of partnership between patients and professionals. For example, in one unit, patients may be referred to as a 'head injury' rather than seen as a person with a unique biography, roles, relationships, and so on. In such settings, it may be difficult for therapists to take partnership working seriously.
- Fragmented teams composed of health professionals who cannot trust or communicate with each other, or who are engaged in power struggles for status and influence, hardly encourage genuine, open partnerships to form between therapists and patients.
- Resource and budgetary restrictions limit appointment times, give rise to shabby environments, place extra pressures upon staff, and affect available services, regardless of clients' needs and preferences. In such situations, therapists may feel stressed and under pressure to take a 'conveyor belt' approach to treatment. Patients may be made to feel 'grateful' for whatever service they receive, rather than perceiving themselves as 'honorary' team members (a position that some health professionals advocate, such as Edwards 2002).
- A strong culture of evidence-based healthcare practice may paradoxically focus therapists' attention on to the 'technical' aspects of therapy and discourage therapists from considering the additional influence of patient-centred ways of working.

The individual therapist only has limited power to deal with these adjuncts to their relationships with patients. However, a more facilitatory context may be established if therapists raise awareness at the team level concerning disabling and disempowering practices, and encourage attention to the quality of relationships among team members. More appropriate, patient-centred services may also be developed by gathering patient evaluations and suggestions, and by disseminating research evidence concerning the influence of communication practices on health outcomes (for example, evidence about the beneficial effects for patients of having translators on the team). Therapists who feel well supported themselves may be able to offer better support to patients. This will be discussed further in the next chapter. Facilitators and barriers relating to teamworking will be discussed in Chapter 9.

CONCLUSION

Partnership between therapist and patient is central to patient-centred communication. An effective partnership depends upon two (or more) individuals having the means to communicate with each other, together with the willingness to share power, the trust to pool their resources, and mutually agreed goals. The nature of effective partnerships between therapists and patients can change over time, for example, as patients become more knowledgeable and confident about managing their conditions. Some common barriers to partnership have been examined in this chapter together with some positive attitudinal, communication and organisational strategies.

Barriers to partnership include therapists' stereotypes of patients, patients' emotional state and beliefs about their ascribed role, and language differences. The adjunctive context – environmental, institutional and cultural – also influences the quality of partnerships, by for example, providing supportive resources or by increasing the stressfulness of the working environment. Although therapists can do much to improve partnership working through attending to their attitudes and communication strategies, structural barriers usually have to be addressed at a systems level, by the whole team or organisation, rather than by the individual therapist alone.

Further Reading

Crepeau E 1991 Achieving intersubjective understanding: examples from an occupational therapy treatment session. American Journal of Occupational Therapy 45(11):1016–1125

This paper gives many examples of sensitive interactions between an occupational therapist and male patient in rehabilitation after a spinal injury. These provide insights into the process of client-centred therapy and partnership-building.

Mead J 2000 Patient partnership. Physiotherapy 86(6):282–284

This provides a clear account of partnership approaches in physiotherapy.

Brooks N, Magee P, Bhatti G et al 2000 Asian patients' perspective on the communication facilities provided in a large inner city hospital. Journal of Clinical Nursing 9(5):706–712

Hines J 2000 Communication problems of hearing-impaired patients. Nursing Standard 14(19):33–37

Both these papers are available in full-text format via the electronic database CINAHL. They provide insights into the communication difficulties experienced in the healthcare setting by people from minority ethnic groups and people with hearing impairments.

Chapter 7

Providing support

CHAPTER CONTENTS

Studies of patients' experiences of illness and health care have uncovered a need for support that is often unmet by the healthcare system. For the person affected, and their families, illness and injury are never 'routine'. Changes in health always carry emotional significance, and yet the traditional, biomedical approach to health care has tended to neglect the 'inner hurt, despair, hope, grief, and moral pain that frequently accompany, and often indeed constitute, the illnesses from which people suffer' (Greenhalgh & Hurwitz 1999 p. 50). In addition to problems such as loss of function and pain, people with chronic conditions often face loss of roles, financial insecurity, and other social and psychological difficulties. The future is likely to seem highly uncertain and anxiety-provoking.

When health professionals are unresponsive to the complex array of emotions that accompany illness, and focus attention only upon the condition, dysfunction or specifics of treatment, they can appear rude, abrupt, or aloof. Some professionals even manage to undermine patients' efforts to cope by the careless use of disparaging remarks or by ignoring their views, implying that patients have nothing of value to add to the consultation (see the disturbing case example reported by Greenhalgh & Hurwitz 1999, and also the paper by Darragh et al 2001). While inadequate communication skills on the part of health professionals are partly responsible for these failures, so too are organisational climates that emphasise cost-cutting and 'through-put' at the expense of patient-centred care (Sourial 1997). This chapter will increase your understanding of the processes and benefits of support through discussion of the following issues and reflective activities:

- Recognising emotional distress in patients
- Forms of support
- What does support offer patients? What difference does it make?
- Supportive communications: addressing the person rather than the patient
- Supportive communications: the practice of empathy
- Supportive communications: containment
- Can empathy be taught?
- Cognitive behavioural approaches
- Other forms of support
- Some barriers to offering patient-centred support
- Support and self-care for therapists.

This chapter should be read in conjunction with the previous chapter, which focused on partnership-building with patients. While collaborative partnerships can be very supportive of patients, we need to be aware that some health professionals are oriented towards forming very task-oriented partnerships. While such partnerships work well in terms of formulating joint goals and acceptable treatment strategies with the patient, they may give patients' emotional needs low priority. Therapists who work in a very task-oriented manner also seem likely to ignore their own personal needs for support, ultimately risking demotivation and emotional burn-out.

This chapter will help you to consider support from the perspectives of patients, families and health professionals, and to identify many ways in which therapists can provide better support to patients. This aspect of patient-centred working is perhaps the most difficult to present in 'evidence-based' terms. This is because 'support' is rarely packaged up as an intervention that can be objectively evaluated. Dean-Barr (2000 p. 82) argues in relation to defining support:

> We know when it's present and when it's lacking but we still haven't advanced far enough in our science of understanding support to be able to define it clearly enough to measure it, systematically study it, and test interventions aimed at closing that gap between needed and available support.

Supportive communications in health care come in many forms and address many needs. Although therapists at times offer deliberately supportive interventions (for example, intentionally engaging in active listening or recommending a patient support group), many supportive encounters are embedded within the very matrix of therapy itself. Both formal and informal interventions can offer the patient much comfort. For example, a simple nonverbal acknowledgement of the patient's distress, or a really pertinent question that reveals the health professional to have a considerable understanding of the patient's difficulties, can help the patient to feel less overwhelmed or alone. The forms of support which are present in the day-to-day interactions between health professionals and patients are difficult to evaluate formally. Thus to make suggestions about ways of increasing support to patients, we have to draw upon not only formal research but also clinical experience and patients' own views.

Research, however, does contradict one popular belief, in indicating that supportive consultations do not *necessarily* take more time. This issue has been widely examined by medical communication researchers and communication skills trainers (e.g. Makoul 2002, 2003).

RECOGNISING EMOTIONAL DISTRESS IN PATIENTS

Patients commonly experience a range of emotions in relation to illness and injury, including sadness, anxiety, frustration, anger, and even shame. While pain and loss of physical function are often distressing in their own right, people can also mourn the wider loss of valued roles and the changes in identity that illness brings about.

Therapists need to be mindful that there is no one correct way for people to manage emotional distress. The following responses are quite common. Therapists will encounter all of these reactions in different patients – or in the same person at different times in the rehabilitation/adjustment process:

- Denial (or other forms of suppression) of feelings
- Anger (and other ways in which distress can be 'acted out')
- Conversion of emotional distress into physical symptoms (including insomnia, headaches, heart palpitations, indigestion)
- Problem-focused coping strategies (dealing with fears and sadness by focusing attention on manageable goals and tasks)
- Emotion-focused coping strategies (including verbal and nonverbal expression of feelings).

Grief has been described as 'the intense emotion that floods life when a person's inner security system is shattered' (Jackson 1974). Although Jackson was referring to the loss of a loved one, serious ill-health can prompt similar feelings of insecurity, loss, and meaninglessness. The emotional distress that follows can take a similar pattern as in other forms of grieving. People often respond to the earliest stages of bereavement and grief with numbness and denial as a self-protective device, when the reality of the loss is too threatening to cope with (Kubler-Ross 1982, Parkes 1972). Later on, once the loss is more fully acknowledged, the person may fear being overwhelmed by feelings of powerlessness and frustration, and may fight back with anger or by trying to 'bargain'. Other people may be blamed unreasonably for failing to prevent the loss or trauma that has occurred. This phase may subside, leaving the person in a state of helplessness, or depression. The person may

ACTIVITY Responding to a patient's emotional distress

Read the following account provided by Bob Penney, a 68-year-old man who is recovering from a stroke.
- Why do you think that Mr Penney experienced heightened emotional distress at *this* point in his recovery process?
- Reflect on your own reactions to tears – are you comfortable relating to a person who is tearful, or not?

'I had a stroke about six months ago and I suppose I have made quite a good physical recovery. Well, I have been really determined to get back to normal. I still have physiotherapy and I do my exercises exactly as I have been advised. I have never allowed myself to feel down about everything that's happened. That was until this week. You see, my wife and I have always loved caravanning. We have our own van, just a small one, that we tow behind the car. We have never had a great deal of money, but we have always valued the small things in life. We always planned to do lots of travelling when we retired, there are so many places in Great Britain that we haven't visited. But I have found that the stroke has affected my concentration, can't seem to take in information in quite the same way as before. My brain feels slower somehow, and apparently I don't always see things on the left side. Anyhow, I went for a driving assessment last week and to cut a long story short, I failed. When I came home and saw the caravan in the drive I just cried. It was the first time I have cried in about thirty years. Then the next day when I went to physiotherapy, she asked me how I had got on with the driving and the tears just welled up again. I think she was a bit shocked as she only knows me as a really determined patient. But she was very good, very supportive. I have tried so hard but I feel quite defeated at the moment. I feel as though I am just standing by and watching as our dreams sink without trace.'

perhaps feel haunted by memories of what has been lost, as well as preoccupied with an altered and uncertain future. A lengthy period of grief-work may be required in order to move through this stage to one of greater acceptance and resolution.

Although therapists need to be sensitive to grief reactions, it is extremely important not to have expectations about what 'should' happen. Not everyone goes through all – or indeed any – of these phases of grieving, and there is no 'standard' or 'ideal' response. Nor is there a fixed or 'normal' timescale for the process. Some people with chronic conditions have expressed irritation when health professionals attempt to classify their complex feelings in simple ways. Michael J. Fox (2003), for example, objects to the ways in which he thought professionals categorised his feelings about having Parkinson's disease:

If this diagnosis was correct, if I had this disease, then I would forever be locked into a prognosis, and with that, an identity I'd had no part in creating … And all the while, I could be counted upon to go through a

by-the-book coping process: Elizabeth Kubler-Ross's five stages of grief
… my most trying personal experience reduced to a common laundry
list by some Swiss woman I'd never even met (p. 177).

Nevertheless, if used with humility, the theory of grief work offers a guide to
the process, helping therapists to understand the emotional volatility that is
all too often an unrecognised part of the rehabilitation experience. The theory
can also help health professionals to cope personally with patients' ostensibly
'irrational' reactions such as denial, or anger towards the healthcare system
and its workers. Such responses can be understood not as consciously chosen
strategies but as unconsciously motivated defence mechanisms that protect
the patient's fragile state of mind during a difficult transition period.

For some patients with chronic conditions, the full recognition of the ways
in which their functioning and roles have been irrevocably altered may occur
relatively late in the rehabilitation process. For example, the full emotional
force may be experienced only on leaving the structured environment of
hospital and returning home, to an array of role demands that can no longer
be accomplished in the same way as before. Grief may also become more
intense on encountering an anniversary. For example, a patient may become
distressed on noting that a whole year has elapsed since having a stroke and
that a full recovery still has not been achieved. Grief may also surface when a
scheduled future event proves impossible (for example, when a planned
return to work, or a visit to a relative living at some distance, cannot take
place because of poor health). As illustrated in the case study of Mr Penney
above, emotional distress can become heightened at such points, and the
patient's need for professional support may then increase.

It is a common saying that time is a great healer, but time alone is not
necessarily helpful. There is some evidence that with conditions that can have
a profound and irrecoverable effect on physical and psychological
functioning, such as stroke, spinal cord injury and head injury, patients can
become *more* depressed over time rather than less. Distress may increase from
encountering ongoing problems, such as cognitive difficulties, stigma and
social isolation (Hammell 1994). Hopes of full recovery, which may have
sustained the patient for some time in the early phases of illness, may
gradually or suddenly give way to an understanding that the pre-illness self
and lifestyle will not be fully restored, and that there is a different future
ahead. Support, both from health professionals and informal social networks,
can make a great deal of difference to patients who are managing emotional
distress, and can assist them in the process of reconstituting a meaningful life.

While we need to be aware of patients' emotional distress, we also need to
recognise that some patients engage in a process of emotional awakening
and personal development following on from the diagnosis of serious illness.
For some, illness – particularly life-threatening illness – brings urgent
spiritual questions, a desire for a more authentic way of being, and a renewed
zest for life. Feelings that may have been locked away by the routines and
responsibilities of life prior to illness, may come to the forefront, in what has
been termed a 'psychic explosion' by Berry (1996). The forcefulness of these

feelings can also threaten a therapist's equilibrium. For example, the therapist may be confronted by challenges to his or her religious beliefs and taken-for-granted ways of living. We need to have as much sensitivity to these energising or transformational emotions as to the more negative ones, as patients can feel quite unnerved by both of these unfamiliar psychological states. Berry (1996 p. 307) offers a vivid description of such an 'awakened state'. While he is referring to people diagnosed as HIV-positive, his comments apply to many others who face life-changing illness:

> ... some newly diagnosed clients speak of feeling as if diagnosis has transported them to a new world where all the surroundings are different: the buildings, the flora and fauna have changed and there are no maps to guide them. Exploring this metaphorical landscape can give valuable insight into such an individual's emotional state.

Metaphors are often used when we attempt to communicate an experience for which 'regular' words do not seem sufficient. Within the metaphor is an image that conveys a core essence of the experience being described.

ACTIVITY Responding to metaphor

Berry in the above statement uses the metaphor of the 'new world without maps'.
- Study the quoted passage and reflect on the meanings that you derive from this metaphor. What feelings does this metaphor suggest to you?

Look again at the account of Mr Penney. His final statement is also metaphorical.
- Free associate to the image of 'dreams sinking without trace', and see whether and how these associations help you to gain further insights into the patient's feelings.
- Does the metaphor reveal anything about this patient's emotional and cognitive state that was not so apparent earlier in his account?

Finally, although patient-centred health professionals need to be alert to patients' distress, they must avoid assuming that patients are necessarily engaged in a process of mourning. Therapists work with many people who have had life-long impairments – and with patients who have had time to adjust to a more recent injury or illness.

Many disabled people are affronted that others assume that they are grieving for loss of function and 'normality', or that they need 'help' to do so (for example, see the discussion by Lenny 1993, about whether disabled people need counselling). Nonetheless, it can be appropriate for health professionals to offer affirmative support, acknowledging for example, their understanding of the social barriers to work and social life that disabled people generally face, and the unfairness of social discrimination.

Clearly, therapists require sensitivity to each individual's construing of illness and disability, to perceive accurately when patients feel defeated by their condition and when they do not, and to assess when the patient's own social network provides sufficient resources for coping and when additional support is required.

FORMS OF SUPPORT

According to the transactional model of stress and coping (Lazarus & Folkman 1984), people experience stress when they judge that the demands placed upon them (for example, by illness) outweigh their coping resources. Coping resources include both personal skills, relevant past experiences, and external sources of assistance, such as social support.

An influential classification of social support was proposed by Kahn and Antonucci (1980), as outlined in Chapter 5. They distinguished practical/instrumental support (which includes providing information as well as giving tangible help); emotional support, including empathy and caring; and affirmative (or esteem) support, referring to communications that strengthen an other person's self-esteem and identity. A further category of 'belonging' support, fostered by one's integration into a social network, has also been suggested (Symister & Friend 2003). Depending on the size of their social networks, and their cultural background, patients may receive all of these forms of support from their family and friends. This is not always the case though. Some patients have very small social networks. Others – even if they have adequately large networks – are determined to protect close friends and family from worry, or from taking on additional caring responsibilities (Stewart et al 2001, Williams & Kent 1996). Research has shown that psychological well-being – especially for women – is closely related to having at least one confidante who is willing to listen to offer emotional support (Crohan & Antonucci 1989, Wenger & Jerrome 1999). Therapists are well placed to offer patients informational, affirmative and emotional support, in addition to assisting patients to extend and harness their own informal social networks.

ACTIVITY Examples of professional support

Provide one or two examples that you have observed in a clinical practice setting to illustrate these different forms of support that therapists or other health professionals provide to patients:
- Instrumental support
- Affirmative support
- Emotional support

(Readers without any clinical experience might reflect on the types of support that they have personally received as patients, from health professionals, for example during minor illnesses, or following an injury.)

From the patient's perspective, instrumental support from therapists includes receiving explanations about the health condition, self-management advice in jargon-free language (see next chapter for further elaboration), receiving a relevant leaflet, an adaptive aid, or advice about entitlement to disablement benefits. Affirmative support includes having one's status confirmed as a person with worth, for example receiving positive feedback from the therapist about one's perseverance, and successful coping. Emotional support, from the recipient's view, includes having one's feelings acknowledged (such as sadness, or frustration), receiving comfort, experiencing the therapist's concern and interest in one's unique situation, and being given sufficient time to express concerns and questions, rather than having the therapist tightly controlling the agenda. Cancer patients with metastatic disease have expressed how much they value sharing thoughts and feelings with a professional who 'truly cares' (MacCormack et al 2001). Supportive communications can also be viewed as engendering hope and meaningfulness (Rustoen & Hanestad 1998).

So far, the patient in emotional distress has been discussed as if he or she is an individual confronting marked changes in health and lifestyle completely alone. A study by Schilder et al (2001) highlights the inadequacy of this perspective, by emphasising that patients are people with complex social identities, and social allegiances. These, in turn, affect their health beliefs and behaviours. All patients are members of wider social and cultural communities, and health professionals need sensitivity to the diversity of beliefs and values in the populations that they serve, if they are to offer effective support. Schilder and colleagues interviewed HIV-positive participants who reported encountering many prejudicial and unsupportive interactions with health professionals. Not surprisingly, participants appreciated interacting with health professionals who were sensitive to their particular sexual and gender identities, who were comfortable with discussing sexual health issues, who offered sufficient emotional safety for disclosing sensitive issues, and who worked in an empowering manner. In the experience of these participants, health professionals all too often failed to offer such forms of support.

Many patients also appreciate support that is offered by peers with direct experience of their health condition, perceiving it to be different but complementary to the support that is offered by professionals (Stewart et al 2001). Support groups and self-help groups enable patients and their partners to share their expertise, preferred coping strategies and useful information, on an equal footing, thereby reducing isolation and uncertainty, and building self-esteem. In support groups, help is both received and *given* to others. This also has beneficial effects on well-being, as a spouse who participated in a support group for couples affected by myocardial infarction explained:

> ... there was always some good feeling that you came away with. You either helped somebody, or you made somebody laugh, or just the comradeship kind of perked you up (Stewart et al, 2001: p. 195).

While emotional support is usually framed in terms of interpersonal communication, Edgman-Levitan (1993) also points out that the physical environment of the hospital and rehabilitation unit also plays a role. She argues (p. 163) that 'clinical staff may become inured to clutter and noise that, to patients, connote disorder, confusion, unknown tortures'. Walker (1993), in the same book, outlines some ways in which the physical environment may be made more comforting. She comments (p. 136):

In the past, healers have recognised the importance of comfortable, supportive surroundings … but modern medical practice has created hospitals designed to accommodate technology, optimise efficiency, and maintain an aseptic environment.

Even though health professionals have little control over the architectural layout, general standard of decoration and large furniture in their place of work, their feedback may be able to influence the use of colour and natural light, the provision of consultation areas that allow privacy, and appropriate control over ambient noise levels. Such features of the environment can exert a significant influence over patients' emotional state. For example, patients who are highly stressed or coping with cognitive impairments (for example, after head injury) find irrelevant sounds particularly distracting. Physiotherapists who have music or radios playing in a gym area need to switch off such background sounds when they are working with these patients, in order to optimise their concentration, limit frustration and enhance feelings of self-efficacy. Even a healthy pot plant can humanise a stark institutional environment and offer the patient a comforting reminder of home (Walker 1993). Whenever major change to the physical environment is planned, patients need to be consulted. Their involvement in the design process can help to enhance the therapeutic qualities of the rehabilitation setting.

WHAT DOES SUPPORT OFFER PATIENTS? WHAT DIFFERENCE DOES IT MAKE?

Certain positive outcomes of receiving support have already been noted in Chapter 5. When adequately supported, patients are likely to report less distress (e.g. less depression and anxiety, greater optimism), higher self-esteem, better quality of life, and improved adherence with treatment (e.g. Platt et al 2001, Symister & Friend 2003). Sharing experiences in a supportive context can help patients to feel less alone and also less judgemental about their own limitations or reactions to illness. They may then feel more able to move on with the process of adaptation. This has been shown by both naturalistic studies of patients' experiences, and by experimental interventions that evaluate the outcomes of providing extra support. For example, in a qualitative survey, one survivor of a myocardial infarction (MI) who attended a support group reflected on his surprise (and relief) at discovering that others who had been through the experience were as angry as he was, 'because nowhere had I read that you could be angry' (Stewart et al 2001 p. 194). A randomised intervention by Herth (2000) followed up patients with a first recurrence of cancer who participated in one of three treatment conditions. The patients receiving supportive interventions designed to enhance hope went on to report a better quality of life and increased hope over the 9-month follow-up period, compared with patients receiving an information intervention, or the 'usual' treatment.

Patients who believe that they have been well supported are more likely to be satisfied with their treatment (as reviewed by Bylund & Makoul 2002). Satisfaction, in turn, tends to increase adherence with treatment as reviewed in Chapter 5. There is some evidence that physical health and even survival can be positively influenced by a supportive context (as reviewed by Stewart Meredith & Brown et al 2000).

Supportive environments open up channels of communication. For example, many patients with life-threatening conditions (such as cancer or heart disease) report attempting to protect their partners from worry, by denying or hiding their own feelings. However, this strategy unfortunately tends to close off mutual support for all concerned when it is most needed during a very stressful life event. Stewart et al (2001) observed that attendance at a support group for people recovering from MI and their partners, not only resulted in the sharing of useful information and coping strategies, it also helped partners to be more open with each other about their fears and frustrations. Openness was the first step in the necessary process of working together to devise a mutually acceptable lifestyle and coping strategies for the emotional and physical consequences of MI. It helped partners to maintain the quality of their relationships, instead of harbouring secrets, worries and resentments from each other. The intervention helped patients to gain or retain a confidante, a resource that is known to promote mental health and physical well-being in stressful situations. Support also seems to enhance self-efficacy (e.g. as shown by Penninx et al 1998), and this topic will be returned to in Chapter 8.

SUPPORTIVE COMMUNICATIONS: ADDRESSING THE PERSON RATHER THAN 'A PATIENT'

Affirmative support begins with basic courtesies, such as using and remembering the patient's name. Although this may seem like 'common sense', many research studies and autobiographies have revealed that patients are not always treated in the clinical setting as 'persons'. Enforced use of nightwear, impersonal dormitory environments, and other aspects of the healthcare system often strip identities away, particularly in in-patient hospital settings. Mattingly (1998) describes how an occupational therapist introduced her by name to a patient seriously affected by a brain injury. Although this seems to be such a basic, and unremarkable courtesy, Mattingly comments:

> Such a little thing, this greeting, but in the world of the hospital it is remarkably rare for a patient, especially one so sick, to be extended this courtesy and invited into the social world of the non-sick (p. 137).

People who are already marginalised in wider society are particularly vulnerable to stigmatising and belittling communications in the healthcare setting. In the study by Schilder et al (2001) referred to previously, HIV-positive individuals described a wide variety of seriously disconfirming experiences at the hands of health professionals. Even though the study was carried out quite recently (when a great deal of knowledge was available about transmission routes for HIV), patients found that their health professionals commonly withheld support by expressing overtly negative judgements about their lifestyles, and by showing reluctance to make physical contact. In one case, the health professional showed complete disregard for the dignity of the patient by throwing off a blanket in a fairly public area of the hospital simply to satisfy his curiosity about the results of a gender re-assignment operation.

Of course, not all unsupportive and prejudicial communications are as striking as this. Frye (1998) wrote of her own struggles with personal prejudice when working with a patient who was outside the norm in many ways. Jim was dirty, had tattoos showing death scenes and had a history of alcohol and drug abuse. Yet she described managing to put aside her prejudices to work intensively with the patient who was in the rehabilitation unit following a head injury. The outcomes of the rehabilitation programme were better than anyone had expected at the outset. She wrote 'I learned many lessons during Jim's rehabilitation stay. In particular, I found out how easy it is to judge a person because of his or her looks, past history, or home situation' (p. 319). She suggested that one should strive to offer patients the same courtesies and respect that one would offer one's parents or close friends.

SUPPORTIVE COMMUNICATIONS: THE PRACTICE OF EMPATHY

The core conditions of client-centred practice have already been described in the previous chapter as they are central to partnership building. Non-judgemental acceptance, genuineness and empathy are highly affirmative of identity, and help patients to work through their feelings about illness and transition in a context of respect. To feel heard and understood, without judgement, is a profoundly supportive experience and one that is much valued when it occurs (as shown by Darragh et al 2001).

Active listening is one of the most potent means of providing support, according to patients (e.g. the head-injured participants in the study by Darragh et al 2001). Active listening involves the therapist being fully present in a psychological sense with the patient, rather than distracted by outside events or internal preoccupations (Burnard 1999). It involves the therapist in making sense both of the 'facts' and also the feelings that the patient is expressing. Active listening is grounded in respect for the patient, and a sensitivity to the way that the patient frames his or her narrative about the illness. Therapists who are skilful listeners recognise that they are not dealing simply with a malfunctioning body, but are also participating in a person's life. The therapist regards both the therapeutic relationship as well as the specifics of therapy as enabling the person to re-engage in valued life plans and projects.

The therapist may understand their role as a 'co-traveller' in the patient's narrative, exploring the illness experience alongside the patient, rather than as a 'miner' who digs out only the specific details deemed 'relevant' to the treatment plan (Kvale 1996, MacLeod 1993). Active listening involves more than a search for 'facts'. As suggested earlier, the therapist who shows sensitivity to the recurrent themes and metaphors in the narrative is more likely to develop an empathic understanding of the patient. Greenhalgh and Hurwitz (1999 p. 48) argue that 'The narrative provides meaning, context, and perspective for the patient's predicament. It defines how, why, and in what way he or she is ill'.

ACTIVITY Attending to narrative

In reading the extract below, attend to Maria's experience of illness. Going beyond the obvious facts of her diagnosis, offer some suggestions into 'how, why, and in what way she is ill'.

Maria is 76 years old. She came to the UK from Italy in 1949 to marry the man she calls her 'sweetheart', a British soldier whom she first met at the end of the Second World War. She has always been a vivacious woman, exuding energy and good humour. She regards herself as the centre of her large family of five adult children and twelve grandchildren, many of whom she cares for on a regular basis. Maria also does voluntary work twice a week as a cook in a day centre for older people.

Her activities have become more difficult in recent months since a fracture, and a diagnosis of osteoporosis. She also has chronic back pain, a problem that has worsened markedly over the last twelve months.

'I have so much pain that I cannot sleep properly. That is making me ratty and tired, not like my usual self at all. I wonder am I going to crumble into a little pile of dust? This problem with my bones, can it be treated? I worry how am I going to support my youngest daughter? At the age of 40, she is going back to college, that's her heart's desire, and I said yes fine I will look after her little boy. Jamie is only two, such a handful, but he keeps me young, and I love his company. I fractured two ribs just lifting him into the car, so I feel so worried that I might break something when I am in the house with him on my own. I cook, clean, look after my dear husband. His health is not so good now. How can he get by if I can't clean the house and look after him? I can't seem to get any advice that tells me what to do for the best. I can't understand why the doctor didn't pick up this problem before, as I've seen him about my back so many times in the last five years. I feel so worried but I do not tell my family as they have enough of their own problems to deal with.'

To be fully present in an interaction, one also needs to suspend judgements about the other person, forgetting about 'oughts', 'shoulds' and any apportionment of 'blame'. The patient's views and goals may be different from one's own, but any dwelling on comparisons only leads one back to one's own frame of reference, and limits the possibility of entering the other's experiential world. When giving full attention to the patient, the therapist also shows awareness of the patient's nonverbal behaviour, in addition to the spoken word. Hesitations, changes in tone of voice, downward gaze or tearfulness, and subtle facial expressions, for example, all provide clues to the patient's psychological state.

While active listening requires cognitive and emotional processing on the part of the therapist, it also requires effective *communication,* enabling the patient to know that the therapist has indeed heard, and understood. Therapists who communicate their developing understanding of the patient's perspective also provide the patient with the opportunity to correct any misinterpretations that are occurring.

ACTIVITY Communicating understanding of the patient's narrative

1. Look again at your interpretations of Maria's narrative above. What feelings and concerns have you identified? If possible, compare your responses with those of another person to check to what extent your interpretations are similar or different.

2. A therapist offered the following summary of what she had understood:
'It sounds to me as though you are beginning to feel reluctant to look after little Jamie, now that you have a lot more pain.'
Maria replied: 'No, I do want to look after him, he is such a sunny little boy, he lights up my life. I am just worried about what might happen if I break a bone when I am with him on my own.'
- Find at least two ways in which it helps Maria to have the opportunity to correct the therapist's understanding of her concerns.
- Why is it so important for therapists to be tentative rather than dogmatic when offering interpretations of the patient's feelings?

There are more and less advanced forms of empathy. Bylund and Makoul (2002) have developed a six-level coding system to classify different forms of empathic response to patient's statements about personal and family issues. This system was based on an earlier classification of comforting strategies devised by Burleson (1994), and was developed originally for communications between physicians and patients. However, the system would appear to generalise beyond the medical encounter. At each level of the hierarchy of response, the health professional communicates a more detailed understanding and acceptance of the patient's perspective.

Hierarchy of empathic communication: based on Bylund & Makoul (2002 p. 210)

Level 0: Denial of the patient's perspective (e.g. patient's statement is ignored or disconfirmed).

Level 1: Perfunctory recognition of the patient's perspective (e.g. a vocal back-channelling response such as 'huh-huh' is given, but combined with other nonverbal behaviour that shows the professional's attention is elsewhere, for example, directed at writing notes).

Level 2: Implicit recognition of the patient's perspective (e.g. the therapist nods and says 'yes' to a patient's statement about an experience without seeking elaboration. The therapist may ask a loosely connected question to elaborate on the 'facts' about the issue raised, rather than the feelings).

Level 3: Acknowledgement (e.g. asking the patient to say more about a feeling or issue that has just been mentioned). Bylund and Makoul give the example 'You mentioned that you've been feeling sad. Would you tell me more about that?'

Level 4: Confirmation (such as making a further inference about the patient's difficulties on the basis of what has just been said; showing insight into the patient's world). Bylund and Makoul give the example of a doctor responding to a sedentary patient who needs to develop a more active lifestyle: 'You sound like you are very busy. I can see why it would be tough for you to find time to exercise.'

Level 5: Statement of shared feeling or experience (finding common ground, disclosing a similar feeling or experience).

Caution may be required in relation to implementing Level 5 in the above classification as many counsellors and psychotherapists advise therapists not to burden clients with their own personal feelings and vulnerabilities (see discussion of empathic responding by Tolan 2003). Such personal feelings can easily be interpreted by clients as blame, disapproval and so on, especially by those who have a poor self-image. Perhaps the level of mutual disclosure that Bylund and Makoul expect to occur in a doctor–patient consultation is quite limited. Nevertheless, the authors illustrate Level 5 with the response 'I understand how scary this must be for you'. In counselling skills training, health professionals are usually advised not to be too dogmatic about how the patient 'must' be feeling, nor too confident about saying 'I understand you'. Edgman-Levitan (1993) for example, points out (p. 157):

> Statements like 'I know how you are feeling' may be very comforting when they come from another patient but infuriating when made by a young healthy nurse.

Deeper forms of empathy can perhaps be phrased more tentatively. For example, one might respond to one aspect of Maria's account (above) by saying 'I get the impression that you are worried about letting your daughter down'. If the therapist also uses a tone of voice that suggests an openness to being corrected, the patient may gain the courage to dispute any misinterpretation offered. Through jointly exploring the subtleties of the patient's experiences, the patient is assisted to think more clearly about her own concerns. Ultimately, this process helps the treatment to focus on the goals that matter most to the patient, increasing the possibility of effectiveness.

ACTIVITY Practising different levels of empathic response to the narrative offered by Maria

- Read Maria's narrative again, and plan some responses that would illustrate each level of the empathic hierarchy, ranging from complete non-empathy (Level 0), to confirmation that you understand her deeper meanings and concerns (Level 4).
- If possible, compare your suggestions with those offered by another person, and discuss any differences in your empathic interpretations, as well as the possible impact of your responses on the patient.
- Note some examples of these different levels of empathy in your everyday interactions – or in the clinical setting if you have the opportunity.

Of course, the effective treatment of a patient such as Maria, with osteoporosis, requires much more than understanding, supportive communications. Nevertheless, in addition to interventions such as medication, falls prevention, strengthening exercises, education about lifestyle management and diet, we may regard psychosocial support as an important means of helping patients to manage the depression and anxiety that so often accompany this condition (Broy 1996).

As well as communicating respect and understanding, the therapist who offers close attention to the patient's narrative, with clarifying summaries and the occasional probing question, helps the patient herself to make sense of her *own* experience. In time, this may help the patient to 're-author' a new story about her life and future. Illness has the propensity to create 'narrative wreckage', throwing the purpose of one's life into question, and making the future that one had previously anticipated seem out of reach (Crossley 2000). Therapists who encourage patients to tell their stories may enable them to discover fresh meanings, and more acceptable 'endings' (Mattingly 1998). Many patients and their families have to work hard to integrate the experiences associated with illness and impairment into their life story, and to imbue the new turn of events with acceptable meaning. Of course, therapists do not necessarily play the most important role in helping patients re-narrate their life stories. Patients' own search for meaning, reflections on self and significant life events, and discussions with family and friends all play a part.

There are many examples of people finding meaning in chronic illness through the process of life review. For example, Michael J. Fox provides a glimpse of how he began to integrate his experience of Parkinson's disease into his life story from watching a videotape of himself as a 6-year-old child cycling in the yard. He started to see the illness as having some positive influence in helping him to re-connect with what he regarded as his earlier, more 'authentic' self:

> It is plain from these scenes [in the video] that in many ways who I am is *who I always was* ... Along the way came distractions and self-doubt, detours and adjustments, but the tape tells me that the adult I am today has more in common with the kid on the bike than with the person I was in between. It's gratifying to know that I somehow found my way back, and it's bracing to realise that my Parkinson's diagnosis played an important part in leading me there (Fox, 2003: p. 52).

Because many patients develop close and trusting relationships with their therapists, sensitive and supportive communications can help patients to find meaningful coherence in the patterns of their lives. Rather than seeing illness as alien and imposed without meaning, patients may come to see illness as having a meaningful part to play in the plot that their lives are following. Therapists can assist in this 're-authoring' process, as the following example shows.

ACTIVITY Responding to a patient's attempt to impose meaning upon her life story

The following encounter occurred between a therapist and Joyce, a 76-year-old woman, at the beginning of her fourth session of rehabilitation following a stroke:

- Consider how the therapist is helping Joyce to think about some deeply personal issues, even though the encounter is quite brief and humorous in places.
- The therapist could have responded to Joyce's opening statement by a 'Level 0' empathic response such as 'Mmm, that's nice, now let's get on with the therapy'. What likely consequences would such a response have had?

Joyce: I have been thinking a lot this week about my mum, how she struggled through the Blitz, our house was bombed during the war but she never seemed to give up.

Therapist: Your mum sounds as though she was made of stern stuff! (Both laugh).

Joyce: (Pause) Perhaps this stroke is my Blitz. (Pause) You know, I'm not going to give up either.

Therapist: (Changing to a reflective tone of voice) You seem to be showing the same grit and determination as your mother did all those years ago. Are you realising that you're made of stern stuff too?

Joyce: Well, stiff stuff anyway. (Joyce laughs, while gesturing to the affected side of her body, showing the first real sign of merriment – and a measure of acceptance of her changed body – since beginning the stroke rehabilitation process.)

This example illustrates three main points about supportive communications:

- Supportive communications do not necessarily take much time, nor are they necessarily reliant on patients offering 'deep' and painful self disclosures.
- Light, humorous exchanges can sometimes help patients to talk about serious issues (although humour must always be introduced with care).
- The therapist can do much to help patients find coherent meanings in their life stories by being attuned to ways in which patients are seeking connections in their lives – for example, finding shared experiences that arise across the generations of their families, and across the different periods of their own lives. In the above case, Joyce has made a connection between the adversities suffered by herself and her mother. She seems to have a growing realisation that, like her mother, she has the attitudes and resources to cope. The therapist has facilitated this way of representing her experience.

SUPPORTIVE COMMUNICATIONS: CONTAINMENT

Finally, consider a further way in which attentive listening and a supportive relationship helps patients to cope with negative thoughts and feelings. The attentive therapist may be understood as offering the patient containment, or a form of psychological 'holding' – that is, a place where feelings may be safely expressed without fear of disintegration or losing control. Some patients have nowhere – and no-one – else safe enough to admit their vulnerability. Berry (1996 p. 312) writes about working with patients who are HIV-positive:

> A client who describes an idyllic landscape which is being rocked by an earthquake may be communicating that the very foundation of their being feels under threat … Whatever the landscape described, understanding and conveying that understanding to clients, seems to help a great deal. A strong here-and-now relationship can be established which helps to hold clients through what is an extremely difficult time.

Although Berry was addressing counsellors, his argument can apply to other health professionals who are responding with empathy to their clients and patients.

Empathic therapists help patients to explore meanings and metaphors, through active listening, the seeking of clarification, paraphrasing and so on. However, patients should not be forced to disclose more than they wish. Reynolds (1994 p. 27) quotes a patient who said of an empathic nurse:

> When I don't want to talk about something she seems to recognise this mood ... She won't persist if I'm reluctant.

Empathy includes respecting the needs that patients sometimes have of hiding feelings such as shame or anxiety, perhaps gaining relief from focusing on the task instead of self. It is not supportive to press patients into disclosure, or to make critical judgements about their preferred coping strategies. It can take time for trust to develop, and some patients prefer to adopt 'task-oriented' coping strategies during their rehabilitation.

CAN EMPATHY BE TAUGHT?

At first sight, it may seem to be difficult to teach people to enter others' subjective worlds with sensitivity, and without trampling all over the other person's subtle personal meanings and concerns. Yet there is some evidence that people can develop more empathic communication skills through various experiences. These include learning about empathy, reflecting on their own feelings and 'blindspots', modelling (that is, observing others who demonstrate the necessary skills), role play and feedback (Oz 2001).

Oz (2001) reported the results of an empathy-training programme lasting for 10 weeks (with two hours per week devoted to training). This quasi-experimental intervention involved a group of 150 nurses divided into empathy training and control groups. Participants in each group were selected from separate teams or units to minimise the possibility of cross-contact and social influence. The participants completed questionnaires before and after the intervention, including offering empathic responses to a number of written case study patients. The researcher distinguished communications that did not show effective empathy (e.g. evaluating the problem as an 'outsider', making criticisms or judgements, giving advice, referring to one's own problems and feelings) and those that did show empathy (e.g. supporting, being prepared to work on the problem jointly with the patient, reflecting back the surface meanings/feelings expressed, showing understanding of deeper feelings). The study found that nurses showed a strong tendency to give advice rather than effective empathy at the outset. However, they did show improvements after training. Such improvements in empathic responding did not occur in the control group, so we can discount the possibility that participants simply learned to perform better on the questionnaire test. Nevertheless, a problem remained in this study in that assessment of empathy continued to rely on pencil-and-paper tests and written cases rather than interactions with complex 'real' patients.

Jenkins and Fallowfield (2002) also support the argument that empathy can be enhanced through training. Their study had the advantage of including observations of the health professionals interacting with their patients. They randomly allocated two groups of physicians into a control group and a three-day residential communication skills training group. The physicians all worked with cancer patients. The researchers observed that not only did the 'trained' group become more positive about discussing psychosocial issues during consultations, they also showed more skilful communications. The group who received training went on to demonstrate more empathic responses, made greater use of open questions, asked their patients for more information about psychosocial issues, and were more responsive to patients' cues.

ACTIVITY Building a partnership through practising empathy

With a colleague/fellow student, spend five to ten minutes with one person designated as speaker and one as listener. The speaker needs to reflect on some difficulty that he/she is willing to share (e.g. students may reflect on any anxieties they are feeling about the next clinical placement). During the five minutes, the listener makes every effort to enter the other's lifeworld. The following strategies may be helpful to listeners in this exercise:

- Be aware of your zone of attention – are you focusing on your partner, on external distractions or on your own thought processes? Try to maintain your focus on your partner, and silence 'internal talk' (Matthews et al 1993).
- Ensure that your nonverbal behaviour communicates attention and interest (e.g. through sitting squarely towards the person, making eye contact, avoiding fidgeting or note writing, using appropriate head nods, and making listening sounds such as 'mmm' and 'huh-huh'. Tone of voice is also a part of nonverbal behaviour. An 'instructive' tone can easily convey 'busy-ness', and lack of interest in the other's perspective (Arthur 1999).
- Attend to the person's choice of words, metaphors, and recurring themes to locate the deeper levels of the person's story.
- From time to time, summarise the main themes in the speaker's account. Rather than being too dogmatic ('You're saying that ...'), it is better to offer a tentative paraphrase (e.g. 'It sounds as though you are saying/feeling ...'), as this invites the speaker to make any corrections that are needed.
- From time to time, try to reflect back the feelings that you believe your partner is expressing (albeit possibly indirectly). Try to attend to the person's tone of voice, facial expression and other nonverbal cues. Again, offer your interpretation quite tentatively so that the speaker can correct you if you have misunderstood the verbal and nonverbal cues.
- Try to ask only a few questions so as not to impose your own agenda. Make sure that any question is pertinent to what the other has been saying, and that it helps you to enter the other's story more fully. Open questions give the partner more scope to reveal personal experience. Questions should not simply reflect your own agenda or 'nosiness'.
- Leave some short silences to encourage deeper thought in both partners.
- Track your own feelings. Are you, for example, feeling anxious during the interaction? Might this feeling mirror your partner's emotional state? Or not? Try to separate your own feelings from those of your partner.
- Allow a period of debriefing, where you encourage your partner to comment on whether she/he felt 'heard' or not, and to point out which of your communications suggested empathy (or a lack of understanding).
- Swap roles and repeat the activity.
- Finally reflect on your own feelings and behaviour during the encounter – what was easy, what was difficult, how might you build more empathic responses into your communication skills repertoire?

Note that in this activity, you are asked to practise certain verbal and nonverbal skills, such as open questioning, or attentive facial expressions. However, the exercise also asks you to monitor your own feelings and responses, termed 'emotional work' by McQueen (2000). This emotional work helps you to 'catch' emotions that the patient may be experiencing but not verbalising. Such awareness also helps you to separate your own responses from those of the patient, potentially helping you to listen more fully. The exercise includes both the perceptual and communicative aspects of empathy. As Tolan (2003 p. 18) argues:

> You can hear, understand and feel very deeply for a client, but if that perception is locked inside your wooden, and unresponsive exterior, it is not available for the client to use.

It is essential for the therapist's empathic understanding to be voiced to the patient, if it is to be supportive.

COGNITIVE BEHAVIOURAL APPROACHES

While traditional definitions of support emphasise the care, nurturance and protection offered *to* the patient *by* the health professional, some authors have outlined further ways in which patients may gain emotional succour through professional interventions. These interventions tend to involve the patient as a highly active and collaborative partner in devising personally meaningful ways of coping with distress. Cognitive behavioural interventions have been shown to help patients with physical health problems to manage distress and uncertainty (e.g. Dudley-Brown 2002). A basic principle of cognitive behavioural therapy is that people's distress is driven not so much by external events directly but by their own thoughts and ways of construing the situation. Gilbert (1992) refers to the client's process of 'meaning-making'. For example, the patient being treated for a facial injury may hold an extremely negative belief that everyone finds a facial disfigurement repulsive and that therefore he will never be able to make any new friends or meet a partner.

If distressed patients can be encouraged to identify such negative thoughts and assumptions, they can go on to test whether their thinking is really valid – or whether, as can happen, the thoughts exaggerate certain threats and difficulties without solid evidence. Depressive thoughts tend to be of an unwarranted dichotomous type – 'all or none' – and can be challenged and changed. For example, patients may represent life following a stroke as without any redeeming features whereas they fantasise that life before stroke was completely 'marvellous'. The patient may also judge progress in rehabilitation in starkly dichotomous terms as either totally successful or a complete failure. The therapist may gently assist patients to view experiences in a more differentiated way, finding the 'shades of grey' in between the contrasts that they are currently working with conceptually.

Another way in which thought patterns elevate distress is through the unreflective application of 'oughts' and 'shoulds'. The therapist who helps the patient to become more aware of these assumptions, may empower more choice and autonomy. Patients can be encouraged to pursue personally meaningful goals rather than being trapped by the 'oughts' that they have internalised from family and the wider culture. A patient with multiple sclerosis (MS), recently interviewed by the author appeared to have challenged some of the 'oughts and shoulds' that she once applied to her lifestyle. This challenge to her taken-for-granted assumptions had clearly taken time and effort:

> [In the early stages of the illness] I felt that I ought to complete my degree because I was in my second year and I owed money and my parents had worked hard to support me financially. I really struggled. But in the end I stopped beating myself up about it and realised that I was just too tired with the MS. The disease is so unpredictable that I cannot know how I will be from one day to the next. I decided eventually that the stress was making me even more ill. (F Reynolds, unpublished work, 2000)

Cognitive behavioural techniques tend to be represented as tackling negative, self-defeating thinking, but they can work well in inspiring hope and a positive approach to rehabilitation. Rustoen and Hanestad (1998), for example, reviewed a number of studies that have invited chronically ill patients (including cancer patients) to reflect on the experiences that inspire hope and lessen distress. From this research, these authors propose that patients gain hope (and better withstand feelings of despair) when they are encouraged to do the following:

- Believe in their own abilities
- Explore and acknowledge their emotional reactions (including grief responses)
- Preserve their relationships with others
- Have an active involvement in treatment decisions and coping strategies
- Clarify religious beliefs and spiritual values
- Take a positive attitude towards the future.

The authors reported an eight-week programme (of two hours per week) in which these various topics were discussed. Small groups of patients, who were being treated for cancer, participated. The intervention followed cognitive behavioural principles, and helped participants to identify and share their problems in coping with illness, and to focus on their preferred goals and choices.

Rustoen and Hanestad (1998) argue that at the cognitive level, patients can be encouraged to identify their negative, self-defeating thoughts and to challenge their validity. For example, the health professional is alert to any statements that the patient makes about being 'worthless', and helps the patient to challenge such a label. Emotional distress may also be reduced if some aspects of the situation can be reframed in more positive terms. For example, if the patient can identify which specific problems they are able to tackle successfully, rather than perceiving problems as piled up into an insurmountable 'mountain' (Rickel 1987). Stress management strategies such as relaxation techniques, and meaningful activities can also help to challenge self-defeating thoughts. Such behavioural coping strategies provide release from unproductive worry, and can help patients to re-invest in their lives. The programme offered by Rustoen and Hanestad (1998) was not formally evaluated, so its effectiveness in providing support cannot be firmly established. However, as a paper that is available in full-text from the database CINAHL, it is worth reading for its many practical suggestions for supportive interventions to patients with serious health problems. Examination of programme content also indicates that support may be most effective when offered by an interprofessional (or multi-professional) team, and that occupational therapists, counsellors, physiotherapists and nurses can each make a complementary contribution.

OTHER FORMS OF SUPPORT

While communications directly between the therapist and patient provide an important channel of support, other strategies can also offer comfort and empowerment. These include:

- Group interventions/therapy
- Support groups
- Telephone support
- Virtual support on the Internet
- Community resources guidebook
- Volunteering
- Education for carers
- Referral to other healthcare professionals, e.g. counsellor.

Therapists sometimes have the choice of providing therapeutic interventions to single patients or to groups. While group treatments are sometimes selected primarily to cut costs, therapists also need to recognise that groups may have an additional value in enabling patients to offer each other mutual support. Group treatment is not *necessarily* more effective than individual treatment, partly because the intervention is likely to be less tailored to any individual's particular needs. Nevertheless, groups have enormous potential for enhancing support, thereby achieving more positive rehabilitation outcomes. Pentinnen et al (2002) compared two 'back school' groups, one in which patients were encouraged to socialise with the other patients, as well as participating in physical exercises, and a control group providing a similar physical intervention without corresponding peer support. They found that the patients in the group with extra support reported better quality of life after 6 months, and better functional capacity at 12 months, compared with patients who attended the control group. Therapists who are debating whether to offer individual or group-based therapy may wish to consult the literature further to evaluate the evidence for the effectiveness of group-based therapy for other conditions (e.g. physiotherapy for MS).

Support and self-help groups can provide people with considerable emotional, informational and practical support. Such groups are often managed by people with direct experience of a health problem, although some support groups are co-led by peers and professionals working in partnership. Co-led groups can work well if the distinct expertise and responsibilities of the professional and lay leaders are defined and agreed, and if professionals are careful not to dominate the group process (Banks et al 1997). There are a huge number of support groups in existence, and their aims are usually both educational and supportive. Support groups help to reduce the isolation and disruption to identity that chronic illness tends to bring about. They help members to acquire knowledge and coping strategies that they might not otherwise gain from books – or indeed, from health professionals who inevitably remain 'outsiders' to the illness experience. However, not all support groups yield measurable benefits, particularly when these are measured through quantitative scales such as quality of life (Kessenich et al 2000). Nevertheless, for the effective treatment of chronic illnesses such as osteoporosis, Kessenich et al argue that support groups should form *one strand* of a multi-strand rehabilitation programme that includes 'education, support, physiotherapy, occupational therapy, and exercise' (p. 90). This emphasises that support comes in many forms, and complements many types of intervention.

People facing an unfamiliar health problem generally have difficulties in finding out information, whether it concerns the condition itself, treatment choices, local support groups in the community, or financial options such as applying for disability benefits. One research study points to the potential value of health professionals putting together a community resources guidebook. Strycker and Glasgow (2002) developed a guidebook on local resources to help people with diabetes more effectively self-manage their diet, and found evidence that patients were satisfied with this resource. The wider application to people with other conditions of such an inexpensive form of support deserves further evaluation.

There is an increasing body of evidence suggesting that telephone support from health professionals can provide a fairly inexpensive intervention with positive outcomes. Telephone contact by a health professional may be supportive in a number of ways. Its purpose may be primarily informative, or it may be motivational, perhaps reminding the patient of dietary or other lifestyle changes that are part of the rehabilitation programme. Telephone support can also be directed primarily at troubleshooting any problems in self-management that are arising, or by promoting problem-solving coping strategies (Roberts et al 1995). The telephone contact can also be experienced as conveying care and concern, with the health professional communicating ongoing interest in the patient's well-being. Telephone support can also be targeted at family caregivers, for example, of people who have had a stroke. Grant et al (2002) found that family caregivers of people with stroke reported many benefits from receiving problem-solving telephone support over three months (weekly during month 1 and once every two weeks during months 2 and 3). The benefits for the stroke patients themselves were not reported but caregivers who are less depressed would appear to be in a better position to provide effective care and support. Low-cost but well targeted communication interventions for caregivers would appear to confer considerable rehabilitation benefits. Again, further research is warranted.

Some telephone supporters are peers rather than professionals. The telephone enables a form of contact that is especially valued by people who find travel difficult, who would otherwise be isolated (for example, people with mobility problems or those who live in rural areas). In one study, patients with osteoarthritis of the knee reported less pain and better functioning when receiving regular telephone support from lay supporters (Rene et al 1992). Ritchie et al (2000) found that parents of children with chronic illnesses reported many positive outcomes from a 22-week telephone peer support service, including better social support, less isolation, enhanced coping strategies and improved confidence. Several quotes from parents showed how the benefits of having informational and emotional support are intertwined. For example, one mother of an adolescent with diabetes explained how acquiring greater knowledge about the condition from the telephone support group had helped her to feel less stressed and to develop a better relationship with her daughter. The telephone supporters also seemed to offer each other a lot of affirmative support. One parent caring for an ill child said:

> Before, I was worrying that maybe I'm not good at this, and [now] I know I am because I am doing the best that I can do. And to have somebody tell you that is good (Ritchie et al 2000 p. 36).

As there are relatively few studies of telephone support, therapists who consider using such a support mechanism are advised to consult the literature further to establish whether there is evidence relating to patients and contexts similar to their own. Directly relevant evidence may be difficult to find, yet the studies to date do seem to suggest that such interventions are worth piloting and evaluating.

The population's increasing access to personal computers and the Internet, has encouraged the formation of a number of 'virtual' support groups. One example in the UK is the award winning site Joolie's Joint (www.mswebpals.org) for people with multiple sclerosis. It might be thought that web-based support would appeal more to younger people with health problems and/or caring responsibilities. However, a study in a rural area of the USA showed that middle-aged and older women with chronic health problems were very favourable about the support offered by a 'virtual' support group. They reported few problems accessing the Internet site and many benefits (Weinert 2000). They found self-worth in offering each other support, gained information that helped them to negotiate more suitable care from health professionals, and learned that their feelings were shared amongst others with a similar condition. Such support would simply not have been accessible had the women been required to travel in person across rural Montana to meet face-to-face. Again, therapists wishing to offer good levels of support to their patients might spend a little time in researching whether there are suitable 'virtual' support groups (as well as community groups) for their patients.

Improved support by health professionals for the family can in turn lead to better support for the patient. Caregivers are all too often isolated and uncertain about their roles and entitlements, and feel unsupported by both health professionals and their own informal social networks (Bergs 2002). Furthermore, lack of support for caregivers can also lead to worse outcomes for the person affected by illness. For example, if caregivers have limited understanding of the patient's needs, they may unwittingly engage in critical, overprotective and infantilising behaviour (Coyne et al 1988; Manne & Zautra 1989). The pressures of caring can eventually lead to the collapse of the whole support system, to the great detriment of everyone involved. Having encountered the fragility of patients' informal support structures, some health professionals argue that family members should be regarded as their 'hidden' clients (Bergs 2002). One study evaluated the outcomes of specifically involving spouses in a programme designed to help patients with arthritis cope with their condition, osteoarthritis of the knee (Keefe et al 1996). The study involved a randomised trial of three conditions, namely pain-coping skills training with and without spouse involvement, and a control group who received education about arthritis and a simple form of spouse support. Each intervention lasted for ten weeks. The pain-coping skills training with spouse involvement produced the best outcomes, with patients reporting less pain, disability and pain behaviour at the end of the treatment programme.

Health professionals can also help patients to enhance their own informal social support, and therefore to maximise their well-being, through encouraging them to think about the quality of their support networks, and to identify ways of strengthening these. Volunteering is one way in which people become part of a wider community, and its psychological importance has been noted by Barlow and Hainsworth (2001). They found that older people with arthritis who volunteered to lead an arthritis self-help group reported a number of emotional and social benefits from taking on this role. They also became less distressed by their pain. Obviously, volunteering does not appeal to everyone, and limited mobility, chronic pain and other problems may prevent this option from being realistic. Nevertheless, evidence such as this suggests that it may be helpful if health professionals help their patients to identify their support needs. Enhanced informal support complements that which is offered by health and social care professionals. Again, therapists with knowledge of local resources (such as adult education classes, exercise classes, women's groups and others) will be in a better position to help patients to extend their support networks.

Referral to other professional services such as a counsellor is another strategy for providing patients with the support that they need. However, some patients with physical health problems prefer to talk about their emotional difficulties with physiotherapists and occupational therapists, believing that there is less stigma attached (Reynolds 1999). A large minority of patients in a general practice setting have expressed reservations about seeing a counsellor from fear that it suggests that they cannot cope (Thomas 1996). Some dislike revealing personal concerns to a person whom they regard as a 'stranger'. Nevertheless, referral is certainly an appropriate option to discuss with patients who require more time for expressing their concerns than is available in the physiotherapy or occupational therapy session, or who reveal psychological difficulties that can be better addressed by a professional with more advanced counselling skills.

BARRIERS TO OFFERING PATIENT-CENTRED SUPPORT

Many barriers to patient-centredness have been discussed in previous chapters, including real or perceived lack of therapy time, limited resources, the domination of the biomedical model which relegates patients' emotional and identity issues to the margins of health professionals' concerns, and the tendency for health professionals to view some health problems as 'routine', when they do not appear this way at all to the patients who are personally affected.

Several additional problems regularly confront health professionals who work with patients suffering emotional distress. Awareness of these may help therapists to remain more open and therefore supportive.

ACTIVITY Reactions to tears and distress: personal reflection

In a previous activity, you read about Mr Bob Penney who became tearful when his physiotherapist asked him about the outcome of his driving assessment following a stroke. You were asked to reflect on your responses to people who are tearful. Take a few moments to reflect more generally on your responses to emotional distress in others – whether expressed nonverbally, through tears for example, or verbally.

- Consider whether or not you usually feel comfortable with expressions of distress, and why/why not.
- What is your first reaction likely to be to another person's distress? Try to identify your first thoughts, feelings and behaviours, without making a judgement about them or offering a 'socially desirable' answer.

Distress in others can be very hard to witness. Rather than listening to the other person and accepting the expression of negative feelings, we may find numerous ways of withholding support, by for example:

- Showing embarrassment.
- Ignoring the subtle signs of distress (e.g. the person's breathy tone of voice, tears welling up, fidgeting) and focusing simply on the task in hand.
- Changing the subject.
- Attempting to 'jolly' the person out of distress, sometimes with empty clichés ('don't worry', 'look on the bright side', 'be positive').

- Treating depression, sadness, worry and so on as a moral weakness that might infect others and which therefore should not be allowed expression.
- Looking for a 'quick fix' solution (perhaps offering glib advice and possibly becoming irritated if this seems insufficient and unconvincing to the other person).
- Focusing on self ('me too' and 'poor me' responses).

These have been termed 'blocking behaviours' by Maguire and Pitceathly (2002).

Failures of empathy may reflect many gaps in one's education and socialisation. Some people grow up in a family culture where expression of distress is rarely tolerated. Perhaps they have been used to family members making fun of or belittling anyone who is vulnerable or seeking help. In some very small families, there is limited opportunity to practise taking on the roles of others, meaning that the person may develop limited insight into others' views and feelings (Oz 2001). Some people live with unresolved issues from the past, and these may lead to misperceptions of the patient's behaviour. For example, a therapist who has never come to terms with a father's anger may magnify the significance of a patient's expression of anger during a difficult session. Gilbert (1992 p. 125) gives an example of such a childhood legacy, quoting an adult client's reflection on his way of dealing with feelings:

> My father used to tease me if I cried. He'd call me poor little baby face or cry baby. I hated him for that … I think most of the time I hold back on feelings. Some think I'm cold maybe but I'm not. I just find it hard to show my feelings. It wasn't done in our family.

A therapist who shares this background may be left feeling vulnerable and childlike if she is reminded about these feelings from the past by the patient's behaviour in the present situation. She is unlikely to be able to offer an angry or tearful patient an 'adult' listening ear. Similarly, therapists who remain locked in mourning for a personal loss (for example, following a childhood bereavement) may find it difficult to listen in a fully focused, non-judgemental and accepting way to patients who are distressed by their own losses or feelings of powerlessness.

By reason of personality or socialisation, some people have difficulties in acknowledging their own feelings of distress, and therefore become very anxious when expected to respond to the feelings of others. The same thoughts, judgements and impatience that they have learned throughout their socialisation to apply to their own feelings (e.g. 'You're pathetic!', 'Grow up!') come readily to the forefront when working with distressed patients. Unfortunately, patients readily perceive signs that the health professional is feeling overwhelmed and unable to go further. Many will control their disclosures accordingly, leaving themselves ultimately with less support.

Some therapists also lack education in empathic responding. Their clinical training may have given priority to imparting knowledge of anatomy, physiology and so on, leaving issues such as empathy and communication skills to seem like frivolous, bolted-on 'extras'. Their training may have provided little opportunity for self-reflection about personal ways of coping with distress and responding to others.

While you are not expected to have advanced counselling skills to work as an effective rehabilitation therapist, it is important to engage in self-reflection and training opportunities that will maximise your capacity for empathy and emotional engagement with patients.

SUPPORT AND SELF-CARE FOR THERAPISTS

Therapists in many settings are exposed to patients' grief – and sometimes anger – day after day. As noted throughout this chapter, some patients with chronic conditions are engaged in a fraught process of mourning their loss of function, and valued roles. Yet engagement with patients' feelings is a relatively unrecognised aspect of practice within biomedical contexts. Mattingly (1998) argues that it is therefore carried out as an 'underground' or 'furtive' practice (p. 22). This can leave therapists largely unsupported, and vulnerable to emotional burnout.

Furthermore, therapists sometimes find that a patient's difficulties closely mirror a personal life event. For example, working with a patient who has been injured in a road traffic accident, or during an assault, may remind the therapist of a personally traumatic experience. A particular older patient may remind the therapist of a much-loved deceased grandparent. Stebnicki (2000) argues that professionals working in rehabilitation settings need to be mindful of possible 'empathy fatigue', or emotional disengagement, and implement strategies of self-care.

Both personal and organisational strategies can be valuable. Personal strategies include health promoting activities such as making time for regular physical exercise, continuing with meaningful and life-affirming leisure activities, and maintaining an acceptable balance between home and work roles. Self-reflection is a vital tool as early awareness of increasing emotional strain can help therapists to act in good time, for example, by talking through problems with colleagues or a clinical supervisor, arranging some holiday leave, or through other strategies.

At the organisational level, the provision of clinical supervision provides the opportunity for therapists to reflect on their work with patients, exploring the difficulties that are arising and identifying appropriate actions. Clinical supervision should be supportive and non-judgemental, to offer most opportunity for learning and personal/professional development. While mandatory for counsellors, it is not always given priority in rehabilitation settings.

There are a few published examples of therapist support and co-supervision groups, in which therapists meet on a regular basis (e.g. weekly or monthly) to reflect on practice, including their relationships with patients. A report of one group, termed a Balint training group, facilitated by a

ACTIVITY Reflection on self-care strategies

- What strategies would help you to maintain your capacity to offer support to others, and to minimise the risk of emotional burnout in the clinical setting?

physiotherapist with psychotherapy training, has been published (Dahlgren et al 2000). In such groups, participants focus on a real case, and reflect on the psychological aspects, the family's needs, and the therapeutic relationship in depth. In the study by Dahlgren et al (2000) participants were all physiotherapists in private practice. They indicated that they had joined the group because they had felt frustrated at their lack of skills for relating to patients, and for managing their own emotional responses to some patients. Through sharing problems and perspectives, they found themselves thinking about patients in a different, deeper way, being more honest in their relationships with patients, and managing their own emotions more effectively. One stated (p. 92):

I think I have become a bit more sensitive, both to my own reactions, to the patient encounter and the patient's reactions ... How they say things, what they do and how they react ... I think I have become a little bit more humble and thoughtful ... I think I dare a little bit more, maybe, to ask that difficult question that felt frightening.

Further training in counselling skills is particularly recommended for therapists working in contexts which have the capacity to be highly emotionally charged, such as spinal injury and head injury units. Not only do such courses help therapists to feel better equipped and more effective in their roles, but also the increased self-knowledge which is usually developed through such training can help therapists to take better care of their own mental health (Reynolds 1999). However, the potential risk of having advanced counselling training is that the team may respond by devolving all 'emotional labour' to the designated 'specialist', thereby increasing the potential strain on that individual. The emotional care of patients and self-care of the professionals involved should be seen as a team responsibility, with at least brief periods regularly set aside for discussing the personal impact of work with patients. It is difficult for therapists to offer patients adequate support if they do not experience at least some emotional care and concern from their colleagues.

CONCLUSION

Various forms of support that can be helpful to patients have been discussed. Some forms of emotional, affirmative and practical support are embedded in the very matrix of interactions between therapist and patient. These do not necessarily take much time but they do require therapists to be sensitive to the process of meaning-making that patients engage in when confronting long-term change in health and functioning. Support can be conveyed through paying close attention to the patient's verbal and nonverbal communications, and showing respect for individual differences in preferred coping strategies.

The embeddedness of support within the therapy process creates difficulties for formal evaluation. Nevertheless, patients have expressed a need for supportive relationships with health professionals, and have also reported that such needs are regularly unmet. Support can be offered informally and also as a formal intervention within the therapy process, for example, telephone support, cognitive behavioural work and information about community support resources. Self-care and teamwork is vital if therapists are to engage with patients' emotional difficulties in the longer term. There is a range of evidence that suggests supportive communications help to maximise the effectiveness of rehabilitation.

Further Reading

Tolan J 2003 Skills in person-centred counselling and psychotherapy. Sage, London
  This book is particularly recommended for detailed further suggestions about person-centred counselling skills, including empathy.
Herth K Enhancing hope in people with a first recurrence of cancer. Journal of Advanced Nursing 32(6):1431–1441
Stewart M, Davidson K, Meade D et al 2001 Group support for couples coping with a cardiac condition. Journal of Advanced Nursing 33(2):190–199
  These two papers are good examples of research into supportive interventions. Both are available in full-text format via CINAHL.
Rustoen T, Hanestad B 1998 Nursing interventions to increase hope in cancer patients. Journal of Clinical Nursing 7(1):19–27
  A detailed account of hope-inspiring interventions. The authors address nurses specifically but an interprofessional team may be able to incorporate these interventions quite successfully. The article can be gained full-text through CINAHL.
Bylund C, Makoul G 2002 Empathic communication and gender in the physician–patient encounter. Patient Education and Counseling 48:207–216
  This paper describes the levels of empathic communication in detail. It is available in full-text format via the electronic database Science Direct.

Chapter **8**

Patient education and empowerment

Chronic conditions inevitably present people with the challenge of coping with a long-term and diverse array of difficulties, including physical symptoms, role and activity limitations, changes in self-image, social discrimination and uncertainty. The previously established patterns of daily life may be irrevocably altered and patients often need to follow treatment recommendations for lengthy periods – or permanently – if these are to improve function and regain quality of life. The effectiveness of a rehabilitation programme generally depends upon patients' understanding of the rationale of the programme and their willingness to adhere to such recommendations in their own environments. Patients need both knowledge and skills to manage the challenges involved. According to Bodenheimer et al (2002 p. 2469), 'optimal chronic care is achieved when a prepared, proactive practice team interacts with an informed, activated patient'.

Patient education has been recognised as making a vital contribution to conventional biomedical care for many years. It perhaps forms an even more important component of rehabilitation. Sluijs (1991) recorded more than 200 physiotherapy sessions and found that teaching, advice and health education of patients occurred in most of these sessions. Various studies have examined the effectiveness of psychoeducation for patients undergoing rehabilitation, although not all have disentangled the effects of the educational component from the 'hands-on' component of treatment (e.g. Moseley 2002). Ley (1988) carried out a major review of the effects of patient education. After appraising a large number of studies, he concluded that patients who receive the information that they need are more likely both to be satisfied with their treatment and to adhere to it. Patient education therefore offers a powerful way of enhancing treatment outcomes.

Traditional approaches to patient education tended to treat patients as 'empty vessels' waiting to be filled by the expertise of their health professionals, especially their medical consultants. Health professionals were seen as having the prime responsibility for determining which information was required by the patient to manage the health problem most effectively (Van den Borne 1998). However, in the last few years, the concept of patient education has been reconceptualised. In this new approach, health professionals still require effective teaching skills for delivering relevant knowledge to patients. However, they also need to develop strategies for working with patients as partners in rehabilitation. This newer perspective on patient education sees it as empowering patients' choice and control, and enhancing their self-management skills, rather than as simply encouraging 'compliance' with treatment. Bodenheimer et al (2002) argue that the concept of patient empowerment 'holds that patients accept responsibility to manage their own conditions and are encouraged to solve their own problems with information, but not orders, from professionals' (p. 2471).

Since about 1999, NHS initiatives have emphasised that patent-focused care involves recognising and developing patients' own expertise in managing their chronic conditions. The concept of the 'expert patient' was included in the document *Saving Lives: Our Healthier Nation* (Department of Health 1999), and developed further in subsequent publications (e.g. Department of Health, 2001). Despite this emphasis, recent studies continue to report that patients encounter difficulties in gaining sufficient information to help them cope with their condition. For example, a large minority of patients in some surveys express disappointment in the quality, quantity and relevance of information received from health professionals during rehabilitation. Tyson and Turner (2000) found that about a third of patients who had undergone rehabilitation after a stroke were dissatisfied with the quality and quantity of information that they had been given. Another recent study of physiotherapy patients, by Trede (2000), asked them to comment on the education that they had received to help them manage low back pain. Almost all regarded their physiotherapist as using a non-flexible information-giving approach, without regard to their particular information needs. Only one therapist was evaluated as patient-centred in her educational approach. Although this was a small-scale qualitative study, it did suggest that therapists in physical rehabilitation might need to learn more about patient-centred educational strategies. However, any idea that limited information-giving is a problem only among physiotherapists is challenged by another recent study. Van Weert et al (2003) analysed videotaped interactions between cardiac surgery patients and various members of the interdisciplinary team, including a health educator, nurse and cardiothoracic surgeon. The study gained a complex array of findings, but notable among them was the observation that more than three-quarters of patients did not receive any information at all about the possible psychological effects of cardiac surgery. Staff asked less than a quarter of the patients directly about their informational needs.

In this chapter, we will consider the following issues:

- What forms of information and education do patients in physical rehabilitation typically value?
- What factors prevent patients from gaining the information they need to empower choice and coping?
- What is the health communication matrix?
- Helping patients learn through maximising attention, comprehension and recall.
- Using a variety of communication media effectively (e.g. leaflets and other supplementary materials).
- Tailoring education to the individual patient.
- Encouraging patients to become more proactive in learning and self-management.
- Behavioural change issues
  - Personal goal-setting
  - Identifying personal barriers to self-management
  - Practice and skill learning
  - Transfer of learning from one environment to another
  - Building self-efficacy
  - Facilitating behavioural change and coping strategies in cognitively impaired patients.
- Widening the context of patient education
  - Expert and lay-led self-management programmes
  - Using community resources – web-sites, local information dossiers, psychoeducational support groups.
- Evaluating the outcomes of patient education and empowerment programmes.

Issues of 'support' and 'education' are discussed in this book in separate chapters, but it is important to understand that these experiences are very much intertwined for patients. Many patients regard information as a vital form of support. Indeed this is one aspect of support as defined by Krause and Markides (1990), who distinguished informational, practical and emotional support. Equally, many patients gain valuable knowledge and empowering coping strategies from people in their informal support networks, especially those with direct experience of similar health problems. There is some evidence, at least for cancer patients, that psychoeducational support groups may have greater effects on well-being than groups which have the primary purpose of providing emotional support (see review by Edelman et al 2000). Some of the processes and outcomes discussed in the previous chapter in relation to support could equally be classed as educational. A good example is the supportive Internet site through which women with chronic health problems in rural Montana shared their experiences, as reported by Weinert (2000).

WHAT FORMS OF INFORMATION AND EDUCATION DO PATIENTS VALUE?

Before considering which forms of information and education are most commonly needed by patients in rehabilitation contexts, consider the following example.

ACTIVITY Questions about living with chronic pain

When you read the following case study, think about the following issues:
- How many questions and uncertainties can you detect in Lucy's account?
- Despite three years of back pain episodes, Lucy is still in need of a lot of information. What do you think have been the most likely barriers preventing Lucy from gaining the information that she needs to manage her condition and maintain her morale?

Lucy has had fluctuating episodes of chronic low back pain for more than three years. She is 45 years old, rather overweight, and works part-time at a supermarket checkout while her children are at school.

She says 'I really don't know what to do for the best. I always thought I should rest my back when the pain got bad but my GP now says that I should try to stay active. But I worry am I doing myself harm? Will I cause some damage to my spine if I do things when my back is hurting? I find it very difficult to sit for long at work, but I don't think I can ask the company for a better chair. I don't like to make a fuss. It's difficult enough around here getting a job that fits in with school hours, and I can't afford to make myself unpopular with the manager. I always think that I really should lose a bit of weight but I can't seem to. I have tried diets but I give up after about two days! Get too hungry! Also, I often feel very down about my back, especially in the evenings when the children have gone to bed, and then I tend to eat for comfort. Something to do to cheer myself up, I can't seem to get out of the habit. The pain is really affecting my life. I used to be quite proud of my garden but now I'm not sure whether gardening will make my back worse. Sometimes I do some digging and then I really pay for it the next day. But then again, sometimes I don't get any lasting effects and I know I feel better for being outside. I really like seeing the improvement that a few hours work makes to the garden. I badly want to get back to normal. Sometimes I think that maybe the doctor would find a treatment for me if I was more insistent. Maybe if I was more educated. He has said something to me about going to a back school at the local hospital but I was thinking that maybe I need an operation. I don't think I need to go to a school to learn about my back and how to lift things. I'm not sure how this back school could help me.'

Research shows that patients (and their families) have numerous questions and uncertainties when they experience a chronic health condition (e.g. Bath et al 1999, in relation to arthritis; Wiles et al, 1998, in relation to stroke). Some questions focus on the causes of their illness, pain or impairment, its likely course and the likelihood of recovery, and the treatment that may be most suitable. People with long-term health problems often express concerns about their likely future, the actions they might take to improve their health and functioning, the financial benefits and legal assistance that they are entitled to, and the coping strategies that could restore some overall quality to their lives (Close & Procter 1999, Wiles et al 1998). They may be uncertain about how to interpret the meaning of their symptoms, such as chronic pain.

Lucy raises all of these issues. She is clearly living in a state of confusion about the behaviours that might help her to cope effectively with her back pain. She is uncertain about whether the medical advice that she has been given is trustworthy. She realises that some of her attitudes and habits are hindering her attempts to manage her back pain, despite having some knowledge about an appropriate strategy. For example, she accepts that losing weight may help alleviate her back pain but feels unable to do this successfully. She is unaware of employment regulations (e.g. in relation to providing suitable seating) and she has not been informed of the purpose of 'back school' and therefore queries whether it is relevant to her needs.

Although patients with long-term conditions often express a need for more information, this alone may not enhance their coping and well-being. Patients can find it difficult to regain an acceptable lifestyle not only from lack of knowledge but because they find it difficult to adapt their behaviour. Negative attitudes, poor self-image, denial, ingrained habits and a limited repertoire of behavioural strategies can all be relevant. Patients also face competing priorities. For example, a person with multiple sclerosis may not wish to pace their activities for fear of 'giving in' to their fatigue, or being seen by others as defeated by their illness. Many individuals with diabetes are not successful in losing weight even though they understand that weight loss would help their condition. People with cardiac or respiratory conditions do not always succeed in giving up smoking even when clearly informed that this is important for their health. In addition to giving up health-risk behaviours such as smoking, people going through physical rehabilitation are often expected to make other long-term behavioural adjustments. They may for example, be expected to use a diary following a head injury that resulted in memory impairment. They may need to adapt to using the non-dominant hand following a stroke. They may be expected to take up more exercise following a myocardial infarction. Yet long-term behavioural change is known to be extremely difficult. Because of the practical, psychological and social difficulties involved, knowledge alone does not necessarily translate into behaviour. Patient education needs to include more than information-giving to be effective.

ACTIVITY Personal reflection on relationship between knowledge and behavioural change

- Do you have a completely healthy lifestyle, or do you engage in any of the following 'risky' behaviours?

Skip breakfast; have much more than/less than 7-8 hours sleep per night; smoke; drink more than the advised number of units of alcohol per day (2-3 for women, 3-4 for men, where a unit is equivalent to a single measure of spirits, or half a pint of beer/lager); eat a diet with fewer than five daily portions of vegetables and fruits; have unprotected sex; cycle without a helmet; take insufficient physical exercise to maintain fitness (at least 30 minutes of moderate activity on most days)?

As a therapist or student therapist, you have a great deal of academic *knowledge* about the behaviours that promote health and the behavioural risk factors for illness. However, you will not necessarily translate your knowledge into health-promoting *behaviour*.

- Consider some of the factors that make it difficult for you to act upon your knowledge of health and health-promoting behaviour. What makes it difficult for you to give up any of the health-risk behaviours that you have identified above?

Long-term behavioural change is difficult for many reasons. These include:

- The possible lack of immediate or visible outcomes (e.g. from efforts at weight loss).
- Lack of social support for change (e.g. family eating habits may make dietary change difficult).
- New behaviours require the effort involved in constant monitoring and decision-making whereas old habits are automatic.
- Some 'old' behaviours are 'tried and tested' coping strategies (e.g. comfort eating), and therefore tend to be most needed in times of stress.

Clearly, to learn new behaviour requires more than simple knowledge about health risks. Self-management education helps patients to develop a larger 'toolkit' of behavioural strategies, including goal-setting, communication and assertiveness skills, and alternative approaches to stress management (Holman & Lorig 2000).

Lorig has pioneered self-management education, originally in the field of arthritis. Her research has compared patients' responses to traditional care, or traditional patient education, with self-management training. She argues that patient education needs to address issues of self-management and behavioural change/adaptation *explicitly*. Such self-management approaches are generally more effective in enhancing well-being, decreasing feelings of powerlessness and in some cases, improving health status compared with traditional patient education (see review by Bodenheimer et al 2002). The programmes seem to influence patients' attitudes towards their symptoms and limitations. Less denial, greater acceptance and a wider variety of ways of dealing with discomfort and activity limitations all help to make the illness less intrusive and frustrating.

Central to self-management education is an interactive 'adult' partnership between health professional (or other facilitator) and the patient (Klaber Moffat 2002). The patient sets short-term and long-term goals, and contracts to engage actively in relevant health-promoting behaviours in order to reach these targets (Bodenheimer et al 2002). There is less emphasis in such programmes on didactic teaching. Didactic teaching describes a form of interaction in which information is passed from teacher to learner, with the teacher occupying the role of expert who determines what is taught and the learner being regarded as a passive receptacle for this knowledge. There is increasing evidence that didactic teaching is relatively ineffective for adults. Instead, adults learn most effectively when they play an active part in the teaching and learning process, guided by their own questions, and encouraged to relate new information to their existing concepts (Ellers 1993). Moreover, such learning seems to have longer-lasting effects. For example, there is evidence of beneficial health outcomes persisting for considerable periods of time following self-management educational programmes (e.g. Von Korff et al 1998).

WHAT FACTORS PREVENT PATIENTS FROM GAINING THE INFORMATION THAT WOULD EMPOWER GREATER CHOICE AND COPING STRATEGIES?

First of all, consider the case study above. Why is Lucy so uncertain about all of the issues that she raises, despite having lived with chronic pain for a long time? Difficulties such as these have many sources, for example:

- Health professionals' limited awareness about effective educational strategies for adult patients, and their cost-effectiveness in improving patients' long-term quality of life (Lorig et al 1999).
- Patients' socialisation into a biomedical approach to health problems (through accepting prevalent cultural and media representations of health care), and therefore taking for granted that the goal of all healthcare interventions is 'cure'. They may not understand the chronic care or rehabilitation model, which aims to promote well-being through self-management, self-reliance and adaptation.
- Patients' reticence about asking questions of health professionals, especially physicians (perhaps because they have been socialised into the role of compliant patient, and/or because they observe that health professionals are busy and have queues of other patients to see, as suggested by Leydon et al 2000, in their study of patients with cancer).
- Having questions ignored or side-stepped by health professionals who have been trained within the biomedical framework and who therefore regard patients as primarily there to receive treatment. They may view questions from patients about how to regain quality of life, and how to re-engage with activities and roles, as irrelevant to their professional

concerns. They may also devalue patients' experiential knowledge (Paterson 2001).

- Patients' difficulties in relating general risk estimates to their personal health. For example, some individuals believe that is only 'other people' who are susceptible to smoking-related diseases. Hence, they may not see any personal need to give up smoking.
- Patients' unfamiliarity with technical terms and the various roles and responsibilities of different health professionals may prevent them from relating as an equal partner during consultations about illness management.
- Patients' capacity to learn and recall information may be impaired by anxiety and by illness symptoms such as pain.

THE COMMUNICATION MATRIX

The above list of barriers to learning shows that health professionals need many flexible strategies if they are to educate and empower patients effectively. In the remaining part of this chapter, we will consider various elements of the communication matrix in which learning takes place, and outline some ways in which patients can be helped to learn more about their health problems, treatment options and self-management strategies.

The health educator Gerjo Kok (1991/2) presented the notion of a communication matrix (see Table 8.1). He developed this matrix from theories of attitude and behaviour change, to help health educators to conceptualise the process of educating people about HIV/AIDS. Despite its specific original focus, the matrix is useful for understanding any form of patient education. In Chapter 6, we examined the PACT communication matrix of patient, therapist, communication medium, and context (adjunctive factors), to establish how each aspect may contribute to partnership working. Here we go further to discuss how these elements of the communication matrix (as well as the informative message itself) influence cognitive and behavioural aspects of learning.

Based on early work in the field of persuasion and attitude change (McGuire 1985), Kok argued that communications that aim to change knowledge, attitudes and behaviour have to achieve several targets along the way. For example, an effective communication needs to attract attention so that it is cognitively processed in the first place (rather than ignored). Secondly, the concepts presented need to make sense to the learner ('comprehension'). For example, new information needs to be linked to the learner's existing concepts, and should ideally answer the learner's own questions. To have any possibility of influence, communications also need to be accepted, rather than rejected – for example, explanations for an illness, estimates of treatment success, or arguments that certain behaviours (such as additional physical exercise) may promote health. Denial, wishful thinking and anxiety may all work against genuine acceptance of the message. Patients also have to find ways of committing information to memory, as learning is not going to have any long-term influence unless it can be recalled.

Table 8.1 The communication matrix (adapted from Kok 1991/2)

	Message	Health professional	Patient	Medium of communication (channel)	Context
Attention					
Comprehension					
Acceptance					
Recall					
Action/ Behavioural change					
Maintenance of behaviour change					

Some forms of education seek to inform and increase the patient's *knowledge*. This is valuable for enhancing the patient's sense of security and control as we have seen above. However, in the therapy and rehabilitation context, patients are often taught and encouraged to implement certain *behavioural changes*. For success, knowledge is necessary but not sufficient. For example, an asthmatic patient may need to learn to use an inhaler effectively, *and* develop a healthier lifestyle (for example, doing more exercise in graded stages and stopping smoking). A patient with MS may wish to implement fatigue management strategies. A patient with a chronic back condition may need to increase physical activity levels in order to manage the pain. Very often in the rehabilitation context, an educational programme cannot be seen as effective unless patients take *action* on the basis of what they have learned. Health professionals can do much to enhance the patient's attention, comprehension, acceptance, and recall of information, as we will see in following sections. Achieving changes in behaviour can be more challenging, and additional strategies will be considered.

The communication matrix reminds us that the communicators have effects over and above the verbal information (message) that they present. Numerous social psychological studies have found that people typically show more attention, acceptance and recall in relation to information given by communicators whom they regard as expert, trustworthy and credible (Gilbert et al 1998). The communicator's status, role and apparent confidence all affect the recipient's judgements of the quality of the information presented. Health professionals tend to be trusted as expert communicators, and even small amounts of information-giving have been observed to influence clients for a considerable period (as noted in a study of GP education/counselling about physical activity by Calfas et al, 1996). Professionals who can discuss the relevant evidence with confidence, and refer the patient to other available sources of expertise may also enhance their credibility. However, we must also bear in mind that some forms of patient education are perceived as more credible and trustworthy when conducted by people with direct experience of the relevant health and lifestyle problems, rather than by health professionals. Health professionals who are aware of the ways in which the communicator influences the acceptance of health information may see the educational value of referring the patient to various sources of supplementary information, including support groups and web-sites designed by people with direct experience of the illness.

Kok's model also reminds us that the communication matrix consists of more than the professional and patient in verbal interaction. Successful communications depend on the whole system of exchange. The medium (or channel) of communication can play a part (such as whether education is based solely on verbal interaction, or additional materials such as audiotapes or written leaflets are used). The context (including the broader cultural context as well as the more immediate social and physical environment) can also enhance or decrease the effectiveness of the educational process.

A variety of strategies will be considered in relation to these broad elements of the communication matrix, supported by reference to theories of adult learning and behavioural change.

ACTIVITY Applying Kok's communication matrix to analysing the process of patient education

Before reading on, think about the various ways in which the educational process in the rehabilitation setting can be influenced positively or negatively. To do this, examine the matrix and provide an example of an effective (or ineffective) communication strategy within each 'box'.

• For example, you might first focus on the message itself (say, a verbal explanation) and consider how it may capture (or fail to capture) the patient's attention and understanding.

• How may the health professional help the patient to attend to important information (or help the patient to better comprehend, or recall information and instructions)? Also consider the converse scenario – how do health professionals distract, confuse and de-motivate the patient?

• Looking at the third column, think about individual patients and how their particular characteristics and motivation may influence their attention to (and comprehension of) educational messages, and their ability to engage in long-term behavioural change.

> • In respect to the fourth column, do you have ideas about how supplementary communications such as leaflets might be used to enhance attention, comprehension, recall and so on?
>
> • Work through the fifth column finding ways in which the context of education (especially the immediate social and physical context) can be influential. For example, how may the context enhance (or diminish) patients' attention, recall or likelihood of taking effective action to manage their condition?

HELPING PATIENTS LEARN THROUGH MAXIMISING ATTENTION, COMPREHENSION, ACCEPTANCE AND RECALL

Therapists have a responsibility to educate their patients. For this aspect of their role, they require not only skills for delivering information, but also an awareness of how patients' learning capacity can be diminished by health problems and the environment. All patients can find it more difficult to learn in the unfamiliar environment of the hospital or rehabilitation setting, and when perturbed by pain and other symptoms. Patients who have acquired a cognitive impairment (e.g. after a stroke or head injury) or who are suffering a high level of emotional turmoil, show greater difficulties in concentration and recall. Even in ideal conditions, every learner has a limited capacity to take on board new information. A large number of psychological studies have shown that in ideal learning conditions (e.g. alert, relaxed and non-distracted) the average person can rarely learn more than seven to nine items of new information in one session, unless the information is repeated several times and/or special strategies are used to connect the items in meaningful 'chunks' (Sternberg 1999). You can check for yourself by testing your ability to learn lists of unfamiliar words, or random digits.

ACTIVITY Test your short-term learning capacity

1. With a partner, draw up some lists of either randomly sequenced digits, or nouns. Try to choose words that are similar in terms of familiarity and which have the same number of syllables (e.g. a list of two-syllable words, such as table, garden, saucer and so on). Vary the list from 4 to 12 in length. Arrange these lists in random order and present these one at a time to your partner. Read the words or numbers aloud and ask your partner to write down the items that he/she can recall immediately after you have finished presenting the whole list. You score how many correct words or digits are recalled. The order of recall does not matter. Do the results indicate that your short-term memory capacity is about 7-9 items, or more, or less? Do not worry if your capacity appears to be much more limited than this – stress, time of day, fatigue and many other factors affect it. The point of this activity is to help you to experience the reality of information overload and memory difficulties when you are bombarded with unfamiliar lists.

2. Again with a partner, each find about 10 words that you anticipate will be *unfamiliar* to the other person (perhaps technical terms from anatomy, medical diagnosis, occupational therapy, physiotherapy and other academic sources). Arrange them in a random list. Make sure that your partner does not see the list while you are preparing it. In a quiet environment, present your list verbally to your partner, asking for immediate recall at the end of the presentation. Your partner will do the same with you as the 'learner'. Score how many words you each managed to recall, discuss your strategies for learning, and the problems in recall that you encountered. Did you recall fewer of these unfamiliar terms than the familiar items in experiment 1?

3. Obviously list-learning is not the same as patient education. However, reflect on what this experience has taught you about the difficulties that patients may encounter when given verbal information about unfamiliar issues from health professionals, particularly when this is unsupported by written reminders.

Ley (1988) reviewed a number of studies that showed medical patients to recall on average four or five items of new information in one consultation, regardless of how many items the health professional offered to them. It seems that patients are even more limited in their capacity to learn than adults in classic memory experiments.

ACTIVITY Barriers to attention, learning and recall for patients in physical rehabilitation

- Before reading on, consider what factors may be responsible for reducing the learning capacity of adults from about 7 items to about 4–5 items during medical or rehabilitation consultations.

Attention and learning may be disrupted by many factors in the hospital setting. Some are associated with the patient's own psychological state, including illness symptoms such as pain, the unfamiliarity or unexpectedness of the issues being discussed, and anxiety associated with illness and injury. Some problems are increased by external factors, such as distracting noise, equipment and bustle in the immediate environment. Learning can also be compromised by the health professional, who perhaps fails to explain terminology that is unfamiliar to the patient. Professional explanations may also differ from the patient's own lay beliefs about illness, affecting comprehension and acceptance (Ley 1988). Because so familiar with the relevant concepts and the rehabilitation environment, the health professional may not realise that the patient may be trying to process an overwhelming volume of information within a short consultation period. Although some health professionals deliver too much information, not realising how overwhelming this can be for the patient, some overestimate the amount and adequacy of information that they provide within a consultation. Patients are also prone to being over-optimistic about how much they have understood, according to a study that observed physicians and patients discussing medication (Makoul et al 1995). Recall may be as low as 50% (as Schillinger et al 2003, noted among diabetic patients). However, as patients frequently do not realise the gaps in their understanding, they do not seek clarification.

Ley (1988, 1989) has made a number of helpful suggestions that therapists can adopt to maximise the attention, comprehension and recall of their patients. In light of the limited capacity of *any* person to learn and recall information from a single interaction, the therapist needs to make sure that they assist the patient by doing the following:

- Emphasising and repeating the most important points.
- Keeping explanations relatively simple (although without patronising the patient).
- Ensuring that the most important information is given at the beginning and ends of the session (as memory shows primacy and recency effects, with forgetting most likely to occur from the middle of a presentation).
- Giving specific rather than general information and instructions (e.g. 'walk a mile in 15 minutes each day', rather than 'take some regular brisk exercise').
- Avoiding jargon.
- Checking the patient's understanding of the most important points (Schillinger et al 2003).

As well as respecting that patients can suffer cognitive overload, professionals also need to be mindful that patients may experience great difficulty in accepting certain pieces of information for emotional reasons. Patients sometimes wish so strongly for a return to their pre-illness lives that they refuse to believe professional views about their diagnosis and prognosis. They may even suspect that relevant information and treatment options are being withheld (Close & Procter 1999). For example, in the case study above, Lucy may find it difficult to accept sound evidence-based advice about pain management until she has accepted that there really is no surgical cure for her back. For patients whose emotional state is fragile, therapists need to approach information-giving as slowly as possible and respect the patient's difficult journey towards acceptance.

The learning that can be achieved will also be improved if the therapist can relate to an *active* patient, rather than simply trying to deliver information to a passive 'recipient'. Therapists can help patients to participate more actively in the educational exchange in various ways, such as:

- Explicitly inviting patients' questions and focusing the exchange of information on these most relevant issues.
- Asking patients about their short-term and longer-term goals and priorities, and orienting education (as well as rehabilitation) around these.
- Setting up a partnership approach to rehabilitation, in which the patient's own resources and expertise are integrated with professionals' knowledge and skills.

Using a variety of communication media (including leaflets and other resources)

Information-giving and education often occur during spoken exchanges between therapist and patient. However, therapists may consider supplementing the information available to patients in a variety of other ways, including leaflets, audiotapes, videotapes, recommended books and appropriate Internet web-sites. Referral to further sources helps patients who wish to develop greater expertise on their condition, enhancing their sense of control, and enabling them to learn at their own pace.

Leaflets and written information

Leaflets and written information sheets are used quite frequently as a supplementary source of information. There is a wide variety of already published leaflets, but according to a study by Sharry et al (2002), occupational therapists often prepare the materials themselves, rather than using commercially sponsored or other ready-made publications. There is a considerable usage of leaflets by health professionals for health education (Chapman & Langridge 1997, Murphy & Smith 1993). However, debate continues about whether written information leaflets are effective or not. Murphy and Smith (1993) questioned whether leaflets are 'confetti, crutches or useful tools' for health professionals, finding in their survey that many health professionals believed they had limited value. On the other hand, Ley's review (1988) suggested that the majority of patients read the leaflets provided by health professionals. However, some caution is needed in interpreting these figures as most of the studies that Ley reviewed concerned written information about *medication.* Patients may feel a strong need to know about safe drug usage and potential side-effects. Unsolicited health education leaflets recommending behavioural change (such as smoking cessation) may be much less appealing to patients.

Not all leaflets offer clear information to patients. A key – and avoidable – reason is that the written English is too complex for the average reader. Leaflets are also likely to be discarded if they present information that the patient does not wish to know about. However, if used as a *supplement* to the verbal consultation, and if the health professional takes time to go through the leaflet with the patient, written materials may provide a useful reference and a reminder of key points. To enable all patients to gain access to similar information, care should also be taken to ensure that leaflets and information sheets are available in the languages of local minority ethnic communities.

How can you tell if your leaflets and patient information sheets are suitable for your patients?

The simplest way is to carry out an informal evaluation by asking patients whether they found the leaflet readable, understandable and useful. However, you need to make sure that your patients do not feel obliged to respond positively. It may be more instructive to ask patients to report more specifically on which aspects of the leaflet – which 'take home messages' – were most useful.

A more technical approach to evaluating the effectiveness of a leaflet is to assess how easy it is to read. Ease or difficulty in reading is not simply reflected by the reader's ability to pronounce the individual words, but by successfully understanding the meaning of the text. The Flesch Reading Ease formula is commonly used but it is difficult to calculate without software assistance. The details can be found in Ley (1988 p. 116). Basically, texts with shorter words and sentences tend to be easier to read, and the corresponding Reading Ease score is higher. The easiest way of checking this score, if you have written the text yourself, is to use the readability check on a word processing package. In Microsoft Word, it can be found by clicking on 'Tools' and then 'Spelling and Grammar'. You need to select under 'Options', 'Check grammar with spelling' and 'Show readability statistics'.

How do you interpret the Flesch Reading Ease score? The scale ranges from 0–100, with higher scores reflecting easier reading. Ley (1988 p. 117) reports that texts with a score of 90–100 are so easy to read that over 90% of the population should be able to manage them. Such easy pieces of writing can be found in some comics. 'Standard' texts tend to score around 60–70 on the scale, and the majority of adults would manage to read these successfully. Academic writing tends to score between 30 and 50, and is suitable for adults who have reached at least Sixth Form or college level. The chapters in this book gain a rating of around 40 on the Flesch scale. This is appropriate as the intended audience is likely to be studying at university. However, this score would indicate that the writing is not suitable for the majority of the population. Very difficult scientific writing tends to score 0–30, and may be read with understanding by less than 10% of the population. Ley (1988) argues that readers tend to give up reading when they face written information that is beyond their reading skills. Even if they persist, they are likely not to understand and remember the information that they have read.

As well as checking the Reading Ease score, you can also check the intended 'grade' of the reader. This broadly correlates with the Flesch score. It is based on the American school system, so a grade of 12 is equivalent to age 18 (Sixth Form or college level). The chapters in this book all require a grade of 12, again reflecting their intended audience. 'Standard' texts require a school equivalent grade of 7–8 (readable by the average 13–14-year-old). It is this level that may be most appropriate for written information intended for the general public. This argument is supported by Butow et al (1998). They compared cancer patients' preferences for five different information booklets. The patients reported greatest satisfaction with the most readable booklet, which required a reading level of approximately grade 8. The somewhat less preferred booklets all required a reading level of grades 11–12 (Sixth Form/college level, as shown above). Obviously, care must be taken in generalising the findings, as it remains possible that the particularly anxiety-provoking nature of the information about cancer might make the material especially challenging to read and comprehend. Nevertheless, the findings are similar to others reviewed by Ley (1988). Chapman and Langridge (1997) recommend that physiotherapists do not use leaflets with a reading grade higher than 9, and noted that two-thirds of the leaflets that they surveyed were more advanced than this.

It is also helpful if you are writing for a general audience to monitor other aspects of the style and presentation. Again, word processing packages facilitate this process. In Microsoft Word, you can use 'Tools' and go to 'Spelling and Grammar' as before. After clicking on 'Options', go to 'Settings'. There you can ask to receive various kinds of further information such as use of passives, wordiness, clichés, sentence length and unclear phrasing. These tools can help you to improve the readability of any patient information that you prepare.

Even without the benefit of this software assistance, you can implement certain strategies to improve the written style of patient information sheets and leaflets. Try the following:

- Use short words and short sentences where possible.
- Explain any technical terms that are used.
- Use plain English and avoid unnecessary jargon.
- Use active tenses and avoid passive sentences. For example, 'You will be treated by a variety of health professionals' is passive, whereas 'A variety of health professionals will treat you' is active, simpler to read and easier to understand.
- Avoid negatives, and especially double negatives, as much as possible. For example, 'You will not benefit from the therapy if you do not give up smoking'. This double negative could be avoided by re-phrasing the message as 'You will gain more benefit from the therapy if you give up smoking'. This is simpler to read and understand, and is therefore more likely to encourage action on the part of the patient.
- Anticipate what information your patients usually require when deciding what to present.
- Aim for an attractive layout but avoid a 'fussy' or 'busy' presentation. While boxes, pictures and cartoons can attract attention, a poor layout can easily detract from the content. The over-use of such features can also trivialise the subject matter. Nevertheless, attractiveness, relevance and quality of information are linked to patients' attention, liking and understanding of leaflets (Bull et al 2001).
- Ensure an adequate font size, especially if your leaflet is designed for older people who may not have their reading glasses with them! Patients with neurological problems, such as multiple sclerosis, often have problems with visual acuity, and also appreciate larger font sizes (e.g. 14 point).

Chapman and Langridge (1997) offer further suggestions to improve the readability of leaflets, focusing on physiotherapy information.

> ### ACTIVITY Improving upon written patient information
>
> - Can you improve the following written information intended for patients with chronic low back pain? It is currently too advanced, with a Flesch Reading Ease score of 28.4 (on the border of very difficult/scientific, and difficult/academic), and a required school grade of 12.0 (Sixth Form to university standard).
> - What changes can you suggest that will make the information easier to read and understand?
> - How can it be written so that it is more interesting and motivating?
> - If possible, compare your work with another person's, and evaluate how successful you have been in creating a readable, user-friendly piece of information.
>
> 'Patients with many different types of chronic health condition, including low back pain, benefit from taking graded exercise. Sedentary behaviour carries the risk of obesity, cardiovascular deterioration, reduced strength and fitness, poor sleep patterns, and many other health-jeopardising problems. Even small amounts of moderate exercise can benefit your health, and help you to manage your pain, so long as you are committed to follow a regular schedule. Current guidelines suggest a minimum period of 30 minutes per day of moderate exercise that raises your heart-rate and which makes you a little warmer (but not necessarily perspiring heavily). You will receive further advice about safe levels of exercise from your therapist, but before the consultation do consider how you might introduce more exercise into your daily life. Consider what types of physical activity you have most enjoyed in the past, what activities might still be accomplished despite your current problems with low back pain, and what forms of social and emotional support might be available to you to help you to reach your goals.'
>
> (A simplified version is given at the end of the chapter for you to compare with your own version.)

Audiotapes

The effectiveness of audiotapes has received some research in the context of consultations between doctors and cancer patients. Many patients who receive an audiotape of the consultation report that it provides a helpful reminder of information that they were too anxious to hear properly in the consultation itself. It can assist patients to assimilate information in their own time and then to seek clarification, as needed, in the next consultation (Ford et al 1995). Audiotapes have also been used for supplementing the information given during consultations, allowing patients to learn at their own pace, in their own environment. For example, Hagopian (1996) compared a random group of cancer patients who received standard care with another group who received information on audiotape. The study found that the patients who received the audiotapes acquired not only more understanding about their treatment but also practised more helpful self-care strategies than the control group. Another study noted that patients discharged following heart surgery achieved better physical functioning if they received audiotaped information about the physical symptoms that they should expect and some suggested ways of managing them, compared with patients who received the usual discharge information (Moore 1996).

Studies such as these show that audiotaped information can be accessible and supportive of patients' coping strategies. However, there appear to be few guidelines to help health professionals make decisions about how to present information most effectively in audiotapes. The previously given suggestions about presenting jargon-free, well structured information would seem to apply. The plan of the presentation probably needs to be made very obvious to the person listening to audiotaped information. A patient can rapidly skim read a written leaflet to find the information that is most relevant, but cannot do so with an audiotape unless the plan of presentation is made extremely clear.

Recommended books and web-sites

There is a wide range of good quality self-help books that health professionals may wish to recommend to their patients with long-term conditions. Some of the better ones have been written by Kate Lorig and colleagues on the basis of their experience of setting up and evaluating self-management programmes (e.g. Holman et al 2000). The material can help patients not only manage their own condition more effectively, but may guide the formation of self-help groups and their educational programmes.

Many patients have access to the Internet, and this offers a huge volume of information in relation to health. Access can therefore help patients become more proactive in managing their own condition. Sharry and McKenna (2001) discuss this resource in relation to occupational therapists and their patients. However, the quality of such information is variable. Professionals may help patients judge the information that they access on the web, by providing them with evaluative criteria (e.g. the DISCERN instrument, developed by Charnock 1998). Many recognised charities (e.g. British Heart Foundation) provide good quality information on their web-sites.

Support groups and learning from others who share the same health problem

Some patients find that their best source of information and advice for living with illness comes from people who share their condition. Support groups have been discussed in the previous chapter, in the context of emotional support. However, it is important to acknowledge the volume of information that is exchanged in such groups. Michael J. Fox (2003 p. 275) celebrates the informational and emotional support that he gained from others once he decided to 'come out' as having Parkinson's disease (P.D.):

My greatest teachers now came from within the P.D. community itself
… It was as if I was looking in a window, and to my comfort and relief,
there were lights on and people inside – people just like me.

Many web-sites are designed and maintained by people with a health
condition to assist others who confront similar issues. As well as providing
support, they often provide links to other sources of information, for example,
sites presenting current research and treatment debates. An award-winning
web-site for people with multiple sclerosis illustrates this approach to virtual
support and education. It can be found at http://www.mswebpals.org. A
lively site (as can be judged from its name) for people with ankylosing
spondylitis can be found at www.kickas.org.

Expert patient programmes

Health professionals are increasingly accepting that the 'activated' patient
(as described by Bodenheimer et al 2002) is a positive asset to the
rehabilitation process. Since 1999, the NHS has encouraged the development
of 'expert patient programmes', designed to encourage patients with chronic
conditions to acquire greater confidence and improved control over their
lives, including their interactions with health professionals. Further details
can be found on the government web site http://www.doh.gov.uk/cmo/
progress/expertpatient/epp3.htm.

In some cases, health professionals facilitate expert patient programmes.
For example, the Heart Manual project assists self-help by people who have
had a myocardial infarction (see the previously named web-site for more
details). Such approaches to patient education have various teaching and
learning components, including lectures, booklets, role play and goal setting,
usually lasting for 4–8 sessions. These various components help patients to
take on the day-to-day management of their illness and to experience greater
choice over daily life. There has also been a considerable development in
self-management programmes with the training of 'lay' facilitators, for
example, people with direct experience of conditions such as arthritis,
asthma, multiple sclerosis and bipolar disorder. Fursland (2001) reports a
lay-led arthritis management programme that included ways of breaking
symptom cycles, managing pain, and promoting relaxation, nutrition,
exercise and emotional health. One lay facilitator who led such a programme
for patients with arthritis commented:

The course was an eye-opener … Rather than seeing themselves as a
problem, people are encouraged to see themselves as a resource. They
are offered tools for living successfully with arthritis (p. 19).

Most studies report that self-management programmes achieve better health
and emotional outcomes than traditional methods of patient education,
including better management of physical symptoms, greater participation in
valued activities and improved psychological well-being (e.g. Barlow, Sturt &
Hearnshaw 2002, Barlow et al 2002, Bodenheimer et al 2002, Lorig et al 1999).

Some studies have found reduced long-term costs and fewer hospital stays and emergency department visits (e.g. Ghosh et al 1998, Lorig et al 1993). Nevertheless, questions remain about how to best educate and empower patients who feel less motivated or depressed about their condition. Health professionals who wish to find out more about supporting expert patients and developing patient self-management programmes can gain information from web-sites such as the Long-term Medical Conditions Alliance (http://www.lmca.org.uk.) and from books such as Holman et al (2000).

Tailoring education to the individual patient

One implication of the discussion so far is that patients in rehabilitation may not benefit from 'standardised packages' of information. Instead, effective communications often need to be tailored to the individual patient's needs. A recent review has examined this issue in the context of tailoring information to the specific needs of individuals with cystic fibrosis (Ireland 2003).

Therapists need to be mindful that different patients require different types of information because they do not experience their illness in the same way. Some cancer patients, for example, report needing a great deal of information around the time of diagnosis and treatment, while others prefer to leave their treatment in the hands of health professionals in the early stages. The latter group perhaps are particularly anxious about their diagnosis, and fear having to deal with additional fear-arousing information that might undermine their morale at such a difficult time (Leydon et al 2000). Some patients point out that the timing of information is crucial. Earlier on in the illness, they may have felt too overwhelmed by pain, anxiety and so on, to bother with questions and explanations. However, later in the treatment or rehabilitation process, when they are less shocked and more accepting about their condition, they may desire more information, and greater involvement in decision-making (Brown et al 2000). One patient with breast cancer explained (Leydon et al 2000 p. 912):

> I think I consciously censored myself [early on]. I didn't look chemo-therapy up on the Internet; I just have recently, and it's really shaken me.

Patients' information needs may also differ according to their health locus of control beliefs. Locus of control refers to whether patients believe that they themselves have the main responsibility for influencing their health (internal locus), or that their health is determined by factors beyond their control (external locus) such as chance or 'powerful others', including health professionals (Wallston et al 1978). However, while it would seem that health-promoting behaviours might be more achievable among those with an internal locus of control, research does not strongly support this association (see discussion by Bennett and Murphy 1997). Many other attitudes, values and behaviours are relevant, such as whether the person feels susceptible to further illness, their levels of social support, their coping styles, and whether they feel convinced by the information that they receive (e.g. about treatment effectiveness).

A growing volume of research suggests that patient education, at least in regards to health promotion, is not only more acceptable but also more effective when tailored to the individual patient's needs and concerns. One way of tailoring information to the individual patient's needs is to be guided by a model of behavioural change. The Stages of Change model (otherwise known as the transtheoretical model of change) was originally developed to explain the different steps that smokers go through in giving up smoking (e.g. DiClemente et al 1991). Since then, the model has been applied widely to understand patients' needs and difficulties when making long-term behavioural changes (such as managing weight loss, making lifestyle adjustments to control diabetes, taking more exercise, adopting safer sexual practices). According to the Stages of Change model, people rarely plunge straight into a major new behaviour or lifestyle change, however strongly they are advised to do so. They tend to progress through stages, as follows:

- *Precontemplation*: not thinking at all about the behaviour change in question.
- *Contemplation*: considering whether to make certain changes; weighing up the benefits and costs involved.
- *Preparation*: actively planning ways to make the behavioural change; working out ways of overcoming the barriers to change.
- *Action*: actively engaged in the behaviour change; successfully overcoming barriers to change.
- *Maintenance*: engaging successfully in the new behaviour(s) for at least three months.

This model also recognises that people do not always make progress in one direction. Temporary lapsing and more permanent relapses are common problems. The person (in the Action stage) who is taking more exercise to improve health can, for example, lose motivation, give up these new exercise habits and regress to an earlier stage. Many factors, including health setbacks, holidays, and stress can lead to lapsing.

ACTIVITY Which stage are you in?

- Look again at any of the health risk behaviours that you admitted in the earlier activity. Identify which stage you are in with respect to giving up the 'risky' behaviour and beginning a more health-promoting lifestyle.

  For example, if you are a cyclist who never wears a head protection, you can be classified as in the 'Precontemplation' stage if you are not considering buying or wearing a helmet, or if you decided some time ago that the bother of wearing and storing a helmet is simply too much for you. You may be in the 'Contemplation' stage if you are actively considering using a helmet. Perhaps you have recently thought more about the risks of not wearing a helmet – for example, from reading about a cycling fatality in your local newspaper. If you have taken some active steps recently to start wearing a helmet (e.g. buying a more comfortable or stylish helmet or solving a problem such as sorting out where and how you could store your helmet after cycling to work), you are in the 'Preparation' stage.

It is unlikely that you are in the Action or Maintenance stage as this activity has asked you to identify *current* risk behaviours. However, some of the other behaviours in the list might have been ones that you have taken action on in the past. For example, if you have recently given up smoking, you are in the Action stage with respect to this behaviour. If you successfully gave up smoking more than three to six months ago, you are in the Maintenance stage for this behaviour.

This model may seem at first sight to be quite descriptive, yet it offers certain useful implications for health promotion and patient education. Firstly, various studies have shown that people in the earlier stages of change are heavily involved in weighing up the potential benefits and costs of the new behaviour, where costs include inconvenience, discomfort, intrusion into normal daily habits and so on (e.g. Boudreaux et al 1998). In these earlier stages, people need information to help in the cognitive decision-making process, including information that helps them to think about how to tackle the barriers to change. They also need to learn more about the health advantages of making the recommended changes. People at the other end of the spectrum, who are in the preparation, action or maintenance stages, require more practical advice concerning behavioural change, and how to develop skills and self-efficacy. The issue for this group is less one of persuasion and decision-making about costs and benefits. Instead, such people have sorted out these decisions and are more concerned with setting goals and gaining a repertoire of behavioural skills to sustain the changes in their lifestyle, to overcome temptations to 'lapse', and to deal confidently with unexpected problems along the way.

ACTIVITY Tailoring information in rehabilitation: an example

- In the case examples below, consider which 'stage of change' each patient is in.
- What *shared* and *distinctive* issues do you think need to be addressed in each patient's programme of education?

A therapist is working with two patients (both males aged around 55) in cardiac rehabilitation. Mr A is overweight and has never exercised for fitness. He is finding it difficult to accept the need for an exercise programme, claiming that he was never 'a sporty type'. His work involves long hours driving and his first reaction to the therapist's description of his long-term rehabilitation programme is that he will never be able to fit in the advised amount of walking into his daily life. Mr B has always enjoyed physical activity, cycling to work, swimming and walking in the countryside at weekends. While his heart problem has come as a great shock to him, he is highly motivated to take part in the graded exercise programme and to play a full and active part in his own recovery.

In the above example, both patients would benefit from developing a clear understanding the role of exercise in rehabilitation. Both may need evidence-based information about the rationale behind the rehabilitation programme. Both may need some information to help manage fears about the likelihood of future heart problems. However, Mr B does not need 'persuasion' about the benefits of physical activity. He already sees himself as active, and seems confident about following the exercise advice. He is already in the Preparation (if not Action) stage. He mainly needs advice about safe levels of exercise, and to discuss his specific exercise plans with the therapist. Mr A is – or has been until recently – in the Precontemplation stage. He will need more information about the role of physical activity in cardiac rehabilitation, the risks of non-adherence, and will need to spend more time planning with the therapist how to build sufficient activity into his daily life once discharged from rehabilitation. For example, he may need to contemplate whether he can do less driving, get up earlier to take a 30 minute walk, or find other solutions to the problem of balancing work responsibilities with his health needs. He may need to consider how to integrate physical activity into his own self-image, as he rejects the idea of himself as a 'sporty type'. If guided by the Stages of Change theory, the educational process will be directed at helping him to dismantle the various anticipated barriers to changing his behaviour, thereby moving him towards preparation and action. He is also likely to need similarly targeted educational support in regards to weight loss.

This example illustrates that different patients can need different forms of educational support during rehabilitation. Knowledge (e.g. of the health risks of remaining sedentary) is necessary but rarely sufficient to motivate behaviour change. Patients differ in how prepared and how confident they are to make recommended behavioural changes. Some of the educational process needs to help patients dismantle their various personal barriers to taking on the new behaviour.

In addition to addressing individual differences in health beliefs, Giger and Davidhizar (1999) remind us that we also need to take into account patients' cultural backgrounds. These authors take a critical position in respect to contemporary patient education, arguing that it reflects Western values promoting active control and independence. Patients from different cultural backgrounds may have different lay beliefs about illness, different attitudes and coping strategies such as fatalism, and different values such as accepting interdependence within their social networks. Giger and Davidhizar argue that some cultures assist people to be more positively accepting of disability and dependence. Nevertheless, health professionals must also be careful to avoid stereotyping people's needs on the basis of perceived cultural difference. A fairly recent study of older Chinese patients following stroke revealed that their information needs were similar to those found in European studies, and were largely unmet (Lui & MacKenzie 1999).

Differences in language can result in some patients from ethnic minorities being excluded from education and information. While family members may offer effective translation at certain times, they may not feel able or willing to communicate bad news or embarrassing information, as discussed in Chapter 6. It is generally preferable for patients to have effective professional translators. Cioffi (2003) interviewed nurses and midwives about their experiences in caring for women from minority ethnic groups. They mostly agreed that it was important to empathise with the patients' potential sense of isolation and powerlessness, and to take their informational and emotional needs seriously. One midwife explained:

> I just try and think 'Well how would I be if I was in China having a baby and couldn't speak to someone? So I really try to get interpreters in for them to explain what's going on ... (p. 302).

Such a simple empathic insight can do much to facilitate appropriate informational strategies for patients with different languages and cultural backgrounds.

ENCOURAGING PATIENTS TO BECOME MORE PROACTIVE IN THEIR LEARNING AND SELF-MANAGEMENT

The educational process can be better tailored to patients' individual needs if the therapist can identify the questions and issues that each patient brings to the therapy process. A meta-analysis of studies of patients undergoing education as part of their cardiac rehabilitation showed that outcomes were better when information was tailored to the patients' interests, needs and questions (Mullen et al 1992). However, patients seem often reluctant to ask questions (Clark & Gong 2000). Patients seem to be particularly inhibited about asking questions when interacting with physicians, perhaps because they perceive a status difference. Alternatively, perhaps they do not wish to take time away from other patients who are waiting to be seen (Leydon et al 2000). Anxieties and discomfort during the consultation session also prevent some patients from remembering the questions that they originally wished to ask (as Rogers et al 2000, observed among patients with chronic heart failure). The patient's relationship with the health professional may also influence their ability to take a proactive role in learning. In some settings, patients seem to be more willing to ask questions of nurses than physicians, perhaps feeling encouraged by professionals who take a more patient-centred approach (Van Weert et al 2003). Close and Procter (1999), however, found that stroke patients reported having more time for discussion with their physiotherapists and occupational therapists than their nurses. Health professionals sometimes cut short discussions by not asking about patients' concerns and fears (Van Weert et al 2003). Health professionals, regardless of role, need to regard every consultation as a potential opportunity for information-giving, and not assume that other professionals are meeting patients' needs in this respect. Tierney et al (2000 p. 860) argue that health professionals should much more frequently ask patients, 'Is there anything you need or want to know?'.

One way of helping patients to become more proactive within the learning process is to encourage them to write down their main questions before the consultation, so that they do not forget them. Maly et al (1999) asked patients in an 'intervention' condition to write down two key questions, which were attached to their clinical notes. This ensured that the physician addressed their most pressing concerns. The 'intervention' patients were also invited to engage in a more active form of collaboration by having access to their own notes. Despite the fairly modest participation involved, a few weeks later it was found that patients in the intervention group (compared with the 'usual treatment' control group) showed small but significant improvements in self-reported health. This group also reported more satisfaction with their treatment, and were more eager to seek health information. The authors suggest that perhaps these patients had developed greater self-efficacy for managing their condition from their experience of a participatory consultation.

Lorig and colleagues regard joint goal-setting and contracting as important steps to engaging patients proactively in the self-management education process (Bodenheimer et al 2002). They ask patients undergoing an arthritis self-management education to set a number of feasible short-term goals, and to draw up contracts, which agreed to some behavioural change. Strecher et al (1995) add to this perspective by suggesting that setting goals which are somewhat challenging to achieve (though nonetheless feasible), may encourage better performance than having no goals, or vague goals. Once goals are set, it becomes easier for the individual to monitor performance and to gain precise feedback about progress.

Other steps that can encourage a proactive approach to learning include providing portable booklets for patients to consult between sessions, and recommending certain resources that can be consulted independently, such as web-sites. For example, Klaber Moffat (2002) refers to materials such as a 'Back Book' for helping patients manage chronic back pain. Kennedy et al (2003) describe the evaluation of a 'guidebook' to ulcerative colitis, written on the basis of consultations with patients about their informational needs. They found that this guidebook improved patients' knowledge, although anxiety and quality of life did not change. Van Weert et al (2003) recommend an interdisciplinary patient information dossier for cardiac surgery patients.

From the health professionals' view, referring patients to other sources of information may be appealing because it saves time during therapy sessions. However, patients should never be asked to look up information in books or Internet sites that could be highly anxiety-provoking (for example, concerning a diagnosis of cancer, or a treatment for which there is limited evidence of effectiveness), even if they seem eager to take an active responsibility for learning. One interviewee with non-Hodgkins lymphoma explains:

> ... even general booklets are too scary and too detailed – my boyfriend looks for me (Leydon et al 2000 p. 912).

Not every patient has a willing partner to help them explore anxiety-provoking information. Health professionals need to be prepared to talk through bad news in a supportive and empathic manner with their patients, and should not expect them to confront such potentially devastating information alone.

BEHAVIOURAL CHANGE AND SELF-EFFICACY ISSUES

The previous discussion has emphasised that patient education and empowerment often involves helping patients to problem-solve and to initiate behavioural change, through, for example, personal goal-setting and working out how to overcome personal barriers to managing their condition (such as pain). A certain amount of didactic teaching and biomedical information (e.g. facts about the disease and recovery process) can be useful if well structured and tailored to the patient's needs. Yet such information-giving often needs to form only part of the process of behavioural change and skill learning within rehabilitation. This is because knowledge, on its own, does not necessarily change behaviour. For example, Hammond and Lincoln (1999) noted how a joint protection education programme successfully enhanced the knowledge of patients with arthritis, but did not increase their joint protection behaviours. Better outcomes may depend upon therapists having a more informed understanding of behavioural change issues (Clark & Gong 2000).

There are many elements to encouraging effective behavioural change. These include patients in the following activities:

- Identifying personal barriers to coping, change and self-management
- Personal goal-setting
- Practise of skills
- Experiencing reinforcement
- Avoiding negative emotional responses to the learning context
- Building self-efficacy
- Practising the transfer of learning from one environment to another.

Behavioural learning theories were originally derived from studies in which animals were trained to make various responses, such as pecking or turning a key. Given such origins, these theories may not, at first sight, seem useful to rehabilitation therapists working in a patient-centred framework. Yet an understanding of behavioural change theories can help therapists to implement more effective techniques (see further details in Bennett and Murphy 1997). Operant conditioning theory suggests that learning new behaviours is best accomplished in gradual stages, with the setting of intermediate goals and the explicit reward of behaviours that reach each stage along the way (referred to as *shaping* the new behaviour). According to operant conditioning theory, an explicit reinforcement (or reward) that immediately follows an appropriate behavioural response is a powerful way of strengthening that response. Without reinforcement, responses tend not to be repeated, or are learned more slowly. Classical conditioning theory further proposes that situational cues can elicit emotional responses by association without the person being aware of the reasons for their reactions. The learning of associations can occur below the threshold of conscious awareness. For example, we may shrink from entering a situation in which we have experienced pain or other trauma, feeling anxious even if we cannot consciously recall the negative events that happened there. For example, Read (1998) discusses the traumatic experiences that many patients associate with being in intensive care, and how recovery afterwards can be complicated by responses that seem equivalent to post-traumatic stress disorder. Such negative emotional responses may not be associated only with intensive care. Patients who have entered the rehabilitation setting in a state of great physical dysfunction or discomfort may find the whole context emotionally upsetting. From a classical conditioning perspective, we might expect such emotional associations to have demoralising effects on some patients' commitment to therapy, inhibiting the subsequent learning process.

Patients seem more likely to learn new behavioural skills from identifying personal barriers to change, and by setting meaningful short-, medium-, and long-term goals. If a new repertoire of behaviours is to be developed, it requires repeated practice. Spaced practice (in which there are shorter sessions with gaps in between) is usually more effective than massed practice, in which the behaviour is repeated many times in a single session (Dempster 1996). In addition to practice, behavioural learning is strengthened through the experience of reinforcement, which can be conceptualised in terms of visible results or rewards. Feedback may be verbal (e.g. praise from the therapist), or in the form of objective evidence. For example, patients engaged in cardiac rehabilitation may be highly motivated by objective evidence about their recovery (e.g. improvements in resting heart-rate), or feedback about progress from their own self-monitoring.

ACTIVITY Planning goals and reinforcements

- Consider how you could modify the health-risk behaviour that you identified in the earlier activity, by planning short/medium/long-term goals for behavioural change. Do not try to implement the whole behavioural change at once, but plan how you could tackle it in stages.
- Think about what reinforcements you could experience that would help you to stick to your behavioural change programme.

The nature of goal-setting is critical to the success of a behavioural change programme. For example, patients who need to implement a walking programme should avoid setting goals that are not feasible. Failure will only be demoralising. If you have been thinking about increasing physical activity in the above exercise, you might decide to set yourself a target of a 30 minute walk twice a week, building up the time, frequency and distance walked to the recommended levels over the next weeks and months. Reinforcements could include feedback about physiological measurements (e.g. resting pulse rate), or other indicators of improved well-being (e.g. better sleep and weight management) and so on. External reinforcements may also be planned (e.g. buying new exercise clothes when a certain target has been reached).

Many theorists and researchers into behavioural change processes argue that self-efficacy predicts who will succeed in learning new behaviours. Self-efficacy is a term that is sometimes used as if it simply means self-confidence. Although this captures its meaning in part, it is a much more *task-specific* concept, referring to confidence that one can carry out a specific behaviour in a variety of circumstances *to achieve a desired goal* (Bandura 1986, Bennett & Murphy 1997, Bodenheimer et al 2002, Marks 2001). A person with generally high self-esteem can have low self-efficacy for a particular task. For example, almost every reader, regardless of general self-confidence, will have low self-efficacy for walking a tight-rope!

A large number of research studies have shown that self-efficacy is highly predictive of achievement. For example, patients in cardiac rehabilitation with high self-efficacy for increasing their levels of physical activity are more likely to modify their lifestyle successfully (Bock et al 1997). There is much debate about why self-efficacy is so predictive of achievement on a specific task. Possibly the belief is grounded in recalling past successes in carrying out the behaviour in question. Perhaps self-efficacy is an attitude or belief that helps to sustain people's resistance to set-backs, whereas the person low in self-efficacy is soon demoralised and gives up when the behavioural change seems difficult. Whatever the reasons, the implication for therapists in the rehabilitation setting is that patients' self-efficacy needs to be encouraged.

ACTIVITY Learning new behaviour: which behavioural strategies encourage better outcomes?

Look at the following account, provided by Richard, a young man who experienced horrific burns in a road traffic accident. He describes a de-motivating experience in rehabilitation.

• Identify some of the ways in which the learning process was poorly managed by the therapists.

• Can you suggest some ways in which the therapists could have incorporated appropriate cognitive and behavioural learning principles to help Richard cope with the programme more successfully?

'Nine months ago, I was severely burned in a car accident. After a long period in intensive care, I started rehabilitation. I had lost muscle and skin in the accident, had numerous operations and I am now really badly scarred, particularly my legs. I couldn't walk, in fact I didn't believe I ever would. Sometimes I went to sleep at night hoping I wouldn't wake up. The pain was constant and difficult to bear. When I started rehab I felt so low. They kept pushing me, pushing me. I had to keep going, for example, walking using the

> parallel bars. No matter what I did, it didn't seem to be enough. They just said, 'that's good, let's do it again'. Over and over again. I couldn't see why I was doing the exercises. Just knew they hurt terribly! And I felt demoralised that I never seemed to do enough, never got far enough to please the therapist.' (Suggestions are found at the end of the chapter.)

Various educational and preparatory approaches can raise self-efficacy. Careful goal-setting, so that success is feasible and visible, can build self-efficacy for the task in question. Patients who have given thought to the barriers that they may encounter along the way, and planned their strategies for dealing with these barriers, increase in self-efficacy. For example, people who need to follow a weight-loss diet to manage their health condition are more successful if they can anticipate common temptations and plan how to manage difficult situations, such as eating in a restaurant with friends (Hunt & Hillsdon 1996). Feedback about successful achievement reinforces the behaviour and builds self-efficacy (Bandura 1986). This is important in cardiac rehabilitation, for example. The results from both behavioural and physiological monitoring can help patients to feel more confident, thereby sustaining their efforts at the various elements of the programme such as exercising, practising relaxation and losing weight. Some patients (for example with cardiac problems or chronic pain) fear that exertion may cause more damage, diminishing their self-efficacy. It is important to offer appropriate reassurance early on to prevent such worries from interfering with the behavioural change programme (Keen et al 1999).

In some settings, patients have to spend much time practising new behavioural skills, or re-learning former skills, for example, walking with an aid, or dressing one-handed. While some forms of learning depend upon cognitive processes such as attention, and declarative (verbalisable) forms of memory, behavioural learning depends much more upon procedural memory. This is a poorly verbalised form of learning. Once learned, behavioural skills seem to be used almost automatically. An everyday example is riding a bicycle. It is difficult if not impossible to say explicitly how one turns a corner whilst riding, yet the behaviour is controlled at the procedural level quite effortlessly. While people with normal cognitive functioning can learn new behaviours with practice and feedback, those with cognitive impairments tend to repeat their mistakes. They encounter difficulties in differentiating past errors from correct responses. They may not therefore necessarily improve with practice as the errors are repeated as often as the appropriate behaviours.

In recent years, research has shown that trial and error learning of new behaviour must be avoided for patients with cognitive impairments (Parkin 1997). Such patients are often found in the rehabilitation setting, having had a stroke, or head injury, for example. Errorless learning techniques provide a much more effective means of teaching such patients new skills than traditional practice, because the patient does not have to remember which of their previous responses was right or wrong, successful or unsuccessful. One approach to errorless learning involves the therapist prompting each behaviour in the sequence, and then gradually withdrawing the prompts (or fading the cues), when the sequence can be performed correctly and without hesitation. Alternatively, therapists can concentrate on predicting errors before they occur. When the patient seems likely to commit an error in the sequence, the therapist steps in to correct the move. Errorless learning, when carried out systematically, is a highly effective method for teaching patients with cognitive problems a variety of new behaviours such as dressing, finding a route through a hospital, or acquiring a procedure relevant to work (e.g. data entry on to a computer). It has been applied in the treatment of dyspraxic patients by occupational therapists (Jackson 1999), but warrants wider recognition. However, it does take considerable time and vigilance on the part of therapists, and generally requires a consistent approach by the whole multidisciplinary team.

Another common problem when teaching patients in the rehabilitation setting, especially those with cognitive impairments, is the hyperspecificity of learning. This term refers to newly learned behaviour that can only be shown specifically in the environment in which it was acquired. Transfer of training to other environments may be slow or non-existent, especially among patients with limited insight or poor explicit memory about their learning. This problem seems to occur because we generally have little explicit awareness of our procedural skills. Just as most people cannot say how they turn corners on their bike (do they shift their weight first, or turn the handle bars?), so cognitively impaired people may not realise that they have learned a skill in one setting that is applicable to another. One way of helping patients to generalise their learning during rehabilitation is to carry out deliberate 'transfer of training' exercises. For example, a patient who has learned to cook a simple meal in the occupational therapy kitchen may need to practise the same skills at home, with support and feedback, until the skills are more securely used in that second environment. This re-learning process can be slow, yet by-passing this stage of rehabilitation risks leaving patients without useable skills in their home environments.

ADDRESSING THE CONTEXT OF PATIENT EDUCATION

The communication matrix alerts us to the context in which patient education occurs. Clearly the immediate physical and social environment can help or hinder learning. For example, noise and clutter are distracting, especially for people whose cognitive abilities are undermined by illness or anxiety.

One important contextual variable in patient education is whether the education occurs in a hospital setting or in the community. Another important aspect of the context of learning is whether the facilitator is a health professional or lay person.

Expert and lay-led self-management programmes

Patient education can be effectively conducted not only by health professionals but also by lay leaders, usually people with direct experience of the health condition (see studies by Barlow et al 2002, Fursland 2001). Lay facilitators are often seen as highly credible and trustworthy communicators. They can use their direct experience of a health condition to help others in a similar situation to learn more, and to explore meaningful coping strategies. Research into arthritis self-management shows that lay leaders are cheaper but no less effective than health professionals. Such leaders also seem to benefit personally from their involvement, such as developing self-confidence and better pain management strategies (Hainsworth & Barlow 2001).

Community resources

Clearly, a considerable amount of patient education is carried out in the rehabilitation setting. Yet, patients can continue to learn at home as well as from health professionals. To this end, it may be cost effective and useful for health professionals to put together packs or dossiers of local community resources that may help their patients to cope with their long-term conditions. These dossiers can alert patients to the presence of support groups, suitable exercise facilities, web-sites, books and so on. Such a portable resource can help the person to rebuild an active, controllable lifestyle, within a better support network.

EVALUATING THE OUTCOMES OF PATIENT EDUCATION AND EMPOWERMENT PROGRAMMES

Therapists who value the educational process as a means of giving the patient back control and purpose will gain much from evaluating whether their efforts are successful. It is relatively unusual for patients to complain directly to health professionals about the information that they have gained. Many seem reluctant to ask further questions even when they feel urgently in need of more information. However, studies that have *asked* patients for their comments on the information and education received from health professionals have generally found that a sizeable minority is dissatisfied (e.g. Tyson & Turner 2000, Van Weert et al 2003). Poorly informed patients may be left in a state of confusion and stress, and may have fewer coping skills than health professionals assumed. There is strong evidence that the educational process influences patients' satisfaction, understanding and commitment to therapy. It influences long-term self-management strategies. These outcomes in turn can determine health status and psychological well-being. Hence therapists need to evaluate the education that they are offering, in order to improve upon it. This will ultimately increase the effectiveness of their rehabilitation programme.

CONCLUSION

This chapter has presented certain cognitive and behavioural principles of learning. Although there are no simple 'cookbook' approaches to patient education and empowerment (Ellers 1993 p. 98), a better awareness of strategies for enhancing patients' attention, comprehension and recall of information can help health professionals to facilitate better patient education. Patients themselves tend to appreciate being treated as a full member of the rehabilitation team, fully entitled to sharing in the information that they need to manage their condition. Patients may experience a greater sense of control and empowerment when they can access information and education from many sources, including written materials, audiotapes, books and web-sites. However, they are likely to need some help to develop skills for appraising the quality of the information that they consult.

Health professionals are not the only source of expertise, and indeed, it is cost-effective to refer the patient to other forms of supplementary information. Patients with similar conditions can be very helpful, especially in sharing self-management skills, and ideas for solving the everyday problems that illness presents. Rehabilitation often promotes motor skill learning, and health professionals may provide a more effective learning context if they incorporate some behavioural strategies. For example, providing feedback and reinforcement is likely to help patients to acquire behavioural skills more readily. Errorless learning can be an effective approach to patients with cognitive problems. Holistic self-management programmes, including those led by trained lay facilitators, have been shown useful to build self-efficacy, and to help patients regain the experience of control and an enhanced quality of life. While this chapter has focused on educating the patient, many of the issues apply equally to educating families and caregivers.

Further Reading

Ley P 1988 Communicating with patients: improving communication, satisfaction and compliance. Chapman Hall, London
A classic in the field of patient education, although it is now a little dated and focuses upon medical encounters. There are many research studies available and it is certainly worth consulting the evidence-base before devising any new educational programmes for patients with a specific chronic condition.

Holman H, Sobel D, Laurent D et al (eds) 2000 Living a healthy life with chronic conditions: self-management of heart disease, arthritis, diabetes, asthma, bronchitis, emphysema and others. Bull Publishing, Boulder
This provides a detailed account of patient self-management education for a wide range of chronic conditions.

Barlow J, Wright C, Sheasby J et al 2002 Self-management interventions for people with chronic conditions: a review. Patient Education and Counseling 48:177–187
A review of research into self-management approaches for people with chronic conditions which is available as a full-text article if you have access to the electronic database Science Direct or have access to the paper format of the journal *Patient Education and Counseling.*

Van den Borne H 1998 The patient from receiver of information to informed decision-maker. Patient Education and Counseling 49(2):105–114
This article looks at the changing role of the patient from recipient of information to informed decision-maker. A full-text version is available via the electronic database Science Direct.

Bodenheimer T, Lorig K, Holman H et al 2002 Patient self-management of chronic disease in primary care. Journal of the American Medical Association 288(19):2469–2475
This review of patient self-management education can be accessed full-text through the electronic database MedLine.

Marks R 2001 Efficacy theory and its utility in arthritis rehabilitation: review and recommendations. Disability and Rehabilitation 23(7):271–280
This provides a clear review of the theory of self-efficacy and its relevance to the rehabilitation of patients with arthritis.

Suggestions in relation to earlier activities

Suggested version of a simplified patient education sheet

An earlier activity asked you to devise a simplified, more readable version of some patient information. One version is given below.
'Regular exercise helps patients with many different types of health problem. As a person with low back pain, you could benefit too. Sitting for too long each day can make your pain worse. You can become overweight, and develop other health problems. Regular exercise can help you to become fitter and stronger, and better able to manage your pain successfully. Do you need to spend hours each day exercising? Do you have to get out of breath, hot, and sweaty? No! You only need to exercise for about 30 minutes each day. You only need to do enough activity to make you feel warm and to make your heart pump faster. How can you fit in some exercise every day? What activities do you like best? Can you ask a friend or person in your family to give you some support to carry on with your new exercise programme? Please think about these questions before you see your therapist. Then you can discuss your ideas together and work out a suitable, safe programme for managing your pain.'

This version has a reading ease score of 72.9 (fairly easy, and readable by the large majority of the population, according to Table 8.3 in Ley (1988 p. 117). It requires a grade level of 6.0 (approximately 12 years old). Of course, your version is likely to be different. You may decide that some of the original information has been omitted in this example above. Perhaps you have included some different information in your version. Do you think that the style here sets the right tone or is it too patronising? Does this style of writing help to attract attention and engage the reader's motivation? Or is it too 'chummy'? All of these considerations are important when evaluating written information and instructions. Only direct consultations with patients can really help to answer such questions with confidence. However, colleagues' opinions can provide a valuable starting-point. In addition, if you type up your version of the information sheet and check it with the software, as described earlier on in this chapter, you will see if you have succeeded in making the information easy enough for a general audience to read.

Motivating Richard – some strategies for more effective learning

An earlier activity asked you to identify some of the ways in which the learning process for a burns patient was poorly managed, and whether you could suggest some ways in which the therapists could have incorporated appropriate cognitive and behavioural learning principles to help Richard cope with the programme more successfully.

Principles of adult learning suggest that adults learn most effectively when they engage in active partnership with educators, rather than being cast into the role of passive receivers of information. Richard needs to feel more involved in goal-setting and in making decisions about his rehabilitation activities. He needs clear information about the reasons for the therapeutic approach, and its likely effectiveness. This information might help him to feel more motivated to participate, for example, through understanding why it may be important to continue with exercises despite pain.

The therapists might also have incorporated more behavioural learning principles into the rehabilitation programme. The following ideas are based on principles of learning theory (operant and classical conditioning). They might assist Richard to develop higher self-efficacy for the tasks involved in walking re-training:

- Preliminary training in coping strategies for the pain (e.g. relaxation techniques) could give Richard more behavioural resources to cope with the pain that arises during movement. This would enhance his self-efficacy for managing the pain associated with walking.
- Setting clear short-term and longer-terms goals, so Richard can monitor his own progress and feel more positively about his gradual achievements.
- Offering clearer reinforcement for progress in rehabilitation – including meaningful praise for specific achievements such as walking for 10 metres (not just routine exclamations throughout the session such as 'good job!', or 'that's fine!'). Other rewards might be scheduled, with Richard's agreement, such as introducing a new activity when a realistic target has been achieved. Above all, regular specific feedback about progress can be highly reinforcing of effort and learning. Such feedback can be verbal, or in a visual format such as a graph of measured progress.
- Ensuring that sessions are not too long. Spaced practice, with more numerous but shorter sessions, may be more effective for learning, and less fatiguing, if the schedule allows.
- Showing sensitivity to conditioned emotional responses. A situation in which the patient has experienced much pain can become, by association, anxiety-provoking or trigger feelings of powerlessness. Such automatic emotional reactions inhibit motivation, learning and progress. If Richard is showing anxious or depressive reactions to the rehabilitation setting, therapists might consider moving some sessions elsewhere, if safe to do so. For example, some activities might be carried out in the hospital garden or another venue. If the patient experiences feelings of achievement in the new setting, he

may feel greater self-efficacy for returning later to the gym or other venue and coping more successfully with the tasks that are presented there.

This example shows that therapists should not treat emotional support and educational interventions as separate issues. The therapist who is empathic about the patient's pain and frustrations is more likely to tailor the educational intervention to meet the client's needs. A therapist who plunges on, regardless, with his or her own agenda will risk being ineffective both in terms of providing emotional support and in terms of teaching the patient new skills.

Chapter 9

Teamwork in the rehabilitation setting

> This team is not patient-led … it is not a needs-led team at all; it is a profession-led team. It's about 'this is my work, and this is your work'; it is not about how we can help this patient.

This comment was made by a staff nurse who was participating in a study of interprofessional teamworking (Miller et al 2001 p. 87). The nurse had observed a team whose members worked in parallel rather than co-operatively, perhaps to the detriment of the patient. Communication barriers and blockages can frustrate the professionals involved in the team, as well as patients. Teams are complex systems, and the factors that are responsible for communication breakdown are rarely clear. As a further complication, each team member may view the functioning of the team in different ways. Atwal (2002b) provided an example of this in a study of multidisciplinary team functioning in relation to the discharge of patients. She found that some nurses reported receiving inadequate information from occupational therapists whereas other nurses considered that they received more information from their colleagues in occupational therapy and physiotherapy than from fellow nurses.

Previous chapters have emphasised that the quality and effectiveness of patient care are shaped by the communication skills of therapists as well as by their technical expertise. This chapter examines how patient-centred practice is also facilitated – or inhibited – by the functioning of the wider team culture. The discussion will highlight some of the ways in which communications among health professionals, and between professionals and patients, are shaped by organisational and group processes. Some possible effects of teamwork on treatment outcomes will also be considered. Specifically, the chapter will discuss the following issues:

- Differences between 'multiprofessional' and 'interprofessional' teams
- Task and maintenance processes in groups
- Group norms
- Communication networks
- Defensive communications in groups
- Limited understanding of each profession's roles and stereotyping/ prejudice
- Geographical dispersal and other 'mundane' barriers to communication
- Leadership styles
- Hierarchy
- Clash of rehabilitation or teamwork philosophies
- Financial barriers to teamworking
- Effective team-working: possible benefits for patients
- Some strategies for enhancing interprofessional teamwork.

DIFFERENCES BETWEEN 'MULTIPROFESSIONAL' AND 'INTERPROFESSIONAL' TEAMS

Collaborative interprofessional teamwork is being increasingly emphasised within the NHS. Many patients, in particular those with chronic conditions and/ or complex needs, require the expertise of professionals from more than one discipline. A good illustration is provided by Nelson et al (2001) who described the distinctive and overlapping contributions of occupational therapy and physiotherapy to patients undergoing rehabilitation following a hip fracture. Effective and efficient teamwork is also seen as a cost-effective means of reducing patients' waiting times for treatment. It can remove unnecessary duplication of assessments and interventions, and help to ensure that patients benefit from a holistic approach.

Although the terms multiprofessional (multidisciplinary) and interprofessional working are sometimes used interchangeably, some authors suggest that the terms have distinctive meanings (e.g. Casto & Juliá 1994). For those who distinguish these terms, a multiprofessional team consists of professionals from different disciplines, such as physiotherapy, occupational therapy, nursing and social work. In such teams, the different professionals may work in parallel rather than collaborating and sharing a common purpose. Even when team members respect each other's contribution to the patient, each may have only a limited understanding of other professionals' assessments, goals and interventions. Interprofessional teams, on the other hand, when working effectively together, collaborate far more extensively and the various members share common goals. A central feature of effective interprofessional (or interdisciplinary) teams is that team members have a good understanding of each others' roles and professional language, and cope positively both with role difference and with role overlap (e.g. Hilton 1995; Miller et al 2001). In well-integrated interprofessional teams, members perceive little threat from others who perform similar roles and therefore feel less need to defend professional 'territories' or undermine the value of others' contributions (Molyneux 2001). Close collaboration is easier to achieve when team members have minimal status differences and hierarchy. However, as we shall see later, when barriers such as hierarchy do occur in teams, they can markedly reduce the team's capacity to offer patient-centred care.

Teams in healthcare settings are not always clearly defined units, partly because individual professionals can be members of more than one team. For example, a dietician may contribute services to different teams each offering specialist interventions for patients with diabetes, multiple sclerosis, and other conditions. Such fluidity of membership sometimes imposes limits on the cohesiveness of teams. Furthermore, in some teams, membership is not well defined even to those involved. Miller et al (1998) found that each member of a diabetes team drew a different diagram of who was in their team and how the team worked together.

TASK AND MAINTENANCE PROCESSES IN GROUPS

To understand whether a team works well, we need to look at more than the individual skills and personalities of its members. Groups function as complex systems, with communication processes serving many functions and operating on many levels. Effective communication at the team level is difficult to define for these reasons.

> **ACTIVITY Identify some effective communication processes in a group**
>
> - Have you been a member of a group or team that has communicated effectively, for example, in a clinical setting, or an educational setting?
> - What kinds of effective communication occurred?
> - How did you know that these communications were 'effective'?

In this activity, you might have reflected that effective communication occurs when the various team members skilfully co-ordinate and integrate their efforts, for example, finding ways of pooling their resources and coming to sound, consensus decisions. Effectiveness may be judged in terms of whether the group achieves the task in hand, accurately and efficiently. Perhaps you also considered the social climate of the group. You might experience a group in which you felt comfortable and ready to contribute as more 'effective'. Skilful communication within a group depends on group members using individual skills such as sensitivity to others' needs, careful listening, taking care to include new members, and appropriate use of humour. These various considerations relate to two basic functions of communication in groups – to achieve the group's task objectives, and to create a positive socioemotional climate in which team members can work together collaboratively.

These distinctive aspects of group functioning have been referred to as the task and the maintenance aspects of group behaviour (Casto & Juliá 1994, Johnson & Johnson 2002). 'Maintenance' communications are those that serve to maintain the group as a social entity whereas task-oriented communications 'get the work done'. In the clinical setting, team members have to co-ordinate their efforts to achieve various tasks such as sharing information, planning treatment priorities, and so on. Groups that are very task-oriented can be emotionally bruising. For example, the group leader may be abrasive to those who hold different opinions, and people who do not speak up and defend their own views assertively may find themselves ignored, belittled or under-resourced.

Maintenance communications refer to any contributions that help to preserve the unity and longer-term cohesiveness of the group. These include expressing respect and interest for other members' contributions, releasing tension with appropriate humour, and inviting quiet members to contribute. In other words, maintenance communications help members to feel emotionally safe within the group, and increase the satisfaction that they gain from working together. Communications that help members to address conflicts and differences openly also help to enhance working relationships and promote the long-term functioning of the group. Casto and Juliá (1994 p. 37) argue that 'to be an effective team member, one must have knowledge about and skills in the group processes that underlie the interaction of team members'. Unfortunately, these forms of knowledge and skills tend to be neglected in professional education (Freeman et al 2000).

GROUP NORMS

Groups are more than collections of individuals, and group processes reflect more than the summation of each member's personal values and skills. There is a great wealth of research into group processes, much of which has been carried out by social psychologists. This research reveals groups to be more than the sum of their parts. Over time, groups develop cultures that influence the behaviour, feelings and attitudes of both existing group members and newcomers. One way of thinking about group culture is to consider the norms that evolve within the group over time. A norm is essentially a social standard or expectation that governs members' attitudes and behaviour.

Norms are rarely written down formally as 'rules', but they still exercise much influence over group members. Indeed, one informal 'test' of whether a certain norm exists within a group is that group members feel as though they risk punishment or rejection if they violate it (Forsyth 1990 p. 160). Various experimental studies confirm such fears by showing that group members who reject a group's norms indeed tend to suffer a loss of status, unpopularity and even ostracism (see reviews in Forsyth 1990 and Brown 1996).

ACTIVITY Norms and their consequences

James is part-way through a rotational post that he took up immediately after qualifying as an occupational therapist. After six months, he has just moved to a stroke rehabilitation team. He is surprised to find that several team members rarely attend the team's weekly meetings. Instead, they report their apologies and continue with other work. Two other members are quite lax about time-keeping and arrive 10–15 minutes late for work on most days. He is also dismayed to find that the team meeting is dominated by a medical consultant who uses most of the meeting to talk 'at' the team. He generally regards contributions from other team members as 'interruptions'. James feels concerned that the other occupational therapists on the team rarely speak up during these meetings, and perceives that their behaviour is undermining his own self-confidence in the situation. James has started to feel quite demotivated, and he has now slipped into a habit of arriving late for work once or twice each week. He even took a 'sick' day recently to avoid the team meeting – something he has never done before.

One way of looking at the dysfunctional team dynamics is to blame individuals – for example the 'authoritarian' leader, the 'lazy' team members who arrive late for work, the 'shy' occupational therapist who does not speak up in meetings. An alternative is to look at the dynamics of the group as a system. The entire system can have powerful effects on group members' feelings and behaviour, almost regardless of their individual personalities and abilities.

- What norms seem to be operating in this work group?
- How are James' feelings and actions being influenced by the norms governing this particular group?
- Suggest some possible reasons why these norms may have developed over time.

Other dysfunctional norms that all too often emerge in groups relate to bullying, racism and sexism. Individuals who would not express such attitudes and behaviours by themselves in isolation, can be persuaded by group norms that such responses are acceptable. To illustrate, research into teamworking by Miller et al (2001) observed some sexist patterns of interaction among health professionals. People can feel very intimidated and isolated when confronted by strong dysfunctional group norms. Yet it is only through awareness of group phenomena such as norms, and by viewing the problem at the system level rather than at the level of the individual, that group members can begin to bring about change in their relationships and working practices.

COMMUNICATION NETWORKS

As well as developing norms, groups also devise communication networks over time. These networks describe the typical patterns of information exchange within the group, and profoundly affect the operation of the team and its effectiveness (Forsyth 1990). For example, some groups operate an egalitarian system of communication in which information is shared among members quite freely, and in which information flows without encountering barriers of status or hierarchy. Other groups have communication networks that look more like a bicycle wheel, with all information flowing from the members on the periphery to the leader in the centre, with little returning in the opposite direction. There is minimal cross-communication of ideas and information among the other group members. Although this system of handling information and decision-making can work quite efficiently in simple tasks, it encounters a number of unfortunate problems in more complex situations. Firstly, the leader in the middle of the 'wheel' can become saturated with information, leading to inefficiency. Secondly, this system has the effect of creating dependence of the group upon the leader who holds most of the information and hence decision-making power. Some group members may become disaffected as a consequence. The system also reinforces the central position and authority of the leader, making it difficult for group members to challenge his or her role in the group, or to learn from each other.

Group members' own socialisation can influence a team culture, and the style of communication within a group. For example, a medical consultant who has been socialised in a very 'adversarial' educational system and who is steeped in the traditional medical hierarchy may not see any problem in using a 'team meeting' to lecture at a group that he regards as 'his' staff. Consultants receive little formal education in social psychology, so they may not realise when they are being demoralising and disempowering to other team members, rather than communicating in ways that enable the group to make maximum use of the expertise available. Other group members, influenced by their own personal and professional histories, may not have sufficient skills or strategies for challenging the social norms of the group. One response to this problem may be to opt out of meetings. The history of a group also affects its cohesiveness and ways of communicating. For example, groups who have worked closely together for many months or years may evolve into such cohesive units that subsequent newcomers feel excluded and even deskilled (as noted by Miller et al 2001).

Miller et al (2001) reported in-depth case studies of six multi/interprofessional teams, each carried out over three months. The research used observation and interview methods as well as document analysis. From the data collected, the researchers distinguished certain different types of group structures within interprofessional teams, from the highly integrated to the highly fragmented. The highly integrated teams formed tight, well-defined entities, characterised by members having an excellent understanding of each other's roles, a clear shared vision, and the smooth flow of information and ideas around all members. Members sometimes took opportunities to reflect on the effectiveness of the group's functioning in order to address promptly any difficulties that were arising. Members' allegiance was primarily to the group rather than to their own profession, possibly because they already enjoyed secure professional identities.

At the other end of the scale, Miller et al observed groups who did not really deserve the title of 'interprofessional team' at all. These fragmented teams were simply loose collections of individuals each pursuing their own uniprofessional agendas, and placing little value on regular meetings or active collaboration. They tended to communicate on a 'need to know' basis, exchanging limited amounts of information, and being dismissive about the learning opportunities that arose during interaction with each other.

The research by Miller et al also located teams that were midway in their characteristics, with a core group that was integrated yet with other members who worked on the periphery in a fragmented way. It might be thought that the latter group of individuals occupied their marginalised position simply because they were only needed occasionally to help the team with specific issues. This was not so. In the groups that the researchers observed, some of the peripheral individuals should have been full members of the team, but as newcomers, they had difficulty breaking into the previously established social unit. The researchers noted in one case that the original group members had developed such a strong allegiance from planning the service together, that they did not easily or willingly admit additional professionals to their group. Certain other professionals found themselves in the peripheral position, because they provided services to other teams as well, and could not therefore prioritise one team alone. While core members tended to communicate freely with each other, based on a good understanding of each other's roles and functions, this did not extend to members on the periphery. In one case, the researchers found that this pattern of divisive teamworking had clearly detrimental effects on patient care.

DEFENSIVE COMMUNICATIONS IN GROUPS

In the discussion above, group interactions have been divided into those that achieve task objectives and those that maintain the group as a social entity. Some psychodynamic studies of groups suggest that deeper, more covert processes can occur, with the primary purpose of protecting group members from anxiety (Morgan & Thomas 1996). Some of the behaviours that serve defensive functions may appear irrational to outsiders, but group members may find it very difficult to see through their own (or their leader's) defensive strategies.

Projection is a defence mechanism that prevents group members from 'owning' their concerns. They therefore cannot address these concerns openly within the group. For example, blame for a 'failure' may be attributed to another group (such as 'out-of-touch' management, or 'non-compliant' patients) or even a scapegoat within the group (Farrell et al 2001). Anxiety within the group (e.g. about taking on a new role or adapting to new policies) may be projected on to one member who is implicitly nominated to carry the anxiety for the whole group. This team member may become seriously stressed as a consequence, while others can more or less disown their own negative feelings.

Splitting is another defensive process that can occur in groups. In some cases, splitting may result in team members being classified into 'good' and 'bad' sub-groups. The energy within the group can be directed towards the opposing half of the group. Splitting is said to be a subconscious way of managing ambivalence. By focusing on the shortcomings of 'other' people, and idealising one's own group (or sub-group), each person's own contribution to a difficult situation can be ignored. Problems can also be 'manufactured' to draw attention away from the real issues that are more troubling for the group. As with projection, this strategy prevents deeper problems and rifts from being addressed rationally and openly by group members. Anxiety is reduced but at the cost of the group's potential development. Individual group members can also find such defensive processes very difficult to deal with, except by avoidant strategies such as taking sick leave or changing jobs. Such processes were examined in a seminal study of hospital nurses and senior staff by Menzies Lyth, cited in Morgan & Thomas (1996). This study also suggested that splitting and other unconscious defensive processes negatively affected patient care. Groups that are consumed with their own defensive strategies would seem to be less able to focus outwards and address patients' needs.

LIMITED UNDERSTANDING OF EACH PROFESSION'S ROLES AND STEREOTYPING/PREJUDICE

Hilton (1995) argues that one of the most important barriers to effective interprofessional teamwork is the lack of understanding that health professionals have about each other's roles. It has been recognised that undergraduate education in the health professions rarely gives sufficient space within the curriculum for students to learn about other professions. Various studies have shown that professionals have a relatively poor understanding of other professional roles (e.g. Atwal 2002a). Co-operation is not only limited by ignorance of others' skills and functions but also by negative stereotypes (Carpenter 1995, Hind et al 2003). It is of concern that some health professionals consider that their negative attitudes towards other disciplines increased during the course of their training (Leaviss 2000).

Carpenter (1995) found that nurses and doctors held both positive and negative stereotypes about each other (e.g. that doctors were confident yet arrogant). Such negative attitudes and stereotypes may affect not only the quality of teamworking, but also patient care. This is because it is only when each professional has a good understanding of other team members' skills and knowledge that they will refer patients appropriately, be able to describe to patients what interventions their colleagues are offering, and explain the rationale of a multidisciplinary team approach. Professionals who have a good understanding of other professional interventions are also more able to carry on with these strategies during rehabilitation, rather than working at odds with them. Waters and Luker (1996) carried out a study showing that nurses in a rehabilitation setting lacked sufficient education about physiotherapy and occupational therapy, and were further hampered by receiving limited written notes from the therapy staff. The researchers argued that these nurses had a great potential to carry on the therapeutic interventions with patients between physiotherapy and occupational therapy sessions and at weekends. However, this potential was largely wasted by the poor communication occurring within the rehabilitation team. The therapists' limited understanding of the nurses' role was also a hindrance to teamwork.

ACTIVITY Which professionals should be involved in planning a patient's discharge home, and why?

For this activity, consider the needs of an elderly patient who is being discharged home after rehabilitation for a stroke.
- Which health and social care professionals are likely to be involved in this process, and what are their usual roles?
- How confident are you in your knowledge of these roles?
- What may happen, from the patient's point of view, if the professionals concerned have a limited understanding of each other's roles?
- If possible, discuss your answer with those of another student or therapist, to check whether your understanding of professional roles is similar or different.

A study by Bull and Roberts (2001) found that effective (or 'proper') discharge planning for elderly patients required excellent co-ordination between health and social care professionals. Yet considerable misunderstanding of certain roles occurred. For example, many professionals expressed uncertainty about the role of the district nurse. Such misunderstandings resulted in community-based professionals being given insufficient notice about the patients for whom they would be taking on responsibility. This left patients and their families with fewer support resources than they needed on arrival home, and with conflicting plans about their discharge. Illegible referral forms were also observed to impede communication across the agencies concerned.

One way of informing professionals about other disciplines is to engage them in regular interprofessional education, before and after qualification. Professionals may, for example, give seminars to others in their team, describing their skills and functions. These educational initiatives may break down stereotypes, as Carpenter (1995) shows, and thereby help people to work more effectively across professional boundaries.

GEOGRAPHICAL DISPERSAL AND OTHER 'MUNDANE' BARRIERS TO COMMUNICATION

Freeth (2001) argues that there are widely recognised 'mundane' barriers to teamwork. An inadequate physical environment provides a good example of a mundane barrier to communication and collaboration. When different team members occupy disparate sites in the hospital or community, making travel and regular meetings difficult to arrange, it is unsurprising that genuine teamwork suffers. Interagency co-operation can be even more difficult to establish, as professionals working in the community are often spread over a large geographical area, reducing the possibility of regular face-to-face meetings. Other structural barriers can also fragment a team. For example, if some team members have access to e-mail whilst others do not, communication will tend to flow more readily around those members who are in electronic contact.

Time pressures also make it difficult for professionals to liase fully with colleagues and attend team meetings. Atwal's study of a multidisciplinary team showed this problem clearly. A staff nurse explained:

... If you are really busy and the whole place is bedlam and the care manager walks onto the ward you just think, 'Oh God no!' and you know that you are going to have to talk and you know that you are going to have to spend time and often you don't have it. It is an inconvenience and, you know, an hour later you are phoning them up trying to get them to come up to the ward so you can speak to them. But if they come at a time when you are not expecting them it is bedlam and you just cringe (Atwal, 2002b: p. 455).

LEADERSHIP STYLES

Leadership styles have a tremendous influence over the functioning and effectiveness of teams. Three basic styles were originally distinguished, by the seminal work of Lewin in the 1930s (see Brown 1996). Authoritarian (autocratic) leaders are highly directive. They tend to use power rather than leading by example or by inspiration. Under this form of control, the team may work quite efficiently. On the negative side, autocratic leaders inhibit disclosure of ideas and dialogue. They therefore lose some of the resources of the group, as there is little sharing of information and ideas and because members can exert so little influence over decisions. Such teams are likely to be very task-oriented and members' emotional needs are readily overlooked.

A second type of leadership is 'laissez faire'. Laissez-faire leaders leave the group to its own devices. This permissive approach can work adequately with highly skilled and well motivated groups, who essentially direct their own group processes. In less ideal circumstances, the group can easily degenerate into unproductive, disorganised chaos. Alternatively, individuals may simply engage in parallel-working rather than co-operating together.

According to Lewin, the preferred leadership style in most circumstances is the 'democratic' type. Democratic leaders tend to encourage the greatest pooling of resources, and help the group to arrive at consensus over goals, tasks and strategies through participative decision-making strategies. This style facilitates not only collaborative work on the task, but also sound maintenance processes within the group (such as care and respect for each other).

More recent research tends to define effective leadership in terms of the demands of the situation as well as the personality or individual skills of the leader. The leader of a group may be most effective when responding flexibly to the demands of the situation and task, whilst also taking into account the quality of relationships within the group (see discussion by Brown 1996). Several studies have noted autocratic leadership and strict hierarchies within certain health service teams (e.g. Miller et al 2001). In illustration, Sweet and Norman (1995) reviewed a number of studies showing that nurses all too often have to 'defer passively to the doctor's authority' (p. 165). It is clearly difficult for individual health professionals who are working in rigid hierarchical structures, with autocratic leadership, to gain sufficient power to bring about a more collaborative group climate (Miller et al 2001). Nevertheless, through greater awareness of group structures and processes, and by working proactively with others at similar levels of the hierarchy, small incremental changes in leadership qualities may be achieved.

HIERARCHY

Hierarchy tends to have an inhibiting or distorting effect upon communication processes in groups. Unfortunately, hierarchy is a strong presence within the healthcare system. For example, traditional biomedical practice has established physicians at the top of the hierarchy, over other professionals such as nurses, who have been traditionally regarded as more lowly 'carers'. Hierarchy appears to be linked to traditional gender roles also, with professions dominated by females tending to have lower status (e.g. Lockart-Wood 2000, West & Field 1995). Even amidst the operation of interprofessional teams, where roles and responsibilities should deserve similar status and equal respect, hierarchies continue to exert influence. Miller et al (2001) note in their research that consultants had a powerful autocratic role in some of the teams that they studied. Nurses in some units express uncertainty about their roles, and feel that therapists do not understand their role in rehabilitation (Dalley & Sim 2001). Whilst hierarchy is partially determined by grades and salaries apportioned by the larger organisation, local factors, values and customs also exert an influence. Newcomers to a team can also influence the nature of its hierarchy. A clinical psychologist observed by Miller et al (2001) seemed to consider that he was so superior to other team members that he refused to share his notes or to attend team meetings. He appeared to introduce a form of hierarchy into a previously egalitarian team, creating suspicion, and negatively affecting working relationships.

Hierarchies have important effects on teamworking because they affect the flow of information from one member to another. Information flowing 'upwards' from the lower status members may be more guarded, as lower status members seek to tell higher status members what they think they want to hear. They also resist telling the higher status members anything that might 'reflect unfavorably on their [own] performance, abilities, and skills' (see discussion by Forsyth 1990 p.133). Higher status members may be sceptical about the information provided from 'below' them in the hierarchy, feeling that they can learn little or nothing from low status team members. Much of the research into the effects of hierarchy on information flow has been based on experimental groups. However, Miller et al (2001) noted some similar effects in the interprofessional healthcare teams that they observed. Some worked within an integrative framework, where there was an accepted pattern of sharing views and information among members of the team. On the other hand, in teams that had a steeper hierarchy, with an autocratic leader, there tended to be minimal debate or exchange of views. All too often, the views of 'lower' members of the hierarchy were dismissed.

ACTIVITY Analyse the potential effects of hierarchy on information sharing within an interprofessional team, and how the patient may be affected

In the following imaginary scenario, professionals in a highly hierarchical rehabilitation team are working with a head-injured teenage girl, Rachel. Rachel has spent three months in the rehabilitation setting. At the end of the week, she will be going home, for the first time since her accident, for a weekend visit. The status of the team members is indicated by a number from 1 to 5, with 1 being the highest status member of the team, and 5 the lowest.

Please note that the team is a *hypothetical example*, and that there is no intention of implying that occupational therapists are always lower in status than physiotherapists, or that nurses occupy the lowest status in a rehabilitation team. Only *in this specific team*, do the various members experience on a personal level this particular 'pecking order'. Nevertheless, research shows that interprofessional collaboration is sometimes problematic because of disparities in the status given to each team member (e.g. Lockart-Wood 2000, Waters & Luker 1996). It would seem therefore that the example is realistic.

- Each team member has a different piece of information about Rachel. Read each comment, and analyse how the hierarchy might influence the way in which the pieces of information are received by the team. Will each observation be given equal weight in the team meeting, and in any decision that the team takes?

- How might any barriers to information-sharing that you have identified affect the patient?

1. Consultant: Rachel is making good progress. It is difficult to make any definite prognosis about anyone with a head injury, but she appears to be medically stable, and will not require any more surgery.

2. Head physiotherapist: Rachel is responding well to treatment. She is mobilising on her own using a wheelchair, and our assessments show that her upper body strength is improving.

3. Senior occupational therapist: Rachel seems rather depressed at the thought of going home this weekend. She has expressed concerns that she will feel more disabled and more different from her previous self when back in her normal home environment. She is not sure how she is going to react.

4. Art therapist: Rachel told me about some of her worries when she was creating a painting. I noticed that she was using swathes of black paint, and I asked her if the blackness said something about her state of mind. She agreed. I think that she has realised that her plans of going to university will have to put on hold until she sees what degree of physical and cognitive recovery she can achieve. She has some worries about the future. On the positive side, she is considering whether she might do a short art course when she leaves the rehabilitation unit as her artwork is giving her much satisfaction.

5. Nurse: Rachel was crying last night. She told me that she feels exhausted by having to put on a brave face to her parents and friends, and that she feels frustrated about her degree of recovery. She is also worried about having frequent headaches. Rachel expressed concerns to me about the strain that her condition is putting on her family.

Based on social psychological theorising about groups, and studies such as that of Miller et al (2001), we may infer that higher status members (1 and 2) will tend not to listen to the information provided by the 'lower status' members. They may feel that they have little to learn from those lower down the hierarchy. Through exposure to these attitudes, lower status members may have been socialised into offering the high status members only very selective information. On the other hand, the lower status members may share information more freely with each other, as well as receiving information from 'above'. One implication of having barriers to information-sharing associated with hierarchy in an interprofessional team context is that the various health professionals may be working to very different goals, instead of collaborating to meet the patient's needs.

In the case above, the highest status professionals are oriented towards the patient's physical functioning, and are trained to evaluate progress in objective, 'outsider' terms. The 'lower' status team members in this example have a more holistic orientation, by virtue of their professional training. They are willing to gain and share information about the patient's psychological and social condition as well as physical progress, and they value the subjective insights given by the patient. In the case example, the patient's account is mixed. On the negative side, the patient is expressing concerns and frustrations about her immediate and long-term future. On the positive side, she is tentatively considering possible occupational goals (an art course once she leaves the rehabilitation unit), and is clearly making progress in her physical recovery. If the 'higher status' members of the team discredit psychosocial information about the patient, rehabilitation is not likely to address Rachel's needs, nor capitalise on her resources. If her emotional vulnerability is not recognised, she may not receive the emotional support that she requires to move forwards in her rehabilitation.

Another consequence of cliques and hierarchy on the team's functioning is that the lower status members may feel deskilled and belittled by the higher status members. Over time, this risks creating hostility and distrust between the two sub-groups (with each person's own status group being perceived as the 'in-group' and the other status group being perceived as the 'out-group'). Such barriers will threaten the unity of the team. If the professionals also work in different geographical locations, it may be tempting for the lower status professionals to opt out of unsatisfactory team meetings, by for example, scheduling other important work on their own worksite. Hierarchies also have a tendency to self-perpetuate. If during team meetings, the high status members reject the ideas of lower status members, or suggest that they are of little concern to the team, the lower status members may choose not to become involved in the meeting, may lose confidence in their professional status, or may shift in their priorities to match those of the high status members. In this case, it is not only the team that becomes self-destructive. Rehabilitation is also in danger of reverting to the strictly biomedical model and becoming less holistic, to the patient's detriment.

CLASH OF REHABILITATION OR TEAMWORK PHILOSOPHIES

Teams are unlikely to collaborate successfully, if individual members adopt very different treatment philosophies (Johnson et al 2003, Miller et al 2001). For example, if some professionals adhere to the biomedical model, they will focus on the patient's physical functioning. They may also take for granted that the professional is the expert and the patient is the passive recipient of treatment. This approach will conflict with professionals who have adopted a biopsychosocial or empowering philosophy of rehabilitation, and the different philosophies are likely to confuse the patient.

Freeman et al (2000) suggest that teamwork can suffer when individual members each bring different philosophies of teamworking. Tensions are likely if some members, for example, adopt an integrative philosophy in which they expect equal sharing of information and participatory styles of decision-making, whilst others take an elective approach to teamwork, favouring minimal contact on a 'need to know' basis, and strong individual autonomy.

FINANCIAL BARRIERS TO TEAMWORKING

It is sometimes unclear where the budget for an interprofessional intervention will come from. This can lead to rivalry within the team, and perceived competition for scarce resources, particularly where health and social care agencies are attempting to collaborate (Johnson et al 2003, Poulton & West 1999). Such uncertainties inhibit the process of decision-making, and commitment to the team's efforts. It may also encourage defensive strategies of communication among team members as each strives to protect their professional 'territory' and its allocated resources. None of these behaviours assist the patient to re-establish control and self-esteem.

SEPARATE ASSESSMENTS, TREATMENT PLANS AND WRITTEN RECORDS

It has been argued that collaborative teamwork requires shared assessments and intervention plans, as well as multiple-entry record-keeping, so that every team member has access to the same written information about patients. Poole and Johnson (1996) reported that integrated care pathways contributed to improvements in teamwork and enhanced patient care in an orthopaedic setting. On the other hand, Atwal and Caldwell (2002) carried out an action research study and found no signs of improvement to interprofessional communications from the implementation of an integrated care pathway for patients with an orthopaedic condition. Gibbon et al (2002) similarly found no improvement in teamworking in stroke care following the implementation of a co-ordinated care protocol. This approach clearly requires further investigation. It is possible that a formal, integrated care protocol will not by itself overcome pre-existing interpersonal problems, or the effects of role confusion, on the team's working relationships.

Shared written records would also seem vital for effective liaison among team members, although it is important that the various health professionals involved agree upon their content and structure. The evolution of suitable documentation for an interprofessional team working with older people has been described by Burnett et al (2002). Casto and Juliá (1994 p. 67) vividly argue that 'records are often the glue that holds multiple entry teams together, permitting interprofessional collaboration'. More research is needed into the effects on teamworking of introducing such shared record systems.

EFFECTIVE TEAM-WORKING: POSSIBLE BENEFITS FOR PATIENTS

Clearly, the whole rationale behind the emphasis on teamworking is that patients benefit from closer liaison among health professionals. Miller et al (2001) argue from their intensive observations of interprofessional teams over three months, that integrated teams provide better continuity and consistency of care for patients, less duplication, fewer ambiguous messages (as team members share information and priorities), more appropriate referrals to other health professionals, and overall, a more holistic approach to the patient. Similar advantages were presented in a case study of an interprofessional approach to an elderly woman who had suffered a cerebral aneurism (Howell & Cleary 2001). Team members who have a good understanding of each other's roles and the rationale for their interventions are also better able to 'carry over' the interventions of other professionals, rather than implementing conflicting plans and priorities. In illustration, Miller et al (2001) describe a patient who expressed gaining a great feeling of security when his occupational therapist explained the rationale for his physiotherapist's intervention.

Despite the good theoretical reasons and several anecdotal reports linking interprofessional teamworking and patient outcomes, there is some debate about whether objective evidence really supports this link. Some authors claim that there really is no evidence that interprofessional teamwork favours patients (e.g. Brown et al 2003) whereas others disagree, albeit with some caution (Schmitt 2001).

ACTIVITY Why is it difficult to gain firm evidence about the effects of collaborative interprofessional teamworking on patients' rehabilitation outcomes?

- On the basis of your understanding of teamwork, developed through reading this chapter, consider why it is difficult to gain firm evidence concerning the effects of interprofessional collaboration on rehabilitation outcomes. You may like to think about this question generally, or in relation to a specific area of rehabilitation (e.g. stroke, head injury).

There are many reasons why it is difficult to obtain evidence about the effects of teamwork processes on patients. The reasons are similar to those discussed in earlier chapters, regarding the impact of therapist communication on patients:

- The process of communication is multi-variate. Many communications are not 'deliberate' interventions but instead constitute part of the taken-for-granted matrix of rehabilitation. These variables make it difficult to evaluate the effects of individual therapist–patient communications. The problems of evaluating therapist–patient communication are magnified considerably when investigating teamworking. Teams vary not only in terms of the skills of their individual members, but also in so many other aspects of their dynamics. Their leadership may be inspiring or problematic; their social climate may be supportive or defensive; the team may have clear or conflicting goals. Group members may differ in how well they understand other's roles. The group may be well resourced, or have an uncertain budget. Team dynamics change over time, with every appointment of new leaders and/or other personnel. It is difficult to tease out the many variables that affect patterns of teamworking, and their various effects on patients. As Schmitt (2001) notes, collaboration is not all-or-none, but is instead a multi-dimensional construct.

- It is difficult to combine outcome data from many teams, as each may function in unique ways, making comparisons of their processes and effects quite meaningless.
- A detailed understanding of the processes that occur within teams requires lengthy, costly research (e.g. the study reported by Miller et al 2001, that took three years in total).
- Patient outcomes are multiple and complex. Studies use a variety of measures including length of hospital stay, return to hospital, functional gains, patient satisfaction, or many other outcomes. Again, it is difficult to link specific team variables to all of the relevant outcome measures.
- It is difficult, and potentially unethical, to vary team functioning deliberately, as part of an experimental investigation into its effects on patients. Nevertheless, some interesting evidence has been gained from studies that compared patients treated by interprofessional teams, with those treated by single professional groups (such as medical specialists).
- It is difficult to isolate the effects of positive team dynamics on the outcomes gained from other aspects of interprofessional working. For example, it is possible that some interprofessional teams achieve more effective outcomes because they attract more specialist staff, provide more intensive treatments, or develop higher level skills from working exclusively with specific groups of patients (e.g. stroke patients). Schmitt (2001) discusses these issues further.

Despite these many difficulties, some studies have examined whether effective teamwork benefits patients in any measurable way. Schmitt (2001), though, reminds us that the question is not simply:

> whether collaboration generally makes a difference, but, also, more specifically what mix of collaborators for what purposes for whom makes a difference for what outcomes and at what costs (p. 47).

It is this question that is so difficult to answer. Schmitt et al (1988) reviewed studies that examined the effectiveness of collaborative teamwork in the care of elderly patients, and found no effect on mortality, but some demonstrable effects on patients' functioning, and in helping patients to become less dependent on services. Stuck et al (1993) carried out a statistical meta-analysis, again in the field of elderly care, and reported that treatment by designated teams tended to improve functioning, helped patients return to their homes, and also decreased mortality rates. High levels of coordination among intensive care staff have been shown to reduce mortality (Knaus et al 1986). Poulton and West (1999) review studies that suggest better outcomes from effective interprofessional collaboration at the primary healthcare level. Schmitt (2001) reviews many other studies which suggest positive outcomes from effective interprofessional teamwork, but she cautions that there is much further research to be done to link *specific* aspects of team functioning with patient outcomes in well-controlled, scientifically robust ways.

SOME STRATEGIES FOR ENHANCING INTERPROFESSIONAL TEAMWORK

A number of strategies for improving interprofessional teamwork can be suggested. It needs to be recognised, though, that individuals working alone have a quite limited power to affect group dynamics. It may be more effective to negotiate possible areas of change with other team members, thereby taking a team approach to implementing new ways of working together. Various strategies can help teams to work together more effectively:

- *Develop clear objectives and goals for the team as a whole:* A study of experts in the field of building healthcare teams provided tips for improving team effectiveness. At the top of their list was the development of clear, explicit goals for the team (Pearson & Spencer 1995). Many other studies of teamwork support this recommendation (e.g. Gilbert et al 2000, Poulton & West 1999, West & Field 1995, Williams & Laungani 1999).
- *Promote ongoing education about professional roles:* Most writers and researchers on interprofessional working emphasise the central importance of role understanding and respect (e.g. Hilton 1995). This need was rated fourth in a list of 20 team-building strategies collated by Pearson and Spencer (1995). Ongoing education about professional roles has been widely advocated as essential for effective interprofessional teamwork (e.g. Atwal 2002a). Such interprofessional education is valuable from the very start of pre-qualification courses (Hind et al 2003), and helps students to feel secure in their own roles, less threatened by areas of role overlap, more appreciative of others' roles, and ultimately more able to focus on patients' (rather than professionals') needs.
- *Take part in education about teamworking and group dynamics*: Professionals need more education about group processes. However, Freeman et al (2000) note that such topics are rarely included in professional training programmes, and Miller et al (2001) observe that undergraduate students tend to devalue such learning about groups and teamworking, believing it to be just 'common sense'. Theory about group processes, including the evolution of groups over time, may challenge this assumption and provide a useful toolkit of concepts (Farrell et al 2001). Team members may benefit from 'away days' in which their team functioning is considered and changes planned to help it work more effectively. Regular reflection on team process and function, especially when newcomers are appointed, may help to improve patterns of communication. Qualified professionals may feel that they have too little time to devote to such matters, preferring to give time to skills development, for example. Possibly professionals become more interested in teamwork issues if they see their relevance to effective patient care and better rehabilitation outcomes.
- *Work in smaller, more cohesive teams, where possible (Miller et al 2001):* On the basis of their research, Miller and colleagues suggest that smaller, better focused teams tend to be more cohesive. Team members, when relatively few in number, can then also become better known to their patients. They

argue that this would 'ensure that patients have a sense of their nurse, or their OT, for example, within the wider framework of their team' (p. 65). Molyneux (2001), also commented on the value of a small team, when reflecting on some of the factors that led to positive working practices in an interprofessional group formed to facilitate the early discharge of stroke patients. Smaller teams (of less than 11) felt safer to participate in, according to professionals participating in a study by Williams and Laungani (1999).

- *Attend to processes of decision-making in the team*: Øvretveit (1995) argues that 'decision-making procedures can bring out the worst and the best in people, and can create conflict, or harness group creativity' (p. 51). Groups need to formulate an explicit yet flexible approach to decision-making if the resources of the whole team are to be used fully yet efficiently, and if conflict is to be managed without injuring working relationships (Freeth 2001).

- *Have shared assessment strategies, shared care pathways, and shared systems of record keeping:* Effective collaboration throughout the rehabilitation process requires team members to liase fully in relation to assessment, treatment planning and written notes. Shared assessment strategies help team members to exchange information and perspectives, and to decide on the key problems to be addressed in rehabilitation. Miller et al (2001) describe how one professional (a clinical psychologist) undermined a child development team's collaborative efforts by carrying out confidential assessments that were not made available to the team as a whole. Previous discussion has suggested that the evidence is mixed for these strategies improving teamworking. If implemented alone, they do not guarantee better teamwork. Many other interpersonal and organisational issues are also involved.

- *Rotate leadership*: An effective way of flattening the hierarchy in a group (or the barriers to communication that are associated with hierarchy), and moderating the effects of any individual's leadership style, is to rotate the leadership of team meetings. Autocratic leadership tends to inhibit team collaboration. It may be advantageous for a person to occupy the role of leader of an interprofessional team on the basis of his/her expertise for the specific task in hand, rather than be placed in post on a permanent basis according to formally assigned status or power. Some interprofessional initiatives have deliberately chosen to rotate leadership among the disciplines represented, in order to encourage equal status and commitment from all members (Freeth 2001).

- *Attend to the 'mundane' barriers to teamwork*, such as poor accommodation and inconvenient timing of meetings. Molyneux (2001) considered that having a shared base contributed to the development of good working relationships in a newly formed team for discharging and supporting stroke patients.

- *Give time and attention to team-building:* Attention needs to be paid to developing the team as an identifiable entity, with clear goals and purpose.

That teams go through evolutionary stages in their functioning is well recognised (e.g. Farrell et al 2001). It is generally more difficult to create a cohesive and productive team if there is a steady flow of team members leaving or joining the group. Movement of staff is difficult to avoid in practice, but with every change in personnel, a little time needs to be spent in re-forming the team, and in reflecting on whether more effective ways of working together can be implemented. Regular time may need to be set aside to discuss any difficulties in communication and collaboration, to explore each members' roles, to develop trust, and to establish team protocols to which members can give their support (Øvretveit, 1995). A brief fortnightly or monthly 'forum' in which team issues are discussed can make a positive difference to team functioning, particularly if 'occasional' or peripatetic team members are given the opportunity to participate. Miller et al (2001) describe several case examples (e.g. Chapter 4). 'Away days' can serve a similar function (Pearson & Spencer 1995).

- *Regard the patient as a member of the interprofessional team:* Several authors suggest that teams who include the patient as a member of the team, tend to be less hierarchical and more oriented towards democratic ways of working. Molyneux (2001), for example, found that team members were increasingly in favour of formulating intervention plans in consultation with the patients, as they learned to become more flexible and open with each other. Edwards (2002) argues that patients should be regarded as honorary members of the team. This 'paradigm shift' helps all concerned to collaborate more effectively, and to take responsibility for their part in the rehabilitation programme.

CONCLUSION

There is mixed evidence that interprofessional collaboration improves patient care. In part, the limited availability of objective evidence may be associated with the considerable difficulties inherent in measuring and linking the many dimensions of both teamwork and patient outcomes. Also, it is difficult – and unethical – to arrange for certain experimental comparisons (such as comparing patients treated by well organised and poorly co-ordinated interprofessional teams). Some reviews do indeed suggest that patients achieve more favourable outcomes when the interprofessional team works effectively together. This issue clearly needs further research.

Effective interprofessional care relies on open and honest sharing of information, including assessments, perspectives and rehabilitation strategies among all team members, and between the team, patient and family. Effective teams have a distinctive identity that members value in addition to their own professional allegiances. They appreciate each other's roles, and agree on the team's common purpose. The group climate is supportive rather than defensive, and conflicts are addressed openly in order to seek a satisfactory resolution. Collaboration is also assisted through facilitatory leadership styles, the relatively equal status of members, and mutual respect.

Effective interprofessional teamwork seems more likely to offer patients (and their families) a seamless service, enhancing the potential for education, motivation, and optimism among all concerned. The team is more likely, through a shared consultation process, to address the patient's and family's needs successfully, with less duplication of assessments, visits and so on. Patients are less likely to receive conflicting messages from the many people involved in their care. These experiences all maximise the likelihood of positive outcomes from rehabilitation.

Further Reading

Bull M, Roberts J 2001 Components of a proper discharge for elders. Journal of Advanced Nursing 35(4):571–581

Recommended for student therapists. This gives a clear and detailed portrayal of the various roles involved in discharging frail elderly people home from hospital, and shows how communication breakdowns and role misunderstanding within the team affect both professionals and patients.

Miller, Freeman M, Ross N 2001 Interprofessional practice in health and social care: challenging the shared learning agenda. Arnold, London

This book describes a three-year in-depth study of various health professionals and health educators, including six interprofessional teams. It provides a rich discussion of the factors that encourage and impede effective interprofessional teamwork, and considers the benefits of teamwork for patients.

Molyneux J 2001 Interprofessional teamworking: what makes teams work well? Journal of Interprofessional Care 15(1):29–35

The paper provides a detailed analysis of the many factors that contributed to positive communications within a newly formed interprofessional team.

Waters K, Luker K 1996 Staff perspectives on the role of the nurse in rehabilitation wards for elderly people. Journal of Clinical Nursing 5(2):105–114

A qualitative study of a rehabilitation team available in full-text from CINAHL – gives a vivid account of role uncertainty and other barriers to teamwork, based on quotations from members of staff who were interviewed.

Chapter 10

Conclusion

RETROSPECTIVE

In earlier chapters, we have encountered a number of patients who have had experience of long-term medical care and rehabilitation. Some have expressed their views in research studies, and some have appeared in case vignettes. Their stories reveal that they all bring complex needs and resources to the process of rehabilitation. Evidence suggests that rehabilitation is most likely to be effective when the patient and therapist are working towards common goals. Yet studies also reveal that mutually agreed goals are not always established. You may recall the account of a paraplegic woman who regarded rehabilitation as focusing only upon the most basic of self-care tasks (Seymour W 1998). Her therapists had overlooked her main priority, which had been to learn how to care for her baby.

Two central questions have been addressed throughout this book. Can therapists take an evidence-based approach to communicating with their patients? Will a 'tutored' approach, based on communication theory, research evidence, clinical sensitivity and personal reflection, enhance the relationship between therapist and patient, and ultimately maximise the effectiveness of therapy?

We have seen that a strictly evidence-based approach to communication is difficult to achieve for a number of reasons. It is often unclear whether research evidence can be confidently applied to guide an encounter with an individual patient in a clinical setting that is different from the original research study. Each person brings different needs and coping styles, so a general approach to communication based on 'group averages' may not be applicable. For example, we have discussed how the stage model of grief can provide a useful guide to people's likely reactions to loss. Yet individuals do vary, and some – as Michael J. Fox (2003 p. 177) commented – are very much aware that their complex feelings cannot be categorised in any simple way. It is also difficult to decide which aspects of the complex 'bundle' of verbal and nonverbal communications that occur in therapist–patient interactions are most effective. A vital piece of information, a facial expression that conveys understanding, or a light touch of humour, can all counteract the depersonalisation that patients often experience in institutional settings, and provide a turning point in rehabilitation. There is another major barrier to applying a strictly evidence-based approach to communication. While there is some evidence about the desirable features of effective *formal* interventions such as educational packages and leaflets, researchers have tended not to study how *informal* interactions during rehabilitation influence health outcomes.

Nevertheless, a research-guided approach to communication is certainly possible. Firstly, therapists need to be mindful of the evidence that some health professionals are poor communicators. Many studies have found that substantial minorities of patients are dissatisfied with the communications they have received during their treatment. Patients particularly dislike being treated as conditions rather than people. Such evidence should counteract any assumption on the part of students and clinicians that communication with patients is simply a matter of common sense, or that their education should focus only on technical knowledge and skills. Research can also guide other communication strategies, as explored in the final case study.

ACTIVITY Isaac: Facing a long-term health condition

Isaac is 22 years old. He was left with a hearing impairment following bacterial meningitis at the age of seven years, but people with whom he interacts rarely notice this. Isaac is in the third year of a Sports Science degree course. He plays hockey for the university but has recently been dropped from the first team. Over the past year, Isaac has been experiencing pain in his back and hips. At first, he tried to ignore the pain, but he sought medical care when it started to affect his performance in hockey and his other sports. Isaac has been diagnosed with ankylosing spondylitis (AS) and has been referred to an interprofessional back pain clinic. Since the diagnosis, and his 'demotion' from the university's most prestigious hockey team, Isaac has been drinking alcohol more heavily than usual. His long-standing career plans – to take a further qualification to teach physical education in secondary school – now seem in doubt and he feels uncertain about the future.

- Based on your reading of earlier chapters, can you put forward some general research-guided strategies that therapists might adopt when interacting with Isaac in order to promote more effective rehabilitation?

Therapists working with Isaac might reflect on their philosophy or model of health, illness and rehabilitation. The traditional biomedical model risks casting the patient into a passive role, devaluing his opinions, experiences and aspirations. A person-centred therapist will view the communication process as one that harnesses the patient's motivation and resources, bringing the therapist and patient into equal partnership.

Therapists who are mindful of research evidence into patients' experiences of health care will be alert to the needs of any person with a hearing impairment. We have seen in an earlier chapter that large numbers of deaf people experience inadequate communications with health professionals. If aware of this evidence, the therapists will follow procedures known to help a hearing impaired patient to focus attention and to lip-read. For example, therapists will be careful not to cover their faces, by looking down or away from the patient. They will try not to have a conversation in a bustling or gloomy environment. Nonverbal gestures will be used to reinforce verbal expression, and not to confuse it. Written materials may be provided to back up verbal explanation. Above all, the therapists will ask Isaac about his needs in relation to verbal interaction, and act on his advice.

Rehabilitation does not provide a cure. A key objective is to help Isaac to manage his condition and to meet his need to put his 'life back together again' (Frank 1995 p. 8). To achieve this, therapists will place great emphasis on effective education. Patients need to have their questions answered. If Isaac is suppressing his concerns about his health, he may particularly benefit from having a therapist who asks explicitly – as Tierney et al (2000 p. 860) suggest – 'Is there anything you need or want to know?' He could be encouraged to write down his most pressing questions before therapy sessions, so that he does not forget them (following the research evidence by Maly et al 1999, that shows a health-promoting effect of such an intervention).

Research-guided therapists will be mindful of evidence, such as that reviewed by Ley (1988), that patients do not take in as much information in a session as they or their therapists like to think. Education needs to be tailored to the patient's own abilities. The therapist may realise that Isaac has excellent knowledge of anatomy and physiology through his study of sports sciences and that as a third year student, he has good skills for searching and evaluating information. The rule of thumb, that written materials should not have a readability level greater than grade 9, may not apply to this particular patient. However, as discussed earlier, some patients feel overwhelmed by anxiety about their condition. When they look up information about their condition, they are not studying pathology in the abstract, but a process that is occurring within their own bodies, and that has the power of affecting their entire lives. Sensitive therapists will provide opportunities to discuss such personal information with the patient, in order to offer emotional support, and to ensure appropriate understanding. They will not expect the patient to learn about the condition and its management alone.

Patients require accurate rather than confusing or contradictory information from the professional team. Studies such as those carried out by Donovan and Blake (2000) and Edwards (2002) show that patients are irritated when the professionals cannot agree on their prognosis or on their treatment recommendations. Such confusion is likely to disrupt the patient's self-management strategies, to the detriment of long-term rehabilitation. Therapists working with Isaac may usefully research AS to establish the best evidence-based guidance regarding his sporting activities (e.g. by consulting papers such as Uhrin et al 2000). Isaac is likely to have questions about whether he can safely continue with hockey and other sports, or whether vigorous activity is likely to damage his health. A sound evidence-based approach is required, and team members will need to liase with each other to establish consensus on this issue.

Working in partnership requires both therapist and patient to communicate freely, to devise a shared agenda and to pool their resources. Barriers to partnership include stereotyping and negative attitudes on the part of the therapist. For example, in the above case, therapists may also be working with severely injured patients whose progress in rehabilitation is slow and tortuous. It may be tempting for the therapists to compare these patients with Isaac and to judge that he is not too badly affected. However, readers may recall the studies by Donovan and Blake (2000), and by Darragh et al (2001), which found, not surprisingly, that patients resent such judgements. For the patient, a condition may not seem at all routine or minor. In Isaac's case, AS may be severely challenging his identity as a sportsman. It is also threatening his long-standing career plans, as well as creating pain and functional difficulties. The person-centred therapist will, through reflection, try to challenge any negative personal stereotypes and develop an empathic understanding of each unique patient.

Support, through empathy, respect and genuineness on the part of therapists, can make a great difference to a patient's ability to cope with the anxiety, changes in self-image, and other problems that long-term illness tends to bring about. Guided by the research evidence that well-supported patients tend to achieve better health outcomes, therapists may also encourage the patient to extend his own support network. The therapist may also notice that Isaac is drinking more heavily. Better clinical outcomes may be achieved if the professional team can integrate health promotion into the rehabilitation programme. Perhaps Isaac is not used to expressing his feelings, and is defending himself against anxiety through using alcohol (Holahan et al 2001). Perhaps he prefers problem-focused coping strategies rather than disclosing his feelings. The therapist will endeavour to get to know the patient's particular style of coping and work with this. Additional support will be required if the patient is going to change maladaptive coping behaviours, perhaps following the Stages of Change model (e.g. DiClemente 2003; Miller & Tonigan 1997).

Evidence suggests that unmarried men are particularly likely to lack confidantes. A disabling condition may threaten the masculinity of a young man who previously took good health for granted, and may lead to his exclusion from his peer group (especially as this largely consists of males who excel at sporting activities). The therapist will need to be sensitive to such social issues. Possibly, a virtual support group and information web-site could meet the needs of this particular patient. The therapist might recommend that Isaac check out web-sites such as www.kickas.org, which offer information and support to people with AS.

As with all forms of intervention, the therapists should evaluate their communication performance as well as their technical interventions, by asking Isaac to comment on these. Open questions during each rehabilitation session to establish what forms of support and information Isaac requires will help to ensure that his feedback at the end of rehabilitation is favourable.

FINAL COMMENTS

Although further research is required, studies suggest that patient-centred communication strategies, including building partnerships, and offering support, education and empowerment, maximise treatment outcomes. Patients who are more satisfied tend to feel more committed to treatment and are more likely to adhere to their therapists' recommendations. Support and information can build morale and self-efficacy, helping patients to resist depression and feelings of powerlessness. Patients are then more able to meet the long-term challenge of adapting and managing their own condition. Patient-centred communication strategies help to counteract the depersonalisation of patients that readily occurs during rehabilitation, especially within in-patient settings.

We need more research into the turning points in rehabilitation, when patients sense not only an improvement in their physical functioning but also regain a familiar self-image. At such points, patients start to believe in the possibility of returning to valued roles, and consider that a good quality of life is within their reach. Therapists' technical expertise, for example in activity analysis and in understanding biomechanics, play a crucial part in achieving effective outcomes, but so, too, do their communication skills.

References

Many journal articles are available in full-text from electronic databases.

MEDLINE includes articles from:
Annals of Internal Medicine
Archives of Internal Medicine
British Medical Journal (BMJ)
Canadian Medical Association Journal
Heart & Lung: Journal of Acute and Critical Care
Journal of Clinical Oncology
Journal of the American Medical Association (JAMA)

CINAHL includes articles from:
Journal of Advanced Nursing
Journal of Clinical Nursing
Journal of Nursing Scholarship
Nursing Standard

Science Direct includes articles from:
Clinical Psychology Review
International Journal of Nursing Studies
Journal of Aging Studies
Journal of Psychosomatic Research
Preventive Medicine

University and hospital libraries may subscribe to additional electronic databases, enabling access to additional research articles.Follow the library's instructions for accessing these electronic databases.

Abbott J, Dodd M, Gee L et al 2001 Ways of coping with cystic fibrosis: implications for treatment adherence. Disability and Rehabilitation 23(8):315–324

Adams N, Whittington D, Saunders C et al 1994 Communications skills in physiotherapist–patient interaction. University of Ulster, Belfast

Admi H 1996 Growing up with a chronic health condition: a model of an ordinary lifestyle. Qualitative Health Research 6(2):163–183.

Agarwal M, Dalal A, Agarwal D et al 1995 Positive life orientation and recovery from myocardial infarction. Social Science and Medicine 40(1):125–130

Ambady N, Koo J, Rosenthal R et al 2002 Physical therapists' nonverbal communication predicts geriatric patients' health outcomes. Psychology and Aging 17(3):443–452

Antonovsky A 1990 Pathways leading to successful coping and health. In: Rosenbaum M(ed) Learned resourcefulness: on coping skills, self-control and adaptive behaviour. Springer, New York, p. 31–63

Argyle M 1990 Bodily communication. Routledge, London

Argyle M, Alkema F, Gilmour R 1971 The communication of friendly and hostile attitudes by verbal and nonverbal signals. European Journal of Social Psychology 1(3):385–402

Arthur D 1999 Assessing nursing students' basic communication and interviewing skills: the development and testing of a rating scale. Journal of Advanced Nursing 29(3):658–665

Atwal A, Caldwell K 2002 Do multidisciplinary integrated care pathways improve interprofessional collaboration? Scandinavian Journal of Caring Sciences 16(4):360–367

Atwal A 2002a A world apart: how occupational therapists, nurses and care managers perceive each other in acute health care. British Journal of Occupational Therapy 65(10):446–452

Atwal A 2002b Nurses' perceptions of discharge planning in acute health care: a case study in one British teaching hospital. Journal of Advanced Nursing 39(5):450–458

Bandura A 1997 Self-efficacy: the exercise of control. Freeman, New York

Bandura A 1986 Social foundations of thought and action: a cognitive social theory. Prentice-Hall, Englewood Cliffs, NJ

Banks S, Crossman D, Poel D 1997 Partnerships among health professionals and self-help group members. Canadian Journal of Occupational Therapy 64(5):259–269

Barlow J, Hainsworth J 2001 Volunteerism among older people with arthritis. Ageing and Society 21(2): 203–217

Barlow J, Sturt J, Hearnshaw H 2002 Self- management interventions for people with chronic conditions in primary care: examples from arthritis, asthma and diabetes. Health Education Journal 61(4):365–378

Barlow J, Wright C, Sheasby J et al 2002 Self-management approaches for people with chronic conditions: a review. Patient Education and Counseling 48:177–187

Barry C, Bradley C, Britten N 2000 Patients' unvoiced agendas in general practice consultations: qualitative study. British Medical Journal 320:1246–1250

Barry C, Stevenson F, Britten N et al 2001 Giving voice to the lifeworld: more humane, more effective medical care? A qualitative study of doctor–patient communication in general practice. Social Science and Medicine 53: 487–505

Basnett I 2001 Health care professionals and their attitudes toward and decisions affecting disabled people. In: Albrecht G, Seelman K, & Bury M (eds) Handbook of disability studies. Sage, London, pp 450–467

Bath J, Hooper J, Giles M et al 1999 Patient perceptions of rheumatoid arthritis. Nursing Standard 14(3):35–8

Bauby J 1998 The diving bell and the butterfly. Fourth Estate, London

Beckman H, Frankel R 1984 The effect of physician behavior on the collection of data. Annals of Internal Medicine 101(5):692–6

Bennett P, Murphy S 1997 Psychology and health promotion. Open University, Buckingham

Bennett P 1993 Counselling for heart disease. BPS Books, Leicester

Bennett P, Mayfield T, Norman P et al 1999 Affective and social-cognitive predictors of behavioural change following first myocardial infarction. British Journal of Health Psychology 4:247–256

Benton D 1999 Clinical effectiveness. In: Hamer S, Collinson G (eds) Achieving evidence-based practice. Baillère-Tindall, Edinburgh, pp 87–108

Bergs D 2002 'The hidden client' – women caring for husbands with COPD: their experience of quality of life. Journal of Clinical Nursing 11(5):613–621

Berkman L, Syme S 1979 Social networks, host resistance, and mortality: a nine-year follow-up study of Alameda County residents. American Journal of Epidemiology 109:186–204

Berry D, Pennebaker J 1993 Nonverbal and verbal emotional expression and health. Psychotherapy and Psychosomatics 59(1):11–19

Berry S 1996 Learning to live with life-threatening illness. In: Palmer S, Dainow S, Milner P (eds) Counselling: The BAC Reader. Sage, London, pp 307–313

Blixen C, Kippes C 1999 Depression, social support, and quality of life in older adults with osteoarthritis. Image – the Journal of Nursing Scholarship 31(3):221–226

Bock B, Albrecht A, Traficante R et al 1997 Predictors of exercise adherence following participation in a cardiac rehabilitation program. International Journal of Behavioral Medicine 4(1):60–75

Bodenheimer T, Lorig K, Holman H et al 2002 Patient self-management of chronic disease in primary care. Journal of the American Medical Association 288(19):2469–2475

Boon H, Stewart M 1998 Patient – physician communication assessment instruments 1986 to 1996 in review. Patient Education and Counseling 35(3):161–176

Boudreaux E, Carmack C, Scarini I 1998 Predicting smoking stage of change among a sample of low socio-economic status, primary care outpatients: replication and extension using decisional balance and self-efficacy theories. International Journal of Behavioral Medicine 5(2):148–165

Brannon L , Feist J 1999 Health psychology: an introduction to behaviour and health, 4th edn. Wadsworth, Belmont, California

Braye S, Preston-Shoot M 1995 Empowering practice in social care. Open University, Buckingham

Brock S C, Kleiber D A 1994 Narrative in medicine: the stories of elite college athletes' career-ending injuries. Qualitative Health Research 4(4):411–430

Brooks N, Magee P, Bhatti G et al 2000 Asian patients' perspective on the communication facilities provided in a large inner city hospital. Journal of Clinical Nursing 9(5):706–712

Broome A, Llewelyn S (eds) 1995 Health psychology: processes and applications, 2nd edn. Chapman Hall, London

Brown R 1996 Group processes: dynamics within and between groups. Blackwell, Oxford

Brown L, Tucker C, Domokos T 2003 Evaluating the impact of integrated health and social care teams on older people living in the community. Health & Social Care in the Community 11(2):85–94

Brown M, Koch T, Webb C 2000 Information needs of women with non-invasive breast cancer. Journal of Clinical Nursing 9(5):713–722

Broy S 1996 A 'whole patient' approach to managing osteoporosis. Journal of Musculoskeletal Medicine 13(2):15–28

Brus H, van de Laar M, Taal E et al 1998 Effects of patient education on compliance with basic treatment regimens and health in recent onset active rheumatoid arthritis. Annals of Rheumatic Diseases 57(3):146–151

Bruster S, Jarman B, Bosanquet N et al 1994 National survey of hospital patients. British Medical Journal 309:1542–1549

Bulger S, Smith A 2000 Message tailoring: an essential component for disease management. In: Wilde M(ed) Patient-centered healthcare. Micromass Communications, Cary, NC, pp 15–22

Bull F, Holt C, Kreuter M et al 2001 Understanding the effects of printed health education materials: which features lead to which outcomes? Journal of Health Communication 6(3):265–279

Bull M, Roberts J 2001 Components of a proper discharge for elders. Journal of Advanced Nursing 35(4):571–581

Burleson B 1994 Comforting communication: significance, approaches, and effects. In: Burleson B, Albrecht T, Sarason J (eds) Communication of social support: messages, interactions, relationships and community. Sage, Thousand Oaks, CA

Burnard P 1991 Using video as a reflective tool in interpersonal skills training. Nurse Education Today 11(2):143–146

Burnard P 1999 Counselling skills for health professionals, 3rd edn. Stanley Thornes, Cheltenham

Burnett V, Cavanagh S, Shearer J 2002 Multidisciplinary documentation in care of the elderly. British Journal of Therapy & Rehabilitation 9(10):382–385

Bury M 1982 Chronic illness as biographical disruption. Sociology of Health & Illness 4(2):167–82

Butow P, Brindle E, McConnell D et al 1998 Information booklets about cancer: factors influencing patient satisfaction and utilisation. Patient Education and Counseling 33(2):129–141

Bylund C, Makoul G 2002 Empathic communication and gender in the physician – patient encounter. Patient Education and Counseling 48:207–216

Calfas K, Long B, Sallis J 1996 A controlled trial of physician counseling to promote the adoption of physical activity. Preventive Medicine 25(3):225–233

Calnan M, Gabe J 2001 From consumerism to partnership? Britain's National Health Service at the turn of the century. International Journal of Health Services 31(1):119–131

Cameron C 1996 Patient compliance: recognition of factors involved and suggestions for promoting compliance with therapeutic regimens. Journal of Advanced Nursing 24(2):244–250

Caris-Verhallen W, Kerkstra A, Bensin J et al 2000 Effects of video interaction analysis training on nurse – patient communication in the care of the elderly. Patient Education and Counselling 39(1): 91–103

Carpenter J 1995 Doctors and nurses: stereotypes and stereotype change in interprofessional education. Journal of Interprofessional Care 9(2):151–161

Casto R, Juli M 1994 Interprofessional care and collaborative practice. Brooks/Cole, Pacific Grove, CA

Chapman J, Langridge J 1997 Physiotherapy health education literature. Physiotherapy 83(8):406–412

Charles C, Gafni A,Whelan T 1997 Shared decision-making in the medical encounter. What does it mean? (or it takes two to tango). Social Science and Medicine 44:681–692

Charles C, Gauld M, Chambers L 1994 How was your hospital stay? Patients report about their care in Canadian hospitals. Canadian Medical Association Journal 150:1813–1822

Charmaz K 1983 Loss of self: a fundamental form of suffering in the chronically ill. Sociology of Health & Illness 5(2):168–195

Charmaz K 1991 Good days, bad days: the self in chronic illness and time. Rutgers University, New Brunswick, NJ

Charmaz K 1999 Stories of suffering: subjective tales and research narratives. Qualitative Health Research 9(3):362–382

Charnock D 1998 The DISCERN Handbook: quality criteria for consumer health information. Radcliffe Medical, Abingdon

Charon R, Montello M 1998 Literature and medicine: an on-line guide. Annals of Internal Medicine 128(11):959–962

Cioffi R 2003 Communicating with culturally and linguistically diverse patients in an acute care setting: nurses' experiences. International Journal of Nursing Studies 40(3):299–306

Clare A 1991 Developing communication and interviewing skills. In: Corney R (ed) Developing communication and counselling skills in medicine. Routledge, London

Clark N, Gong M 2000 Management of chronic disease by practitioners and patients: are we teaching the wrong things? British Medical Journal 320:572–575

Cleary P, Edgman-Levitan S 1997 Health care quality: incorporating consumer perspectives. Journal of the American Medical Association (JAMA) 278(19):1608–1612

Close H, Procter S 1999 Coping strategies used by hospitalised stroke patients: implications for continuity and management of care. Journal of Advanced Nursing 29(1):138–144

Colman A 2001 A Dictionary of Psychology. Oxford University, Oxford

Corker M, French S (eds) 1999 Disability Discourse. University Press, Buckingham

Coulter A, Fitzpatrick F 2000 The patient's perspective regarding appropriate health care. In: Albrecht G, Fitzpatrick R, Scrimshaw R (eds) The handbook of social studies in health and medicine Sage, London, pp 454–464

Coyne J, Wortman C, Lehman D 1988 The other side of support: emotional over-involvement and miscarried helping. In: Gottlieb, B (ed) Marshalling social support: formats, process and effects. Sage, Newbury Park, CA

Crepeau E 1991 Achieving intersubjective understanding: examples from an occupational therapy treatment session. American Journal of Occupational Therapy 45(11):1016–1125

Crohan S, Antonucci T 1989 Friends as a source of social support in old age. In: Adams R, Blieszner R (eds) Older adult friendship: Structure and process. Sage, Newbury Park, CA, pp 129–146

Crossley M 2000 Introducing narrative psychology: self, trauma and the construction of meaning. Open University, Buckingham

Dahlgren M, Almquist A, Krook J 2000 Physiotherapists in Balint group training. Physiotherapy Research International 5(2):85–96

Dalley J, Sim J 2001 Nurses' perceptions of physiotherapists as rehabilitation team members. Clinical Rehabilitation 15(4):380–389

Damush T, Weinberger M, Perkins S et al 2003 Randomized trial of a self-management program for primary care patients with acute low back pain: short-term effects. Arthritis & Rheumatism

49(2):179–186

Darragh A, Sample P, Krieger S 2001 'Tears in my eyes 'cause somebody finally understood': client perceptions of practitioners following brain injury. American Journal of Occupational Therapy 55(2):191–199

Davidhizar R, Giger J 1998 Patients' use of denial: coping with the unacceptable. Nursing Standard 12(43):44–46

Davis G, Hiemenz M, White T 2002 Barriers to managing chronic pain of older adults with arthritis. Journal of Nursing Scholarship 34(2):121–126

Davis K 1993 On the movement. In: Swain J, Finkelstein V, French, S (eds) Disabling barriers – enabling environments. Sage, London, pp 285–292

Dean-Barr S 2000 How can we define and measure support? Rehabilitation Nursing 25(3):82

Dempster F 1996 Distributing and managing the conditions of encoding and practice. In: Ligon Bjork E, Bjork R (eds) Memory: handbook of perception and cognition 2nd edn. Academic Press, New York, pp 317–344

Denscombe M 1998 The good research guide for small-scale social research projects. Open University, Buckingham

Department of Health 1992 The patient's charter. HMSO, London

Department of Health 1996 Promoting clinical effectiveness: a framework for action in and through the NHS. NHS Executive, Leeds

Department of Health 1998a Modernising health and social services: national priorities guidance. HMSO, London

Department of Health 1998b Partnership in action. HMSO, London

Department of Health 1999 Saving lives: our healthier nation. HMSO, London

Department of Health 2000a The NHS Plan. HMSO, London

Department of Health 2000b Meeting the challenge: a strategy for the allied health professions. HMSO, London

Department of Health 2001 The expert patient: a new approach to chronic disease management for the 21st century. HMSO, London

Diamond J 1998 C: because cowards get cancer too. Vermilion, London

Dickson D, Hargie O, Morrow N 1997 Communication skills training for health professionals: an instructor's handbook, 2nd edn. Chapman Hall, London

DiClemente C, Prochaska J, Firhurst S et al 1991 The process of smoking cessation: an analysis of precontemplation, contemplation, and preparation stages of change. Journal of Consulting and Clinical Psychology 59(2):295–304

DiClemente C 2003 Addiction and change: How addictions develop and addicted people recover. Guilford, New York

Do Rozario L 1997 Spirituality in the lives of people with disability and chronic illness: a creative paradigm of wholeness and reconstitution. Disability and Rehabilitation 19(10):427–434

Donovan J, Blake D 2000 Qualitative study of interpretation of reassurance among patients attending rheumatology clinics: 'just a touch of arthritis, doctor?'. British Medical Journal, 320(7234):541–544

Dudley-Brown S 2002 Prevention of psychological distress in persons with inflammatory bowel disease. Issues in Mental Health Nursing 23(4):403–422

Duggan C, Dijkers M 1999 Quality of life – peaks and valleys: a qualitative analysis of the narratives of persons with spinal cord injuries. Canadian Journal of Rehabilitation 12(3):179–189

Edelman S, Craig A, Kidman A 2000 Group interventions with cancer patients: efficacy of psychoeducational versus supportive groups. Journal of Psychosocial Oncology 18:67–85

Edgman-Levitan S 1993 Providing effective emotional support. In: Gerteis M, Edgman-Levitan S, Daley J et al (eds) Through the patient's eyes: understanding and promoting patient-centered care Jossey-Bass, San Francisco, pp 154–177

Edwards C 2002 A proposal that patients be considered honorary members of the healthcare team. Journal of Clinical Nursing 11(3):340–348

Egbert L, Battit G, Welch C 1964 Reduction of post-operative pain by encouragement and instruction of patients: a study of doctor – patient rapport. Paper re-printed in Steptoe A, Wardle J 1994 Psychosocial processes and health: a reader. Cambridge University, Cambridge, pp 386–392

Ellers B 1993 Innovations in patient-centered education. In: Gerteis M, Edgman-Levitan S, Daley J et al (eds) Through the patient's eyes: understanding and promoting patient-centered care. Jossey-Bass, San Francisco, pp 96–118

Ellis-Hill C, Horn S 2000 Change in identity and self-concept: a new theoretical approach to recovery following a stroke. Clinical Rehabilitation 14(3):279–287

Elwyn G, Edwards A, Kinnersley P 1999 Shared decision-making in primary care: the neglected second half of the consultation. British Journal of General Practice 49(443):477–482

Engel G 1977 The need for a new medical model: a challenge for biomedicine. Science 196:129–136

Esterling B, L'Abate L, Murray E et al 1999 Empirical foundation for writing in prevention and psychotherapy: mental and physical health outcomes. Clinical Psychology Review 19(1):79–96

Evans P, Hucklebridge F, Clow A 2000 Mind, immunity and health: the science of psychoneuroimmunology. Free Association Books, London

Farrell M, Schmitt M, Heinemann G 2001 Informal roles and stages of interdisciplinary team development. Journal of Interprofessional Care 15(3):281–295

Farrell C 2004 Patient and public involvement in health: the evidence for policy implementation. Department of Health, London

Fisher K, Hardie R 2002 Goal attainment scaling in evaluating a multidisciplinary pain management programme. Clinical Rehabilitation 16:871–877

Fleming M 1991 The therapist with the three–track mind. American Journal of Occupational Therapy 45:1007–1014

Ford S, Fallowfield L, Hall A et al 1995 The influence of audiotapes on patient participation in the cancer consultation. European Journal of Cancer 31A:13–14, 2264–2269

Forsyth D 1990 Group dynamics. Brooks Cole, California

Foss C, Sundby J 2003 The construction of the gendered patient: hospital staff's attitudes to female and male patients. Patient Education and Counseling 49(1):45–52

Fox M J 2003 Lucky man: A memoir. Ebury, London

Frank A 1995 At the will of the body: reflections on illness. Houghton Mifflin, Boston

Frank A 1997 Illness as moral occasion: restoring agency to ill people. Health: an interdisciplinary journal for the social study of health, illness and medicine 1(2):131–148

Frank A 2001 Can we research suffering? Qualitative Health Research 11(3):353–362

Frankel R, Beckman H 1989 Evaluating the patient's primary problems. In: Stewart M, Roter D (eds) Communicating with medical patients. Sage, Newbury Park, CA, pp 86–98

Freeman M, Miller C, Ross N 2000 The impact of individual philosophies of teamwork on multi-professional practice and the implications for education. Journal of Interprofessional Care 14(3):237–247

Freeth D 2001 Sustaining interprofessional collaboration. Journal of Interprofessional Care 15(1):37–46

French S 1993a Can you see the rainbow? The roots of denial. In: Swain J, Finkelstein V, French S et al (eds) Disabling barriers – enabling environments. Sage, London, pp 69–77

French S 1993b What's so great about independence? In: Swain J, Finkelstein V, French S et al (eds) Disabling barriers – enabling environments. Sage, London, pp 44–8

French S 1997 The attitudes of health professionals towards disabled people. In: French S (ed) Physiotherapy: a psychosocial approach, 2nd edn. Butterworth-Heinemann, Oxford, pp 86–99

French S 1999 The wind gets in my way. In: Corker M, French S (eds) Disability Discourse. Open University Press, Buckingham, pp 21–27

French S, Reynolds F, Swain J 2001 Practical research. Butterworth-Heinemann, Oxford

Frye A 1998 Prejudiced? Me? Lessons learned from a challenging patient. Rehabilitation Nursing 23(6):318–319

Fursland E 2001 Patient's angle. Nursing Standard 15(48):18–19

Gallant M, Beaulieu M, Carnevale F 2002 Partnership: an analysis of the concept within the nurse–patient relationship. Journal of Advanced Nursing 40(2):149–157

Gerteis M, Edgman-Levitan S, Daley J (eds) 1993 Through the patient's eyes: understanding and promoting patient-centred care. Jossey-Bass, San Francisco

Gething L 1992 Judgements by health professionals of personal characteristics of people with a visible physical disability. Social Science and Medicine 34(7):809–815

Ghosh C, Ravindran P, Joshi M 1998 Reductions in hospital use from self-management training for chronic asthmatics. Social Science and Medicine 46(8):1087–1093

Gibbon B, Watkins C, Barer D et al 2002 Can staff attitudes to team working in stroke care be improved? Journal of Advanced Nursing 40(1):105–111

Giger J, Davidhizar R 1999 Transcultural nursing: assessment and intervention, 3rd edn. Mosby, St. Louis

Gilbert D, Fiske S, Gardner L 1998 Handbook of social psychology, 4th edn. Vol. 1. McGraw-Hill, Boston

Gilbert J, Camp R, Cole C et al 2000 Preparing students for interprofessional teamwork in health care. Journal of Interprofessional Care 14(3):223–225

Gilbert P 1992 Counselling for depression. Sage, London

Godin G, Shephard R 1990 An evaluation of the potential role of the physician in influencing community exercise behavior. American Journal of Health Promotion 4(4):255–259

Granshaw L, Porter R 1989 The hospital in history. Routledge, London

Grant J, Elliott J, Weaver M et al 2002 Telephone intervention with family caregivers of stroke survivors after rehabilitation. Stroke 33(8):2060–2065

Gray R, Fitch M, Phillips C et al 2000 Managing the impact of illness: the experiences of men with prostate cancer and their spouses. Journal of Health Psychology 5(4):531–548

Greenfield S, Kaplan S, Ware J et al 1988 Patients' participation in medical care: effects on blood sugar control and quality of life in diabetes. Journal of General Internal Medicine 3(5):448–457

Greenhalgh T, Hurwitz B 1999 Narrative-based medicine: why study narrative? British Medical Journal 318:48–50

Haerkaepaeae K, Jaervikoski A, Estlander A 1996 Health optimism and control beliefs as predictors for treatment outcome of a multimodal back treatment program. Psychology and Health 12(1):123–134

Hafsteinsdottir T, Grypdonck M 1997 Being a stroke patient: a review of the literature. Journal of Advanced Nursing 26(3):580–588

Hagopian G 1996 The effects of informational audiotapes on knowledge and self-care behaviors of patients undergoing radiation therapy. Oncology Nursing Forum 23(4):697–700

Hainsworth J, Barlow J 2001 Volunteers' experiences of becoming arthritis self-management lay leaders: "It's almost as if I've stopped aging and started to get younger!" Arthritis & Rheumatism 45(4):378–383

Hall J, Roter D 2002 Do patients talk differently to male and female physicians? A meta-analytic review. Patient Education & Counseling 48(3):217–224

Hall-Lord M, Larsson G, Steen B 1998 Pain and distress among elderly intensive care unit patients: comparison of patients' experiences and nurses' assessments. Heart & Lung: the Journal of Acute and Critical Care 27(2):123–132

Hamer S 1999 Evidence-based practice. In: Hamer S, Collinson G(eds) Achieving evidence-based practice. Ballière-Tindall, Edinburgh, pp 3–12

Hammell K 1994 Psychosocial outcome following severe closed head injury. International Journal of Rehabilitation Research 17(4):319–332

Hammond A 1998 The use of self-management strategies by people with rheumatoid arthritis. Clinical Rehabilitation 12:81–87

Hammond A, Lincoln N 1999 The effect of a joint protection education programme for people with rheumatoid arthritis. Clinical Rehabilitation 13(5):392–400

Harbaugh G 1994 Assumptions of interprofessional collaboration: interrelatedness and wholeness. In: Casto R M, Juli M C (eds) Interprofessional care and collaborative practice. Brooks-Cole, Pacific Grove, CA, pp 11–21

Hawks S, Hull M, Thalman R et al 1995 Review of spiritual health: definition, role, and intervention strategies in health promotion. American Journal of Health Promotion 9(5)371–388

Heckman T, Somlaj A, peters J et al 1998 Barriers to care among persons living with HIV / AIDS in urban and rural areas. AIDS Care 10(3):365-375

Heim M, Wershavski M, Arazi-Margalit D 1998 The will to walk: a partnership involving dual dynamics. Disability & Rehabilitation 20(2):74–77

Heisler M, Bouknight R, Hayward R et al 2002 The relative importance of physician communication, participatory decision-making and patient understanding in diabetes self-management. Journal of General Internal Medicine 17(4):243–252

Hellstrom K, Lindmark B 1999 Fear of falling in patients with stroke: a reliability study. Clinical Rehabilitation 13:509–517

Henbest R, Stewart M 1990 Patient-centredness in the consultation: 2. Does it really make a difference? Family Practice 7:28–33

Henkin A, Dee J, Beatus J 2000 Social communication skills of physical therapy students: an initial characterization. Journal of Physical Therapy Education 14(2):32–38

Herth K 2000 Enhancing hope in people with a first recurrence of cancer. Journal of Advanced Nursing 32(6):1431–1441

Hickey G, Kipping C 1998 Exploring the concept of user involvement in mental health through a participation continuum. Journal of Clinical Nursing 7(1):83–88

Hilton R 1995 Fragmentation within interprofessional work. A result of isolationism in health care professional education programmes and the preparation of students to function only in the confines of their own disciplines. Journal of Interprofessional Care 9:33–40

Hind M, Norman I, Cooper S et al 2003 Interprofessional perceptions of health care students. Journal of Interprofessional Care 17(1):21–34

Hines J 2000 Communication problems of hearing-impaired patients. Nursing Standard 14(19):33–37

Hogan A 1999 Carving out a place to act: acquired impairment and contested identity. In: Corker M, French S (eds) Disability Discourse. Open University. Buckingham, pp 79–91

Holahan C, Moos R, Schaefer J 1996 Coping, stress resistance, and growth: conceptualising adaptive functioning. In: Zeidner M Endler N (eds) Handbook of coping: theory, research, applications. Wiley, New York, pp 24–43

Holahan C, Moos R 2001 Drinking to cope, emotional distress and alcohol use and abuse: a ten-year model. Journal of Studies on Alcohol 62(2):190–198

Holman H, Lorig K 2000 Patients as partners in managing chronic disease: partnership is a prerequisite for effective and efficient health care, British Medical Journal 320:526–527

Holman H, Sobel D, Laurent D (eds) 2000 Living a healthy life with chronic conditions: self-management of heart disease, arthritis, diabetes, asthma, bronchitis, emphysema and others. Bull, Boulder

Horne R 1997 Representations of medication and treatment: advances in theory and measurement. In: Petrie K, Weinman J (eds) Perceptions of health and illness. Harwood Academic, Amsterdam, pp 155–188

House J, Landis K, Umberson D 1988 Social relationships and health. Science 241:540–545

Howell D, Cleary K 2001 Benefits of an interdisciplinary approach: a case of collaboration. Physical and Occupational Therapy in Geriatrics 20(1):73–83

Humphris D 1999 Types of evidence. In: Hamer S, Collinson G (eds) Achieving evidence-based practice. Ballière-Tindall, Edinburgh, pp 13–40

Hunt P, Hillsdon M 1996 Changing eating & exercise behaviour . Blackwell Science, Oxford

Hunter K M, Charon R, Coulehan J 1995 The study of literature in medical education. Academic Medicine 70(9):787–791

Hurst R 2003 The international disability rights movement and the ICF. Disability and Rehabilitation 25(11–12):572–576

Iezzoni L 1998 What should I say? Communication around disability. Annals of Internal Medicine 129 (8):661–665

Ireland C 2003 Adherence to physiotherapy and quality of life for adults and adolescents with cystic fibrosis. Physiotherapy 89(7):397–407

Jackson E 1974 Concerning death: A guide for the living. Beacon, Boston

Jackson T 1999 Dyspraxia: guidelines for intervention. British Journal of Occupational Therapy 62(7):321–326

Jacobs M 1998 The presenting past: the core of psychodynamic counselling and therapy. Open University, Buckingham

Jenkins V, Fallowfield L 2002 Can communication skills training alter physicians' beliefs and behavior in clinics? Journal of Clinical Oncology 20(3):765–769

Jennings B, Loan L 2001 Misconceptions among nurses about evidence-based practice. Journal of Nursing Scholarship 33(2):121–127

Jensen L, Allen M 1994 A synthesis of qualitative research on wellness-illness. Qualitative Health

Research 4(4):349–369

Jha A, Patrick D, MacLehose R et al 2002 Dissatisfaction with medical services among Medicare beneficiaries with disabilities. Archives of Physical Medicine and Rehabilitation 83(10):1335–1341

Johns C 2000 Becoming a reflective practitioner. Blackwell Science, Oxford

Johnson D, Johnson F 2002 Joining together: group theory and group skills. Allyn & Bacon, London

Johnson P, Wistow G, Schulz R et al 2003 Interagency and interprofessional collaboration in community care: the interdependence of structures and values. Journal of Interprofessional Care 17(1):69–83

Kadner K 1994 Therapeutic intimacy in nursing. Journal of Advanced Nursing 19:215–218

Kahn R, Antonucci T 1980 Convoys over the life course: attachment, roles and social support. In: Baltes P, Brim O (eds) Life-span development and behavior Vol. 3. Academic Press, New York, pp 253–286

Kamwendo K, Askenbom M, Wahlgren C 1999 Physical activity in the life of the patient with rheumatoid arthritis. Physiotherapy Research International 4(4):278–292

Keefe F, Caldwell D, Baucom D et al 1996 Spouse-assisted coping skills. Training in the management of osteoarthritic knee pain. Arthritis Care Research 9(4):279–291

Keefe F J, Brown G K, Wallston K A et al 1989 Coping with rheumatoid arthritis pain: catastrophising as a maladaptive strategy. Pain 37:51–56

Keen S, Dowell A, Hurst K et al 1999 Individuals with low back pain: how do they view physical activity? Family Practice 16(1):39–45

Kennedy A, Robinson A, Hann M et al 2003 A cluster-randomised controlled trial of a patient-centred guidebook for patients with ulcerative colitis: effect on knowledge, anxiety and quality of life. Health & Social Care in the Community 11(1):64–72

Kessenich C, Guyatt G, Patton C et al 2000 Support group intervention for women with osteoporosis. Rehabilitation Nursing 25(3):88–92

Kirklin D, Richardson R 2001 Medical humanities: a practical introduction. Royal College of Physicians, London

Kizer K 2001 Establishing health care performance standards in an era of consumerism. Journal of the American Medical Association (JAMA) 286(10):1213–1217, 1249–1250

Klaber Moffat J 2002 Back pain: encouraging a self-management approach. Physiotherapy Theory and Practice 18(4):205–212

Klaber Moffat J, Richardson P 1997 The influence of the physiotherapist – patient relationship on pain and disability. Physiotherapy Theory and Practice 13:89–96

Kleinman A 1988 The illness narratives: suffering, healing and the human condition. Basic Books, USA

Knapp M, Hall J 2002 Nonverbal communication in human interaction, 5th edn. Wadsworth, Belmont, CA

Knaus W, Draper E, Wagner D et al 1986 An evaluation of outcome from intensive care in major medical centres. Annals of Internal Medicine 104:410–418

Kok G 1991/2 Health education theories and research for AIDS prevention. Hygie X:32–39

Krause N, Markides K 1990 Measuring social support among older adults. International Journal of Aging and Human Development 30(1):37–53

Kreuter M, Lukwago S, Bucholtz D et al 2003 Achieving cultural appropriateness in health promotion programs: targeted and tailored approaches. Health Education & Behavior 30(2):133–146

Kreuter M, Oswald D, Bull F et al 2000 Are tailored health education materials always more effective than non-tailored materials? Health Education Research 15(3):305–315

Kubler-Ross E 1982 On death and dying. Tavistock, London

Kvale S 1996 Interviews: an introduction to qualitative research interviewing. Sage, London

Lackner S, Goldenberg S, Arrizza G et al 1994 The contingency of social support. Qualitative Health Research 4(2):224–243

Lane J, Khan S, Diwa, A 2000 Osteoporosis: current clinical trends. Clinical Geriatrics 8(8):30–31, 35–6

Law M 1998 Client-centered occupational therapy. Slack, New Jersey

Law M, Baptiste S, Mills J 1995 Client-centred practice: what does it mean and does it make a difference? Canadian Journal of Occupational Therapy 62(5):250–257

Lazarus R, Folkman S 1984 Stress, appraisal and coping. Springer, New York

Leaviss J 2000 Exploring the perceived effect of an undergraduate multiprofessional educational intervention. Medical Education 34(6):483-486

LeFort S, Gray-Donald K, Rowat K 1998 Randomized controlled trial of a community-based psychoeducation program for the self-management of chronic pain. Pain 74(2–3):297–306

Lenny J 1993 Do disabled people need counselling? In: Swain J, Finkelstein V, French S et al (eds) Disabling barriers, enabling environments. Sage, London, pp 233–240

Ley P 1979 Memory for medical information. British Journal of Social and Clinical Psychology 18:245–256

Ley P 1988 Communicating with patients: improving communication, satisfaction and compliance. Chapman Hall, London

Ley P 1989 Improving patients' understanding, recall, satisfaction and compliance. In: Broome A (ed) Health psychology: processes and applications. Chapman Hall, London, pp 74–102

Leydon G, Boulton M, Moynihan C et al 2000 Cancer patients' information needs and information-seeking behaviour: in depth interview study. British Medical Journal, 320:909–913

Little P, Everitt H, Williamson I et al 2001a Preferences of patients for patient-centred approach to consultation in primary care: observational study. British Medical Journal 322:468–472

Little P, Everitt H, Williamson I et al 2001b Observational study of effect of patient-centredness and positive approach on outcomes of general practice consultations. British Medical Journal 323:908–911

Lloyd C, Maas F 1992 Interpersonal skills and occupational therapy. British Journal of Occupational Therapy 55(10):379–382

Lo R 1999 Correlates of expected success at adherence to health regimen of people with IDDM. Journal of Advanced Nursing 30(2):418–424

Lockart-Wood K 2000 Specialist nursing: collaboration between nurses and doctors in clinical practice. British Journal of Nursing 9(5):276–280

Lorig K, Mazonson P, Holman H 1993 Evidence suggesting that health education for self-management in patients with chronic arthritis has sustained health benefits while reducing health care costs. Arthritis & Rheumatism 36(4):439–446

Lorig K, Sobel D, Stewart A et al 1999 Evidence suggesting that a chronic disease self-management program can improve health status while reducing hospitalization: a randomized trial. Medical Care 37:5–14

Lorig K, Sobel D, Ritter P et al 2001 Effect of a self-management program on patients with chronic disease. Effective Clinical Practice 4(6):256–262

Lui M, MacKenzie A 1999 Chinese elderly patients' perceptions of their rehabilitation needs following a stroke. Journal of Advanced Nursing 30(2):391–400

Lund M, Tamm M 2001 How a group of disabled persons experience rehabilitation over a period of time. Scandinavian Journal of Occupational Therapy 8(2):96–104

Lyons R, Sullivan M, Ritvo P 1995 Relationships in chronic illness and disability. Sage, London

MacCormack T, Simonian J, Lim J et al 2001 'Someone who cares': a qualitative investigation of cancer patients' experiences of psychotherapy. Psycho-oncology 10(1):52–65

McCrum R 1998 My year off. Picador, Basingstoke

McDonald H, Garg A, Haynes R 2002 Interventions to enhance patient adherence to medication prescriptions: scientific review. Journal of the American Medical Association 288(22):2868–2879

McGuire W 1985 Attitudes and attitude change. In: Lindsey G, Aronson E, (eds) Handbook of social psychology, 3rd edn. Vol. 2. Random House, New York

McKinnon A 2000 Client values and satisfaction with occupational therapy. Scandinavian Journal of Occupational Therapy 7(3):99–106

MacLeod M 1993 On knowing the patient: experiences of nurses. In: Radley A (ed) Worlds of illness: biographical and cultural perspectives on health and disease. Routledge, London, pp 179–197

McQueen A 2000 Nurse–patient relationships and partnership in hospital care. Journal of Clinical Nursing 9(5):723–731

Maes S, Leventhal H, De Ridder D 1996 Coping with chronic illness. In: Zeidner M, Endler N (eds) Handbook of coping: theory, research, applications. Wiley, New York, pp 221–251

Maguire P, Pitceathly C 2002 Key communication skills and how to acquire them. British Medical Journal 325(7366):697–700

Makoul G 2002 The SEGUE Framework for teaching and assessing communication skills. Patient Education and Counseling 45(1):23–34

Makoul G 2003 Communication skill education in medical school and beyond. Journal of the American Medical Association 289(1):93

Makoul G, Arnston P, Schofield T 1995 Health promotion in primary care: physician–patient communication and decision-making about prescription medications. Social Science and Medicine 41(9):1241–1254

Malchiodi C 1999 Medical art therapy with adults. Jessica Kingsley, London

Maly R, Bourque L, Engelhardt R 1999 A randomised controlled trial of facilitating information-giving to patients with chronic medical conditions: effects on outcomes of care. Journal of Family Practice 48(5):356–363

Manne S, Zautra A 1989 Spouse criticism and support: their association with coping and psychological adjustment among women with rheumatoid arthritis. Journal of Personality and Social Psychology 56(4):608–617

Mannerkorpi K, Kroksmark T, Ekdahl C 1999 How patients with fibromyalgia experience their symptoms in everyday life. Physiotherapy Research International 4(2):110–122

Manns P, Chad K 2001 Components of quality of life for persons with a quadriplegic and paraplegic spinal cord injury. Qualitative Health Research 11(6):795–811

Marks R 2001 Efficacy theory and its utility in arthritis rehabilitation: review and recommendations. Disability and Rehabilitation 23(7):271–280

Matthews D, Stuchman A, Branch W 1993 Making 'connexions': enhancing the therapeutic potential of patient–clinician relationships. Annals of Internal Medicine 118(12):973–7

Mattingly C 1988 Perspectives on clinical reasoning for occupational therapy. In: Robertson S (ed) Mental health focus: skills for assessment and treatment. AOTA, Rockville, pp 185–188

Mattingly C 1998 Healing dramas and clinical plots: the narrative structure of experience. Cambridge University, Cambridge

Maxwell K, Streetly A, Bevan D 1999 Experiences of hospital care and treatment seeking for pain from sickle cell disease: qualitative study. British Medical Journal 318:1585–1590

May S 2001 Patient satisfaction with management of back pain: part 2: Qualitative study into patients' satisfaction with physiotherapy. Physiotherapy 87(1):10–20

McWhinney I 1995 Why we need a new clinical method. In: Stewart M, Brown J, Weston W et al (eds) Patient-centred medicine: transforming the clinical method. Sage, Thousand Oaks, pp 1–18

Mead J 2000 Patient partnership. Physiotherapy 86(6):282–4

Mead N, Bower P 2000 Patient-centredness: a conceptual framework and review of the empirical literature. Social Science and Medicine 51:1087–2013

Mead N, Bower P 2002 Patient-centred consultations and outcomes in primary care: a review of the literature. Patient Education and Counseling 48(1):51–61

Mead N, Bower P, Hann M 2002 The impact of general practitioners' patient-centredness on patients' post-consultation satisfaction and enablement. Social Science and Medicine 55(2):283–299

Metcalfe C, Lewin R, Wisher S et al 2001 Barriers to implementing the evidence base in four NHS therapies: dieticians, occupational therapists, physiotherapists, speech and language therapists. Physiotherapy 87(8):433–441

Miller C, Freeman M, Ross N 2001 Interprofessional practice in health and social care: challenging the shared learning agenda. Arnold, London

Miller C, Ross N, Alderton J 1998 Becoming a member of the diabetes ward team. Journal of Diabetes Nursing 2:59–62

Miller W, Tonigan J 1997 Assessing drinkers' motivation for change: The Stages of Change Readiness and Treatment Eagerness Scale (SOCRATES). In Marlatt G, VandenBos G (eds) Addictive behaviors: Readings on etiology, prevention, and treatment. American Psychological Association, Washington, DC, pp 355–369

MMWR 2001 Prevalence of disabilities associated with health conditions among adults – United States 1999 Morbidity and Mortality Weekly Report 50(7):120–125 [published in full-text in MEDLINE – see local subscriber instructions]

Mohr D, Dick L, Russo D et al 1999 The psychosocial impact of multiple sclerosis: exploring the patient's perspective. Health Psychology 18(6):376–382

Molyneux J 2001 Interprofessional teamworking: what makes teams work well? Journal of Interprofessional Care 15(1):29–35

Moore S 1996 The effects of discharge information intervention on recovery outcomes following coronary artery bypass surgery. International Journal of Nursing Studies 33(2):181–189

Morgan H, Thomas K 1996 A psychodynamic perspective on group processes. In: Wetherell M(ed) Identities, groups and social issues. Sage, London pp 63–117

Morisky D, DeMuth N, Field-Fass M et al 1985 Evaluation of family health education to build social support for long-term control of high blood pressure. Health Education Quarterly 12(1):35–50

Morris J 1991 Pride against prejudice: transforming attitudes towards disability. The Women's Press, London

Morris J 1993 Prejudice. In: Swain J, Finkelstein V, French S et al (eds) Disabling barriers – enabling environments. Sage, London, pp 101–106

Moseley L 2002 Combined physiotherapy and education is efficacious for chronic low back pain. Australian Journal of Physiotherapy 48(4):297–302

Mullen P, Mains D, Velez R 1992 A meta-analysis of controlled trials of cardiac patient education. Patient Education & Counseling 19:143–162

Mullins L, Cote M, Fuemmeler B et al 2001 Illness intrusiveness, uncertainty, and distress in individuals with multiple sclerosis. Rehabilitation Psychology 46(2):139–153

Murphy S, Smith C 1993 Crutches, confetti or useful tools? Professionals' views on and use of health education leaflets. Health Education Research 8(2):205–215

National Health Service Executive 1999 Patient and public involvement in the new NHS. Deptartment of Health, London.

Natterlund B, Ahlstrom G 1999 Experience of social support in rehabilitation: a phenomenological study. Journal of Advanced Nursing 30(6):1332–1340

Nelson D, Cipriani D, Thomas J 2001 Physical therapy and occupational therapy: partners in rehabilitation for persons with movement impairments. Occupational Therapy in Health Care 15:35–57

Nichols K 1995 Institutional versus client-centred care in general hospitals. In: Broome A, Llewelyn S (eds) Health psychology: processes and applications, 2nd edn. Chapman Hall, London, pp 99–107

Nieuwböer A 1992 Attitudes towards working with older patients: physiotherapists' responses to video presentations of post-amputation gait training for an older and younger patient. Physiotherapy Theory and Practice 8(1):27–37

Niven N 1994 Health psychology: an introduction for nurses and other health care professionals, 2nd edn. Churchill- Livingstone, Edinburgh

O'Connor B, Vallerand R 1998 Psychological adjustment variables as predictors of mortality among nursing home residents. Psychology and Aging 13(3):368–374

Ogden J, Ambrose L, Khadra A et al 2002 A questionnaire study of GPs' and patients' beliefs about the different components of patient centredness. Patient Education and Counseling 47(3):223–227

Oliver M 1990 The politics of disablement. Macmillan, London

Oliver M 1993 Re-defining disability: a challenge to research. In: Swain J, Finkelstein V, French S et al (eds) Disabling barriers – enabling environments. Sage, London, pp 61–67

Oliver M 1998 Theories in health care and research: theories of disability in health practice and research. British Medical Journal 317(7170):1446–1449

Osborne M, Smith J 1998 The personal experience of chronic benign lower back pain: an interpretative phenomenological analysis. British Journal of Health Psychology 3(3):65–84

Otte D 1996 Patients' perspectives and experiences of day case surgery. Journal of Advanced Nursing 23(6):1228–1237

Øvretveit J 1995 Team decision-making. Journal of Interprofessional Care 9:41–51

Oz F 2001 Impact of training on empathic communication skills and tendency of nurses. Clinical Excellence for Nurse Practitioners 5(1):44–51

Pakenham K 1999 Adjustment to multiple sclerosis: application of a stress and coping model. Health Psychology 18(4):383–392

Pargament K 1997 The psychology of religion and coping: theory, research, practice. Guilford, New York

Parkes C M 1972 Bereavement: Studies of grief in adult life. International Universities, New York

Parkin A 1997 Memory and amnesia: an introduction, 2nd edn. Blackwell, Oxford

Parsons T 1975 The sick role and the role of the physician reconsidered. Health and Society 53(3):257–278

Paterson B 2001 Myth of empowerment in chronic illness. Journal of Advanced Nursing 34(5):574–581

Pearson P, Spencer J 1995 Pointers to effective teamwork: exploring primary care. Journal of Interprofessional Care 9(2):131–138

Peloquin S 1993 The depersonalization of patients: a profile gleaned from narratives. American Journal of Occupational Therapy 47(9):830–837

Pennebaker J, Kiecolt-Glaser J, Glaser R 1988 Disclosure of traumas and immune function: Health implications for psychotherapy. Journal of Consulting and Clinical Psychology 56(2):239–245

Penninx B, van Tilburg T, Boeke J et al 1998 Effects of social support and personal coping resources on depressive symptoms: different for various chronic diseases? Health Psychology 17(6):551–558

Penninx B, van Tilburg T, Deeg D et al 1997a Direct and buffer effects of social support and personal coping resources in individuals with arthritis. Social Science and Medicine 44(3):393–402

Penninx B, van Tilburg T, Kriegsman D et al 1997b Effects of social support and personal coping resources on mortality in older age: the longitudinal aging study. American Journal of Epidemiology 146:510–519

Penttinen J, Nevala-Puranen N, Airaksinen O et al 2002 Randomized controlled trial of back school with and without peer support. Journal of Occupational Rehabilitation 12(1):21–29

Petrie K, Buick D, Weinman J et al 1999 Positive effects of illness reported by myocardial infarction and breast cancer patients. Journal of Psychosomatic Research 47(6):537–543

Petrie K, Weinman J, Sharpe N et al 1996 Predicting return to work and functioning following myocardial infarction: the role of the patient's view of their illness. British Medical Journal 312:1191–1194

Peveler R, George C, Kinmonth A et al 1999 Effect of antidepressant drug counselling and information leaflets on adherence to drug treatment in primary care: randomised controlled trial. British Medical Journal 319:612–615

Pillemer K, Suitor J, Henderson C et al 2003 A cooperative communication intervention for nursing home staff and family members of residents. The Gerontologist 43:96–106

Platt F, Gaspar D, Coulehan J et al 2001 'Tell me about yourself': the patient-centered interview. Annals of Internal Medicine 134(11):1079–1085

Poole P, Johnson S 1996 Integrated care pathways: an orthopedic experience. Physiotherapy 82(1):28–30

Post S, Puchalski C, Larson D 2000 Physicians and patient spirituality: professional boundaries, competency, and ethics. Annals of Internal Medicine 132(7):578–583

Potter J 1996 Attitudes, social representations and discursive psychology. In: Wetherell M (ed) Identities, groups and social issues. Sage, London, pp 120–173

Poulton B, West M 1999 The determinants of effectiveness in primary health care teams. Journal of Interprofessional Care 13(1):7–18

Pound P, Ebrahim S 2000 Rhetoric and reality in stroke patient care. Social Science and Medicine 51(10):1437–1446

Pound P, Gompertz P, Ebrahim S 1999 Social and practical strategies described by people living at home with stroke. Health and Social Care in the Community 7(2):120–128

Rachman S 1998 Anxiety. Psychology Press, Hove

Radley A (ed) 1993 Worlds of illness: biographical and cultural perspectives on health and disease. Routledge, London

Read C 1998 Patients' information needs in intensive care and surgical wards. Nursing Standard, 12(28):37–39

Rebeiro K 2000 Client perspectives on occupational therapy practice: are we truly client-centred? Canadian Journal of Occupational Therapy 67(1):7–14

Reece A, Simpson J 1996 Preparing older people to cope after a fall. Physiotherapy 82:227–235

Reeves P, Merriam S, Courtenay B 1999 Adaptation to HIV infection: the development of coping strategies over time. Qualitative Health Research 9(3):344–361

Rene J, Weinberger M, Mazzuca S et al 1992 Reduction of joint pain in patients with knee osteoarthritis who have received monthly telephone calls from lay personnel and whose medical regimes have remained stable. Arthritis and Rheumatism 35:511–515

Reynolds B 1994 The influence of clients' perceptions of the helping relationship in the development of an empathy scale. Journal of Psychiatric and Mental Health Nursing 1:23–30

Reynolds F 1996 Models of health and illness. In: Aitken V, Jellicoe H (eds) Behavioural sciences for health care professionals. W B Saunders, London, pp 120–173

Reynolds F 1997 Coping with chronic illness and disability through creative needlecraft. British Journal of Occupational Therapy 60(8):352-356

Reynolds F 1999 When models of health care collide: a qualitative study of rehabilitation counsellors' reflections on working in physical health care settings. Journal of Interprofessional Care 13(4):367–379

Reynolds F 2003 Conversations about creativity and chronic illness I: Textile artists coping with long-term health problems reflect on the origins of their interest in art. Creativity Research Journal 15(4):393–407

Reynolds F, Prior S 2003a "A lifestyle coat-hanger": a phenomenological study of the meanings of artwork for women coping with chronic illness and disability. Disability and Rehabilitation 25(14):785–794

Reynolds F, Prior S 2003b "Sticking jewels in your life": Exploring women's strategies for negotiating an acceptable quality of life with multiple sclerosis. Qualitative Health Research 13(9):1225–1251

Rickel L 1987 Making mountains manageable: maximising quality of life through crisis intervention. Oncology Nursing Forum 14:29–34

Rimmer J 1999 Health promotion for people with disabilities: the emerging paradigm shift from disability prevention to prevention of secondary conditions. Physical Therapy 79(5):495–502

Ritchie J, Stewart M, Ellerton M et al 2000 Parents' perceptions of the impact of a telephone support group intervention. Journal of Family Nursing 6(1):25–45

Roberts J, Browne G, Streiner D et al 1995 Problem-solving counselling or phone-call support for outpatients with chronic illness: effective for whom? Canadian Journal of Nursing Research 27(3):111–137

Robinson I 1990 Personal narratives, social careers and medical courses: Analyzing life trajectories in autobiographies of people with multiple sclerosis. Social Science and Medicine 30(11):1173–1186

Rogers A, Addington-Hall J, Abery A et al 2000 Knowledge and communication difficulties for patients with chronic heart failure: qualitative study. British Medical Journal, 321:605–607

Rogers C 1951 Client-centered therapy. Houghton-Mifflin, Boston

Rogers C 1967 On becoming a person. Constable, London

Rosenberg H, Rosenberg S, Ernstoff M et al 2002 Expressive disclosure and health outcomes in a prostate cancer population. International Journal of Psychiatry in Medicine 32(1):37–53

Roush S 1995 The satisfaction of patients with multiple sclerosis regarding services received from physical and occupational therapists. International Journal of Rehabilitation and Health 1(3):155–166

Rumrill P, Roessler R, Koch L 1999 Surveying the employment concerns of people with multiple sclerosis: a participatory action research approach. Journal of Vocational Rehabilitation 12(2):75–82

Rustoen T, Hanestad B 1998 Nursing interventions to increase hope in cancer patients. Journal of Clinical Nursing 7(1):19–27

Sackett D, Richardson W, Rosenberg W et al 1997 Evidence-based medicine: how to practice and teach EBM. Churchill Livingstone, New York

Sacks O 1984 A leg to stand on. Harper & Row, New York

Santana M, Dancy B 2000 The stigma of being named "AIDS carriers" on Haitian-American women. Health Care for Women International 21(3):161–171

Saxton M, Howe F (eds) 1987 With wings: an anthology of literature by women with disabilities. Virago, London

Scherer Y, Bruce S 2001 Knowledge, attitudes and self-efficacy and compliance with medical regimen, number of emergency department visits, and hospitalisations in adults with asthma. Heart & Lung: Journal of Acute and Critical Care 30(4):250–257

Schilder A, Kennedy C, Goldstone I et al 2001 'Being dealt with as a whole person'. Care seeking and adherence: the benefits of culturally competent care. Social Science and Medicine 52(11):1643–1659

Schillinger D, Piette J, Grumbach K et al 2003 Closing the loop: physician communication with diabetic patients who have low health literacy. Archives of Internal Medicine 163(1):83–90

Schmitt M 2001 Collaboration improves the quality of care: methodological challenges and evidence from US health care research. Journal of Interprofessional Care 15(1):47–66

Schmitt M, Farrell M, Heinemann G 1988 Conceptual and methodological problems in studying the effects of interdisciplinary geriatric teams. The Gerontologist 28:753–764

Schneidert M, Hurst R, Miller J et al 2003 The role of environment in the International Classification of Functioning, Disability and Health (ICF). Disability & Rehabilitation 25(11–12):288–295

Schwartz C E, Sendor, Rabbi M 1999 Helping others helps oneself: response shift effects in peer support. Social Science & Medicine 48:1563–1575

Schwartz C E, Daltroy L H 1999 Learning from unreliability: the importance of inconsistency in coping dynamics. Social Science & Medicine 48:619–631.

Seers K, Friedli K 1996 The patients' experiences of their chronic non-malignant pain. Journal of Advanced Nursing 24(6):1160–1168

Senior M, Viveash B 1998 Health and illness. Macmillan, Basingstoke

Seymour J 1998a The unsound barrier: availability of rehabilitation services for older people. Nursing Times 94(20):56–58

Seymour W 1998b Remaking the body: rehabilitation and change. Routledge, London

Shakespeare T 1999 Art and lies? Representations of disability on film. In: Corker M, French S (eds) Disability Discourse. Open University, Buckingham, pp 120–173

Sharry R, McKenna K 2001 The world wide web as a patient education resource for occupational therapy personnel. British Journal of Occupational Therapy 64(10):509–516

Sharry R, McKenna K, Tooth L 2002 Occupational therapists' use and perceptions of written client education materials. American Journal of Occupational Therapy 56(5):573–576

Simpson J 1994 This game of ghosts. Vintage Books, London

Sissons Joshi M 1995 Lay experiences of the causes of diabetes in India and the UK. In: Markova I, Farr R (eds) Representations of health, illness and handicap. Harwood, London, pp 163–188

Sitzia J, Wood N 1997 Patient satisfaction: a review of issues and concepts. Social Science & Medicine 45(12):1829–1843

Slevin O 1991 Ageist attitudes among young adults: implications for a caring profession. Journal of Advanced Nursing 16(10):1197–1205

Sluijs E 1991 Patient education in physiotherapy: towards a planned approach. Physiotherapy 77(7):503–508

Smart J, Smart D 1995 The use of translators/interpreters in rehabilitation. Journal of Rehabilitation 61(2):14–25

Sourial S 1997 An analysis of caring. Journal of Advanced Nursing 26:1189–1192

Southwell M, Wistow G 1995 Sleep in hospitals: are patients' needs being met? Journal of Advanced Nursing 21(6):1101–1109

Sparkes A 1998 Athletic identity: an Achilles' heel to survival of self. Qualitative Health Research 8(5):644–664.

Stack S 1999 I am more than my wheels. In: Corker M, French S (eds) Disability Discourse. Open University, Buckingham, pp 28–37

Stansbury J, Mathewson-Chapman M, Grant K 2003 Gender schema and prostate cancer: veterans' cultural model of masculinity. Medical Anthropology 22(2):175–204

Stebnicki M 2000 Stress and grief among rehabilitation professionals: dealing effectively with empathy fatigue. Journal of Rehabilitation 66(1):23–29

Steptoe A, Wardle J 1994 Psychosocial processes and health: a reader. Cambridge University, Cambridge

Sternberg R 1999 Cognitive psychology. Harcourt Brace, London

Stewart M 1995 Effective physician – patient communication and health outcomes: a review. Canadian Medical Association Journal 152(9):1423–1433

Stewart M, Brown J, Donner A et al 2000 The impact of patient-centered care on outcomes. The Journal of Family Practice 49(9):796–804

Stewart M, Brown J, Weston W et al (eds) 1995 Patient-centred medicine: transforming the clinical method. Sage, Thousand Oaks, CA

Stewart M, Davidson K, Meade D et al 2000 Myocardial infarction: survivors' and spouses' stress, coping and support. Journal of Advanced Nursing 31(6):1351–1360

Stewart M, Davidson K, Meade D et al 2001 Group support for couples coping with a cardiac condition. Journal of Advanced Nursing 33(2):190–199

Stewart M, Meredith L, Brown J et al 2000 The influence of older patient-physician communication on health and health-related outcomes. Clinics in Geriatric Medicine 16(1):25–36

Strecher V, Seijts G, Kok G et al 1995 Goal setting as a strategy for behavior change. Health Education Quarterly 22(2):190–200

Strycker L, Glasgow R 2002 Assessment and enhancement of social and community resources utilization for disease self-management. Health Promotion Practice 3(3):374–386

Stuck E, Siu A, Wieland G et al 1993 Comprehensive geriatric assessment: meta-analysis of controlled trials. The Lancet 342:1032–1036

Sumsion T 2000 A revised occupational therapy definition of client-centred practice. British Journal of Occupational Therapy 63(7):304–309

Sumsion T, Smyth G 2000 Barriers to client-centredness and their resolution. Canadian Journal of Occupational Therapy 67(1):15–21

Sutherland B, Jensen L 2000 Living with change: elderly women's perceptions of having a myocardial infarction. Qualitative Health Research 10(5):661–676

Swain J, Gillman M, French S 1998 Confronting disabling barriers: towards making organisations accessible. Venture, Birmingham

Sweet S, Norman I 1995 The nurse – doctor relationship: a selective literature review. Journal of Advanced Nursing 22(1):165–170

Symister P, Friend R 2003 The influence of social support and problematic support on optimism and depression in chronic illness: a prospective study evaluating self-esteem as a mediator. Health Psychology 22(3);123–129

Talvitie U 2000 Socio-affective characteristics and properties of extrinsic feedback in physiotherapy. Physiotherapy Research International 5(3):173–188

Tepper M 1999 Letting go of restrictive notions of manhood: male sexuality, disability and chronic illness. Sexuality and Disability 17(1):37–52

Theobald K 1997 The experience of spouses whose partners have suffered a myocardial infarction: a phenomenological study. Journal of Advanced Nursing 26:595–601

Thomas C 1999 Narrative identity and the disabled self. In: Corker M, French S (eds) Disability Discourse. Open University, Buckingham, pp 47–56

Thomas P 1996 Patients' perceptions of counselling within general practice. In: Palmer S, Dainow S, Milner P (eds) Counselling: The BAC Reader. Sage, London, pp 570–584

Thompson N 2001 Anti-discriminatory practice, 3rd edn. Palgrave, Basingstoke

Thorne B 2003 Carl Rogers: key figures in counselling and psychotherapy. Sage, London

Tickle-Degnen L 1998 Using research evidence in planning treatment for the individual patient. Canadian Journal of Occupational Therapy 65(3):152–159

Tierney A, Worth A, Watson N 2000 Meeting patients' information needs before and after discharge from hospital. Journal of Clinical Nursing 9(6):859–860

Tolan J 2003 Skills in person-centred counselling and psychotherapy. Sage, London

Trede F 2000 Physiotherapists' approaches to low back pain education. Physiotherapy 86(8):427–433

Turner P 2001 Evidence-based practice and physiotherapy in the 1990s. Physiotherapy Theory and Practice 17:107–121

Tyson S, Turner G 2000 Discharge and follow-up for people with stroke: what happens and why. Clinical Rehabilitation 14(4):381–392

Tyson S, Turner G 1999 The process of stroke rehabilitation: what happens and why. Clinical Rehabilitation 13(4):322–332

Uhrin Z, Kuzi S, Ward M 2000 Exercise and changes in health status in patients with ankylosing spondylitis. Archives of Internal Medicine 160(19):2969–2975

Union of the Physically Impaired Against Segregation 1976 Fundamental principles of disability. UPIAS, London

Van den Borne H 1998 The patient from receiver of information to informed decision-maker. Patient Education and Counseling 34(2):89–102

Van Weert J, van Dulmen S, Bar P et al 2003 Interdisciplinary preoperative patient education in cardiac surgery. Patient Education and Counseling 49(2):105–114

Von Korff M, Moore J, Lorig K et al 1998 A randomised controlled trial of a lay person-led self-management group intervention for back pain patients in primary care. Spine 23(23):2608–2615

Wade D, Halligan P 2003 New wine in old bottles: the WHO ICF as an explanatory model of human behaviour. Clinical Rehabilitation 17(4):349–354

Walker J 1993 Enhancing physical comfort. In: Gerteis M, Edgman-Levitan S, Daley J et al (eds) Through the patient's eyes: understanding and promoting patient-centered care. Jossey-Bass, San Francisco, pp 119–153

Wallston K, Wallston B, DeVellis R 1978 Development of the multi-dimensional health locus of control. Health Education Monographs 6:160–170

Wallston K A 1989 Assessment of control in health care settings. In: Steptoe A, Appels A (eds) Stress, personal control and health. Wiley, Chichester, pp 85–106

Waters K, Luker K 1996 Staff perspectives on the role of the nurse in rehabilitation wards for elderly people. Journal of Clinical Nursing 5(2):105–114

Weinert C 2000 Social support in cyberspace for women with chronic illness. Rehabilitation Nursing 25(4):129–135

Wenger G C, Jerrome D 1999 Change and stability in confidante relationships: Findings from the Bangor Longitudinal Study of Ageing. Journal of Aging Studies 13(3):269–294

Wensing M, Jung H, Mainz J et al 1998 A systematic review of the literature on patient priorities for general practice care: Part 1: description of the research domain. Social Science and Medicine 47:1573–1588

West M, Field R 1995 Teamwork in primary health care. 1. Perspectives from organisational psychology. Journal of Interprofessional Care 9(2):117–130

Wetherell M 1996 Life histories/social histories. In: Wetherell M (ed) Identities, groups and social issues. Sage, London, pp 299–342

Whitehorse L, Manzano R, Baezconde-Garbanati L et al 1999 Culturally tailoring a physical activity program for Hispanic women: recruitment success of La Vida Buena's salsa aerobics. Journal of Health Education 30(2):Suppl S18–24

Wikstrom I, Isacsson A, Jacobsson L 2001 Leisure activities in rheumatoid arthritis: change after disease onset and associated factors. British Journal of Occupational Therapy 64(2):87–92

Wiles R, Pain H, Buckland S et al 1998 Providing appropriate information to patients and carers following a stroke. Journal of Advanced Nursing 28(4):794–801

Williams B 1994 Patient satisfaction: a valid concept? Social Science and Medicine 38(4):509–516

Williams C 2000 Doing health, doing gender: teenagers, diabetes and asthma. Social Science and Medicine 50(3):387–396

Williams G, Laungani P 1999 Analysis of teamwork in an NHS community trust: an empirical study. Journal of Interprofessional Care 13(1):19–28

Williams G 1993 Chronic illness and the pursuit of virtue. In: Radley A (ed) Worlds of illness: biographical and cultural perspectives on health and disease . Routledge, London, pp 92–108

Williams S, Kent G 1996 Patients' disclosure of a diagnosis of cancer: issues in obtaining social support. Journal of Cancer Care 5(4):135–139

Wilson J 1999 Acknowledging the expertise of patients and their organisations. British Medical Journal 319(7212):771–774

Wong-Wylie G, Jevne R 1997 Patient hope: exploring the interactions between physicians and HIV seropositive individuals. Qualitative Health Research 7(1):32–56

Worden J W 1986 Grief counselling and grief therapy. Tavistock, London

World Health Organization 1980 International classification of impairments, disabilities and handicaps: A manual of classification relating to the consequences of disease. WHO, Geneva

World Health Organization 1984 Health promotion: a discussion document on the concept and principles. WHO, Regional Office for Europe

World Health Organization 2001 International classification of functioning, disability and health. WHO, Geneva

Wressle E, Eeg-Olofson A, Marcussin J et al 2002 Improved client participation in the rehabilitation process using a client-centred goal formulation structure. Journal of Rehabilitation Medicine 34(1):5–11

Wressle E, Lindstrand J, Neher M et al 2003 The Canadian Occupational Performance Measure as an outcome measure and team tool in a day treatment programme. Disability and Rehabilitation 25(10):497–506

Yates B 1995 The relation among social support and short-and long-term recovery outcomes in men with coronary heart disease. Research in Nursing and Health 18(3):193–203

Young J, McNicoll P 1998 Against all odds: positive life experiences of people with advanced amyotrophic lateral sclerosis. Health & Social Work 23(1):35–43

Websites

http://www.doh.gov.uk/cmo/progress/expertpatient/epp3.htm
http://www.doh.gov.uk/cmo/progress/expertpatient/epp4.htm
http://www.lmca.org.uk

Index